S0-AKH-103

Mail-Order Marriage

5 Historical Stories of Marriage Arranged
by Letters Between Strangers

Mail-Order Marriage

Tracie Peterson
Mary Davis, Denise Hunter
Judith Miller, DiAnn Mills

BARBOUR BOOKS
An Imprint of Barbour Publishing, Inc.

Cinda's Surprise © 2000 by Barbour Publishing, Inc.
His Brother's Bride © 2000 by Denise Hunter
Changes of the Heart © 1998 by Barbour Publishing, Inc.
Mail-Order Husband © 1996 by DiAnn Mills
Forever Yours © 2002 by Tracie Peterson

Print ISBN 978-1-63409-273-9

eBook Editions:
Adobe Digital Edition (.epub) 978-1-63409-394-1
Kindle and MobiPocket Edition (.prc) 978-1-63409-395-8

All rights reserved. No part of this publication may be reproduced or transmitted for commercial purposes, except for brief quotations in printed reviews, without written permission of the publisher.

All scripture quotations are taken from the King James Version of the Bible.

This book is a work of fiction. Names, characters, places, and incidents are either products of the author's imagination or used fictitiously. Any similarity to actual people, organizations, and/or events is purely coincidental.

Published by Barbour Books, an imprint of Barbour Publishing, Inc., P.O. Box 719, Uhrichsville, OH 44683, www.barbourbooks.com

Our mission is to publish and distribute inspirational products offering exceptional value and biblical encouragement to the masses.

 Member of the
Evangelical Christian
Publishers Association

Printed in the United States of America.

Contents

Cinda's Surprise

by Mary Davis

To Zola who planted the throught in me to get published, then watched it grow. Thanks mom! To my sister who graciously plucked the weeds in my writing. And to my husband who encouraged my writing into full bloom!

Chapter 1

*S*mile, Cinda."

Cinda stopped just short of running into David Swan in his own front yard. In her worry, her gaze had been focused on the ground and not on where she was going. Now, she looked up at her best friend's new husband with an apologetic smile.

"Oh, hi, David. Is Allison inside?"

Cinda had rushed over to see her friend as soon as the mail had arrived. Normally, she strolled along, enjoying whatever pleasures the day had to offer; however, today in her haste, she had heard nothing but her own rushing thoughts and had seen even less. She hadn't even seen David until he spoke to her.

David was just over six feet tall, broad across the shoulders but lean in build, with a kind face and thin, sandy blond hair. He stood firmly in her path. "I won't tell you until you smile. You'll never get a husband with that scowl."

Cinda gave him a quick, forced smile. The last thing she felt like doing today was smiling.

"You're a pretty girl, Cinda. If you smiled more often and looked up once in awhile, you'd catch a husband in no time."

Her cheeks warmed at his compliment. She could see that look in his eyes—*help poor, shy Cinda so she doesn't become an unhappy old maid.* Why were all old maids assumed to be miserable? Wasn't it possible for a spinster to be happy? "Now, who said I was fishing for one, anyway?" she asked him.

"Aren't all young ladies looking for a man to put a ring on their finger?"

Here he was playing big brother again; she was irritated by his teasing, but if she could choose a brother, he would be David. She could see now he was amused. Putting her hands on her hips, she stood up to her full five feet, eleven and a half inches. Like this, she could intimidate most men unless they were young, handsome, and unmarried—then it was

Cinda who was intimidated. She was tall, but she never felt she could measure up in the eyes of a potential suitor.

Less than two inches shorter than David, she was almost eye to eye with him, as she was with most men. "No, David. Some of us are independent souls and don't need marriage to feel complete." Her own words hurt her because she wasn't so sure she was an independent soul.

David opened his mouth as if to counter, but Cinda spoke quickly. "Allison? Is she inside?"

David's hesitation made her uncomfortable. She hoped he wouldn't harass her further. She had had enough for one day. "Yes. She's in the kitchen," David said finally with half a grin.

Allison glanced up at her friend lurking in the doorway and smiled. "Don't just stand there. Peel me some apples." Allison stood at the kitchen worktable, stirring the ingredients for a piecrust. "You can help me make these pies for supper."

Cinda had no siblings while Allison was the only girl of five children. The two had developed a special sisterly bond rooted in friendship.

"I'll just spoil it. You know I can't cook," Cinda countered, staying out of the way by the door.

"Nonsense. That's your aunt talking." Allison set a paring knife on the table next to a bowl of last year's apples she had brought up from the cellar.

Cinda sat down in one of the kitchen chairs. She thought Allison painted the perfect picture with her white apron over a light blue blouse and navy skirt and her blond curls pulled back with just a wisp dangling beside the smudge of flour on her cheek. She obviously enjoyed being a wife and mother-to-be.

Cinda forcefully pushed the thoughts away. She picked up an apple and started peeling. "How are you and the baby doing?"

Allison patted her growing stomach. "Great. He's an active one." Allison put a glob of dough on the floured end of the table. "David fusses over us already. He's going to be a great father."

"It's hard to believe you are six months along. You hardly show."

"Seven. It's this skirt and the apron over top." She smoothed the layers of fabric tightly at the top and bottom of her rounded tummy. She was definitely pregnant.

Cinda peeled apple after apple.

When Allison had the crusts rolled out, she sat down and sliced the peeled apples. "Out with it."

"What?" Cinda looked up from the apple she was peeling, surprised.

"You're frettin' over something. You might as well tell me before it spoils these pies." Allison waved her knife in the air.

"I'm sorry. I don't mean to bring my troubles down on you, but I'm in an awful fix. I don't know who else to turn to." Cinda let out a heavy sigh.

"What has your aunt Ginny done now?"

"It's not her this time, but I hate to think what she will say when she finds out." Cinda wiped her hands on the dish towel and laid it back on the table, then pulled a letter from her pocket. "It's this letter."

"Who's it from?"

Cinda lowered the letter to her lap and looked down. "A man."

"A man? Who?"

"I don't know."

"Didn't he sign it? Are you sure it's from a man then?" Allison picked up another apple and sliced it.

"Mr. Rawlings is definitely a man!"

"How do you know this Mr. Rawlings?"

"I don't," Cinda exclaimed. "That's just it. I've never heard of him until today when I opened this letter." She waved the letter in the air.

"It's probably just a mistake then. Take it back to the post office and tell them to return it to Mr. Rawlings." Allison let out a sigh of relief.

"I can't do that." Cinda could tell her friend was brushing this off as inconsequential.

"Then write to Mr. Rawlings yourself and tell him he made a mistake."

"I can't do that either."

"Why not?" Exasperation coated Allison's heavy sigh. "It would be the proper way to deal with it. Honestly, Cinda, when there's a man concerned, you can make a problem where there is none."

"He's coming here—today." Cinda's voice squeaked. "He's coming for me!"

When Allison's eyes widened, Cinda's stomach flipped. Cinda could tell her friend was trying to hide her surprise.

"Now, why would this Mr. Rawlings, whom you don't even know, be comin' after you?"

"I don't know." Cinda twisted her hands together in her lap. Her aunt had convinced her she was no good for any man; her tall stature had confirmed it in her own mind.

"It can't be all that bad." Allison patted Cinda's hand. "Read the letter aloud, and let's see what Mr. Rawlings has to say."

Cinda unfolded the letter and drew in a deep breath. "'Dear Miss Harrison,'" Cinda started calmly. "That's me. There is no mistaking that. I'm the only unmarried Harrison in town. In fact, I'm the *only* Harrison in town."

"Just read on."

"'I have enjoyed your letters and feel I know you well.'" She stopped and looked at her friend. "Did you hear that? Letters. With an *s*, meaning more than one. He has *letters* from me! *I* didn't write any letters. How can he know me?"

"Go on," Allison said.

Cinda looked back to the letter. "'After these months of correspondence, I look forward to finally meeting you.' *These months!*" Cinda choked out the words and looked wide-eyed at Allison. "He says he has been corresponding with me for months!"

"So far, there is nothing so terrible to have you so worked up."

"Oh, it gets worse. A lot worse."

"Just finish the letter. Or I'll be havin' this baby before I find out what all the fuss is about."

Fuss? Allison thought she was making a fuss over nothing. Well, she would soon see there was a great deal to fuss over. Cinda's hands shook as she continued.

> *Since we have come to know each other through our letters, and due to a deficiency of time, if it's all right with you, we will need to be married immediately and return for the spring planting.*

Cinda's voice was fairly shaking by now.

> *I will arrive in the afternoon on the second of April.*
>
> *Yours truly,*
> *Lucas Rawlings*

Cinda meticulously refolded the letter. "That's what all the *fuss* is about."

The two women sat in silence for a few moments.

"The postman simply delivered it to the wrong house."

"No!" Cinda showed her the address. There was no mistake; the letter was meant for Cinda. "I'm a mail-order bride! What am I going to do?" This kind of thing might happen up north in Chicago—but not in their sleepy little town.

"There has to be a good explanation for all this," Allison said as she put the tops on the two pies and trimmed the edges. "Someone must have been writing to Mr. Rawlings using your name. Would you open the oven for me?" She picked up the pies and slid them into the oven.

Cinda closed the oven door. "Who would do that to me?"

The women fretted over that question while the pies baked. Finally, Allison jotted down something on a piece of paper and sent it off with the freckle-faced boy next door.

Chapter 2

*a*n hour after the note was sent, Vivian and Eve came prancing up onto the porch in a fit of giggles. Cinda and Allison were sitting in wooden rocking chairs on the front porch. Allison was knitting some booties for the baby, and Cinda was working on a half-sewn baby shirt. This was the first spring day warm enough to be outside, and despite their anxiety, they were enjoying the fresh air.

"Allison, it's good to see you looking so fit," Vivian said cordially.

"Yes. You do look fit, Allison," Eve echoed.

Eve wore a low-cut green velour walking dress with her shawl hanging around her elbows. Her black hair was pulled back in the front with ringlets cascading down behind. Vivian's tawny hair was done up in a stylish chignon with jeweled combs. She was dressed in a peach walking dress with a mass of ruffled lace about the neck, upper chest, and sleeves. Vivian could wear all that flounce because she was small, as were Eve and Allison. Cinda seemed to be the only one inflicted with height; she could never get away with all that frill on her tall frame. Suddenly, she drooped her shoulders and pulled her head down between them, feeling overly large.

Vivian and Eve turned simultaneously to Cinda. "How do you do, Cinda?" Eve said in greeting. She turned to Vivian and giggled again. A mischievous smile played on Vivian's lips.

"Sit down you two, and tell us all about Mr. Lucas Rawlings." Allison's irritation was evident in her tone.

The chastised Vivian and Eve sat down dutifully, one on a wooden bench and the other on a straight-back chair. "How did you find out about Lucas?" Vivian asked.

So these two are behind the mysterious letter. Had they written to Cinda pretending to be this man—or was there really a Lucas Rawlings? Cinda pulled out the letter. "I received this from him this morning."

"Vivian!" Eve scolded. "How did that get past you?"

"I haven't been at the post office much lately. My wedding is only two weeks off." Vivian folded her hands in her lap.

"Vivian, maybe you should tell us the whole story," Allison said.

"Oh, do let me tell it. It really is quite amusing," Eve jumped in, eager to tell all. "You remember when we stayed over at your parents' house the night before your wedding, Allison?" She paused until the others nodded, then continued. "Remember that advertisement in the ladies' magazine for finding a husband? Remember the letter we wrote? We sent the letter, Viv and I."

"It was just for fun. You said you weren't going to really mail it. *I* threw that letter away." Cinda was trying to convince herself that this couldn't be happening. Marry a stranger? The thought was appalling.

"I was the one who took it out of the trash. Viv and I rewrote it." Eve's grin widened as she pointed to herself. "We improved it."

Cinda felt the blood drain from her face. "I knew something bad would happen. I never should have agreed to let you use my name." She slumped in the chair and put her head back.

"Who else was there?" Vivian said. "Allison was getting married the next day. I had just gotten engaged. And Eve already had three beaus buzzing around her. It wouldn't have been fair to add another one to her hive when you had none."

"What happened after you sent the letter?" Allison's voice was tinged with annoyance.

"We didn't send it right away," Eve went on. "But about a month after we did send it, we received the first letter from Lucas. We wrote back to him, and before we knew it, we had a regular correspondence with the man."

"Regular correspondence!" Cinda gasped, confirming her fear. Her stomach knotted and lodged in her throat.

Allison gave Cinda a sorrowful look. "Where are the other letters?" Allison demanded.

Eve pulled a bundle of letters out of her reticule. "There are four of them." She handed them to Cinda.

Cinda stared at the stack, too paralyzed to take them from Eve. If she didn't touch them, they weren't real. It was all a bad dream, a nightmare.

Allison reached over and relieved Eve of the collection. "Shall I read them aloud, or do you want to read them in private?" she asked Cinda.

Cinda found it difficult to speak. All she could do was shake her head. She didn't want to know any more about the man. She wanted it not to be true. This couldn't be happening.

Allison took the top letter and opened it.

Dear Miss Harrison,
I acquired your name through the Matrimonial Agency.

15

Cinda grimaced. She closed her eyes to block out Eve's and Vivian's excited faces.

Allison hesitated a moment then continued.

> *I would very much like to begin correspondence with you. Since we live some distance apart, I'll have to court you by mail. If this arrangement is satisfactory with you, I will expect to receive your correspondence.*
>
> *Sincerely,*
> *Lucas Rawlings*

Cinda shook her head. No, it wasn't satisfactory.

"He's not very verbose," Vivian acknowledged, "but he does sound educated and refined."

"Educated and refined! He could be a desperado for all you know," Cinda shot at them.

Allison opened the next letter.

> *Dear Miss Harrison,*
>
> *I'm sorry to say that I don't have a way with words as you do, but I will do my best to answer your many questions. I live on a prosperous farm outside a small town called Buckskin. Montana is the most beautiful country you will ever see. Majestic mountains that reach clear up to the big blue sky. Sparkling rivers and fertile ground. A man could grow just about anything here he put his mind to.*
>
> *I am twenty-eight years old and share your love for the Lord. Life has not always been easy, but God has been good to me.*
>
> *I have never been married, and so I have no children of my own. I do like children and hope to have some one day. Family is very important to me. It is the backbone of this country, God's own design.*
>
> *I anxiously await your next letter.*
>
> *Respectfully,*
> *Lucas Rawlings*

Cinda could feel Vivian's and Eve's eyes on her. Allison opened the next letter.

No, no, Cinda wanted to shout. She didn't want to hear any more, but all she could do was sit there.

Dear Miss Harrison,

I do so enjoy your letters. To answer your further questions, most folks in town consider me tall, though I am not overly so. I have dark hair and blue eyes. Buckskin has a population of two hundred people, more or less, mostly cattle ranchers spread out across the rolling hills. We have a general store, telegraph-post office, church, and we even have a local doctor.

My farm lies to the south of town and supports six horses, twenty-five laying hens, a rooster, a milking cow, and a sow with nine piglets. There are also five apple trees, two peach trees, two cherry trees, and one plum tree, a large garden area, and even a water pump in the kitchen, as well as one outside.

The house is two stories with four bedrooms and a large front porch with two rocking chairs. Not far from the house are wild blackberries and huckleberries. The farm does quite well and provides a good life.

I look forward to your next letter.

Cordially,
Lucas Rawlings

He sounded like a peddler selling his wares. Cinda sucked in a small, quick breath as Allison unfolded the last letter. Wouldn't she ever stop this torture? Cinda bit her bottom lip, knowing that this was the one where he asked *the question.*

Dear Miss Harrison,

I feel as if I know you so well from your letters and have come to the conclusion that we would be most compatible. I can provide well for you and give you a good life.

Cinda buried her face in her hands and shook her head as Allison went on.

I hope you don't think it improper of me to ask without our ever having met, but as I said, I feel as if I know you. Would you do me the honor of accepting my proposal of marriage?

Warm regards,
Lucas Rawlings

Cinda heard Allison fold the last letter and heard the shuffle of papers as she added it to the others. The silence hung heavy in the air.

Eve impatiently broke the silence. "So, what does our—or should I say, *your* dear Lucas have to say in his latest letter?" she crooned.

"How could you two accept his marriage proposal?" Allison scolded.

"Don't get huffy with us, Allison." Vivian preened the ruffles on her sleeves. "You want to see Cinda happily married as much as anybody. We were only trying to do a favor for a friend. She is our friend, too."

"I'm going to get hysterical if someone doesn't tell me what is in that last letter," Eve said, coming off her seat.

Cinda heaved a sigh and relinquished the letter as Eve plucked it from her hand. Cinda moved her lips to the words as Eve read the dismal letter aloud. "Why, isn't today the second of April?" Eve's cheery tone settled a cloud of gloom and doom over Cinda.

"Yes," Cinda moaned. It was true then. She was expected to marry a stranger whose arrival was imminent.

"We certainly didn't expect this." Eve's eyes brightened with excitement. "For him to rush out here as soon as he got a positive reply, I mean. I can't wait to finally meet him."

"Just what did you expect?" Cinda snapped.

Vivian shifted in her seat. "We expected to break the news to you first...slowly...gently. Then we'd giggle over wedding plans."

"He must be pretty desperate to rush out here, grab his bride, and vamoose." Eve's thoughtless words were out before she could stop them. She quickly gave Cinda a wide-eyed look. "I'm sorry. I didn't mean...oh." She stopped before she made things worse.

Is that what my friends really think of me? Cinda wondered. *That I could only be the wife of a desperate man?*

"You heard what he said in the letter. He has to get back for spring planting." Vivian sat rigid as she tried to smooth things over. "If he is desperate, it's only to be a good provider. He's being a perfect gentleman by coming all this way to escort you safely back to his home. He could have simply sent you train fare and let you travel all by yourself out to the wilds of Montana. That's the way it's usually done."

"Why are you pushing this, Viv?" Allison asked, eyeing her suspiciously.

"Because," Vivian said tightly, "because I want to believe Lucas is the right man for Cinda." She straightened the skirt of her dress, then her voice softened. "I don't want her to turn into an unhappy old maid. There! I've said it. I've said the terrible words we have all been thinking...old maid."

"Vivian, I had no idea you cared so much!" Allison said with surprise.

"Well, I do." Vivian looked off across the lawn, but Cinda could see the sincerity on her face.

"I don't have to be married to be happy, Viv." Cinda stood and laid a hand on Vivian's shoulder. She could tell there was more to this for Vivian than a practical joke. Vivian placed her hand on Cinda's. "I don't even want to get married, ever."

Allison sputtered behind her, and Cinda turned to her. "What?"

Allison's mouth hung open in disbelief. "What do you mean 'what'?"

"Not every woman wants a husband."

Allison straightened in her chair. "Ever since the day we met, we've dreamed of getting married. When we were fourteen, we even planned our weddings. Remember?"

"That was *your* dream, Allison, not mine," Cinda interrupted before Allison could go on with any more unpleasant truths. "I just went along to make you happy."

She knew it was a lie, and she felt a rush of shame. Her whole life she had wanted a man to love her more than life itself, the way her father had loved her mother. But she knew now she would never have a love like that; she had given up that unattainable dream several years ago. Now, an inch and a half taller, the dream was even more impossible.

"I don't believe you. I know you better than that." Allison was near tears.

"I don't believe you either," Vivian stated matter-of-factly.

"I believe it. Give her a stack of dusty old books, and she'd be happy," Eve said.

"Eve!" Vivian scolded.

"If we are being honest here, then let's be honest," Eve said, a little indignantly. "This is the first time in three years I've seen her without a book in her hand."

Eve wasn't normally so blunt, but Cinda knew she never had understood Cinda's reluctance with men. Cinda walked to the end of the porch so no one would see the tears welling in her eyes.

"Didn't you ever think all that reading was to cover the pain?" Allison whispered, but Cinda could still hear.

"What pain?" Eve asked innocently.

"Eve, sometimes you are so impossible. You are so caught up in yourself you can't see anyone else," Allison said.

"Well, how do you like that. You try to be honest and this is the thanks you get," Eve said.

"Eve, hush!" Vivian said.

Cinda wiped her cheeks as Allison came over to where she leaned on the rail. "Is everything all right?"

"Fine. I just had something in my eye."

"Did you get it?" Allison asked.

Cinda nodded. If her friend knew there was nothing in her eye except tears, she didn't say anything. For that Cinda was grateful. The two returned to the rocking chairs.

"Cinda, Eve and I are sorry." The sincerity in Vivian's voice touched Cinda. "We never meant to hurt you. We just wanted to make you happy."

"I am happy, just the way I am," Cinda said.

"You should at least give him a chance, after coming all this way," Eve said. "You never know, he may be your Prince Charming."

Cinda could tell Eve was trying to be encouraging, but her stomach was too knotted for her to respond.

Chapter 3

*a*s the four women continued their conversation on the porch, Cinda tried focusing on the beautiful spring weather. Vivian and Eve went on about the virtues of Lucas Rawlings and what they thought he was really like. "I think he's quite tall. Certainly tall enough for Cinda," Vivian said.

"He said he didn't consider himself tall. I think he could be short. He just didn't want to say so in his letters. Even if he is average, you know most men like a small—" Eve tried to soften the blow. "I mean a shorter woman for a wife."

"It doesn't matter one way or the other. We have it in writing, his offer of marriage. That's almost as good as a contract," Vivian said.

Cinda's stomach reeled and flipped. Some stranger was going to show up at her house to claim her. Fortunately, she would not be at home and Aunt Ginny would send him away. Still, she would have to face him sooner or later. How would she tell him she couldn't—she wouldn't—marry him, and that it was all a big mistake? What would he do when he found out he came all this way for nothing? She hoped he didn't have a violent temper. What if he insisted on her sticking to their agreement? But *she* hadn't agreed to anything; it was Eve and Viv who had done it all. A terrifying thought popped into her head. What if he forced her to marry him? He, too, had it in writing.

Cinda looked at Allison. Allison was shaking her head at something Eve had said. Cinda wanted to ask if she thought Mr. Rawlings could actually force her into marriage when a tall figure crossing the lawn caught her attention.

His dark hair curled up from under the back of his bowler. He wore a white linen shirt, a faded green waistcoat, and a dark brown suit that looked like it had been years since it fit properly. If he moved too fast, the stitches would likely pop for the coat stretched taut across his wide shoulders. She couldn't help but think he was handsome, in an odd sort of way, even if he did look out of place in his old clothes and the stylish new bowler perched on his head.

"Good afternoon, ladies," the tall man said, tipping his hat. "I was told I could find Miss Harrison here."

Cinda drew in a quick breath. *Me? Why would he want to see me? I don't know this man.*

"Who is it that wants to know?" Eve cooed, leaning on the porch rail.

"Lucas Rawlings, ma'am." He removed his bowler, revealing his unfashionably long hair.

Cinda's eyes grew large. For a moment she forgot how to breathe. She couldn't help but notice his clear blue eyes even from a distance. But what was he doing there?

Cinda and Allison exchanged glances. Allison patted her arm as she rose and went down the steps to greet him. "Mr. Rawlings, it's nice to finally meet you."

Lucas looked at the blond, bewildered. He was expecting a redhead instead of this delightful blond smiling up at him. She'd probably blow away in a good strong wind. He smiled back. "Miss Harrison?"

He took her hand and was about to kiss it when he felt a hand clamp down hard on his shoulder. He whirled around and caught the first punch in the palm of his right hand. His hand engulfed the other man's fist and held it firmly. "I don't think you want to do that," Lucas said through gritted teeth. A muscle in his jaw twitched. He clenched his left fist still at his side.

A fight would not make a good impression on his bride-to-be. He would avoid it if possible. He stared at the smaller man in front of him, willing him to back down.

"David, stop it!" the blond practically screamed. "I can explain everything—later. Now let him go."

David yanked his hand free and stepped backward. "Keep your hands off my wife." David ground out each word.

"I understood that *Miss* Harrison wasn't married," Lucas said while his focus never left the smaller man. He didn't come for a fight, but he could certainly finish one if necessary.

David wrapped a possessive arm around the woman and said, "This is Mrs. David Swan."

"My mistake, Mrs. Swan." Lucas gave the woman a nod and slight smile.

Two other women slid up next to Mrs. Swan. "Ooo, you're a tall one," the black-haired woman cooed.

An elegant smile slid into place on the other woman's face, and she held out her hand to him. "I'm Miss Vivian Van Dornick." Her tawny hair was pulled up in a sophisticated twist.

Lucas declined the offer of her hand. He dipped his head as he said, "Pleased to meet you, Miss Van Dornick."

"Soon to be Mrs. Alvin Pratt," the black-haired woman said, slipping in front of her. "I'm Miss Eve Weston. Do call me Eve." She held out his hat that he had flung to the ground when David had abruptly arrived.

Lucas's blue eyes flashed to the immodestly dressed Eve. He slowly shrank away from her as he reached for his hat. "Thank you, Miss Weston." Lucas had a little difficulty getting it from her grasp. She had offered it to him but now seemed to be reluctant to give it up. He was relieved she hadn't introduced herself as Miss Harrison. He couldn't imagine spending his life with her purring around.

"I came to see Miss Harrison." Lucas raised his hat to his head. "If she's not here, I'll be on my way."

"She's here," Mrs. Swan said quickly and turned to call her down from the porch. But the porch was empty. She turned back around slowly and said with a polite smile, "Miss Harrison is indisposed at the moment."

Lucas looked toward the house. He remembered there had been four ladies on the porch when he arrived. He couldn't recall what the fourth woman looked like; everything happened so fast. He did recall her letter said she had auburn hair.

"Mr. Rawlings, would you be so kind as to come back for supper? Miss Harrison would be glad to see you then," Mrs. Swan offered.

Lucas glanced at David, who still had his arm wrapped protectively around his wife. His piercing glare continued to drill Lucas. "I don't think your husband would approve of that, ma'am."

"David, tell Mr. Rawlings he's welcome in our home." When David remained silent, the little blond jabbed her husband in the ribs with her elbow and said through a forced smile, "David! Tell him."

David let out a gust of air. "You're welcome to come for supper." David's glare never wavered.

Lucas could tell by the man's look that he didn't want him to return. "Until then." He dipped his head. "Ladies. Mr. Swan, Mrs. Swan. Good day."

"We eat at seven," Mrs. Swan called after him.

"I'll be here." Lucas walked down the street.

Cinda had watched in disbelief as Allison went down the steps and greeted Mr. Rawlings on the lawn. David seemed to appear out of nowhere, and the two men were instantly locked in a confrontation, David's hand engulfed by the tall stranger's. Cinda's hand flew to her mouth as she gasped. *That brute is going to hit sweet David,* she thought. He could easily whip poor David.

But after a verbal reprimand from Allison, the men disengaged. Everyone was safe. Now if he would only leave, Cinda could breathe easily. She hoped Allison would just send him away. She watched as Vivian and Eve got up. *Where are they going?*

Mr. Rawlings's rich, deep voice reverberated up to the porch, though she couldn't hear what he or anyone was saying. But she knew it was only a matter of time before she was called down to join the group gathered on the grass. That was one trip she was not ready to make. She slipped inside the door and hoped no one noticed her unladylike escape.

She leaned against the wall next to the door. With her hands clenched at her chest, she held her breath and waited for someone to call after her. No one called her name. She let out her breath but stood frozen to the wall, listening to the muffled voices outside, unable to hear what they were saying. Curious as to what was going on, she peered around the edge of the front window, being careful to remain unseen. Mr. Rawlings said something, then left. *Good, the ruffian has gone.* She couldn't help but watch and wonder about him as he walked away.

Cinda hoped and prayed Allison, Vivian, and Eve had the good sense to tell Mr. Rawlings it was all a mistake. Then she would never even have to face the man or explain the unfortunate situation to him.

Chapter 4

Cinda had barely stepped through the door before her aunt started in on her. "Where have you been all day?" Cinda's aunt Ginny dried her hands on her apron. Her tone was accusing, her lips pinched. "I've been working all day by myself while you have been off doing who knows what."

"But you don't like anyone in your kitchen," Cinda said, her nerves still frayed from the day's events. She hung up her hat and shawl on the wall pegs by the door.

"Well, you could have done a little fetch and carry for me. I can't be expected to do everything around here. With all the cooking, there is so little time left to do the other house chores." Aunt Ginny liked making elaborate meals that kept her busy in the kitchen, far busier than she needed to be.

Cinda had come to live with her aunt and uncle eleven years ago when she was twelve. Her father had just died and her mother had died three years earlier. Uncle Barney and Aunt Ginny, being her only relatives, took her in. Uncle Barney welcomed her warmly with open arms, but Aunt Ginny had always kept a cool distance.

Cinda knew if she had been home today her aunt would have found fault with her, saying she was in the way and useless. It didn't matter what she did, it was always wrong in her aunt's eyes. "I would be happy to help you with the cooking if you would only—"

Her aunt cut her off. "Do you know how to knead bread dough so it rises properly for baking?"

"No, but—"

"Can you mix up piecrust and roll it out even and make up a pie so the crust is flaky?"

"No." Cinda sighed. It was the same old argument, over and over.

"What about roast a chicken tender so it almost falls from the bone and isn't scorched and shriveled?"

"No, but—"

"Then what use would you be in my kitchen?"

"I could learn if you would teach me." Cinda spoke quickly so she

25

wouldn't be overridden again.

"I have too much work to do to be wasting time teaching you what your mother should have." Aunt Ginny straightened her apron and headed back to the kitchen. "You could at least set the table for supper," she said over her shoulder.

Cinda walked into the dining area just off the kitchen. "I'm glad to help in any way I can." She automatically removed three plates from the cupboard, then put one back. There would be one less for supper tonight. What would her aunt have to say about that?

"You say that now; but put hard work in front of you, you will crumble," her aunt called from the kitchen. "Mark my words. No man wants to marry a girl who can't cook and keep a house."

No man? Cinda sighed, dropping her shoulders and head simultaneously. The strong, dark-haired stranger who came to claim her as his bride flashed before her eyes. He wanted her, or at least he thought he did.

"Stand up straight," her aunt said, strolling into the room. "Ladies don't slouch. Haven't you learned anything?"

Cinda snapped to attention

"A man stopped by this afternoon. A very tall man."

Cinda's eyes got large. That was how Mr. Rawlings had found her. He had come here first. What had he said to Aunt Ginny? What had she said to him?

"I didn't like the looks of him. He's not from around here. But then it's none of my business what you do."

Cinda rolled her eyes.

"I told him you were probably over at Allison's. But then how was I to know where you were, you went flying out of here so fast this morning." She waved her hand as if shooing a fly. "Did he find you over at Allison's?" She turned to face Cinda with her hands perched on her hips.

"Yes," was all Cinda could manage. She wasn't sure what to say. How much did her aunt know?

"Who is he?"

"I really don't know. It was all some sort of a mistake." Cinda hoped her aunt wouldn't grill her any further.

"He seemed sure he knew you." Her aunt pointed at the table. "You forgot a plate."

Cinda decided to ignore her aunt's prodding and take advantage of the opportunity to change the subject. "Allison invited me over for supper. I hope you don't mind."

"Why should I mind? You spend more time at her house than you do here. I don't know why you even bother to come home at all sometimes."

Cinda dropped her head and turned to leave the room.

"Stand up straight!" her aunt called after her.

Cinda snapped up straight and went to her room to slouch in solitude. She pulled out the green dress Allison had suggested she wear. Allison said it would enhance her green eyes, but Cinda didn't want to enhance her eyes. She wanted to calm the fluttering in her stomach by backing out. She still couldn't believe her best friend had betrayed her, but she had promised she would have supper with Mr. Rawlings at Allison and David's, so she would go and be perfectly miserable.

Cinda stood in the kitchen doorway. Even though she wasn't sure what to do, she wanted to be in the kitchen doing something to keep busy. David was even put to work, but Allison wouldn't let Cinda help with supper because she might spill something. "Allison, I thought you were on my side."

"I am." Allison paused from her work at the stove. "You just haven't realized yet that this *is* your side."

"He nearly hit your husband, and you want him inside your home?" Cinda hoped she could talk her friend out of this.

"No. David nearly hit him." Allison waved a wooden spoon in Cinda's direction. "He was only defending himself, and nobody got hurt."

"Did you see his clothes? They weren't well tailored and they are out of style. And what about his hair?"

"Give the poor man a chance. He came all this way. The least you can do is talk with him a little. If he is completely repulsive, I'll have David throw him out."

"Just say the word and I'll throw him out before he steps inside," David said with a smile on his face.

"David, you wouldn't."

Cinda stood back, nearly forgotten as the two argued over her future.

"If Cinda doesn't want to see him, he's not coming in." David's words were stern and not to be questioned.

"This is no different than your inviting over suitors for Cinda," Allison said, her attention focused on her husband.

"Except this man expects a little more than supper conversation. He's planning on a wedding!" David was clearly irritated at what his wife had roped him into.

"This is better. The hard part is done. They already know each other, so to speak. Cinda just has to carry on polite conversation. We'll have a nice meal and learn a little about him. If Cinda decides she doesn't want to marry him, she can tell him about the little misunderstanding." Allison turned her pleading eyes on Cinda. "Please."

Lucas stood outside the gate at the Swans' residence. He pulled out his pocket watch and looked at the time once again, one minute to seven. He had come early to make sure he wasn't late and ended up wandering around to kill time. He didn't want to be early and seem overly eager.

He looked down at his ash gray suit and shifted his coat. This suit fit almost as poorly as the one he had worn that afternoon. On the farm he didn't have much use for a suit. He was going to save it for the wedding, but he had decided making a good first impression was more important. Now he wished he had bought a new suit.

He strode up to the door. His hands felt oddly empty as he looked at them. *Flowers!* Women liked flowers. He fisted his hands. Why didn't he think of it before? Or candy. He could have gotten candy. It was too late now. He swallowed hard and knocked on the door. He wasn't sure what kind of a reception he would get after this afternoon.

The door opened. The moment of truth. Mrs. Swan's friendly smile greeted him. She graciously invited him in. At least one person was glad to see him.

Lucas shook David Swan's outstretched hand and met his disapproving stare. Mr. Swan's words and actions were welcoming, but his glare told Lucas he wasn't. Obviously, Mr. Swan was cordial for his wife's sake, but Lucas refused to be intimidated. He backed down once to a man much less threatening than this David Swan when he was young, and he had regretted it ever since. Never again.

Allison drew his attention away from David. "This is who you really came to see," she said, motioning toward Cinda. "Mr. Rawlings, this is Miss Harrison."

Before him stood a beautiful woman in a modest green dress. Her dark auburn hair was neatly pulled back and swept up on her head. She was the picture of femininity and not at all too short either. He wouldn't spend the rest of his life looking down at the top of her head. Why would this stunning woman need to be a mail-order bride? Surely she had several beaus. He had expected a homely, somewhat plump, unmarriageable woman.

"Pleased to meet you," Cinda said with a slight nod of her head but her gaze didn't quite meet his.

"The pleasure is mine." Lucas watched as her cheeks flushed.

He was glad to see his intended was modestly dressed—not like Miss Weston with her low-cut dress and forward manner.

Allison kept the meal from being eaten in complete silence by plying him with question after question. He answered attentively, but his attention kept drifting back to the quiet young woman across from him.

"Miss Harrison told us about all your animals and that large house. It all sounds really nice. I would love to have all those fruit trees," Allison said, filling the silence. Lucas wished she had used his fiancée's first name, but everyone was acting stiff and formal.

"A mighty big house for just one man," David said skeptically, insinuation in his tone. He had remained silent until now, but Lucas figured he was about to do a lot more talking before the meal was over. "And an awful lot of livestock and fruit."

Lucas shifted uncomfortably, looking down at his plate to take another bite. "I took the place over from the previous owner, lock, stock, and barrel." He raised his eyes in time to see Allison admonish her husband with a scolding look.

At that moment, he caught Miss Harrison looking at him. He had guessed her eyes would be brown, and he couldn't have been more pleased to be wrong. She had the most brilliant green eyes he had ever seen. They were greener than any emerald. He had never seen a real emerald, but no gem could be as beautiful as those sparkling green depths. She quickly diverted her gaze back to her plate.

"So, Mr. Rawlings, do you run that big farm of yours all by yourself?" Allison asked.

He cleared his throat. "I have help. We hire extra hands when it gets busy."

"We?" David said, clearly looking for anything to question.

Lucas looked him squarely in the eyes. "I have a couple of guys who are pretty regular out at the place."

"Sorta like family?" David said in a condescending tone.

"I suppose you could say that." He swallowed hard. "This is delicious beef, Mrs. Swan." He turned back to his plate and took another bite. He hoped that would terminate Mr. Swan's accusing questions. He much preferred Mrs. Swan's polite, dignified ones.

"I thought Montana was cattle country." David said.

Lucas had to give Mr. Swan credit for his persistence. "Most of it is."

Before he could elaborate, Mrs. Swan, bless her soul, jumped back in the conversation.

"We aren't interested in cows and farming. We want to know more about you, your family."

Family? That was a subject he would like to avoid for the time being. Thankfully his mouth was full and he had a moment to think while he chewed slowly.

"Where are they from?"

"Virginia," he said upon swallowing.

"It must be really lonesome in Montana for you," she said, giving a sly sideways peek at his intended.

Lucas stole a glance, too. His bride-to-be sat staring at her plate with flushed cheeks. "It's not so bad," he said.

"Then why come all this way to get a wife?" David folded his arms across his chest, a challenge in his eyes. "Aren't there any women in Montana?"

"David."

He ignored his wife and went on. "Certainly there must be one that would want all you have to offer? This is all a little too good to be true. Maybe the Montana women know something we don't?"

"David!"

"What's wrong?" David leaned forward across the table. "What aren't you telling us?"

"Dessert anyone?" Miss Harrison's voice cracked as she pushed away from the table, successfully terminating the conversation. Allison cleared the dinner plates and served dessert.

"This pie is delicious, Mrs. Swan," Lucas said, breaking the long silence.

"Your fiancée helped," she said, indicating Miss Harrison. He looked at her and saw her blush. Again her first name wasn't used.

He had hoped to get to talk with her, but she kept her eyes on her plate and said nothing unless she was directly asked. Even then, her answers were short and to the point.

She wasn't at all like her letters. Her letters had been lengthy, flowing from one subject to another. But then he supposed he wasn't much like his letters either. He glanced at David, who glared back at him. What kind of a hold did this David Swan have on his fiancée? Once away from him, it would be easier to talk with her; he was sure of that.

But David drilled him with a menacing stare all night. What was his problem?

"May I escort you home, Miss Harrison?" Lucas asked after dessert. Maybe she would open up more when not under Mr. Swan's scrutiny.

Lucas didn't like how protective David was over *his* soon-to-be wife. She seemed to be shy with David around. She didn't seem so shy in her letters, but confident and self-assured.

Cinda didn't know what to say. She dreaded the thought of being alone with Mr. Rawlings, but how could she gracefully decline? Fortunately, David came to her rescue. "A walk sounds nice. We'll all go." He reached for his wife's coat.

Cinda was relieved she wouldn't be left alone with him.

"David, I'm not feeling well." Allison lowered herself to the sofa and rested her hands on her stomach. "We'll have to pass on that walk tonight."

"If you're not feeling well, I can stay," Cinda offered, seating herself next to Allison. She wanted to stay as much for herself as for her friend.

"Nonsense. You go on home. I'm just a little tired. We've got David to look after us." She patted her belly.

Cinda reluctantly accepted Lucas's offered arm. She didn't know what to say to this stranger. Should she tell him flat out what Vivian and Eve had done? He would think she was childish and backward. She could always tell him she changed her mind. Then he would think she was fickle and petty.

Lucas and his betrothed walked along in silence. The first half of the walk he tried to decide the best way to bring up the wedding. This wasn't as easy as he had thought. He had imagined strolling into town, getting hitched, and hopping on the next train out of town with a bride in tow. He had proposed. She had accepted. Everything had been settled. Hadn't it? Now he felt like he was starting all over—courting! If marriage weren't necessary, he would call the whole thing off and hightail it home.

She shivered in the cool night air. Lucas quickly shed his coat and draped it around her shoulders. When she looked up at him, he thought she might refuse it, but instead she pulled it around her more tightly. "Thank you." She spoke so softly he almost couldn't understand her.

The silence was finally broken. Lucas decided to take advantage of it and start a conversation. "You know I don't even know your first name." He succeeded in making his question light and inoffensive.

"You don't?" She looked up at him, startled.

He smiled down at her, seeing her face clearly in the moon light; long dark lashes framed her green eyes. "Your letters were all signed Miss Harrison," he said in a musing tone.

"Oh." She looked away. "I didn't realize."

"You do have a name, don't you?" he teased.

"Yes," she said, smiling. "Cinda."

"Cindy. That's pretty. I like it." He was making headway; at least she was talking to him. She looked at him sideways as if to say something, but she remained silent.

He was considering bringing up the wedding when they reached her house. He held the gate open for her. Cindy whisked through the gate and turned, closing it behind her. "Thank you for walking me home." She held out his coat to him.

He took the coat and looked down at the gate that was obviously meant to keep him away. "My pleasure." His bride-to-be was more reserved than her letters. She was a nice blend of grace and dignity, a real lady. Just what he was looking for.

Unsure of what he had done to make her skittish, he decided to take it slow. He wanted this to work. He would wait until tomorrow to broach the subject of the wedding. That gate wasn't the only barrier between them. "Until tomorrow," he said, tipped his hat, and left.

When Lucas got a little way down the street, he noticed the figure of a man leaning against a maple tree. *David Swan!* Lucas was furious. He strode up to David and stopped. "You followed us?"

David stood silent against the tree with his arms folded, suspicion etched on his face.

Lucas shook his head and walked on. He knew David didn't trust him. It didn't really matter. Once he and Cindy were married, the man would be out of their lives for good.

Cinda leaned against the porch rail and let out a sigh of relief when Mr. Rawlings disappeared into the night. Even though he had been polite all evening, she was uncomfortable. If she hadn't closed the gate on him, she was sure he would have insisted on coming up to the door, or worse, wanted to come inside.

Cinda crept into the house, careful to close the door without a sound. She wanted to slip upstairs undetected.

"That's the same man who was here this afternoon," her aunt called from the parlor when she was only three steps up the staircase.

She couldn't avoid her aunt now. Cinda put on a smile and glided into the parlor. Her uncle sat in a winged chair, puffing on his pipe. She greeted him with a kiss on the cheek. "Good evening, Uncle Barney." She turned to her aunt and said formally, "Aunt Ginny."

Aunt Ginny nodded as she poked at her sewing. "I didn't see a chaperone." Her words were clipped. "It's not proper for a young lady to be escorted without a chaperone."

Aunt Ginny usually referred to her as a lady but treated her like a child. Cinda knew her aunt wouldn't give up until she explained Lucas Rawlings. Cinda took a deep breath. "Allison invited Mr. Rawlings to supper. He's visiting."

"Does he have relatives in town? Who is he visiting?" her aunt asked, prying as usual.

How was she going to answer that question without lying? She certainly couldn't tell her aunt he was here to marry her. "He has friends in town." In a way, he did.

"I don't like this. I don't like this one bit," her aunt said between pinched lips.

"Oh, leave the poor girl alone," Uncle Barney said, waving his pipe in the air. "So she has a beau." Her uncle popped his pipe back in his mouth and sucked on it.

"Umph." Her aunt went back to jabbing at her sewing.

Thank you, Uncle Barney. He often stood up for her when her aunt got difficult.

Cinda retreated to her bedroom and readied herself for bed. She found sleep elusive and needed desperately to talk about the sufferings of the day. The stress-filled day swirled in her mind. She closed her eyes and lifted her ordeal up to her heavenly Father. A calm settled around her. She got out the letters from Mr. Rawlings and reread them with curiosity. Her fears renewed, she prayed again until she finally succumbed to sleep.

Chapter 5

*C*inda sprang out of bed. The sun had been up for some time. She rushed about, trying to dress as quickly as possible. She wanted to visit Allison and be back before Mr. Rawlings came to call. If her aunt got hold of him again, there was no telling what she would get the unsuspecting man to confess. She skipped breakfast, giving herself enough time for a quick visit with Allison.

When she heard her aunt's voice outside, Cinda peered out her bedroom window. She sucked in a quick breath and blinked several times. This couldn't be happening—Aunt Ginny and Lucas Rawlings. . .talking! Cinda quickly pinned her hat on and rushed down the stairs with her shawl draped over her arm.

When Cinda came up to the pair, Lucas was speaking. "Mrs. Crawford, I assure you, your niece and I had chaperones all evening. Mr. Swan was kind enough to accompany us and remain a distance back when I escorted Miss Harrison home."

David had followed them! Cinda wanted to turn around and hide in the house, but it would be more embarrassing if Lucas Rawlings stated his real reason for being there and her aunt said she knew nothing about it. Cinda didn't think their conversation had gotten around to it—yet. Her fear of her aunt finding out about Lucas Rawlings won over her trepidation of Mr. Rawlings.

"Mr. Rawlings, it's nice to see you again." Cinda wrapped her shawl about her shoulders. Although she managed to speak pleasantly, her stomach tightened. She turned to her aunt and said, "I'm going to look in on Allison. She was feeling poorly last night when I left her. I want to make sure she's doing better today."

Lucas replaced his hat and opened the gate for Cinda. "Good day, Mrs. Crawford." When the gate closed, Lucas offered his arm to Cinda. She took it and the two left the annoyed Aunt Ginny behind.

"You spend a lot of time at your friend's house, don't you?" Lucas said.

"Yes. We've been best friends since we were twelve. I don't know what I would do without her." Lucas's arm tensed.

Cinda felt as though the eyes of the whole town were on her as she walked along with this tall handsome stranger. She had wanted to talk to Allison before she saw him again. Last night in her sleeplessness, Cinda decided to tell Mr. Rawlings she couldn't possibly leave her best friend in her time of need. She would tell him she would come along later, then write a letter saying she had had a change of heart. She would tell him she was terribly sorry for his inconvenience and wish him well. But she needed to talk to Allison first to gain her courage. Allison could even tell him how much she needed Cinda to be around, this being her first baby.

Lucas drew in a deep breath. "Cindy."

She cringed slightly at the mispronunciation of her name. Her whole life she had corrected people on her name.

"I feel like I know you fairly well from your letters."

She knew him a little, too, through his letters that she had read three more times last night. It was evident he worked hard, loved God, family, and his land.

"I think we should talk about the arrangements. . .for the wedding, I mean."

Cinda bit her bottom lip. He had done it now. She couldn't avoid it any longer. He sounded as uncomfortable as she felt. What should she say? "Yes, I suppose we should" fell out of her mouth. Her knees went soft, and she hoped they didn't give out on her before she reached Allison's.

"I'll find a minister for this afternoon. . .if that's all right with you?"

"No!" This afternoon definitely was not all right. "I mean," she took a moment and a deep breath to calm herself, "the ministers are usually very busy on weekends."

"I suppose we can wait until Monday if we have to," Lucas said. "I was hoping to be on our way home by Monday."

Home? "You may not be able to get anyone until Tuesday." The longer she put it off, the more time she had to think.

He stopped her on Allison's lawn and said, "You haven't changed your mind, have you?"

Since she never agreed to marry him in the first place, she could honestly say no. "No, I haven't *changed* my mind."

He walked her up to the door. Cinda hoped he wouldn't stay; she couldn't very well talk about him to Allison with him there. He knocked on the door.

Allison answered the door and her usual friendly smile broadened. "Good morning."

"Good morning, Mrs. Swan. I hope you're feeling better this morning," Lucas said, removing his hat.

"Much better, thank you. A good night's sleep was all I needed." Her eyes flitted back and forth between Lucas and Cinda.

"I'm glad to hear that." He turned to Cinda and said, "I'll see you here later then."

Cinda nodded with a forced smile, and he was gone.

The two women sat in the parlor. "You seem to be getting along fine with Mr. Rawlings." Allison still smiled, quite pleased. "Last night, now early this morning, and he'll see you later. I take it things are going well with you two."

"It's awful. He's going to make arrangements with a minister." Cinda's voice cracked as she spoke.

"Then I take it you didn't tell him the truth?"

"I sort of told the truth," Cinda confessed. "I told him I hadn't changed my mind."

"Giving him the impression you are going to marry him."

"Allison, I know when I was younger I thought I could only be happy if I married and had children, but I have realized since then I can be happy by myself as well."

"I know you can, but isn't this an answer to your prayers?" Allison asked.

"I never prayed for this." Cinda's anguish painted every syllable. "I can't. I don't know how to be a wife. I can't even cook. What did Vivian and Eve tell him about me? Do you think he knows I can't cook?"

"You can learn."

"Who will teach me? Mr. Rawlings? I can't very well ask him to teach me to cook. He's expecting me to be the one who can cook."

"You're smart. You'll learn."

"No, I can't."

"Remember when Mrs. Pennywell had her baby? You went over and helped her with the housekeeping and her other three children while she was gaining her strength back. And what about Miss Stern? She was sick for nearly three weeks, and you took over her schoolroom. I believe her comment was 'If I'm not careful, Cinda Harrison, you'll steal my job right out from under me.' She was glad she had someone dependable and competent to call on. You didn't know what you were doing those times either. There are a number of other times you have helped out in a pinch. I don't believe there is anything you couldn't do. You always seem to rise to the occasion."

"That was different. I already knew those people. This is permanent."

Allison shook her head. "I thought I knew David well before we married. We grew up together, but I find out more and more about him all the time. The more I find out, the more I realize I don't know."

Allison's words did nothing to settle Cinda's anxiety.

Later, Vivian and Eve showed up to find out what had happened the previous night. The four women were chatting out on the porch when David returned home.

"I can't go through with it," Cinda said.

"Go through with what?" David asked.

"Marrying Lucas." Eve answered for her and giggled.

Eve sounded so chipper about this whole thing. After all, she wasn't the one expected to uproot herself and move hundreds of miles away and perform tasks she had never done before. He would find out and be angry with her. "I can't. I just can't."

"If you don't want to marry him, don't. I would be happy to break the news to Mr. Lucas Rawlings." David normally didn't like to speak on someone else's behalf, but since his wife was partly responsible, even in a small way, he would step in if Cinda wanted him to.

"Oh, David," Allison said.

Cinda wrung her hands in her lap. "I don't know what to do."

"You had better decide quickly because here comes Prince Charming," Vivian said.

David looked across the lawn at Lucas then back at Cinda. "Do you want to marry him?" His tone was urgent.

She pressed her teeth into her bottom lip. She wasn't sure what she wanted anymore. "No," she said, "I don't think so."

David bounded off the porch and stopped Lucas from coming any farther. "You are not welcome here."

Lucas took a controlled breath. "I'm here to see Miss Harrison. She's expecting me."

"She doesn't want to see you—ever again." The emphasis David put on "ever again" carried an unmistakable message.

The two men glared at each other for several minutes, then Lucas looked up at Cinda on the porch. She diverted her gaze, unable to look him in the eye. Lucas turned and walked away.

On her way home, Cinda couldn't stop worrying about whether or not she had done the right thing. She wrapped and rewrapped the end of her shawl around her hand. Mr. Rawlings was never ill-mannered and his intentions were honorable. She feared he might insist upon seeing her when David sent him away, but he left without making a scene. A scene David probably wanted. Why was David so itchy to get in a fight with a man so much bigger than himself?

Near her home, she saw Lucas Rawlings leaning casually against a tree, watching her approach. Her heart lurched up in her throat, and she came to a sudden halt. Had he really waited all this time for her? She continued walking slowly, not looking at him. When she was almost to him, he said, "Mr. Swan said you don't want to see me. I assume that means the wedding is called off?" His voice was level and calm, controlled.

Cinda stopped and sunk her head lower. "I–I'm sorry. I–I can't marry you." She nearly choked on each word. He said nothing. *What must he be thinking? Is he mad at me?* She inched her gaze up until she met him eye to eye. He didn't look mad, only disappointed and maybe hurt. She regretted her tactlessness.

"I thought you were the right woman. Obviously, I was mistaken."

A sudden pang inside her made her want to be that right woman. He turned and walked away without saying another word.

How could she have hurt the poor man? He had been kind and gentlemanly. She in turn cut his heart out. Tears burned Cinda's eyes as she ran into the house.

Chapter 6

I saw you out there with him again." Her aunt's curt words stung. "Don't tell me there is nothing. Twice yesterday and then twice again today. He's got designs on you. You shouldn't encourage the likes of him."

Cinda wanted to ignore her aunt and go to her room, but her aunt was insulting an innocent man. It wasn't his fault. She turned to face her aunt. "What do you mean the likes of him? There is nothing wrong with. . .Lucas." She felt funny using his first name when she hardly knew the man, but she did it to irritate her aunt. "And I'm not encouraging him."

"Lucas is it now?" Aunt Ginny said with shock in her voice. "If that isn't encouraging a man, being so familiar with him, I don't know what is."

"Yes, Lucas." Cinda swallowed hard, then blurted out, "He's my—fiancé."

"Fiancé!" Her aunt glared at her. "Then there has been something going on and for sometime, I would say."

"We've been corresponding for months, and he has now come to marry me. You have no say about it." Cinda had no idea why she was saying such things. She wanted her aunt to see she couldn't run her life entirely.

"I have plenty to say about it." Aunt Ginny perched her balled fists on her hips. "Your father would be very disappointed in you, sneaking around like this."

"I'm not sneaking around, and you leave my father out of this. You have no idea what he would think." She hated it when her aunt mentioned her father. She did it to get Cinda to do what she wanted her to do. Not this time.

"You don't think he would actually approve of that. . .that giant?"

Cinda walked across the room and said tersely, "He's just the kind of man my father would have chosen for me. He's a hardworking farmer, conscientious, and a perfect gentleman, too." In fact, Cinda thought him a lot like her father.

"Gentleman!" Her aunt shook her finger in the air as she spoke. "A true gentleman would never wear such an ill-fitting suit. He may have a few manners but no real sophistication. Your father was a true gentleman, and I know he would never—"

Cinda turned on her aunt, leveling her gaze. "My father was a caring, forgiving man who saw the good in people, who could see the good in anybody—even you." Her sharp tone surprised even herself.

"Your father spoke kindly of me?" Aunt Ginny's voice suddenly became soft.

Cinda noticed the change in her aunt but ignored it because of her own anger. "Of course. He never had a bad word to say about anyone."

After a moment, her aunt took a quick breath. "I still don't think he would approve of this Mr. Rawlings."

"You know nothing about Lucas, but you can easily judge him." Cinda shook her head and turned to leave the room.

"Well, you can't think much of him or you would have mentioned him before now. You must be embarrassed by him. Why else wouldn't you have introduced him to your uncle and me? I don't believe one word of this, not one word," her aunt called to Cinda's back.

"Believe what you like. You will anyway," Cinda shot back over her shoulder as she ascended the stairs.

Cinda closed herself in her room and ignored her aunt's knock at suppertime. Her stomach churned with misgivings, and she didn't have the vigor for another round with her aunt. She wanted to be alone.

She flitted from the dresser, to the window, and over to her writing desk, finally landing on the edge of the bed. As quickly as she sat down, she was up again making the rounds.

This was all Vivian's and Eve's doing. They were the ones who got Lucas and her mixed up in this. She felt sorry for Lucas Rawlings. He hadn't asked for their cruel joke. They hadn't meant for it to be cruel, but it had turned out that way. He believed every word they wrote and got caught in the snare with Cinda. Eve might have done it for the sheer thrill, but Cinda believed Vivian actually wanted to help. But Lucas Rawlings was innocent in all this. He had been led along and ended up with nothing. Cinda could give him one thing—the truth. It was the least he deserved.

If he really was in such a hurry, he would probably be on the first train he could catch. There was no reason for him to stick around now. She would have to go tonight before he left town, if he wasn't gone already. She whisked down the stairs.

"It's about time you came down," her aunt called out to her before she could reach the door. "I want you to tell your uncle what you told me this afternoon. He won't like it any better than I, and don't expect him to believe you either. Go on, tell him."

"Ginny," her uncle said, "if you want Cinda to tell me something, hush up so she can speak."

"You won't believe it, I tell you." Her aunt paused briefly. "Well, go on and tell him, or are you too ashamed?"

"Virginia! Not one more word from you until Cinda has spoken."

Ginny pinched her lips together.

Cinda looked from her aunt's accusing face to her uncle's kind, gentle face. He waited patiently until she had her thoughts collected and was ready to speak. "What Aunt Ginny is talking about is. . ." She hesitated. Where should she start—with Mr. Rawlings himself or with Vivian and Eve?

"The gentleman caller you had yesterday?" he asked when Cinda had trouble continuing.

"And today. He called again—" Her aunt stopped short when Uncle Barney shot her a look of reproof.

Cinda, too, had looked at her aunt but now she turned back to her uncle. "Yes, the gentleman caller. His name is Lucas Rawlings. He has a farm in Montana." Cinda tried to keep her tone even, unsure of how to say everything. She knew her aunt wouldn't let her get away before she had told him the whole story.

"Montana? He's a long way from home. What's he doing way out here?" her uncle asked. "Does he have business in town?"

Cinda looked over at her aunt. She had a smug look on her face. Cinda took a deep breath and turned back to her uncle. "He came to see me." Cinda dropped her gaze to the floor. "To marry me."

"Cinda? Why would Mr. Rawlings come all this way to marry you?" Her uncle's words were filled with shock and concern.

"We've been corresponding, sort of."

"You've been writing back and forth, and now he has come to ask you to marry him without consulting with me?" Her uncle's tone wasn't one of anger but rather concern.

"Not exactly." Cinda nervously told her uncle about the letters and Vivian's and Eve's part in the whole thing.

"I knew there was more to this than you were letting on," Aunt Ginny said, then shut her mouth and folded her hands primly in her lap.

"So you've decided to marry him?" her uncle asked.

"I don't know what to do, Uncle Barney." Cinda looked at her uncle, almost pleading for the answer. "I don't think I want to marry him, but I feel awful he came all this way for nothing. It's not right what they did to him."

"What are you going to do?"

"I think I should tell him the whole truth before he leaves. He at least deserves that." She didn't sound convinced.

Maybe she just wanted to see him one last time. She felt a little sad at the thought of never seeing him again. She felt a tugging, a longing where he was concerned. Now that she had had a chance to catch her breath, this was kind of exciting, like something she might read in a book. He was a nice, Christian man and deserved a good wife, whoever she was.

"Honesty is always best. Do you want me to walk you over?" her uncle said, offering to give Cinda a little courage.

"No. It's not far. I can manage by myself. I need to think about what I'm going to say."

"She can't go by herself," Ginny scolded.

Cinda was exasperated with her aunt and spoke curtly, "Of course I can. I'm a grown woman, not a child."

"Ginny, leave her be," Barney said.

Cinda swung her cape around her shoulders and caught a glimpse of her aunt's critical glare.

Cinda marched down the street. The gall of her aunt telling her what to do. Cinda was twenty-three years old. By most, she was considered an adult, but her aunt insisted on treating her like a child, telling her what she could and couldn't do, what to wear, and how to stand. As the thought crossed her mind, Cinda purposefully slouched. She had had it with her aunt; she would like to do something to prove to her aunt she was in control of her own life. She should run off and marry Mr. Rawlings, a stranger, just to show her aunt.

The more she thought about it, the more it appealed to her. She would have her own life then and do what she wanted. She could get out from under her aunt's thumb. It would be just her and Lucas. She would be far from her meddling aunt, though Cinda would miss her uncle. Cinda liked the idea, getting away from her aunt and caring for a man who maybe loved her, someone with whom she could possibly fall in love one day and build a life.

Was she crazy? Marry a stranger?

Other women had done it. Why not her?

No, the idea was absurd.

She prayed for him as she walked, that he would not be too angry with her and for the Lord to send him the right woman to be his wife.

Maybe she could think of someone suitable for him, so his trip wouldn't be a waste. Eve certainly was interested, but she didn't think Eve was his type. What was his type? The images of her unmarried friends and acquaintances skipped through her mind. None seemed right.

Not only did she feel a pang of jealousy when she unsuccessfully tried to picture him with someone else, but when she prayed she got the distinct impression she should be the one to go with him. If he left without her, she would be thwarting God's plan.

What a ridiculous notion. God might work in mysterious ways, but there was no mystery about this. It was Vivian's and Eve's doing. And it was downright odd. That's how she felt. . .odd.

She turned and headed for Allison's. A talk with her would straighten out her turbulent emotions.

"I mean, it is a good thing that he was willing to come and all," Cinda said, fidgeting with her skirt folds. "He has that big farm to run and all those animals to look after. It must be a lot of trouble to find someone to look after things."

Allison raised her eyebrows. "It sounds to me like you are trying to talk yourself into this."

"I am not! I just feel bad for him coming all this way for nothing."

"It doesn't hurt that he is the proverbial tall, dark, and handsome gentleman. May I emphasize the *tall* part. You'd not find another man like him if you searched the rest of your life. He has a lot to offer a woman. He has a lot to offer you."

"I'm not interested in—"

"You are too," she interrupted with a dismissive wave of her hand. "But that is neither here nor there. He's probably left town by now."

Cinda didn't tell her friend she was sure he hadn't. If he had left straight from Allison's when David turned him down for her, he could have. But he waited to hear the bad news from her. She was sure the next train wouldn't be until tomorrow, probably not until the afternoon. She also didn't tell her friend she was on her way over to see him.

She left Allison's more confused than when she arrived. Was she the right woman for Lucas Rawlings? When she again tried to imagine him with someone else, like Eve or Vivian, the pang of jealousy startled her. Why did she keep thinking of herself being with Lucas? Was it a leading from her heavenly Father. No! This couldn't be from God—just her confused imagination playing tricks on her. She might have a few wayward emotions, but one thing was for sure, she was not marrying Mr. Rawlings.

Chapter 7

*T*omorrow's train was not soon enough for Lucas. He had just come from the station to find out when the next train would leave. He entered his hotel room, shed his coat, and flung it to the floor. Next he shucked off the tight suit pants and slipped into a comfortable pair of Levi's.

He bathed and washed the grease from his hair. He hated having his hair slicked down, but it was necessary to keep his wavy hair out of his eyes and under control. He normally liked to run his hand through his hair, but he wouldn't touch it with that junk in it. He had been an idiot running around for two days in a suit with that stuff in his hair after a woman who probably never had any intention of marrying him.

The whole trip was a waste of time. He should have known he couldn't pull it off. At least one good thing had come from today—he wouldn't have to wear those tight suits or put grease in his hair again. He ran his hands through his hair just because he could. His room was warm, so he took off his shirt and stood by his open window to breath in the fresh air. He couldn't wait to get back to the wide-open space of Montana.

Where had he gone wrong? He had worn his best clothes so the lady wouldn't think him uncivilized. He slicked back his hair so she wouldn't think he was unkempt. He was a gentleman and acted politely, and he was sure he hadn't said anything offensive, not even to the intolerable David Swan.

From the start, jealousy churned in Lucas where Swan was concerned. The man obviously had a close relationship with the woman he had come to marry. Lucas had hoped she would trust him that much someday. Now there wasn't a chance of that. He had come all this way just to make sure she didn't change her mind. The farm and everything else was suffering because of his fool-hearted notion of getting married. He should have been more certain, waited a little longer. Why was he so impatient? Maybe he had been isolated on the farm far too long. He obviously didn't know how to properly act around a pretty woman. He had made a muck of the situation and would go home emp-ty-handed, though he wasn't quite sure what he had done wrong. Now who could he marry—Eve? He shuddered at the thought.

He looked into the night sky. *What do I do now, Lord? My way failed. I want to do Your will. I thought that's what I was doing. I guess I answered my own prayers and claimed it was You. I'm staying out of it from now on. I'll do the best I can with what You've given me. If You have a woman out there for me, You will have to bring her to me. I'm not chasin' after another one.*

A knock at the door interrupted his prayer. He didn't want to see anybody. Should he even bother to open it? It was probably one of the hotel staff. He raked his hands through his clean hair as he strode over to the door. Just as he reached it, he heard a second, lighter knock. He grabbed the doorknob and yanked the door open. "What?" he barked.

Miss Harrison stood in the hallway; long dark lashes framed her wide green eyes. Her mouth dropped open. "Oh my!" She covered her gaping mouth with her hand.

Lucas's mouth hung open as well. He couldn't help but stare. "M–Miss Harrison, Cindy. . .I–I mean Miss. . ." He took a slow breath to calm his rattled nerves. She was the last person he expected to see at his door and looking so pretty. "Won't you come in?" he offered politely, motioning with his hand into the room.

"Oh," she squeaked and looked away blushing.

"No. I didn't mean that." Inviting an unchaperoned woman into his hotel room, especially at this late hour, would be scandalous and certainly tarnish her reputation. Flustered, he continued, "What I meant was—I don't know what I meant. Wait there while I get my shirt." He retrieved his shirt, but when he turned back around, she was gone.

He fumbled with the buttons and crammed the tails into the waist of his jeans. He would have to hurry to catch her. He raced down the stairs and headed straight for the doors, but stopped when he saw her sitting in a lobby chair hunched over with her face in her hands, shaking.

Why do women always cry when they are in stressful or awkward situations? Lucas walked over to her and took a deep breath. "Miss Harrison? Are you all right?" he asked softly. "I didn't mean to scare you."

She drew in a quick breath and held it, trying to control herself. She looked up slowly.

Her smile surprised him. In fact, she looked as though she was struggling not to laugh. He smiled instinctively. "Did I miss something here?"

"It's this whole situation." She almost laughed again.

"You find this funny?" Lucas pulled his brows together.

"I was just looking at this whole situation from your point of view." She looked down at her reticule, fussing with it to avoid looking at him.

"You wrote those letters and came out expecting to find a willing bride. Instead you find me shying away and putting you off. Then I show up now, at night, and you half dressed."

"I assure you I find nothing humorous in all this." A hard edge crept into his voice. "I paid good money to travel all the way out here. I have a farm to run. I have obligations. There are things to be done. This isn't a joke."

Cinda took a deep breath. "I know. Mr. Rawlings, I truly am sorry about all your troubles. You must think me capricious. You have to understand, I received your letter yesterday only hours before you showed up. It was quite unexpected, I assure you." For some reason the nervousness she had felt the past two days melted away.

Lucas Rawlings had every right to be very cross with her for all the trouble he thought *she* had put him through, but he was gentle and was clearly trying to be understanding. She knew she wasn't making that easy for him. He had always spoken politely and with respect, even to her aunt and David, and never once had he tried talking her into anything.

There was no pretense in him now. He looked comfortable and no longer out of place in his clothes. He was much more suited to Levi's than a suit. His wavy hair around his face was less stiff. He looked more...natural. It was time to confess the truth and let him be on his way in peace. She couldn't make more a fool of herself than she already had.

Cinda looked him straight in the face to tell him the whole mixed-up story, Vivian and Eve included. When she gazed deep into his blue eyes, she saw her future. Lucas Rawlings was in that future. She imagined being on the porch of a small farmhouse, arm in arm with Lucas looking out at their spread. Lucas's deep voice pulled her back from her reverie.

"Miss Harrison, you were going to say something?" He combed a hand through his thick dark hair. She wondered if it felt as nice as it looked.

For a brief moment her dream was within reach. Could she find the courage to reach out and grab it? "Yes," she whispered. She couldn't push aside the feeling this was from the Lord.

"You certainly had a purpose in coming all the way down here," he paused and looked around the empty lobby, "alone."

Cinda snapped out of her daydream. "I've changed my mind." She forced the words out in one big gasp before she could change her mind again.

"I know. You made that clear this afternoon."

"No. I mean, I've changed it back." Cinda could feel her cheeks flush and her heart race.

"Are you sure?" Lucas furrowed his brow. "You said this before. Don't feel you have to. I don't want you to do this unless you are sure."

"I'm sure this time," she said, barely able to keep the quiver from her voice. She wondered if Lucas suspected how nervous she was at this moment.

Lucas looked at her for a moment, not sure if he should believe her this time. "It's getting late. Maybe we should talk about this in the morning. Here." He pointed to the lobby. "Just you and me. No Mr. Swan and no aunt."

"I can't in the morning."

Lucas rolled his eyes. She was putting him off again. "I'll walk you home, Miss Harrison."

She stood up to walk with him out of the hotel. "Tomorrow's Sunday. I have church."

"My train leaves in the afternoon. I'm not changing it again." The sooner he got out of town the better.

"I understand."

Lucas stopped and turned to her, studying her face. "You understand what?" He narrowed his eyes.

"You no longer want to marry me. . .after everything I've put you through." She shifted uncomfortably.

He wondered if she was playing some sort of game with him or if she had genuinely had a change of heart. "It's not that. I'm not sure you really want to get married. I don't have the privilege of idle time to dillydally in town to be turned down again." He raked a hand over the back of his neck. "I have a farm to run."

"I won't change my mind; I give you my word."

"We'll talk tomorrow." He would leave it at that, and if by God's grace anything came of it, there might be a wedding after all.

Chapter 8

*Y*ou are going to what?" Aunt Ginny had an irritating shrill in her voice.

"I'm going to marry Lucas Rawlings." She had made up her mind.

"Are you sure about this?" Her uncle's loving concern had always been a comfort.

"Yes, I'm very sure," she said to him. "I feel this is somehow in God's divine plan. I know this sounds all a bit...well, strange, but I believe in my heart this is God's will for my life."

"Just when do you plan on marrying this stranger? I remind you, he is a stranger." Her aunt tilted her nose in the air, her lips pinched.

Cinda turned slowly to her aunt. "Tomorrow." She swung her gaze back to her uncle and said with a touch of urgency in her voice, "It has to be tomorrow, Uncle Barney. He's leaving on the afternoon train."

He studied his niece's face for a moment, trying to read her heart. He always could. "If this is truly what you want," he said slowly and paused. Cinda nodded. "Then we had better get busy. There is a lot of work to be done." Her uncle took her by the hand and led her upstairs. Dumbfounded, her aunt remained behind in the parlor.

Her uncle opened the door to the third room that they used for storage. Cinda had seldom been in this room. He pointed to two trunks and told her she could pack her belongings in them. Then he took her over to the corner where a dusty old trunk sat.

He knelt down beside the trunk and patted it lovingly. "These were your mother's things." He opened the lid and turned to look up at Cinda, still standing. "Now they're yours." Cinda's mother was Uncle Barney's younger sister.

Cinda caught her breath. She touched the cameo at her throat as she slowly sank down beside her uncle at the treasure chest. She skimmed her hand over the beautiful quilt that topped the trunk.

"These have always been yours. I was never sure when to give them to you. Now seems like the right time." His voice was heavy with emotion.

Cinda turned to her uncle and hugged him. "Thank you. Thank you so very much." Pulling away she asked, "But how did you do this? I thought

49

everything was sold at auction to pay my father's debts?"

"I managed to save a few things. I couldn't let my baby sister's whole life be sold off to strangers." Tears welled in his eyes, threatening to spill over, but he kept them in check.

However, Cinda's tears ran free as she hugged him again. Cinda wanted to sift through her mother's things, but she knew she didn't have the time to dwell on the past. Her future was at hand.

Closing the trunk, her uncle said, "Let's get those empty trunks. You have a lot of packing to do."

Lucas arranged to meet his fickle bride immediately after church. He came in a little late to the service and stood in the back. He chose to wear olive green pants with a matching green and tan plaid shirt. He debated whether or not to wear one of his ridiculous suits. He decided if these clothes were good enough for church back home, they were good enough here. He was tired of pretending to be someone he was not.

He leaned against the back wall, resting one foot on it. He looked around until he spotted the back of Cinda's head. She was seated near the front with her aunt and a middle-aged man Lucas assumed was her uncle. If the aunt was any indication of what the uncle was like, he wasn't so sure he wanted to meet him.

He supposed the sermon was good. His thoughts bounced back and forth between his bride-to-be and praying for guidance. Was marriage to this woman the right answer? He thought it was, but maybe in his eagerness to solve his own problem, he was stepping on God's toes. When he left Montana, he was sure of God's will. Now he wasn't as confident.

When the service ended and people filed out, he watched Cinda as she made her way down the narrow aisle, greeting friends along the way. She wore a white linen dress with a touch of ruffles and lace at the neck, elbow cuffs, and the skirt hem—a lovely vision. Was it possible that she was really going to marry him?

He remained against the wall, gazing at her. When she finally caught sight of him, he smiled and tipped his head to her. She blushed and bit her bottom lip. She turned away and headed back up the aisle.

He had his answer. She had changed her mind once again and didn't even have the courage to tell him. He shoved away from the wall and exited at the tail end of the masses, though several people remained inside.

Halfway across the church lawn he heard a female voice call his name. "Mr. Rawlings!"

He turned to see Cinda coming toward him with her aunt and uncle and Mr. and Mrs. Swan. He surveyed the small mob descending on him and braced himself, for what, he wasn't sure.

The group stopped in front of him. Cinda looked from him to Allison and David. "You've already met my very best friend and her husband, Mr. and Mrs. Swan." Lucas nodded at Allison and shook David's outstretched hand. Distrust still lingered in David's eyes, but he said nothing. Cinda drew Lucas's attention. "You've met my aunt, Virginia Crawford."

The aunt's condescending expression told him she probably had a thing or two to tell him, but she held her tongue.

He nodded to her. "Ma'am."

Then Cinda's smile broadened. "This is my uncle, Barney Crawford."

Lucas shook the man's hand. "Good to meet you, Mr. Crawford." At least he hoped it was a good thing.

"It's good to finally meet you, too, and it's Barney." Barney's casual nature and warm smile put Lucas at ease.

Lucas scanned the group and settled his bewildered gaze on Cinda. He wasn't sure what this little get-together was about.

"We should be getting along. Pastor Cooke doesn't have much time," Allison said.

"We'll meet you two inside." Uncle Barney guided the group toward the church.

With raised eyebrows, Lucas looked down at Cinda. She understood his unspoken question of *What is going on?*

"Pastor Cooke can perform the ceremony, now, before he goes off visiting." Cinda diverted her eyes to the buttons of his shirt. "If you want, Mr. Rawlings."

"Get married right now?"

Cinda nodded, looking up only as far as his chin.

"How did you manage that?" Lucas folded his arms across his chest. "I thought your pastor was too busy on the weekends."

"Pastor Cooke and my uncle have been best friends since they were babies." Cinda looked him in the eye with a boldness he had not seen in her yet.

Lucas gazed into those rich green eyes and lost himself. She was going to marry him. Somehow he knew he didn't deserve her. After a few moments of silence, he said, "If indeed we are getting married, Cindy, I think you should start calling me Lucas."

Her cheeks tinged pink and her gaze dropped back to his chin. "Then...Lucas...you should start calling me Cinda."

"What?" He had gotten caught on the melodious way his name sounded on her lips, so he didn't quite catch what she said.

"My name is Cinda, not Cindy."

"Cinda," he said to himself, to establish the sound of it. "Why didn't you tell me I was saying your name wrong?"

"It didn't seem important."

"Because you weren't planning on marrying me, and I would soon be gone."

Cinda nodded.

They walked side by side back to the church. Lucas wasn't sure if he should really believe she was going to go through with it this time.

Uncle Barney was waiting for them at the door. Another man ushered Lucas to the altar, across from where Allison stood as matron of honor. Lucas looked out over the curious crowd.

In the front sat Cinda's aunt, Mr. Swan, Miss Van Dornick, and Miss Weston. A half dozen others Lucas didn't know were huddled in the first few pews. Was this really going to happen? Or was this the grand finale to the whole big joke? He should cut and run while he had the chance.

The first note of the wedding march startled him. The door at the back of the church opened. Barney Crawford proudly escorted his niece down the aisle. Lucas realized she had a specific reason for wearing that white linen dress today. A piece of lace covering her head and face served as a veil. Since there were no flowers in bloom yet, her bouquet was a nicely done bundle of white ribbons and lace.

The woman coming down the aisle would be his wife now and forever. Should he really do this? She was sweet, and he could see she had gone to a lot of trouble since her change of heart last night. But then, he, too, had gone through a lot of trouble to come all this way for her. He hoped he was doing the right thing.

Lord, right or wrong, please bless this marriage.

Cinda tried to calm the butterflies swarming in her stomach. This was it. She couldn't—wouldn't—back out now. She was really getting married. To think, three days ago she had never even heard of Lucas Rawlings, and now their lives would be forever entwined.

The ceremony rushed by in a blur. Lucas placed an aged silver wedding band on her finger. Her stomach danced at the thought it could be a family heirloom.

When Pastor Cooke said, "You may kiss the bride," she drew in a quick breath. She knew this was coming. She had been to weddings before. The groom usually grabbed his bride and kissed her passionately. Once she even saw one groom who kissed his young bride for a whole minute while his friends whooped it up. The poor girl was red-faced before he let her go.

Lucas lifted the veil, put his finger under her chin to lift her face, and softly pressed his lips to hers. The tingling started at her lips where they touched and spread like wildfire throughout her body. She hadn't expected such gentleness from this large man. Much to her surprise, she found she liked his tender kiss.

Cinda stood on the train platform with her friends and family.

Eve waved a gloved hand in the air. "I can't believe you got to the altar before I did. I had better hurry up or I'll be the only one not married. Can you imagine me an old maid?" Eve giggled.

Vivian shook her head and rolled her eyes. She gave Cinda a quick hug and whispered in her ear, "You take good care of *our* Lucas."

Cinda wanted to laugh but settled for a smile.

Allison handed Cinda her copy of the *American Frugal Housewife*. "All my favorite recipes are marked."

"I can't take your cookbook."

Allison leaned into her so only she could hear. "You need it more than I do."

Cinda took a deep breath. "What am I going to do?"

"You'll do great. Just don't worry about it."

"Thank you, Allison. Good-bye, David, Eve, Vivian. I'm going to miss you all." Cinda turned to her aunt and uncle who were waiting a few feet away.

Aunt Ginny handed her several envelopes bundled together, each containing a different type of vegetable seed. "Here. You should plant a garden right away."

"Thank you." Cinda gave her aunt a quick peck on the cheek.

Her aunt had a shrewd look on her face and gave her head a little shake. "I hope you don't regret your hasty decision."

Cinda noticed a sad expression skim across her uncle's face as he looked at his wife.

"All aboard!" the conductor yelled.

Lucas put his hand on the small of her back. "We need to get going."

Cinda kissed her uncle on the cheek and hugged him. "Good-bye, Uncle Barney. I'll miss you most."

"I'll miss you, too, Sweetheart. You're like my very own daughter." He couldn't keep a tear from falling to his cheek and quickly brushed it away.

Cinda's tears cascaded down her cheeks as Lucas assisted her onto the train. She kept turning her head away trying to hide the tears. Her lacy handkerchief wasn't sufficient enough to capture all the moisture.

Lucas pulled out his and handed it to her. "If you're going to have a proper cry, you need a proper handkerchief."

"I'm sorry. I don't mean to cry all over the place." She sniffled. "I'm just going to miss everyone."

"My mother used to say, 'If you don't let the tears free, they will singe your heart until you have no feelings left.'" He pointed his finger and shook it in the air at an invisible person and said in a false voice, "'You can't rightly be human without feelings now, can you?'"

She took the handkerchief with a smile, but somehow she didn't feel like crying any more.

Chapter 9

*a*fter the train was underway, the conductor came by to check for tickets. While Lucas showed their tickets, Cinda rested her head and closed her eyes for a second. The events of the past three days had caught up to her.

"Are you all right? Is anything wrong?"

Lucas's concerned voice woke her. The conductor was just passing. She hadn't realized it possible for a person to fall asleep that fast. "I'm fine. I'm just tired. I was up all night packing and getting ready."

Lucas's concerned look softened. "Rest your head on my shoulder." He wrapped his arm around her slender shoulders and drew her close.

Cinda knew she should protest. A lady never slept in public. But she was exhausted. She would rest her tired eyes for a few minutes; there would be no harm in that.

As his new bride drifted off to sleep, her hand slipped from her lap to his. Startled by the sudden touch, he realized she was already asleep. He wrapped his big calloused hand around her slender, feminine one. He wasn't sure how he would feel about the added responsibility of a wife. It surprised him that he kind of liked it. Had he made the right decision? Was this really the only solution? It was the only one he could think of at the time. He still couldn't think of a better one. It was now done, and he would do what he could to make her happy. He gently squeezed her hand.

Cinda descended from the train, relieved to be off of it. Two days of rattling around on a train had made her joints sore. "How many more days will it take to get to your farm?"

"Our farm," Lucas corrected. "We should be at *our* farm the day after tomorrow if all goes well."

"If all goes well?"

"Sometimes travel out west can be. . .unpredictable."

Unpredictable? Just what did that mean?

She was glad to hear they wouldn't catch the stagecoach until the morning. The worst of the trip was over, she hoped. They stood at the front desk of a local hotel.

"One room, sir." The desk clerk confirmed Lucas's request while pointing at the register book.

Lucas, poised to sign, suddenly turned to Cinda. "Unless you would prefer two? I have money enough for separate rooms."

She looked up into his caring face and saw understanding in his blue eyes. It was still difficult to get used to having to look *up* to him.

"This isn't that kind of hotel," the desk clerk said sharply. "We don't rent rooms to unmarried couples."

Lucas ignored the clerk's curt remark, patiently waiting her reply.

She was his wife; he was her husband. There was no point in wasting money or putting off the inevitable. "One room will be fine," she replied softly.

Lucas studied her a moment before turning back to the registry, signing their names, Mr. and Mrs. Lucas Rawlings. He plucked the key from the speechless clerk, and they headed up the stairs with their bags.

He knew he should have automatically suggested they get two rooms until they knew each other better, but he wanted to make her completely his before. . .things. . .got difficult. The more he had to tie her to himself, the more she would feel as though she belonged with him. He wouldn't have pressed if she wanted separate rooms, but she had agreed to one. As it was, they lay in bed next to each other and did nothing more than sleep.

Lucas and Cinda took the last two seats on the crowded stagecoach. After an hour of bouncing and rocking along, Cinda concluded this was definitely worse than the constant rumblings of the train. Lucas seemed unaffected by the jouncing and kept his arm securely around her to keep her from bouncing off the seat.

As the morning wore on, the road got bumpier. She would rattle to pieces if this kept up. The jarring made it impossible to have any kind of conversation. Everyone sat in silence, if you could call the knocking and banging silence.

"You can trade seats with me, ma'am," offered a heavyset man with dark hair and a full face of whiskers. He wore a business suit and sat in the front seat that faced the rear of the coach. "It's a little less bumpy up here."

Cinda's eyes widened with hope. Less bumpy sounded wonderful.

"No thank you, sir," Lucas answered before Cinda could accept. "We'll stay put."

How dare he speak for her! She wasn't a child. Didn't he realize how uncomfortable she was? Besides she was offered the seat, not him. "But Lucas—" she started to argue, then decided a full stagecoach wasn't the proper place to question her new husband. She would suffer for now and discuss it with him later. She hadn't thought she might be going from Aunt Ginny telling her what to do to another.

Lucas pointed to the slender blond man also seated in the front. "Most people get sick riding backward."

Cinda stared at the peaked man just as he lunged for the window and heaved his breakfast. She looked up at Lucas. "Oh."

Lucas shrugged his shoulders. "Change if you think your stomach can handle it."

Cinda raised her eyebrows. "I–I think I'll stay put." She realized Lucas wasn't trying to treat her like a child but was protecting her from further discomfort.

Just then the coach tipped down on one of the front corners and came to an abrupt halt. Everyone piled out. A wheel had broken. After the driver and the rest of the men helped in the repairs, they were on their way.

It was only a quarter of an hour before they stopped at a station for lunch and to change the team. The driver would only allow a fifteen-minute stop. They had lost much time with the broken wheel.

At the station they were served a barely palatable meal. Cinda could only choke down half a biscuit at Lucas's insistence. Getting back on the stage held little appeal, but she was glad they weren't staying at the station longer than necessary. She just wanted the trip to be over. She would have to endure this the remainder of today and again tomorrow.

The stage went faster than it had in the morning, while the ride got rougher and bumpier. She feared the coach would shake apart. Cinda noticed Lucas's grip grow tighter around her. She wondered if the jolting trip was finally getting to this strong, seemingly calm man next to her.

Since they had stopped for food and fresh horses, the old lady in the back had repeated in agony, "We be over. We be over." The woman's words grated on Cinda's nerves. She also wished for the ride to be over. When Cinda thought she couldn't take any more of the jarring, the coach teetered. Lucas wrapped both arms around her, cradling her protectively against himself and whispered, "Here we go."

Cinda held on tightly and heard herself scream as the coach toppled over onto its side. They quickly came to a stop. The horses couldn't drag the overturned coach far.

Lucas quickly pushed people off Cinda. "Are you all right? Are you hurt?" People were moaning and groaning all around them.

"I–I'm f–fine." At least she thought so. She was not quite sure what had happened, but at least the bouncing had stopped.

"Is anyone hurt?" Lucas asked the whole group. The responses were all negative.

Someone flung open the side door that was now on top, and the driver helped pull out the passengers. Lucas helped Cinda and the others before he climbed out.

Once outside, Lucas rushed over to Cinda. "Are you sure you're not hurt?"

"I'm fine." Cinda looked at him, amazed. "You knew the stagecoach was going to overturn." She was both astonished and accusing. "Why didn't you warn me?"

"It doesn't always happen. I didn't want to worry you unnecessarily. The trip is hard enough without worrying about that, too."

He reached out to touch her, but she pulled away. Anger rose in her. How could he not warn her?

"If you've ever ridden a coach before, you would already know it could happen." He lifted his shoulders slightly.

She glared at him.

"And if not," he held his hands out palms up, "there is no sense worrying about it needlessly."

Consoling her would do no good. She was too shaken and angry, as much at him as herself for letting it scare her so.

He looked uncomfortable and pointed back to the stage. "I should help the others right the coach so we can be on our way again."

After the bone-jarring box was set on its wheels, Lucas came to escort Cinda.

"It's time to get back on that thing, isn't it?" Cinda sneered at the stage.

Lucas nodded with a sympathetic smile. "I'm sorry."

"That was the most terrifying experience in my entire life. I will not soon forget it." Cinda took a shuttered breath to keep the tears at bay and shook her finger at him. "And I'm mad at you for not warning me. I don't like surprises." She strode off in a huff, not really so much mad as scared.

They bumped and bounced along mile after mile. Three more people got sick, one inside the coach. But at least they stayed upright the remainder of the day. Cinda's stomach had knotted from worry. Lucas had been right not to forewarn her. At least she had half a day with peace of mind. When they finally stopped in a town slightly larger than the one the night before, Cinda was so overwrought she could hardly stand, let alone think about food.

She clutched Lucas's arm as she got off. "I can't do that again."

"You don't have to."

She looked up at him. "Really?" Didn't they have another day of travel before they reached their destination? Relieved, she hung onto his arm, still unable to stand on her own.

"Really." He smiled down at her. "We'll take my wagon."

Cinda snapped up straight and let go of him. "You had a wagon and made me ride on that awful stagecoach?" Why would he do that to her?

"I didn't have a choice." He held his hands out in front of him. "The axle broke on the way. If I had waited for it to be fixed, I would have been late in arriving at your place. I didn't want you to think I wasn't coming. I wanted to have the wagon waiting in town when we got off the train, but traveling out west is unpredictable."

Cinda nodded. She was beginning to understand these unpredictabilities. "Lucas, are there any other surprises I should know about? I would like to prepare myself. There isn't anything else you're keeping from me, is there?"

Lucas raised his eyebrows but remained silent.

Cinda put her hands on her hips. "Is there anything else I should know about on this trip? Any more traveling unpredictabilities?"

"No. The wagon should be a better ride, and I promise not to turn the wagon over." His smile asked for forgiveness.

They checked into the hotel for the night, but Cinda refused to eat. Her stomach was still in knots from the trip.

Though they got only one room again, he let her go to sleep undisturbed. She was frazzled after her harrowing day. She needed sleep and looked so peaceful in her slumber. He hated to wake her for another day of travel.

She seemed better in the morning, and he was glad to see her eat a healthy breakfast.

The wagon was loaded with Cinda's trunks, some food and water, blankets, and a few tools. Cinda hesitated, staring at the wagon, when

Lucas reached out his hand to help her aboard. "You promise this will be better?"

Lucas smiled. "I promise. We can stop whenever you want."

With a heavy sigh, Cinda climbed up and sat on the thin cushion on the seat. At least by tonight the grueling trip would be over.

True to his word, the trip was calm and smooth. Lucas even made a place for her to lie down in the back if she wanted. After the noon meal, they walked in silence alongside the horses for awhile.

She wondered if her new husband felt he had made a mistake in marrying her. He hadn't tried to touch her at night as was his husbandly right or even kiss her since the wedding. Was he disappointed in her?

Lucas rolled his eyes as he thought about how different today's travel was from yesterday's. If the lady was mad about not being warned about an upset coach, she would be livid before long, because the end of this journey was full of little surprises.

She wasn't very much like her letters. She was better, so much better in every way. She wasn't nearly as uppity and high-strung but every bit a lady. It was like getting to know her all over again. She was so quiet. He had expected to be plied with questions like in her letters. He was glad he wasn't. There were some questions he wasn't ready to answer just yet. There was nothing stopping him from asking the questions, though.

"How did you come to live with your uncle and aunt?" He wanted to know as much about her as he could.

Cinda snapped up straight. She looked up at him, staring for a moment before answering. "My mother died when I was nine and my father three years later. Uncle Barney and Aunt Ginny are my only relatives, so I came to live with them."

Her answer came out smooth, without a drop of emotion. Then she turned the question back on him. "What about you? Do your parents live near you? Will I be meeting them?"

"They passed away nine years ago," *and left me with the farm and everything that goes with it.* He noticed his answer also came out sounding rehearsed and emotionless. He wondered what thoughts tailed her answer.

"I'm sorry to hear that," she said, her voice full of emotion now. After a pause and a breath, she asked, "How much farther to your farm?"

Lucas looked down at her. "Our." He had to get her thinking of the place as hers, that she belonged there with him.

Cinda smiled shyly. "All right. How much farther to *our* farm?"

Lucas smiled. "I suspect just after lunch tomorrow."

"Tomorrow?" She halted. "But I thought we were going to get there today. No more traveling unpredictabilities. You said there was nothing more about the trip I needed to know."

"We aren't traveling at the same reckless speed as the stagecoach. I thought you would appreciate the slower pace." Also he could use the extra day to get her used to the idea of belonging on the farm with him. He didn't want this peaceful time with her to be over so soon.

"I do." Cinda's gaze dropped to the dry prairie grass. "I just thought the trip would finally be over."

"Well hop in, little lady," he said in an old-timer drawl, thumbing his hand back to the wagon, "and I'll see if we can make it home before the moon is high in the sky. You'll have to hold on tight. I can't promise we'll stay upright, but I'll do my best."

Cinda laughed at his antics. "No, thank you. I think I'll walk."

Cinda knew Lucas was a man with whom she could and would fall in love and they could build a life together. She found she was comfortable around him. He made her laugh and feel at ease, never pushy, always letting her make her own decisions, like where to sit in the stage. It was a small thing, but it was the type of thing her aunt wouldn't have let her do—end of discussion.

She couldn't remember the last time she walked with someone who could match her own natural stride. It was her father, she supposed, but then he had generally altered his gait to match hers as she normally did for others. Her new husband was probably doing the same for her. His long legs glided along smoothly. He didn't seem to mind slowing down for her. In fact, he stopped for breaks before she needed them. For a man who was in an all fire hurry to leave town, he wasn't in much of a hurry now.

Lucas gave her the option of going a little out of their way to a town to stay the night in another hotel or cutting across the countryside and sleeping in the wagon. She opted for the shortcut. Lucas wouldn't have suggested it if it weren't safe, and he had a feather mattress in the wagon that would be as comfortable as any hotel. She felt rather adventuresome and seemed to surprise her husband.

They stopped by a babbling creek among the trees and ate beans, potatoes, and biscuits Lucas amazingly cooked over the open fire. She caught him staring at her again. While he was doing every little chore, whether building the fire or tending the horses, he stole glances at her. What was on his mind? She felt her cheeks warm as he came closer.

"If you're tired, you can go to bed." He pointed to the back of the wagon. "I know the traveling has been hard on you."

"I'm not tired. I slept well last night, and today's travel was pleasant as you promised."

His mouth curved up slightly, seemingly pleased at the fact she noticed he had tried to make today more enjoyable. "Montana is a might prettier place now that you're here."

She smiled at his compliment.

His gaze softened. "You're very beautiful."

"Me?"

"Yes, ma'am. You are the only one here. Hasn't anyone told you that before?"

Her uncle and friends had, but she didn't think that counted. "I didn't think you thought so. I mean you never—I mean, you don't exactly get to choose a mail-order bride on looks. It's a sight unseen deal."

"Oh, I noticed," he said with a grin. "Don't get me wrong, I've wanted to make this marriage real. It's just that you have been so overwrought and tired from the journey. I thought it best to wait; but I don't want you to think I don't want you, because I do."

She diverted her gaze to her husband's chin, his shirt front, the trees in the distance behind him. "I'm not tired tonight."

He stepped closer and caressed her upper arms. "Are you sure?"

She looked up at his tender face and nodded.

He kissed her tenderly before taking her in his arms.

Chapter 10

*L*ucas pointed to the horizon. "There it is. Our farm." He wrapped his arm lovingly around her shoulder and drew her close. "We're home."

Home. That sounded nice. Her very own home. A place for the two of them to build their lives together. She looked up at her new husband and straightened herself. For the first time in years she didn't feel tall. In fact, next to Lucas she felt short... almost.

As they got closer, Cinda could see the house was quite large. The other homes they had passed on their journey were considerably smaller. "It's so much larger than I expected."

"My father built it for my mother. Most of what my father did was for my mother." He gave her shoulder a little squeeze. "She said when they were first married, she was afraid my father would go broke. He would get her everything she said she liked. She quickly learned to keep quiet except for her deepest heart's desires. This was her deepest of all desires—a home in which to raise a family."

He looked down at her, warmth in his bright blue eyes. "Now it's our turn." He paused then said, "How many children do you want?"

"A whole house full," she said shyly and looked away. "I was an only child. I always wanted brothers and sisters. I was very lonely when my parents died. I would dream about belonging to a big family. That probably sounds silly to you."

"No, it doesn't."

He sounded so sincere she was drawn to look back up at him. His smile consumed his entire face, even his eyes were smiling. She couldn't help but smile back.

"A big family sounds real nice." His soft tone caressed her.

As they pulled into the quiet farmyard, Cinda took in the full view at once. She could see the weathered two-story house was missing curtains in the windows and probably a woman's touch on the inside as well. Across the yard stood a great barn with a chicken coop nestled next to it. There were several chickens wandering free around the yard pecking at the ground. On the other side of the barn was a corral with two horses at the water trough. When the wagon rolled in the yard, the two corralled horses raised their heads and nickered a greeting. The team hitched to the wagon snorted in response and bobbed their heads.

They recognize each other. How cute.

Lucas pulled the wagon to a halt with a "whoa." He seemed anxious, looking around for something. He jumped down and turned, lifting Cinda to the ground. She noticed he had a strange look on his face, like he was nervous, expectant.

He probably wondered what she thought of the place. She wouldn't keep him waiting any longer. "It's wonderful, Lucas."

He gave her half a smile before the barn doors burst open. Two identical, carrot-topped, ragamuffin girls ran across the yard squealing, scattering squawking chickens. Their worn dresses were too small for them and so dirty you could hardly tell the dresses were once yellow. At least Cinda thought they were yellow.

Lucas took a few steps forward and knelt down on one knee with open arms. They plowed into him, but he remained solid and scooped them up.

"We missed you soooo much," they said in unison, then smothered his cheeks with kisses.

"I missed you both soooo much." His voice thick with adoration.

A young man exited the barn and came toward them. He was built a little more slender than Lucas. In his Levi's and tan shirt he could pass for Lucas's twin at a distance. As he reached Lucas, Cinda could tell he was a couple of inches shorter and didn't have quite the same pronounced features as Lucas. He was a younger version.

"We expected you back two days ago," the young man said. She realized he must be Lucas's brother.

"It looks like you were expecting us," Lucas said, letting his gaze run up and down his dirt-covered brother. "We ran into a few snags."

The brother looked past Lucas and eyed Cinda. "She's a pretty one. Didn't expect that. Tall too. Have you sampled her cooking? I can almost taste a good home-cooked meal."

He was in for a surprise the first time he came visiting for supper and found out she couldn't cook. What Cinda really wanted to know about was the two dirty five-year-old girls in Lucas's arms. He said he had no children, but these two greeted him with a great deal of fondness, and he returned the feelings. Were they the brother's girls?

Cinda was rooted in place next to the wagon. She wanted to know who these people were, but she couldn't get herself to move forward.

Lucas turned around with his arms still brimming with the two wiggly little girls and led his brother over to her. She took a deep breath.

"Trev, this is Cinda."

"Howdy," he said, touching his thumb and finger to his hat.

"Cinda, this is my brother, Trevor." Lucas looked at Cinda, waiting.

"It's nice to meet you, Trevor." Why hadn't she thought to ask if he had any siblings? "Are these your girls?" she asked Trevor. It would set her mind at ease when he said yes.

"Nope," was his simple reply.

No? Then who did they belong to? She wasn't sure what to say to the unexpected brother, but she wanted to be polite. "Do you live near here?"

Trevor looked to Lucas, then back to Cinda. "Not near. Here." He said it so matter-of-factly, like Cinda should have known already.

Cinda looked up at Lucas. He had a look that Cinda could only interpret as *surprise*.

Lucas seemed uncomfortable and couldn't hold her stare. He jiggled the two girls in his arms and asked, "Who is who?" He looked from one redheaded little girl to the other and back again.

The girls giggled and said together, "You know."

Lucas moved each girl up and down as if weighing them and said to the one in his left arm, "You feel like you weigh just enough to be Davey."

The little girl giggled a yes.

Lucas turned to the girl in his right arm and said, "That must make you Dani."

"Yes," the girl chuckled.

He looked hesitantly back at Cinda and said, "These are my nieces."

Cinda was relieved. They weren't his.

Lucas raised the girl on the right a little higher and introduced her. "This is Daniella." Then he raised the other girl a little. "And this is Daphne."

"Hello, Daniella. Hello, Daphne. It's a pleasure to make your acquaintance." She curtsied slightly to the girls. "And where are your mommy and daddy?"

"They died," Daniella said.

"Bofe of them," Daphne said sadly.

She noticed Lucas eyeing her cautiously.

Cinda's insides tightened. "The girls live here, too?" It was more a statement of recognition than a question.

Lucas nodded.

Surprise!

Two bachelors trying to raise a pair of little girls must be hard. She could understand why they wanted a woman around. She just wished her husband had forewarned her.

At that moment, a horse and rider came racing across the pasture. Everyone turned to watch the rapid approach. The pair entered the farmyard at full speed. When they were almost upon the group, the rider pulled up the horse. Cinda let out a little yelp as the horse skidded to a halt, spraying her dress with dirt. The boy jumped down off his mount before it came to a complete stop. Horse and rider panted. He slapped the dirt from his denim pants.

"Marty, this is Cinda," Trevor offered with an eager grin.

"Howdy," Marty greeted gruffly.

Another brother. Surprise.

"Marty, take off your hat," Lucas reprimanded. The boy did as he was told. "Cinda, this is my sister, Martha."

Sister! There was absolutely nothing about her that would give anyone reason to believe she was a girl. She was dressed like her brothers, including the hat. Her curly, dark hair was cropped just below her ears and tucked behind them. She walked like a boy. She behaved like a boy. And she looked like a boy.

"Hello, M—Martha," Cinda stammered out.

"Marty," the girl spat back.

"Aunt Marty, can we ride Flash?" Daniella asked.

Marty looked to Lucas for approval.

"Please?" Daphne begged, lacing her hands together.

Lucas nodded and raised each of the girls up onto Flash. "You go slow with them. No trotting."

Lucas gave Cinda a quick, shy glance as he went to the back of the wagon and carried her trunks and the other supplies to the porch. Trevor offered to take care of the horses and led them off to the barn.

Lucas took Cinda inside the house to show her around. There was a sitting room with a couple straight-backed chairs, a worn settee, and a wooden rocker. The dining area had a large wooden plank table with a bench along each side and a chair at each end.

Next to the dining area was the kitchen. It was obvious this was not a room they cared much for. The small worktable was dirty like the rest of the room and piled with semi-clean dishes. The sink had the really dirty dishes. The few shelves were either broken or looked unstable. The whole house looked like all traces of a woman's care had been erased over time.

Lucas looked ashamed at the house, like he was seeing it for the dump it had become. He probably had been so busy in the fields, with other farm chores and his nieces, that the inside of the house never mattered as long as the roof didn't leak.

As Cinda looked around the kitchen dumbfounded, Lucas's brother came in through the kitchen door. He certainly made short work of caring for the horses. He came skidding to a halt and hollered, "Yahoo, home cookin'."

He surely had a one-track mind.

"Did you leave your manners in the barn?" Lucas glared at his brother.

He removed his hat and held it to his chest. "Howdy, ma'am. It's nice to meet you."

Cinda looked at him, confused. Had he forgotten they had already met in the yard?

"Cinda." The tentativeness in his voice caught her attention. "This is my brother Travis."

Cinda looked up at Lucas. "I thought his name was Trevor?"

"No. I'm Trevor," came a voice from behind them in the dining area.

Cinda whirled around to face Trevor smiling back at her. Then she looked to the smiling face of Travis. Twins!

Surprise!

"Most people cain't tell us apart, so we'll answer to either name," Travis offered.

Cinda looked one more time at the smiling brothers and didn't know how she would ever tell them apart. She looked up at Lucas, who gave her a half-hearted smile, as if to say, *please don't be mad*.

Mad? How could she be mad? She was too overwhelmed.

Chapter 11

*L*ucas showed Cinda the upstairs. There were four bedrooms; the largest one was theirs. He left her with her trunks so she could rest awhile before getting supper ready.

Rest!

She plopped down on the bed. She would never rest again. She put her hands to her cheeks. Oh, what had she done? What had she gotten herself into? Too much was expected of her. Mother to a pair of dirty little girls she couldn't tell one from the other. She was sure they would have fun fooling her. A tomboy for a sister-in-law. Her hands dropped into her lap. She assumed she was supposed to make a lady of her. A pair of indistinguishable brothers with a single mind—home cooking. Cooking! She couldn't cook. She had hoped to start out slowly cooking for just one man and hope she didn't make a mess of it. Instead, she had a whole family that expected her to cook edible meals. Besides the washing and mending, there was the cleaning. This house needed a good scrubbing from top to bottom. She noticed Lucas seemed to realize how bad it was.

It was too much. How could he do this to her? She balled up her hands. Hate and anger vied for dominance, which was unlike her, but she couldn't help herself. She wanted to go home and leave this place far behind. But that was out of the question; she was married now, and this was her home, like it or not. Her aunt's words came back at her and slapped her in the face. "I hope you don't regret your hasty decision." She did regret it. Had her aunt known something she didn't?

So much was expected of her. It would be hard enough to learn to care for and keep house for one man, but now there was suddenly a house full. She ran a hand over the threadbare quilt. No doubt they all needed new quilts and clothes, and she was expected to make them. She had no experience. She couldn't do it. Anger rose in her as she contemplated all there was to do. She wouldn't do it. She would go down right this minute and inform her new husband that they must live in their own house. His family could stay here, but she would not.

She would demand it.

She got up, straightening her dress, and smoothed her hair. Drawing in a deep breath of courage, she glanced in the mirror on the dresser to give herself a quick nod of encouragement. Horrified by what she saw, she stumbled back to the bed and sat down. Her face now had the same scornful look her aunt had worn for years. The pinched lips. The knitted brow. The cold, squinty, disapproving eyes.

She was turning into her aunt!

Still able to see herself from where she sat, she stared for several minutes at her reflection in the mirror. She opened her eyes wide, raised her eyebrows, and rubbed at the corners of her mouth. She refused to turn into her aunt.

Her aunt's words came crashing back to her. "Put hard work in front of you and you will crumble. Mark my words." Was her aunt right? Was she crumbling at the work put before her?

And whatever ye do, do it heartily, as to the Lord, and not unto man, the calm voice of the Lord whispered to her soul.

That was in Colossians. She had memorized it years ago. But could she really do all this family expected and needed her to do? *Lord, what have I gotten myself into? What am I to do?*

She got up and walked over to the mirror and said to her reflection, "You got yourself into quite a pickle, Cinda Harrison. What are you going to do about it?" She stared at herself for a minute mulling over the question. "I guess I go downstairs and get that kitchen cleaned up, then pretend to cook supper."

She put on an old calico dress she rarely wore but thought it would be good for the job ahead. She dug through her travel bag and clutched the cookbook Allison gave her. "Thank you, Allison," she whispered and trudged down the stairs.

Cinda surveyed the kitchen, trying to decide where to begin. The counter and the dishes in the sink—that needed to be done first. She marched over and removed a stack of dirty metal plates from the sink. When she turned to put them on the worktable with the other dishes, an old man stood between her and the table. Instinctively, she screamed. Plates clattered to the floor as she braced herself against the counter.

"A rose, a rose," he began but stopped when she screamed.

Lucas was the first to race into the kitchen. He scanned the room and came over to her. "It's okay. It's only—"

The others quickly piled into the kitchen. "What's the matter?" Trevor asked.

"Dewight scared Cinda," Lucas explained.

"Why's she afraid of Dewight? He wouldn't hurt no one," Martha mocked.

Cinda stepped away from Lucas. "If someone," she shot Lucas a wicked glare, "had bothered to tell me about your grandfather, I wouldn't have been so terrified when he appeared out of nowhere."

"He's not our grandpa," Travis said. "Lucas found him two winters ago caring for a hog of ours that got out and wandered away. We don't even know if Dewight's his real name."

"He's really harmless. He'll do pretty much anything you ask him," Lucas explained.

Cinda settled her hands firmly on her hips and turned her glare on Lucas. He shrank back from her slightly. "Is there anyone else? Any more brothers or sisters lurking around the corner? Any other relatives or non-relatives," she gave a quick glance at Dewight, "that are going to pop up out of nowhere? Anyone at all that I haven't met yet? Anyone?"

"No, this is all of us," Lucas said sheepishly.

"Then unless you want to be put to work," she said to the whole group, "get out of the kitchen." She pointed to the open door.

Martha, Trevor, and Travis practically fell over each other to get out. Lucas scooped up Dani and Davey and exited without another word.

Dewight stood rooted in the place he had been standing. He stared at her, cocking his head to one side. She supposed he was waiting for something, so she dropped her hands from her hips and said, "It's nice to meet you, Dewight."

He said nothing. He just stood silent, staring at her.

What was he waiting for? His constant gaze made her nervous. She replaced her hands on her hips. If he really wanted to stay, she would put him to work. "Fine, Dewight. I need some wood to start a fire in that stove," Cinda pointed to the stove without looking at it. "Could you get some for me?"

He didn't move or speak.

Cinda threw up her hands in resignation. She would just clean around him. She knelt down to collect the plates that had crashed to the floor. When she stood again, Dewight was gone. Cinda shrugged her shoulders. She piled the plates and other dishes from the sink on the table. Dewight came back in with an armful of wood and built a fire in the stove while Cinda cleaned the kitchen. He prattled on about a rose dying in the desert or some such nonsense.

It took Cinda two hours to get the kitchen clean enough to attempt cooking. She found the root cellar and took stock of its contents. With supplies in the kitchen and root cellar in mind, Cinda sat at the kitchen table and began to read her recipe book.

Daniella and Daphne came skipping in the kitchen and took a big whiff.

"Mmm. Smells good," one of them said.

"Mmm. Smells good, too," the other echoed.

Cinda eyed the pair suspiciously. The brothers had probably sent these two in to find out when supper would be ready. *Cowards.* She bent down and said, "Supper's just about ready. Can you two tell everyone to wash up and get to the table?" She heard immediate scrambling outside the kitchen door, and the girls scampered out to wash up at the outside pump.

One by one they clambered to the table and sat, waiting. Lucas came in last and sat down at the head of the table with Trevor and Travis on either side. Cinda placed a pot of slightly burned succotash on the table with the not-quite-done boiled potatoes and a mound of overdone biscuits. She sat at the other end of the table with Daniella and Daphne on either side. Martha and Dewight sat on the middle of the benches across from each other. Although their faces and hands were clean, there was a perimeter of dirt around each of their faces where the water hadn't quite reached. Lucas was the only one without any dirt showing. They all bowed their heads while Lucas said grace.

Cinda watched while the food made its way around the table. She took very little. Her appetite had left her long ago. She held her breath as Trevor and Travis shoveled in their first mouthful. They looked across at each other, then glanced at Lucas who ate heartily, ignoring them. Cinda could tell it wasn't quite what they expected. She almost felt sorry for them as they ate in silence. The only ones she could have pity on were the innocent five-year-olds. They so desperately needed a woman's care.

When the meal was over, his beautiful bride stood to clear the table. *Oh, no. That won't do.* Lucas took the dishes from her hands and put them back on the table. He reminded his brothers and sister how they used to do the supper dishes while their parents had taken a walk around the farm after supper. He was reinstituting that tradition. He guided Cinda outside where they walked in silence.

What could he say to her after all the surprises? She had taken it well, considering she hadn't left. . .yet.

They stopped by the corral. Lucas leaned against the fence. "Supper was good."

Her mouth dropped open and she swung her gaze to him. "It was awful. I can't cook, if you didn't notice."

"That's okay. You'll learn." He kicked at the ground. It hadn't been that bad. He had eaten a lot worse.

"In the meantime, everyone will starve." She shook her head. "Isn't that why I'm here, to cook and clean for the masses?" She swept her hand about to encompass the whole farm.

He shook his downcast head. He could see how she could think that.

"If you don't care that I take perfectly good food and turn it into slop not fit for the pigs, then why am I here?" Frustration and impatience coated her words.

"It wasn't that bad." He took a deep breath. "I was just nineteen when my folks passed on." At times like these, the ache in his heart was fresh and painful. "I had to look after a farm and four younger brothers and sisters. Lynnette was barely fifteen. The twins were eleven, and Marty was only four."

Cinda couldn't help but feel sorry for Lucas saddled with the enormous responsibility at a young age.

He took another deep breath and continued, "The next year Lynnette married a man on a wagon train heading for Seattle. Trevor and Travis had to quit school to help out here. I didn't know how to raise a little girl, so I raised Marty like a boy, as you can see." All he could do was shrug in excuse for his actions.

He had been so caught up in running the farm, he hadn't noticed when Marty had grown up. He turned around one day and found his baby sister was a boy. He couldn't tell her from his brothers. The irreparable damage was done.

Lucas stared out over the corral. "About nine months ago, Lynnette came home to die. I looked at her girls and saw Marty all over again. Lynnette was feminine and ladylike, like you. I couldn't do to Lynnette's girls what I did to Marty. I had a choice this time. I could make it different, better."

"Why didn't you just tell me about everyone and everything?"

"Would you have come if I had?"

Cinda looked to the ground, giving his question serious consideration. He waited.

"No."

He appreciated her not giving a quick, easy lie to placate him. "They need a mother. I know you'll be a great mother." He wanted to convince her it was going to be all right.

He was uncomfortable with her silence. Should he say more? Had he said too much? "You can go ahead on in. I'm going to put the animals to bed."

Cinda nodded but remained silent as she turned toward the house.

He wanted to make everything right for her, make it all perfect. But what in life was? "Should I be sleepin' in the barn with Dewight tonight?" Lucas called after her tentatively.

Cinda stopped but didn't turn around. After a moment she shook her head and continued to the house.

Though Cinda felt sorry for the nineteen-year-old boy who had a great burden placed on his young shoulders, she couldn't help but be angry with the man who had thrown his burdens upon her. At least she wouldn't have to worry about the supper dishes.

When she entered the sitting room, the conversation ceased. Travis, Trevor, and Martha were busy playing with the little girls. And who knew where Dewight was? He seemed to appear and disappear in a snap.

Cinda looked at the cluttered table. They hadn't even moved one dish. She could tell they were waiting to see what she would do. Cinda gathered up the dishes and took them to the kitchen. She would let Lucas deal with them when he came in and found her doing what they had been told to do. They were *his* family.

Lucas came in just after she had finished and was taking the little twins up to bed. He gave an approving nod at the clean kitchen. He never knew. Cinda dressed the still dirty girls in their too-small night shirts and tucked them in bed. Tomorrow they would get baths and something different to wear.

Although Lucas slept soundly, sleep eluded Cinda. She lay awake, nervous about having to fix a proper breakfast for everyone when they rose. She prayed but couldn't seem to give up her anxiety. She didn't even know what to make, so she got up and took turns reading her cookbook and the Psalms by candlelight until dawn. The struggles and praises of King David always comforted her.

Chapter 12

*L*ucas leaned on the doorjamb and watched Cinda rush about the kitchen. He admired her diligence. She was trying so hard to please everyone, and it was important to her that she did. As the sun peeked over the horizon, it streamed in the kitchen. Her straight auburn hair blanketed her back down to her waist. Whenever her hair fell forward, she pushed it back over her shoulder. When she crossed the stream of sunlight, it set her hair ablaze. Lucas couldn't help but stare.

"Oh." Cinda startled when she saw Lucas grinning in the doorway. "Is everyone getting up already? I'm not ready yet. I don't have anything cooked."

He felt like a schoolboy caught gawking at the saloon gals. His mother had given him a month of extra chores the one time that had happened. She said if he didn't have enough to keep busy, she would see to it he didn't have time to think about those strumpets.

"Don't worry about it. There are morning chores that need to be done before breakfast." He wanted to soothe her worries. "The cow needs to be milked, the chickens fed, and the eggs gathered—" He was going to continue, but Cinda jumped in.

"I already collected the eggs." She nervously pointed to a bowl of eggs. "I didn't know I was supposed to feed them. I'll do that later and remember it tomorrow. I don't know how to milk a cow, but if you show me I—"

Lucas shook his head, stopping her in mid-sentence as he stepped up close to her. He placed his hands on her shoulders to stop her flitting about. "You don't have to do everything. Marty takes care of the chickens and eggs, and I'll continue to milk the cow. Don't worry so much."

"But I don't know anything about farms. There is so much to learn." She rubbed her scratched and pecked hands.

Lucas took her hands in his and caressed the red marks. "My brothers, Marty, and I will run the farm. You just have to take care of Dani and Davey. Everything else will work itself out."

Cinda wasn't as confident as her husband. There was so much she didn't know. He said she didn't have to do much, but what did he really expect?

She noticed him staring at her disorderly hair. She pulled her hands from his and scooped up her wayward mane. Pulling it over one shoulder, she began twisting it. Her hair was straight as a board and difficult to do anything with—a constant burden to her. "I'm sorry it's a mess. I haven't done a thing with it today. I didn't want to disturb you."

He took the bundle from her grasp and rubbed it between his fingers. "It shines like fire in the morning sun." He studied each feature of her face and settled his gaze on her mouth. As he leaned closer, Daniella and Daphne came bounding into the kitchen. Lucas took a deep breath. "I had better go milk that cow."

Cinda spent that first morning after breakfast trying to figure out how to tell the little redheads apart. She sat down with them and studied their giggling faces. She discovered that Daniella had a distinct freckle, larger than the others, slightly off center on the bridge of her nose. Daphne had a similar freckle high on her left cheek under her eye. Now, as long as they were facing her, she could tell them apart.

Later in the afternoon, Cinda made Daniella and Daphne lie down to rest, and she ignored the filthy house while she explored her mother's treasures. She pulled out a worn wedding-ring quilt that had graced her parents' bed. She spread it across her own bed. Beneath it in the trunk was a new wedding-ring quilt top her mother had been piecing together before she died. Cinda caressed the new quilt as memories of helping her mother flooded back. She pushed away tears and vowed to finish it.

Among the items below the two quilts were her mother's Bible, a handful of other special books, a rag doll, and wrapped in a blue cloth were the pieces to her mother's once beautiful ceramic jewel box. It was smashed into a million teeny, tiny pieces, no doubt broken when the stage overturned. Cinda's heart was crushed as well. The box had been a wedding present from her father. He promised her mother on their wedding day that he would fill it with jewels for her, and he had, but they had all been sold at auction to pay the debts. Cinda saw a glimmer of gold and carefully flicked through the shards and rescued her mother's wedding ring.

"Don't cry."

Cinda looked toward the doorway as Daphne and Daniella rushed in the room.

"She hurted herself," Daphne said on the verge of tears.

"No, no. I'm not hurt," Cinda said, trying to console the pair. "I'm just sad. This box belonged to my mother. She died when I was young, and I miss her." Remembering the girls' loss as well, she added, "Do you have anything of your mother's?"

Both girls scrunched up their face as if thinking. "I got her eyes and Dani got her nose."

"Don't worry 'bout your box," Daniella said, patting Cinda on the shoulder. "Uncle Lucas can fix it. He can fix anything."

"He fixed the pitchfork Aunt Marty busted, and he made a cradle for our dolls," Daphne said.

"And he fixed the corral so the horses couldn't get loose no more," Daniella added.

Cinda smiled. Neither one wanted to be left out when there was a story to tell. "I think this is beyond repair, even for your uncle Lucas."

Daniella looked at her real serious. "What does 'yond pair' mean?"

"Be–yond re–pair," Cinda said slowly so they could hear each syllable, "means it can't be fixed."

"Uncle Trevor and Uncle Travis say that we are quite a pair," Daphne said with big eyes.

Cinda smiled.

Yes, she had to agree. They were quite a pair and had a way of jumping straight into your heart.

She held her arms open and they plunged into her arms, enjoying a group hug.

Cinda threw out the pieces of the destroyed box so the girls wouldn't get hurt when curiosity got the better of them.

The rest of the week, she spent her mornings cleaning up the twins and making them dresses from one of her old calico dresses. She spent the evenings, after her quiet walks with Lucas, doing the dishes.

She would heat bath water during breakfast and bathe Daniella and Daphne right after they ate. Within two hours they were filthy again, even when they remained in the house. The inside of the house was as dirty as the outside.

Lucas, Trevor, Travis, and Martha spent long hours preparing and planting the fields. Dwight mulled around the house and farmyard doing odd little chores and talking to himself. When Cinda was within earshot of him none of his words made sense. He would go on about a rose wilting, an apple tree blooming, and fighting some war. Those were only the ones she understood.

One morning she took the bathtub out behind the house and filled it with warm water. Dewight happily helped her until she informed him it was for him to bathe in. Cinda didn't know when he had bathed last, if ever. Dewight made himself suddenly scarce. Cinda hoped she hadn't scared him. But when it was time for supper, Dewight was seated at the table as usual, bathed and wearing clean clothes, though they were wrinkled.

Everyone looked at him oddly. Cinda just smiled.

One evening on their nightly walk, Cinda looked out at the budding fields. "Lucas?"

"Yes."

"What's out there?"

"What?"

"What do you grow? Everyone else has cattle around here. Why don't you?"

"We grow alfalfa." He looked at her. "And we grow alfalfa because everyone else around here has cattle. Cattle eat alfalfa."

Cinda smiled to herself. She noticed the way he stressed *we*. He wanted her to know what was his was hers, that she belonged here. She just didn't feel like the farm was hers. She felt like she was visiting on some terrible vacation. She didn't feel like she belonged, on the farm or with *his* family.

On Sunday morning Martha's howls could be heard all the way to the barn. "I ain't wearin' no dress." She turned defiant eyes on Lucas. "You cain't make me. My clothes was always good enough fer church before she come. They are just as clean as theirs." She motioned toward her twin brothers. She rammed her hat down on her head and stormed out, planting herself in the back of the wagon.

Cinda had taken one of her dresses that was a little small for her and altered it to fit the begrudging Martha. She figured Martha never wore a dress because she didn't have one. Evidently not.

A sad expression settled in Lucas's eyes. "Let's get going or we'll be late." He walked outside with a look that showed his heartache over what he thought he had done to his baby sister.

Cinda decided she would spend more time with Martha and transform her into a lady for Lucas. He shouldn't have to feel badly. He did the best he could under the circumstances he had faced. All Martha needed was a little feminine intervention. Once Martha saw how pretty she looked in a dress, she would feel differently about wearing one.

The sparsely populated small church building stood at one end of town. The circuit preacher came around every four weeks, weather permitting. The other weeks they gathered for a prayer meeting and sing-along. A select group of men took turns leading the prayer and singing.

Cinda's cheeks warmed at all the people staring at her and whispering among themselves.

Lucas stood to lead this week's meeting. He raised his hands to hush the group. "It seems that before we begin praising the Lord in song, I should make an introduction or none of us will have our minds where they should be. You all are wondering who this beautiful young woman is." Lucas cupped Cinda's elbow and brought her to her feet. The whispers of speculation started up again. "I'm proud to introduce you to my wife, Mrs. Lucas Rawlings."

Cinda smiled politely as the group became louder in their discussion.

"The Lord's been answering your prayers," called a man from the back. Hoots and hollers came from around the room.

Lucas quieted the group again. "Let's get back to the reason we are here—worship. There will be plenty of time afterwards to meet my beautiful bride. Jed, will you open in prayer? Then we'll sing 'Amazing Grace.'"

After church, the congregation crowded around her, many people speaking at once.

"Cinda, this is my good friend Lem Dekker," Lucas said, introducing a tall, handsome blond man.

A scuffle off to the side cut the introductions short and shifted the group's attention off Cinda. Three boys were rolling around in the church-yard, fighting. No, there were only two boys. . .and Martha! Apparently they had teased her, telling her she would turn into a sissy now that Cinda was around, and she was getting the better of them.

Lucas, Trevor, and Travis pulled apart the group. The two boys gave up more easily than Martha—after all, it was her pride on the line. She kept swinging, trying to get away from Lucas as he held her by the scruff of her shirt collar, depositing her in the wagon. Cinda doubted it would be as easy as she thought to transform Martha.

Because of Martha's fighting, they left town before the noon meal, instead of eating in town as they normally did. Would every Sunday be this challenging?

That night on their after-supper stroll, Cinda brought up the painful subject of Martha. "I don't think Martha should be out in the fields with you and your brothers."

"But she's a big help. She really pulls her weight out there. We need her."

Cinda realized that before Martha could see herself as a girl, her brothers needed to see her as a girl. "She's your sister, not another brother. She'll never become a lady if you don't start treating her like one." Lucas was silent. "I think for starters she should be called by Martha. Marty sounds too boyish."

Lucas shook his head. "That will go over about as well as the dress."

"But it is something we can control. Do you want her rolling around on the ground fighting with boys?" she asked in earnest.

He shook his head. "No, of course not."

"We can't force her into a dress; I realized that this morning, but we can get her used to the feminine sound of her name. When we get her to start thinking of herself as a girl, it will be easier to get her to look and act like a girl." Cinda wanted to soothe his guilt.

Lucas hesitantly nodded in agreement but didn't look convinced. He seemed willing to give it a try, probably to undo the damage he had done.

"I'm glad you're here," he said and caressed her cheek.

"Thank you." Strangely, part of her was happy to be here with him and the other part wanted to wake up from this nightmare.

Lucas went to take care of the livestock while Cinda went inside to do the dishes.

Trevor and Travis looked up at Cinda expectantly as she entered the house. Martha had a smug, contemptuous look on her face. Cinda looked over at the cluttered table. If she thought for one minute that they would have already done the dishes, she was fooling herself. She took a deep breath and started clearing the table.

They thought they were so smart getting out of the chore of washing the dishes. She felt like leaving the dishes but figured they would probably leave them for her to do in the morning when they would be twice as hard to clean. She couldn't face a dirty kitchen in the morning. Cinda didn't so much mind the task, it was the air of power they felt they had over her. Cinda continued to stew and fume. By the time she finished, she was downright mad. She grabbed the dishpan and marched to the open kitchen door. She would heave the water as far as she could. Maybe that would make her feel better.

The dishpan was already in motion when she saw Lucas in her line of fire. Lucas was passing by the door. It was too late. She couldn't stop the dirty water from heading straight for her husband. Lucas looked up in time and jumped back. The water sloshed on the ground in front of him, splashing his boots but sparing the rest of him.

At first he looked merely startled. When his shock faded away, it was replaced with what she could only determine as anger.

Cinda was too shocked to move as Lucas strode toward her and into the kitchen. He glanced around, then yanked the dishpan from her and examined her shriveled hands. He pulled her along after him out by the fruit trees.

"I—I'm sorry, L–Lucas. I—I didn't know y–you were there," she stammered as she trailed in his wake.

He stopped and faced her. "You washed the dishes?" It was more an accusation than a question.

Cinda nodded. "They can't be left till morning."

"Have you been doing the supper dishes all along?" His voice was harsh and demanding.

Cinda nodded again. She didn't understand why he was so upset with her. She certainly hadn't meant to douse him with the dirty water. "I—I didn't know you were there. I wasn't trying to throw dirty water at you."

"You are not to clean up the supper dishes," he commanded gruffly.

"But they have to be cleaned before I can prepare breakfast."

"Then don't fix breakfast," he snapped.

"But Lucas—"

He turned to her and put his hands gently on her shoulders. "I told my brothers and sister that it was their responsibility. I won't have them defying me," his voice softened, "or taking advantage of you. Now promise me you won't do the supper dishes, no matter what."

Cinda searched her husband's face. "But—"

"Promise me."

Cinda reluctantly nodded. She knew a pile of dirty dishes would await her in the morning if Lucas enforced this.

He pulled her into his warm embrace and held her close. "I'm sorry for being cross. I'm not angry with you. I'm angry with Marty and the boys."

The next night Lucas took Cinda with him to the barn to see to the livestock. When Cinda entered the house, she looked at the table of dishes. What was Lucas going to do? She looked at the triumphant trio. How would he confront them? The usual expectant expressions faded quickly when they saw Lucas enter behind her. They stole glances at each other. Lucas didn't acknowledge the table. He walked over and scooped up Daphne and handed her to Cinda. He scooped up Daniella in his arms and said, "It's time for you two to be getting to bed." Then he marched upstairs with a casual good night to the stunned trio.

As Cinda suspected, the following morning the dirty dishes were waiting for her, still scattered across the table. She rolled up her blouse sleeves preparing to dive into the chore, when Lucas came in with a pail of fresh milk. He set the pail on the kitchen table and hooked an arm around her waist. "No you don't," he said and guided her into the sitting room. He sat her in the rocking chair and handed her a book from the nearby shelf.

"But Lucas, everyone will be hungry."

"It says in the Bible, in Second Thessalonians, chapter three, 'if any would not work, neither should he eat.' I believe that's verse ten. Hunger spurs one to work harder when the reward is food." They heard footsteps on the stairs. From where they sat, she could see Trevor and Travis stop before they reached the bottom.

Another set of footsteps trotted down the stairs. "What's for breakfast?" It was Martha's voice. "I can't smell—"

Cinda heard an umph. Martha had evidently bumped into Trevor and Travis who stood frozen on the third step from the bottom.

"Do you think she's sick or something?" Travis asked.

"They'll never get done with the three of you gawking at them," Lucas called from the sitting room. They spun around to see Lucas, Cinda, Daniella, and Daphne cozied up together sharing a book. Lucas continued, "Call us when breakfast is ready." They were speechless, as was Cinda. "Could you hurry it along? We're hungry, and there's a heap of work to be done around here today."

The trio went groaning into the kitchen. They knew better than to argue and understood that the sooner they got to it, the sooner they would all eat.

Daniella and Daphne started whining about their hunger pains. Cinda's heart went out to them. "Lucas, this isn't fair to them."

"You're right, this isn't fair." He turned to Daniella and Daphne. "You two go in the kitchen and let them know just how hungry you are until they have fed you." The two girls skipped off to the kitchen, and soon the moans and groans increased.

"Lucas, how could you?"

Lucas smiled. "They'll not leave the dishes for you again. I promise you that."

Cinda hoped that was true. Caught off guard by Lucas's intense gaze, she smoothed back a lock of hair from his forehead.

He leaned over and kissed her gently. "I dare not continue or I'll never want to stop."

She smiled back at him and felt as if it had suddenly gotten warm in the house.

The next night and every night thereafter, the supper dishes were clean when she and Lucas returned from their evening walk.

Chapter 13

*M*artha sulked in a kitchen chair with her arms folded across herself. Lucas had left her to help Cinda, but she would have nothing to do with it. Cinda could feel Martha's piercing glare on her back as she finished up the breakfast dishes. She wouldn't push Martha into doing much this first day. At least she was in a more ladylike atmosphere. One step at a time. Cinda had to take it slow.

Cinda turned with a smile on her face. "Who would like to help me?"

"No one," Martha snarled.

"I wanna help," Daphne offered with excitement in her small voice at the same time Martha had spoken.

"No, you don't," Martha snapped at the girl and glared at Cinda.

Daphne stuck out her bottom lip and looked away.

"Dani, Davey, and me are going outside to ride Flash." Martha shot Cinda a gloating smile as the three left the room. Daphne looked back forlorn.

Two could play at this game. "Since no one will help me bake the cake, I guess I will be forced to lick the bowl all by myself," Cinda called lazily to their backs as they reached the front door. She had never made a cake before but thought since her cooking was improving, they could have fun trying. Following a recipe wasn't as hard as she had feared.

Daphne and Daniella came racing back. "I wanna help," they both called out.

"Great. But I think we need one more helper. Don't you?" Cinda looked up at Martha, hoping she would relent and join in the fun.

Martha narrowed her eyes and tightened her mouth into a narrow line. She flung open the door and stormed out to the barn. Cinda was sure this wasn't the last battle with Martha. She might have resigned the twins for now, but she wasn't through yet.

They made a mess of the kitchen and themselves trying to make the cake, but Cinda couldn't remember having more fun.

She realized that with Martha around it would be a constant battle of wills for the twins' allegiance. A battle. What was it that Dewight said about battles? "A war is won, one battle at a time." Yes, this was definitely war, and with God she could win this war one battle at a time. Now, which battle should she approach first? It needed to be an easy one—one she knew she could win. She needed success early on to have the courage to endure.

The most difficult battle would be Martha. She would save that one for last. If she put off doing anything with Martha, then she really would have no trouble with the girls. The most important battle she had to win was for Daphne and Daniella. They desperately needed a mother's guidance, and they already looked to Cinda quite naturally.

Cinda marched out to the barn to free Martha from her sentence of housework. She found her lounging in the ceiling rafters. She was so far up, Cinda shuddered with fear for the girl's life.

"Martha, would you come down here? I would like to talk to you," Cinda tried to be calm, but she couldn't keep a slight quiver from her voice.

"My name ain't Martha, Cindy," she called from her lofty perch.

"Your given name *is* Martha, mine however, is *not* Cindy," she retorted.

"If you say so—Cinderella."

Cinda took a deep breath. O*ne, two, three, four, five, six, seven, eight, nine, ten,* she rattled off in her head. She wasn't going to get into this just now, but she knew Martha thought of her as a work maid. "Would you please come down here so I may speak with you without shouting?"

"If you want me, come and get me."

Cinda really wasn't up to playing these games with her. But Martha wasn't coming down until she was good and ready. "I came to tell you that you may help your brothers in the fields, if you like."

"What?" Martha shifted positions.

"You heard me."

"If this is some sort of trick to get me down, it won't work. Lucas would just send me back, and you know it. Then I would be in trouble with him. You would love that, wouldn't you?"

"I assure you this is no trick. Tell Lucas that I told you to go, and tell him I will explain my actions this evening. If he still doesn't believe you, remind him his wife has been known to change her mind. . .often." On that note, Cinda turned and left the barn. She wasn't sure if Martha would go or stay up in the barn. It really didn't matter as long as she didn't try to come between Cinda and the twins. This was the one battle she had to win for Lucas's sake. She couldn't fail him. They were the reason Lucas brought her here in the first place.

A few minutes later, Cinda saw Martha race out of the barn on Flash full speed ahead. At least she didn't kill herself climbing down out of the rafters, but she might on that horse.

At supper that night the haggard work crew filed in. Cinda wondered if they even stopped at the pump before coming in. Maybe tonight wasn't the best night to start this. No. They shouldn't eat with all that filth on them. Cinda wondered how long it would take them. They looked around the table and at each other.

"We ain't got any plates," Trevor moaned.

"We don't have any plates," Cinda corrected. "And you won't get one as long as I can see dirt on your face, neck, and arms." She looked over each of them and shook her head. "Nope. None of you will get a plate until you're cleaned up properly." Lucas had shone her how motivational food was with his family, and her cooking was actually edible now.

"What about Lucas? Aren't you gonna check his face and hands?" Martha asked with a smug smile. She and her brothers glanced past Cinda.

Lucas had come in just after his brothers and sister. She could feel his presence behind her. He had heard the whole conversation.

Oh, no! Lucas. Cinda swallowed hard. She had forgotten about him. She couldn't very well humiliate him in front of his siblings by treating him like a child, but if she allowed him at the table unwashed, they might not take her seriously.

Cinda took a plate from the stack she held in her hands and handed it over her shoulder to Lucas. "Your brother always washes thoroughly." She hoped and prayed tonight he hadn't been careless and was still grimy.

The three filed out grudgingly. Lucas took his place at the table. Relief swept through her when she saw he was washed and clean.

"What would you have done if I hadn't been washed up?"

Died of humiliation, she thought but said, "You, my husband, have always washed up properly."

Lucas gave her a broad smile, flashing his dimple, as she strode down the table giving a plate to Daphne and one to Daniella. The others filed back in like whipped puppies—clean whipped puppies.

After supper Cinda explained to Lucas that too many changes would be hard on a fourteen-year-old girl. She remembered what it had been like at twelve, being uprooted and having her entire world turned upside down. She would need to go slow with Martha, very slow. She had to accept Cinda first, so for now only her name would change.

Chapter 14

*a*fter three days of chasing Daniella and Daphne, Cinda was at her wit's end.

Just this morning she had read in the twenty-seventh Psalm, "Hear, O LORD, when I cry with my voice: have mercy also upon me, and answer me." She had cried out for mercy and answers and felt as if God weren't listening. In her loneliness and desolation, the Lord brought to mind a promise in Matthew, "Ask, and it shall be given you; seek, and ye shall find; knock, and it shall be opened unto you." She had asked for guidance and was fervently seeking a solution. Where was the answer?

She studied the girls, trying to figure out why they had a change in demeanor. They had been compliant before and enjoyed helping her around the house. Now they were defiant and downright disobedient. Occasionally, Daphne would look at her like she wanted to be with Cinda, but she remained glued to Daniella's disobedient side. They refused to answer to Daniella and Daphne, only to Dani and Davey. They had been fine and enjoyable until—until Martha had been forced to stay behind. She was reaching back from the fields and interfering. Cinda turned thankful eyes to the Lord.

Cinda knew she had to break Martha's hold on the girls. First, she had to find out what Martha was holding over them, and Daphne was just the one to tell her.

The girls were still at the breakfast table. Everyone else had left for their day's work. The twins were the last ones to finish, picking at their food. Cinda took hold of Daphne's hand, helping her off the bench.

"Where are you taking my sister?" Daniella asked, alarmed.

"I just want to talk to her. You stay here," Cinda said.

"No!" Daniella screamed, jumping off the other bench. "You can't have her." She came around and grabbed Daphne's other arm. Daphne became the object of a tug of war and started crying.

Stunned by Daniella's reaction, Cinda released the sobbing girl's hand. Daniella draped herself around Daphne. Cinda put her arms around the stiff, crying pair.

"Oh, please don't eat us," Daphne wailed.

"Eat you? Why would you think I wanted to eat you?" Cinda asked, horrified that they would think such a thing.

"Because trolls eat little girls," Daniella cried.

Trolls? "You think I'm a troll?"

The two bleary-eyed girls nodded.

"What makes you think that?"

"Aunt Marty said so," Daniella said bravely.

Martha. She should have guessed. *These two probably believe everything she says.* "How could I be a troll? I'm much too tall for a troll, you know. They are no taller than this." Cinda stood up and held her hand at shoulder height. For once she was glad she was so tall. "And they are this wide." She held her arms out well beyond her sides. "Their hair is really short and curly." Cinda took the pins from her hair and let it fall over her shoulder. "Any curl here?" She knelt down and held out her glossy hair to the girls to touch. They each caressed it gingerly, shaking their heads. "And trolls have long, pointy noses and drool all the time. Have you ever seen me drool?" They both shook their heads again. "Then how could I be a troll?" she concluded, holding her arms open. She wasn't sure if they believed her.

Daphne rushed into Cinda's embrace. Daniella held back with a pout.

"What's wrong, Daniella? Do you still think I'm a troll?"

She shook her head. "I don't want Mama to cry in heaven."

"Your mama won't cry."

"Yes she will," Daphne said emphatically, pushing away from Cinda. "She will think we don't love her anymore."

The poor girls had been so scared that they were denied love from the one person they were around all day. In Martha's attempt to get at Cinda, she clearly hadn't realized what she was doing to Daphne and Daniella. She couldn't know the effects it was having on them. Martha loved those little girls, Cinda was sure of that. It was Cinda who Martha disliked—just why, Cinda wasn't sure.

Cinda didn't want to frighten them any more than they already were. She let them play in their room with their dolls the rest of the day.

Martha and her brothers returned early from the fields. They came in through the kitchen door.

"Martha, I would like to talk with you," Cinda said, trying not to reveal her anger.

Martha completely ignored her and strode on by.

Cinda knitted her brows together. "Travis, would you stir this for me?" she asked, without even looking at him.

"I'm Trevor," he said awkwardly. Cinda had asked them to correct her when she called them by the wrong name. She wanted to learn their right names and couldn't do that if they allowed her to use the wrong name.

"I'm sorry," she said, looking at him. If she had bothered to look at him before she spoke, she would have noticed his bangs down as Trevor always wore them. If they ever changed and wore their hair the same, she would be at a loss to tell them apart. "Trevor, could you stir this for me and not let it burn?" She absently plopped the wooden spoon in his hand and took off after Martha.

"Martha, let's talk in your room where we won't be bothered," Cinda said.

Martha continued to pretend she didn't exist, thumbing through a book.

"You can talk to the *troll* now or Lucas later."

Martha's head popped up, her eyes wide.

"Now," Cinda commanded.

Martha silently stalked up to her room with Cinda on her heels. Martha crossed through her room and stared out the window.

Cinda closed the door firmly and stared at Martha's defiant back. She was waiting for Cinda to say something. Cinda wasn't sure where to begin. "How could you do it? How could you tell those sweet little girls I was trying to fatten them up to eat them?"

Martha shrugged her shoulders.

"Do you know that they have hardly eaten a thing in three days?"

Martha snapped around in surprise to look at Cinda. She was genuinely concerned.

"Yes, that's right. They are the ones suffering, not me. They are scared to death all day with no one to comfort them because you have taken that away from them. I know you don't like me, but please leave them out of it."

Martha could no longer hold Cinda's stare. Obviously, she had never meant to hurt the girls.

Cinda let her words sink in awhile before continuing. "I don't want to bring Lucas into this if I don't have to, and I don't think you want that either." Martha shook her head. "Then you better convince those two I'm not a troll and won't eat them. You better be so convincing they eat a hearty supper. Do you understand me?"

Martha nodded and made a move for the door.

"I'm not through with you yet. If they don't eat well, I will talk to Lucas after supper."

"I'll tell them," Martha said softly with downcast eyes.

"One more thing. Daniella and Daphne need all the tender loving care we can *all* give them. To make them think their mother is crying up in heaven because they hug me is hurting them as well. You let them know that no matter what they do, their mother and father will always love them. Always. Have I made myself clear?" Cinda's words were stern and not to be questioned.

Martha nodded. "Yes," she said barely above a whisper then jumped at the rap on the door.

"Marty, is Cinda in there?" came Lucas's voice through the door.

Martha looked at the door in a panic, then she looked back at Cinda.

"Yes, Lucas, I'm in here," Cinda called back and then opened the door. She smiled up sweetly at her husband, trying to douse the flames of anger she had felt moments before.

"I don't want to interrupt," Lucas said with uncertainty, looking from her to his sister and back again.

"You're not interrupting a thing. Martha was just on her way to play with the girls before supper," she said.

Martha took the hint and slipped past Lucas and Cinda without a word.

Lucas watched her go into the little girls' bedroom. "What was that about?" Lucas asked, swinging his gaze back to Cinda.

"Girl talk."

Lucas raised his eyebrows and smiled at the promising prospect. She swept past him and went down to check on supper.

Daniella and Daphne ate, but Martha spent the meal nervously watching them and Cinda. The days that followed, however, were filled with happiness and hugs for the two little girls. Martha seemed as relieved as Cinda.

Cinda focused a lot of her attention on the girls. She made new dresses for their dolls, replaced the yarn hair, and drew new faces with almond-shaped eyes, long lashes, and smiling mouths. She opened a jar of cherries they would have at supper and painted the lips red.

Next it was time to get back to the chore of scrubbing the house and making curtains. Cinda took the girls and Dewight into town to buy some scrub brushes and window fabric. Cinda also bought fabric for two more dresses for each of the girls. Dewight disappeared when they got into town and magically reappeared when Cinda was ready to leave. Cinda was grateful for the break from his annoying, nonsensical rambling.

No one was really sure of Dewight's real name, but someone in town thought he might be a man who once had a place in the hills. They thought the man's name was Dewight and his homestead burned to the ground some thirty years ago, killing his family. He'd been wandering ever since.

"Ooooo," Daphne sighed.

"It's soooo prettiful," Daniella crooned.

The girls were eyeing a white handkerchief with a delicate lace border that Cinda had put up as a prize for the best wall scrubber. Armed with scrub brushes and a pail of soapy water, the girls went to work. They each had a wall to scrub, and Cinda cleaned the other two walls in their little room. Cinda helped them reach the high areas, but they worked diligently for an hour. Each would check out how the other was doing, then go back to her wall and work harder. Cinda had finished two walls and half the floor when both girls were finally satisfied.

Cinda studied both walls carefully. They had both done such a good job she couldn't reward one and not the other. "It seems as though we have a tie."

"A tie?" Daphne asked, raising her eyebrows up and down, and up and down again.

"I don't want a tie. I want the handkerchief," Daniella whined.

"A tie means you both win. Let me find another prize."

"But I don't want another prize. I want the prettiful handkerchief," Cinda heard one of them say on her way out. She was certain it was Daniella.

Cinda returned a minute later with her hands in her pockets. She pulled out the white handkerchief with the lace from one pocket and handed it to Daniella. She snatched the handkerchief from Cinda's hand and said to Daphne in an encouraging tone, "You get the other prize."

From her other pocket Cinda removed a lavender handkerchief with a purple iris embroidered in one corner.

Daphne's eyes got as round as her mouth. "Ooooh. It's beautiful." She cuddled it to her face. "I love it."

They raced each other to the barn, trying to be the first one to show Lucas. When Cinda caught up with them, Lucas was praising their work and complimenting their dainty prizes. He looked up at Cinda adoringly. His eyes sparkled with a hint of moisture. She could tell he was pleased, and it warmed her heart that he cared so much. This big, strong fortress of a man seemed as soft as a baby chick on the inside.

Two nights later Daniella and Daphne came to the table after everyone was seated. Lucas had had them doing something for him. After supper they made Cinda close her eyes. When she opened them, before her sat a cake with a single lit candle and a wrapped present.

"What's this for?" Cinda asked, confused.

"It's your birthday, May seventeenth," Lucas said.

Cinda was astonished. Had time really passed so swiftly that it was her twenty-fourth birthday already? She had been there for a month and a half. "How did you know?"

"I asked Allison on the train platform before we left." Lucas held her gaze for a long moment.

"Open your present," Daphne begged.

"No, blow out the candle," Daniella countered.

"We have to sing first," Daphne corrected.

After a round of "Happy Birthday," the candle was extinguished and Cinda untied the green ribbon from the gift.

"The ribbon is for your hair. It matches your eyes. That's what Uncle Lucas said." Daniella rubbed the ribbon.

Cinda glanced up at Lucas and gave him a smile of approval. He could be so thoughtful. She looked at the gift and peeled back the paper. It was a small ceramic jewel box like her mother's, the one that had broken in transit. Cinda bit her bottom lip, trying to hold back the tears.

"See, we told you Uncle Lucas could fix anything," Daphne said.

"He certainly can," she said and looked at him not only with her eyes but with her heart as well. She felt something there. Could it be love?

"Open it," Daniella called out.

Cinda raised the lid slowly. Inside was a single strand of pearls, just longer than choker length.

"They belonged to my mother," Lucas said apprehensively.

That was it. The dam burst and the tears flowed freely. "They're beautiful," Cinda murmured through quivering lips.

Martha got up swiftly and stormed out of the house.

"What's her problem?" Travis asked, clueless.

Cinda had seen that loathsome look on Martha many times, but just now she finally understood it. The girl was jealous and hurt of the time and attention Lucas showed Cinda. Lucas was more like a father than a brother to Martha, and now Papa had a new bride. She was no longer the only woman in his life. Cinda unknowingly was taking everything that was hers—her brother, her nieces. . .her pearls. She had expected to get her mother's pearls; she had never thought they would be given to a stranger. One day Cinda would relinquish them to her. Martha's caring about something as feminine as a string of pearls was a glimpse of the woman hidden deep within.

Lucas came around the table and fastened the pearls around Cinda's neck. "Thank you," was all Cinda could manage.

Chapter 15

$\mathcal{T}$hat night Cinda and Lucas took their usual walk. Cinda couldn't keep her hand from fingering the pearls. He had been so thoughtful from the beginning to think to inquire about her birthday, then to surprise her with a cake and such thoughtful gifts. This was just like the kind of romantic love she read about in so many books. Could this big, strong man really love her? Or was he just grateful she was raising his nieces to be ladies? She liked to think that maybe he could love her. . .someday.

They stopped at their usual spot next to the corral. After a moment of silence Lucas said, "Do you know what's the most beautiful sight to a man?"

His wife? she hoped. "What?"

"The land he owns stretched out before him," he said, making a sweeping gesture with his arm, "growing green and lush. It's your land, too, now. Isn't it a wondrous sight?"

Cinda, disappointed, looked out at the swaying green land. To her it was just a green field like so many others she had seen. Nothing special about it. She supposed she had read too many romance stories where the man falls in love with a woman and can't live without her. Real life wasn't like that. She should be happy to have a good man with whom to grow old.

She had seen love. David and Allison certainly loved one another. Alvin was in love with Vivian. Eve loved men—period. And Cinda's father had loved her mother with his whole heart. He loved her so much that life without her was impossible. Yes, a deep lasting love did happen in real life, but it was reserved for a precious few. She felt fortunate to have seen such a devoted love in her parents, but for her it was unlikely. How could it be with everything happening around here? Except for their short nightly walks, Cinda and Lucas were rarely alone or spoke to each other. His days were filled with caring for the fields, the livestock, and providing for everyone. Her days were filled with two active little girls and enough household chores to keep her busy for a lifetime. No, there would be no time for love here.

That night Cinda took off the pearls and put them in her new jewelry box with her mother's cameo, her mother's wedding band, and a small emerald ring her uncle had given her on her eighteenth birthday. She knew there would be very little opportunity to wear any of them. She had worn her mother's cameo only once since the day she arrived. If she were back home, she would have had many occasions to wear each of them.

Cinda had heard Trevor, Travis, and Martha talking about Dewight's odd behavior. Travis said they had never seen so much of Dewight. Normally, he would disappear for days at a time except in the dead of winter. That was the only time he generally stayed close to the farm. Trevor said he was acting different because Cinda always set a place for him at the table. He knew he was welcome with her.

Cinda thought Dewight was odd indeed but not for the same reasons the others thought so. They seemed not to notice his talking to himself and not making sense, or maybe they just ignored it. Cinda couldn't ignore it when she was around it so much.

"The apple tree always blooms in spring. Always in the spring," Dewight mumbled as he came in through the kitchen door, walked through the dining area and out the front door.

Cinda could only stare after him. He seemed to have a purpose in coming in with his message and back out again, but even the little twins ignored him. He had carved each of them a beautiful wooden pony, and that said to Cinda that he didn't have the mind of a crazy man. What he did, he did with purpose. It only made sense that what he said, he said with purpose.

Cinda looked at the apple tree already losing blooms, sprinkling petals in Martha's short, dark curls as she sat below its limbs. Sure enough, it bloomed in the spring. She wondered if in the summer he would mention the fruit, and in the fall the leaves turning, and in the winter the bare branches. Maybe he was just a senile old man ranting.

Cinda watched as Martha stood and pulled down a branch, drinking in the sweet fragrance of the blossoms. Cinda hadn't expected her to do that. Dewight's words rolled around this vision of Martha. She, like the apple tree, would bloom. She was on the verge of her own spring, and bloom she would in her own time and her own way. Next, Cinda saw Martha racing off on Flash. She was afraid of nothing. Cinda decided not to worry any more over Martha's impending womanhood. She might not have traditional feminine qualities, but she would have special qualities all her own.

Cinda's reverie was interrupted by a sudden squawking of the chickens in the yard. She ran out to see what had them fussing so. She hoped it wasn't a fox or something dangerous—the girls were out there playing. Daniella and Daphne were there indeed, watching their uncles, Trevor and Travis, duke it out. Why were they fighting? Determined to find out, Cinda marched over to them. She tried to get their attention by calling out their names. It was no use. What on earth would make them fight each other like this? Brother should not be fighting against brother. Not having any brothers or sisters, she knew siblings were something to be treasured.

Cinda stepped closer to them, ready to shout and command their attention. Before she could, one of them drew back a fist, catching her mouth with his elbow. At the same time the other one swung, grazing his brother's face and popping Cinda in the cheekbone. Cinda's hands flew to her face. Daniella and Daphne started screaming. Trevor and Travis froze in horror. When Cinda got over the initial shock, she went over to the little twins to calm their fears.

"I'm okay," Cinda said to the weeping pair.

"You have a bleed," Daphne screeched.

Cinda touched her mouth where the frightened girls were pointing. Sure enough, there was a little blood at the corner of her mouth. After she calmed the girls, she turned back to the stunned pair of fighters.

"Why'd you step into a fight like that?" Travis ventured to ask.

"Because I wanted to find out why the two of you were fighting."

"He took my biscuit and ate it," Trevor explained.

"If you would eat faster, then I wouldn't have taken it," Travis replied.

Cinda balled up her fists. "You mean to tell me that you two were fighting over a biscuit?" Two nearly grown men fighting like wild animals over a silly biscuit. "Get in the house, both of you, now."

They immediately obeyed.

"Lucas is going to kill you," one said to the other.

"Me? You hit her, too," the other shot back, backhanding his brother in the chest. Unless facing them, she couldn't tell them apart, but she could tell from the tone of their voices that they were genuinely scared about what Lucas would do to them when he found out.

"I didn't know she was there. I couldn't see her. You should have told me she was there."

"It's not my fault. I didn't see her until it was too late."

"We're both going to get it." They hung their heads.

Oh my. What would Lucas do? Travis and Trevor certainly hadn't meant to hit her. She was the one at fault. Well, maybe they could be blamed a little for fighting in the first place. She would tell Lucas it wasn't their fault, or she could just say she fell or something.

"Do you still want a biscuit?" Cinda asked Trevor once inside the house. Trevor gave a little nod. These two were like a pair of two-year-olds. She could deal with two-year-olds. Cinda set a full bowl of biscuits and another cookie sheet full of biscuits on the table. "Good. You and your brother get to eat biscuits. Every last one. Do I make myself clear?"

They both nodded and sat down. "Are you gonna tell Lucas what we done?" Trevor asked.

"Just what is it you two don't want me to know you have done?" Lucas asked. He was just returning from town, no doubt hungry for his own lunch. He looked closely at his brothers and gave a half smile. "You two fighting again? Well, I guess it was only a matter of time. The peace couldn't last forever."

They stared wide-eyed at him. Cinda almost felt sorry for them.

"They fighted because Uncle Travis took Uncle Trevor's food," Daphne explained.

"And he ate it, too." Daniella didn't want to be left out of this exciting story. "Then they hit Cinda."

"They did what?"

Cinda tried to escape into the kitchen, but Lucas caught hold of her arm and turned her to face him. He lifted her face to examine the damage. He studied the split in the left corner of her mouth and the shine on her cheek. Fire flashed in his eyes.

"Which one? Which one did this?" Lucas demanded. He turned to his brothers and brought his fist down on the table. "Which one of you?"

Oh dear. What was Lucas going to do? There had been enough hitting for one day. "I did it," Cinda said. "I was foolish enough to walk into the middle of a fight. I am the one to blame."

"A man never hits a woman for any reason, ever!" Lucas was yelling. "I want you two outside. Now!"

"Sit down," Cinda barked when they started to stand like sheep going to the slaughter.

"Stay out of this," Lucas growled.

Though startled by Lucas's gruffness, she couldn't let him harm them. "I'll not have brother fighting brother. That's why this whole thing started. Unless you want to be the next one hitting me—"

Lucas spun around to face her. She flinched slightly. His face contorted. "I would never hit you."

"If you raise a hand to either one of them, I will step in between you and them. You'll have to knock me out of the way." Cinda could feel the anger heat her face, and her voice trembled.

Lucas's face was red as well and his nostrils flared. He stormed out of the house.

Cinda turned around to see two wide-eyed young men staring at her. "Eat," she barked. They shoveled in the biscuits.

Shaken, Cinda went into the kitchen. She had never heard Lucas speak with such harshness to anyone. He hadn't seemed upset that his brothers were beating on each other, so why had he gotten so angry?

A sudden realization hit her. He got mad when he learned they hit her.

Lucas stormed out and grabbed the reins of his horse from where it was tethered to the hitching rail. He marched to the barn and threw open the door as hard as he could. It slammed against the wall. The horse nickered and pulled back.

"Come on, Boy." Lucas pulled on the reins.

He led the hesitant horse into his stall and yanked at the strap to loosen the saddle. How could his foolish brothers get themselves in a position to hit Cinda? The thought of her hurt tore at him.

"What's got you spittin' nails?" Marty said behind him.

He spun around to see her leaning over the side of the stall. He glowered at her. She was no better.

She held up her hands in mock surrender. "Whatever it is, I didn't do it. I swear."

He pointed at her. "Your brothers did." He turned back to the horse. He had never before not claimed any of his siblings. He had spent his whole adult life looking after them and keeping them together. But right now he felt like there were a few too many Rawlings around. "Why can't they solve their problems without using their fists?"

"They was fightin'?" Marty said astonished. "You're riled up because they was fightin'? Since when?"

"They weren't just fighting." He yanked the saddle from the horse's back, then flung it over the stall rail and brought his fist down on it. "They hit Cinda, both of them. She's going to have a black eye and a fat lip."

"Is that all?"

"Is that all!" he bellowed.

"A lot worse has happened to me in fights, and you never got this mad."

Lucas ignored the hurt tone in her voice. "This is different." He stomped over and grabbed a brush.

"Why? Because it's sissy Cinderella. She'll live."

"Because she didn't deserve it." He shook the brush at her with each word. "You, on the other hand, pick your fights." He turned to the horse and made a long, quick stroke down his back with the brush, then shoved the brush in Marty's hand. "Take care of my horse." He strode out of the barn.

There was one too many Rawlings in the barn for his liking. He needed to be alone. Marty was right, of course. Cinda would be fine, but just the thought of her being hurt twisted his insides something fierce—not just because she was a woman to be protected and taken care of but because she was Cinda, his wife, whom he cherished and cared for. His insides twisted more when he recalled her flinching when he hollered. How could he have yelled at her? She wasn't at fault. It was his pigheaded brothers he was angry with.

As he took off up the hill as fast as he could, he tried unsuccessfully to pray. He needed to run off some of his fury.

Lucas was gone the rest of the day and didn't show up for supper, and Trevor and Travis weren't hungry after all those biscuits, so they skipped supper. The meal seemed quiet with so many missing, even though Daniella and Daphne couldn't tell Martha enough times about Trevor and Travis hitting Cinda. Cinda just wanted to forget the whole horrible situation.

After supper, Trevor and Travis showed up to do the dishes. Lucas came in as well.

Cinda grabbed his plate. "I'll fix you up some food."

"I'm not hungry." He motioned her toward the door and took her outside for their walk. They walked in silence around the yard and ended up at their usual spot by the corral.

"I'm sorry for yelling at you. It was my brothers I was mad at, not you." Lucas didn't look at her.

"It really was an accident. They didn't know I was so close to them."

"I know, they told me."

"Oh, Lucas, you didn't. . .hit them?"

He faced her. "No, I didn't. And I wouldn't have this afternoon either."

"But you were so mad, I thought. . ."

"My brothers may talk with their fists from time to time, but I prefer not to. I was just going to talk to them. I wanted to know how they could get in such a fool position."

"Just talk?" she questioned.

He smiled slightly. "All right. I would have yelled the roof off the barn, but I wouldn't have hit them—not that they knew that for sure."

"I don't think they will be fighting again."

"At least not anywhere near you," Lucas said, and they both laughed.

Lucas became serious again. "Please know that I would never strike you." His eyes were pleading with her. He held out his hand for her to take.

She took his hand and smiled. "I know."

With his other hand he tilted her head up to look at her injuries. "Does it hurt much?"

"No, not really. A little when I smile. Your brothers knew just what to do. It seems they have had some experience tending these kinds of wounds."

"They've had a lot of experience." He gently touched the bruise on her cheek. His touch was so light it left her skin tingling. His eyes lowered to her split lip. He softly kissed the unharmed corner of her mouth.

She was once again surprised by the gentleness in this big, strong, proud man. Wrapping her in his arms, he held her in silence for a long while. She felt safe in his tight embrace.

Before falling asleep that night, she prayed.

Father God in heaven, I praise Thee for the grace you have bestowed on me and Thy loving mercy. Keep Daphne, Daniella, Lucas, Trevor, Travis, and Martha safe. . .and, oh yes, Dewight, too. I worry about him wandering off and getting hurt. Teach Travis and Trevor to settle their disagreements in a different way.

She paused and took a deep breath. *I know I should be thankful for this family, but I can't quite find the gratitude in my heart yet. Please continue to work in me. I always prayed for a large family. I never imagined this is how You would answer that prayer.*

Lucas rolled over in his sleep and draped a muscular arm across her waist. *Lucas is a good, kind man. I thank You for that.* She yawned. *I better end or I'll fall asleep before I finish. One more thing, could You please do something about Martha? Amen.*

Chapter 16

The rooster crowed, announcing the beginning of a new day. Cinda pulled the covers over her head. No, it couldn't be morning already. Hadn't she only just dropped into bed? Why were the noisy, chaotic days so long and the peaceful nights so short? She wanted to ignore the wake-up call. To sleep in just once would be so delightful, but she knew she couldn't do that. Lucas was already up milking the cow and would expect to greet her as he always did when he came in the kitchen with the pail of milk and a kiss. Then everyone else would slowly get up and the day would be underway, not stopping until after dark when it was time to fall back into bed.

Today she wanted to finish the church dresses for Daniella and Daphne, shirts for Lucas and Travis needed mending, and Trevor had a pair of pants that required a patch. Keeping the house clean was a constant battle. The kitchen floor definitely needed a good scrubbing. Then there were the daily chores of cooking and keeping up with a pair of active five year olds.

Cinda readied herself and went down to the dreary kitchen. Although she had cleaned it several times, it still looked dull. She had made some yellow gingham curtains to cheer up the window, but the rest of the kitchen was still drab. The broken and uneven shelves still wobbled. She had attempted to fix them but only ended up with a battered thumb and frazzled nerves. As soon as Lucas was not so busy, she would ask him to fix them. He'd already had so many burdens placed on him from such a young age, but never once did she hear him complain nor would she.

She wanted to do a little decorating to make the house seem more homey, but there was never time. Today would be no different.

Martha was the first one down. "What's for breakfast, Cinderella?"

Cinda took a deep breath. "I'll make a deal with you. You call me by my name, Cinda and I will call you Marty instead of Martha."

Marty looked at her for a moment, then shrugged her shoulders on her way out of the kitchen.

After a noisy breakfast, Cinda sat down and completed the mending and sewing while Daniella and Daphne played quietly at her feet. It was a nice change from their usual squabbling. Lunch was noisy as well but uneventful. Afterward, Cinda worked on the kitchen floor. With Daniella and Daphne outside with their aunt and uncles, she finished the task in no time.

Suddenly, Cinda found herself with what looked like an hour to herself before she should start supper. She spent about ten minutes walking around the house making a list of the things needed to spruce up the place—curtains, doilies, maybe a rug for the sitting room. Then she settled herself in the rocking chair in the sitting room. She sighed. It was good to get off her feet and rest. She picked up a book she had been wanting to read, one she had started several weeks ago when she had a spare minute but hadn't been able to get back to until now. This was her chance to escape to another world for a little while. Even Dewight's annoying ramblings wouldn't spoil her solitude.

She reread the beginning to refresh her memory. Just as she became engrossed in the story, however, chaos sounded in the kitchen. Cinda ran in and found a muddy piglet and two muddy five year olds scrambling across her clean floor.

Daphne and Daniella squealed as much as the pig. Their mud-drenched clothes sprayed everything as the girls spun around, chasing the pig.

Cinda's first thought was to stop the flying mud. The only way to do that was to stop that grubby swine. As the squealing hunk of ham came toward her in the doorway, threatening to muddy the rest of the house, she reached for it. She fell half on it, capturing it in her grasp. "Somebody take this thing," she said, stunned by what she had done.

Marty waltzed in and took the piglet from Cinda. "Sorry, Cinderella. It just got loose," she said with a shrug.

Cinda clenched her fists. She was *not* Cinderella and obviously the chat she had with *Martha* this morning fell on deaf ears or a cold heart. Then there was her floor. Her beautifully clean floor now was smeared with mud. The cupboards were splattered as well. She gritted her teeth. *One, two, three, four, five, six, seven, eight, nine, ten,* she rattled off as fast as she could under her breath.

Lucas blocked Martha's escape. He surveyed the muddy scene and took the piglet and pointed to the twins. "See to it that those two get cleaned up."

"But Travis was the one who let them play with Chuckie."

"Now! Take them down to the creek and get as much mud off as you can." Lucas left no room for argument.

Martha huffed and held out both her hands. Daniella and Daphne each claimed one.

Lucas left with the pig, leaving Cinda sitting on the dirty floor in a muddy dress. If she got started right away, she would be done in time to fix supper.

She got a scrub brush and filled a pail with water. Her arms and shoulders were still sore from cleaning it the first time. Well at least she would be off her feet. Tears stung her eyes.

Just when she thought she had a moment to herself, it had been viciously ripped away. Cinda clenched her fists and growled. "I can't take it any longer. There's always one more thing to do, no one to talk to, no one to confide in, no one to lean on." She rubbed her hand on the muddy floor. Frustration boiled under the surface. "Does the dirt never end?" She slapped the floor and blinked as a mist of mud sprayed her face.

Cinda angrily scanned her dismal surroundings. She marched over to the shelves. Afraid to put anything on them for fear they would fall down completely, she lifted the edge of one rotting board and let it drop on its support. The support pulled out of the side board. Cinda jumped slightly as the shelf crashed to the bottom. "Kindling, that's all they're good for."

Still fuming, she surveyed the entire kitchen. "A kitchen without a pantry is like a house without a roof. This is pathetic. There isn't a mixing bowl left that isn't chipped and cracked." She looked at the dented and bent metal plates; pushing them aside, she shook her head. They had obviously been pounded out a time or two. She held up two wooden spoons, the only cooking utensils. One had a piece missing and the other's handle was broken. "What use are these?" How was she supposed to cook decent meals under these conditions? She glanced at the room as a whole. "This whole kitchen is a joke. One big joke," she yelled, half laughing and half crying.

The anger built inside her as she scanned the room, looking for something, anything about the kitchen that was good. Even the pump creaked and was difficult to use. She turned and heaved the pair of broken spoons at the wall. She should count to ten, but this felt so much better.

Then she caught her breath. Out of the corner of her eye she saw a stunned Lucas standing in the doorway. She faced him and stared in horror. How long had he been there? She hoped it wasn't long, but from the pained expression on his face, he had heard enough. He went back outside without a word, looking dejected and downtrodden.

How could she have said all those things? She had criticized his mother's kitchen. She hadn't meant to hurt him. Could she take it all back? No. Once spoken, words can never be retrieved. The damage was done.

"But the tongue can no man tame; it is an unruly evil, full of deadly poison," the Bible said. Her tongue had certainly spewed poison, and Lucas was its victim. She fell to her knees next to the pail of water, defeated, and started scrubbing.

Chapter 17

*L*ucas rose earlier than normal and milked the cow before leaving for town in the wagon.

He never spent much time in the kitchen, and he hadn't realized how pathetic it really was. It used to be a nice kitchen, one his mother had been proud to show off to occasional visitors.

Cinda hadn't complained once about it. She had asked him to repair the shelves when he had time, but the job didn't seem urgent, and he forgot. He couldn't blame her if she wanted to up and leave. He certainly hadn't provided a very appealing home for her. But that would change. Starting today, he would make it her home too—change whatever she wanted to make her feel like it was hers. He wondered if this was how his father felt when his mother wanted something. He had always gone to the ends of the earth to please her.

Lucas pulled into town and headed straight for the mercantile. He bought all the lumber Jed Overman had on hand, which wasn't much, and ordered more. It would be enough to get started. He bought paint, nails, and more of that yellow yard goods Cinda had at the window. At least he had noticed that much. While he was there he picked up the food supplies, so he wouldn't have to make an extra trip into town.

"You're cleaning me out, Lucas," Jed said with a whistle. "What you doin', building a whole new house or something?"

"Or something," Lucas said smiling. "You got any cooking spoons?"

"Over there." Jed pointed to an area to the back. Jed was near fifty, with one arm stumped just below the elbow. He had lost it during the War Between the States. Now he ran the store with his wife and daughter.

Lucas sifted through the kitchen stuff and came up with a metal spoon. "Is this all the kitchenware you have?"

"What are you looking for?" Jed said as Lucas moved back to the counter.

"I don't know. What do you need in a kitchen?"

"That's not my domain." He turned toward the back. "Maggie, got a customer who needs your help."

Maggie appeared from the back room and went through the catalog with Lucas. Lucas ordered everything she suggested.

"That's one lucky lady you got yourself, Lucas. Hang on to her," Maggie Overman said and returned to the back.

"I intend to, but I'm the lucky one."

"Tell me how a no-good scoundrel like you got a beautiful, refined, citified wife," Lem Dekker said, slapping him on the back. Lem had arrived a few minutes before and had leaned over watching what Lucas chose from the catalog.

Lucas had gone to school with Lem, and he took his good-natured harassing for the fun it was. "All I can say is I don't deserve her," he began but was cut off.

"We already know you aren't worthy of such a delicate flower. Whatcha do, hog-tie her?" Jed teased.

"I know, it was a shotgun weddin'," Lem jumped in with a chuckle. "That's the only way a pretty thing like her would have anything to do with a ugly mug like him." He chucked his thumb toward Lucas.

Lucas stood there with a smile and took their ribbing.

Maggie appeared from the back room again with two old dresses their daughter Becky had outgrown years ago. The fabric was still good and could be made into dresses for the twins. "I think it was Lucas's good looks and charm that won her over." She handed the dresses to him.

Lem and Jed looked at Lucas, then at each other and said, "Naw."

"Thank you, Mrs. Overman," Lucas said, tipping his head to her. "I believe it was the good Lord Himself who saw fit to bless me."

Lem's smile faded. He shoved his hands into his pockets and walked out. "Hi, Lem," Becky said sweetly as he brushed past her without a word. Lem had had eyes for Lucas's sister, Lynnette, and was just as heartbroken as Lucas was when she married and ran off to Seattle. The two men had been through a lot together. Only Lucas was blessed many times over and Lem had nothing.

Lucas shed his smile as well. He knew Lem felt cursed by God at every turn and struggled to hold on to his faith. Most of the time he simply ignored God and pretended all was well. It pained Lucas to see his friend in such agony.

"I best be getting along." Lucas picked up a sack of flour and swung it over his shoulder.

"You tell that bride of yours to come by for a visit and a cup of tea. Becky and I are dying to get to know her," Maggie said. "We have too few womenfolk around these parts."

"And the ones we do have are looking after men who aren't looking back," Jed said, staring at his daughter's back as she gazed out the window at Lem.

Lucas headed for the door. "Lucas," Jed called after him, "Sam over at the post office said to tell you to stop in if I saw you."

"Thanks, Jed. I will."

Cinda regretted her little explosion the day before. She told herself it was just because she was so tired. She hadn't meant to hurt Lucas. She didn't even know he was there. She wished she could take it back at least a hundred times. If she had only closed the kitchen door, the pig wouldn't have gotten in. But she had left it open so the floor would dry faster. As it turned out, it didn't get a chance to dry at all. She looked at the floor and could see several spots she had missed in her fury. She would have to get down on her hands and knees again today to get them.

Lucas came in with a box of canned goods. "There's a letter here for you." He set the box on the table and handed her the letter. The good news quickly edged out her bad feelings.

"It's from Allison." She sat in a chair excited to read the news. "I wonder if she's had her baby." She could hardly open it fast enough.

Lucas went out and returned with a sack of flour draped over his shoulder. "I hope it's good news." He put the sack down by the flour barrel. He turned to her when she didn't answer. He asked again. "Is it a girl or a boy?"

Cinda looked up at him with tears stinging her eyes.

Lucas came over and knelt in front of her. "What is it? It's not her baby?"

Cinda shook her head. "I—It's my. . .m—my. . .my uncle."

Lucas wrapped his arms around her and held her close as she cried. When Cinda composed herself, she said with a quivering lip, "Allison says he's really sick. The doctor doesn't think he is going to make it." The tear dam burst again.

"I'm so sorry," Lucas said, holding her. "It's okay. Please don't cry."

He seemed worried by her tears so she did her best to collect herself. "I'm fine now." She struggled for control. "I don't want to keep you from your chores." Lucas didn't seem to know how to handle a distressed woman. It would be best if she found someplace private to cry. She didn't want him or anyone else fretting over her. He just nodded and got up to leave.

"Thank you for getting the provisions," Cinda said. He made two more trips to bring in the rest of the food he bought, then disappeared until supper.

Cinda tried to get her work done but caught herself staring blankly into space several times. She never knew how much time passed from her last conscious thought to when she jerked back to reality. She drifted through the day not completely aware of her surroundings.

Why did it have to be her uncle? He couldn't die. He had been a second father to her. She still needed him, and now he needed her. Almost as if coming out of a dark closet into the sunlight, she knew what she had to do. She had to go to him. But would Lucas let her? Would he keep her from going? She wouldn't ask, she would just tell him. . .after supper during their walk.

Supper went along as if nothing had happened. Why shouldn't it? For his family, nothing had happened. It wasn't their uncle on his death-bed. None of them had even met him, except Lucas the day they were married and hastily departed. Cinda lost what little appetite she had. She couldn't sit there any longer and pretend everything was fine. She shoved away from the table and put her plate in the sink. She slipped out the kitchen door. She was leaning against the peach tree when Lucas joined her a moment later. He stood silently next to her.

"He is like a father to me," Cinda said with a cloud of melancholy surrounding her. "He comforted me when my father died. I was always soaking his shirt with my tears. He was my strength. I can't imagine him sick. He's never sick, or at least he would never admit it. He can't be dying. He just can't." Tears streamed down her face.

Lucas encompassed her with his big arms. "Shh. It will be all right." Now her tears drenched his shirt.

Cinda appreciated his trying to comfort her, but she knew it wouldn't be all right. Her uncle was dying. The only person on earth who loved her was dying, and she was so far away.

"So when do you leave?" he finally asked, his voice heavy.

"Oh, Lucas, could I?"

"If you need to."

In the depths of his blue eyes she could see he wanted her to say no. "Yes. He needs me."

Cinda refused to pack her black dress for the impending funeral. She had to think positive. Her uncle would be fine. She did pack her dark gray traveling suit, just in case.

Lucas leaned against the wall, watching Cinda pack her trunk.

Did he have to stand there watching her every move? He was always so busy around the farm. "I'm really not sure what to pack."

"When are you coming back?" Lucas asked.

Cinda ignored the forlorn tone in his voice. She couldn't think about him right now, only her uncle. "I don't know. It depends on how sick Uncle Barney is." She heard him shift positions. When she returned to the dresser for another garment, she glanced over at him. He was leaning on the window frame, staring out the window. He was usually so confident and in charge, but right now he looked like an insecure boy.

"Are you coming back?"

Cinda froze, staring unseeing at the folded nightgown she had retrieved from the drawer. Coming back? She tried to swallow the sudden lump in her throat. How could she answer him when she didn't know herself? All she had thought about was getting away from this wretched place and seeing her uncle…going home. She hadn't thought about coming back or the future. She should say something. But what?

His heavy footsteps crossed the room. The door creaked open, then quietly swung shut. She quickly turned to the door. She was alone, empty and alone. His slow, even footsteps faded down the stairs. Each one stabbed at her pounding heart.

Her uncle needed her. She couldn't think about anything else right now. She forced Lucas out of her thoughts and finished packing, but she wasn't sure who her tears were for—herself, her uncle, or Lucas. It didn't really matter. She was going and going with her husband's consent, that's what mattered. She *was* going.

She went to the jewel box Lucas had given her for her birthday and caressed the top of the ceramic box before opening it. She put her emerald ring on her right hand and pinned her mother's cameo at her throat. For a moment, she held the pearls in her hand, rolling their smooth, glossy texture between her fingers and thumb. She let them pour out of her hand and back into the jewel box, and then she took her mother's wedding ring and slipped it in her reticule. Like closing a coffin, she slowly closed the lid of the jewel box.

When she opened the bedroom door, Trevor was propped up against the wall, waiting for her. He took her suitcase, and she followed him downstairs. She expected Lucas to be in the wagon, but he was nowhere in sight.

"Where's Lucas?"

Trevor shrugged and helped Cinda aboard. He climbed in after her. "Isn't Lucas driving me into town?"

"Guess not. He told me to take you and see you got on the stage-coach all right," he said, like it was perfectly normal for her husband not to take her.

Dewight appeared next to the wagon, holding out a single meadow daisy for Cinda. When she took it, he bowed and left without his usual rambling.

Trevor snapped the reins and the wagon jerked into motion. Cinda took one last look at the farm. She thought she saw someone standing in the shadow of the open barn door. The shadow disappeared before she could make out who it was. Was it Lucas or just wishful imagination?

She got on the stage and waved to Trevor. Cinda was not looking forward to the bone-rattling ride. The coach managed to stay upright, barely, the only good thing about the trip.

After two days of bouncing around in the stage, Cinda was relieved to step aboard the train. As the train pulled out of town, Cinda noticed a lone rider on a hill. She hoped it wasn't a train robber—another traveling unpredictability. Then he disappeared. Cinda looked nervously for a robber and his buddies to appear. They never did. It was probably just her active imagination running wild because of the stress of traveling alone, her uncle being so ill, and too little sleep. She let go of the image and focused on the remainder of the trip.

Chapter 18

*S*tepping off the train, her eyes moistened. The familiar sights and sounds were refreshing. She had never noticed before, but there was even a distinct aroma to her home. She drank it all in.

"Cinda," a familiar voice called.

Cinda turned to see Allison sitting in a nearby buggy, waving her arm. She rushed over to her dear friend whose stomach was as big and round as a watermelon. After a quick hug, David loaded Cinda's trunk into the back of the buggy, and they were off to Cinda's old house.

As they drove through town, Cinda took in the faces of those she knew growing up. The places seemed more wondrous than she had ever realized. The simple school building she graduated from brought tears to her eyes, and when they passed her church, her heart quickened. She and Lucas were married there. Why had that thought popped into her head? It happened so quickly, she wouldn't have thought it would have made a lasting connection with her church of many years. Of all her memories of her childhood church, why did that one memory come to mind? *Probably because it was my last memory of the building,* she told herself.

Her thoughts turned to her uncle. "How is he?"

"He's failing fast. The doctor doesn't think he'll hang on much longer." Her friend patted her hand. "It's a good thing you got here when you did."

When they pulled up to her aunt and uncle's house, Cinda's first thought was. . .*home.* Funny, she had never thought of it that way before. Being away made it seem different somehow—less cold and lonesome.

She looked woefully at the doctor's buggy parked in front of the house.

"If you need anything, just let me know," Allison said as Cinda went through the gate.

Cinda nodded. "I will. Thanks."

David and Allison drove away as Cinda closed the gate. Lucas's face flashed before her. The night they first met, she had barricaded herself behind the gate. She left the memory lingering there as she continued up the front walk.

An eerie chill swept over her as she entered the deathly quiet house. Was the house always this quiet? Or had it been such a long time since she had been in absolute quiet that now the silence seemed loud?

She set down her suitcase and went up the stairs slowly, cautiously. Each step was one step closer to her uncle's passing. If she stayed on that last step, maybe she could stop time itself and her uncle's imminent demise. She stood as still as a statue, staring at her uncle and aunt's bedroom door. That would be where he rested, if. . .

When the bedroom door opened, Cinda caught her breath. The doctor exited with his medical bag and a grim expression. He held the door open for her. She moved slowly to the doorway, her feet dragging like lead. Her stomach twisted.

"It's only a matter of time," the doctor said as Cinda passed him at the door. "Send for me when he gets worse. I can't do anything for him but ease his pain. I'll be back in the morning to check on him." He closed the door and left.

There was no hope then. She walked in and sat at her uncle's bedside. Her aunt stared out the window.

"I don't know why you bothered to come. He's not likely to wake again," Aunt Ginny said toward the window.

Cinda ignored her and scooped her uncle's hand in hers. He would know she was there whether he woke or not. "I'm here, Uncle Barney. Your little Cinda is home." The words seemed odd to her somehow—because she was calling herself little or because of the tightness in her chest when she said home? This would never feel like home again without her uncle to warm it.

When he gets worse. The doctor's words kept echoing in her head, louder and louder.

WHEN.

It was a foregone conclusion—Uncle Barney *was* going to die. If she could only accept it, maybe it would make it easier.

She hoped and prayed for God to grant her this one miracle and spare her uncle's life. If he would wake up so she could talk to him one last time, maybe she could will him to live.

Cinda clutched her uncle's hand. Exhausted from her jarring trip, she laid her cheek on his hand and fell asleep.

Some time later, she was startled awake by her uncle's moving hand. She lifted her head and looked into her uncle's droopy eyes. His first look was one of recognition and joy, then he furrowed his brows and frowned.

"You shouldn't be here." He struggled with each word.

What? Of course she should. Did her uncle really not want to see her? Or was it delirium from the illness and medication?

"I couldn't stay away when you were sick," Cinda begged.

"I'll live or die whether you are here or not." He strained for breath. His energy sapped. "Go home, child. Go back to your hus—band." With that he slipped back asleep.

"I am home," she whispered. A tear rushed down her cheek.

Her aunt looked tired and weary. Cinda wondered how much sleep she had gotten since her uncle fell ill. It didn't look like much. With fretting over arriving in time and the arduous journey, Cinda hadn't slept much either.

The house was as spotless as ever and the kitchen sparkled. Cinda finally figured out the eerie feeling in the house. There were no smells except the heat of the approaching summer and the ensuing death. No baking bread, no simmering stew, no pie cooling in the window with its scent drifting in on the afternoon breeze. Nothing. The air was stripped bare. If death itself had a smell, this was it.

Cinda's tears came and left like waves. Aunt Ginny, on the other hand, hadn't dropped a single tear; her eyes remained dry. She stayed close to her husband except to prepare simple meals.

Cinda tossed and turned as sleep evaded her. She kept wondering if her uncle would still be with them in the morning or if their heavenly Father had called him home during the dark hours of the night. It was doing her no good lying there, flipping back and forth. She rose with a foreboding feeling and donned her robe. She crept down the hall, cracked open the other door, and peered in.

Aunt Ginny was seated in the chair alongside the bed. Her uncle was awake and Ginny was reading to him by lamplight. Her aunt quit reading and looked up at her, and her uncle's gaze followed. He limply patted the bed next to him. He was glad to see her.

"Doesn't my Ginny have a beautiful voice?" he strained to say. Cinda nodded. Virginia Crawford had a melodious tone in her voice when she spoke kindly, and her singing was the loveliest in church.

As Cinda sat down, she exchanged glances with her aunt across the bed. Aunt Ginny stood and crossed to the window. It was still black as midnight. Cinda wondered just what time it was. It had to be close to dawn.

Barney Crawford tried to speak. Cinda stopped him. "Don't talk. Save your strength."

He smiled knowingly. "I have no strength left. My time has come."

"Don't say that."

"I have something important to say to you. You must listen." He was insistent, a sense of urgency in his frail voice.

Cinda bit her quivering bottom lip and nodded.

"Forgive her." He glanced over at his wife's back.

Just what did her uncle expect her to forgive Aunt Ginny for? For being cold and indifferent? For making an orphaned twelve-year-old feel unwelcome? For treating her like an unwanted stray mutt? For squelching her dreams? If her aunt did ask for forgiveness, could she give it to her? She wasn't sure.

He squeezed her hand. "If I can, so can you." Barney Crawford drew in a final, labored breath and was gone.

"No," Cinda sobbed. She looked up with tear-filled eyes at her stone-faced aunt.

Virginia Crawford never displayed excessive emotion in public. She left without a word or a tear.

Cinda looked sadly at the doorway through which her aunt had escaped. *This isn't public,* Cinda wanted to shout after her. *We can cry together. How could she not cry? Didn't she love him? How could she be married to this sweet, caring man for all these years and not love him? Everyone loved Uncle Barney.*

Maybe not everyone. Cinda shed a tear for her bitter aunt.

Chapter 19

ncle Barney's friends crowded the cemetery. Cinda cried because she would miss her uncle. She also cried because of the throng of good people who were touched by her uncle's life. She never thought that so many people would attend. Allison had delivered her baby the morning Uncle Barney died and was unable to come, but David was there. Cinda told him she would come by next week to see Allison and David Junior.

After the funeral service, Cinda and her aunt accepted the condolences of friends and neighbors.

"For goodness sake, stop slouching. I would have thought you would have outgrown that by now." Aunt Ginny handed her unused handkerchief to Cinda, who had long since soaked hers.

Next, her aunt would be scolding her for crying in public. Cinda straightened her shoulders and held her chin up. It had been awhile since she felt so tall. She noticed it actually hurt to slouch.

During the somber ride home, Cinda could hear the echo of her uncle's sweet voice in her ear. *"Forgive her."* She looked over at her stoic aunt sitting stiff and proper, without so much as a moist eye.

"Forbearing one another, and forgiving one another, if any man have a quarrel against any: even as Christ forgave you, so also do ye." The words filled her soul.

No, she couldn't forgive her, not this heartless woman. There had been too much hurt at her hand.

"Then came Peter to him, and said, Lord, how oft shall my brother sin against me and I forgive him? till seven times?

"Jesus saith unto him, I say not unto thee, Until seven times: but, Until seventy times seven.

It was too much to ask of her. She couldn't.

"And when ye stand praying, forgive, if ye have aught against any: that your Father also which is in heaven may forgive you your trespasses. But if ye do not forgive, neither will your Father which is in heaven forgive your trespasses."

She had done nothing wrong. She didn't need forgiveness. She focused on something else so she wouldn't have to listen to the little voice in her thoughts any more. Her heart hardened. The voice was silenced.

That night a noise woke Cinda. She had a hard time waking herself enough to recognize the sound. *Crying?* More than crying, she realized, a heart-wrenching sob. *One of the twins probably had a bad dream.* She sat on the edge of her bed and pried open her eyes, shaking off the confusion.

Daniella and Daphne weren't there. The only one in the house was her aunt. Cinda walked groggily to her aunt's room and found her sitting in the middle of the empty bed she had shared with her husband for years. She was hunched over her bent knees, sobbing uncontrollably.

Cinda wanted to wrap her arms around her aunt to comfort her, but she wasn't sure her aunt would let her. She never had before. In fact, Cinda could not remember ever being hugged by her aunt. Cinda sat on the edge of the bed and tentatively put her arms around her aunt. Aunt Ginny didn't resist and leaned into her niece's embrace. In the lonesome darkness they mourned side by side, yet separately.

When the tears stopped, her aunt said through sniffles, "I did love him. I loved him so much."

Really? What should Cinda say? What could she say? She had never heard her aunt say she loved her uncle before. She had never seen her show love to anyone. She had never witnessed her display this much emotion. This was not the heartless aunt she knew.

"I know you don't believe me," Aunt Ginny said, getting off the bed, drying her face with her hands. She crossed to the window and looked into the empty blackness that mirrored her heart. "I didn't love him when I married him, of course. I was in love with another man. . .or at least I thought I was at the time. Only he had married someone else. I convinced myself he did it just to hurt me. Two weeks later, I married Barney to prove to him and myself he couldn't hurt me."

All these years her aunt had settled for second best. The other man must have been quite exceptional to be considered better than her uncle, who Cinda thought was the best. . .next to her own father of course.

She obviously needed to get this off her chest. Her aunt stared out the window. "I was hurt and could never quite let go of it. When his wife died, I left Barney and went to him. I was so sure he wanted me." Her voice was far removed from this time and place. "It was all in my head, of course. He never said he wanted me. He never asked me to come. He never wanted me, even from the beginning. He couldn't even see me through his grief. He wasn't the man I thought he was, the man I thought I had fallen in love with. I realized Barney was the man I had thought the other was. I came back to Barney, begged for forgiveness, and asked him to take me back."

It was like the dam had broken and every pent-up emotion was freed to rush forward. "We were actually doing well for awhile. Now there is no time left to make it up to him."

When did this all happen? While Cinda was in Montana? No, she spoke as if it all happened long ago.

"I don't know why you are crying over him. You don't have to worry, you'll see him again." The confidence in her aunt's voice both comforted and confused her.

"What do you mean? You'll see him in heaven, too."

"God doesn't let the wicked in heaven."

"We are all sinners in God's eyes."

"I don't think even God could forgive my wicked heart when my own husband couldn't. Oh, he said he did. But in his heart," she thumped on her chest, "where it counted, there was no forgiveness there."

"But he did forgive you, from deep down in his heart. The last thing he said was 'Forgive her. If I can, so can you.'" Her uncle had known his wife had a deep need to be forgiven. She didn't know why her aunt needed her forgiveness, but Cinda felt she could finally forgive this hurting woman. "I forgive you, too, Aunt Ginny."

Aunt Ginny let out a shrewd, knowing laugh. "You don't even know what you're forgiving, do you? If you knew, you wouldn't throw your forgiveness around so easily, you impudent child."

"Don't tell me what I can and can't forgive. I'm long past being a child, if you haven't noticed." Cinda was regretting coming in to comfort her grieving aunt.

"Easy for the ignorant to say, hard for the knowledgeable to do." Her eyes narrowed and her expression hardened.

"Then enlighten me," Cinda snapped back.

Her aunt turned fiery eyes on Cinda. "It was your fault he couldn't forgive me. You were a constant reminder—of him." Cinda looked at her curiously, shaking her head, confused. "Don't tell me you haven't figured it out? I thought you had known since you were a child. Everett, your father, he was the one. Didn't you ever wonder why Barney never visited your home? And when you visited here, you came with only your mother."

Her father! Her aunt had been in love with her father? "My father would never—"

"You're right. Everett never would, despite my efforts," her aunt said cutting her off. "I accepted Barney's proposal to have a reason to be near his brother-in-law. I tried my best to break your father and Olivia up. He was always a perfect gentleman—and an absolute sap over your mother."

Her aunt was like an erupting volcano, spilling over, destroying everything in its path. Why was she saying these hurtful things now that they didn't matter?

"I'm the reason they moved away from here." She pointed to herself. "Then when Olivia died, I took advantage of it and tried to trick Everett into marrying me for your sake. 'A girl needs a mother I told him.'"

"Stop it! Why are you doing this?"

"You're just like Olivia, too caring and forgiving. Olivia and I were best friends until I ruined it. I was a fool for so many years. She should have hated me, but she didn't. God sent you here to punish me and hate me for her."

Is that how her aunt saw her, a constant thorn in her side? The poor woman was tormented by her own guilt. She couldn't forgive herself or accept that others could. She was trying to finally make things right with her own husband. Then Cinda's father died and she was thrust upon her aunt as a reminder of her evil deed. No wonder her aunt never made her feel welcome. With Cinda in her home, Ginny could never escape her past.

Cinda felt like she should hate her aunt for everything she tried to do and did. She always wanted to hate her aunt, but there was nothing to base it on. Now she had something to hate her for, but she found compassion instead. Anything her aunt might have done, she had long since punished herself for.

Her aunt stood there, waiting for Cinda's hatred. Cinda walked across the room and stood before her aunt.

Forgive, and ye shall be forgiven.

Cinda's heart softened toward her aunt, and the bitterness melted away. "I don't hate you, and I do forgive you." Cinda couldn't blame her for falling in love with the most wonderful man in the world. . .Everett Harrison, Cinda's own father.

"How can you?" her aunt asked through tear-filled eyes.

"There is nothing for me to forgive." Cinda found tenderness for her aunt. "Uncle Barney forgave you years ago. So did my father and my mother. God has forgiven you. You need to forgive yourself and accept our forgiveness." She hadn't realized until now that to her uncle she was always his little sister's child, but to Aunt Ginny she was always Everett's daughter.

Ginny buried her face in her hands. "I'm sorry for everything. I'm sorry for not treating you better."

Cinda's eyes teared up, and she threw her arms around her aunt. They mourned together for an uncle and husband who would be dearly missed. They mourned for years of denied love. They mourned for a friendship long overdue.

Chapter 20

*a*llison, he's beautiful. David must be so proud," Cinda cooed over the newborn baby she cradled in her arms.

"David can't stop talking about him. He's a good papa." Allison smiled broadly. She, too, was proud of her little bundle of joy. "David fusses over us something terrible. He won't let me do a thing." She leaned close to Cinda and whispered in a teasing tone, "You won't tell him I'm out of bed, will you?"

The two laughed.

Allison grew serious and patted Cinda's arm. "How are you doing?"

"I'm doing fine. It is hard to believe Uncle Barney is really gone. I keep expecting to smell his pipe smoke filtering through the house." Cinda got a mischievous look on her face. "I even lit it yesterday just to be able to smell it. I thought Aunt Ginny was going to faint when she came in and saw me. I think she actually expected to see him in his chair."

Cinda went on to explain about Aunt Ginny having been in love with her father. She told Allison about them crying and talking together and how they were getting along wonderfully now. Her aunt's guilt had been between them all those years. Now that it was confessed and forgiven, they could be friends.

Cinda fixed some tea and poured them each a cup.

"How long will you be staying?" Allison asked her.

Cinda sipped her tea, putting off the question. "I haven't decided." She couldn't look at Allison.

After a moment of uncomfortable silence, Allison said, "You're not planning on going back, are you?"

Cinda looked up. "I don't know, Allison. What should I do?"

Her friend shook her head with a look of sympathy and understanding.

Cinda let out a heavy sigh. "I went into this thing in such a rush. I thought it was God's will, but now I wonder. I don't know that I made the right decision. Maybe God wasn't calling me to marry Lucas. Maybe I was just trying to escape Aunt Ginny. . .and. . .being an old maid. I think

I made a terrible mistake."

"Was he really awful?" Allison held compassion in her eyes. "He seemed nice enough."

"Lucas? No, he's not awful at all." Cinda drew in a long, thoughtful breath. "Lucas is wonderful. He's caring, tender, giving, and loving."

"He sounds perfect," Allison said, raising her eyebrows in question. "I don't see what the problem is."

"He has one major flaw," Cinda said tight-lipped. "Travis, Trevor, Martha, Daniella, Daphne—and Dwight."

Allison looked at her hands and moved her fingers. "I count six flaws."

"I always wanted to have a big family—and I wouldn't mind them so much, if they weren't all so impossible." Cinda huffed and closed her eyes for a moment, conjuring each one up in her mind. "Martha doesn't even know she's a girl. Excuse me, Marty. She calls me Cinderella. She knows I hate it. Then there is Dwight. He rambles and appears from nowhere."

Allison shivered. "It gives me the creeps just thinking about him."

"He's not all that bad. I figured out that most of what he says actually makes sense if you have the time to figure out what it means. He really is harmless, unlike Travis and Trevor."

"Those are Lucas's twin brothers you can't tell apart?"

Cinda nodded. "They fight each other over the most ridiculous things. They were actually fighting about their food. I ended up with a black eye and a split lip."

"They hit you?"

"They didn't mean to. I really shouldn't have gotten so close."

"Was Lucas mad?"

"Furious, but he didn't lay a hand on them. Despite his size, he is really very gentle. You should see him with Daniella and Daphne. They can be quite a handful at times. He's a good father to them."

Cinda paused for a moment, then focused on her friend. "I feel really wicked for not wanting to go back. It would be so much easier if I stayed here."

"Maybe. But you'll never be at peace."

"You think it's peaceful there?"

"I'm not talking about peace on the outside. I know you won't be content here, not really. The Lord won't let you. You don't belong here anymore."

That's just what her uncle had told her. "I thought you would want me to stay."

"I do, but more than I want to satisfy my own selfish desires, I want you to be happy. You won't have the joy of the Lord going against Him."

"I told you, I'm not sure it was God's will. I think I acted hastily without the Lord's blessing."

"Mistake or not, Lucas is still your husband, and God wants you at your husband's side. It's not like Lucas has hurt you. You admitted that yourself."

"No. He has never hurt me. He's always been so..." Her words trailed off as she thought of Lucas. No doubt he was out in one of the fields seeing to it nothing got neglected. Or riding out on his horse, sitting tall in the saddle. Or hunting for food to put on the table. Or tending to a scraped knee. She took a deep breath and exhaled. "Selfless. That's what Lucas is. Everything he does is for someone else."

"I'll miss you." Allison had a wistful expression.

"What?" Cinda asked, coming out of her dreamy state.

"When you leave, I'll miss you."

"Am I leaving?" She had hoped for someone to make the decision for her, though she knew it was hers alone to make.

"Yes. You'll go. You're only putting it off for a little while."

"How can you be so sure, when I'm not?"

"I just know, and I know you. It's something in your eyes when you talk about them. . .about him. They are a part of you now. They're your family, and family has a way of getting under your skin."

Cinda didn't remember her bed being so terribly uncomfortable and cold. She pulled the covers around her neck. How could she be cold? It was almost summer. It had been colder in Montana, but she had never felt it.

Cinda had unconsciously slipped back into the routine of being "home." She thought the peace and quiet was wonderful, and she enjoyed being able to sleep in. She actually got to read a book, and she was getting along with her aunt better than she ever imagined possible. With the barrier of guilt stripped away, they had nothing to stop them from being friends, at last. Her aunt even let her in the kitchen. All the while, though, Cinda couldn't shake the uneasy feeling, like something bad was going to happen; but hadn't it already?

Cinda took her place in the doorway of the kitchen. She watched her aunt kneading bread dough.

Aunt Ginny caught sight of her. "Come help me make these pies for the church social tomorrow." She turned the kneaded dough into the greased bowl and draped a towel over it to let it rise.

Cinda stood dumbfounded in the doorway. Had Aunt Ginny really invited her into the kitchen? Maybe she had imagined it. . . wishful thinking.

Aunt Ginny heaved a bowl into Cinda's arms. Cinda clutched the bowl and cautiously stepped into the room, afraid to disturb anything or make a mess in the spotless shrine. Her aunt gave her the ingredients and guided her through the steps of preparing the piecrusts. Cinda soon relaxed and the two spent the afternoon in the kitchen baking and talking pleasantly. Cinda cherished the time they spent together and would savor it forever.

They both conveniently avoided mentioning Lucas or Cinda's leaving.

Cinda went to a schoolmate's wedding. Sally was three years younger than Cinda, and now she was marrying Emery, a boy who had been in Cinda's class. As long as Cinda could remember, Sally had been in love with Emery. Love. What was love? Cinda couldn't put a finger on it.

After the wedding ceremony, Cinda gathered with her friends— Allison and David, Vivian and Alvin, and Eve and her banker fiancé, Leon Livingston. They stood together under an oak tree in the churchyard.

Eve held out her hand so everyone could see her grand engagement ring. "Isn't it gorgeous? We're getting married next month. I couldn't let you have all the fun."

"Next month?" Vivian asked. "Isn't that a little fast? I mean, to get a proper wedding together."

"Leon says he loves me too much to wait any longer than that to make me his wife." She flashed the ring in the sunlight to show everyone just how much Leon loved her. Leon stood proud. Proud of the expensive ring and proud of being the one to catch the beautiful Eve Weston. *Love?* Cinda wondered. Was this love?

"My wedding will be the most splendid this little town has ever seen. Too bad you'll be going back soon," Eve said to Cinda.

Cinda looked away, not knowing what to say, but she knew Allison understood.

Chapter 21

Cinda wandered around the empty, quiet house. There was no arguing. No talking. No conversation at all. No playful laughter. No giggling girls chasing after one another. No love crossing the table between the many occupants. Nothing—just peace and quiet. Very quiet. She should have been happy in the stillness. It was what she had longed for ever since she left, wasn't it?

She found herself thinking more and more about Lucas and his entire family. They were loud, sloppy, and sometimes even a bit rude. Chaos always reigned in that house—and love. There was no mistaking the love that enveloped the house. They were a tight-knit family. Any one of them would go out on a limb for another. She missed the love that seemed to be floating about in the air in that crowded, rundown house.

She couldn't believe she had been here for three weeks already. At times it seemed as though she had never left this home. At the same time, it seemed like she had long since overstayed her welcome. Her uncle was right. She didn't belong here anymore. It was time to go *home*. Home to Lucas.

I struggle against my own flesh, Father, my selfish worldly desires. I am so weak. I must confess what You already know. I don't want to go back. I know You want me to return, so I will. I will try with Your help to do so with a cheerful heart. Believe it or not, I actually miss them, and I think I have come to love the husband You gave me. Thank You for letting me not grow old alone. Amen.

She seemed happier somehow knowing she was going home. It felt as though a weight had been lifted from her soul.

Cinda sat at the writing desk in her room. She would write Lucas a letter, letting him know she was returning—immediately. She wasn't quite sure how to say it. She mulled it over so long, she noticed the mailman heading down her street before she had written one word.

"Oh, I don't have time to run to the post office, and it must go out today." Cinda scribbled, *Dear Lucas, I'll be home soon. Love, Cinda.*

It wasn't at all what she wanted to say, but the mailman was almost at her door. She rushed down and caught him just as he had turned to leave.

The next day, a letter from Lucas arrived. Cinda tucked herself safely up in her room before opening it in private. She took a deep breath.

Dear Cinda,

    I'm sorry to hear about your uncle. I hope your aunt is doing well under the circumstances. Everyone here misses you.

Everyone?

    The twins are asking when their mama is coming home. The boys miss your cooking, even your biscuits. I even caught Marty looking at that dress you fixed for her. I've done some fixing up myself, around the place.

What about you, Lucas? Do you miss me?

    Looking around, I can see that there's something missing. It's hard for me to believe what you took.

What?

He was accusing her of stealing? She took nothing but her own clothes. She didn't even take the pearls he gave her. She left more behind than she took. All her mother's treasured things. Now she wished she hadn't written that letter saying she was coming back. Just what did he think she had stolen? Whatever it was, she would be sure to return it. She read on with fury burning in her eyes.

    When I sat down to write that very first letter to you nearly a year ago, my thoughts were not of myself. All I could think about was Lynnette's girls. They needed a mother, nothing else mattered to me. Now it seems I can only think of myself.

    I know I'll never get back what you took, for how does one retrieve his heart when it has been stolen? For that is just what you've done. My heart is yours, now and forever.

                      Lovingly,
                        Lucas

Cinda slipped her fingers across the word "lovingly," caressing each letter. A tear dropped on the paper, smearing Lucas's signature.

"Oh no." She pulled out her white handkerchief and dabbed at the drop. The ink came off, ruining her best handkerchief. She didn't care. The signature was almost illegible. She clutched the letter to her chest.

"I'm coming, Lucas," she whispered, hoping it wasn't too late. *He loves me!* She dashed down the stairs.

"Really, Cinda. Ladies do not run," Aunt Ginny said in disgust.

"Well, maybe they should." Cinda smiled broadly and pecked her aunt on the cheek. "I'll be back later to pack."

Cinda raced in a most unladylike way all the way to Allison's to show her the letter and to say good-bye.

Chapter 22

*C*inda entered the house and smelled the familiar aroma of freshly-baked bread. She went to the kitchen door. The sight of her aunt in the kitchen warmed her, but something seemed wrong. Her aunt stood still at the sink with her back to Cinda. She wasn't washing dishes, though it looked like she was going to. She wasn't even looking out the window over the sink.

"I'm home, Aunt Ginny," Cinda said with a cheerful lilt in her voice.

Her aunt jumped slightly and brought her hands to her face. If Cinda hadn't been looking at her, she would have missed it.

"Aunt Ginny?" Cinda walked over to her and touched her shoulder.

"I didn't hear you come in," she said in a shaky voice.

"What's the matter? Did something happen? Did you get some bad news?"

Her aunt shook her head to all the questions.

"What is it?"

"I'm going to be alone." A tear ran down her face. She wiped it away. "All alone."

Cinda hadn't thought that her aunt might be lonely when she left. She couldn't leave her now. She also knew she couldn't stay. It was simple. There was only one solution. "Pack your things. You're coming with me."

"Where are you taking me?"

Cinda smiled. "Montana, of course."

"I couldn't. That's your home."

"And now it's your home, too. I can't leave you here alone, and I can't stay," she said with a shrug. In Cinda's mind it was easy and settled. She ignored her aunt's protests and started deciding what they would take with them. She remembered the list she had made a few days before she left Montana—the items she wanted to get for Lucas's house. She located all of them and more from her aunt's house.

"What we don't take with us and can't sell, we can give to the church." There were a few larger pieces Cinda knew she could sell to interested parties.

"Are you sure this will be all right with him?" Aunt Ginny asked.

"Most men wouldn't take to their wife's relations being put upon them unexpectedly."

"*Him* has a name. It's Lucas." Cinda smiled to herself. "And Lucas will make no arguments. I can guarantee that." Not after his little surprises when she first arrived in Montana.

Three days later, they stood on the train platform. Cinda was glad her uncle and aunt had rented their house. Now she didn't have to worry about selling that, too.

The two-day train trip seemed to take forever. Cinda was anxious to get back to Lucas. She had herself so worked up, her stomach flipped and turned the entire train ride.

"The first thing we are going to do when we get off this train is find the town doctor," Aunt Ginny said.

"Are you feeling ill?" Cinda hoped not. She didn't know if she could handle more trouble after her uncle's death.

"No. But you obviously are." She had a no-nonsense look on her face. "The doctor can give you something to settle your stomach."

"I'm fine." Cinda tried to assure her. "I'm just anxious."

"You haven't eaten a thing since we got on the train. It won't do any good for you to faint into your husband's arms. Mr. Rawlings will think I have been neglectful in taking care of you."

Cinda didn't think it would do any good to argue, and it would be nice for her stomach to settle.

After seeing the doctor, they went to the livery to rent a wagon and horses. Cinda wasn't going to trust their precious cargo with the stagecoach or some other freight service she didn't know about. Fortunately, Lucas's name was known throughout the region or the liveryman wouldn't have even bothered with them.

They started out early the next morning with their loaded wagon. Cinda hoped their journey wouldn't take more than three days. She also hoped they wouldn't get lost. She didn't think she could cut across the prairie like Lucas did. If she followed the road the stage took to the town south of Lucas's land, then headed north, she couldn't miss. She hoped.

Mid-morning they stopped at a stream to water the horses. When they climbed back aboard and got on their way again, Cinda noticed a horse and rider on the next rise. The silhouette looked vaguely familiar. She soon realized it was the one she had seen when she left on the train. *Please don't see us.* Visions of bandits raced through her mind.

He hadn't really threatened the train Cinda was on. Maybe he wasn't really a bandit but a regular person out for a ride. Cinda racked her brain about what to do, turn and run or continue on, hoping he stayed put. The road forked up ahead. In case he wasn't a figment of her imagination and posed a real threat, she would take the south fork. It led away from him. Then she would loop back around to the northwest.

As soon as she veered to the south, the rider prodded his horse in motion and headed straight for them. Cinda snapped the reins, urging the horses faster. The rider would overtake them in no time. He came at them so swiftly, his hat swept off his head and bounced on his back.

Cinda could see his brown hair bouncing in time with his hat and his strong, determined jawline. *Lucas!* Cinda reined the horses to a halt as he caught up to them. His horse was lathered from being ridden hard for some time, not merely the short distance he just closed between them.

"You're going the wrong way," he said, jumping down from his mount.

"Lucas!" Cinda exclaimed as he pulled her down off the wagon seat.

He was out of breath from the ride and cupped Cinda's face in his hands. He studied her and then pulled her close. She could hear his racing heart. He pushed her away. "Are you all right? You're not hurt are you?" Concern etched his face. Before Cinda could answer, he was squeezing her again. He pushed her away again and looked around. "What are you doing out here alone?"

"I'm not alone." Cinda pointed up to the wagon seat. "Aunt Ginny is with me."

Lucas frowned. He obviously wasn't comforted by that fact. "Don't you know it's dangerous for women to travel alone in the West?"

"I didn't—" Cinda started, but Lucas pulled her into his chest again. The back and forth motion turned her stomach. She wished he would make up his mind, hug her or hold her at arm's length.

When his breathing slowed, he stepped back from her and cradled her face in his hands. "You're really safe?"

Cinda nodded with a weak smile.

Lucas looked deep into her eyes. "They're greener. I couldn't remember if they were greener than alfalfa or not. They are definitely greener." He leaned down, kissing her long and hard. Then he tied his horse to the back of the wagon.

Cinda thought about Lucas up on the hill on his horse before he raced down. Was he the man she thought was a train robber? Were they one and the same? "Lucas, did you follow me to the train when I left?"

His broad mischievous smile emphasized his dimple. He kissed her again. She had her answer. He had seen her safely to the train. Now he helped her up onto the wagon seat and climbed aboard.

"It's good to see you again, Mrs. Crawford." Lucas replaced his Stetson.

"Not as good as it is to see you, Mr. Rawlings," Aunt Ginny said with a formal air.

He turned the wagon north and headed across the prairie. "This is a good pair of horses you got here. I'm surprised they didn't try to push some plugs on you."

"If it weren't for Aunt Ginny, they would have."

Lucas leaned forward and eyed the older woman.

Her aunt kept her gaze forward, sitting properly. "My father was a horse breeder."

Lucas raised his eyebrows. "You made wise choices."

The corners of her aunt's mouth turned up ever so slightly at the compliment, and she sat a little taller.

Chapter 23

Three days later, they pulled into the quiet farmyard. The only activity was the chickens mulling around, pecking at the ground. It was just like the last time. Lucas helped Cinda down and then her aunt. All was quiet, but Cinda knew it wouldn't last. She eagerly waited, listening for that first sound.

There it was!

Cinda's smile broadened. "Here they come."

"Here who—" Aunt Ginny started to ask when the barn door burst open, and Daniella and Daphne, dirty from head to toe, raced full speed toward them, scattering the chickens.

"Mama, Mama," they yelled.

"I hope you don't mind?" Lucas removed his hat. "They asked if they could call you Mama. I said it was all right."

Cinda nodded. Tears filled her eyes as she knelt down to catch the racing pair.

"We missed you sooo much," Daphne said with Daniella chiming in on the sooo.

"I missed you both, sooo much." Cinda hugged and kissed them both.

Trevor strolled out of the barn just like last time. "We weren't sure what happened to you, Lucas. Jed said you got a letter and raced out of town." He looked at Cinda and her aunt. "I see everyone's all right."

Lucas nodded in agreement and introduced Trevor to Cinda's aunt. Cinda had already introduced the twins.

Travis and Marty came racing toward them on horseback. They were neck and neck until Travis veered around a pyramid of three bales of hay at the edge of the yard. Marty sailed over them and into the lead. She skidded to a stop. "Yee haw." She jumped off Flash. "Better luck next time," she gloated to Travis, who was just coming to a halt. "You do my chores for a whole week."

"Mrs. Crawford, this is my other brother, Travis, and my sister, Martha," Lucas said, pointing to the pair.

Aunt Ginny had a horrified expression on her face that she quickly replaced with a sterner one. "I have never seen such rowdy behavior from a young lady."

Martha stepped directly in front of the older woman and planted her balled fists on her hips. "I ain't no lady."

Aunt Ginny stood taller. "That's obvious." The battle of wills had begun. It was a toss-up as to who might win.

Cinda knew her aunt wouldn't back down as easily as she had. In fact, her aunt wouldn't give up at all. She would have Martha in a dress if it were the last thing she did. And it just might be, if Martha had anything to do with it. Life would be interesting with those two.

Aunt Ginny stepped away from Cinda when she saw Dewight approach, eyeing him suspiciously.

"A rose, a rose. To see its beauty. At last it wilts in the desert sun." Dewight looked up to the clear blue sky, smiling and shouted, "The rain comes!" He began twirling around with outstretched arms. "The rose will bloom again." He spun away.

Daniella grabbed one of Cinda's hands and pulled her toward the house. "Come on. You gotta come see the new kitchen."

Daphne quickly grabbed the other hand and pulled as well. "It's so beautiful. Hurry, hurry."

Cinda allowed herself to be dragged in and through the house to the kitchen with everyone tagging along behind. She stopped and caught her breath at the sight.

The worn floorboards were replaced, and the whole floor and the walls had been whitewashed. Cinda ran her hand along the worktable that had been sanded and refinished. Her gaze settled on what used to be the broken-down pantry. The old shelves were gone and replaced with what appeared to be new pantry shelves draped in yellow gingham. Cinda stared at the bright, cheerful room.

Daniella and Daphne pulled back the curtains of the pantry to reveal the shiny new metal mixing bowls and new ceramic serving bowls. The tears Cinda was trying hard to hold back broke free. She tenderly touched the bowls.

"And new spoons, too." Daphne held up an array of metal and wooden spoons.

Daniella snatched a spoon from Daphne's grasp and handed it to Cinda. "Uncle Lucas carved this one hisself."

Cinda clutched the spoon with tear-stained cheeks. He had done all this for her.

"It isn't much, but I guess it will do," her aunt said, looking around.

Lucas looked down.

"No. It's perfect. Absolutely perfect." Cinda smiled lovingly at Lucas when his eyes met hers. "Thank you."

He smiled back.

Chapter 24

*O*ver the next couple of days, Lucas became more and more distant. He was scarce all day. He didn't come in for either lunch or supper. He didn't even come in after supper for their walk. Cinda's stomach twisted, wondering what was wrong. She fixed a plate of food and took it out to the barn where Lucas stood, brushing his horse.

"I brought you something to eat." She held out the plate for him.

"I'm not hungry." He kept stroking his horse.

"You haven't eaten since breakfast. You need to eat."

Lucas yanked the plate from her hand and plopped it on a nearby crate. "I said, I'm not hungry."

Cinda realized she had been wrong—it did bother him that she brought her aunt without asking him first. "I'm sorry for bringing Aunt Ginny without asking you first. I just couldn't leave her all alone."

"You're sorry. *You're* sorry." He dropped his head, shaking it. "It's not your aunt. She's welcome, if you want her here."

"Then what is it?" Cinda was confused. "What have I done to upset you?"

"You haven't done anything," he said softly. "And you have done everything."

Cinda cocked her head sideways. Her confusion was compounded with each passing moment.

"You have done everything I hoped for in a wife and more. I deceived you and dumped my whole family on you. I only heard you complain once. I don't deserve you." He paused, struggling with his emotions. "Why did you come back? There certainly isn't much for you here."

"You're here."

He stopped her before she could say more. "I know you never wanted to marry me."

"But I did. It was my choice."

Lucas pulled a stack of letters out of his back pocket. "I've been asking God what I should do about these. He keeps giving me the same answer. . . 'Ask her.' So I'm asking." He divided the letters into two piles. He held up the group of four letters. "These were written before we were married. Those two were written after we were married. Your handwriting changed." He weighed the two stacks. "Who are you? You're not the woman I asked to marry me."

Cinda reached for the four letters Lucas held. He gave them to her. The writing was Vivian's.

"Are you really Cinda Harrison? Is our marriage even legal?" he asked, sounding as though he really didn't want to know.

Cinda felt bad she hadn't told him about the letters. "Vivian," was all she could manage to whisper.

"Your name is Vivian?"

Cinda shook her head. She looked up at him. "It's Vivian's handwriting."

"Then you are Cinda Harrison?"

Cinda shook her head again and stood up tall. "I'm Cinda Rawlings." Lucas stared at her suspiciously, waiting for her to continue. "Vivian and Eve decided to find a husband for their shy friend before she became an old maid." A tear splashed on her cheek. "It was kind of a joke. I didn't know anything about it until I got your letter the day you arrived."

Lucas caressed the tear away. "Why didn't you tell me? I wouldn't have bothered you any more. You know that."

"I was terrified. I didn't know you then. I didn't know how you would react to being tricked like that. How do you tell a stranger he came a long way for nothing? When I got to know you a little in those few days, I felt God leading me to you. I thought maybe life with you would be easier than with my aunt."

"But it wasn't, was it?" Shame coated his words.

"No, it wasn't. It was hard in a different way. But something strange happened. I was needed here. I needed to be needed. I was an only child and wasn't used to all the commotion of a large family. I'm still not used to it, but I do know this is where I want to be—with you."

Lucas grabbed her and held her tight. "Whatever did I do to deserve a blessing such as you? The more I get to know you, the more convinced I am I don't deserve you." He stepped back from her. "When I married you, I wasn't thinking of you as a person with feelings. To me you were the solution to a problem. And if you were the woman of character I hoped and prayed you were, you would stay out of a sense of duty even after you met my family."

He leaned against a stall post and looked down at his boots. "I always wanted to have a loving relationship like my parents, but I had to give that up a long time ago."

"When your parents died?"

He nodded and continued. "I didn't have time for anything. My brothers and sisters needed me. The farm needed me. Then Lynnette and her girls needed me. I thought if I could find a good mother for Lynnette's girls, that was all that was important. I didn't have to have love as long as they did." He turned his focus back to Cinda. "I'm sorry for not being honest about my family. I have always felt bad for not telling you. Can you ever forgive me?"

"Of course, Lucas." Cinda stepped up to him, wrapping her arms around his waist.

He held her close for a long while. "I thought I was going to die when you left. I never expected to love you."

"I love you, too." She could feel Lucas's arms tighten around her. "You really don't mind about my aunt? I just couldn't leave her all alone."

"If you can live with my family, I can live with yours. You only have one relative, I sprang five on you. Six if you count Dwight."

Dwight definitely counted. Cinda decided now was a good time to spring another one on him and held up two fingers. "Two relatives."

"Two? I thought your aunt and uncle were your only ones?" Lucas pulled his brows together. "You have another relative coming? When?"

Cinda shrugged her shoulders and smiled. "In about seven months. But it's not just my relation, it's yours as well." She patted her stomach.

Lucas looked from her stomach up to her face and smiled broadly, his eyes bright with hope. "You're going to have a baby?"

"*We* are going to have a baby."

Lucas picked her up and spun her around. "I'm so happy."

"Me, too."

"You know what this means?" he asked, putting her down.

Cinda shook her head.

"No more my family and your family." He gently put his hand on her stomach. "This baby ties us all together as one big family. *Our* family."

Cinda nodded. They headed to the house. She hadn't slept well since she left, but she would tonight. She didn't know if it was the hard work or the company—maybe both. She didn't care. She was home with her family and the man she loved.

Mary Davis is a full-time writer whose first published novel was *Newlywed Games* from Multnomah. She enjoys visiting schools and talking to kids about writing. Mary lives near Colorado's Rocky Mountains with her husband of over thirty years and two cats. She is thoroughly enjoying her new role as a grandma. You can find her online at www.marydavisbooks.com.

His Brother's Bride

by Denise Hunter

Dedicated to Colleen Coble and Kristin Billerbeck, my awesome
critique partners and superb witers in their own right.
You are my eagle eyes, my encouragement, my sounding board,
my travel buddies, and my dear friends. Love Ya!

Chapter 1

*E*mily Wagner untied the handkerchief from around her nose and mouth, breathing the undiluted dust for the first time of the day. The stage rocked over a rut, and she jostled the woman beside her. She thought to excuse herself, but after six days together and hundreds of such bumps, they were beyond such niceties.

Emily resituated herself as best she could in her fifteen inches of space—less than that when she accounted for the heavy man on one side whose body overlapped onto her. She tried to wipe away the dirt she knew covered her face. When she'd dreamed of seeing Thomas for the first time, never had she envisioned her face streaked with dust and her hair powdered gray.

She felt a trickle of sweat slip down her temple and wiped it away with the dirty handkerchief. To think she'd spent the last of her money on this ride.

It is money well spent, though, for it will bring me to Thomas. She smiled, her thoughts on her betrothed, then realized she was grinning stupidly at the scoundrel seated across from her. His knees, dovetailing with hers in the tight space, knocked softly against hers in a movement she suspected was not altogether necessary.

She wiped the smile from her face and looked down at her white fingers clutching her reticule. Thankfully, she was almost to Cedar Springs and her new life. She vowed she could not endure another day on this stage.

That was not entirely true, she admitted to herself. In truth, she would endure anything to save her grandmother from her uncle Stewart's clutches. And this wasn't such a sacrifice at all.

She was eager to meet Thomas and have a real family at last. Thomas would be a wonderful father; she didn't have to see him in person to know that. They would have many children, and at last, she would have a real family, all her own. She cared not that the land Thomas farmed with his brother was not prosperous.

She'd had little enough in Denver under Uncle Stewart's negligent care. She would make sure her new home was filled with laughter and warmth—and one day, the pitter-patter of tiny feet.

But first, though, I must find the gold. And soon, for Nana's sake. She closed her eyes and tried not to think of what was at stake. She would not think of sad things today—when she was about to meet Thomas.

It couldn't be long now until they reached the town. She opened her reticule and withdrew the letter she'd saved for last. She'd reread one each day of her journey as a small reward to mark the time and lift her spirits.

She unfolded the paper, her insides buzzing at just the thought of Thomas's words. His bold, slanted script brought her familiar comfort. She held the page close to her, an effort to hide the private note from the woman seated beside her. Miss Donahue was quite beautiful but had a propensity to be somewhat nosy.

Focusing her thoughts on her intended, Emily read the words she'd nearly memorized.

> *Dear Emily,*
>
> *I am so pleased and honored that you have agreed to join me in marriage. I know you will make a fine wife and, Lord willing, a loving mother to any children we bear. I hope I will not be a disappointment to you, Emily, for you are deserving of the finest things in life.*
>
> *Cade is happy for me, and we both look forward to your arrival. It was generous of you to offer to look after Adam during the daytime. It has been hard on my brother, both losing his wife, and caring for a child and a farm all at once.*
>
> *Every day I thank God that your uncle found my grandfather's letter. It is astounding that but for that one missive, we would never have begun our correspondence.*
>
> *I so look forward to meeting you in person. You have been a great encouragement to me these two years.*
>
> *I will expect you in Cedar Springs, then, on the eighteenth of May. I will be the man wearing a proud smile.*
>
> *Fondly,*
> *Thomas*

Emily sighed happily and folded the letter. How many women got to marry their dearest friend? She closed her eyes and pressed the paper to her chest.

Thank You, Jesus. Thank You for this man, for his willingness to marry me. Forgive me for my role in this deceit. Help me to find success for Nana's sake. Bless my union with Thomas, and Lord, bless us with children. My heart fills to overflowing with thoughts of our babe in my arms!

The stage hit a rut and lurched. Emily grabbed the hanging leather strap, her only means of support in the center seat.

"Well, I'll be plumb tickled when this misery is over, I can tell you that," Miss Donahue said.

"Shan't be long now, if your destination is Cedar Springs, Kansas," said a gentleman behind her.

Emily's heart thudded heavily in her chest at the words. Her limbs felt weightless and jittery with anticipation. She turned, a difficult task with the heavy man at her side. "How long do you think?"

The man looked beyond her out the front of the stage. "We're coming up on the town even now, Miss. And 'tis glad I am to see it."

Emily turned quickly and looked just over the crest of a hill. A small town of mostly one-story structures loomed ahead. A few tall buildings and a church sat perched on a grassy hill at the far end of town.

Her mouth grew dry as her eyes scanned the approaching town. There were folks here and there, and numerous wagons, some parked, some moving. Where would the stage stop? Was Thomas waiting even now, as he'd promised?

She glanced down at her watch pin. They were nearly forty-five minutes late, but that was to be expected. They entered town, passing over a bridge, the horses' hooves clopping loudly. The heat was forgotten. The dust was a dull memory as she looked ahead.

They approached a tall, white structure—Cooper's Restaurant and Boardinghouse, according to the sign—and the horses slowed to a walk. A few folks lingered on the porch, and her stomach fluttered at the sight of a tall, dark-haired man among the others.

It was him, it must be. He was the only man except for an elderly gentleman. His skin was darkened like a farmer's, though she would not have described him as gangly, as he had in one of his letters.

The stage drew to a sudden halt, and Emily was forced to take her eyes off Thomas long enough to steady herself with the hanging strap. Her torso pitched forward then back as the carriage settled in place. The woman next to her stood, eager to exit the stage, and Emily could see Thomas no longer.

She withdrew her hanky one last time and tried to wipe the dust from her face. When she brushed at her skirt, dust billowed from it. Oh, how she wished she were wearing clean clothes!

The driver opened the door, and the passengers began filing out, though most would be staying only long enough for the noon meal. Emily stood when there was room, then inched along the aisle, stooped over like an old woman because of the low ceiling.

Her stomach stirred with anxiety. What if Thomas thought her plain or homely? What if he changed his mind when he saw her? The thoughts tumbled through her mind and settled heavily upon her heart.

When she reached the stage door, the driver assisted her down, and Emily immediately sought Thomas's gaze. His own eyes, though, had settled on Miss Donahue, who was in front of her. The woman wore a hat over her dark hair, and Emily realized Thomas had mistaken the comely woman for her.

A cold, hard lump formed in her stomach. Of course he'd be hoping the beautiful Miss Donahue were his wife-to-be.

When the other woman rushed past Thomas and embraced the elderly man and woman, her betrothed's gaze left and scattered around the remaining travelers. His gaze settled upon hers when she stopped a few feet shy of him.

He was handsome; there was no getting around that. His dark hair reached just below his jawline on either side of his face, and his eyes, just below the rim of his hat, were a curious mix of blue and green.

A smile tilted her lips; she was unable to suppress her delight at meeting him at last. Everything in her wanted to embrace him. She knew him so well, and he her. She'd bared her heart to him on many occasions.

"Miss Wagner," he said loudly, speaking over the crowd of people. He removed his hat, and Emily noticed for the first time that he was not smiling. His lips were drawn instead in a tight line.

Her smile faltered. Surely they had progressed beyond the formalities. "Emily," she corrected. They were to be married, after all.

He nodded once. "Emily. I hope your trip was uneventful. I'm afraid I. . ." He cleared his throat, his gaze breaking contact with hers. He twisted the brim of his hat between strong fingers.

His awkwardness was beyond endearing. She found herself smiling once again. Of course, he was simply nervous, just as she. Emily cupped his arm with her hand. "Oh, Thomas, I am so glad to be here." She tilted her head and affected an impish grin. "And not just because the ride was most dreadful."

"Emily, I have to tell you—"

"These your bags, ma'am?" The driver set two satchels at her feet.

"Why, yes, thank you."

The stage crowd bustled into the restaurant leaving her alone with

Thomas. The sudden quiet pressed in around them. Something was wrong; she could see it in his eyes. Perhaps he was disappointed; she was no Miss Donahue, after all. The thought stung, but she could imagine what the heat and dust had done to her average appearance.

"I must look a mess." She tucked a stray hair behind her ear.

"You're fine, it's not—I'm afraid I—"

For the first time, a fire of dread burned within her. His hollow eyes spoke of more than uneasiness or disappointment. Liquid heat surged through her limbs and up her spine. "What is it, Thomas?"

His eyes were shrouded with emotion. She tried to read them, tried desperately to determine what had him so upset.

"I'm not Thomas." He cleared the raspiness from his throat.

"Not Thomas?" Was that all? Did Thomas have to stay behind at the farm? Perhaps he was afraid she'd be offended. Suddenly she realized who he must be. "Cade?" A hesitant smile formed. Relief began flowing through her, cooling the raging fire of dread.

"Yes, ma'am, Cade Manning." He held out his hand, and she clasped it with her own.

His hand felt big and strong, his grasp firm, yet gentle. "Was Thomas unable to get away? I understand completely. Please don't think I'm upset." Her reassuring smile was not returned.

"Miss Wagner—Emily." He met her gaze directly, and she realized he had not let go of her hand. "Two days ago Thomas's wagon tipped over into a deep ravine. He was thrown off. Apparently his head struck a stone or tree. . . ."

Emily's thoughts slurred. She tried to focus on what he was saying, but panic reverberated in her mind. *Wagon tipped. . .struck a stone. . . No. No, it can't be.* She shook her head and forced herself to speak. "What are you saying?"

His eyes were laced with sadness and something else. Pity, she realized through a fog of fear.

"I'm sorry, Emily, but there will be no wedding." His Adam's apple bobbed once, and shadows danced in the hollows of his cheeks as he clenched his jaw. "Thomas is dead."

Chapter 2

*D*ead? Emily's mind faltered on the word. Her thoughts swam. Her knees buckled.

Cade caught her arm with a strong grip. "Whoa, there."

She felt his hand at her back, was aware of him guiding her away from the street. He was speaking, but his words came as if from some deep cavern.

Not Thomas, Lord! Not her dear friend. The only godly man in her life. What would she do now without him? She'd spent all her money to get here, and now there was no Thomas to meet her. No friend to marry.

Her thoughts careened wildly before coming to an abrupt halt. If Thomas were dead, she wouldn't be able to search his house for the map.

She didn't even have a way back to Uncle Stewart and Nana. She would have to tell her uncle she'd failed. That his plans were ruined. And what would he do then?

Poor Nana. How could Emily let Uncle Stewart put her in the asylum? But what choice would she have when she'd failed to find the gold?

"I'm sorry," Cade said. "I shouldn't have told you so sudden-like."

Emily looked at him. She was sitting on a bench beside him and wondered idly how she'd gotten there. Her satchels sat at her feet.

Her eyes stung as she looked into eyes that were probably very like Thomas's had been. This man had lost his brother not two days hence, and the pain was still written plainly on his face. She remembered his wife had died in childbirth a few years back, leaving him and his little boy alone.

Guilt swarmed her mind. How could she be so selfish as to think of her own predicament?

"I'm sorry for your loss," she said. "You must be missing him mightily."

He propped his elbows on his knees, and his gaze found the planked porch. "He was a good man. A faithful man." His fingers played with the worn brim of his hat. "He cared a great deal for you."

Emily felt her face grow warm at his perusal. She'd cared for Thomas, too. She had never known a person could care so much for one they'd yet to meet.

"He was chomping at the bit about your arrival. Couldn't talk of much else for days."

Emily let the silence fall around them. She thought of the letters in her reticule and pulled the satchel closer to her body. It was all she had left of her friend. She felt like part of her had died. And in a way, it had. For Thomas had been dear to her, and she'd dreamed of a new life with him. And now that dream was dead.

She looked around the town, trying to clear her mind. She had to think practically. She was on her own in a foreign town with no money and no family. *I have to get back to Nana and somehow explain to Uncle Stewart what's happened.*

"You must be hungry."

Her stomach recoiled at the thought of food. She shook her head.

"Well, you'll be wanting to head home, I reckon. I'd like to pay for the stage back to Denver and a room for tonight, if need be."

Her heart caught at his thoughtfulness. Did he know she was nearly penniless? But she knew Thomas and Cade barely made ends meet with their farm. "I couldn't let you do that."

"Thomas would have wanted me to."

She opened her mouth to argue but closed it. What choice had she? "Thank you kindly," she whispered.

He stood. "You stay right here, and I'll make arrangements."

She managed a smile of gratitude before he turned and walked into the establishment. Her heart felt smothered with sadness. She would never meet Thomas. He would never hold her or give her the children she so desperately wanted. Tears stung her eyes. She'd thought to have a new life, but she would be going back to her old one. Only this time it would be far worse, because she had failed her uncle.

Oh, Nana, I'm sorry. I tried my best, but I've already failed you, and now Uncle Stewart will send you away for good.

It wasn't fair. Her grandmother wasn't dangerous to herself or anyone else. She was only befuddled from time to time. There was no help for that. But she deserved to be loved and cared for, not locked up like a mad woman. Her uncle didn't care about her grandmother, though. He'd gained guardianship so he could acquire her home and possessions.

Emily watched a wagon clatter by on the dirt road. The white chapel, perched on the grassy knoll, seemed to watch over the town like an eagle watches over her young. Across the street, two men loaded sacks onto their wagon bed, their muscles straining against their shirts. She could picture Thomas here, in this quaint town of Cedar Springs. He'd described it to her in his letters, and his words came alive before her very eyes. His house and farm would have been no different. *You'll love the grassy meadows and rolling hills,* he'd written.

When Cade appeared again at her side, he took her hand and helped her from the bench. She scarcely reached his shoulders.

"It's all arranged. There's no need for you to stay here tonight. The stage leaves right after the noon meal for Wichita. From there, you can catch another stage back to Denver. If you'll follow me, I'll take you to Mrs. Cooper. She'll take care of you."

She followed him to a counter where an attractive middle-aged woman stood. After introductions, the woman picked up Emily's satchels. "Cade said you might like to clean up. You can rest a bit until your stage leaves, if you like." She turned and made for the stairs. "Right this way, Miss."

Emily turned awkwardly to Cade. He replaced his hat and extended his hand. "Good luck to you, Emily."

His hand surrounded hers with warmth. She could feel calluses against the softness of her palm. "And to you." With that, she turned and retreated up the stairs.

After closing the door behind the kindly woman, Emily sank onto the soft bed and stared at the patterned wallpaper. Its swirls and whirls seemed to echo the directions of her thoughts. Even sitting here now, she couldn't believe it was true. Thomas was dead.

"Why, God?" she whispered to the empty room. He was so young, with a full life ahead of him. She'd been so looking forward to meeting him in person. They would've been so close, she just knew it. And she longed for a close relationship. She'd been so lonely since her mama had passed on. Even Nana, dear though she was to Emily, had not filled the empty place in her heart because her confusion and memory loss prevented a normal discussion.

She detected the aroma of fried chicken in the air, and her stomach turned. Though she'd not eaten since dawn, she knew she couldn't force down a single bite. She needed to gather her thoughts, to figure out what she was going to do.

She reached into her reticule and pulled out her diary. Whenever she needed to sort her thoughts, that was what she did.

Dear Diary,
I scarcely know how to write the words that I heard only minutes ago. I don't want to write them, for I fear putting them

into print will make it more real. But that is what needs to happen. Perhaps then the truth will begin to sink in.

Thomas is dead. I learned the dreaded news upon my arrival in Cedar Springs. Thomas's brother, Cade, met me at the stage stop. He looks a bit as I thought Thomas would, though he's sturdier than Thomas described himself. I will never forget the look in Cade's eyes. I have never seen such emptiness. And as I remember the loss of his wife several years ago, I know that Thomas's death must have dealt a harsh blow to him.

I have only minutes to decide what I am to do. Though, I suppose, there is really little choice in the matter. Cade has graciously agreed to pay my fare back to Denver. It's a good thing, too, because I am nearly penniless at the moment.

Only the thought of facing Uncle Stewart makes me question my decision. What will he do when he discovers I have not been able to follow through with his plan? Never mind that it is no one's fault. He will somehow find a way to assign blame to me. I don't fear for myself, but I do fear that he will take his anger and disappointment out on Nana.

From below, she heard the sounds of chairs scraping across the floor and knew her stage would be leaving soon. She packed the diary back into her bag and took a few minutes to freshen her appearance before leaving the room.

"Gee-up!" Cade snapped the reins, and the horses began walking, kicking up the dry Kansas dirt. He paid no heed to the direction he went; his bays knew their way home.

The familiar knot in his stomach coiled tighter the farther he got from town. He hated leaving the woman there alone. She'd walked away from him, following Mrs. Cooper up the stairs, her shoulders slumped, her head down.

Thomas had not told him much about Miss Wagner's life in Denver, but he wondered if she had much to return to back home.

When she'd gotten off the stage, he'd been taken with her obvious awkwardness. Her chin had tipped down, and he'd dreaded telling her about Thomas. She'd come all that way thinking her future was secure.

And when she'd mistaken him for Thomas, his own heart clenched. He shook his head. It had been one of the most difficult moments of his life. These past two days had been almost more than he could bear.

Of course, he was acquainted with grief. When he'd lost Ingrid, he'd thought his body would wither up and die with the pain of it. But he'd had Adam to care for and raise. And the women in town helped out a great deal. Some of the townsfolk cared for baby Adam while Cade resumed farm work, but they had their own lives, their own families to care for. Eventually, Cade assumed full responsibility for Adam. And his brother was there to pick up the slack around the farm when he had to tend to his son.

But now Thomas was gone. It was only he and Adam. How would he manage the farm and his busy five-year-old? Even if he got neighbors' help for a while, how would he manage every day, month after month, year after year?

He tried to picture his daily routine without Thomas. He would prepare breakfast as usual. But Thomas had always milked the cow, collected the eggs, and slopped the pigs while he'd fixed breakfast. Now he'd somehow have to do all that. And the laundry, mending, cleaning, and butter-making. And, with spring arriving, the land had to be plowed and the seed planted. That alone was a dawn-to-dusk job, if he wanted to have enough harvested to keep them all winter. How could he manage Adam with all that? He and Thomas together had scarcely managed to get the work done.

Lord, I can't do all that by myself, he prayed.

He rubbed his chin and felt the scruff from the past couple days. His mouth was dry, his throat tight. He sighed heavily, rocking on the seat as the wagon cleared the ruts in the road.

Sara McClain was at the house with Adam now, and he knew she would offer to help. But he needed more than help. He needed a full-time worker. He needed someone to care for Adam while he worked in the fields. He needed someone to do some of the chores around the house. He needed. . .

A wife.

The word hit him square in the gut. He didn't want a wife. He felt as if he still had one. Ingrid. His heart still belonged to her. It seemed wrong to even think of taking another woman. It seemed like a betrayal.

She's gone. I know that, and losing her was too hard. Too painful. I don't want to go through that again. Loving hurts. Hadn't he loved Ingrid and lost her? Hadn't he loved Thomas and lost him, too?

But he needed help, there was no denying that. There were practical matters to consider here. He didn't have the luxury of getting his life the way he wanted it. If he did, he would be on his way home to Ingrid even now.

One of his bays whinnied and scuttled around a deep groove in the road. The afternoon sun beat down on his skin, and a trickle of sweat rolled down his face from beneath his hat.

What was he to do? If he took a wife, it would have to be an arrangement of sorts. He couldn't give himself to her the way he had to Ingrid. But what woman would marry under those circumstances?

Emily.

His grip tightened on the reins. He thought of Thomas's words about his intended. He'd read parts of her letters aloud, so Cade knew a little about her. And somehow, he knew, Thomas would have approved of Cade taking care of Emily. He'd once mentioned a strain in her relationship with her guardian uncle.

He rubbed his chin. Could this be the answer? Would Emily agree to such an arrangement? His heart caught in his chest even as his thoughts bounced to and fro. It might work. She might agree to marry him, and then Adam would have a woman to nurture him the way only a ma could. He wanted that for his son.

He would do it. He would ask her. The worst thing she could do was say no. He noted the sun's position in the sky and drew in a quick breath. The stage was leaving after the noon meal. And Emily would be on it.

He pulled the reins to turn the horses. He had to get back to town and fast.

"Yaw!" he cried, and snapped the reins.

Emily made her way out to the porch with her two satchels in hand. She felt clean after washing the dust off her skin and brushing the dirt from her hair. She'd wanted to change her dress, but the other two in her case were in no better condition. So she'd made do and beat the dirt from the material with her brush.

Her fellow travelers were entering the stage, so she handed her satchels up to the driver. She would wait until the very last minute to board. The thought of three more days on the stage was almost as daunting as the thought of returning home to her uncle.

"Board!" the driver called as he hoisted himself up onto his seat.

She reluctantly stepped up into the stage and took the only seat left, the uncoveted middle bench. She settled the folds of her skirt and tried to avoid the gaze of the man across from her.

The stage jerked forward as the horses were spurred on. A clatter at the side of her stage caught her attention. She looked out the window and saw a wagon pulled alongside the stage.

"Stop the stage!"

The words came from Cade, who balanced on the edge of his seat as if willing to cut the stage's horses off with his own.

The stage slowed to a stop. The curses from the driver were muffled by the roof over her head.

"Whatever's the trouble?" Miss Donahue asked.

A man behind her sighed. "We're already behind schedule."

But Emily's mind spun with confusion. What was Cade up to? What if he'd changed his mind about paying for the stage? She would be stranded here with nothing, with no one.

Her traveling companions watched as Cade leaped off his wagon bench and hurried to the stage door.

"Oh!" Miss Donahue said.

The door flung open. His gaze darted around the stage and settled on hers. She saw a twitch of surprise and realized the last time he'd seen her she'd been a filthy mess.

"Can I have a word with you in private, Miss Wagner?"

"Well, I—"

"Get off and let us be on our way," one man said.

"I'm not leaving until I have a word with her." His gaze didn't leave hers.

Emily, drawn by the intensity of his gaze, began to rise.

"Then say your peace and be done with it," said someone behind her.

"Yeah, Mister, you're holding us up."

Emily settled back in the seat and tried to read his face.

"Very well." He removed his hat and looked down at where his foot was perched on the door ledge.

His gaze found hers again. "Look, Miss Wagner, it's like this. You came here needing a husband, a home. My brother can't offer you that anymore."

Emily's heart stomped a hoedown in her chest. Her stomach tightened.

"I need a wife. My son needs a ma."

Out the corner of her eye she saw Miss Donahue's fan begin fluttering.

"We don't have much to offer." He looked down again, and Emily's throat constricted. "But we have a home where you'd be welcomed."

Emily could scarcely believe it. It was an answer to her prayers. Cade was a godly man; she knew that from Thomas's letters. He would be a good husband to her. She opened her mouth.

"Before you say anything—" He stopped and took in their rapt audience.

Emily, too, glanced around her. Miss Donahue leaned forward, her fan twitching erratically. One impatient man rolled his eyes, and two of the men in the back stared unabashedly, their arms crossed impatiently. She looked back at Cade.

"This could solve both our problems. I need to explain a few things, though—"

"Enough already!" the impatient man said. He glared at Emily. "Answer the man, and be done with it."

Her body felt weightless, and her mouth went dry. "I. . ." She looked at Cade. "I—yes, I accept your offer."

She heard Miss Donahue draw in a sharp breath.

A smile spread wide across Cade's face. "I'm honored, Miss Wagner." He held out a hand and assisted her off.

"Get your own bags," the driver snapped.

Cade hefted down her satchels and set them at her feet as the stage lurched away.

"Best of luck to you!" Miss Donahue called out the window.

Emily turned to Cade, her face growing warm under his gaze.

"I'd like to find Pastor Hill and get this settled tonight, if that's agreeable to you."

She nodded. "Of course."

He walked her to his wagon and set her satchels in the wooden bed. As he helped her onto the bench and walked around to mount up beside her, Emily couldn't stop the glimmer of hope that spread like sweet honey through her veins.

Chapter 3

*P*astor Hill winked at Cade. "You may kiss your bride."

Emily felt her face flood with heat as her new husband leaned toward her. His lips touched her warm cheek, and she pushed away a niggle of disappointment. He might be her husband, but they had only met today, after all. Still, she was not so naive that she didn't know the intimacy they would share tonight. The heat in her face flooded outward to her ears, and she hoped they didn't glow red.

"Congratulations, dear," Mrs. Hill, who'd graciously served as their witness, said. "You're most welcome to come back to the house with us; I made two pies this morning."

"Thank you kindly, Mrs. Hill," Cade said. "But I need to get back to Adam."

After they bade farewell to the older couple, Cade helped Emily onto the wagon bench, and they made their way to the farm. On the way there, Cade told her about Adam. Emily already knew he was five, and she was looking forward to taking care of him. She laughed when he told her Adam's favorite activity was playing in the dirt with sticks. "He's right fond of his marbles, too," he said.

He told her about their farm. They had a milking cow, chickens, pigs, and the two horses that pulled the wagon. He was a wheat farmer, and they had a garden to the side of the house where she would grow corn, tomatoes, onions, and anything else she wanted to plant.

Cade seemed relaxed and serious as he spoke. But excitement stirred within Emily. She was a married woman now. Tonight, she and Cade would begin their lives as husband and wife. Soon, she would carry a child of her own. Not that she wouldn't love Adam. She thought she would love him as her own. But everything in her longed to carry a baby within her womb, to deliver a son or daughter and nurse the babe at her breast. And she wanted lots of children. She wanted a house full of laughter and teasing like she'd had as a child.

Cade turned the horses onto another road. "This is it."

The long road was packed dirt with tall grass on both sides. In the distance, a two-story white clapboard house sat, flanked by a barn on one side and a grove of trees on the other.

As they pulled up to the house, a boy burst through the door, followed by a petite woman with lovely dark hair. Immediately, Emily cringed as she thought of her own haphazard appearance.

"Pa!" Adam hardly waited for the wagon to stop before he clambered up into Cade's lap for a hug. "Who's she?"

"Adam, where's your manners?"

Cade introduced her as Emily but didn't mention she was his new wife. Emily figured it was probably best to wait until they were at least in the house before telling the boy.

He introduced the woman as Sara McClain, a neighbor, and the two women exchanged pleasantries. Emily knew the woman must have wondered who she was and why she'd come to Cade's home, but to her credit, she didn't pry.

After the horses were put up and Mrs. McClain left, Cade took her into the house. Immediately, she could tell it was a man's home. There were no fripperies or bric-a-brac lying around. The furniture looked sturdy, but the room seemed almost barren. It was, however, recently swept, probably by Mrs. McClain.

After she'd looked around, she noticed Cade was speaking to Adam. "So now she's going to live here with us."

Adam glanced at Emily, and she smiled tenderly. "I hope we can be friends, Adam."

"I already have lots of friends." A thoughtful frown puckered his brow. His eyes were an expressive blue, and she watched as they studied her seriously. "I don't have a ma, though."

Emily's heart caught at the innocent expression on the boy's face. She sensed Cade going still at Adam's side. Was he afraid Adam would forget his real mother? Emily didn't want to do anything to hurt Cade, but the boy clearly longed for a ma.

She squatted down to his level. "You don't have a ma, and do you know what? I don't have a little boy. Maybe we can fill the gap for each other. Would that be all right?"

Her gaze darted up to Cade's. He seemed to approve.

"Do you know how to play marbles?" Adam asked.

"No, I surely don't. Perhaps you can teach me."

Adam nodded. "Okay. I can teach you what boys do, and you can show me what a ma does."

Emily held out her hand, her heart squeezing tightly. "It's a deal."

Later that night, as Emily and Cade tucked Adam into bed, she hugged the boy. The straw ticking crackled with the movement. "Good night, Adam. Sweet dreams."

"Night, Emily."

She left the room, leaving Cade to say good night, and made her way down the stairs to clean up the mess from supper. As she pumped water into the basin, her thoughts drifted to the man upstairs. *My husband,* she thought, a giddy feeling racing through her. Thomas's brother. It was strange, how it had all happened. While her heart ached with the loss of her dear friend, she was married to his brother.

She shook her head, willing away the sadness over her loss. She had a husband and child now to look after. And a treasure map to find.

She chased the thought away. She wouldn't think of it now. Tonight was for her and her new husband to become one. Heat simmered in her belly as she considered what lay ahead for her. Her mother had told her very little on the subject, but what she had shared with Emily left her anticipating the night ahead. If she could only settle her nerves. She wondered how long it would take her to conceive. She hoped it would be soon.

She scrubbed the crust of okra from the pan and rinsed it under a flow of cold water. She heard a floorboard creak above her head and knew Cade must be leaving Adam's room. Her belly tightened as she anticipated his appearance.

She began scrubbing another pan and tried to calm herself. By the time she'd finished the dishes and dumped the water, Cade had still not joined her. Maybe he was waiting for her to join him. Warmth kindled in her stomach, and her breath caught in her throat. She leaned over the kitchen lamp and blew out the flame.

Cade threw the last pair of trousers from the armoire into the bag at his feet and sat on the edge of his bed. All his personal belongings were ready to be moved into Adam's room. Emily's bags were still downstairs, and he needed to bring them up for her. He would let her have this room, and he would sleep in Adam's bed, as he'd just told him. His son had been tickled pink.

He would have to go back downstairs, but he needed a few minutes to gather himself. It felt awkward having a woman in the house again. And not just any woman, but his wife. Not in the true sense of the word, he reminded himself.

He looked at the bed where he and Ingrid had spent many cold nights huddled together beneath the covers. It had brought him some comfort over the past five years to sleep in this bed, as if he could recapture her here. But now, Emily would sleep here, and he would have to leave Ingrid behind. He knew it was time. Past time. Five years was too long to hold on to someone who was gone.

A tap sounded on the door. Emily probably needed her things brought up to her room. He stood, walked to the door, and turned the metal knob.

Emily stood on the threshold, a vision in white. A smile trembled on her lips. The simple nightgown she wore was modest, but his face grew warm, and his gaze dropped to the floor. There, ten bare toes peeked from beneath a white lace hem. His mouth felt suddenly dry.

Emily forced her eyes to meet Cade's when he opened the door. Everything in her wanted to turn and flee. Her breath came so rapidly that her chest heaved beneath the gown.

His eyes widened, his jaw went slack, then he looked down. His discomfiture only served to embarrass her further. She should have waited for him to come to her.

His body blocked the door, and she wondered why he didn't move to let her in. She should say something, anything. "Is Adam settled?"

He nodded, though his gaze avoided hers. "He's fine."

Silence filled the hallway again. "Supper's all cleaned up."

He nodded. "Good, good. Find everything all right?"

"Yes."

Her skin was growing warmer by the minute beneath the gown. She felt flushed and wondered if he could tell. No, he would have to look at her to tell, and he was looking anywhere but at her. Wasn't he going to take the lead? Isn't that what husbands were supposed to do? She bit the inside of her cheek. She would just have to say it. "May I come in?"

He looked at her then. His eyes widened again ever so slightly, and his lips parted as if he were about to speak. Instead, he stepped aside. Far aside, giving her a wide berth.

She stepped through the door into the small room. One lantern by the bed cast a dim light in the room. Shadows danced across the quilted bedspread, across the wooden floors. The room was clean and sparse, even more so than the rest of the house, so her eyes went automatically to the bags that sat on the floor. Clothes spilled from one bag while the other was topped with a daguerreotype in a wooden frame. The woman in the picture stared somberly back at her.

His things were all bundled up together there on the floor. She cast another glance around the room. There wasn't a single item on the armoire or night table. Her gaze found the bags on the floor, then Cade's face. He'd packed up all his things. But why?

A cold dread settled heavily in her stomach.

"I thought you might be more comfortable in here."

In here? Of course she'd be more comfortable in here; where else would she go? The barn? She searched his face, but his eyes were avoiding hers.

"I'm fixin' to move to Adam's room."

He was moving out? But why? Her thoughts tumbled back to the scene on the stagecoach—mere hours ago. *Before you say anything. . .I have some things to explain. . . .*

Is this what he'd wanted to explain on the stage? That he wanted a marriage in name only? He should have told her so right then and there!

She'd come to him wanting their marriage to start right. She'd come to him wanting to please him. She'd come here. . . .

She looked down at herself, clothed in a thin nightgown, and remembered the way he'd averted his gaze upon opening the door. Her skin grew warm until she thought she might glow. She'd all but thrown herself at him, and he didn't want her.

She bolted past him, wanting to escape the stifling room.

He grabbed her arm as she passed. "Emily." There was gentle coaxing in his voice.

"Let go." *Lord, please just let me melt in a puddle and sink through these floorboards.*

"I'm sorry, I thought you understood."

She looked away from him—couldn't bear to let him see her face. *What a brazen woman he must think me, coming to him dressed so.*

"I tried to explain on the stage," he rasped. "But the others. . ."

Her legs felt weak, and she wondered that they supported her at all. His grasp gentled on her arm, and the skin beneath it felt so feverishly hot.

"It's not you, it's—I just can't. I'm sorry."

Her eyes stung, and she knew tears would soon follow. She would not let him see her cry. Hadn't she humiliated herself enough this night?

She gave a nod and tore away from him, dashing through the door and down the stairs. She wanted to run outside and keep going until she had no breath left in her. She settled for the porch instead.

The door creaked behind her as she closed it softly. Her eyes still stung, though they were as dry as the prairie after a long, hot summer. She walked on wobbly legs to the porch swing and dropped into it.

Please, Lord, don't let him follow me out here.

She'd never in her life been so humiliated. What had possessed her to go to him that way? They were strangers. No matter that they'd been joined in holy matrimony, they'd only met that very day.

Who am I to presume what he wants? Perhaps he finds me repulsive.

Her heart caught at the thought. The hollow ache in her stomach filled with pain. She wasn't very comely, she knew that. Her uncle had reminded her often enough.

She remembered the daguerreotype she'd seen in Cade's room. The woman—his former wife—had been lovely. She'd had golden hair and petite features. And those haunting eyes.

What did Emily have? Drab brown hair and plain features. She must look as appealing to him as a garden weed. She crossed her arms, feeling exposed. The night air had grown chilly, but it felt good against her warm skin. She wanted to stay out here all night. She wanted to stay out here forever.

How would she ever face him again? She'd gone to his room practically begging.

She closed her eyes. She didn't want to think about it anymore. She was his wife now—even if in name only—and she had a job. She still had to find the treasure map for Uncle Stewart. She still had to take care of Adam.

For the first time, it occurred to her that if there were no intimacy, there would be no child. She would never feel her baby kick her from within. She would never bring her own child into the world. She would never hold a suckling babe in her arms. Her throat constricted with the pain of it.

Oh, no, Lord Jesus, what have I done? In marrying Cade, she'd given up her one true desire, and there was no treasure in the world worth that.

Chapter 4

Dear Uncle Stewart,

I'm sorry it has taken so long to write. There have been some changes you need to be aware of. When I arrived in Cedar Springs, I found, to my sorrow, that Thomas had recently perished in an accident. Before you get riled up, I will tell you that I have married his brother, Cade. I am living in his grandfather's farmhouse, so I have been looking diligently for the map these past three weeks.

I have many other responsibilities as well. Cade has a five-year-old son I am looking out for.

Emily paused, her hand steadied over the paper, and watched Adam out the window playing with a pail beside a pile of dirt. She wanted to tell her uncle how sweet and precocious the boy was and how much his presence warmed her heart. But her uncle would not care about that. She continued.

In addition, there are animals to feed and care for, a garden to start, and all the household chores. I spend every spare moment looking for the map. Cade plows the fields from sunup to sundown, so I am able to do so without suspicion.

Emily cringed even as she wrote the words. Guilt had built up within her more each day. It felt wrong to search through Cade's private things. *Well, isn't it wrong of him to deny me of my own children?* She would never realize her dream because of his decision. Was it so wrong of her to help Nana? Her gaze focused on the paper.

I have asked Cade some questions about his grandfather, but he doesn't seem to know anything about the robbery. He describes his grandfather Quincy as a "scoundrel" and says he disappeared one summer day and was never heard from again. This must have been the day he and my great-grandfather stole the coins. Cade doesn't seem to know Quincy and Grandpapa stole the gold or that they were hung for it the following week.

Emily rubbed her hands over her face. She hated thinking about the past and her involvement in this mess. She sighed and began writing again.

How is Nana? Does she still lie awake singing "Listen to the Mockingbird"? Please tell her hello and let her know I'm thinking of her.

She closed her eyes against the sting. Uncle Stewart would do no such thing; she could almost guarantee it. Was he making sure she was eating properly? Was he being kind to her? She knew better than to ask.

I promise to let you know as soon as I find the map. Until then, please take good care of Nana.

Sincerely,
Emily

She looked over the last line and knew she was pushing things. He didn't like to be told what to do. But she was keeping her end of the bargain, and it was only fair that he did as well. She folded the note, tucked it into an envelope, and addressed it. Now she had only to take it to the post office.

As she and Adam rode to town on the wagon, they sang songs together. She taught him "Camptown Races" and "Pop Goes the Weasel." He had his pa's dark hair and coloring, but his eyes were clear blue, and she wondered if they were like his ma's.

Once they arrived in town, she parked the wagon outside the mercantile and went to post her letter in the adjacent building. She left Adam on the porch with another boy while she entered the mercantile for a few things. It was not her first trip to the store, but she still felt like a stranger in town.

There were a few women in the store, two she recognized from church.

"Emily." One of those women set down the bolt of fabric she'd been eyeing and approached. "Good afternoon. I'm Mara, we met at church."

"Of course." Emily smiled, and wished she'd taken time to fix herself up. She must look a mess after gardening this morning.

"I'm glad to see you. I've been wanting to invite you over to tea one morning."

"That would be delightful."

They set a time for the next day, and Emily finished her shopping. It wasn't until Mara had extended the invitation that Emily had realized she was lonely for adult company. A friendship would be like a balm to her soul.

That next week, Emily finished up the supper dishes while Cade repaired a chair on the sitting room floor. She could hear him driving in nails and knew Adam was probably sitting beside him, taking in everything Cade did. She admired the relationship between Cade and Adam. The boy watched his pa so closely and imitated everything he did.

Emily dumped the dishwater behind the house and gathered up her sewing. Even as she dropped into the sitting room chair, her eyes felt heavy with weariness. Her busy days were catching up with her. Trying to run the house, look after Adam, and search for the map were taking their toll. She'd barely gotten started on the garden, and she knew she'd have to focus her efforts on that soon.

She threaded the needle and grabbed a shirt of Cade's from the little pile.

In front of her, Cade drove a nail into the arm of the chair.

"Can I try, Pa?"

Cade shook the arm to test its strength then turned the chair. "Here, hold the nail like this."

Emily peeked up from her stitching. Cade molded the boy's fingers around the nail's body then picked up the hammer. "Put your other hand here." Adam put his hand on the hammer, though Cade didn't let go. Together, they drove the nail into the wood.

"I did it!" Adam said.

Cade set down the hammer and squeezed his shoulder. "I reckon you did."

"Look, Emily, I did it," Adam said.

Emily smiled. "You're growing up. Before you know it, you'll be as big as your pa."

The proud smile on the boy's face was a picture that made Emily want to chuckle. Her gaze found Cade's, and they exchanged a smile. He looked away before she had time to enjoy the private moment. It was the most attention he'd given her since that fateful first night of their marriage.

She poked the needle through the fabric and pulled it out the other side. It was strange, their relationship. Cade cared for Adam and gave him affection, and the boy clearly adored his pa. And Emily had grown to care for Adam even in the short time she'd known him. Adam was starting to return her hugs and search her out when he did something he was proud of.

But Cade and Emily—their relationship was hardly a relationship at all. It was more as if they were acquaintances who shared a house. They said "good morning" and "pass the potatoes" and "good night" and little else. And yet, they were husband and wife.

Each night as she lay in bed waiting for sleep to come, she thought of Thomas and how different her life would be if he were still alive. They'd have shared their lives in a way that she and Cade hadn't. He would've shared her bed and given her a passel of children.

Stop it, Emily. It does no good to think of what cannot be changed.

"Why you making a chair, Pa? We have enough already."

Adam leaned over Cade's shoulder, almost smothering him with his closeness. Most men, she suspected, would have nudged him back. Cade just kept working as if it didn't bother him.

"It's for Mr. and Mrs. Stedman. They need another chair, and I remembered we had one in the attic just needed a little fixin'."

The attic. Why didn't I think of that? Emily had searched all over the house for the map, and she'd come up with nothing. But the attic would be the perfect place to look. There were probably trunks of old things up there, and surely she'd find the map among the relics.

"—over there, did you?"

Emily felt Cade's gaze on her and raised hers to meet it. She'd not been paying a lick of attention. "I'm sorry, what did you say?"

"Adam said you went over to the Stedmans' the other day."

"Yes, Mara had us over for tea."

He nodded and talked around the nail in his mouth. "Glad you're making yourself some friends."

Emily was glad, too. She and Mara had struck up an easy friendship, and the afternoon had sailed by before she'd known it. Afterward, she'd felt guilty that she'd been making small talk with a neighbor instead of doing her work or looking for the map. But she hadn't realized the depths of her loneliness until she'd started talking to Mara.

Cade set the chair upright and gave it a shake. "That should do it." He grabbed Adam and tickled him, then swung him up in his arms. Adam's belly laughs filled the room. "All right, Mister, it's time for bed."

"Aww."

Another round of tickling quickly put an end to the complaint.

Chapter 5

*E*mily tossed aside an old quilt, and a cloud of dust rolled up around her like a prairie storm. She coughed as the dust settled on her damp skin, clinging to her and making her itch. She'd already searched through three trunks in this stuffy old attic, and there was much more to go through. So far, her search had turned up no map, but the historian in her wanted to go slowly through each batch of letters and box of collectibles.

There was no time for that, though. Already, she was putting off much-needed garden work. The laundry, too, awaited her, and the downstairs was in dire need of a good sweeping.

She constantly worried that Cade would notice her neglect of other chores. So far, he hadn't said a word, but she knew by looking at her neighbors' gardens that she was behind.

"I'm thirsty, Emily." Adam looked up from his spot on the floor. His eyes peeked out from under an old beehive bonnet that was perched on his head. An old Prince Albert overcoat swallowed his body. She nearly laughed.

"I see you've found some new clothes."

"These ain't new, Emily, they's got too much dust on 'em for that."

"These aren't new," she corrected.

"That's what I said. Can I have a drink now?"

Emily drew in a deep breath then coughed at the dust she sucked in. She could use a break herself, but she wanted to finish this one trunk before she started supper.

"Tell you what. Do you think you could get your own glass of water if I let you go down to the kitchen by yourself?"

Adam stood up and the bonnet fell off. "Yes, ma'am!"

"All right then, let's get you out of here." She helped him over all the piles of relics then went back to work.

She felt like she was getting to know Cade's ancestors just by going through their things. The clothes were mostly homespun. Trousers and linsey-woolsey for the men and calico for the ladies.

She'd come across old bank papers and coins, simple jewelry, and an old Bible. She'd found a lamp that was perfectly good and decided she'd take it downstairs. Cade had complained the sitting room was too dark.

By the time she finished going through the trunk, she sat back on her heels and sighed. Would she never find it? The faded remnant of the map Uncle Stewart found in his father's things said the more detailed map was hidden in this house. It was the only way he'd known there was hope for finding the gold. And her uncle's map indicated the gold was buried on Manning property. But it would be impossible to find it among the miles of hills and caves that encompassed the property. Why, the gold could be buried anywhere.

She looked around the dark room. The lantern she'd hung from a nail shed dim, yellow light on the stuffy space. There were a few little tables to look through and still a couple trunks she'd yet to open, but those would have to wait until tomorrow. It was getting late, and she needed to get supper on.

She began putting things back into the empty trunk, taking care not to rip the fragile fabrics. She'd just stuffed the last gown on top when a sound at the door reminded her she'd forgotten about Adam.

"Did you get your drink of water without spilling?" she asked, tucking the clothing into the trunk.

"What are you doing?" The voice was no young boy's.

Her gaze swung to the doorway. Cade's large frame filled it, his face washed in a glow of lantern light. A frown puckered his brows.

Emily's mouth felt as dry as the dirt that coated her gown. "Cade, I—why, you're back early, I don't even have supper on yet."

He looked around the room as if to make sure everything was still there. She felt her face flush.

"Adam said you were up here."

"Yes, I—I wanted to sort through things." Her mind fished for a plausible excuse. Why hadn't she thought of this before? "I found a lamp for the sitting room." She held it up by the metal handle, but she felt the smile on her lips wobble.

He nodded, but the frown remained.

She must look a sight, evidence she'd been up here far too long to justify the finding of a single lamp. "Well, I'd best get supper on."

She began to rise, but her feet had fallen asleep and refused to support her. She reached out to grab hold of something, but there was nothing but air. She tried to take a step toward the wall, but her foot connected with something, and she tripped.

Cade stepped forward and caught her as she fell into his arms. Her hands found the hard flesh of his arms. His chest was a rock-hard wall against the softness of her cheek. Her pulse skittered.

He felt warm against her already heated body. She pulled back and realized his hands encompassed her waist. The glow of the lantern light flickered over his face, revealing something new in his expression. Her mind was too befuddled to put a word to it.

Her thoughts swirled in her mind in a heated frenzy. She felt his hands tighten on her waist, and it brought the oddest of sensations to the pit of her stomach. Her heart, too, reacted to Cade's nearness.

As his gaze roamed over her face, she became aware of how she must look. Dust and cobwebs probably coated her hair. She wondered if there were streaks on her face where drops of sweat made trails through the dirt.

She looked down, and her gaze locked on a button on his shirt. She felt his hands leave her waist, felt him pull back, both physically and emotionally.

Whatever she had seen on his face before was certainly gone now.

Her gaze darted to his, and she saw her suspicions confirmed. A deep shadow had settled into the plane of his jaw and shifted as his muscles twitched. His eyes too had grown distant, hard.

Silence swelled around them, and she wished he would say something, anything. Because she couldn't seem to form a rational thought.

She backed away a step, and her foot connected with something on the floor. She caught herself quickly.

"Pa," Adam called from somewhere downstairs.

Cade glanced at the door, then back to Emily. "Be right there," he called to Adam. His voice sounded loud in the confinement of the attic. He cleared his throat. His posture was stiff, his gaze harsh. She wondered what had caused him to go from warm and pliable moments before to rigid and withdrawn.

"I told him I'd take him for a ride while you get supper on." His voice was clipped.

Emily nodded, her tongue stuck to the roof of her mouth.

He started for the door, and Emily felt a physical relief that he was leaving. Before the breath she'd inhaled found release, he turned.

In the shadows, his expression was unreadable. "In the future, you might spend more time tending the garden than sorting through junk."

The words hit their mark. Her face went hot and her skin prickled. She heard his heavy boots thudding down the stairs and thought her heart must surely be as loud. Shame uncoiled in the pit of her stomach and snaked through every part of her. She looked down at the floor where the silly lamp sat. Her excuse for being up here seemed absurd.

He must think her lazy or incompetent or daft. Why else would she let chores go undone while she snooped about in an attic? And all for nothing, too, since she'd come up empty-handed.

She heard the front door slam and was relieved he was out of the house. A quick glance of the room reminded her there were still trunks to go through. And like it or not, she would have to go through them.

But first, she had to get cleaned up and get supper fixed. And if it killed her, she would get it done before Cade returned.

Cade balanced Adam in front of him and kicked Sutter into motion. His heart still thudded heavily in his chest even while guilt flooded his soul. He relived the moment in the attic, then shook his head as if to dislodge the thoughts. Never in his wildest dreams would he have thought he was capable of those feelings again. It was wrong.

But it had felt so right for just those few moments. Right and good.

Stop it, Manning. He clenched his teeth and kicked Sutter into a gallop. Adam laughed as the wind hit their faces.

When Emily's eyes had widened in the glow of the lamplight, his gut clamped down hard. Her dirt-streaked face had looked adorable, had reminded him of the first time he'd seen her, getting off the stage.

Then Ingrid's face had come into his thoughts. Her golden hair and sad blue eyes. Sad because he'd been thinking of Emily the way a man thinks of a woman.

She's my wife.

In name only, his spirit rebutted. What would Ingrid think of him now? She'd loved him and given birth to their precious son. What right did Cade have to carry on with another woman when his wife had lost her life bearing him a son?

"Faster, Pa, faster!" Adam's voice mingled with the wind.

"This is fast enough." Cade held his son close to him and allowed himself to enjoy the softness of his little body. Before he knew it, Adam would be too big to ride tandem with him. One day, he would leave home and go off on his own. The thought tugged at his heart. And then where would Cade be?

Emily will still be with you.

Yes, she would still be here, Lord willing, but they would be like brother and sister sharing a house. His heart denied the idea. A man's skin didn't flush and prickle when he held his sister in his arms.

He shifted in the saddle, feeling suddenly discomfited. No, she hadn't felt like a sister at all, but more like a—

Wife.

His mind rejected the thought. No matter that his heart had felt alive for the first time since Ingrid had died—he would not let himself fall for Emily. Hadn't he loved Ingrid well, and what had that gotten him? A broken heart. He'd grieved for months like he hadn't thought possible. He'd never imagined such pain as he felt when he'd lain his head on her pillow and smelled her lilac soap. Or held his baby in his arms, knowing Ingrid would never have that chance.

He didn't want to feel that way again. Ever. No amount of pleasure was worth that, and if necessary, he would put up walls twenty feet high around his heart to keep her out.

Chapter 6

*E*mily,

I'll not waste time with pleasantries as you did in your letter. It seems you have settled in that cozy little farmhouse with a husband and his brat and forgotten why you're there to start with. You are not there to be a wife or ma. You are there to find the map and gold.

Since you have become so lax in your thinking, I am going to save you from your laziness by setting a deadline. You have until winter's first frost to find the gold. Anyone with any wits about them could manage that. Unless you want your grandmother to be sent away, you'd best get to work.

Uncle Stewart

Emily's belly clenched, and her fingers trembled on the page. She sat down on the settee, glad she'd sent Adam out to play. She was beginning to despair of ever finding the map. She'd finished looking in the attic and around the house. It was only spring, but winter would be here before she knew it. What if she couldn't find the gold by winter? What if the map was not even here? Someone could have found it and thrown it out long ago for all she knew.

She heard Adam squealing outside and peeked out the window. He sat in the dirt watching some bug crawl along the ground. He coaxed it onto a stick and squealed again. Emily smiled. She longed to go outside and play with him, but now she felt compelled to search for the map.

She looked around the room for some area, some piece of furniture she hadn't searched already. She'd looked everywhere.

Maybe she was going about it all wrong. Maybe Cade knew something that would give her a clue as to the gold's whereabouts. Maybe he even knew of the map but didn't know its significance.

That's it. I'll see if I can find out something from him.

It sure beat looking for a needle in a haystack. Especially when she didn't even know if the needle existed.

Emily put another spoonful of potatoes on Adam's plate and smiled at him.

"Thank you," he said.

Her eyes met Cade's, and she read the approval in them. She'd been working with Adam on his manners. He was a fast student, ready to learn and eager to please. Keeping him clean, though, was a task she'd given up on. She'd learned to let him get as dirty as he pleased, then have him get washed up for supper.

She glanced at Cade, who was serving himself another slab of ham. He could put away food, that man, but still stayed slim and solid. Well, it was no wonder with the hard work he did all day. Her gaze fell to his hands, so strong and tanned. His fingers, squared at the tips, were long and so. . .masculine.

And still.

Her gaze found his, and she saw he was studying her. She'd been staring at his hands, she realized, and knew he must think her odd. She picked up her fork and worked a piece of ham onto it, her face burning.

He'd never said a thing about their embrace in the attic a while back. But she'd thought about it more than she cared to admit. If Cade had thought much of it, she couldn't tell, for he'd been as distant as he ever had.

Her uncle's words flashed in her mind. *You are there to find the map and gold.* The weeks were slipping away, and she had to start questioning Cade, like it or not.

She glanced in his direction and realized Adam was telling him about a game they had played today. How could she steer the conversation toward the map without drawing Cade's suspicion? Then an idea occurred to her.

"Perhaps tomorrow we could play a different game," she said to Adam.

His dark eyebrows popped up high. "What game?"

"Well, seeing as how you like dirt so much, perhaps I could bury some treasure. I could make you a map with pictures and see if you can find it."

"Real gold?"

Emily laughed and hoped it didn't sound as brittle as she thought. "Well, I don't have any real treasure, but maybe we could use buttons and just pretend it's real."

Emily glanced at Cade, hoping to jog some memory. If he'd seen a map lying around somewhere, maybe he'd think of it now.

"Can we do it now?" Adam asked.

"Finish your supper," Cade said. "Tomorrow's soon enough." He glanced at Emily then back to his son. "You might help Emily with the garden before you think of asking her to play."

Her cheeks burned. Now he thought she was putting off her chores to play games with Adam. He must think her completely slothful.

She tried to regain her composure. "We'll do our work first, won't we, Adam?"

"Aww."

"None of that," Cade said. "If we don't grow a garden, what do you reckon we'll eat all winter?"

This was getting her nowhere. He'd not taken the hint about the map at all, and now they were on a different topic altogether.

"How about if I draw up the map tonight, Adam?" she asked. "Then as soon as we're finished with our chores, I can bury the treasure for you."

"Yippee!"

"Finish your peas," Cade said.

"Yes, sir."

Later that night after Adam was in bed, Emily sat with a piece of paper, mapping out the backyard. Her trees looked more like inverted pitchforks, but she supposed Adam would be able to make it out.

She glanced at Cade where he sat reading his Bible. She needed to get him talking about his grandfather or the map. Surely he knew something that would be of help.

She marked the spot on the map where she would bury Adam's treasure and held it up. Would Adam be able to understand the pictures?

"What do you think of it?" She held up the picture for Cade. Across the room, his gaze lifted from the Bible to the picture she held up. He squinted, and she realized he couldn't see well from across the room.

She got up and walked over to the settee where he sat. Feeling brave, she sank down beside him and handed him the picture.

His lips twitched as he looked at it.

She felt amusement well up in her. So her picture did look like

Adam had drawn it. Had she ever claimed to be an artist?

His lips twitched again.

"And what's so funny, Mr. Manning?" she asked, feeling suddenly playful.

He glanced at her then back to the map. "Why's there a porcupine in the middle of the yard?"

She swatted his arm and wondered if she'd overstepped her bounds. "That's a bush."

His laugh was disguised as a cough.

"And I suppose you could do better?"

He looked at her then, and the amusement on his face made her feel warm and cozy all over. "I'm not the one who offered to draw a treasure map."

His smile slid away slowly like the ocean's tide, but his gaze remained locked on hers. She felt her own fade away. The mantel clock ticked off time, and so did her eager heart.

He cleared his throat and looked back at the paper. "It's fine, really." He handed it back to her. "You've been real good to Adam."

She accepted the paper and suddenly realized how close they were sitting. Her calico gown draped over his knee, and she realized she liked the intimacy the image invoked.

"I've grown fond of him. He's a good boy."

Cade settled against the back of the sofa, and she was relieved he didn't seem to mind her closeness. "He is good. But I've been a little neglectful of the manners and such. He's learning a lot from you."

His approval brought a wave of pleasure to her belly. "He's a delight to me, I assure you." All this talk was wonderful, but she couldn't help but think of her uncle's last letter and his deadline. Perhaps now, while they were talking so nicely, was a good time to probe.

"Adam's been asking about his ancestors lately." It was true. He'd had a barrelful of questions about who owned the clothes and trinkets in the attic.

"That a fact?"

"Umm." She worked absently on the map. "I didn't know what to tell him."

He closed the Bible on his lap and laced his fingers behind his head. "Not much to tell, really. We're farmers, going back at least three generations."

He went on to tell her about his own parents. They'd been hard workers and plain folk who'd done well to raise a family and provide the necessities. When he mentioned his grandparents, Emily's ears perked up.

"Don't know much about Grandpa Quincy 'cept he didn't much like to work. My pa said he was gone a lot and would turn up out of the blue. One day he just disappeared, and they never did know what happened to him. Eventually, they figured he was dead and put a grave marker on the hill out back."

She'd seen it weeks ago and had wondered about it. "Do you remember him at all?"

He shook his head. "I was young when he disappeared."

"You must have missed having a grandfather."

He shrugged. "It was odd. Nobody liked to talk about Grandpa Quincy much. When I'd ask my pa about him, he'd get all snippy. Grandma didn't cotton to talking about him either. I just figured her feelings had been hurt by his desertion. She had a hard life, trying to keep up the farm without his help."

"What do you suppose he did all those times he went away?" She glanced at his face.

His eyes squinted as if he could see into the past. "Don't know. I guess I figured he wandered around, liked his freedom."

He didn't know. She could see the honesty on his face.

Unlike me. A wave of shame washed over her. *I'm doing this for Nana, though. I have no choice.* She shifted in her seat and watched the material of her skirt slide off his leg.

"Have you ever looked through his things? In the attic, I mean?"

His gaze fixed on her, his brows hiked up beneath his dark bangs. "No. Grandma must've put some things up there, but I've never gone through the stuff." His eyes narrowed, and their depths were laced with suspicion.

She grew warm under his scrutiny and adjusted her skirts around her legs.

"Why? Did you find something up there?"

"No." The word, too emphatic, popped out of her mouth before she could stop it. But at least that question she could answer honestly. "No, I just—I just wondered if you'd ever looked through his things and found some kind of explanation of what he'd done while he was away," she finished lamely.

"Don't reckon there's much to find. He was just a wanderer who didn't much want to be tied down to family and work."

She nodded, not wanting to agree verbally. It would be too much like a lie, and she'd had her fill of dishonesty. She decided to turn in for the night. As much as she'd enjoyed her talk with Cade tonight, it didn't take a genius to recognize the suspicion that lingered on his face. And she'd just as soon hit the hay before he started asking questions.

Chapter 7

"I found another one!" Adam called from behind the big oak in the backyard.

"Good job, Adam. There are only two more marbles." She wiped a dirt-coated hand across her sweaty forehead and caught Adam's look. "Silly me," she called. "I mean only two more nuggets of treasure."

She grabbed a weed and gave it a mighty yank, feeling satisfied when the whole thing came up, roots and all. The spring sun beat down on her dark hair with such intensity, she wished she hadn't left her bonnet on the front porch.

Adam dug through the dirt a stone's throw away. Though she'd wanted to hide buttons for treasure, Adam had wanted to use his marbles. She hoped they didn't lose any of them. He carried them everywhere he went; you could hear them jangling together in his pockets as he walked.

"My aggie!" Adam called.

Emily saw him hold his favorite marble up in the air, wearing a proud look on his face.

"You mean your treasure," she corrected, relieved that he'd found his favorite. "One more to go!"

He attacked the dirt with vigor, and she moved down the row of tomato plants, plucking another weed.

She'd reached the end of the row when Adam jumped up. "I found it, Emily!"

The marbles that had sat in his lap spilled to the ground. He reached down to collect them and ran to her. "Will you hide 'em again?"

"Tell you what, if you fetch me my bonnet, I promise to hide your treasure again tomorrow."

"Yippee!"

"It's on the front porch."

He ran toward the house, his marbles cupped in his hands. Emily watched him go until he rounded the corner, then, turned back to her work.

She'd only uprooted two more weeds when she heard his cry.

"Emily!"

She jumped up from the dirt, her legs faltering from having been bent so long. She could hear him crying, and though it didn't sound like an emergency cry, it sounded serious.

She came around the front corner of the house to see him lying facedown on the wooden steps, still, except for the heaving of his torso. Had he twisted his ankle on the steps? Hit his head on the porch rail?

Please, Lord, let him be all right.

"What is it, Adam?" She squatted down beside him.

"My aggie!" He pointed at the gap between the rise and tread of the step.

A heavy dose of relief flowed through Emily. She put a hand to her booming heart.

"Oh, Adam, you scared the wits out of me."

"It fell out of my hand and rolled down there." Another wail escaped his lips, and he turned his tear-trailed face to hers.

"It's all right, Sweetheart, we'll get it." She sat on the step beside him and patted his shoulder.

He turned into her arms and melted into her embrace.

"It's all right," she said.

"It's my best one."

"I know, Honey, we'll get it." She pulled away and surveyed the crevice. There was no way a hand would fit through there. She grabbed the step ledge and tried to pry it up, but it didn't budge.

"Let's get Pa," he said.

She tried to loosen the board again and failed. "I'm sure I can do it. I just need to find the right tool. Stay here."

As she walked to the barn, she looked back and saw there had been no need to tell him to stay put. Adam was not going to leave his marble.

When she sat down beside him again, she had a heavy hammer in her hand. "Move back, now." She whacked under the ledge until it lifted. As she pried up the board, the rusty nails squeaked as they loosened their grip on the plank.

Sunlight poured into the cavity, bathing the stale space with light. Emily set the step tread on the porch.

"There it is!"

The green glass marble lay nestled in dirt below. She reached in through strings of cobwebs and grabbed it. As she pulled it out, something alongside the inner wall of the steps caught her eye.

She handed the aggie to Adam, and he threw his arms around her.

"Thanks, Emily." With that, he ran into the house, the door slapping behind him.

Emily reached back into the crevice and grabbed for the canvas against the wall. Once she had it in her hands, she quickly withdrew it, dropping it beside her, and plucked off all the webs on her arm. She set the plank in place and hammered it back down.

Picking up the rumpled canvas, she stood and walked up the steps.

On the top step she froze. The canvas, browned with age and blurred by water damage, was a map.

She eagerly scanned the page. Yes. She could see where a crude house was drawn.

I've found the map!

At the top right-hand side of the page, an X was very clearly marked, though the drawings in the area around it were blurred. She flipped the map around. If this were the front of the house, then the X was behind the house to the west. But how far?

She studied the lines and indistinct images. There was simply no way of telling how far. But it looked like. . .yes, it looked like the lines around the X depicted a cave or a cliff wall. The gold might be buried in a cave on Cade's property. But there could be many caves. How would she ever find the right one? And once she did, how would she retrieve the gold?

She scrutinized the picture again, then hugged it to her chest. At least she had an inkling now of the direction it was in. And maybe there were only a few caves out that way. She could ask Cade a question or two and then start searching. Hope welled in her chest. Maybe she could find the gold and be done with this whole mess before winter. Uncle Stewart would release Nana to her care, and surely Cade wouldn't mind if Nana came here to live.

She so wanted to get this over with. She was tired of deceiving Cade. Perhaps he withheld his affections because he sensed her dishonesty. Perhaps when all this was finished, he would find it within himself to love her as a wife. Somehow, even though she cared greatly for Adam, she couldn't seem to let go of the desire for her own children. Her heart harbored frustration because of Cade. What were a few white lies when he was denying her dream?

Finding the map put a hope in her heart the rest of the day. Later that night as Emily tucked Adam into bed, she ran her fingers through his soft, dark hair. He had a new freckle on his nose, a result of the hours spent in outdoor play. She wondered idly if a child of hers would have freckles. Probably so, since her own skin was fair and prone to them.

"I forgot to get your bonnet," he said.

"I think we both forgot, Sweetheart."

"Does that mean you won't bury the treasure tomorrow?"

She chuckled and ruffled his hair. "I'll still bury it. But not until after chores."

A shuffle sounded behind her, and she turned to see Cade in the doorway.

She leaned down and planted a kiss on Adam's cheek. "Sweet dreams, Adam. Good night."

Suddenly, he pulled her into his little arms. "Night, Ma."

The word caused her breath to catch in her throat. Her eyes stung, and as she pulled back from the boy, the sweet smile on his face stole her heart.

She squeezed his arm and stood, turning to leave the room. But before she took a step, her gaze connected with Cade's. His stricken expression impaled her. She couldn't move for a moment, caught in the steely web of his gaze. His displeasure was evident in the tight bunching of his brows, the rigid set of his shoulders.

Quickly, she brushed past him and down the stairs. She grabbed her sewing basket and busied her fingers with a holey stocking. Why was Cade so distressed that Adam had called her "Ma"? Was it so awful that he had grown to love her, that she had grown to love him? A child needed a mother, and she was the only one this child would ever have. That was his reason for marrying her, after all.

She realized the hurt she'd read on Cade's face must be on Ingrid's behalf. Of course that must hurt. But it had been five years, and it was only right that Adam should have a ma.

She stuck the needle through the material and pulled it out the other side. The look on Cade's face bore into her with more force than she'd like to admit. Wasn't she good enough for his son? Did he see something in her he disliked so much that he wanted distance between her and Adam? Wasn't the distance between her and Cade bad enough?

She heard his feet on the stairs and stiffened as he entered the room and settled across from her, his Bible in his lap. She kept her gaze fixed on her work. Her heart jumped against her ribs.

Cade's presence in the room was thick and tangible. The very air had changed when he'd entered, and her spirit squirmed. Did he regret marrying her? Her gut clenched at the thought. Did he dislike the influence she had over his son? When had she come to care so much what he thought of her?

Her gaze darted to him, and in the brief instant, she knew why she cared so much. She was falling in love with him.

She glanced at him again, her fingers trembling with the discovery. Was it somehow written on her face, in her posture? She felt sure it was and wished she could evaporate right then and there. She poked the needle through the stocking, and it poked her finger.

She sucked in her breath.

He looked at her then.

She looked at her finger, where a dot of red bloomed, and blotted it with a handkerchief from her pocket.

"You all right?" he asked.

She nodded, holding the cloth to stanch the flow of blood.

Quiet settled over the room like a heavy fog. She wondered if he looked at her still, but hadn't the nerve to check.

Upstairs, Adam shifted in his bed, and the straw ticking crackled. The mantel clock ticked off time.

"I'm sorry about how I acted upstairs."

She looked at him then, her heart in her throat. His expression was soft in the glow of lamplight, and her breath came in shallow puffs. He was so strong and masculine, yet sometimes she caught a glimpse of this gentle side and wondered at it.

"It's good for him to call you 'Ma.'" There was a glimmer of sadness in his eyes.

A dark cloud of jealousy spread through her, but she pushed it away. It was only normal that Cade would be sad for his loss. For Adam's loss.

Cade wondered if Emily could see the heavy thumping of his heart through his shirt. When she looked at him like that, with her doe-brown eyes all defenseless, he remembered that time in the attic when he'd held her in his arms. The familiar stab of guilt stopped the thought.

He had to think about Adam now and his need of a mother. He'd wanted his son to have a mother. But hearing him call Emily "Ma," seeing him embrace her, had sent an ache deep into the pit of his stomach. Though it hurt to see Ingrid replaced, he had to admit Emily was a fine substitute. She would love him and nurture him the way a child needed.

Emily's face was a mask of vulnerability. Did she think he was angry with her? *Admit it, Manning, you were angry with her. Angry that she's replaced Ingrid in Adam's eyes.*

"You've been good to Adam," he said, wanting to allay her fears. "I reckon he's taken to you like we both hoped he would."

She pulled the handkerchief off her finger and surveyed the pinprick, then twisted the white material in her hands. "I've grown fond of him."

She wetted her lips, and he wished for a moment that she'd said the words about him. Had she grown fond of him as well? The thought made his heart jump.

As if she could read his mind, her face turned pink, and she looked down at her hands. "He's a good boy. You've done well by him."

The words struck a note of pride in his father's heart. He'd done his best, but Emily had given Adam something he'd badly missed. Gratitude for her swelled up within him. He'd gotten a mother for his child and a woman to care for all their needs, and what had she gotten in return? A place to live? How could he repay her for her sacrifice? He felt a deep longing to do something for her.

"I appreciate everything you've done for him. For us." He nodded and hoped the words hadn't been spoken too brusquely. Words were not his specialty, especially flowery ones.

"It's a privilege to care for Adam." She avoided his gaze, and he thought he'd embarrassed her with his gratitude.

He wished briefly that she'd included him in her words. Did she count it a privilege to care for him as well? He knew the thought went beyond their relationship, but he wanted it to be true regardless.

"You don't mind then?" Hope lit the velvet brown of her eyes.

His thoughts, scattered as a whirlwind, missed her meaning.

"If he calls me 'Ma,' I mean," she said.

He shook his head. "I think that'd be best."

She gave a short nod and picked up her sewing. Somehow, allowing her to be a real mother to his son made him wonder what it would be like if she became a real wife to him. His gut clenched.

With a clamped jaw and a tenacious spirit, he tried to call up pictures of Ingrid. Pictures of their own wedding, of her standing over a hot griddle, of her reading by lantern light. Deep down, in the shadows of his mind, he admitted that these days, those pictures were fading from his memory. And he wondered what would take their place.

That night before Emily snuggled up under her quilts, she pulled her diary from its drawer and sat back against her pillows.

Dear Diary,

What an eventful day this has been! Quite by happenstance, I found the map under a step on the porch. It is, unfortunately, damaged by water and weather, but it gives me the general idea of the gold's hiding place.

A while ago, when I tucked Adam into bed, he called me "Ma" for the first time. My heart wanted to weep with joy. He is the child I always longed for, and though I didn't carry him in my womb, he is every bit the child of my heart. It was distressing for Cade to hear his son call me "Ma," but now, I think, he has decided it's best.

I hope this will bring our little family closer together. For right now, I don't feel like we're a family at all, but rather like three people sharing the same abode. I can't help but think Adam feels this, too. Perhaps with time, Cade's heart will soften toward me, and we will be a real family at last.

Chapter 8

Dear Uncle Stewart,

I have good news for you. I found the map that Quincy Manning hid. It was beneath the porch for all these years. Although it has significant water damage, I was able to tell the general direction to search for the gold. It looks as if they buried it in a cave. I have inquired of Cade about the caves on his property as much as I can, but I don't want him to become suspicious. Because of the map's condition, I'm not sure how many caves there are to search, but most of them appear to have numerous tunnels.

Though the summer is well under way, I'm hopeful that I will meet your deadline. When I find the gold, I will notify you right away. Perhaps then Nana can come here, and you won't be burdened with her care any longer. Please take good care of her for me and give her my love.

Sincerely,
Emily

Emily stashed the letter in the envelope and sealed it. A dose of guilt trickled through her veins, and she knew Sunday's sermon was the cause of it. Had Pastor Hill's sermon on Potiphar's wife been just for her? It had been a while since she'd heard the story of Joseph and how Potiphar's wife had tried to seduce him. Although Joseph had turned her away, she deceived her husband and told him Joseph had tried to seduce her. The sermon had focused on how God had blessed Joseph regardless of the evil done against him, but a different point poked Emily in the heart. She was deceiving her own husband just like Potiphar's wife had.

But this is different. I'm doing it for Nana's sake. Potiphar's wife was doing it out of her own selfishness.

It wasn't as if Emily was after the gold herself. She wanted nothing to do with the stolen gold. She wanted only Nana's safety.

But I'm deceiving Cade.

She couldn't get around that no matter how hard she tried. Did the end justify the means? It was a question she wasn't sure how to answer. She felt like the raccoon she'd seen two dogs chase up a tree this week. What choice had she? Was she supposed to let her uncle put her grandmother in the asylum? Dear, gentle Nana? Her stomach twisted.

Help me, Lord.

But even as the words formed in her mind, she snatched them back. There was no easy answer here, no easy way out of this dilemma. She would just find the gold as quickly as possible. Then she could get on with her new life here. Life as Adam's mother and Cade's—she couldn't quite bring herself to say the word. She was not Cade's wife at all. But in the depths of her heart, she knew she longed to become his wife in every sense of the word.

Emily took a sip of the tea Mara had poured her and watched Adam playing with Abbey, Mara's little sister-in-law. Though Abbey and Mara weren't related by blood, it was obvious they shared a mother-daughter bond.

Mara settled in the swing and dragged a hand across her forehead. For the first time, Emily noticed that her normally peachy skin was blanched.

"Are you feeling peaked?" Emily studied her friend, noticing a bead of sweat roll down her temple even though the summer day was mild. "You seem tired."

Mara sent her a private smile, then her gaze swung to Abbey who was showing Adam how to balance his marbles on the fence post. "I'm fine, really. In fact, I—" Her face reddened. "I'm in the family way." Her smile widened, and her face softened with excitement.

A baby. Mara would be having a baby. Emily's heart caught with a mixture of joy and envy. "Oh, Mara, that's wonderful!" she exclaimed, feeling a prickle of guilt for the seed of jealously that instantly sprang up.

Mara laid a delicate hand on her flat abdomen. "I just told him last week." She giggled. "He's so excited. Abbey, too."

Emily took a sip of her tea, wishing for the world she could swipe away the ugly envy she felt. She already had Adam, loved him; why couldn't that be enough?

"I just can't get over it sometimes. God has blessed us so much. I feel so undeserving."

Emily had heard others talk about the change Mara had experienced when she'd become a Christian. She had trouble believing the woman beside her used to be as self-serving and uppity as they said.

"I hope the good Lord blesses us with a whole passel of children." She laughed. "I know, it's easy for me to say now. I have yet to experience even one."

"You'll be a wonderful mother. You already are. Look at Abbey. She adores you."

"She's a joy, sure enough. I count her as my own." Her gaze bounced off Emily. "But—I don't know if I should even say this. It's probably wrong but . . ."

"What is it?" They hadn't known one another very long, but already, Emily felt close to Mara.

"Well, as much as I love Abbey, I've longed for a baby of my own."

Emily felt her skin prickle with heat. She grabbed Mara's hand. "Oh, Mara, I'm so relieved to hear someone else voice the same feelings I have." Her eyes stung with the fervency of her feelings. "I love Adam, I do. But—"

"But there's something about carrying your own child, about the thought of seeing a part of you in another being."

"Yes, that's it exactly. I so long for a child . . ."

Mara nodded. "After Clay and I got married, it was all I thought of. After waiting so long for a child, I finally told God I would be content with just Abbey. I truly thought I couldn't have a baby." Her blue eyes brightened, and Emily thought they must rival the clear sky at the moment. "But look at me now. It'll happen for you, too, Emily, I just know it."

Emily felt her jaw go slack then snap back in place. It couldn't possibly happen for her. Cade had seen to that. Her heart squeezed tight as if gripped by a vise.

"I'm sorry, I didn't mean to upset you."

Suddenly, the deep longing and disappointment welled up within her until she felt she would explode if she didn't give the feelings release. She tried to push back the feelings, and a knot formed in her throat.

Mara's hand settled on her arm. "What is it, Emily?"

Her throat worked, trying to dislodge the lump, but it was going nowhere. And neither were these stubborn longings of hers. "I—" She tested Mara's expression with a glance then plunged ahead. "Cade and I won't be having children. We—we're husband and wife in name only." Her flesh grew warm at the confession. She remembered their wedding night and the way he'd rejected her.

"Oh, Emily. I didn't know."

She gave a dry laugh. "Neither did I."

Next thing she knew, she was spilling the whole story starting with Cade's proposal on the stage and ending with his continued distance from her. Part of her wanted to tell Mara about the gold and her uncle's threat on her grandmother, but she was too ashamed. Besides, it was hard enough just sharing her humiliation about Cade.

"Do you have feelings for him?" Mara asked.

Emily fidgeted with her skirts, wondering if she could admit the fullness of her feelings for her husband. One glance at Mara's face convinced her she could. "I think I'm falling in love with him."

Mara squeezed her arm. "That's wonderful."

"No, it's not." Her throat constricted. "He doesn't return my feelings, and I'm so weary of hiding mine from him."

"How do you know he doesn't feel the same?"

"He—he's distant with me, as if he doesn't want there to be anything between us. It's like he holds a shield in front of himself every time he's near me. I think he's still in love with Ingrid."

Mara looked away, her gaze moving off to some distant place.

"Did you know her? Ingrid?"

Mara nodded. "I got to know her a bit while she was carrying Adam. Just before she passed on. He did love her, Emily, but it's been five years now. That's a long time to be without love, especially when he's had a son to raise alone."

Her heart twisted as she thought of Cade loving Ingrid. She longed for him to feel that way about her. "Well, he's not raising Adam alone anymore." She watched the boy shoot a marble through the dirt. Abbey squealed and patted him on the shoulder.

"That's not right," Mara said. "You're taking care of Adam and the house for Cade, yet you've sacrificed your heart's desire."

Emily was starting to wonder exactly what her biggest heart's desire was: a child of her own or her husband's love. She wondered if she'd ever have either.

Emily wiped her face with the back of her hand and knew she'd only smudged the dirt that coated her skin. She sat back on her haunches.

The lantern light flickered against the cave walls, casting eerie shadows on the dirt floor. Behind her, Adam dug for his own treasure in the dirt. She looked at the hole she'd spent the last hour digging and felt a surge of hopelessness. It was as empty as the last dozen holes she'd dug in this endless cavern of tunnels and halls. Who would have guessed that the little opening in the cliff wall would have so many corridors and rooms? Her back ached from stooping under low ceilings. Her arms ached from digging in the packed earth.

She rubbed her neck and decided to call it a day. They would both need to get cleaned up, and she needed to get supper on before Cade got home.

After helping Adam find the remainder of his marbles, she grabbed the lantern from the stone ledge and began walking. Behind her, Adam's marbles clattered together in his pockets.

"I'm thirsty, Ma."

Even through her weariness, she smiled at the word. "Here, Sweetie." She handed him the canteen and waited while he drank. The coolness of the cave felt good against her warm flesh.

They continued until they came to a fork. She turned right. When they came to the next fork, she turned left.

"What's for supper? I'm starved."

She thought about the contents of their pantry. "How about beans and ham?"

As they wound through the cavern, they talked about all Adam's favorite meals. Emily was laughing at his description of zucchini when her gaze fell on the wall up ahead. Her heart stopped. She held the lantern up as the wall came into the fringe of light. A dead end.

Her heart jumped back to life even as her mouth dried up.

Adam bumped into her then wrapped an arm around her leg. "Why we stopping?"

Why was there a wall here? There was supposed to be another fork that would take them to the cave's entrance. She turned around and looked back where they'd come from. She must've taken a wrong turn.

"Let's go back this way."

When they reached the last fork, she turned left, hoping it would set them back on track. But at the end of that corridor, there were three tunnels branching off in the darkness.

I think we're lost, Lord.

"Which way, Ma?"

Which way? Which way? What if she couldn't find the way? What if they wandered around this cavern until their lamp flickered out for good?

Oh, help me, dear God.

Chapter 9

*E*mily?" Cade wandered into the kitchen and dried his hands on a towel hanging from a hook. "Adam?" He glanced out the window toward the garden where bright green plants sprung up from the soil. Except for the leaves quivering in the wind, there was no movement there.

Where could they be? Normally Adam barreled over to him before he got his horse put up for the night. Today he was nowhere to be seen.

Cade opened the oven door. Cold, gray ashes lay in a heap. She didn't even have a fire on for supper. He closed the oven door and walked to the foot of the stairs, scratching his stubbly chin.

"Emily? Adam?" His words echoed off the walls, then silence.

He paced across the room, hunger clawing at his stomach. She always had supper on when he got home—usually had it on the table. Except the one time when he'd found her in the attic.

His stomach did a hard flop at the thought, and he told himself it was hunger. Maybe she's in the attic again. He trotted up the stairs and to the attic door, but it was closed. When he opened it, the pitch-black emptiness greeted him.

Had they run into town for something? He tried to remember if the wagon had been in its place when he'd put away Sutter. His mind had been elsewhere, and he couldn't be sure.

He went out to look. When he opened the barn door, the wagon sat off to his left in its usual spot. Sutter stirred in the hay, and Cade went to rub his nose. "Now where'd they take off to, boy, huh?"

Sutter nudged his nose up in the air and neighed.

That's when Cade noticed. Bitsy's stall was empty. "Now, how'd I miss that?" He walked over to the empty stall as if it would give him some clue where Emily went. "Huh."

He heaved a sigh and went back into the house. After waiting awhile, he gave in to his hunger and slathered a piece of bread with marmalade. Had she gone to the mercantile for something? Or over to Mara's?

He chawed on the bread, his mind beginning to wander off to places he didn't want it to go. What if they'd fallen from Bitsy, and Emily or

Adam was injured? What if Emily were hurt, and they were too far from home for Adam to get help? What if Adam were trying to find his way and had gotten lost?

Stop it, Manning. They'd probably just lost track of time, that's all. Like she had that day in the attic. He scooted back his chair and brushed the crumbs from his lap. They were fine. It wasn't that late.

An hour later, he walked out to the porch, peering out into the growing darkness. He could still make out the silhouette of trees and hills, but soon the night would cover the land like a heavy shroud. If Emily or Adam were lost, they would never find their way in the dark.

His feet beat a path to the barn. He had to do something. Enough of this sitting around and waiting. He couldn't take it any longer. Once inside the barn, he grabbed the tack and headed to Sutter's stall. The horse blinked lazy eyes his way.

Where would he go once he got saddled up? To Mara and Clay's house? She couldn't be there. If she'd lost track of time, it surely would have dawned on her when Clay arrived home for supper. The mercantile was now closed.

Where is she, Lord? Keep them safe. The thought of Adam hurt or worse twisted his gut. Fear sucked the moisture from his throat, and his heart quivered in his chest. Calm down, it's going to be all right.

But memories of another night assaulted him. Another night when he'd thought everything was going to be all right. And that night had ended with a dead wife.

Blinded by worry, Cade opened the stall door and tossed the saddle blanket over Sutter's back. As he smoothed the blanket flat and saddled her up, his mind played cruel tricks. What if he found them dead somewhere? Ingrid's still form flashed in his mind, and his limbs grew cold. He couldn't lose Adam, he couldn't.

And Emily. The thought of something happening to her made his heart hurt. He didn't know where he would look, but something had happened or Emily would have brought them home. He would search all night if he had to. Maybe he should go to Clay and Mara's house first and get some help.

He heard the noise just as he pulled Sutter from the stall. He stopped, going still to listen. Hoofbeats. His heart gave a jump of hope. He left Sutter and trotted to the barn door.

Darkness had swallowed the yard, and the only light came from the lantern he'd lit in the barn. His gaze detected a shadowed movement, and he focused on that spot until the object moved into the circle of light.

His breath left his body in a sudden gush. Bitsy sauntered toward him, Emily and Adam perched on her back. He searched their bodies for any sign of injury, but found no evidence. Even in the dim light, he could see they were both coated with filth.

When Emily noticed him, her eyes widened, then her chin tipped down.

"Pa!" Adam's weary shoulders straightened, and he held out his arms for Cade.

When Bitsy stopped, Cade pulled his son into his arms, holding him tighter than necessary. *Thank You, Jesus.* "Are you all right? Are you hurt?"

"Nuh-uh. We got lost in the cave, and it was dark!"

Cade's gaze found Emily, but her gaze was averted. "A cave?"

"We were looking for treasure!" Adam said.

Emily's gaze darted to his this time, and he studied her face.

Adam dug into his pocket and pulled out some marbles. "And I found 'em all again, didn't I, Ma?"

As the relief drained away, something rose up in its place. Something deep and unsettling. She'd taken his boy on some foolhardy treasure hunt and gotten them lost so he could fret for hours? So he could sit around and worry that they were hurt or—or dead? It was dark and late, and who knows what could have happened to them, traipsing around the countryside all alone?

Heat coursed through his veins, penetrating his limbs. He narrowed his gaze on Emily. "You'd best get inside and get yourself cleaned up." His voice grated across his throat. What he'd like to do is put her over his lap and give her a sound whipping.

She clambered down from the horse and pulled Adam from his arms. When Cade set him on the ground, she whisked him off for a bath.

By the time a simple supper was on the table, Cade was too angry to eat. Did she have any idea the fright she'd given him? He glanced at her over his glass of lemonade. She'd hardly spoken two words all through the meal. But then she didn't need to with Adam here. The more details the boy gave about their little outing, the more he wanted to give Emily what for.

She met his gaze then, and he gave her a look that promised a heated discussion later.

Emily eyed Cade across from her, the ache in her stomach spreading outward and filling her with dread. Her relief at finding their way out of the cave had only lasted as long as it had taken to arrive home. Once she'd seen the worry and anger on Cade's face, she'd known she was in for a dressing-down.

"Get on upstairs and get ready for bed," Cade told his son.

Obediently, Adam wiped his mouth then trotted up the stairs.

Cade's chair scraped loudly across the plank floor, and Emily jumped.

Without a word, he left the table, and Emily began gathering up the dirty dishes.

She drew in a deep breath, exhaling loudly. She was plumb tuckered from the long day. Putting in chores, then searching for the gold, then getting lost... She smothered a yawn.

Just before the lantern had flickered out, she'd seen the cave opening with the moonlight streaming in. If the light had gone out earlier, she and Adam might still be lost in the belly of the cave. She shuddered at the thought. After tonight, the thought of going back into the dank cave was more than she could bear. She could still smell the stale moisture of the rock walls, still feel them closing in on her.

The floor creaked above her head, and her stomach twisted. Cade was waiting until he had her alone to confront her. He hadn't had to tell her that. It was plain in the look he'd given her.

She dried off the last plate, hung the towel to dry, and dumped the dirty water.

She passed Cade on the stairs as she went up to bid Adam good night. He avoided her gaze, and her heart sank. She was dreading the confrontation. She was guilty, after all, of causing him worry. And what if he'd become suspicious? What else had Adam told him about their adventure today? Would Cade believe she'd taken Adam there solely as a diversion for him?

In Adam's room, she sat on the edge of his bed and told him a story she made up as she went along. The story grew so long, she realized she was stalling. Finally, she tacked on an appropriate ending and smiled as Adam clapped with glee.

After kissing the boy on the cheek and ruffling his dark hair, Emily blew out the flame in the lantern and pulled his door shut.

She turned and faced the stairs with equal measures of dread and resolve. Might as well get this over with.

He was waiting for her by the hearth when she entered the room. He turned, his face a mask of anger, his hand grasping the rough-hewn mantel.

He wasted no time with trivialities. "Do you have any notion of the worry you caused me tonight?"

She opened her mouth, but he wasn't finished.

"At first I thought you'd just lost track of time. But when it started getting dark and you still weren't back, that's when I really fretted." He crossed his arms over his broad chest.

Her legs quaked under her, and she sank onto the couch, hating the way he now towered over her.

"What do you think you were doing in that cave? What if you hadn't found your way out? What if it had collapsed on you—those things happen, you know. Or maybe you don't know. Maybe you just went on your frivolous adventure all willy-nilly, never mind the chores that were waiting or the dangers of the cave. You took my son, my son, and risked his life."

"I'm sorry, I—"

Cade continued, mentioning dangers of caves she hadn't even known existed. Her gaze clung to her skirts like a cat clinging to a tree. He was right. She never should have taken Adam into the cave. She wouldn't have, if only she'd been aware of the risks. Still, it had been an innocent mistake.

"And it was irresponsible. If you can't take care of him proper-like, maybe I need to find someone else." He turned toward the fireplace, but she heard him muttering, "Gallivanting all over the countryside..."

If you can't take care of him proper-like.

A bubble of heat welled up in her stomach. Hadn't she taken good care of Adam for weeks now? Hadn't she loved him like her own son? She'd taught him, played with him, nurtured him, and now he was accusing her of being a neglectful mother?

He continued muttering to the mantel. "A mistake all along. Should've sent her packing that day."

Deep within her, the rolling heat gave birth to an inferno. How dare he criticize her when she'd kept her end of the bargain! She'd cared for his son, done all the daily chores, cooked his meals, washed his clothes, cleaned up his messes, and what had she gotten in return? Nothing, that's what. She'd made all the sacrifices, and he'd gained all the benefits, just like Mara had said. He had gotten all he wanted from her yet he had denied her the desire of her heart.

"How dare you." Her voice sounded deep and harsh in the quiet of the room. Somehow, she'd come to her feet.

"I have cared for Adam like he was my own. Don't you dare say I have neglected that child." Her eyes stung with the fervency of her feelings for Adam. "I made a mistake today. A mistake. Am I not entitled to one every now and again?" Her voice quivered as it grew louder. "But I would never do anything to endanger that child. I have done nothing but wait on you, hand and foot. I have washed your clothes, cooked your food, mended your garments. . . ." She picked up the sewing basket and threw it at his feet.

His expression was laced with surprise, though his planted feet didn't budge.

"And what have I gotten in return? You have denied me the joy of ever holding my own child in my arms. Never mind that you didn't even tell me this before I married you! And now I'll never have a child of my own, never!"

He blurred in front of her, and she knew her eyes had filled with tears. Her throat ached, and her stomach felt hollow. She turned from him, crossing her arms, feeling suddenly exposed and strangely relieved. It was all true, and why shouldn't he know it? He was being selfish and cruel.

A long moment later she felt his touch on her shoulder. Every muscle in her body tensed. His touch was gentle yet strong, and she hated the way it made her heart lurch.

"Emily . . . I'm sorry."

His voice sounded in her ear, and suddenly she realized how close he was. She could feel the heat of his body.

"I lost my temper. I shouldn't have said what I did."

As he spoke, the curls on her nape whispered softly against her skin, sending gooseflesh up and down her arms.

"You never told me about wanting a child."

It was true, she hadn't. But didn't every woman want children? He should have known.

His hand squeezed the flesh of her arm, and heat kindled there. "I wasn't thinking straight that day on the stage. All those people watching. . . I just didn't know how to say it."

Her lips trembled, and she put a hand against them.

He turned her around, and her heart caught. His broad chest was inches from her face, and she focused on one of the pearly buttons on his shirt. She couldn't bring herself to meet his gaze, though she felt it as sure as a touch. She closed her eyes, then felt his hand on her chin, tipping it up.

When she opened her eyes, his gaze burned into hers, and her legs trembled under her. His eyes darkened to a deep bluish green. Their depths held a mix of sorrow and something else she was afraid to define. His thumb moved along her jaw, blazing a trail of fire. Her heart threatened to escape her chest. She closed her eyes again lest he see the depth of her feelings.

Chapter 10

*H*is thumb traced the curve of her lip, and she thought she'd surely faint dead away. Why was he doing this? It was sweet torture.

There were no words, and no world around them, just the touch of his hand and the fire of his gaze. Though she'd never been kissed, she knew this man, her husband, wanted to kiss her now. And she longed for it with all her heart.

He leaned closer until she could see the tiny flecks of color in his eyes. She wanted to drown in their depths, but more than that, she wanted to feel his lips on hers. Even now, she felt the heat of his breath caress her lips.

"Ma?" Adam's voice echoed down the stairs.

She froze in place, as did Cade, and her heart beat out an emphatic complaint.

"Pa?"

Cade's hands fell to his side, and the flesh they'd left went suddenly cold.

His eyes flitted to hers, and she read the reluctance in them. He walked to the stairs and spoke from there. "What is it?" His voice sounded raspy and mildly irritated. Was he as disappointed as she at having been interrupted?

"I got a question 'bout heaven."

Cade tossed her a look, and she suddenly felt silly standing alone in the middle of the room.

Before she could move, he went up the stairs. The moment was gone, and she feared there would never be another like it.

That night, she pulled out her diary from its secret spot and put her thoughts on paper.

> *Dear Diary,*
>
> *I feel compelled to broach a subject I have avoided all these weeks here in Cedar Springs. It's silly of me, but somehow I felt if I didn't write my feelings in these pages, they would vanish. I'm speaking of my feelings for my husband.*

Such a whirlwind of emotions are even now flooding my mind. Moments ago, I was so angry with him I could have screamed.

I have never seen him angry like he was tonight, and as much as it distressed me, I realize how different his anger was from Uncle Stewart's. I had no fear tonight of harm coming to my own person.

Still, his anger bothered me in a different way. I think it's because I care so much what he thinks of me. And to think that he was disappointed in me was most distressing.

But I couldn't let him think as badly of me as he did. In his anger, he'd said things that weren't justified, hence my own temper flared. But somehow, just a kind word and a touch from him, and I was as pliable as dough.

My face heats as I write this, but, Diary, tonight he nearly kissed me. My heart has still not recovered, nor has my deep disappointment that we were interrupted before his lips met mine. Has another woman ever felt so overwhelmed at her husband's touch? I wonder if it's inappropriate to feel so much desire.

Well, these questions won't be answered tonight, and right now, I long to curl up on my bed and dream sweet dreams.

Cade pulled his chair back with a scrape and let his weary body fall onto it. He could hear Emily at the stove scraping breakfast from the skillet. Next to him, Adam rested his chubby cheek against his palm, his eyes closed against the morning.

Cade rubbed his own eyes. Sleep had been slow in coming last night on account of his confused thoughts. By the time he'd answered all Adam's questions about heaven and hell, Emily had gone to bed. A part of him had been relieved, but another part was disappointed. He'd wanted to kiss her, no denying that.

He picked up the pitcher and filled their cups with fresh milk.

Was it so wrong of him to want his new wife? To have feelings for her? Those were the questions that had kept him awake for the better part of the night. The kitchen door creaked open, and Emily appeared, a basket of biscuits in her hand. He rose and took it from her, setting it square on the table, and she turned back to the kitchen.

He watched her go, her calico skirts swinging in rhythm with her steps. He admired the way the material clung to her narrow waist then flowed out from the flare of her hips.

Heat flooded his face at the direction of his thoughts. All last night, he'd seen her face behind his closed eyes—those deep brown eyes and cherry lips, trembling with anger. He'd come so close to kissing them. Would they have softened under his ministrations?

Emily came through the door, this time holding a platter filled with ham and eggs. He rose briefly until she settled into her seat then he said grace.

She scooped some eggs onto Adam's plate while he speared a slab of ham.

She had yet to meet his gaze, and he knew she felt just as awkward about their embrace as he did. As they ate the meal, the strain was thick. Only Adam spoke, finally wakened by the tasty food in his belly.

"We going to the cave again today?"

The question was directed at Emily, but the answer slipped from Cade's mouth before he could stop it. "No."

Adam turned to him with an argument on his lips, but Cade put a stop to it. "You're not allowed going into the caves again. It's not safe."

"But me and Emily—"

"Answer's no, and I'll not hear another word about it, understand?"

His son's eyes flashed blue then his gaze fell away. "Yes, sir."

Cade looked at Emily, but she studied the eggs on her plate as she moved them around with her fork.

Even Adam fell silent after that, and Cade wondered if Emily was thinking that he didn't trust her. He remembered her emphatic words from the night before and how he'd hurt her feelings. He still felt bad about that, even after apologizing. He hoped she understood about the caves.

His gaze darted her way just in time to catch hers. They held for a memorable moment.

With a loud clank, Adam's glass turned over and milk flowed across the table. Emily got up for a towel, and the moment was lost again.

All that afternoon, Cade couldn't get Emily from his mind. He hadn't been without a woman for so long that he didn't recognize the feelings that had been building in him. Emily was no longer a mere boarder in his home. She was no longer just a fill-in mother for his son. She was coming to be special to him. A part of his heart, a part he'd thought long dead, was coming alive again. And as much as that scared him, it excited him, too. He wondered what his brother would have thought of this.

Would Thomas approve of my feelings for Emily?

He nodded thoughtfully and pulled Sutter's reins until he stopped. Thomas would approve. He probably would've thumped Cade on the forehead for being stubborn about it so long.

He led the horse to the creek and let him drink his fill, then squatted beside him and filled his canteen. As the clear water rushed into the small opening, Cade knew he'd made a decision he wouldn't go back on. He would pursue this relationship with Emily. Slowly, carefully, he would try to win the heart of his son's mother—his wife.

Emily picked up the yellow yarn and started working on what was going to be a blanket for Mara's baby. She'd settled on the most delicate colors and though she'd barely started, she knew it was going to be the perfect gift.

Upstairs, the floor creaked where Cade no doubt stood beside Adam's bed. His announcement over breakfast that she wasn't to take Adam into caves had left her reeling. What was she going to do now? How would she search for the gold and obey Cade's wishes? She couldn't leave the boy at home or even at the cave's entrance all alone. He was too young to stay out of trouble, and she would never forgive herself if something happened to him.

Cade was right. A cave was no place for a child. But that left her in a quandary. The only person whom she knew well enough to ask for help was Mara, but what reason could she give to her friend why she needed help with Adam so often? She couldn't bring herself to lie. All the deceptions with her husband were a heavy enough burden. She couldn't sully her relationship with her only real friend.

And perhaps if she gave up the search, her relationship with her husband would improve. Cade had cast strange glances her way during both breakfast and supper until she wanted to set down her utensils and ask him if she had preserves on her chin.

And over supper, he'd talked to her. To her, not just to Adam. He'd asked her about the garden and told her he'd chop more wood for the stove. And besides that, he'd looked at her when he'd spoken.

Her insides got all quivery just thinking about it. She looked at the spot across the room where they'd stood together last night—and she'd lost her temper in a way she had never done. She felt bad about it now.

She could hardly believe she'd bared her soul that way, told him of her disappointment. Now he knew how badly she wanted children.

That's it. He's being kindly toward me because he feels guilty.

A lump of disappointment formed in her stomach. He feels sorry for me. Only when she felt the keen stab of regret did she realize she'd been hoping for something else. She'd been hoping all day that he was growing fond of her.

Did he embrace her the night before because he pitied her? Because he felt bad that he'd ruined her dream of having children? Her face flooded with heat, and she was glad he was upstairs at the moment.

Lord, this marriage is a mess. I'm so confused, Father, and I'm so tired of hiding my feelings from him.

The creaks on the stairs alerted her to Cade's entrance. She pretended to be absorbed in her knitting, but every nerve in her body was aware of his presence, of his movement across the room.

He settled in his chair in the corner by the fireplace. "Adam's all tucked away for the night."

The needles trembled in her hands, clacking together. "Good." Was her voice as wobbly as she thought?

Why wasn't he picking up his Bible from the mantel? Why was he just sitting there? She could feel his gaze on her.

"He said you went into town today."

From the corner of her eye, she could see him cross his legs. "Picked up some yarn for this blanket."

"Clay told me they were expecting."

Her skin prickled with heat, and she wondered if her face bloomed with color. Why had she mentioned the baby blanket? Now he must be thinking of her words last night.

"Corn's coming up good. Old man Owens said he thought this might be the best crop in years, barring a drought."

"That's good." Why couldn't she think of anything else to say? He must think her addlepated.

"If we get a good price on it, I was thinking to build on a water closet on the east side of the house."

She glanced at him then back to her work. How wonderful it would be to have a necessity. Especially in the cold of winter.

"Parnell said he could get me good price on one of those bathtubs, too."

"A bathtub?" Oh, how nice it would be not to haul water to the stove and heat it up for each bath.

His eyes sparkled in the lantern light. "If we have a good crop."

She worked her needles, and they clicked together, breaking the silence.

Finally, Cade retrieved his Bible from the mantel and settled in the chair. As she knitted, her mind spun. Was he offering to build the necessity out of kindness to her? Men didn't care about such things, did they? Her heart skittered in her chest. Would he do that for her?

Even as she worked, she could feel his gaze on hers, but she couldn't bring herself to meet it. Either he was feeling sorry for her, or he was growing fond of her, and she couldn't bear to expose her feelings until she knew for sure one way or the other.

Chapter 11

*D*ear Uncle Stewart,
    I hope this letter finds you and Nana well. I'm finding the life of a farmer's wife is both exhausting and rewarding.

Emily leaned back and read the lines. Her uncle had a disliking for small talk, but the next words she wrote must be exactly right. *Help me say this in a way he'll accept, Lord. I'm so tired of this awful game, of deceiving Cade. Let this be the end of it, please.*

> *I'm afraid I have some bad news. Last week Adam and I became lost in one of the caves while I was searching. It's only by God's grace that we found our way out. The caves here seem endless with many tunnels leading in many directions. One could disappear into one of them and never come out alive. I have spent many hours searching that particular cave to no avail. There are so many places the gold could be hidden, and no way of knowing where it is. There are several other caves in the area where the gold could also be buried. I could search for years and never find it.*
>
> *In addition to that, I have found it's very dangerous work. Caves can collapse, leaving a person buried alive. Wild animals are known to make their homes in these caves. And, as I recently discovered, one can become hopelessly lost.*
>
> *In all honesty, I cannot risk Adam's well-being by taking him into these hazardous caverns anymore. After last week's disaster, his father has forbidden it anyway.*
>
> *Because of these safety reasons and because of the hopelessness of ever finding what you seek, I think it would be best to discontinue the search. Please be reasonable about this, Uncle. I know you are displeased to hear this, but please know that I have given it my best effort.*
>
> *You needn't be burdened with Nana any longer. I would love to take care of her here if you will only send her to me. I will gladly*

*pay her fare, and you will not have to care for her anymore. Please
write soon. Until then, know that I care for you and am praying for
you both.*

*Love,
Emily*

She sighed and covered her mouth with a trembling hand. Would
her uncle accept her words? *Please, Lord, help Uncle Stewart be fair-
minded.* What other hope had she?

"Did you know my mama?" Adam asked.

His question stilled the breath in Emily's body. Her hands, too,
stilled on the lump of dough before they resumed their kneading. "No, I
didn't. I know she was very special, though, and that she loved you very
much."

Adam squished the small wad of dough she'd given him to play with.
"She died when I was borned."

"I know." She wished she knew what else to say. Was the boy missing
his real ma? The thought brought an ache to her own stomach.

Something had happened once she'd written that letter to her uncle.
It was as if it had freed her. There was no wall of lies between her and her
husband and no tricking Adam into going on treasure hunts. Somehow
it seemed she was truly his mother now and not just playing a role.

"Pa said she's in heaven." He flattened the dough.

"Sure enough. She had Jesus in her heart just like you." Emily smiled
down at him, but when she saw his wide blue eyes gloss over with tears,
her heart caught.

She knelt down and put her hand on his arm, mindless of the sticky
flour that coated it. "Oh, Sweetheart. What is it?"

His chin quivered, and a tiny frown puckered between his brows.
"What if you go away, too?" His eyes scrunched up, and he dove into
her arms.

She embraced him, her own eyes stinging. He was worried he was
going to lose her like he had lost his ma. She remembered when her own
mother had died. Consumption, they'd said, but it had seemed so unfair.
At least she'd known her ma. Adam had never gotten that chance.

"I can't promise that bad things won't happen, Adam. But God has it
all under control, and He has a purpose in everything He does."

She pulled back and looked him in the eye. "Why, just look at us.

Didn't God bring you into my life? What would I do without my special boy?" Her throat ached with a knot that seemed lodged there. "And you needed a mama, and didn't God send me to you? You see, He cares for us and provides for us."

She smiled through her own tears and wiped Adam's cheeks. Flour from her hands dusted his face. She chuckled. "You've got flour on your face now."

A smile wobbled on his lips, and he put a powdered finger on her nose. "Got you back."

She laughed and hugged him tight, her love for him welling up in her.

"I love you, Ma."

Warmth enveloped her like a thick, cozy quilt. "I love you, too, Son." And she realized then that she truly did love this child of her heart the way she would love a child of her body.

"Look, Ma, a matatoe!"

Emily looked up from the straggly weed she'd gripped and laughed. "Sure enough, it's a tomato."

"Can I pick it?"

"Oh no, not yet. See how green it is? It won't do for cooking until it's red as a cherry." She yanked with all her might, and the weed came uprooted. "You keep an eye on it, though. It'll be red before we know it."

The garden was coming along nicely, and she took pride in the plants she'd tended so carefully. Come winter, they'd have a cellar full of vegetables to last through the cold months. She'd have a lot of canning to do.

In the two weeks since she'd written to her uncle, she'd felt like a whole new woman. Though she was anxious to hear from him, she felt sure he would come to his senses. He should know it was futile, and he's surely eager to be rid of Nana.

She would have to broach the subject with Cade soon. It wouldn't be too hard given the way he'd taken to talking to her. Twice now, he'd even touched her shoulder as he passed by in a way that had made her skin heat and her heart sigh. In church last Sunday, he'd put his arm across the pew behind her shoulders, and she scarcely heard a word Pastor Hill uttered from that point on.

Is he really starting to care for me, Lord?

It seemed so impossible that he would, but wasn't God capable of anything? Even changing the heart of her stubborn husband?

Having not heard Adam making any noise, she glanced up to see what he was up to. He was splayed out on his belly in front of the same tomato plant, his gaze fixed earnestly on the green vegetable.

A smile tilted her lips, and she sat back on her haunches. "Adam, what are you doing?"

He spared her a glance. "Keeping an eye on the matatoe."

"But why?"

"You said it'd turn red soon."

Emily chuckled, delighted at his earnestness. She scooted over beside him and tickled his belly. "I'll bet I can make you turn red sooner."

He laughed and rolled away, but she crawled after him on her knees. "Gotcha!" She sprinkled his ribs and knees with tickles, and he laughed until his face colored. Before she knew it, she was lying in the dirt beside him, a tomato plant crowding over her shoulder.

"Well, now." The voice from the edge of the garden made her shoot upright. Cade stood there, silhouetted by the sun. His hands rested on his hips. "I think I see a couple nuts ripe for pickin'."

Adam jumped up beside her. "Pa!" He ran across down the row of plants, leaving footprints behind him. "We didn't plant no nuts."

As Cade swung Adam into his arms, Emily stood and dusted the dirt from her skirts.

"Is it that late?" she asked. The sun was behind the house, but it seemed too early for Cade to come home. Was he angry she'd been goofing off instead of working?

Why does he always seem to catch me at the worst possible moment?

"Nah, came home early today. Thought I might know a young 'un that'd like to go wading in the creek."

Adam squealed and squirmed until Cade set him down.

Emily walked toward them feeling a bit out of place. Her bonnet had slipped off and hung from the ribbons tied at her neck. She felt her hair and tried to tuck away the damp strands that had come loose.

"Will you teach me to swim, Pa? Please?"

"Not tonight. Thought we'd go to that shallow spot by Bender's Meadow."

Emily turned toward the house. She supposed she could get the floor mopped up while they were gone. Hearing the happy chitchat behind her made her feel strangely empty inside. She felt like a fifth wheel. Cade and his son were a pair. Where did she belong?

While Cade went to hitch up the wagon, Emily filled the tin pail with water from the pump and shaved some soap into it. She looked across the length of the house and felt a sigh well up in her.

No use moaning about it, Emily Jane, it needs to be done.

As she dipped the mop into the water, Cade entered the house.

"What are you doing?"

She pulled the sopping mop from the water. "Mopping the floor."

His expression seemed to fall, and she wondered what she'd done now.

He tapped his hat against his thigh, his gaze scanning the floor. "You don't want to come along?"

Her heart sailed high at his words. He'd assumed she would come with them.

"I thought you might pack us a little supper, and we'd picnic alongside the creek. If you want to, I mean."

Her hands tightened on the mop handle, the soppy weight of it bearing down on her arms. A picnic. She felt a smile tugging on her lips. "That sounds just fine. Let me just. . ." She looked back toward the kitchen, wondering what she'd fix for their picnic, but turned back, realizing she still had a mop in her hands.

"Here, let me get that." Cade took the mop from her hands and picked up the full bucket. "Something quick and easy's just fine."

She nodded and scurried off to pack the meal.

Before long, they were at the bend in the creek. She selected a spot on the high bank under a weeping willow tree, its graceful branches dipping down around them like a veil. Adam slipped off his shoes and stockings and slid down the grassy incline.

"Careful you don't fall," she called.

While Cade gathered the basket from the wagon, she spread the colorful quilt over the grass and sank down in the cool shade. She slid off her bonnet, and the evening breeze ruffled the stray hairs. She patted it, wishing she'd taken the time to put it up again. The knot was loose, and some of the pins were sliding out.

Cade set the basket beside her. "You should take it down, now that it's cooling off."

She lowered her hands, and heat crawled up her neck at having been caught primping.

"Come on, Pa!" Adam called from the edge of the creek. Sunlight broke through the leafy canopy and kissed the water here and there with splotches of light.

"Comin'," Cade called. He tugged off his boots and socks and began rolling up the ends of trousers. His calves were thick with muscle and covered with hair as black as the ones on his head.

"You coming in?" Cade's gaze was fixed on her, his lips tilted in a crooked grin, his eyes sparkling with amusement.

He'd caught her staring. She began unpacking the basket. "I'll just stay here and get everything ready."

In the fringes of her vision, she saw him stand to his feet. "Suit yourself."

It didn't take long to set out the simple fixin's of bread, apples, and cheese. Once she did, she watched Adam and Cade playing together in the water, reluctant to interrupt.

When they walked downstream a ways, she lay back against the soft, worn quilt and closed her eyes. She could hear a bird chirping in a tree above her, and the wind sighing through the leaves. She drew in a breath and let the day's worries and frustrations slide away. The last thing she remembered hearing was a squirrel chattering off in the distance.

A faint tickling sensation on her nose tugged her from someplace warm and lazy. She brushed at it, drifting away once again.

Again, something tickled her nose, and she reached up to swat it away. She gradually became aware of a cricket chirping somewhere nearby. Her eyes opened. Above her, Cade's face hovered, and she could feel the heat from his body so near her own. She looked around.

The picnic. I fell asleep.

"Adam." She started to sit up, but Cade put a hand on her shoulder. "He's fine. Just trying to catch tadpoles."

She noticed the willow twig in his hand, its feathery leaves dangling down toward her stomach. "You were tickling me."

His smile made her heart skip a beat. "Guilty." But he didn't look guilty at all. In fact, he looked completely unrepentant. His jaw was shadowed with a day's worth of stubble, and she thought for the first time that it only added to his rugged good looks.

"Shame on you," she said, studying for the first time the way the sun had tanned his skin, leaving only fine white lines bursting around the corners of his eyes.

"You're pretty when you're sleeping."

"Only when I'm sleeping?" *Did I just say that?* She sat up and felt the heavy mane of hair tumble down her back. The pins had finally come loose. In her hair and her brain.

She didn't know how close she was to Cade until she felt the whisper of his breath across her face. "No," he said.

She looked him in the eye, and her heart stilled at his nearness. "What?"

"You're right pretty all the time."

He picked up a length of her dark hair and ran it between his fingers. Chills shot down her neck and across her arm.

"I'm hungry!" Adam called.

She turned to see him running up the incline, his britches wet and soggy and splotches of darkness flecking his shirt.

"I caught me a tadpole, Ma!"

She gathered her wits. "Where is it?"

"Got away. We eating soon?"

Emily busied herself smoothing out the blanket. When she reached Cade's corner, he remained unmoved, staring at her, a smile on his face that would melt ice. She moved to the center where Adam sat with a plate already filled with the picnic fixin's.

After they filled their bellies, Emily packed the basket and blanket while Cade untied the horses. The ride back seemed longer somehow than the ride there, but perhaps it was only because Adam was not separating them this time. Cade's thick thigh rubbed up alongside hers until she could think of little else.

By the time they'd arrived back at the farm, the sun had sunk below the horizon, leaving only a sliver of moonlight to see by. Cade lifted Adam down from the wagon and handed him the basket and blanket. "Think you can carry all that?"

"Yes, sir!" Adam swaggered into the house, clearly pleased to be a helper.

Cade turned then and gave her a hand down. His hand felt large and warm in hers. It would have been comforting if not for the way it set her heart to racing. She turned to the house.

"Stay out here awhile."

She turned to look at him.

"Light a lantern for me?" he asked.

She moved into the barn where the lantern hung on a peg and lit it. She turned and watched as he unhitched the horses with sure, strong movements. He was an enigma, this man. This brother of her dear friend,

Thomas. How she wished she'd had a brother or a father who'd been alive long enough for her to figure out how a man's mind worked. As it was, she was at a loss. Surely most men were nothing like Uncle Stewart.

One day Cade's like a stranger living in the same house, and the next he's like a friend who wants to be my—

Her throat grew dry at the thought, and her traitorous heart beat a jig she was sure Pastor Hill would disapprove of.

You're being silly, Emily. He's just a man. He only wanted you to light the lantern, and here you stand staring after him like a wallflower at a barn dance. Why he'd probably think you were daft if he even knew the directions of your—

It was only then she'd noticed he was standing in front of her. Not just in front of her but right in front of her. Surely no more than a whistle away. The glow of light hit his face at all the right angles, kissing his upper cheekbones, letting shadows seep into the recesses of his jaw. His dark lashes had lowered to nearly his cheekbones, leaving just a sliver of those sparkling eyes in view. She'd give the baby quilt she'd worked on for weeks for just an inkling of what was going on behind them.

"I've been praying, Emily."

"Oh?" If her heart jumped any harder, surely it would bump his chest.

"You know . . . about us."

She nodded as if she knew what he was talking about. He'd long ago slid the hat from his head, and the dark strands of hair framed his face, the light glimmering off them.

"You've been a gift to Adam and me. A gift from God, and I got to wondering how He'd feel about how accepting I've been of that gift." He lowered his head, the shadows enshrouding his face. "I reckon it must look to God like I took the gift He gave me, put it on a shelf, and said 'no thank You.'"

Her face heated at his words. Her heart kept tempo with the music in her soul, and she held her breath waiting for the words she hoped to hear.

Chapter 12

*L*ast night I told God 'thank You,'" Cade said. "He's sent me a wonderful mother for my son and a wonderful woman to be my wife." The flesh of his palm found her cheek, and his thumb rubbed across her lips until she thought her knees would give way.

"When we married, I didn't know you wanted young 'uns. Shoulda known, I guess, but I didn't give it much thought. I was too wrapped up in my own needs." His other hand found her face, and she felt wonderfully surrounded by the comfort of his flesh.

"What I'm trying to say, I suppose, is that I'd like to give this marriage a fighting chance—if you're willing, that is." Eyes the color of a blue spruce questioned her in the glow of the lamplight.

Her heart took flight.

"I've come to care for you a great deal, Emily. I think we make a good match, you and I. And I'd like to . . .I'd like to court you the way a man courts a woman. I don't know much about you, but I want to learn everything. I want to know whether you wore hair ribbons as a girl and if some boy ever broke your heart. I want to know how you feel about moving here to Cedar Springs, and—I want to know if you could ever care for me."

His last sentence ended in a whisper she felt all the way to her toes. His lips, inches away, begged to be kissed. She looked deeply into his eyes, hoping he'd read her feelings there, because suddenly, not a word would squeak from her parched throat.

His lips lowered onto hers, slowly, maddeningly slowly. Her heart quickened, and she met his lips with a desperation born of loneliness and desire. His lips teased with soft brushes, tasting, testing, until she feared she'd go mad for want of him.

Finally, he embraced her, pulling her closer to him than she had ever been. Her skin heated up like a stoked bonfire. She wondered if her ears glowed orange with the warmth of it. His hands curved around the back of her head, holding her firmly, lovingly.

Her hands worked up his strong chest and rested there.

A moment later, he pulled away, though they still embraced one another. Their breathing came quickly. Cade's eyelids were half shut, a lazy surprise in his eyes.

She pulled away. She could hardly believe his effect on her. Weren't women supposed to be subdued? And they certainly weren't supposed to be so. . .so needy and eager.

Her gaze found the hay-strewn floor even as heat crept up her neck. What must he think of her now? She'd behaved like a wanton woman instead of a wife doing her duty. She was still breathing heavily. Shameful.

She felt his knuckle tip up her chin. His lips tipped in a crooked smile, but she noticed he, too, had not yet caught his breath. "You are some woman, Emily Manning," he rasped.

She looked away. What had he meant by that? Had she shamed him as well as herself?

He stepped closer again, this time wrapping her up in his arms like a big, cozy quilt. He planted a kiss on her nose.

What was he thinking? Oh, that she could read his mind and have done with it.

He laid his cheek against hers. She shivered, and he wrapped his arms more tightly around her.

"Stop fretting," he whispered in her ear. Then he took her hand and placed it against his heart. She could feel it beating under the plaid shirt, beating as fast as hers. What was he saying?

The answer came softly in her ear. "This is what you do to me, Emmie."

She smiled at the name her father used to call her.

"This is a good thing."

"I'm scared." *I can't believe I admitted that.*

His arms tightened. "It's all right. I am, too."

He held her for several moments of bliss while their hearts settled back into a steady rhythm beneath their homespun clothes. He pulled away. "I reckon Adam must be wondering what's become of us."

She nodded, still dazed.

"Let's take it a day at a time, all right?"

She nodded again.

He drew her hands up to his mouth and laid his firm, soft lips against them. "All this is new to me, too, you know. It's been so long . . ."

Ha, she thought. *He could coax a bear from a honey hive!*

He curled his warm hand around hers, and together they went into the house to begin again.

Several days later, Emily scraped the bacon grease from the pan while Adam dried off a plate. Behind her, Cade's chair grated across the wooden floor. She was ever so aware of him these days. He was like a cool breeze when he entered the room, and her skin shivered in his presence.

"I'm going to town this morning. Be back in a few hours," he said over his shoulder.

She turned, but he was already through the doorway. She dried off her hands and chased after him.

"Cade."

He turned, that handsome, lopsided grin tilted on his face. Her heart flopped.

"What is it, Emmie?"

The nickname still made her tremble. "I was—I want to go with you if it's not too much trouble."

Was it her imagination, or did his smile widen a fraction?

He gave a nod. "I'll hitch up the bays while you finish the dishes."

She smiled. "All right." She watched him all the way to the barn, his long legs eating up the distance quickly, then returned to the kitchen.

Once the dishes were in order, she went to the pantry and picked up her real reason for going into town. Her marionberry preserves. She'd topped the lids with a circle of cloth and had tied thin ribbons around the necks of the jars. When Mrs. Parnell had bragged on her preserves at the church social and asked for a few jars for the mercantile, Emily had felt so proud. Now, maybe she'd be able to earn a few pennies of her own and please Cade, too.

She packed the three jars in a basket and called for Adam to come.

Outside, Adam scooted onto the center of the bench, and Cade lifted Emily up. Her insides ached to be seated next to her husband. The past few days, he'd touched her often, though he had yet to kiss her again. But he had said he'd wanted to take it slowly. Was she brazen for wanting him to go faster?

As they bumped along the dusty road, with Adam's little body tossing against hers, she realized God had given her everything she'd wanted. Adam was a child of her own heart, and as much as she wanted Cade's love, it wasn't because of what he could give her.

A warm, soft feeling tickled her insides. She loved Adam so dearly. He was her son in every way that counted. She reached over then and pulled him close to her. He looked up, those big blue eyes so trusting and vulnerable, and smiled sweetly. She laid a kiss on his hair.

When they arrived in town, Cade helped them down from the wagon then he ran over to the feed store, promising to meet them shortly. Emily carried her basket of preserves into the store with Adam trailing closely behind.

The door jangled their entrance, then Emily approached the table where Mrs. Parnell was tidying up a bolt of cloth.

"Well, good day, Mrs. Manning," she said.

"How do, Mrs. Parnell." Suddenly she wondered if the woman had really meant what she'd said about selling her preserves. Perhaps she was only being friendly. She wished she could hide the basket behind her, but its bulk prevented that.

"Can I help you find something?" she asked.

"I—well, I brought these preserves." She held out the basket. "That is, if you still have need of them."

Mrs. Parnell put her age-spotted fingers to her face. "Oh, that's wonderful. Let's see what you brought."

She set the jars on the counter, marveling over the pretty cloth and ribbons. "These'll fetch a fine price. I'd love to try your strawberry and boysenberry as well, if they're up to the same standards as your marionberry."

"They're yummy!" Adam said from her side. "Sometimes I want to skip the biscuits and eat the preserves right from the jar."

Mrs. Parnell laughed.

"Adam." Emily scolded.

"Well, it's probably true, dear. Your marionberry is mighty fine indeed."

They settled on a price, and Emily left the store, eager at the thought of making money of her own. They shopped a bit, then went out to where Cade waited for them. After he assisted them up, they started off.

As they passed the post office, the postmistress came running out the door. "Mrs. Manning," she called.

Cade slowed the horses to a stop while the postmistress ran into the road. "You've a letter, dear." She handed up a well-handled envelope.

"Thank you," Emily said.

As she looked at the heavy scrawling on the envelope, she could feel Cade looking over her shoulder. "From your uncle?" he asked.

She nodded, anxiety worming through her and drying her throat.

As Cade gave the reins a yank, she tucked the letter into the pocket of her skirt. Part of her wanted to rip the package right open, but the smarter part of her knew she'd better wait until she was alone. There was no telling what Uncle Stewart had to say, but she was certain it was nothing that would benefit her fragile relationship with her husband.

Chapter 13

*O*nce Cade set off to the back pasture and Adam got settled with his marbles, Emily sat at the desk and ripped open the envelope. Her uncle's handwriting was scrawled hastily across the paper, and she read quickly.

> *Emily,*
>   *I'm advising you that I have put your grandmother in the asylum.*

Emily sucked in a breath, her heart beating against her ribs in fear.

>   *As you know, her health has continued to decline so I am no longer able to take care of her here. You have expressed interest in taking care of the old woman, but you have failed to fulfill our agreement. Until you find the gold, which I might remind you is the reason you were sent there in the first place, your grandmother will remain in the institution. As her legal guardian, I will do with her as I see fit since she is not of her own mind.*
>   *If you will bring yourself to continue the search, I will consider handing over guardianship to you. Though, I must admit, I'm growing increasingly irritated by your games.*
>
>   *Uncle Stewart*

Emily covered her face with trembling hands. Oh, sweet Nana in the institution! Emily had been there once to visit a friend's mother and had seen the deplorable conditions of the facility. And the treatment of the patients was something to be feared. Some had their hands bound about their waists, and some were strapped to their beds and left moaning with nary a soul to comfort them.

Oh, Nana, have they done this to you as well?

She brushed away the tears that had fallen on her cheeks. How selfish of her to become so taken with her life here that she actually thought

Uncle Stewart might give up on getting his gold. She'd been thinking only of herself.

She laid her head against the hard surface of the desk and allowed herself a good cry. When she finished, she smoothed the letter and stuffed it back into the envelope. She had to find that gold, that's all there was to it.

Outside the window, Adam picked up a stick and used it as a gun toward the grove of trees. "Pow, pow, pow!"

How could she search the caves when she'd promised Cade she'd not take Adam there again? Besides her promise, she couldn't risk his safety.

Her heart grew heavy at the thought of deceiving her husband again, just when things were starting to go right. The heaviness turned leaden when she thought of justifying the hours she'd spend away from the house. Would Cade grow to mistrust her? How could she keep up such deceit?

Lord, I know it's wrong to deceive my husband, but what choice have I?

"Tell him."

But I can't! I can't tell him the truth. That I'd only come to marry his brother because of the gold. He'll never trust me again, and rightly so.

"Tell him."

I can't!

There must be some other way. If she could only find that gold, all this would be over with and she and Cade and Adam could go on as if all this never happened. Cade would never have to know, and he would be free to love her, to trust her.

Yes. That was the best thing to do.

But how to search the caves when she had to protect Adam. That was the problem. If she could just solve that, her dilemma would be over. If she could just figure some way to keep Adam safe while she searched the caves.

Mara.

It was late afternoon by the time Emily made it over to Mara's house. She found her friend bent over an onion plant, knees planted firmly in the rich soil. Down the row, Abbey stood and stretched, her skirts billowing in the breeze.

Adam ran ahead. "Abbey!"

The girl walked toward them, and Mara stood, stretching her

shoulders back with her hands on her hips. Her bonnet flapped in a mock wave, and Emily saw the smile that bloomed on her face.

"Emily, Adam, to what do we owe this pleasure?"

"I wanna show Abbey my new aggie!" Adam said. The two youngsters ran to a spot under a shade tree and started a game of marbles.

Fear sucked the moisture from Emily's mouth as she thought of what she must tell her new friend. The relationship was too new to be tested in this way. What if Mara wanted nothing to do with her or her rotten scheme? What if Mara told Cade what she'd been up to all this time? Her insides quaked with the weight of it.

As the women approached each other under the hot summer sun, the smile slipped from Mara's face. "What's wrong?" Mara took her arm.

Emily tried for a smile. "Everything's fine. I just . . .I have some things to tell you. I need your help." She said the last with all the desperation she felt.

Mara squeezed her hand. "You know I'll do anything I can. Come inside; let's have a glass of lemonade."

As they entered the house, Emily's stomach churned with doubt. Maybe there was some other way. Sure, Mara was willing to help a friend, but that was before she knew that Emily had married Cade under false pretenses. Before she knew that she'd been deceiving her husband all these weeks. What would she think of Emily when she knew the truth? At the thought of losing her only friend, a heavy weight settled in her middle.

She took a seat on the sofa while she waited for Mara to fetch the lemonade. There was no way of knowing how Mara would react, especially since she really hadn't known her that long. But even so, she felt their bond of friendship was strong. And Emily had already gone over all her options. This was the only one she had. The safest one she had. She had to find that gold without Cade knowing.

If the thought of losing Mara made her sad, the thought of losing Cade just when things were coming along sent prickles of terror through her. No, she must do what she'd come to do.

Mara entered the room and set down the lemonade. Emily took a long sip and complimented Mara on the taste.

"Enough small talk, Emily. What's going on? You look as if you're being chased by a band of renegades."

Emily tested Mara with a glance, then fastened her gaze on the glass in her hands. "I have some things to tell you that will surprise you. I'm afraid what I say will be a bitter disappointment to you. And I'm afraid you'll think me a horrible person."

"Nonsense." Mara squeezed her arm. "Nothing you can say will make me think that. We all do silly things sometimes. Believe me, I should know about that with all the shenanigans I've pulled."

Emily remembered some of the stories she'd heard about Mara. Maybe she would understand. With trembling hands and a quaking spirit, she told Mara the truth. All the way from her uncle finding the map to her agreement to marry Thomas in order to have access to the farm. From finding out about Thomas's death to accepting Cade's proposal; then her refusal to search for the gold and her uncle's news that he'd put Nana in the asylum.

Throughout the story, Emily carefully avoided Mara's gaze, but when she mentioned that her grandmother was now in an asylum, she heard Mara gasp. It was all the encouragement she needed to meet her friend's gaze.

Mara's sky-blue eyes were widened, her delicate skin drawn. "That's awful," she whispered.

"I know what I've done is wrong, but I only did it for Nana's sake, don't you see?"

Mara's gaze found her lap. "I understand why you did it, truly." She met Emily's gaze. "It was wrong, mind you, what you did to Cade, using him that way."

"I know. I know." Guilt bore into her stomach, filling it with a week's worth of shame and embarrassment.

Mara brushed a smudge of dirt from her skirt. "Well, there's only one thing to make this right."

Oh, thank You, Lord, she understands! If I only find the gold, all this deceit will be over and done with. She felt a deep urge to hug her friend.

"You must tell Cade, of course," Mara said.

Emily settled back into the sofa, feeling her the skin on her face sag with disbelief. No. No, she couldn't do that. He'd never forgive her, never trust her.

"No," Emily said, but the word came out a croak.

"Emily, you have to. You can't go on deceiving him anymore. It's not right. God is displeased with—"

"Don't you think I know that?" The words were too loud, and she immediately regretted them. Especially when Mara shifted uncomfortably.

"I'm sorry," Emily said. "I have no aught against you." She grabbed Mara's arm, desperate for her friend to understand. "Cade is finally starting to care for me. After all these weeks, he's tender with me, and he's treating me like his wife." She looked down. "Well, almost." The heat she felt in her face left no doubt Mara understood.

"Still, Emily, it's lying." Mara shook her head and looked away. "You have no idea who you're talking to. I'm the queen of lies. Or at least, I used to be."

"I've heard stories," Emily admitted, berating herself for listening to the gossip.

"They're all true, I'm sure, every last one. I shamed myself time and time again, and believe me, I made no friends in doing so."

"But you got Clay."

She gave a brittle laugh. "That was God's work, rest assured. I began our relationship under pretense, just as you have done with Cade." Her face filled with color. "He needed a housekeeper and caretaker for Abbey, and I pretended I was up to the task."

"How is that pretense?" Emily knew Mara to be a fine homemaker and mother to Abbey.

"Oh, Emily, you've no idea how I've changed since then. I was raised in the lap of luxury with nary a thought for anyone other than my own self. I'd never cooked or cleaned, and certainly never fed hogs."

A smile sneaked up on Emily's face as she tried to imagine Mara doing those things for the first time.

"It was a disaster, I assure you. Oh, I was able to hold it together for a while, but eventually things came crashing down around me. Clay found out the truth, and I was caught."

"This is different, though. I'm doing this for Nana. I can't allow my uncle to leave her in the asylum!"

Mara squeezed her hand. "Of course you can't. But as hard as it will be, you must be honest with Cade."

"No. I won't do it, Mara."

Didn't her friend understand how delicate Cade's feelings for her were? If he found out how she'd tricked him all this time, it would ruin things for sure.

Her eyes stung with tears. "Yes, I married Cade for all the wrong reasons. But I've come to love him. And finally, after all these weeks, he's beginning to care for me, too." Emily stood and walked to the window, letting the sunlight warm her skin.

There was only silence behind her, and she wondered if Mara was beginning to come around. The thought sent hope bubbling to the surface.

She turned. "I know it's not right, but I just need to get this over with.

I need to find the gold and give it to my uncle, then I can get my grandmother back, and Cade won't have to know about any of it."

"All this aside, the stolen loot belongs to the bank, Emily. Giving it over to your uncle is stealing."

Emily blinked. "What else am I to do, Mara?"

"Why did you come to me, Emily?" Mara asked quietly.

In her rush to tell the story, she'd forgotten to tell Mara about Adam. "A while back, Adam and I got lost in a cave, and Cade became very worried. He forbade me from taking Adam into the caves anymore." She walked to her friend and knelt at her feet. "But that's where the gold is buried. I can't take Adam to the caves anymore, and I thought perhaps . . ."

Mara tucked in the corner of her lip. "You want me to look after Adam while you search."

"Yes." She took her friend's hand and let the desperation she felt in her soul shine in her eyes. "Please, Mara. Just in the afternoons. I'll be back before you get supper on, and he won't be any problem, I promise."

"I know he won't be any trouble. Adam's a fine boy." Mara looked away, and Emily knew she was weighing her options.

"It won't take me long to find the gold, if I can just focus on that. Then all this will be over. Nana will come here, and Cade. . .Lord willing, Cade will find himself falling in love with me, too."

The tears that blurred her vision slipped quietly down her face. Her insides froze with Mara's indecision, and, at the same time, she felt gooseflesh tighten her skin.

Mara sighed deeply. "All right. I'll do it."

Emily embraced her friend, gratitude welling in her.

"I'll do it, Emily, but I still think what you're doing is wrong."

Emily squeezed Mara's shoulders. "You won't regret it, I promise."

Chapter 14

*C*ade watched Emily scrubbing the dishes through the open kitchen door. Her slim shoulders tapered down to the narrowest of waists, and, for just a moment, he wondered how her waistline would look thickened with the pregnancy of their child.

Heat rose up in his gut and coiled around, loosening a pleasurable sensation. His heart thudded against his ribs at the thought. Emily with child. With his child.

Just as quickly, his gut clenched tightly, almost painfully. He remembered the way Ingrid had died after birthing Adam, and fear rose up in him like a whirlwind.

He rubbed his face with roughened hands. Emily was not with child, he reminded himself. He would face those fears when the time came, and he knew—trusted—that time would come.

Though she'd behaved mighty strange this evening, he knew things would work out between them. It was painful, putting the past behind him. Putting Ingrid behind him. But in truth, her face had dimmed more each day, replaced by Emily's vivid features. And each day, he looked forward to coming home to Emily, looked forward to her smiles and tender glances.

Yes, his heart had opened to her, despite his reluctance, and he found his gaze swinging toward her more and more. Even now, his hands itched to touch her. He stood up, draining the last of his coffee and took it into the confines of the kitchen. In the sitting room, he could hear Adam playing with the toy soldiers he'd given him on his last birthday.

When he approached Emily, he reached around her, setting the cup in the water.

She jumped, clearly not hearing his approach over the sloshing water. "Oh!" She gave a stiff laugh. "I–I didn't hear you."

Maybe he should back away, but the way her face softened, the way her lips curled up so sweetly made his body move closer as if it had a will of its own.

His hands found her shoulders and slid slowly down to her waist.

As his hands came around her, the longing for her welled up in him so strongly, his breath caught in his lungs. His hands lay against her abdomen, and despite the fear he'd felt moments earlier, he knew a fierce desire to see Emily carrying their child.

When she laid her head back against his chest, he nearly groaned. Oh, how he wanted this woman as his true wife. How he wanted them to be a real family—he, Adam, and Emily.

He nestled his face in the curve of her neck and felt her shiver. There was nothing in their way now. He was ready to let go of the past and give their relationship a real chance. It was what God intended, he was sure, and what he himself had come to desire above all else.

He turned her in his arms, and when her hands clung to his biceps, he hardly noticed the dishwater that seeped through his shirtsleeves.

He lowered his head toward her and tasted her lips. His heart filled with something sweet and hot, and when she moved her lips tentatively against his, a joy welled up in him that belied all reality. He wanted to lose himself in her, had already done so—

A twitter of laughter pulled him reluctantly from a world that contained only the two of them. He turned toward the sound.

"Yer kissing Mama." Adam giggled again. "Abbey said kissing's ucky, and her ma and pa do it all the time."

This time the giggle came from Emily.

"Well, that's her opinion," Cade said. "And besides, you're not to be sneaking up on folks like that."

"Why do grown-ups like to kiss so much, Pa?" His wide blue eyes stared back at Cade as guileless as a dove.

"Why do—well, they just do, is all." By the heat coursing under his skin, he felt sure Emily must see a rising tide of red on his face.

"Abbey said grown-ups kiss a long time, like you's just doin' with Ma. But when Ma kisses me, it's just a little one. Why's that, Pa?"

He shifted away from Emily and rubbed his neck. "I think you've been talking to Abbey too much is what I think. Go get your nightshirt on, it's your bedtime."

"Aww."

"Get on with you now."

"Yes, sir." Adam slumped away, his toy soldiers in hand.

Cade dared a glance at Emily. Her eyes brimmed with mirth, and her still-damp hand covered her mouth.

"You think that's funny, do you?"

"Mmhmm." She giggled again, and the sound of it tweaked his

funny bone. He reached out and poked her in the ribs where he knew she was ticklish.

She jerked away.

"Well, if you're gonna be laughing anyway, I say, let's give the lady a real reason." He dodged toward her again, hands outreached.

She bolted around him and out the kitchen door, squealing like a little girl. He scrambled after her, joy lighting his insides, mindless of the chair he overturned in the process.

Emily nudged the horse, and he jolted into action. In front of her, Adam squeezed his marbles tight in his little fists. He was eager to go play with Abbey, but Emily was dreading going back to the caves.

After last night's embrace and the tickle fight that had led to another embrace, the very last thing she wanted to do was go behind her husband's back again. He was falling in love with her, and the thought brought a warm, stirring sensation in her middle that was goodness itself. She already loved him more than life.

Looking at the boy as she drew alongside him, she felt her insides turn to mush. Her son. She so loved the way he nudged the hair from his eyes with the jerk of his head. The way his blue eyes turned dark and stormy when he didn't get his way. Yes, he was her son in every way that counted. And, Lord willing, Cade would soon be her husband in every way that counted.

If she could just get this gold found. She nudged the horse again, making him pick up the pace. Last night she'd had an awful dream about Nana. She had been strapped down to her bed whilst all the doctors and nurses stood laughing around her. Emily's heart beat heavily in her chest. It wasn't true, she knew that. But what was going on at that place so far away? Was Nana crying her name in the night as she had in her dream?

Lord, help me find that gold and fast! I can't bear for Nana to be there any longer.

After she left Adam with Mara, she rode back toward the area the map indicated. It seemed futile to search in the cave she'd been in before. Hadn't she dug up practically every scrap of dirt in there?

She rode past the cave's entrance for a while and around a grove of trees where an open meadow ended into a cliff wall. She looked down at her map, and her heart surged. Was this oblong circle on the paper the meadow? If so, the cave where the gold was buried would be in that cliff wall across the way. She wished the markings were clearer, but the water damage had smeared so much of the map.

Her breaths came in gasps as she trotted the horse across the open field.

Please, Lord, let this be it.

Reaching the other side seemed to take forever, but when she did, she rode along the face of the cliff looking for an opening. The wall was jagged and tall, jutting out this way and that and covered with weeds and bushes. Tumbleweed had blown up against the face of the cliff and lay trapped against the rocky surface. The cliff went on for quite a distance, varying in height, but her heart sunk as it began to grow shorter and shorter until it was barely over her head.

Then she saw it. Behind a scrubby bush, no higher than a dog's back, and nestled in the rock wall was a little black hole.

Chapter 15

*E*mily stabbed the shovel into the dirt once more and pulled up a small pile of ancient earth. She wished the map had been more specific as to the whereabouts of the buried loot, but she was certain she was at least in the right cave.

A whole week had passed without finding the gold, but Emily was sure she would find it soon. This cave was much smaller than the one she'd searched before. Only one open chamber and two short tunnels.

She hated that her relationship with Mara was strained each day when she dropped off Adam, but she rested assured that when everything worked out, Mara would see Emily had done the right thing.

She stopped digging, noting that it must be growing late. She walked the short distance outside the cave to check the sun's position. She should leave now if she wanted to get home in time to get supper on.

She stooped down to enter the cave, wishing the ceilings were a bit higher so she could straighten fully in the main room. She would finish this hole before she left. Just a few more shovelsful, then she would get Adam.

She struck the earth with the shovel once, twice, then three times. She should go a few inches deeper, just to be certain. She hurried, not wanting to take the chance that Cade would return home before she did.

On the last thrust of her shovel, she heard a solid thump. She stopped a moment, wondering if her ears were playing tricks on her in the echoing confines of the cave. She struck the dirt again. Thump. A rock? No, she knew very well by now the way the shovel clanked, not thumped against rock. Her heart accelerated.

Oh please, Lord, let it be!

She removed more dirt and held the lantern above the hole. Something was buried under there. Hopefully not a big log. She ran her fingers ran along the surface and felt chills snake up her spine. This was no log.

It was smooth to the touch, with straight grooves across the surface. A chest.

She sat back on her haunches, her hands trembling, her insides churning. It was late; she had to get Adam and go home. She straightened as much as she could under the damp ceiling. It would take too long to dig out the chest tonight. She would have to wait until tomorrow. The thought nearly killed her. She'd waited so long to find it, and now she had to leave it here!

She dusted off her skirts. Well, there was no help for it. Besides, the gold had been here for ages, it certainly wasn't going anywhere.

As she left the cave and rode to collect Adam, she sent up prayers of thanksgiving. Soon this would be over, and she and Cade and Adam would be a real family at last. Cade would never have to know the ugliness that had brought her here to begin with.

Later that night, when the house was quiet, and she was alone in her room, she pulled her diary from the bottom of a drawer.

Dear Diary,

I have found the gold at last. I am so excited that this ruse is almost over. I wish I could give Nana a hug and assure her she'll be in my care soon, but alas, that is impossible. It's all I can do to wait until tomorrow.

The gold is buried in a chest, and though I have yet to unearth it, I could see its rounded top buried a foot or so under the ground. I'm so thankful to Mara for watching Adam for me.

Diary, my heart beats rapidly even now as I think about finishing this job. I can hardly wait for it to be done so I can focus solely on my husband and child. Oh, to be a regular farmer's wife! I will be so relieved not to have this dreadful search hanging over my head.

Emily took the eggs she'd collected from her basket and, one by one, cracked them into the skillet. They sizzled and smoked, their yolks staring up at her like the bright sun dawning outside. A course of energy had flowed through her veins all night and every moment since she'd awakened. Chores had been done in record time. She could not wait to get back to the cave. But wait she must because Mara had plans this morning and couldn't watch Adam.

She would just have to bide her time until the afternoon. Part of her couldn't believe she'd found the treasure so quickly. For that she was so thankful to God! Soon, her uncle would have his gold, she would have Nana, and Cade would have the wife he thought she was.

A niggle of guilt coursed through her at the thought of Cade.

Don't be silly. What he doesn't know won't hurt him.

It would be a disaster for him to find out now. It would ruin everything.

She flipped the eggs, letting the underside cook just a moment before scooting them onto a platter. She checked on the biscuits and saw they had a few minutes left to cook. The ham was already on the plate and the table set. She'd just—

Cade's arms circled her waist, and she jumped. Turning her head, she saw Cade's clean-shaven jaw only inches from hers. Her heart did a happy jig. "You mustn't sneak up on me like that."

"Can't help myself." The smile in his voice sent shivers up and down her arms.

She tried for an indignant voice. "Oh, and why is that, Mr. Manning?"

His hands flatted on her sides, shooting hot darts straight to her belly, and she sucked in a breath.

"I've got me a beautiful woman in my kitchen. How am I supposed to keep my hands to myself?" If she was about to take offense at his answer, it was forgotten when he planted the gentlest of kisses on her temple. Immediately, heat flared in the spot his lips touched.

Somewhere in the house, she could hear Adam singing, but her eyes were only for her husband at the moment. The green in them had come out to play, as his boyish lashes drooped lazily over them.

He turned her in his arms, and she could feel his thighs pressed up against hers. Fire kindled in her belly and spread rapidly through her limbs.

He tipped her chin up.

"You are some woman."

The words brought more pleasure to her heart than she'd felt in a long time. She feasted on them like a starving animal and was hungry for more.

His thumb moved tenderly across her chin, and she wondered if he knew he was causing a riot inside her. Oh, how she loved this man. How she longed to be loved by him.

"I have some things I want to tell you, Emmie," he whispered. His breath fanned the curls loosened beside her face, and the movement sent shivers across her scalp.

She wondered what he wanted to say. She wished she could drag the words from his mouth, but she had to be patient.

She was vaguely aware of tromping on the stairs and knew Adam would be coming down for breakfast. Cade must've heard it, too, for she felt him withdrawing.

His hands moved down to her arms. "Plenty of time for this later, I reckon."

Disappointment turned the fire in her belly cold, and her legs felt as wispy as smoke.

Behind her, she heard Adam scooting his chair out from the table. She smothered a sigh.

"But tonight," her handsome husband said, "when Adam's in bed, and I've got you all to myself, I got some things I need to tell you." His eyes promised so much. Love and—dare she hope—the fulfillment of their marriage vows.

She was suddenly so grateful she'd made the decision not to tell Cade about the gold.

She nodded, mesmerized by the intense look on his face. "I'll be here."

When he left the kitchen, she started getting breakfast on the table, and despite the delay of Cade's words, she knew she had reason for that extra spring in her step.

She almost croaked when Adam asked if they were going over to Abbey's again today. When she said yes, Cade had looked at her and said, "Sure are spending lots of time over at the Stedmans'."

She buttered her biscuits to busy her hands. "We've become fast friends," she said, hoping he wouldn't disapprove. "But I always finish my chores first."

She waited while he finished a bite of eggs. "I think it's good you've become friends."

She breathed a silent sigh of relief and quickly changed the subject to the coming harvest.

The day dragged by so slowly, Emily thought she'd go mad with the waiting. She kept herself busy with her chores, especially the garden. She picked the ripe tomatoes, mopped the floors, wiped down the doors, and made two loaves of bread.

At last, it was time to take Adam to Mara's. She trotted the horse through the meadow, taking the shorter route. The shovel thumped against the horse's side, and Adam bounced in front of her.

When at last they reached the Stedman ranch, Emily whisked Adam down from the horse and hurried to the door. She knocked, her limbs trembling with anticipation. When several moments went by, she knocked again. Maybe Mara was around back tending the garden. She was just about to check when the door squeaked open.

"There you are," Emily said. "I was just about—Mara, what's wrong?" Her friend's face was flushed, her nose an uncomely shade of red, and her eyes look glazed.

Mara put a hand to her head.

"You're sick." The realization left her both sympathetic for her friend and worried that she wouldn't be able to watch Adam. But then, there was always Abbey. Perhaps . . .

"I'm so sorry," Mara said. "I'm not up to watching Adam today."

"Of course you're not. You need to be in bed." She wanted to ask about Abbey, but felt ashamed to be so selfish. Still, she could have that gold in her hands today.

"I'd have Abbey watch him, but she's at the McClains' today helping Sara. I'm sorry, Emily."

She fought the flood of disappointment that flowed through her. "Don't be silly. Get yourself to bed. Can I make some tea for you?"

"No, no, thanks. I'm sure it's nothing serious, but you don't need to be catching it."

She gave a wan smile. "I'll check on you tomorrow, then. Take care of yourself and get plenty of rest."

Mara nodded and shut the door, and Emily and Adam returned to the horse. Adam whined about not getting to stay until Emily felt impatient with him. What was she going to do? She needed only one more day to unearth the gold, and it would be over.

And the timing couldn't be better. Tonight her husband was going to tell her he loved her, she was sure of it. How wonderful it would be to have this mess cleared up beforehand. And there was Nana, too. She didn't want her staying in that asylum one day more than she had to. She had to unearth that chest today.

She helped Adam mount the horse, then mounted behind him. Was there anyone else who could watch Adam today? Her mind sifted through the town residents, and she tried to imagine herself asking each of them for the favor. Slowly she eliminated everyone she knew. What reason could she possibly give?

Perhaps . . .

No, you promised you wouldn't.

Still the thought formed fully in her mind. Maybe she could take Adam just this once. After all, the chest was buried only feet from the cave entrance. He could play outside, by the mouth of the cave where she could hear him. Why, he wouldn't even have to set foot inside.

She nudged the horse, a tentative smile forming on her face. "Adam, how would you like to go on an adventure today?"

Chapter 16

*E*mily scooped another shovelful of dirt and tossed it in the growing pile. Even in the shade of the cave, her skin dripped with sweat. She stopped, letting herself rest against the shovel's handle, and caught her breath. Excitement raced through her veins until she trembled with it. She could see the chest now and had dug until the rounded top was exposed.

The trunk appeared to be wooden and about three feet long, smaller than she had imagined. The color was a rich brown, though since it was dirt-stained, there was no telling its original color.

She picked up the shovel and began digging again. Outside, she could hear Adam talking to himself as he played in the grass under a tall tree with his soldiers. She couldn't believe how perfectly everything was working out. Even with Mara sick, with the digging site so close to the cave entrance, it was easy enough to listen for him.

She dug deeply on the side of the chest and saw the dark metal loops attached to the side. Her heart thumped heavily in her chest, both from exertion and anticipation.

"Whatcha doing?" Adam's voice came from inside the doorway of the cave.

"Adam, you're not to be in here."

"Why does that tree have arms?"

"What? What are you talking about?"

He pointed out toward the spot he'd been playing in. "It goes like this." He forked his hands showing her how the tree was one trunk that split into two.

She had to get him out of here. "It's called a schoolmarm tree, Honey. It just grows that way. Now, you need to go back outside."

"Did you find treasure?" he asked.

For a moment a dash of anxiety prickled her skin, then she remembered all the times she'd buried his marbles and knew the child couldn't know the truth.

She stepped around the hole, not wanting him to see there really was something under the dirt. Something very big and valuable. She wondered idly how she would get the chest out of the cave and to her uncle.

"Let's go back outside," she said, ushering the boy through the little opening. "I shouldn't be much longer, then we'll go home and have supper."

"Can we have corn cake?"

"We'll see." Emily slipped through the doorway and resumed her digging. She would have to leave the chest here and come back for it when Adam wasn't with her. And how would she get it to her uncle? How did one go about shipping a chest full of stolen gold coins?

Perhaps she should wire her uncle and have him come get it. Yes, that would be the safe thing to do. But first, she would insist he take Nana out of the asylum. He could bring her with him when he came for the gold. She wouldn't give him his precious loot until he brought Nana safe and sound.

She moved to the front of the chest and began digging. Her mind wandered back to this morning when Cade had embraced her. Shivers ran up her arms even as heat curled in her belly. What had he been about to say when Adam had come downstairs? It was torture having to wait an entire day to hear his words, but the promise in his eyes left little doubt that he'd fallen in love with her.

Her heart skittered faster, and a smile tilted her lips. Would tonight be their first night together as man and wife? She could hardly believe it was happening, and yet she'd seen the love shining in Cade's eyes. Why, she might yet get to experience the feeling of a child growing within her. Cade's child.

Her stomach clenched at the thought. A baby brother or sister for Adam would be just the thing.

"I'm bored." Adam's whine from the cave's entrance scared her.

"Adam. You're supposed to be playing outside."

"I wanna come in here with you."

When he approached, she stepped in front of the hole. She had to keep him occupied safely, outside the cavern, if she ever wanted to get this gold dug up. "Would you like me to bury some marbles for you?"

"In here?" He dug the marbles from his pocket.

"No, Adam, your pa said—"

Adam threw down his marbles and stomped a dirty boot. "I wanna stay in here with you, Ma." Even in the cave's dim light she could see his tears. "Please. . ."

Emily sighed and looked over her shoulder at the chest, still half covered with dirt. Well, she knew there were no wild animals in the cave, and that had been Cade's biggest concern. Besides, it wouldn't take long at all to finish.

"All right. But just this once."

Adam clapped his hands and bounced on his feet.

"But you have to stay over there near the entrance." She wanted to add that he couldn't tell his pa but couldn't bring herself to do it. Lying herself was bad enough. She wouldn't teach Adam to do it too.

She walked over with her shovel and began digging. "Turn around, so you can't peek."

When he did as she said, she continued digging until she had each marble hidden, then she covered the spot with the fresh dirt. "There you go. Stay over here, understand?"

"Yes, Ma'am!" Adam was already on his hands and knees pawing through the dirt.

She walked back to her hole, keeping the lantern closer to Adam so he couldn't see the chest. She worked hard, removing the packed earth from around the wooden exterior. Every few minutes, Adam would let out a squeal when he found another marble.

Soon she had all but one corner of the chest unearthed. There seemed to be a rock or something equally hard against this side of the chest, for she made very slow progress. Finally, she began stabbing harder and harder at the dirt with her shovel blade. Sweat beaded on her forehead, and her back strained with every downward slice. She grunted under the effort, her arms aching.

Then she heard something. Something that started quietly, like the rumble of a stampede off in the distance. But it grew louder. She stopped and listened, holding her shovel still.

Gravel slid down the wall beside her as the rumble grew louder, and all of a sudden it dawned on her. The cave was going to collapse.

She threw down her shovel just as larger rocks began to fall around them. The rumble was so loud she had to shout as she ran toward Adam. "Get out!"

Adam stood, his eyes wide with fright, and his feet rooted to the ground. As if in slow motion, she saw a rock break loose from the wall above him.

"Moooove!" She reached out and shoved him out of the way, toward the entrance. Her feet found the hole he was digging, and she stumbled, falling just feet from the cave's entry.

"Ma!"

Her head smacked the hard floor of the cave, and the rock that had fallen hit her calf with the force of a cannonball. She cried out, barely recognizing her own voice. The rock's rough edges tore into her skin, the weight of it crushed her bones.

Chapter 17

*M*a!" Adam knelt beside her.

"Get out," she rasped. "Hurry!" The rumble had turned to a loud roar.

"You're hurt!"

He tried to tug on the rock, but she knew it was too heavy for him. "Get out, Adam!" What if a rock fell on him, too? She couldn't bear the thought of her boy being hurt or worse. It was only then she realized the roaring she heard was in her head, and that the rumbling had stopped. No more rocks fell, only bits of gravel. Fear still rattled between her ears and pumped through her veins.

She wet her lips, her cheek smashed into the dirt. "Adam, listen to me."

The boy kept trying to dislodge the rock, and each time it moved a tiny fraction, she moaned in agony.

"Adam, stop!"

He sat back on his haunches, then crawled up where he could see her face. "It's stuck, I can't move it." Tears streaked through the dirt on his face, and his little lips quivered.

She reached out and took his hand. The pain got the best of her, and her teeth began chattering. It was taking all her effort not to cry out. "Listen, Adam. I need your help. You have to go home. Get your pa and show him where I am, can you do that?"

He shook his head. "I don't know how."

"I'll tell you how," she said, stopping for some quick breaths. "But you must listen carefully."

Cade sat on the front porch chair, his elbows propped on his knees. Where were they? He'd been home for a long time, and the sun was finding its home on the horizon already.

He told himself she'd lost track of time. He told himself she was only running late. But a thought kept snagging him like a burr on fleece.

A thought he tried to avoid until now. He recalled the words he'd spoken to Emily this morning. He'd made it clear he had something to say to her tonight. Something important.

He was going to tell her he loved her. That he wanted them to be a real family; that he wanted her to be his real wife. All day long he'd thought of little else. But the thought that had lingered in the back of his mind since he'd come home to an empty house, the thought that he'd shoved away each time, surfaced with the stubbornness of a mule.

Maybe Emily didn't want to hear what he had to say. Maybe he'd scared her off with his promise of something important to say.

No, he wouldn't let the thought linger. Not yet. The sun still had a sliver poking up over the land. There were a dozen reasons she might be late.

Cade watched the sun melt silently into the prairie grass. He watched the darkness fall over the ground like a smothering shroud. He heard the crickets and cicadas start their oscillating songs.

Maybe she really didn't have feelings for him.

She probably went over to the Stedmans' again today and—

Mara. If Emily weren't over there, her friend might know where she was.

He ran to the barn and saddled up Sutter, noticing for the first time that Bitsy wasn't in her stall. Now worry clawed at his insides. This was just like last time when she'd taken Adam to a cave and gotten lost. At least he could scratch that worry from his list. She wouldn't go against his decision to keep Adam away from the caves.

He swung himself up on Sutter and took off across the field toward the Stedmans'. His heart threatened to burst from his chest as he rode. He was starting to think either she or Adam had hurt themselves. She knew better than to be riding at night.

When he arrived at the Stedmans', they were just finishing supper.

"Cade, what brings you out tonight?" Clay asked.

"Can I get you some coffee?" Mara asked. Her cheeks were too pink, and her eyes drooped tiredly.

Cade stepped through the door and shook his head no. "Have you seen Emily today, Mara?"

She looked down at the floor before meeting his gaze again. "What's wrong, Cade?"

"She isn't home. Wasn't there when I got home and still isn't. Adam's with her. Have you seen her?"

She looked at her husband before answering. "She was by this afternoon. Around three o'clock."

"Did she say where she was going?" Cade asked.

Her jaw went slack, and Cade thought her face grew even more red. When she wavered on her feet, her husband led her to the sofa.

"She's been sick today," he explained to Cade. "I told her she shouldn't be up fixing supper. You all right, Angel?" he asked his wife.

"I'm fine." Mara settled back against the sofa and closed her eyes, rubbing her face like a tired toddler. Abbey must've been washing the supper dishes, for he could hear the clanking in the kitchen.

"Sorry to bother you like this, but I'm worried about Emily and Adam."

"Of course you are. I–I think I might know where they went," Mara said. "I think they went to a cave out toward the cotton tree grove."

Cade shook his head. "I told her not to take Adam to the caves. She wouldn't do that."

Mara studied her hands as they picked at the ribbon on her dress. There was only one word for the expression on her face. Guilt. Could Emily have gone against his decision? No, she wouldn't risk Adam's safety any more than he would.

"I was supposed to watch Adam this afternoon, but with me being sick . . . I think she went ahead anyway."

Cade's thoughts seemed to be flowing as slow as molasses. He couldn't make sense of what Mara was saying. The Emily he knew wouldn't go against him that way for no good reason.

He shook his head again. "She must've gone someplace else. Emily wouldn't defy me like that."

"Mara?" her husband asked. His gaze trained on his wife's face, he seemed to see something Cade was missing. "What's going on?"

Mara wet her lips, meeting her husband's gaze, then Cade's. "I promised I wouldn't tell."

At her words, hope stirred in his heart even as dread twisted his gut. "They might be in danger, Mara. I need you to tell me anything you know."

Mara bit her lip then met his gaze. "She's been looking in the caves for some stolen loot that was buried there years ago by your grandfather and hers. She didn't want to take Adam—she hasn't since you told her not to," she said in defense of her friend.

"Stolen loot?" Cade wondered if Mara's fever had gone to her head. Even her husband was looking at her funny. But it was getting late, and Emily and Adam might be hurt.

She sighed, clearly reluctant to go any further. "I guess I better start at the beginning."

Cade cut her off. "I want to hear all about this, but not right now. If you're right about the cave, there's no time to lose."

Clay stood up. "I'll go with you. You be all right, Mara?"

She nodded.

"Thanks," Cade said to Mara.

"I'm sure they're fine," Mara said.

Emily and Adam would be home if they were fine.

The two men rode their horses out across the Stedman property toward the cotton tree grove. There was a cave on a small cliff over there. He'd never been in it, but he feared it was the one Emily had gotten lost in before. Maybe her lantern had burnt out, and they were just lost, like before.

When they reached the cave, they dismounted the horses and untied the lanterns. He couldn't see or hear anything suggesting Bitsy was tied up nearby, but he had to search the cave anyway.

"We'll need something to mark our way; this is a deep cave with lots of tunnels," Cade said.

"I think I have some corn kernels in my pocket." He checked and nodded. "We can drop them as we go."

They split up inside the cave, each with a handful of kernels and a lantern. Cade called out for Emily and Adam, but all Cade heard was his own echo and Clay's calls. He got almost dizzy with all the turns and twists in the tunnel. In places he had to crawl. He could see footprints in the dirt, but he knew they could be weeks old. When he finally worked his way back to the entrance, Clay waited there.

"They can't be in there," his friend said.

Cade shook his head, knowing he was right.

"Where else?"

"There are plenty of caves." He tried to ignore the hopeless tone in his voice. "Hard to tell which one they might have gone to." It was pitch-black out now, and he realized he'd been gone for a couple hours. "Maybe they're home now."

"I can go check if you've a mind to keep looking."

He nodded thoughtfully. "I'll be at the cave by the fallen oak back by Shanty Creek," Cade said as he mounted his horse.

"If they're at your house, I'll come for you. And if they're not, I'll come back and help you look." Clay took off on his mare, and Cade set off for Shanty Creek.

As he rode, he called out for his wife and son. If anything had happened to them . . .

A long while later, he exited the cave. It had opened only to one small room, and there was no sign Emily had even been in this one. He waited outside the entrance, his back propped up against the rough, moss-covered stone.

God, please help them to be all right. Take care of Emily and my boy, and please help me find them.

It was torture waiting here for Clay's return. He fought the urge to go and search other caves, but the truth was that he wasn't sure of their whereabouts. He'd seen other caves in passing, but this land was not as familiar as his farming acreage. How would he find them in the dark with only a lantern to guide his way?

I need Your help, Father.

He laid his head against the hard stone and closed his eyes. What was that loot Mara had mentioned, and why had Emily been looking for it? Why had she taken Adam along? It just didn't add up, and he wished he'd let Mara finish the story. A lot of good it had done him to rush off. Now here he sat just waiting—

"Pa!" The cry came from a short distance away and accompanied the sound of hoofbeats.

His heart thudded in his throat. He rose to his feet, his legs trembling beneath him. When Clay's horse came into view, he saw his son, safe and sound in the circle of his friend's arm. Adam's face was wet, streaked with dirt and tears, but otherwise he looked all right.

He felt the sting of tears in his eyes at the sight. "Adam."

"You found them." Cade said as the horse drew to a halt in front of him.

Clay shook his head, but his son spoke. "Ma's hurt, Pa. R–real bad." The tears started again as he drew his son off the horse and into his arms. The boy's little arms wrapped around his neck.

"I g–got lost, and it got dark."

"I know, I know, you're all right now. Papa's got you." He met Clay's gaze.

"Best I can tell," his friend said, "they were in a cave, and it started to collapse. He said a rock fell on Emily's leg, and it was too big to move."

His gut clenched hard. "How bad is she hurt?"

Clay shrugged. "She was conscious at least."

His son loosened his hold and leaned back to meet his gaze. "She said to go home and get you, but I g–got lost."

Hope stirred when he realized Adam knew where she was.

"Do you think you can find the cave, son?"

"I don't know."

At Cade's request, he described the terrain, narrowing down the location to a few areas. His description of the cliff made him think right off of Potter's Ridge.

He looked at Clay. "Let's mount up. I think I might know the area he's talking about."

They rode the short distance to the ridge, Adam safe in his arms, and Cade thanked God for his son's safety. But Emily's injuries. . .

Lord, keep her safe till we find her.

"It's no use," Cade whispered. They'd searched the ridge over and again, and there was no cave there. Adam had said the entrance was small, but even so, they'd searched the walls on foot, even looking behind all the brush.

Clay had stopped, his lantern hanging in his hand, his gaze trained on Cade. Shadows played over his features, and Cade thought how weary his friend looked. Pity shone from the depths of his eyes.

"Your boy's tuckered," Clay said.

Cade looked down and saw his son had slumped against a rock and fallen asleep. He sighed. She wasn't here at Potter's Ridge. Worry filled his belly with a burning sensation. He hated thinking of her lying in the dark somewhere suffering.

"We can keep looking if you want to," his friend said.

Cade's gaze swung across the darkened land. The trees were black against the starlit sky. It would be like looking for a needle in a haystack to continue searching tonight. Maybe Mara had information that would help them locate the cave. Or maybe Adam would be able to find his way back to it in daylight.

"No," Cade said. "It's useless." He hated even saying it. Felt like he was betraying his wife to leave her out there all night.

Dear Lord, protect her tonight. Be there for her in a way I can't.

"Why don't I take the boy back to our house?" Clay said. "You can come by at dawn, and we'll head out again."

Cade shook his head. "I'd like to talk with your wife tonight, if it's all right. She might know something helpful." If she did, he could come back out by himself.

They mounted up and headed back for the Stedman ranch. Adam slept all the way and barely stirred when Cade swung him off Sutter and carried him up to a spare bed.

Mara had waited up, and her face broke out in a smile of relief when she saw Adam in his arms. But tears gathered in her eyes when Clay told her they hadn't found Emily.

After putting his son to bed, Cade sat in a chair across from Mara and her husband. "It was just too dark," Cade said to Mara. "I was hoping you might know something. . .anything that might help us find Emily tonight."

Mara put a trembling hand to her lips and shook her head. "I just know she was west of your house. She never said exactly where she was looking. What did Adam say? Is she hurt bad?"

Cade filled her in as best he could, and together the group prayed for Emily's safe return. It filled him with regret to think he might have lost the chance to tell Emily he loved her. Sorrow welled up in him like a big, black storm.

The prayer ended, and suddenly he remembered what Mara had said earlier about the stolen loot and something about his grandfather.

"I don't understand what you were saying earlier," he said to Mara. "What's this loot Emily was looking for, and how was my grandfather involved?"

Mara closed her eyes briefly. He was asking her to betray her friend, but he knew she must be weighing out the benefits of finding some clue that might help find her. "Apparently your grandfather and hers robbed a bank years ago. Her uncle found a map that showed your farm as the burial spot. A note on the map indicated there was another map hidden at your house."

"I don't know anything about this." He wanted to deny his grandfather's involvement, but remembered the man's absence and eventual disappearance. "What's Emily got to do with it?" An ugly feeling was stirring in his gut, and he almost didn't want to hear the answer, knew instinctively he wouldn't like it.

Mara seemed reluctant to answer, and the feeling of foreboding grew until his head swam with it.

"Her uncle forced her to come here," Mara said. "She was supposed to marry Thomas, as you know, but then he died, and you asked her to marry you."

"Forced how?" Cade asked.

"Has she told you about her grandmother back home?"

"A little."

"Well, apparently her uncle is her grandmother's guardian, and she has some problems with her memory and such. I didn't get all the details. But her uncle is no gentleman. At first, he threatened he would put her grandmother in an asylum if she didn't go through with the marriage."

He knew she'd written Thomas a letter originally, and that had started their correspondence. Had she done all that to finagle a marriage proposal? Just so she could get at the map and have access to the caves?

His heart sank to his boots, and he felt like he'd swallowed a walnut for the ache in his throat. She'd wormed her way into Thomas's heart, tricked him into proposing? She'd wormed her way into his heart. Into his life. Into his son's life. All for the purpose of digging up some stolen gold?

"It's not what you're thinking, Cade," Mara said. "She did it for her grandmother, whom she loves dearly. She hated having to do it."

Hated being married to him? Hated having to pretend. . .

He rubbed his hands over his face to stop the stinging in his eyes. Had she pretended all along? Pretended to care for him, pretended to enjoy his kisses?

"She cares about you, truly." Fervency shone from Mara's eyes. "I'm not explaining this well." Tears escaped her eyes and coursed down her face. "She had stopped looking for the gold after you told her you didn't want Adam in the caves. She had written her uncle and told him she wouldn't do it anymore. She was starting to . . .care for you. She didn't want to deceive you anymore—"

"Then why didn't she just tell me?" His voice boomed louder than he'd expected.

"She was afraid she'd lose your trust. Can't you see, she valued that so much. Her uncle wrote her back that he'd put her grandmother in the asylum and wouldn't take her out until she found the loot. She felt trapped."

His jaw clenched. "So she started searching again."

Mara nodded, dabbing at the tears on her face.

He could hardly believe this. The lies she must've told, the deceit. Maybe she didn't care for him at all. Him or Adam. Maybe it was all just a giant ruse to get at that loot. The thoughts came quickly, each blacker than the one before it, swirling like a twister.

He got up and walked to the window. His temples throbbed with pain, his jaw clenched tightly. How could this be? When he'd thought he loved her?

"Please, Cade, you have to believe me." Mara had approached and took hold of his arm. "She cares deeply for you. She was so afraid of losing your. . .trust."

"So afraid she's lied to me all these months?" He set his hat back on his head. He looked up the stairs where his son slept. How would this affect his boy? He lay upstairs as innocent as a lamb. He'd been in tears over the thought of losing his ma.

Cade sighed. As hopeless as it seemed, as angry as he was with Emily, he would go back out looking tonight. For Adam's sake.

Chapter 18

*E*mily heard a moan and tried to move. Her leg screamed with agony. Her eyes opened. At least she thought they did, but the darkness didn't recede. Her arms tightened with gooseflesh, and she felt damp.

She remembered now. She was in the cave, and she'd sent Adam home to his pa. But how long ago was that? The lamp must have flickered out sometime during the night, using up all the oil in the reservoir. There had been hours of light in the oil. Adam should've been back by now.

Please, dear God, let Adam be all right!

What if he'd never made it home? What if he was wandering alone in the darkness? Her eyes stung with silent tears.

What have I done? Oh, dear Lord, what have I done?

She'd endangered her son's life and her own, too. A sharp stab of pain shot up her leg, and she gasped. She cradled her head in her arm, smelling the dirt and mustiness of the cave, tasting it in her mouth. Fear snaked up her spine and branched out to every part of her body.

What if Adam never made it home? What if he died because of her? She deserved it herself. It was her own fault for going through with this awful plan. Her fault for deceiving Cade.

He would be worried sick by now and surely was out searching for them both. She struggled to think straight, in spite of the searing pain. Her brain seemed stuffed with fog, and she waited a moment until it passed.

How would Cade know where to find them? Perhaps Adam had found his way home but he couldn't find the cave in the darkness. Oh, please let it be so! If only Adam made it safely through, she would be ever so grateful.

What would Cade do if Adam couldn't find the cave? How would he find her? A thought sprung up, bringing with it both hope and despair. Would he go to Mara's? Would she tell him everything about her uncle and the loot?

At first she denied it. Mara was a loyal friend, and she wouldn't betray her confidence.

But Emily's life was at risk, and that changed everything, didn't it?

Her heart raced at the thought of Cade learning everything. She closed her eyes and buried her face in her arm. If he found out everything, it was all over. He wouldn't trust her. Wouldn't love her. How could he when she'd deceived and betrayed him so?

God, I was so wrong! Wrong to deceive my husband and wrong to sin against You. Forgive me, Lord.

She should have refused to do her uncle's bidding or confided in her husband from the beginning. Why was it always so easy to see wrong choices when it was too late to change them?

Another pain shot up her leg, and her head spun with dizziness. She fought the sensation, but the wave overtook her.

Cade drew Sutter to a halt, letting the feelings he'd held back for hours come flowing over him like muddy river water. She'd lied to him about everything. Their marriage was a lie. Their life together was a lie.

Clay's horse drew up beside him, and Cade could feel his friend's gaze on him.

"It's time we call it a night." Hadn't he tried his best to find the woman? It was useless looking in the dark. And even though his heart still longed for her, he knew she'd killed his love for her as surely as he sat here.

"Maybe she'll somehow make it home on her own," Clay offered.

Or maybe she'd never make it home at all. Even though he was angry, even though he knew his feelings had been mocked, he couldn't bear the thought of Emily gone.

"Your boy told me something when I found him tonight. Seeing as how you're so angry right now, I thought you'd best know."

"What is it?"

"You might not like what Emily did. It was wrong, I'll give you that. But if you're questioning her love for the boy, or for yourself, I'd guess you're wrong about that."

Tired as he was, angry as he was, Cade met his friend's gaze in the lamplight. "What are you talking about?"

"Adam told me what happened when the cave-in started. The boulder landed right where he was standing. . . Emily pushed him out of harm's way, Cade."

Cade's tongue wouldn't seem to move.

Clay ran his hand through his hair. "Rock that size would've killed the boy. Seems your wife risked her own life for the young 'un."

The news made the anger stirring in his gut slow a fraction. Was it true? His mind swirled with the thought.

"Don't know if that changes anything, but I thought you should know," his friend said. "You can come by at dawn for me and Adam. We'll be saddled up and ready to go. Let's pray Adam will be able to find the cave in the daylight."

Cade nodded. "Thanks, friend."

By the time Cade reached the house, he was feeling tuckered himself, but his mind worked like a dog that wouldn't let go of a bone. Even after hearing what Emily had done for his son, anger ate at his soul. She'd still deceived him. Maybe she did cotton to his son, maybe she had saved his life, but that didn't change what she'd done.

As he lay alone in Adam's room, he thought back to all the times he'd touched her, kissed her. She'd set his blood aboil with her tentative responses, but what had been going through that mind of hers? Had she been recoiling in disgust? Had she forced herself to respond?

No. He didn't want to believe it. His gut tightened painfully at the very thought. Even Mara was convinced of Emily's loyalty. But with all the lies that had been told, all the secrets, how could he believe anything anymore?

He turned over and punched his pillow hard, trying to settle into a comfortable position. It was only a matter of hours before dawn, and if he wanted to be ready to search, he'd best get some sleep.

But try as he might, even though his body was weary, his active mind wouldn't oblige. He sat up in bed and ran a hand through his hair.

Emily.

Oh, Lord God, I love her.

No matter what she'd done, what she'd said or hadn't said, he loved his wife. And she was out there somewhere, likely suffering in pain while he was cozy in this warm bed. If only there was some way of finding out where she—

The map. Mara had said she'd found a map here somewhere. Maybe it was in her room.

He tore off the blanket and ran to his old room, throwing open the door so hard it bounced against the wall. He scrambled in the darkness to light the lamp then carried it over to the bedside. The top drawer of her night table turned up her Bible, stationery, and a book.

The second drawer held nothing of help, and he slammed it closed. What if she'd taken the map with her? He ran his hands over his weary eyes. She probably had, of course. He looked around the dimly lit room, watching the shadows flicker in the light. Maybe there was something else.

The letters. Of course, Mara had said she'd been corresponding with her uncle. Perhaps she'd kept them. He tore through her drawers, feeling only a smidgen of guilt at the invasion of privacy. This could be a matter of life and death, and if he could help it, his wife would live, never mind what she'd done.

He scrounged through her clothing, realizing she may have hidden them away.

From you.

He brushed the thought away. He needed to focus on more important matters right now. His hands searched, the lamp on top of the chest providing him a glimpse of articles of clothing he had no right to see. Suddenly, his fingers closed on something hard. He pulled it up through the filmy clothing. Two bundles of something. Letters. A book.

A rush of excitement buzzed through him, giving him a second wind. One bundle had a letter from Thomas atop the pile. The other stack was from Denver. He sat on the foot of the bed and tore off the ribbon. The letters scattered around him, and he saw they were all from the same man. It had to be her uncle. He opened the first one he grabbed.

Emily,

I'm advising you that I have put your grandmother in the asylum.

As you know, her health has continued to decline so I am no longer able to take care of her here. You have expressed interest in taking care of the old woman, but you have failed to fulfill our agreement. Until you find the gold, which I might remind you is the reason you were sent there in the first place, your grandmother will remain in the institution. As her legal guardian I will do with her as I see fit since she is not of her own mind.

If you will bring yourself to continue the search, I will consider handing over guardianship to you. Though, I must admit, I'm growing increasingly irritated by your games.

Uncle Stewart

Cade set down the letter, an ugly feeling growing in his middle at the words scrawled on the page. What kind of man . . . ?

The date was recent, and it fit with Mara's story. Perhaps Emily had been a helpless pawn in the whole mess.

He read the rest of the letters and felt such frustration well up in him that he realized he wanted to slug this Uncle Stewart. After he read the last letter, he picked up the hardbound book with a plain brown cover. Was it Emily's diary? His heart pounded heavily against his ribs. Did he want to know her innermost thoughts?

Fear sucked the moisture from his mouth. What if her heart was contrary to everything she'd said to him? What if inside she had laughed at his bumbling efforts to court her? Could he stand knowing it, if that were the truth?

He nearly laid the book aside, unwilling to face the possibility, but his friend's words played in his mind.

You might not like what Emily did. It was wrong. But if you're questioning her love for the boy, or for yourself, I'd guess you're wrong about that.

Slowly, he opened the book. The first page was dated almost a year ago, and he saw Emily's graceful handwriting slanted across the page. If this were her diary, he needed to see if there was anything that might hint of her location. Any clue what cave she was lying in.

He thumbed through until he came to a more recent date. It was dated the same day as the first letter he'd read.

Chapter 19

*D*ear Diary,

My heart is overflowing with so many thoughts and feelings. The first of which is my love for my dear husband. He kissed me tonight, and when he touched me, I thought surely I'd burn up from the inside out. Somehow, when little Adam came around, Cade and I ended up in a tickle chase that reminded me of childhood so long ago. But I have gotten ahead of myself.

Even as these wondrous feelings of love consume me, I am torn apart with guilt and shame. Today I received a letter from Uncle Stewart. He has put Nana in the asylum and threatened to keep her there unless I find the gold. So you see, dear Diary, I am in the most precarious of positions.

While Cade has not professed his love for me, I have sensed it in his touch, in his glorious eyes. I can't for the life of me work up the courage to risk losing his trust. So I must continue that dreadful search tomorrow.

My heart fights the thought. I want so much to go forward with our wonderful life here. Cade and Adam have become my precious family, yet Nana needs my help. My heart cries out for the injustice done against her.

It is only because of Mara that I can continue the search without going against Cade's order that Adam stay out of the caves. She has agreed to help me, though she says I should tell Cade the truth.

Oh, Diary, my heart longs to do exactly that, but I just can't risk losing his love when I have longed for it for so long. So tomorrow I will search again, and may God help me find it quickly for all our sakes.

Cade let the diary fall to his lap, his eyes stinging with tears. His heart pummeled his ribs as relief washed over him.

Thank You, God.

Even though there was no clue about her whereabouts, at least her feelings for him, for Adam, were there in black ink for him to see. He suddenly felt like a doubting Thomas, needing to see proof in order to believe.

He reread the words of love, feeling warmth flow through him. She had deceived him, she had made wrong choices, but she loved him. His wife loved him, and he wanted to jump onto the rooftop and shout it to the world. She hadn't wanted to lie and keep secrets from him. She'd felt she had to for her grandmother's sake. It was just as Mara had said.

He heard a rooster crow and looked toward the window. The sun would be rising soon, and he would be able to search for Emily. He thumbed through the pages of the diary, reading excerpts, hoping for some clue as to where she was. Her words were balm for his soul, a glimpse of the woman he'd known all along. A woman who had become mother to his son, keeper of his heart.

Even though her words brought him comfort, they provided no information as to her whereabouts. It was all up to Adam. But would his son remember the way they'd gone?

He stopped right there on the foot of the bed and whispered a prayer for Emily's safety. His gut twisted at the thought of her lying on the cold cave floor in pain. Was she even conscious now? What if it were already too late?

He wouldn't allow himself to think like that. Dropping the diary on the bed, he went to gather the supplies he and Clay would need. By the time he saddled up, the first light should be chasing away the darkness.

When he arrived at the Stedmans', Clay and Adam were ready to go. His son gave him a hug and turned wet eyes toward him. "We have to find her, Pa."

Cade patted him on the back. "We will, son."

Mara waved them off then Cade spoke to Adam, who was snuggled against his belly. "Can you remember anything? You left here yesterday and went in this direction right?"

"I think so."

Cade sighed and exchanged a glance with Clay. "Do you remember anything at all about the cave?" Cade asked. "Think hard, it's important."

"I wasn't supposed to go inside it. Ma said so. She said to play near the doorway where she could keep her eye on me."

She'd tried to keep her word to him. The thought tightened his gut.

It was then he noticed Adam sniffling. "It'll be all right. We'll find her." He wrapped his arm tightly around his son.

"If I'd a listened, maybe Ma wouldn't be dying."

The word struck something deep within him. He stopped Sutter and turned Adam in his arms, shaking his shoulders. "Now you listen here. Your ma's not dying. She's not." The ache in his throat cut off his words.

Everything went still around them as Cade watched his son blink back tears, his little chin quivering.

Cade gentled his voice. "We'll find her. Everything's going to be fine, you understand?"

Adam's head bobbed against Cade's chest. He met Clay's gaze and saw his friend blinking hard, his jaw clenched tightly.

They headed in the general direction Mara had told them about, bringing their horses to a gallop. It seemed Adam wouldn't be able to help them find the cave, and he really shouldn't have expected it of a young boy anyway. When they neared the first cave they'd searched the previous night, the mammoth one, Adam perked up.

"I've been here!"

Cade's heart did a heavy flop. "Is this the cave, Adam? Is this where you and Emily came yesterday?"

Adam shook his head. "Not yesterday. We got lost in there."

His hopes shriveled up like a decaying leaf. What if they never found her? What if it were already too late? No, he wouldn't think it.

He looked at Adam who'd perked up, sitting straight up on the horse, looking around with a frown puckered between his brows. Maybe he could jog his son's memory.

"Tell me what the area looked like, where you were yesterday. Outside the cave, where you were playing?"

He shrugged. "It was a big grassy field, and there was a cliff. That's where the cave was."

It was nothing more than he'd said the night before. "What were you playing with?"

"My soldiers. The bad guys were behind the tree, and the good guys came and got 'em. Pow, pow, pow!"

Beside him, Clay ran a hand through his hair. "Why don't we split up? I can go a ways south—"

"Wait a minute," Cade said. Hadn't Adam said twice now he'd been in a grassy meadow? And then he said there was a tree. It was probably nothing, but. . . "Adam, were there lots of trees? You said it was a field before."

"No, there was just one. It was shaped funny too."

"Shaped funny, how?"

He scrunched up his eyes. "Ma said it was a . . .school tree. . .or some such."

"A school tree?" Clay asked.

Adam shrugged. "Somethin' like that. It was like this." He put his forearms together, letting his hands branch out.

"A schoolmarm tree," Cade said. A schoolmarm tree. In a meadow, by a cliff. His heart pounded like a fist inside his chest. "I know where she is."

They rode hard all the way there. Cade's heart felt as if it were thumping as fast and hard as the horses' hooves. It had to be the right place. He'd noticed the tree several times before because it didn't split into two trunks until a good ways up, and he'd always thought it looked like a giant slingshot.

He'd never noticed a cave there in the cliff, but if the entrance was as small as Adam was saying, it was no wonder.

He whispered a prayer, his heart in his throat.

"That's it!" Adam called. "There's the tree!" His voice carried away on the wind.

They pulled up to the tree, and Cade dismounted before Sutter reached a full stop, steadying Adam as he did.

"It's over there." Adam pointed.

Cade ran for the child-sized hole, and Clay was close behind. It was a squeeze getting through and once he did, the dimness of the cave prevented him from seeing much but the rubble at his feet.

"Get a lantern," he said to Clay. His eyes adjusted to the darkness, and he carefully made his way through the rubble. "Emily?"

Then he saw her—lying facedown several feet away. Her hair was gray with dirt and gravel, and she lay as still as a corpse.

"Emily!" He rushed to her side, a knot the size of cannonball forming in his throat. Why wasn't she moving? Why wasn't she answering? Dread welled up quick and heavy, and his heart sank like a stone.

Chapter 20

a sudden light burst in front of Emily, and she wondered if she were in heaven. A sharp stab of pain relieved her of that notion. She moaned.

"Emily."

She felt someone's hands caressing her face, and she opened her eyes. Blinking against the bright light, she saw a person kneeling beside her. Then she recognized him. "Cade," she whispered. Her parched throat protested.

"It's going to be all right." He asked Clay to go after the doc. "Take Adam with you, will you?"

At his words, she felt relief that Adam had found his pa. She shivered, her body starting odd little tremors that made her leg move and pained her something awful.

"Adam," she whispered.

"He's fine." His voice sounded odd. "I'm going to try to move the rock."

She nodded her head, and the bits of gravel dug into her face with the movement. She sensed him moving toward her feet and braced herself.

"This is going to hurt."

Already the pain had taken her under at least twice. She wondered how much time had passed since—

The weight came off her leg, and searing pain ripped through her. She choked back the scream that came up in her throat.

Please, God, please help me!

A wave of blackness flooded through her, and she fought it with all her will. Her other leg moved restlessly as if it could carry her away from the throbbing limb.

She heard Cade saying something through the fog of pain, and she struggled to focus.

"Doc'll be here soon," he was saying.

Suddenly she wanted to release the tears she'd held for however long she'd lain in this dark chamber. She wanted Cade to take her in his arms

253

and tell her everything was all right.

"It's broken, for sure," he said. "Try to lie still."

As if she could do anything else. She tried to say it, but her tongue felt like it was pasted to the roof of her mouth. "Thirsty."

Cade got up and left, and she felt a sea of hysteria closing over her at the thought of being alone again. Her breath came in shallow puffs. The pain actually seemed worse now that the weight was off.

Moments later, he returned and held a canteen to her lips. She drank eagerly of the cool water, though half of it dribbled down her chin and cheek and dripped onto the dirt.

"Be right back." He left her again, and she felt stung once again at his detached tone. Of course he was upset. Worse than upset, and he had a right to be. Hadn't she taken his son where he'd told her not to? Risked his very life?

He must be furious with her. She deserved a broken leg. Why if the boulder had fallen on Adam—she didn't want to think about it. But Cade must have. He blamed her for this, and well he should. How would he ever trust her with Adam again?

It seemed like an eternity before he returned with a blanket and spread it over her wordlessly. She wished he would say something. Hot tears leaked from her eyes and seeped into the soil under her cheek. She'd been so foolish to bring Adam here. Why hadn't she seen it then?

"I'm sorry," she whispered. "I'm so sorry."

"Hush, now."

A clatter outside drew Cade's attention, and she felt alone and cold when he left her again, despite the heavy blanket.

The tremors started again, shooting pain up her leg in fiery darts. She blinked against the pain and tried to call out to Cade, but her lips moved vainly.

The last thing she heard was Doc Hathaway's voice.

Someone was crying and moaning quietly. A low, rumbly voice talked in soothing tones.

A stab of pain brought her fully alert, and she smothered the scream in her throat. Bright lantern light flickered on the armoire at her feet. She was at home in her room.

Doc Hathaway. Cade.

"That oughta do it," the doctor said to Cade.

She looked down at her leg and saw it was splinted. Then she noticed her skirt was pulled clear up to her knee exposing her healthy leg which had ugly blue bruises and several scrapes. Her face grew warm, and she wished she could reach down and cover herself.

"Ah, Mrs. Manning, you're back with us," Doc Hathaway said. An opening in his gray beard exposed his tight smile. To her relief, he pulled the bed's cover up over her legs. "You're going to be just fine. Lucky your husband found you. I've got you all set here and have given you something for the pain."

"Thank you," she whispered.

He smiled and began putting his things in his black bag.

Cade came close, and it was then that she became aware that her face was wet. Tears. She remembered the moaning and crying she'd heard upon awakening and realized it had been her. What had she said in her delirium? Judging from the expression on Cade's face, she'd said something she shouldn't have. No doubt he was still angry.

"I'm so sorry, Cade." Whatever she'd revealed, she owed him an apology. A million apologies. "I know I shouldn't have taken Adam to the cave." How could she even explain why she'd done it without exposing everything about the gold and her uncle?

He nodded. "I already know. About everything—"

"Well," Doc Hathaway said, "I'll be going now. Cade, if I can speak with you a moment."

With one glance back toward her, Cade followed the doctor from the room even as Emily's entire being froze with fear. He knew about the loot. About everything, he'd said. No wonder he was so distant when he found her. He must've gotten the truth from Mara.

Fresh tears welled up in her eyes and clogged her throat. He knew she'd married him only for the gold. He knew she'd used him. She'd found the treasure she'd searched for, but in doing so she had lost what she valued most of all. Her husband's love. He would never have her now. How could he?

And Adam. She would lose the boy she'd come to love as her own son. She put her hands over her face at the realization. An ache, thick and heavy started in her belly at the thought of losing the two people she'd come to love so dearly. Would he turn her away from his home? It was what she deserved.

Others knew where the gold was now, and it would likely be returned to the bank it had been stolen from. How would she save Nana now?

God, I've made such a mess of things. Why didn't I ask You for guidance?

I took it all in my own hands and didn't give You a chance to direct me. And now look what I've done.

Downstairs, Cade listened to nary a word Doc said about medical instructions. But it hardly mattered since he was scrawling it all on a tablet of paper for Cade.

All he could think about was his wife, lying upstairs in her bed. The most pitiful look had come over her face when he'd told her he knew about everything. He felt awful that he hadn't had time to set her mind at ease before the doctor had called him from the room.

Fact was, he hadn't wanted to talk of the loot at all until she was in a better frame of mind. But her mindless ramblings and tears had gotten to him. He could see she was tormented with the secrets she'd held from him. He'd only wanted to set her mind at ease.

When he'd seen her leg in the cave, all purple and blue and bent in a place that had no business bending, he'd wanted to cry himself. But he'd had to be strong for her. He'd seen she was suffering something awful. And as much as he'd wanted to take her in his arms and smother her with kisses, he couldn't deny the guilt he'd felt at having read her diary, at having been privy to her innermost thoughts.

Besides, he'd been afraid to touch her, afraid the slightest movement would pain her even more. He'd been mighty grateful when Doc had given her the morphine.

He looked up the stairs, eager to go check on her, to put her mind at ease about everything. Maybe she was even sleeping soundly now, what with the medicine she had in her.

"Should be about it," Doc was saying as he picked up his bag.

Cade ushered him to the door, thanking the man for his care before heading up the stairs to his wife.

Emily smothered a yawn and forced her eyes to stay open. Despite all the turmoil going on within her, she felt like she could sleep twelve hours. *Must be the medicine.*

Then she heard sounds outside her door and realized someone was coming up the stairs. Cade, she knew, from the heavy, confident thuds. She wiped her face dry, her heart in her throat. Was he coming to tell her it was over? Would he ask her to leave and never come back?

The door opened, and her husband entered. She absorbed him with her gaze, trying desperately to read him.

He approached the bed. "Doc's gone."

She nodded, her heart pummeling her ribs. The edge of the bed sank as he sat carefully, slowly. A strand of his dark hair hung alongside his stubbled cheek. How could she lose this man, her beloved Cade? Her eyes stung with tears.

"How's your leg feel?"

She was taken back that he still cared enough to ask. "It's not paining much really."

"Good. Doc left more medicine for you when you need it."

The room grew so quiet she could almost hear her fearful heart beating.

"I have some things I need to tell you," he said.

She nodded, unable to speak past the knot that clogged her throat. She must be strong. She mustn't make him feel guilty for his decision. It would only make things harder on him, and she deserved everything she got. She sat as straight as she could against the pillows and steeled herself.

"Last night," he said, "we searched for you for a long time. Adam couldn't find the cave in the dark, and Clay and I . . . well, we did the best we could." He clenched his jaw.

Emily wondered where he was going with this. Her gaze took in his precious face, and she wanted so badly to touch his cheek one last time.

"When we quit for the night, I went back to the Stedmans' and asked Mara some questions. As I said before, I know everything about the loot and your grandmother. About your uncle's plan to get the loot back through you."

He met her gaze just then, and she was shamed by his knowledge. She tucked her chin, and her gaze found the worn quilt. "I'm so sorry," she whispered.

He was quiet so long she wondered if he were going to speak again. Finally, he did. "After that, I came back home. I was angry and I couldn't sleep. I got to thinking maybe the map was in your room someplace, and maybe I could figure out where you were."

She shook her head. "I took it with me."

"I know. I didn't find the map, but I found some other things."

She met his gaze, and his blue-green eyes flickered with something she couldn't identify.

"Your uncle's letters and . . . and your diary."

Her heart did an awkward flop. If he read the letters, he really did know everything. But her diary had private thoughts. Thoughts about him. Her face flooded with heat as she recalled specific things she'd written about her husband.

"I read all the letters—enough to know the sort of man your uncle is." His jaw clenched again, and she wondered if the anger she saw was directed at only her uncle or at her, too.

Then he took her hand, and she thought her heart might up and quit right then. What was that shining in his eyes? Dare she hope that—

"I did read a few pages of your diary, and I'm real sorry for poking around in your private things, but. . ." His eyes narrowed with fervency. "You have to understand how confused I was. I was so angry. I felt used. I thought you'd been pretending with me—"

"Pretending?" Her heart caught.

He looked at their joined hands. "I thought you were just using me to get at the loot. That everything was a lie. That your feelings for me were false."

"No. No, that's not true."

He looked at her then. "I know that now. And I can't say that I'm really sorry about reading your diary, either. Because if I hadn't, I wouldn't have believed the truth."

Her blood fairly burned with the velvety heat that flowed through her. "I'm not, either." And she realized she meant the words. Who cared if he'd read her innermost thoughts if they'd proven her feelings true?

"I was going to tell you something last night, if you recall."

She remembered the embrace they'd shared before she went off to the cave. It seemed so long ago, like so many things had gone wrong between then and now. Yet, here her husband was, sitting inches away from her with the same gleam of love in his eyes.

He wet his lips, and she noted how dry her own throat was. "When I married you, as you know, it was to be a marriage of convenience," he said.

His gaze sought confirmation, and she nodded.

"At the beginning, I fought any sort of relationship between us. I guess I was afraid after losing Ingrid and all."

"That's understandable."

His gaze locked on hers, a promise shining in their depths. "Somewhere along the way, I told God I'd put my fear aside. And after that, my heart didn't stand a chance." A smile tilted his lips, and she felt it all the way to her heart.

"I love you, Emmie."

She felt her own lips stretch in a smile as joy filled her heart. How could it be, with all the mistakes she'd made, that this man loved her anyhow? She'd lied, used him, risked his son's safety, and still he loved her and wanted her.

Her heart full to overflowing, she blinked back tears. "I love you, Cade. So very, very much."

He leaned toward her then, his lips grazing tenderly over hers, and heat swept through her. Would her pounding heart ever grow accustomed to her husband's touch? She couldn't imagine such a thing. Especially when he touched her cheek so gently.

He broke the kiss, and she almost pulled him back in her arms.

"I want us to be a real husband and wife," he said.

Warmth bathed her face at his meaning.

"I want us to be a real family. The three of us. . .and your grandmother, Lord willing."

Her heart clenched at the thought of Nana. It seemed so hopeless. How could she get Nana back now? The gold would have to be returned to the rightful owners, and rightly so. Her uncle would remain Nana's legal guardian, and after she'd failed to deliver the gold, he would leave Nana in the asylum to spite her.

"Wipe that frown off your face," he said. "I have an idea."

Hope stirred inside her and she searched his eyes. "What is it?"

He shook his head and gave her a tender smile. "Not now, Sleepyhead. There'll be time for that later. You need to get some rest—doctor's orders."

"But I want—"

He held a finger over her lips, and she couldn't resist kissing it. His eyes took on a new look she hadn't seen before. She decided she rather liked it.

"Don't you go doing that, woman."

"Whyever not?" she teased, fighting another yawn.

"Save it for about. . ." He looked pointedly at her splinted leg. "Oh, about six weeks."

She groaned, but he broke it off with a quick kiss. "Doctor's orders."

Epilogue

*E*mily struggled to remove the wedding veil from her elegantly styled up-do. It had been a long, wonderful day. And it wasn't over yet.

"Here, my darling," Cade said from behind her. "Allow me."

She smiled at her husband's reflection in the mirror, taking in the breadth of his shoulders under the crisp, white shirt. His suspenders already dangled from his waistband as if he couldn't wait to shuck the fancy clothes.

"Did I tell you what a beautiful bride you are?"

"Only a dozen times or so." She smiled, content to let him remove her veil. It had been thoughtful of Mara to plan a real wedding for them. Especially for Nana's sake.

As Cade worked the pins out, he bit his lip in concentration. As if reading her thoughts, he asked, "Is Nana settled for the night?"

"Mmhmm. She's looking better, don't you think?"

He handed her another pin. "She's filling out, that's for sure."

"She needed to." Just thinking about how Nana had looked when she'd stepped off the stage with Cade was enough to bring tears to her eyes. It had taken months, even with the attorney Cade had hired in Denver, but Nana was home at last.

"It must've been pretty bad at the asylum," he said.

With the veil finally removed, she placed it on the bureau and turned to face him. "Have I told you how thankful I am for what you did?"

"At least a dozen times," he said with a humble smile. "Thanks be to God that the judge saw reason and gave us guardianship of her."

She wrapped her arms around his waist and laid her head on his chest. "Using Uncle Stewart's letters was a brilliant idea."

"I don't know about brilliant, but it worked. His own words were the best proof of his disregard for her."

He tipped her chin up for a peck that lengthened into a satisfying kiss. So much so, that it almost distracted her from the news she'd been waiting to share.

When she pulled away, he caressed her with his gaze. "Something wrong?"

"Not wrong, no."

He tilted his head. "What is it then?"

She soaked in his gaze, eager to see the change that would come over him when he heard the news. "I do have something I need to tell you."

He waited, albeit impatiently if his antsy fingers were anything to go by.

She'd only known for sure for a couple weeks, but somehow, waiting for today seemed right. Suddenly, she giggled.

"What? What is it?"

She put her fingers over her lips. "I never thought I'd say this on my wedding day, much less be thrilled to do so."

"What?" His brows drew low.

"I–I'm in the family way, Cade."

She wished she could forever preserve the expressions that danced across her husband's face. She reveled in each emotion with him.

Finally, he lifted her up off her feet in an airborne embrace and whooped so loudly she feared he'd awaken Adam and Nana.

"Shh!" She swatted him on the shoulder but couldn't hold back the bubble of laughter that welled up in her.

When he was finished whirling around, he let her slide down him until her stockinged feet reached the planked floor. Then his gaze swept over her face in a reflective, serious way.

"I wonder sometimes," he said, "what Thomas would think about all this. You were to be his bride, after all."

She gazed at her husband's precious face, from his clean-shaved jaw to his sea-green eyes, and had trouble imagining herself married to anyone but him. Even her dear friend, Thomas.

"I'm your bride now," she whispered. "and I couldn't love you more." She let the desire she felt for him blaze from her eyes and was quickly rewarded with that expression she was becoming so wonderfully familiar with.

"Thank you, ma'am, for that timely reminder," he said. And then he took her into his arms once more.

Denise Hunter is the award-winning author of six novels and three no-vellas. A voracious reader, she began writing *Stranger's Bride* in 1996, and it was published two years later. Her husband Kevin claims he provides all her romantic material, but Denise insists a good imagination helps, too. She and Kevin live in Indiana with their three sons, where they are very active in a new church start-up.

You can learn more about Denise and her books by visiting her web-site at www.denisehunterbooks.com.

Changes of the Heart

by Judith McCoy Miller

Prologue

June 1847

*L*uther Buchanan sucked in a breath and squared his shoulders. His father's angry eyes and curled lip were proof Josiah Buchanan considered his son the town's laughingstock. "I suppose I'd be packing my bag and heading out of town, too, if I'd been left standing at the church. Folks hear tell of a bride that's left standing at the altar, but I don't believe I've ever heard of a groom being made the fool,"

"I don't particularly think of myself as a fool, Father, but I realize that if I'm going to make anything of my life, I must leave you and this town." Josiah swallowed hard to force the pain from his voice.

"As usual, you're going to be late." His lips drooped as he pulled a gold timepiece from his vest pocket and shook his head. "After twenty-five years, I might as well just give up. Day after day I've told you that if you're ever going to amount to anything, you've got to be punctual. Why do you think I bought you that expensive pocket watch?"

"The stage doesn't arrive for another hour, and although you refrain from believing facts, I am seldom late for anything." Luther longed for his father to leave the room and give him time to complete packing his valise in solitude. But he knew that wouldn't happen. Until the stage door was closed and the horses were urged into motion, his father would be at his side, reminding him of his failures and berating him as a son.

His father leaned his shoulder against the doorframe. "I just can't imagine what got into that girl. I went and talked to her parents, did I tell you that?"

Luther sighed. "No, you didn't tell me, but I wish you hadn't done that. I'm sure it only served to make them uncomfortable. It's not their fault that Elizabeth ran off with someone else."

"Well, she's their daughter. Her behavior decries their ability to rear a child. I told them that, too." His father's straightened, and his large belly puffed out even farther than usual. "Besides, I wasn't overly concerned about their discomfort. Look what I had to endure last Saturday when that little snippet didn't appear for the ceremony. Everyone express-ing their sympathy and then laughing behind my back," the older man recounted as his thick neck reddened above his stiff white collar.

"This isn't about you, Father. If people are laughing, they're laughing at me. You can rest easy now. My departure should assure you that you've suf-fered your last embarrassment at my expense." Since last Saturday, Luther had been forced to endure his father's harsh remarks, and he'd grown weary of his father's self-centered viewpoint.

"I still think you're making a mistake. Not about leaving Virginia, but going out west to California. Everyone's rushing out there thinking they're going to get rich overnight. It doesn't happen that way. People get ahead by hard work, making sound decisions, and being punctual." His father tapped his vest pocket.

"I've already explained that I'm not going off in search of gold. I plan to open a mercantile and perform the same work I've done in your store for all these years." Luther turned away from the older man and placed several folded shirts in his valise.

"Yes, so you've told me. Once you've set up your own store, you'll soon find that there is much you don't know about operating a business. You'll be racing home with your tail between your legs before two years have passed; that is my estimate. I'll hold your job for you."

It would serve no purpose to respond, but Luther silently vowed he would never return to his father's house. Since his mother's death fifteen years earlier, he had silently endured his father's sarcasm and tongue-lashings. Endured a childhood that had molded him into an angry man who already believed that he was destined to become a failure. Endured Elizabeth's recent rejection, which now served to reinforce what his father's behavior had taught him as a child—he was unlovable.

Chapter 1

May 1852

Maura Rebecca Thorenson slipped her fingers into the service-able brown leather bag she was carrying and touched the packet of letters nestled in its depths. They were carefully bound with a blue grosgrain ribbon, along with a new journal and the small Bible that had belonged to her grandmother. A shiver ran down her spine as she and her parents, Walt and Bessie Thorenson, stood on one of the docks scattered along Boston's harbor.

"You sure you're ready for this, Maura?" Her father's voice was laced with concern. His eyes remained fixed on the ship that she would board in a few short minutes.

"I'm not as sure as I was last week." Maura wished she could snatch back the comment, for her mother's tears immediately increased ten-fold. "Mama, I was only joking. Please don't cry anymore. This is my chance for a new life. We've been over this so many times that I thought you were finally in agreement," she said, leaning down to embrace her mother. Bessie was six inches shorter than her twenty-eight-year-old daughter, and it never seemed more evident then when the two women hugged each other. Maura had been blessed with the thick auburn hair of her father and the creamy complexion and blue eyes of her mother. Classic beauty, that's what her mother used to say—you have classic beauty, Maura. As a child she delighted in that particular compliment; but, as she'd neared adolescence, she decided classic beauty was not what inter-ested boys.

"I've accepted the fact that you're leaving, Maura. Please don't ask me to remain dry eyed when my only daughter is leaving home. I'll proba-bly never see you again." Her mother's sobs soon resulted in hiccoughs, which caused both women to giggle.

Her parents had been dismayed when Maura first informed them she had answered an ad for a mail-order bride. They had given her all the arguments against doing such a thing. Initially, she had conceded to their request that she not make a hasty decision, and when she wrote her letter of introduction to Luther Buchanan, she inquired if he would correspond with her for a year. Maura had carefully penned the letter, telling him of her life in Boston. She'd enclosed her photograph, as requested in his advertisement. The likeness had been taken when she turned twenty-one years old, and although she didn't think she'd aged much since then, she was careful to advise Mr. Buchanan the picture was seven years old.

Maura's parents had reasoned that a year would at least give their daughter an opportunity to become acquainted with this stranger's views and expectations for a wife. After receiving the letter and photograph of Maura, Luther had reluctantly agreed to wait for six months. Although more mail had been sent from Boston to Placerville, California, than the reverse, Luther Buchanan had kept his promise and answered all of the questions Maura listed in each of her letters to him. After several months of corresponding had elapsed, and without solicitation from Maura, Luther sent her a photograph of himself standing outside the Buchanan General Mercantile.

The picture had been taken at a distance and Luther's features were blurred, but Maura didn't care. She had never put much stock in physical attributes, which was the reason she hadn't requested a picture of her husband-to-be. It did appear that he was tall enough to overshadow Maura's height, but pictures could be as deceiving as actual appearances. Early in life, Maura had learned that some of the most attractive people could be the most disagreeable and thoughtless.

Having lived all her life in the same place, Maura found the prospect of moving to California as exciting as it was frightening. Maura had worked with her parents in their bookstore and bindery business since she was a young girl. During her school years, she and her brother, Dan, had been expected to spend at least two hours after school and all day Saturday helping in the family business. Daniel, three years her senior, had left home years ago. After attending Harvard, he'd read law under the tutelage of a highly respected Boston attorney and was eventually asked to become a partner in the practice. Married and the father of four small children, Dan and his family were frequent visitors at the Thorenson household. It was Amanda, Dan's wife, in whom Maura had first confided her plan to answer the ad. And it was Amanda who had become her strongest advocate in persuading the senior Thorensons to agree.

After several hours of listening to the two women, her father had voiced his reservations about the arrangement but added that he realized Maura was certainly old enough to make her own decision to leave home and marry.

Later, after Luther had agreed to the six-month waiting period, Walt hadn't told his daughter that he felt compelled to make inquiries regarding the voyage she would be taking. After extensive investigation, her father had personally written to Luther Buchanan, setting forth what he considered mandatory arrangements before he would allow Maura to make the journey. Walt had failed to advise his daughter of that information also.

Nor had he divulged all of his findings to his wife, Bessie, knowing she would become even more distraught about the situation. He was, however, inordinately forthright in describing the facts to Maura.

Several days after returning from a trip to the docks, her father had taken Maura aside. "You realize the journey could take up to eight months?"

"Yes, but Luther wrote that some of the ships make the voyage in as few as four months. It just depends upon the weather, Father."

"Did he also tell you about the bad food, seasickness, and boredom?"

"No, but I'm not a picky eater, and I'm sure I can pass the time reading and writing in my journal. As to seasickness, I suppose we'll be at the mercy of the weather, and there's not much I can do about that."

Her father's brow had creased with concern. "I realize you're not finicky about your meals, Maura. But I'm talking about concoctions of a stringy paste made from salted meat, potatoes, and hard bread, or something the sailors call hushamagrundy—made of turnips and parsnips with a bid of codfish thrown in. That's the good meals—before the supplies run low. When that occurs, they resort to three bean soup, which is mostly water, three beans, and a tiny piece of rusty pork. I was also told the water becomes foul after being stored in vats for several months. It attracts bugs and insects, and folks sometimes resort to adding vinegar and molasses just to kill the horrid taste. I'm not trying to discourage you, but I think you need to know what lies ahead."

"It sounds worse than I had imagined, but Luther said it was the best of the three options available. He said the trip overland was much more difficult, and he hadn't talked to anyone who recommended the sea-land-sea route across the Isthmus of Panama. I trust his judgment on sailing around the Cape."

"I trust his judgment on that also. I'm not suggesting that you change your route. But I talked at length to a sea captain who told me that if his daughter were making the trip, he'd not let her travel on any ship but the Edward Everett. It's a luxury ship that serves decent food and has excellent accommodations for its passengers. It is more expensive but more suited to genteel travelers." he'd explained.

"It does sound much more inviting, but Luther is planning on the voyage costing only five hundred dollars."

"If he wants you as a wife, I feel certain he will be more than willing to pay for you to travel in the most comfortable and respectable manner." His words had been gentle, yet firm.

"I suppose I could write to him, but I doubt the letter would reach him and give him enough time to send the additional funds before my departure date," she had thoughtfully explained to her father.

"No need to write. I did that some time ago."

"You wrote to Luther without telling me? What did you say?"

"I merely explained to him what I've just told you—along with the fact that he'd have to send the price of a ticket on the Edward Everett, or I'd not allow you to make the journey."

"Papa, how could you do that?" Her voice had been strained with anger.

He'd been unapologetic. "How could I not? You are my child, and no matter what your age, I have an obligation to seek what is best for your welfare. I couldn't live with myself if I did less than that."

It was impossible for her to argue with such a reply. He had opened his arms, and she had willingly gone to him, returning his hug. It was during that moment she had realized more than ever before how much he loved her.

Luther had written to Walt, agreeing to pay for Maura's passage on the Edward Everett. Although he had made sure Walt knew the cost was more than double what he had planned, his willingness gave Walt a sense of confidence that Luther was a good man and one who would treat his daughter well.

Her mother had dried her tears as they continued along the dock. "Now I know why the name of the ship sounds so familiar." Bessie rested her hand on her husband's arm. "Walter, isn't the president of Harvard named Edward Everett?"

"Indeed he is. I'm told the ship was named after him, although I'm not sure why. Perhaps the owner is a Harvard graduate. I feel certain, however, that Edward Everett wouldn't permit it to carry his name unless it was a fine vessel." Walter patted her hand and smiled down at his wife.

There was little doubt her father was doing his best to reassure her mother, a fact that pleased Maura. If her mother succumbed to another bout of tears, Maura would likely join her.

The crowds along the dock were beginning to swell. Some of the passengers had already boarded the ship, but Daniel and Amanda had not yet arrived with the children and Maura had no intention of leaving without bidding them good-bye. The gathering multitude of travelers and well-wishers were, for the most part, in jovial spirits. Mixed among them were a few teary-eyed women bidding their male companions farewell, as boisterous children raced between clustered groups of friends and family.

"There they are." Walter waved his arms to signal his son and family. It took several long minutes for the group to wend their way through the throngs of people, but soon the children were circling around Maura, caught up in the excitement of the voyage.

Daniel, Jr., the oldest of Dan's children, grasped Maura's hand. "Can we go on board and see the ship, Aunt Maura?"

"I'm not sure. Let's go and ask." She took the lead and when they neared the gangplank, she turned toward her brother. "Perhaps if you ask, they'll be more agreeable."

Daniel nodded and moved forward. "Excuse me, sir. We've come to bid my sister farewell, and the children would like to board the ship to examine her accommodations. Would that be possible?" Dan glanced toward his four chldren.

"I don't think I have the authority to give permission for that." The sailor touched his pocket and winked.

"Would this help you obtain enough authority?" Daniel slipped the man several coins.

The sailor glanced into his hand and smiled. "You folks enjoy yourselves. Just be sure and get off before we set sail. Otherwise, you'll all end up in California," He laughed, apparently amused by the possibility.

Dan, Jr., and his brother, Samuel, led the group on board while the two girls clung closely to their mother and Maura. "Are you sure you want to go, Aunt Maura? How can you leave everything you know and go live with a stranger?" Ruth's eyes shone with concern.

"Ruth! You have no business questioning your aunt's decision." Amanda's reprimand didn't appear to deter Ruth, for she continued to stare at her aunt.

"It's all right, Amanda. Why shouldn't she ask the very thing everyone else is wondering?" Maura turned toward her niece. "Ruth, it's difficult to explain. I'm not sure beyond all doubt that this is what I should do. On the other hand, I've prayed about it and feel that my life in Boston is leading me nowhere and that God has a plan in mind for me elsewhere. It's going to be very difficult not having all of you around, and I hope one day your parents will bring all of you for a visit. I want to believe I'll see all of you again, but I know there is a strong possibility that may not happen. I'm going to have to depend upon you, your mother, and grandmother to keep me aware on all the news. Do you think you could help with that?"

"Yes, I'll write to you, but what happens if you don't like this man you're supposed to marry?" Ruth remained unrelenting in her pursuit of answers.

"Well, his letters have revealed that he's a Christian man and that he's anxious for my arrival. If I don't like him, I'll have to depend on God to give me a change of heart."

"But what if He doesn't?" Ruth continued to question her while Jenny, the youngest of the four children, clung to Amanda's skirt.

"Then I suppose He'll do something else to change my circumstances. I'm not trying to escape answering your questions, dear. I just don't know the answers." Maura longed to give the girl an answer that was truthful and would satisfy the child's curiosity, but she simply didn't have one. In truth, the same questions had muddled her own thoughts over the past months.

"Thank you for trying, Aunt Maura. I want you to be happy, and I'm sure God will take care of everything. After all, He knows how special you are." Ruth smiled and wrapped her arms around Maura's waist.

Amanda smiled over her daughter's head into Maura's eyes. "Did you tell him?" Her sister-in-law's mouthed the question.

Maura shook her head and looked away.

Amanda touched her daughter's shoulder. "Ruth, why don't you take Jenny and the two of you go find the rest of the family and tell them we've located Aunt Maura's quarters? Ask them to come along and join us."

The two women watched as the girl departed the cabin and skipped down the passageway on her assigned mission.

"Maura, I can't believe you didn't tell him. Each time I asked, you told me you were going to in your next letter." Amanda tightened her lips into a thin line.

"I meant to, Amanda, truly I did. But the longer I put it off, the more difficult it became. I was afraid he'd ask why I hadn't told him when I originally answered his ad. Then, as time passed, I didn't want to tell him for fear he'd be angry and break the engagement." Maura swallowd hard in an attempt to hold back tears that threatened to spill at any minute.

"I'm sorry, Maura. I didn't mean to make you unhappy." Amanda leaned to the side and pulled her into a quick hug. "I'm sure it will be fine. How could he not love you? You're the finest person I've ever known—except perhaps for your brother," she quickly added.

Maura's forced a weak smile. "Please don't tell my parents. They think Luther knows and has accepted my 'affliction,' as they call it."

"I won't mention it. Just promise that when you write to me, you will tell me the truth about your new life." There was a pleading tone in her voice.

"I'm sure that everything will be wonderful and my letters will overflow with only good news to all of you. However, should something arise that I don't want the others to know, I'll send along a separate page addressed just to you. I trust you'll not reveal the information to anyone."

"You have my word." Amanda offered a mock salute.

"It makes me feel better just knowing I'll have a confidante should I need one." Maura smiled and attempted to ignore the twinge of doubt that lurked deep inside her heart.

Moments later, Daniel appeared at the cabin door. "You two certainly appear to be deep in conversation," He stepped into the cabin followed by the rest of the family. "I don't think we'll all fit in here at once, children. Why don't you wait until we've looked around and then you can come in?"

Her mother peered around the cabin, and clasped her arms around her waist. "It's awfully small, dear. Do you think you'll be able to live in this tiny space for eight months?" A tour of the vessel hadn't seemed to assuage her mother's concerns.

Maura chuckled. "Mother, I won't be confined to my cabin."

"Of course, she won't." Her father shook his head and frowned at his wife, "Bessie, you've talked to almost every member of the ship's crew. She'll have weekly papers to read, and there are concerts to attend as well as a variety of other activities. There's a board of health and a police department should she have medical problems or need protection of any sort. This room is elegant, and the bill of fare sounds better than what most of the Boston restaurants serve. You must quit your fretting."

Her mother's lips trembled. "I know, I know, but it doesn't make it any easier to see my daughter leave home."

Not wanting her mother to once again turn tearful, Maura stood and gestured toward the door. "Let's allow the children to see the cabin." As soon as her parents had stepped into the hallway, Maura waved the children forward. "You're next. Come in and see my living quarters."

"It's as beautiful as I told you, isn't it?" Ruth nudged her sister as they entered the room.

"Oh, yes." Emily's voice was filled with awe. "I wish I could come with you, Aunt Maura. I would be happy forever in this room."

"I seriously doubt that, Emily," her father said. "You grow tired of everything within a few hours. Just imagine if you had to stay on this ship for six months. I think you would probably change your mind."

Maura nodded her head. "Your father is right, Emily. Although the room and ship are lovely, I'm sure the trip will be long and sometimes very boring. I would love to have your company on the voyage, but I think you'll be much happier playing outdoors with your friends all summer rather than being a captive on this ship."

Maura's father poked his head just inside the door of the cabin. "We've got to leave the ship now. They're about ready to set sail."

All of them quickly gathered together and moved with the other visitors toward the gangplank. Maura followed along with them, a sense of fear beginning to creep into her consciousness. Now that the time of departure had finally arrived, she didn't want them to know she was filled with anxiety. Pasting a smile on her face, she hugged each of them and watched as they walked down the gangplank and back to the dock. As the ship slowly moved out of its berth, she stood transfixed on the deck while attempting to emblazon a picture of each of them in her mind. The minutes passed, and their figures became smaller and smaller until they were no longer in view. She could neither force herself to move from the railing nor take her eyes from the spot where she had last seen her family's waving arms. Nothing but water remained in sight, but she held her vigil until the sun began to set.

Chapter 2

*D*espite her fears and new surroundings, Maura slept soundly. She awoke the next morning just as the sun was rising and peeked out her cabin window. The scene was beyond expectation. The sun appeared as a blazing ball rising out of the water and the sky a mixture of soft aquamarine and burnished red dipping down to meet the bluish-black depths of the ocean. She continued to revel in the sight until her growling stomach served as a reminder she had not eaten since departing the previous day. Although a light evening meal had been offered, Maura had preferred to remain at the ship's railing staring toward the beauty of a distant horizon. Now, almost twenty-four hours since her last meal, she realized she was famished.

Deciding upon a white muslin dress with a pattern of roses scattered about the border, Maura prepared herself for her first full day at sea. Weeks earlier, her mother had hand stitched the three-tier skirt, each layer emphasizing the delicate rose-patterned border. The bodice was a fashionable V-neckline exhibiting a modest inset of white embroidered muslin. Gathering her auburn tresses in a pale green ribbon that complemented the green leaves in her dress, Maura decided upon carrying her green silk parasol. It would provide her creamy complexion ample protection from the sun, should she decide to linger on deck after breakfast.

"Are you going to the dining room?" Maura turned to see a small, white-haired woman walking toward her.

Maura glanced about and seeing no other passengers, assumed the woman was speaking to her. "Yes, I've not eaten since we set sail, and my stomach is beginning to protest."

"Would you mind very much if I joined you? I can't tolerate eating by myself, and it seems most of the passengers are men who prefer talking to each other rather than an old woman. I'm Mrs. Windsor." The woman extended her hand as she reached Maura's side.

"And I'm Maura Thorenson. I would be delighted to have your company at breakfast." Maura matched the older woman's gait as they continued toward the dining salon.

"I'll try not to bore you to tears or make a nuisance of myself, although I'm sure you'll be glad to see the last of me once we reach California." Mrs. Windsor chuckled as they entered the dining room. "Where are you going?" The older woman stayed Maura with a touch of her hand.

Maura arched her brows. "I thought we could be seated at one of those tables on the far side of the room."

Mrs. Windsor shook her head. "I forgot that you weren't at dinner last evening. We serve ourselves. The food is placed on that large table close to the kitchen." She pointed toward the far side of the room.

Maura hadn't noticed the line of people waiting at the other side of the room and was embarrassed when she noticed several passengers staring at the two of them. Hesitating for a moment, she placed her parasol on one of the benches and moved with Mrs. Windsor to the end of the line.

Mrs. Windsor glanced at Maura's arm. "Do you need assistance? I can fill my plate and come back for yours."

"No, I'm more than capable of taking care of myself." Her tone had been sharper than she'd intended. Noting the look of remorse on the older woman's face, Maura apologized. "I didn't mean to be so abrupt. I'm sorry if I hurt your feelings."

"No apology is necessary. Now, let's see what they're serving for breakfast." The older woman turned her attention to the menu.

After helping themselves to generous portions of ham, eggs, biscuits, fresh fruit, and steaming cups of coffee, the women seated themselves at the table where Maura had earlier placed her parasol.

Mrs. Windsor glanced at the other diners at their table. "As far as I'm concerned, these tables certainly make eating difficult. I understand the need for this edge around the table, but you'd think someone would invent one that could be removed when the seas are calm." She lifted her short arms over the wooden rim.

A gentleman seated across from them nodded. "Know what you mean. By the end of the meal, my arms feel as though they have permanent dents in them."

A woman seated to his left curled her lip. "Perhaps you should try lifting your arm to your mouth instead of leaning over your plate

He shot an angry look at the woman. "You're not my mother, and I don't need your advice on how to eat."

"I didn't mean to cause an argument." Mrs. Windsor touched her napkin to her lips, then gestured toward the windows along the east side of the dining salon. "If the sunrise is any indication, it looks as though there's a beautiful day awaiting us,"

"Think I'll see if I can find a game of cards," The man picked up his plate and pushed to his feet.

His companion frowned. "It's a little early in the day for you to begin your gambling, isn't it?"

"I'll be glad when we get to Rio de Janeiro." He shot the woman a look of disdain as he turned away from the table.

The woman carved a piece of ham from the slice on her plate. "Let's hope you haven't lost all of our money before we get there."

Obviously unflappable, the woman offered no apology or explanation to those remaining at the dining table. Instead, she popped the piece of ham into her mouth, and continued with her meal as though nothing out of the ordinary had occurred.

Although Maura tried to engage Mrs. Windsor in conversation several times, the older woman remained somewhat subdued for the remainder of the meal. Finally Maura gave up and ate in silence, relieved when the breakfast was finally completed.

When they neared her cabin, Maura glanced toward Mrs. Windsor. "I believe I'll gather my writing materials and return to the deck. It's such a beautiful morning, and I want to add a few paragraphs to the letter I'm writing my sister-in-law and make notations in my journal."

Mrs. Windsor grimaced. "I believe I'll read in my room for a while. I think I've stirred up enough trouble for one day."

"What occurred between those two wasn't your fault. They obviously fight all the time. It was apparent they had no respect for each other or the rest of us, for that matter." She hoped her words would provide a bit of comfort to her new acquaintance.

She gave a slight nod. "You're probably right, but I still feel uncomfortable for any part I played in that altercation." She hesitated a moment. "Perhaps I'll join you later this morning. If not, I'll see you at dinner."

Maura watched the older woman stride down the passageway, head held high, shoulders thrown back, a picture of determination and self-reliance. No one would guess she was retreating to her room for any reason other than a brief respite after her morning meal.

The days soon became a monotonous routine, and had it not been for Mrs. Windsor and Georgette Blackburn, Maura was doubtful she could bear another three months aboard ship. Mrs. Windsor's penchant to discuss literature, philosophy, and spiritual matters and Georgette's carefree disposition had proved advantageous to all three of them. Georgette, with her oval face, full cheeks, pouty lips, and lush blond curls, never failed to coax them into laughter. Her flair for making a humorous story out of everything offset Mrs. Windsor's sober, reflective manner.

But even the intermittent concerts and literary discussion groups became tiresome after a while, with most of the passengers preferring gambling to a scholarly conversation about the literary genius of Shakespeare or Chaucer.

Maura stepped from her cabin, planning to join Georgette for a few hours of visiting, but she quickly returned for her woolen cape and bonnet.

She nodded to one of the crew who was a short distance from her door. "It has certainly turned cold, hasn't it?" She gathered the warm cape tightly around her.

The fellow nodded. "It will only get worse."

Surprised by his remark, she stopped to quiz him. "What do you mean?"

"It may be summer in New England, but it's winter where we're headed. The closer we get to the Cape, the colder and rougher the weather becomes. Didn't anyone tell you that before you left home?" He appeared surprised at her lack of knowledge.

She shook her head. "Nobody I know has made this voyage."

He arched his bushy brows. "Then why is it you're going to California?"

"I'm getting married. My husband-to-be is already there."

"Seems he would have told you what to expect." He gave a slight shake of his head and continued on his way.

"What do you mean—what to expect?" She quickened her step, and hurried after him.

"Like I said, it's winter down here. The winds get bad; the temperature gets frigid; and stormy seas are the general fare. Sorry, but I don't have time to talk. The first mate's waiting on me." He scurried off leaving her with a multitude of unanswered questions.

Casting her head downward against the harsh wind, she finally arrived at Georgette's cabin and pounded on the thick wooden door. "Georgette," she called out, "hurry, it's cold out here!"

When Georgette finally opened the door, Maura rushed inside, the cold biting at her hands and feet. "I can't believe how quickly the weather has turned on us." When she finally looked up, she saw why Georgette had been so slow to answer.

"Georgette, what's wrong? You look positively dreadful." The young woman's complexion was sallow and her hands trembled as though she was the one who'd been out in the cold.

"I think I'd better lie down for a while. Suddenly, I'm feeling. . ." Georgette winced as though she were in pain and fell upon the bed.

"Feeling what?" Maura coaxed.

Georgette didn't immediately answer and Maura's concern heightened when she noted the girl's swollen belly.

"Georgette! Are you going to have a baby?" Stunned that she hadn't previously realized the girl was pregnant, Maura drew close to the bedside.

"Yes." She offered a feeble smile. "I've kept it well hidden, haven't I? I bet you and Mrs. Windsor wondered why I was always wearing a long cape around me, even on those horribly warm days, didn't you?"

Maura shook her head. "I assumed you were cold-natured, Georgette. You told me you weren't married, and quite honestly, I never gave a thought to the idea that you might be expecting a child. As for Mrs. Windsor, she has never mentioned your attire and speaks only good of you."

Perspiration dotted the young woman's forehead. "It doesn't matter. I don't know how I thought I could keep this a secret until we arrived in California anyway." Georgette's voice had grown weaker.

"When is your baby due?" Maura took hold of Georgette's hand.

"Not for another ten weeks. I'm so afraid, Maura. Please don't leave me." She clung to Maura's hand like a child who feared the dark.

"I won't leave, but I think we should try and get you into your nightgown and under the covers. I've always heard bed rest was the best thing if there was fear the baby would arrive early." Memories of the difficulties Amanda had encountered during her last pregnancy flooded Maura's mind. She had stayed with Daniel and Amanda during those trying weeks when her sister-in-law had been required to remain abed. In the end, it had been worth every minute. After those long boring days of lying in bed, Amanda had finally given birth to a healthy, beautiful daughter—sweet little Jenny.

Digging deeply into one of Georgette's trunks, she found a warm nightgown; and after what seemed like an eternity, her young friend was tucked into bed. The cramping had finally subsided, and Georgette slipped into a restless sleep under Maura's watchful eyes.

Several hours later, Georgette awakened and discovered Maura sitting beside her bed reading a small Bible.

Georgette extended her hand to Maura. "I'm feeling much better. The pain seems to have completely gone away. I'm sorry to have frightened you, but I think it was a false alarm."

"Perhaps, but I think it would be best if you remained in bed for at least the next several days. I'll see that your meals are brought to your cabin and explain to Mrs. Windsor you're just a bit under the weather."

"But what if Mrs. Windsor wants to come and visit?" Georgette's eyes shone with concern. "I don't want her to know I'm expecting a child. What will she think of me? She knows I'm not married—or even engaged, for that matter. I feel somewhat stronger, and it will be better if I just try to carry on as I have been."

"Absolutely not! If you care nothing about yourself, think of what damage you may do to the unborn child if you don't take care of yourself. I can handle Mrs. Windsor, and if and when the time comes that she insists upon visiting you, we'll make advance arrangements so that your condition will be hidden from her view. I'll not argue about this, Georgette."

"You're not my mother! What makes you think you can tell me what I must do?"

Maura flinched at the angry retort, but she wasn't going to relent in her decision. "It's certainly a fact I'm not your mother, but I'm as close to any female assistance as you'll find when it comes time to have your child. Besides, you know I'm only doing what's best for the two of you."

Georgette was quiet for several minutes, and Maura rose from the chair and picked up her bonnet and cape.

"Where are you going? I haven't gotten out of bed. I'll do whatever you think is best. Really I will, I promise."

Maura turned her head to conceal the smile that played on her lips. "I'm going to go and get us something to eat. Do you think you can keep down a meal, or would you prefer just a bowl of soup?"

"I know this will probably surprise you, but I'm ravenous." Georgette failed to hide a sheepish grin.

"That's a good sign. I'll see what I can do about solving that problem." Maura gestured toward the bed. "You stay under those coivers so nothing happens while I'm gone."

Fortunately, Mrs. Windsor and the other passengers hadn't arrived for dinner when Maura entered the dining room. Spotting one of the cooks coming from the galley, she crossed the room as swiftly as possible and approached him.

"Excuse me, but would it be possible for me to have two trays prepared and delivered to Miss Blackburn's cabin?"

"Dinner won't be ready for another half hour, but I'll have the trays delivered before we begin serving. If the winds become any stronger, you may want to keep to your cabin after dinner. From the looks of things, this could turn into a rough night."

"Thank you, I'll keep that in mind. Is there reason for great concern?"

"Nah, nothing out of the ordinary. The closer we get to the Cape, the worse the weather is this time of year, but we'll be in for quite a ride over the next week or so."

His words didn't provide the comfort Maura had longed to hear. "But you've never had a problem with this ship while rounding the Cape, have you?"

"There's not a ship that doesn't have problems rounding Cape Horn in the middle of winter. But if you're asking if you think we're going to go down at sea, the answer would be no." He nodded toward the galley. "I got to get back to work."

On her return to Georgette's quarters, it seemed the ship might be rocking more arduously. *Now stop that*, she chastised herself. *You're allowing your thoughts to be controlled by a simple cautionary comment.*

By the time dinner arrived, there was no doubt that they had entered rougher waters. When Maura opened the door, the cabin boy tumbled into the room, somehow managing to keep their food within the confines of the covered trays while overcoming the obstacles of a lurching ship and Georgette's open trunk sitting just inside the doorway. He wasted no time depositing the items, bidding them good night, and scurrying back to the passageway.

"Let's see what's on the trays." Georgette plumped several pillows behind her and wiggled into a sitting position.

"Are you sure you want to eat? This turbulence has caused me to lose my appetite completely." Maura eyed the girl in disbelief.

"Not me. I could eat a cow". Georgette giggled at her own remark.

Maura smiled weakly, feeling as though she would retch when the smell of the food reached her nostrils.

"Oh, how wonderful." Georgette sounded like a small child at Christmas. "Roast pork and potatoes. Oh, look, Maura, there's even apple pie with cheese for dessert. I can't remember the last time I had roast pork."

Moving across the room to avoid smelling the food, Maura positioned herself in a high-backed chair with cushioned arms and leaned her head back.

"This is delicious, Maura. Can I have your pie if you're not going to eat it?"

Closing her eyes, Maura nodded her head. Several minutes passed, and it seemed that the bow of the ship was going to touch the very depths of the ocean before it rose back up and violently descended in the opposite direction.

"Are you going to bring me the other tray, or should I get up?" Georgette arched her brows when Maura remained in the chair.

Maura forced her eyes open a mere slit. "You're not to get up, and I'm not bringing you anything else to eat right now, Georgette." Maura gulped as the prow of the ship took yet another dive into the swirling waters.

"It's getting rather exciting, isn't it?" Even when her dinner tray went crashing to the floor, and scraps of food and dishes tumbled helter-skelter, Georgette's enthusiasm remained intact.

Maura attempted to rise, but the swooping motion of the ship immediately threw her back into the chair.

"You're positively green, Maura. It seems strange, doesn't it? Just a short time ago I was the one in need of medical attention; but now, I believe, you are in worse condition than I was."

"Our ailments are completely dissimilar, Georgette. I am suffering from seasickness due to this horrendous weather. As soon as the weather clears, I'll be fine. Your ailment, however, won't disappear with the passing of a storm." She'd spoken with more rancor than she'd intended, but how could Georgette compare seasickness with the possibility of a premature birth?

Seeing Georgette's pained look, Maura immediately regretted the outburst. "I'm sorry, Georgette. I didn't mean to hurt your feelings. Why don't you rest while you can and I'll do the same."

"Papa always did tell me God must have given me a double helping of good looks to make up for my lack of common sense. I'll be quiet as a church mouse, and I'm sure that we'll both be feeling wonderful by morning." Georgette mustered a weak smile before she made certain the rail on her bed was secure.

During the next four days, the weather roared with a violence that neither of them could have imagined. One of the crew members had come to Georgette's cabin the second day and told them to remain inside. He'd advised that a crew member would deliver what food he could as the weather permitted. Maura was unable to eat anything during the four days, but she did force herself to drink liquids to keep from dehydrating. Georgette, however, remained the epitome of good health and devoured every morsel of food each crew member delivered to the room.

The seas finally calmed, although the weather remained frigid for another week, but at least Maura was able to return to her cabin and assume a somewhat normal routine. One of her first priorities had been to find Mrs. Windsor and see how she had fared throughout the storm. Discovering her cabin unoccupied, Maura had gone to the dining room and then the library in search of the older woman. Failing to locate her, Maura had finally inquired of the ship's captain, who revealed Mrs. Windsor had come out on the deck during the storm, appearing to be delirious. Before any of the crew members could reach the older woman, she had been swept overboard.

"Our attempts to save her or recover her body went unrewarded."

Maura gasped at the news.

"Are you a relative?"

"No, no, but she was a lovely lady. We had just met on the ship, but I felt as though I'd known her for some time."

He nodded his understanding. "Do you know if there is someone I should notify—a family member in California, perhaps? We found nothing in her belongings to indicate why she was aboard the ship or if she had family elsewhere."

"She told me that her family was all deceased and she wanted a bit of adventure in her life before she died. Having heard stories of the excitement in California, she decided to sell her home and move west. Apparently she was known for her excellent cooking and was planning to open a restaurant when she reached her new home." Maura's chest ached as she recalled Mrs. Windsor's plans for the future.

"I'm sorry she didn't live to see her dream through. Since you're probably the closest thing she had to a relative, why don't you take her belongings when we get to California? She'd probably prefer that over my men scavenging through them."

Maura nodded. She wasn't sure she wanted to claim the belongings of a deceased woman she barely knew, but any further discussion of the subject seemed abhorrent.

Slowly making her way back to Georgette's cabin, Maura wrestled with thoughts of how to break the news to her young friend. The three of them had grown close during the voyage, and although Georgette was somewhat intimidated by Mrs. Windsor's maturity and sophistication, her respect for the older woman's Christian standards and beliefs was obvious. While Maura and Mrs. Windsor studied and discussed passages of scripture, Georgette would often sit nearby listening intently. In turn, Mrs. Windsor always attempted to draw Georgette into their Bible studies.

"Her questions make it apparent she's trying to find what's missing in her life. I hope somehow I can play a small part in helping her find it," Mrs. Windsor had once confided to Maura.

Maura was pleased that Mrs. Windsor had found that opportunity and led Georgette to the Lord. Mrs. Windsor could have taught Georgette so much more about God's love, Maura thought as she entered the doorway.

Georgette looked up when Maura stepped inside the cabin. "Did you visit with Mrs. Windsor while you were gone? How did she make it through the storm?"

"Not very well, I'm afraid. You see. . ."

"Did you tell her about the baby? What did she say? Do you think she'll ever speak to me again? Oh, I hope so; I hope she'll find it in her heart to forgive me. What's wrong, Maura? You look positively ill. I'm sorry. Here I am just rambling on with my questions and you're sick. Why don't you sit down and rest? Can I get you something?"

"Georgette, I don't know how to say this, so I'll just come straight out with it. Mrs. Windsor died during the storm. The captain told me she had come up on deck during the squall. Apparently she was ill and had become delirious. She was hit with a giant wave and washed overboard. They weren't able to save her."

"No! That can't be true. Surely they've made some mistake, Maura. Tell me this isn't so." Tears glistened in Georgette's eyes.

"I wish I could, but there's no way to change the truth."

"She told me once that she didn't fear death because time on earth was only a short delay on the path to eternity and that she was looking forward to heaven. I wish I could feel that way; but whenever I think about death, I still become frightened."

"As you grow in your faith, you'll find that same assurance." Maura hoped her words would encourage the young woman.

"Perhaps, but it's difficult for me to remember that God has forgiven all the terrible things I've done in my life. Somehow it just seems too simple to ask for forgiveness and receive it. Look at what my family did to me when I asked for their forgiveness! They sent me off to California so that they wouldn't be humiliated." Georgette's voice trembled. "It's truly amazing that God will forgive me when my own flesh and blood has disowned me!"

Maura sat down beside the girl. "But don't you see, Georgette—your parents are human—just like you and me. You can't compare them to

God and His perfect love. I know it seems too simple that this gift is ours, free for the taking. Perhaps that's why so many reject it—because it is a sovereign gift, straight from God through His Son."

"I'm just thankful that God sent you and Mrs. Windsor into my life to explain all of this. Had I remained at home with my family, I may have never accepted the Lord. Perhaps one day I'll have the opportunity to lead someone else—maybe even someone in my family."

Chapter 3

*S*o you're finally off to San Francisco to get your woman. I was beginning to think it was..."

"Was what? A lie?" Luther clenched his fists in an attempt to hold back his anger, but his voice betrayed him.

The two old men had been sitting in the corner of the store playing cards all afternoon, just as they did most afternoons. The only difference between today and the countless other afternoons was the fact that they were taking great pleasure in baiting the proprietor about his approaching marriage.

"Don't get yourself all riled up, Luther. You know Aaron's only funnin' with ya."

"I'm tired of listening to both of you. If you want to sit and play cards, that's fine. But don't sit in my store and call me a liar."

Aaron ran his fingers through the gray, scruffy beard that surrounded his haggard face. "I'm sorry, Luther. Hank's right, ya know. I'd never call you a liar. You're a good man, and I wish you only the best."

Hank nudged his card partner and nodded toward the door. "We'd best be getting out of your way."

"Oh, yeah, we got things to do. We'll see ya when you get back from San Francisco." Aaron waved and followed Hank toward the front door of the Buchanan Mercantile.

"Sorry, Aaron. I'm just a little nervous—don't hold it against me." Luther lifted his hand in a half-hearted wave. "Great! At this rate, I won't need to come back to Placerville. If I keep this up, I'll run off all my customers." Luther walked through the store and checked the shelves one last time.

He disliked leaving the store, but going to San Francisco to pick up supplies was a necessity. Collecting goods at the wharf wasn't a chore he could entrust to anyone else. He'd learned that it took a careful eye to avoid having one's cargo shorted. There were always beggars and thieves on the quay, men down on their luck as well as those who were too lazy to work for a living. They prowled among the cargo as it was unloaded, helping themselves to anything they could carry off.

Shortly after his arrival, he'd traveled to the docks to collect his first shipment of goods. To his amazement, several thieves had been successful in joining forces and hauling off large crates while the unwitting crew was aboard ship fetching the remaining shipment. From that day forward, Luther made every effort to be present on the wharf when his cargo was being unloaded, and he didn't leave until it was completely accounted for and secured.

Luther soon devised a plan to successfully protect his cargo and haul it to Placerville. After inquiring about various ships' captains, he engaged Captain Nedrick Wharton, a man of good reputation, to transport his supplies. Captain Wharton had delivered all of the cargo for the Buchanan Mercantile for the past five years. The two men had a gentlemen's agreement that Luther's cargo was never to be unloaded until his arrival at the dock, and, in exchange, Captain Wharton would receive several gold coins for the added service. The process had worked admirably, and Luther could boast that no thief had ever pilfered any of his stock.

Likewise, Luther had made painstaking arrangements with a local livery where he boarded his horses and wagon while in the city. He would rent two additional wagons and drivers to assist in hauling the supplies back to Placerville. The drivers varied from trip to trip, but the owner of the livery vouched for any man he hired out, and Luther had never met with any complications.

His attention to detail and unfaltering determination to disprove his father's prediction of failure had caused a transformation. From an insecure, yet trusting human being, Luther had slowly evolved into a man with a penchant for success and a lack of tolerance for obstacles that might delay his achievements.

As his business flourished in the small gold mining town, Luther had realized that an extra pair of hands would allow him to move even more rapidly toward achieving his goals. And, in his methodical calculations, he came to the conclusion that the best way to gain another pair of hands was to marry. There were abundant benefits to the plan. Aside from the obvious advantage, he would have additional help without the added expense. Granted, he would have to feed and clothe a wife, but that would cost less than hiring a full-time employee. Besides, he would no longer be required to send out his laundry or cook his own meals; he could train her to balance the ledgers, a chore he despised; and, as she bore children, there would be even more hands to help! The only problem would be finding a woman. California was home to an abundance of men, but women—at least good Christian women—were nowhere to be found. In order to resolve his problem, Luther had once again devised a plan.

A little over a year ago, Luther had traveled to San Francisco and requested Captain Wharton deliver an advertisement for a mail-order bride to several East Coast newspapers. The responses had been less than he had hoped for—one from a woman almost twice his age, another from a married woman wanting to escape a cruel husband, and one from Maura Thorenson. Although Miss Thorenson came the closest to meeting his requirements, he wasn't entirely satisfied. In her first letter, she avowed to be twenty-eight years old. He would have preferred a woman of eighteen or nineteen years of age, young and healthy, who could earn her keep and give him many children. But at least she appeared in good health and somewhat comely in the picture she had sent.

Of course, the request by the woman's parents that she correspond with him for an entire year before setting sail for California had been totally unacceptable. He had begrudgingly conceded to a six-month delay, arguing that his bride's traveling time of at least six months would require him to wait over a year for her arrival in San Francisco. Throughout the six-month correspondence period, he had continued to hope that some younger, more suitable prospect would contact him and be willing to make immediate arrangements to marry him. Those hopes had heightened even further when Luther received a letter from Walter Thorenson practically demanding that his precious daughter travel aboard a luxury ship to California. Luther was aghast as he had calculated the additional cost, but he had bleakly agreed when he was unable to devise a logical plan to avoid the request. If Mr. Thorenson thought him a miser, he'd likely entice Maura to cancel their wedding. And Luther didn't want that to occur!

Now, after a year of anticipating the arrival of his bride, Luther was leaving Placerville as a single man for the last time. When he returned, he would have a wife—a helpmeet.

"I'll expect an accounting of everything when I return." Luther frowned and tapped the ledger book as he spoke to Clem Halbert, the man he had hired to look after the store during his absence. "As usual, I've completed an inventory of all the merchandise, so I'll know if you attempt anything underhanded."

"The preacher vouched for me, Mr. Buchanan. I'm an honest man, and I worked in the general store in my hometown for ten years before coming to California. We've been over this for the past two weeks. If you don't trust me, find someone else to tend the place." Clem folded his arms across his chest and frowned in return.

"I'm sorry, Clem. It's just that I don't like leaving my business in the hands of someone else. Every time I go to San Francisco, I've got this problem. Used to be Johnny Weber would take care of things, and I was finally getting used to him. Now that he's up and left, it's, well—"

"I understand, Luther, but you got two choices. Either trust the store to me or stay home. Makes me no difference at this point. Course, if you decide to stay in Placerville, I may ride down to San Francisco and see if I can talk your intended into marrying me," he joked.

Luther laughed weakly in return. "Never know, she just might marry you if that happened. Women have been known to reject a man for less!"

"Aw, ain't no woman gonna jilt you, Luther. She's coming halfway around the world to marry you. Now, you better get going before the sun's any farther up in the sky."

After checking the store one last time, he hoisted himself onto the seat of the wooden freight wagon and slapped the reins. "Giddyup." The horses followed Luther's command without hesitation--he hoped his new bride would do the same.

Georgette and Maura stood on the deck of the ship as it slowly maneuvered between the numerous vessels in the San Francisco harbor, many of them in a terrible state of disrepair, obviously having been deserted for a long period of time.

When one of the crew members drew near, Maura quizzed him. "Why are all those ships in the harbor in such dreadful condition?"

"Them? Oh, once they dock, the sailors get gold fever and never return. The ships remain in the harbor until the captain can hire another crew. But that doesn't happen very often, so the ships sit here and rot." The sailor's gaze settled on the decaying wreckage. "You'll find some of them have been towed and placed between other buildings. They're used as hotels and general stores or saloons—looks strange at first, but you get used to it. I better get back to work."

Georgette touched Maura's arm. "So you think your Luther Buchanan will be waiting on the dock for you?"

"I really don't know. He said if he wasn't at the dock, I should stay at the Ashton Hotel." Maura forced a smile and attempted to calm her nerves. She felt as though a million butterflies had encamped in her stomach.

"Are you frightened?" Georgette arched her brows. "I know I would be. Marrying some complete stranger, not knowing if he'd like the way I look or act." She shivered. "Does he know about that?" Georgette nodded toward Maura's left side.

Maura stiffened at the question. "No. I didn't think it was important."

Georgette looked at her friend in astonishment. "Do you really believe that?"

Maura swallowed hard. "Why is it that everyone thinks the most important thing about me is the fact that I was born with a withered arm and leg, and that I walk with a limp and have difficulty using my left hand? Is that any more important than the color of my hair or how much I weigh—or perhaps how tall I am?"

"Did you tell him the color of your hair and how tall you are?" Georgette's soft voice didn't abate Maura's anger.

Maura clenched her jaw. "Yes, but only because he asked."

"I don't suppose it entered his mind to explore the possibility of some infirmity. He probably assumed you would have been candid about anything like that."

"Well, it makes no difference to me if he has an ailment of some type, so I didn't think there was any need to address the matter." Maura squared her shoulders as if ready to do battle. "There's nothing I can do to change my appearance. I was born this way and have had to deal with it all my life."

"Please don't misunderstand. I know that once Mr. Buchanan gets to know you, he won't even notice that you're. . ."

"Different?" Maura arched her brows.

"Yes, different. You know you're different, and so do I. But once people get to know you, they no longer notice. I just thought you would tell Mr. Buchanan so that he would be prepared to accept you as you are. Oh, no matter what I say, it comes out wrong." Georgette slapped her hand on the ship's railing.

"The fact is, he doesn't know that I'm crippled, and it's too late to tell him now. But you're right—I was afraid he'd reject me if he knew." Maura hiked a shoulder. "Guess I'll find out just what's important to him in the next hour or so."

The passengers were beginning to disembark when the captain rushed over to where Maura and Georgette were standing in line.

"I had my men place the other trunks with yours. They'll be together on the dock," he said. "Hope the trip wasn't totally unbearable, ladies. We strive to provide the finest service and consider ourselves a luxury ship, unlike most of those," he said, indicating toward the other ships in the harbor. "Unfortunately, we have no control over the weather, although it wasn't too bad this voyage."

Maura extended her thanks and kept her thoughts about the storm to herself. Truth be told, she hoped she'd never again have to endure such horrid weather. Meanwhile, Georgette rattled on about how exciting the trip had been, apparently forgetting that her unborn child had threatened to make an early delivery. Maura had been surprised and extremely thankful that the girl had suffered no further difficulty with the pregnancy. By now there was no hiding her impending condition, and by Georgette's calculations, the baby had been due the previous week.

The two women walked arm-in-arm down the unsteady gangplank, Maura keeping her eyes on Georgette, not wanting a last-minute disaster. When they finally reached the dock, Maura spied a man holding a picture and peering among the passengers who had disembarked. Leading Georgette in his direction, she took a closer look. The man resembled the picture of Luther Buchanan, but she couldn't be sure.

She watched as he caught sight of them. His eyes darted back and forth between the two women and then slowly moved up and down the length of her. He was holding her picture in his hand, looking at the picture and then at her. For several minutes he didn't say anything; he just stared until they came to a stop in front of him.

The man stared at Maura for a moment before he nodded toward Georgette. "Who's she?"

"Georgette Blackburn. Georgette, I believe this is Luther Buchanan." Maura tipped her head to the side as she looked up at him.

Georgette offered a slight smile. "Pleased to meet you, Mr. Buchanan. Maura and I met on the ship. She's such a wonderful lady that I don't know what I would have done without her. You're very fortunate she's agreed to be your wife, but I suppose you already know—"

Maura nudged her friend. "Georgette, you need not extol my virtues to Mr. Buchanan. You are Luther Buchanan, aren't you?"

"Of course, I'm Luther." His gaze rested on her left arm. "I've been here two days waiting on the ship and already made arrangements with the preacher and rented a room at the hotel. We'll leave in a couple days after I've gotten all my supplies loaded. Where's your belongings?"

Maura pointed out her trunks as well as those that had belonged to

Mrs. Windsor. Without further comment, he nodded and hoisted them one by one onto a wagon.

"He doesn't seem to talk much, does he?" Georgette whispered.

He turned toward Georgette. "Someone coming for you?"

"No, I don't think so."

Luther frowned. "What's that mean—you don't think so? Either you got someone coming or you don't."

Luther's blunt remark caused tears to form in Georgette's eyes, and Maura stepped forward to protect her. "There is no one meeting her. She's come to California to begin a new life."

"Looks to me like she's running away from her old life." Luther's gaze settled on the protrusion beneath Georgette's cape. "If you want a ride to the hotel, you can come with us." His voice was void of compassion.

Georgette bowed her head. "That would be very nice of you. Those are my trunks."

Maura thought she heard him make a comment under his breath, but she chose to ignore it. Although the hotel wasn't far, the escalating tenseness among the three passengers made the short trip seem like hours. Luther helped Georgette down and then reached up to assist Maura.

"We need to talk about that." He gestured toward the left side of her body.

Maura felt herself stiffen and she quickly moved away from him. The two women walked into the hotel, followed by Luther.

"I'm already registered. I'll need a room for Miss Thorenson." He turned toward Georgette. "Are you renting a room, Miss Blackburn?"

"I suppose, so." She peeked at Maura from beneath her bonnet.

Maura smiled at the hotel clerk. "She won't need a separate room. She can stay with me tonight."

Luther edged to Maura's side. "Why don't you freshen up and then we'll go to dinner—alone."

"I'll need a little time." If Mr. Buchanan's behavior didn't soon change, she doubted she'd ever be ready to spend time alone with him.

"I'll make arrangements for the trunks to be delivered to your room. Meet me here at five o'clock—without her."

Maura gave a slight nod. "I understood she wasn't invited the first time you told me to come alone." She could feel his gaze on her as she walked away.

"You look lovely. That dress was a wonderful choice." Georgette fluttered around Maura arranging the forest green edging that bordered the deep pink flounces of the skirt. The deep green bodice accented her auburn tresses that fell in soft waves around her face. Georgette had fashioned the remainder of her hair into a large bun surrounded by a matching green ribbon.

"Thank you, Georgette, but I don't think Mr. Buchanan will be overly impressed." She retrieved her long wool cape and placed it over her shrunken arm.

At exactly five o'clock she walked into the hotel foyer, where Luther was impatiently pacing back and forth. She was pleased to see that he had changed from the rumpled attire he'd worn to meet her. This evening he wore gray wool trousers, a white shirt with gray cravat topped by a double-breasted waistcoat, and a black alpaca frock coat. He carried a black beaver felt top hat and his chestnut hair was cut short and parted on the side. A dark brown mustache showed a hint of gray, making him look older than his avowed age of thirty years. Although his face appeared permanently etched in a frown, he wasn't altogether unpleasant in his appearance.

"Have I kept you waiting long?"

He pulled his watch from his waistcoat. "It doesn't matter how long I've been waiting. You are exactly on time. It's five o'clock."

Once again she felt as though his eyes were boring through her. The silence was deafening. When he said nothing further, she glanced toward the dining room. "Are we dining here?"

"No." He offered her his arm. "There's a restaurant a short distance away. I thought we could walk. That is, if you're able to walk that far?"

"You'd be surprised just how far I can walk, Mr. Buchanan." She wanted to add that if she weren't so far from home, she'd walk right out of his life. Instead, she held her tongue and took his arm.

Not another word passed between them until they were seated in the restaurant and Luther had ordered dinner for both of them.

"Now, then, how is it you failed to mention in your letters that you're a cripple—or didn't you think I'd notice?" Sarcasm laced his words.

"Unless you have a problem with your vision, I was sure you would notice, Mr. Buchanan." Any attempt to hold her temper in check had failed.

"Well, I don't have a problem seeing, and if I did, I would have told you. In fact, I would have told you if I suffered from any infirmity." His lips thinned into a tight line.

"Mr. Buchanan, I do not suffer from anything. I happen to have an arm and leg that are somewhat shriveled. My left leg causes me to limp, and I am somewhat limited in the use of my left hand and arm, but I do not consider myself a cripple—wasn't that the word you used—cripple?"

"It seems to me if you weren't afraid I'd have rejected you, you would have told me. You were careful to send a picture that hid your imperfection and just as careful not to write me about it. Is that why you've never married? No one would have you?"

Maura stared back at him for just a moment and then very quietly replied, "It's very likely that the reason I remain unmarried is because I have visible physical differences. You're right. I was afraid you would find me unacceptable because of that divergence from what the world considers normal. I'm sorry that I didn't tell you, because it's obvious you find me outwardly displeasing. Unfortunately, I must tell you that I find you even more unsuitable. You don't realize it, Luther, but you are much more crippled than I—inwardly crippled by a cruel spirit and vicious tongue. Now, if you'll excuse me, I've lost my appetite." She pushed up from the table.

"No, I won't excuse you. This matter needs to be settled, and walking out of here isn't going to resolve anything. Please, sit down." He gestured toward the chair. "Please."

His voice had softened a modicum, and she knew he was right. The problem between them must be resolved. Her stomach lurched at the thought of food, but their disagreement hadn't bothered Luther. He ate as though he hadn't had a meal in weeks.

When he finally looked up, he gestured toward her plate. "You need help cutting your meat?"

She stiffened at the question. "No, I don't need help cutting my meat, or combing my hair, or washing dishes. I lead a perfectly normal life, although I'm sure you find that hard to believe."

"No need to get on your high horse. I was just offering to help."

Maura held her emotions in check. Anger was not going to serve her well in this situation. "I think it would be best if I returned to Boston."

"Now hold up just a minute." Luther held a forkful of mashed potatoes and gravy in mid-air. "I think you're forgetting how much money I've already spent getting you here. Not to mention the fact that I've lost a whole year what with waiting the six months you requested and then almost six months for your voyage."

"As far as your capital outlay is concerned, I could send you monthly payments until you're reimbursed. There's nothing I can do to replace your time."

"You have money for your return voyage?" He watched her as he shoved the forkful of potatoes into his mouth.

She met his eyes. "No, I don't. You'll have to advance it, and I'll repay that also."

"Sorry, but I don't have that kind of money right now. I'm in San Francisco not only to meet your ship but also to purchase the supplies I ordered to restock my store. I don't have an extra thousand dollars to send you home. In fact, I don't think there are too many choices available to either of us. The preacher's already been paid and agreed to conduct the wedding tomorrow morning. I'll honor my word that we'll be married, but in name only."

How dare he? All attempts to remain calm now failed her. "Do I have any say in this?"

"Not really. You don't have the money to return home; you don't have any family here; you can't support yourself; and even if you could, no self-respecting single woman would want to live alone and unprotected in San Francisco. The town is swarming with men—most of them with very little regard for a lady." He picked up his knife and cut a piece of pork roast.

"In other words, I should be thankful that you're willing to sacrifice yourself and marry me?"

"Well, I wouldn't exactly put it in those words, but—"

She couldn't believe her ears. "I'll say one thing for you, Mr. Buchanan. What you lack in character you certainly make up for in arrogance."

"If you can think of another way to solve this, I'm willing to listen."

"If and when I do, you'll be the first to know. I'd like to return to the hotel now if you've finished your dinner."

When he'd eaten the last biscuit and swallowed the last of his coffee, they walked back to the hotel in a deafening silence. "I'll meet you here at ten o'clock in the morning. The preacher's expecting us at ten-thirty." Luther removed his watch from the pocket of his waistcoat.

"Counting up your hours of freedom?" Maura shouldn't have baited him, but she couldn't resist. He wanted to be free of her and she wanted free of him, yet in the morning they'd stand before a preacher and promise to love and cherish each other. Such hypocrisy, but what else could she do?

He didn't respond to her question. Instead, he turned and proceeded down the hallway. He'd gone only a short distance when he abruptly turned and came back. "Did you bring a wedding gown?"

She nodded, surprised by the question.

"Wear it," he commanded and once again walked away from her. "And you can bring that Blackburn woman along if you want," he called back over his shoulder, surprising her even further.

When he finally disappeared from sight and Maura was sure he wouldn't reappear, she returned to her room. Georgette was sitting in a large overstuffed chair that appeared to have her submerged in its depths.

"Wouldn't that other chair be more comfortable?" Maura gestured toward the chair as she removed her cape.

"I think so, and I would certainly like to try it, but I can't seem to get out of this one." Georgette giggled. "Every time I attempt to stand up I'm thrown off balance and land right back where I started from. It seems my legs are too short and my belly is too large. I was beginning to fear I would have to spend the night in this chair. I don't know what I would have done if you hadn't returned."

"Here, let me help you." Maura extended her good arm to the girl and helped her up. Georgette ungracefully waddled across the room and lowered herself into the smaller chair.

"Oh, this is much better. Now, tell me what happened at dinner."

Not wanting to relive all of the painful exchanges that had transpired earlier in the evening, Maura related only a portion of the events.

"This is so exciting! Obviously, I'm not a good judge of people. When we met Mr. Buchanan on the dock he seemed so sullen that I was fearful he would be mean-spirited about—well, you know. . ." She glanced at Maura's arm.

"You mean about my being a cripple?"

Georgette folded her arms and rested them atop her protruding belly. "I never called you any such thing."

"No, you didn't—that's what Luther Buchanan calls me." She couldn't withhold her pain any longer. Until that moment she hadn't realized the wounds he had reopened. All the old sorrow from years gone by came rushing back to haunt her, and she was unable to hold back the racking sobs that spilled forth from deep within.

Georgette moved as quickly as her ungainly body would allow and embraced her friend, smoothing her hair and attempting somehow to relieve a small portion of Maura's agony.

"I am so very sorry, Maura. He can't even begin to imagine what a wonderful person you are. It will all work out. You'll see." She crooned the words like a mother attempting to soothe a child.

Georgette had barely spoken the words when her fingers dug deep into Maura's shoulder and a sharp cry escaped her lips. "Oh, Maura, I think I've begun my labor." She released Maura's shoulder and doubled over in her attempt to reach the bed.

Chapter 4

The next morning Luther doggedly paced back and forth in the lobby, pulling out his pocket watch every thirty seconds. It was almost ten o'clock, but Maura hadn't appeared. He'd told her they were to meet the preacher at 10:30 am, and now they were going to be late. Fear slowly crept into his mind. Perhaps she'd fled during the night, after deciding marriage to him was a worse fate than fending for herself in unknown territory. His thoughts raced back to the small church in Virginia where he had stood waiting for Elizabeth five years earlier.

"It's happened again." Once again he peered at the timepiece.

Snapping the watch closed and returning it to the pocket of his embroidered blue satin waistcoat, which had been specially ordered for this occasion, he resolutely walked toward Maura's room and rapped loudly on the door. Several minutes had passed when, just as he raised his hand to knock once again, the door swung open.

Maura stood before him in the same dress she had been wearing when they had parted company last evening. It appeared wet in places and stained in others; her hair was damp, and the waves from the night before were now straight and unkempt. Dark circles rimmed her eyes, and her limp seemed even more exaggerated than he remembered.

"Come in and close the door if you care to stay." She didn't wait to see if he'd accepted her offer.

"Would you care to tell me what's going on?" He pushed the door closed with a slam.

His answer came from the adjoining room—the lusty cry of a newborn.

"I've been acting as Georgette's midwife all night. Obviously, I'll not be ready for a wedding at 10:30 am."

Luther clenched his jaw in an attempt to control his rising anger. "You mean we're going to be held up until tomorrow? I don't even know if the preacher is available then. How long will it take you to get ready? I can go and see if he'll wait another hour. Can you be ready by noon?" Hands resting on his hips, he'd fired the questions in rapid succession.

Maura walked back and stood directly in front of him. "Luther, I just told you that I've been up all night. Look at me. Do I look like I can be ready for a wedding in less than an hour? As soon as things quiet down, I plan to clean up and then get some much-needed rest. If you're determined to get married today, you'll have to find another bride." For the first time, she looked directly into his eyes.

"Well, can you give me some idea when you'll be able to find time to attend the wedding?" He raked his fingers through his thick brown hair while meeting her gaze.

She suddenly appeared quite calm. "I'd prefer to wait for at least two weeks."

"Two weeks!" His shouted protest was quickly followed by the robust cries of the infant.

"Would you please refrain from raising your voice and slamming doors? I'm sure that Georgette would appreciate it, and I know I certainly would." Her features tightened into a frown.

"My humble apologies, Miss Thorenson. It would be nice if you'd remember who is paying for these rooms. It isn't Miss Blackburn or her newborn. It would also be appreciated if you would remember just why you came to California!"

"I know who is paying the hotel bill, and I know why I came to California. How could I forget? But you see, Mr. Buchanan, I would be failing miserably if I were to leave this girl alone with a newborn. She has no one. Who will help her? To be honest, I don't know if I'll be able to force myself to leave her in two weeks."

She made the announcement with the same newfound calmness she'd exhibited a short time ago. Did this woman not realize he had a schedule to keep and commitments to honor?

Luther fell into the large wing chair. He folded his hands together and then leaned forward and rested his elbows on his knees. "It seems as though we're once again going to be forced to make some difficult decisions."

"We? I believe your idea of joint decision-making is different than mine. As I recall, you didn't suggest any choices."

"Well, in that case, why don't you tell me your plan for resolving this matter. Believe me, I'd love to hear your solution."

Maura sat down on the brocade settee. "I've had little sleep and my mind is barely functioning, but I believe the easiest solution would be to wait for several weeks before we leave for Placerville. Why wouldn't that work?"

"Why? I'll tell you why. I own a store in Placerville that is being operated by a man who is more interested in returning to the gold fields than taking care of my business. When I left, I was sorely in need of supplies, and I've already been gone three weeks, what with my travel time and waiting for the supplies and your ship to arrive. I was expecting to be back before now, and you want me to remain here several more weeks? Time is money! I have a schedule to keep. For some insane reason, I thought having a wife was going to help me run my store more efficiently. If I listen to you, I won't have a business left to run!"

He'd hoped to maintain civility with this woman, but she seemingly couldn't understand that he had obligations that required his attention. How could one woman be so difficult?

She leaned forward and glared at him. "Is that what I'm to be, then? Someone to act as your hired help in the mercantile?"

"Let's not even get into that right now. We're supposed to be looking for a solution, not finding additional problems to argue over. If you have any other ideas, this is your chance to air them, because it is out of the question for us to remain here." He leaned back in the chair and waited. This would be her last opportunity to solve the matter.

Moments later, she sighed. "If the preacher is available to marry us tomorrow, we can leave shortly after the ceremony. Before we depart, you'll need to make a bed in the back of the wagon for Georgette and the baby. That's my solution."

"What?" He jumped up from the chair. "You think I should take that woman and her baby with us to Placerville? Are you planning on them living with us, too? I can't believe this." He paced back and forth in the small sitting room while he continued to rant.

"You want to return immediately, and I can't leave her here alone. It's going to be difficult for her to make the trip so soon after the baby's birth, but I think she'll agree."

"You think she'll agree? You think she'll agree? Well, of course she'll agree. Why shouldn't she? All of a sudden she has an instant family to take care of her. If it isn't being too inquisitive, might I ask just what this woman had in mind when she set sail for California in her condition? Or is she totally mindless?"

"Keep your voice down. She doesn't need to hear your mean-spirited remarks; it's quite enough that I must tolerate them. She's young and made a mistake. Her family disowned her, and her father's final gift to her was passage on the Edward Everett with the admonition never to contact the family again. Someone told her that men greatly outnumbered women in California, so I suppose her plan was that she would find a husband after the baby was born."

"If, and I'm just saying if, I agree to take her with us, what then? Do you plan on her living with us? Because I'll not agree to that." His retort had a weak ring to it, and she hadn't missed it He could see it in her eyes.

Her smile appeared forced, but she rebutted in a strong voice. "She'll have to stay until she's able to make other arrangements."

He slowly shook his head. "Maura, you know I've got to return, and I'm bound to my pledge to marry you. I'll take them with us, and they can stay for two months. If she has any money, I expect her to pay for her board. I want your promise that at the end of two months, Miss Blackburn and her child will move from our home—with no excuses, no extensions, and no argument from you. Do we have a deal?"

Maura nodded. "You have my word. After you've talked with the preacher, let me know when I'm to be prepared for the marriage ceremony. I'll be on time."

"I'll not come back until dinner time so that you can rest. Hopefully, I'll have completed the arrangements by then." He reached into his pocket, withdrew his pocket watch, and checked the time. He should have ample time to make the arrangements.

Once he'd left, Maura leaned against the closed door, unable to believe that he had agreed to her terms but too tired to delight in the victory. She tiptoed into the bedroom, where Georgette and the baby were sleeping. Quietly she poured water into the china washbowl and bathed herself and, even though it was past noon, slipped into a soft cotton nightgown.

Several hours later, the baby's vigorous cries and Georgette's voice pulled her out of a deep sleep.

"What time is it?" She'd napped on the small settee, and arched her back as she sat up.

"I don't know, but I'm getting terribly hungry. Is there anything here to eat?" Georgette's voice drifted from the bedroom.

"No, but I'll get you something as soon as I get dressed." Maura rubbed her back as she pushed up from the settee. She hurried into the bedroom, certain that it must be close to five o'clock.

Panic seized her. She didn't want to be late. Moving quickly, she removed a pale blue silk dress with navy piping and a lace collar from her trunk and pulled her hair into a chignon at the back of her head.

Somewhere in her trunk were blue ribbons that matched the dress, but in her haste she was unable to find them. Giving up, she grabbed her silk bonnet from the dresser as a knock sounded at the door.

Her jaw went slack when she opened the door. Luther stood before her holding a covered plate of food and pot of steaming tea he had carried over from the restaurant. "I thought Miss Blackburn would be hungry." He extended the plate toward her as he entered the room.

"Thank you, Luther. I know Georgette will be most appreciative." She accepted the offering, both pleased and surprised by his thoughtful gesture.

He shrugged. "I just didn't want you rushing me through dinner so that you could get her meal back here. I knew that was what would happen

Now, that's more in his character. What I momentarily mistook for kindness is not kindness at all—merely a continuation of his self-serving attitude. Maura took the platter to Georgette and waited until the new mother was settled with her dinner before returning to the sitting room. He shot her a look of irritation, no doubt upset he'd had to wait an extra few minutes. Maura was tempted to tell him that she needed to change the baby's diaper before they could leave but then thought better of further annoying him.

The restaurant wasn't crowded when they arrived, and Maura requested that they be seated near one of the windows.

"Being able to look outdoors while you're dining is nice, don't you think?" Perhaps they could have a civil conversation while they ate dinner.

He shook his head. "Personally, I don't like people watching me eat."

"So much for civil conversation," she murmured.

He leaned closer. "Excuse me? I didn't hear you."

"Oh, nothing. Were you able to find the preacher?" She'd try another approach.

"Yes, and I might add that he wasn't very happy. Apparently he sat around for several hours waiting on us. He said he'd meet us at the church at eleven o'clock tomorrow and not a minute later. Of course, he expected extra compensation for his inconvenience." His comment bore a hint of anger.

"Of course." She forced a smile. Anything more would likely lead to another disagreement.

He waited, but when she said nothing further, he leaned forward in his chair. "You will be ready on time, won't you?"

"Yes, Luther, I'll be ready on time. You will have the wagon prepared for Georgette and the baby, won't you?" She widened her smile.

"I've already seen to it."

He shot her a smug look that heightened her irritability.

Why is it I allow him to make me so quarrelsome? It seems as though he takes pleasure in making me angry. How can I spend the rest of my life with this cantankerous man?

"The supplies are already loaded, so we'll be able to leave shortly after the ceremony. We'll be taking three wagons."

His comment about three wagons jolted her back to the present. She arched her brows. "Three wagons? How can we do that?"

"I've hired a couple of men. It's got nothing to do with you and Miss Blackburn. I always need at least three wagons to get my supplies back to Placerville."

"Well, it's good to know that at least one thing isn't our fault," she replied, but then was sorry for not holding her tongue.

Morning arrived all too soon, and Maura carefully prepared herself. She had slipped into her chemise when Georgette offered to lace her corset, explaining that she could easily perform the task without leaving the confines of her bed.

"You don't even need this corset. I believe your waist is just as small without it." Georgette looked at her own figure in the mirror and curled her lip in disgust.

"Don't worry, Georgette. You'll be back to a tiny waistline in no time." Maura picked up her brush and pulled it through her hair.

"Let me do your hair." Georgette wiggled toward the edge of her bed. "I'd like to do something for you after all you've done for me."

Maura smiled and handed her the hairbrush. "Let me pull the chair close to the bed so that you can manage."

Patiently Georgette fashioned the thick auburn hair into long, plump curls that would accentuate Maura's coronet headpiece of crystal-beaded flowers and waxed orange blossoms, which held her three-quarter-length veil. "There. It looks beautiful." Georgette handed Maura her brush.

Maura glanced in the mirror. "It looks lovely. Thank you, Georgette." She clasped a hand to her chest when she took note of the time. "I must hurry. I don't want to be late."

She carefully stepped into the silk wedding gown. Ivory silk lace edged the pleated bertha, and the gusseted bodice formed an exaggerated

V-shape just below her waist. Ivory lace accented the long sleeves. She brushed her hand down the front of the dome-shaped shirt that was held in place by whalebone hoops. She slipped her lisle-stockinged feet into a pair of low-heeled ivory shoes decorated with tiny lace bows. In her hand, she carried a small bouquet fashioned from ribbons, lace, and waxed orange blossoms that matched her headpiece.

"Oh, Maura, you look gorgeous. You even thought to make a bouquet before leaving home."

She glanced over her shoulder as she dug deep into one of her trunks. "Actually, my mother made it." She sighed and lifted her head. "I can't seem to find my handkerchief or netted mitts."

"May I help you look?" Georgette scooted toward the side of the bed. Maura shook her head. "Don't you dare get out of that bed." Maura pulled a silk reticule from the depths of the trunk. A sense of relief washed over her as she dangled the drawstrings from her fingers. "Oh, look—my mitts and handkerchief are inside."

She took a fleeting look in the mirror. "This certainly isn't the wedding I imagined when mother and I were spending hours choosing fabric and lace. But I suppose it really doesn't matter."

"Of course it matters. You get married only once, and you're a beautiful bride. I just wish I could be there." Sadness shone in Georgette's eyes.

Maura sighed. "I may be a bride, but it doesn't appear I'll ever be a wife or mother. This whole thing is a mockery, and if I had any sense at all, I'd tell Luther Buchanan that I'm not willing to settle for half a marriage. Please don't waste your time wishing you could observe this travesty. I'd better leave. Mr. Buchanan is quite a stickler for being on time." She leaned down to place a kiss on the baby's soft cheek.

"I've decided to name her Rachel Rebecca Blackburn. I named her after you and Mrs. Windsor. I thought we could call her Becca," Georgette said, her eyes filling with tears. "You can't begin to imagine how much I appreciate all you've done for me. How will I ever repay you?"

"You named your baby after me, and I'll have the pleasure of being with the two of you a while longer. How could I ask for anything more? I think that Rachel Rebecca Blackburn is a beautiful name, and I know Mrs. Windsor would be pleased as punch to have this beautiful child as her namesake. Now, get some rest and enjoy the comfort of that bed while you can. Soon you'll be riding in a wagon and won't think I've done you such a favor. I'll be back in an hour or so." She hurried toward the door, holding the bouquet in her withered left hand.

As expected, Luther was pacing back and forth through the foyer when she arrived. He looked up as she approached him at the end of the hallway.

"You look. . ."

"I look what?" Did he disapprove of her gown?

"Oh, nothing. Hurry or we'll be late. There's a carriage outside. I thought we would look odd walking down the street in our wedding attire." He directed her toward the front door.

The hotel clerk hurried to the front door and held it open. He smiled at Maura. "You make a beautiful bride."

She nodded and smiled in return. "Thank you, sir."

Luther made no comment, but she noticed that his face and neck reddened at the man's flattering remark. *Either he doesn't think I look nice enough to receive a compliment, or he's embarrassed since he failed to mention my appearance.* She lifted her head, and straughtened her shoulders. She wouldn't dwell on the thought.

It was a brief and unremarkable ceremony, each of them pledging to honor and obey the other, followed by the minister pronouncing them man and wife. Maura noticed the preacher's perplexed look when Luther didn't take advantage of his announcement that he could now "kiss the new bride."

Enjoying his apparent embarrassment, Maura couldn't resist making the situation even more difficult for him.

She curved her lips in a winsome smile and looked up at him. "Luther, didn't you hear the minister say that you could kiss me?" She fluttered her lashes and glanced back and forth between Luther and the preacher. She hoped Luther would experience at least an iota of the humiliation she was bearing due to his oafish attitude.

"I'm sorry. A kiss—is that what you're wanting?" Anger flashed in his eyes.

She'd gone too far with her childish behavior. She'd opened her mouth to apologize but before she could say a word, Luther crushed his body against hers. The fullness of his lips covered hers with a reckless intensity that left her breathless. Leaning into him, she felt a passion rise inside that she'd never before experienceed. Her body turned weak, and her knees threatened to buckle at any moment. Without thought, she placed her hand around the nape of his neck and pulled his head toward her. She never wanted this moment to end.

Reaching back, Luther removed her hand and shifted away from her. "I believe one kiss was the requirement." Ice dripped from each word.

Blood rushed to Maura's face, and she wanted to run from the church—as far away from his cruel remark as her legs would carry her. *Seeing me run would really give him cause for laughter.* If only she could quell the fury raging inside her.

With a modicum of dignity remaining, Maura turned and quietly limped toward the doors of the church. *This is my husband, till death do us part. Lord, when will I ever learn to control my tongue?* It would have been much easier had she never experienced the wonder of that impassioned kiss.

Chapter 5

*S*tanding behind the counter of the Buchanan Mercantile Store, Luther watched as Maura laboriously measured and cut fabric for one of the few women who lived at the diggings with her husband. The customer probably hadn't seen another woman for six months, and her mouth had begun moving the minute she eyed Maura and still hadn't stopped. Maura gave the woman a smile every now and then or nodded her head, but the stranger didn't seem to want conversation, merely a set of female ears to hear all the unspoken thoughts she'd stored up in the past six or eight months.

Maura led the woman through the store while pointing out or suggesting different items, all of which the customer agreed to purchase. Walking toward the counter, Maura looked toward Luther.

"Have you sold all of the Christmas nutcrackers?" She looked at the empty space on the shelf behind him.

"I'm afraid so. I didn't expect they'd be so popular, or I'd have ordered more." He hiked a shoulder. "They were all sold just a few days after Thanksgiving."

The woman lowered her head and sighed. "I've been saving a little money each week to buy one." Disappointment laced her words. "I saw some last Christmas when we came to town, and I've been wanting one ever since."

Maura had been listening to the woman talk for almost an hour. It was obvious that she had come searching for a better life and was hungry for an existence beyond the gold diggings. It seemed so pitiful. *Not so much different from my circumstances,* Maura thought. *I came searching for a life beyond what I had, and I've settled for being a wife in name only—while giving my time to work in this store, in addition to caring for the house and tending to his needs.*

She touched the woman's hand. "I'll be back in just a minute. Please don't leave." She gestured to Luther. "You'll need to figure up her bill, while I'm gone."

The woman was outside loading their wagon with her purchases, and Luther was helping her husband carry out some of the heavier provisions from the back of the store when Maura returned a short time later. She stepped to the woman's side and extended a package to the woman.

The woman's eyes grew large as she pulled back the brown paper wrapping. "Oh, I can't take this."

"Of course, you can. I want you to have it. Believe me, it will give me far greater pleasure in your possession than in mine."

"If you really insist." The woman's voice faltered as she reached forward and wrapped her arms around Maura. "Thank you, thank you so much. I don't remember the last time someone did something for me, not expecting anything in return. God love ya." A tear slipped down her cheek as she released Maura from her embrace.

"Look, Jed! Look what she gave me." The woman hurried to her husband on the other side of the wagon.

Maura didn't look toward Luther as the woman proudly displayed the brightly painted nutcracker. "Ain't it just grand?"

"That it is, that it is. I'm not sure why you think having one of those things is so important, but I gotta admit it's good to see you smile." He turned and tipped his hat toward Maura. "Thank you for your kindness, ma'am."

"You're quite welcome. It was my pleasure." Embarrassment seized her as they continued to express their thankfulnes, and she backed toward the mercantile. "I'd better get inside. Have a safe journey."

"Thanks again, and Merry Christmas!" The woman waved with the enthusiasm of a child.

Maura stopped short upon hearing the wish for a merry Christmas. The words were a reminder of what she'd been attempting to forget. Soon it would be Christmas—the deadline for Georgette and Becca to move from Luther's house. Merry Christmas no longer seemed like a joyous greeting but, instead, a quickly approaching ultimatum.

She entered the front door with the woman's wishes still ringing in her ears. Her gaze settled on the fabric that needed to be arranged. on a nearby shelf. She'd folded only a few of the woolen pieces when she felt Luther's breath on the back of her neck.

"Would you like to tell me why you gave that stranger my nutcracker?" His voice was low and steady.

She glanced over her shoulder. "I didn't realize it was your nutcracker. You brought it home shortly after I arrived, and as I recall, you said something to the effect that I might find it either useful or decorative during the holidays."

"That's right. But I didn't mean it was yours to give away. I meant exactly what I said—that it might be useful as a decoration and to crack nuts during the holidays."

"Since I find nutcrackers rather unattractive, I wouldn't want to use one as a decoration, and using one to crack nuts is more for novelty than quick results." She sighed. "I'm sorry we've once again misunderstood each other. It seems that's what we do best."

"Those nutcrackers aren't cheap, you know. And you just gave it to her—a complete stranger." He followed after her when she moved to another shelf.

She shrugged. "Consider the nutcracker payment for the privilege of working in your store."

"Working? You think the little bit you accomplish around here is work? As slow as you move, it's about the same as having no help at all. It took you twice as long to measure and cut that material as it would a normal woman." He fired the words at her with the precision of a talented marksman.

She flinched, but quickly recovered. "Normal woman? First I'm a cripple, and now I'm abnormal. Well, Luther, I'm going to take my crippled, abnormal body out of your store. Since I'm of little assistance, it's good to know I won't be causing you any great loss." She limped toward the door, tears forming in her eyes as she slammed the door behind her.

"Maura! Wait up a minute..."

She heard Luther shout, but chose to ignore him.

"Maura!" The urgency in his tone caused her to stop and turn. He took a few steps toward her. "Since you're going home, why don't you empty those extra trunks so that I can get them out of the house. There's always folks needing steamer trunks. Most likely I'll be able to sell them in short order."

His request left her speechless. As she continued toward home, she silently berated herself for thinking Luther Buchanan would ever apologize for anything. The man was without compassion.

Entering the house quietly, she was careful not to disturb Georgette or Becca. Georgette would question her about why she was home in the middle of the day, and the last thing she wanted to do was answer questions. Although Georgette had been aware of Luther's attitude before the wedding, Maura didn't discuss their ongoing problems with the young woman. Such discussions would be improper now that they were man and wife. When all of them were together, Maura and Luther remained civil, and Georgette was left to assume the two had resolved their earlier problems. Anyone who was around them for any length of time could see they weren't deeply in love, yet they appeared to be adjusting to married life—at least to everyone else.

Hanging her coat on the peg inside their bedroom door, Maura's eyes fell upon Mrs. Windsor's trunks. Except for dusting, she hadn't touched them since Luther placed them along the west wall of the room when she'd arrived. Pulling the wooden rocker from the corner, she sat down and unlatched the largest trunk. Although feeling like an uninvited intruder into Mrs. Windsor's life, she methodically inspected the items and placed them in piles--those she would keep, those Georgette might want, and those that could be given to the needy. The stack to be given away was by far the largest, since Mrs. Windsor's clothing was styled for a woman of differing proportions and age than Maura or Georgette. Just as Maura was completing the chore, Georgette walked into the room carrying Becca.

She glanced at the various mounds. "I thought I heard someone in here. What are you doing?"

"Luther thought I should go through Mrs. Windsor's belongings so that he could move the trunks out of the bedroom. I've picked out some items that may appeal to you. Why don't you look at them, and if you're not interested, I'll put them in that stack." Maura gestured toward the pile to be given away.

"Don't you want any of this?" Georgette held Becca on her lap and began to pick through the jewelry.

"I've already looked at it, and I did choose this one pin as a remembrance, but if you like it, I'll take another. I've also kept her journal. She has a lovely Bible, Georgette. I'd like you to take it. That way you'd have your own for our daily Bible readings and for church services. Mrs. Windsor had marked so many wonderful passages and made little notes along the margins. I think it will become a real blessing to you as you explore God's Word." Maura picked up the Bible and extended it toward Georgette.

"I'd be honored." Georgette took the book and clasped it to her chest.

Shortly after they had met on the ship, Mrs. Windsor had suggested the three of them join together for a daily Bible study. Embarrassed by her lack of spiritual training, Georgette had confided in Maura that her father did not believe in God. Even worse, he had forbidden any members of the family to attend church or study the Bible. It was the one rule all of them had kept.

It hadn't been an easy task convincing Georgette that Mrs. Windsor would view her lack of religious training as a challenge presented by God himself. Maura had carefully explained that Mrs. Windsor would find it a privilege to introduce Georgette to the Lord. And she had. Before her untimely accident, Mrs. Windsor had spent many hours nurturing, explaining, and guiding Georgette in God's Word. Through Mrs. Windsor's loving spirit and God-given patience, she had led Georgette down the path of salvation.

It had been a wonderful experience for Maura to observe the changes that continued to take place in Georgette's life since her introduction to God's grace and love. Much as Becca was thriving in her mother's love and adoration, Georgette was flourishing in God's loving acceptance of her as one of His children.

"Are you thinking about our Bible studies with Mrs. Windsor?"

Maura looked up and smiled. "Yes. She was such a fine lady, and I miss her. It was such a privilege to meet her, but I'm sure the Lord is showering her with rewards as we speak."

"Do you think she would have forgiven me for having a child out of wedlock? I wish now I would have told her, but I was afraid she wouldn't want to associate with me."

"She would have forgiven you, Georgette, and she would have told you that if you seek God's forgiveness, it is there for the taking. Do you remember how excited Mrs. Windsor was when you accepted Jesus?"

Georgette nodded her head.

"Being an unwed mother wouldn't have changed any of that. Jesus knew you were going to have a child, but He didn't turn you away. Surely you know in your heart that Mrs. Windsor would have done no less."

"You're right. She would have been loving and supportive, just like you. I guess it was easier to talk to you since you're younger."

"Perhaps, but if you recall, you didn't tell me, either. I only found out because of your illness. I don't think you were all that trusting of me, either." Maura patted her friend's shoulder. "I'd better finish up before Luther gets home. Do you feel good enough to sit at the table and peel some potatoes?"

"Of course I do. You go ahead and finish up in here. I'll put Becca back in her cradle and have those potatoes ready in no time."

Going through all of Mrs. Windsor's belongings had been more of a chore than she'd expected. She lifted the lid of the remaining trunk, pleased it was the smallest. This one appeared to be filled with Mrs. Windsor's family mementos and knickknacks. Picking up what appeared to be an old leather reticule, Maura was surprised at its weight when she lifted it from the trunk. Placing it on her lap, she struggled to untie the leather thongs that held it tightly closed.

She gasped and then turned toward the kitchen. "Georgette! Come here, right now!"

"What is it? What's wrong?" Georgette rushed into the room still holding a paring knife in her hand.

"Look in here." She held open the leather bag.

The knife dropped from Georgette's hand and clanked on the floor. "Oh, Maura! I wonder how Mrs. Windsor came by all that money."

"She told me she had sold just about everything she owned. She must have owned quite a bit from the looks of what's in this bag."

Georgette shook her head. "What are you going to do with it?"

Maura hesitated. "I'm not sure. She had no family left, so I guess it's ours. We'll split it. You can do what you want with your half, and I'll do what I want with mine."

"It's not half mine. The captain gave the trunks to you—it's yours." Georgette flitted her hand at the leather reticule as she backed away. Her eyes shone with fear.

"Why are you looking so frightened? We didn't steal this. There's nothing to be afraid of." Hearing Luther's footsteps on the wooden porch, she leaned close to Georgette's ear, "Please don't say anything about this in front of Luther, at least not just yet."

Georgette hurried from the bedroom while Maura placed the bag beneath several articles of clothing in the carved oak chiffonier.

"Where's supper?" Luther stepped into the bedroom only moments after she'd closed the doors of the chiffonier.

"I thought you wanted me to clean out these trunks." She nodded toward the open trunks. "I realize a normal person could have finished by now, but as you can see—"

"Stop it. You've made it quite clear that I hurt your feelings. In fact, you always make it abundantly clear when you're unhappy. Which, I might add, is most of the time. I told you the first time I laid eyes on you that I needed a wife to help in the store—someone that could keep up at a regular pace. I'm aware that you try, but there is no way you're ever going to be able to perform as much or as quickly as someone without your..."

He hesitated, apparently knowing whatever word he used would be wrong.

Maura didn't fill in the word for him. "Luther, if I don't meet your needs in the store, perhaps you should hire someone."

"I've been thinking along those lines." He leaned against the doorframe.

She leaned back, startled by his response. "You have?"

He gestured toward the hallway. "Let's go out to the kitchen."

Georgette was busy mixing cornbread when the two of them entered the kitchen. "I'll be done with this in just a minute and then I'll be out of your way."

Luther shook his head and smiled at her. "No, sit down and join us."

Georgette looked at Maura and arched her brows. When Maura dipped her head in a slight nod, the girl sat down.

Luther cleared his throat. "Maura and I have been talking about how difficult it is for her to meet my expectations as a wife. In helping at the store, that is." Both of the women's heads simultaneously jerked up and their mouths dropped open.

"I meant, you know, with her. . .ailment, it's uh. . .harder for her than a. . ." He glanced back and forth, obviously at a loss for words.

A deafening silence followed.

Finally, Luther leaned forward. "What I'm trying to say is that you've been living here with us, Georgette, and although you haven't said anything to me outright, I'm sure you've been feeling you owe us something for all we've done for you and your baby."

"Luther! How dare you say such a rude thing to Georgette! I thought you wanted to talk about hiring someone to work at the store." Just as she had uttered her last word, the realization hit her like a bolt of lightning. "Oh—I see, I see." She began to rise from her chair while Georgette gaze darted back and forth between the two of them.

"Sit down, Maura." Luther's forehead creased into thin, hard lines. "I'm not proposing anything illegal or immoral, so you best just settle down." He paused momentarily and looked at Georgette. "I feel it would be well within your Christian duty, Georgette, to repay us for our kindness by working at the store for a period of time. That way Maura could take care of the house and care for Becca while you're working. It would be much easier on Maura, and I'm sure you'd prefer to make life easier for her." Luther turned toward Maura. "You see? It's not what you expected at all, is it?"

"It's exactly what I expected! I've learned what's most important to you in the short time we've been married, and it's not a wife. What you want is free labor to work in your store, and Georgette is a perfect solution. By creating feelings of guilt and indebtedness, you believe she'll consider herself obligated to work for you. Tell me, Luther, how do you sleep at night?" Maura's stomach clenched. In the past, she'd hidden their marital discord from Georgette. She silently chided herself for airing marital differences in front of the girl.

Luther's lip curled. "Don't make me out to be the villain. If you'd been honest with me in the beginning, none of this would have happened."

"You're right, Luther. What I did was misleading and dishonest, and if I had it to do over again, I'd certainly change things. But before there are any decisions made, I think all three of us need to think and pray on this matter. It's not a decision that should be made in haste," she said, her voice quiet and subdued, a stark contrast to her earlier diatribe.

"I don't know what to say." Georgette's eyes glistened as she jumped up from the table and rushed from the room.

Maura hadn't returned to work in the store since the evening that Luther suggested Georgette replace her. During the following days, she and Georgette had spent much time in prayer, but only one answer had come to them. Although Maura had doubts, she had stepped out in faith when she'd boarded the ship in Boston. She had believed coming to California to marry Luther had been an answer to prayer.

"I'm going to talk to Luther tonight, Georgette." Maura forced a weak smile. "He's insisting upon an answer, and we're as ready as we can be under the circumstances."

"If you're sure. I don't want God holding me accountable for anything that's not in His will."

"I'm the one who will be held accountable for my own actions, Georgette. You haven't influenced me, and I truly believe that God's hand is at work in this. After dinner, why don't you take Becca into your bedroom while I talk to Luther in the kitchen."

Before Georgette could reply, Luther strode in the front door. After grace had been offered, the only conversation at the dinner table was the little that was needed to get through the meal.

Georgette rapidly downed her food and gulped a glass of milk, then rose from the table. "Sorry to rush off, but I need to check on Becca." She hurried from the room without waiting for a response.

Luther glanced after her. "She sure seems skittish tonight."

Maura placed her fork on her plate and looked him in the eyes. "We need to talk."

"Good, it's about time. Why don't you pour me another cup of coffee, and I'll have a big slice of that apple pie while we talk." He gestured toward the pie safe.

Maura complied with his requests, then seated herself across from him. "I think you'd agree that this is not the marriage either of us intended."

"Don't even start with that kind of talk. I don't hold with divorce, and I'll not be hearing of it. Is that the solution you've come up with after two weeks of praying?" He glowered at her.

She wished that just once he wouldn't interrupt her. "No, it isn't. As I said, this isn't the marriage either of us planned, and I don't think it's what God wants for us, either. I've prayed steadfastly for an answer and believe I've received one. I don't intend ever to speak of divorce, Luther, but I believe it would be best if we separated for a time. What I plan to do is move out of your house, but I'll remain here in town. I'm hopeful that one day soon we will be able to resolve our differences and begin our married life anew. Until then, I expect nothing from you and will take only the belongings I brought with me from Boston. I'll be leaving tomorrow, and, of course, Georgette and Becca will be moving at the same time."

He sat looking at her as though she hadn't spoken. After what seemed an eternity, he lifted his cup and took a drink of coffee. Carefully placing the cup on the table, he looked directly into her eyes.

"Just how do you and Georgette plan on supporting yourselves and Becca? Or am I allowed to ask?"

"We'll be just fine, Luther. I'm much more capable than you think, but be assured that I truly want to make our marriage work. I just don't think it's possible right now."

"You avoided answering my question, so I guess that means it's none of my business. What if I told you I forbid you to leave—that you are my wife and you'll do as I say?"

She looked up and met his gaze. "If you went so far as to say that, most likely I would stay. But you're not going to forbid me, are you, Luther?"

"No, I'm not going to forbid you. In fact, I'm not even going to ask you to stay. But when you've had your fill of trying to make it on your own, you need not ask permission to move back in. The house will be here, I'll be here, and your place will always remain here."

"Why, Luther?" A lump lodged in her throat.

"I committed myself to this marriage. You're my wife, and your place is with me."

"Thank you for your honesty." An overwhelming and undeniable sadness filled her. His proclamation revealed what she already knew in her heart. The marriage was a contractual bargain he must fulfill—not out of love and affection for her, but out of duty to God's Word.

Chapter 6

The morning dawned crisp and cool with large puffy clouds lazily floating across a clear blue sky. Luther had been gone only a short time when a wagon pulled by two large draft horses drew in front of the house. Two men from the church loaded the trunks and belongings of the women and then urged the horses forward with a familiar "Giddyup."

Their destination was a house previously owned by Frank Millard, a banker who had become ill and died a short time after his arrival in Placerville. Maura had been told that his family moved back East and the house had remained vacant for almost six months. But now it belonged to Georgette and Maura, thanks to a measure of the money found in Mrs. Windsor's trunk.

The women had spent a goodly portion of their time during the past week cleaning the house and preparing a list of necessities. It had been exciting, and Maura had been surprised that Luther hadn't gotten wind of their activities.

"There you are, ladies." The younger of the two church menbers announced while placing a trunk in the east bedroom. "That's the last of it. Looks a little sparse, but I'm certain it won't take long before you'll have everything you need."

"I'm sure we'll manage just fine for now, but we'll be glad when you've completed the rest of our furniture."

Michael Blanchard was an excellent carpenter and furniture maker. Georgette had approached him after church last Sunday with their order, and he had worked feverishly to complete several small items. Rather sheepishly, he'd offered to loan them some of his own furniture in exchange for home-cooked meals. Maura suspected the handsome young man was more than a little interested in Georgette, although she seemed oblivious to his overtures.

Georgette gestured toward the dinner table. Two place settings and their dinner awaited. "Well, what do you think?"

Maura offered a smile and sat down. "I think it's going to be fine." She didn't want to admit she would miss Luther's presence at the table.

When she added nothing further, Georgette sat down and spread her napkin across her lap. "Do you really think we can be ready to open by the first of the year?"

"What? Oh yes, at least the restaurant. If Michael can complete all the tables and chairs, we can sew the curtains and tablecloths. It won't matter that the serving dishes don't match. Most of our customers will be single men who care more about the quality and quantity of their food. I doubt they'll notice whether their dinnerware matches."

Georgette wriggled in her chair like a child on the first day of school. "It's almost too exciting to believe. I'm half owner of a business."

"It won't seem so difficult to believe when we're cooking, washing dishes, and waiting tables." Maura sighed. "I think it's probably a good thing we won't be opening the rooming house part of our business until later."

Maura bowed her head and offered a prayer of thanks for their food and the means to purchase their new home. The moment she'd said amen, Georgette spooned a helping of green beans onto her plate and passed them to Maura. "Maybe it won't seem so overwhelming by taking on one boarder at a time. Michael said he'd finish the furniture for the bedrooms one by one, instead of doing all the beds and then all the washstands. He mentioned we might be taking on too much, but I think the idea of making ten bedsteads before moving along to something else had seemed daunting."

"I'm sure he prefers a little variety in his work." Maura grinned. "Sounds like the two of you have been chatting a good deal lately."

"Only about business." Georgette bristled and shook her head.

"I was only teasing, Georgette. Besides, Michael is a fine young man who seems to be devout in his Christian beliefs. Furthermore, he's a hard worker, and I certainly admire his ability to withstand the gold fever that plagues the majority of the people in this area."

Georgette nodded. "He is a nice man, but I've had enough experience with men for now. Besides, I think Becca and our business will be more than enough to keep me occupied."

Later that afternoon, Maura left the house and walked the short distance to Luther's store. They needed fabric to make tablecloths and curtains for the restaurant, and Georgette had made it abundantly clear she wanted Maura to make the choice. Maura's apprehension mounted as she neared the store. Luther hadn't attempted to contact her since she'd moved, so there was no way to judge how he might react to her visit. A gust of wind caught her woolen cloak, and she grasped the flap before entering the store. The familiar tinkling of the bell and the warmth from the stove seemed almost welcoming as she stepped inside. Except for two men inspecting the supplies, the store appeared empty.

Removing her cape and hanging it on the peg, she walked to the yard goods and automatically began straightening the shelves.

A middle-aged man tapped Maura's shoulder. "Excuse me, ma'am, but could you possibly help us? The owner said he'd be back shortly, but he's helping someone out in back."

"I can try." Maura smiled at the man. "What is it you're looking for?"

"We've just arrived and need to purchase supplies before we go to find our gold." The man tucked his thumbs behind his suspenders and spoke with assurance. He obviously thought gold was sitting on top of the ground awaiting his arrival. "Placerville appears to be a quiet little town. I heard this place used to be called Hangtown. Is that true?"

"I haven't been here long myself, but I'm told that story is true. Originally the town was called Dry Diggings, but my husband told me that back in 1849 three men were caught red-handed attempting to rob and murder a gold rusher. It seems most of the miners were drunk and a kind of vigilante attitude overtook the mob. When someone asked the crowd what should be done with the three perpetrators, the crowd yelled, 'Hang them!' It turned into a chant and shortly thereafter the three men were hanged. After that, the town became known as Hangtown. Just last year, the town was renamed Placerville." They followed her throughout the store while she continued to select items for them.

One of the men stopped to examine a shovel. "Someone told me they serve something called 'Hangtown Fry' around here. What's that?"

Maura smiled, recalling that she and Georgette had decided they wouldn't put "Hangtown Fry" on their menu when the restaurant opened. However, when Michael Blanchard overheard their discussion, he'd told them it was a mistake.

"People come here for the first time and they want to try 'Hangtown Fry.' At least put it on the menu and if you see I'm wrong. You can always remove it," Michael had said. He'd quickly convinced them his advice was sound.

"Do you know what it is?" the other man asked when she hadn't immediately answered.

She nodded. "Oh, yes. It's a fried mixture of oysters, eggs, and bacon."

"Is there a story behind that, too?" The man picked up the shovel and carried it with him.

"Yes." She smiled. "It appears there's a story behind most things around here. Would you like to hear it?"

They nodded their heads. "Sure."

"It seems there was a hungry miner who had struck gold and came to town fresh from his claim and went to the hotel. Apparently he was feeling quite prosperous and asked for the most expensive meal the cook could prepare. He was told the most expensive item was oysters, followed by eggs. After thinking for a moment, he told the waiter to fry a mess of both and throw in some bacon. It's been a popular dish in these parts ever since."

One of the men patted his belly. "We'll have to try some of that after we strike it rich."

"You be sure and do that. I think I've gathered most of the items you'll need. Are you going to share a pan and rocker? They're rather expensive."

"I guess we'll just take one to start. What else have you put together for us?" The men didn't appear to have much knowledge about what they needed or what the future might hold for them, but even if she attempted to tell them, they would doubt her. Every man who entered the store thought he was going to strike it rich.

"You'll need beans, pork and bully beef, coffee, pick and shovel, bucket, frying pan and eating utensils. Do you have knives and sidearms?"

Both of them nodded affirmatively to that question.

"I don't know if you'll be interested in chewing tobacco, whiskey, or playing cards. A lot of the men request those items, although I'd advise against all of them."

Before they'd had an opportunity to answer, Luther walked in the back door. "Sorry to keep you waiting so long, gentlemen." He stopped short when he noticed Maura.

"We've been doing just fine. Your wife has kept us entertained while gathering our supplies." One of the men gestured toward Maura.

"I'll let you finish up, Luther. I wanted to check some of the fabric for tablecloths and curtains." She hurried toward the shelves of fabric and took a position where she could see Luther.

Luther turned his attention to the men. "Let's see what you've got here. Appears she's just about got you outfitted. Will you be needing any weapons, ammunition, or whiskey?"

The younger man stepped forward. "Don't think we'd better be spending what little money we've got left on whiskey, but I'd like a pouch of chewing tobacco and some playing cards."

Once Luther and the men had loaded all of the supplies into the wagon, they returned to the store. Maura was measuring and cutting the fabric she'd decided upon. Although she could feel Luther's eyes on her as he calculated the men's purchases, neither of them said a word.

"Thanks for your help, ma'am," one of them called out to Maura.

"And for the fine storytelling, too," the other added.

"You're more than welcome. Best of luck to both of you. Stop by again when you need supplies," she answered, giving them a wide smile.

Maura had just completed folding the last piece of material when Luther returned.

"I really appreciate your help with those customers." His tone was warmer than usual.

"You're welcome. I think I've tallied this correctly." She withdrew several coins from her reticule and counted out what she owed him.

He pushed the coins back across the counter. "You don't need to pay for it."

"Yes, Luther, I do need to pay for it. You'll need to replenish your stock, and that costs money. I promise to allow you the same privilege if you eat a meal in our restaurant." She smiled and gently pushed the coins back toward him.

"No free meals, huh?" His lips curved in a lopsided grin.

"I'm afraid not. At least not until we see if we can make a go of it."

"There's no doubt in my mind you'll make a go of it. There's plenty of hungry men in these parts, and once they've tasted your cooking, the word will spread like wildfire."

Maura felt a blush rise in her cheeks. It was the first time he had ever acknowledged she was a good cook. Not that he hadn't eaten with a hearty appetite, for he'd surely done that. But it was the first compliment she'd received from him. Although she wasn't sure why, it pleased her immensely.

He gestured toward the other side of the store as she turned toward the doors. "I've got the coffee on. Would you care for a cup?"

She crossed the short distance and retrieved her cloak from the peg. "Thanks, but I'd better be getting back. We plan to get started on our sewing this evening."

Luther arched his brows. "Some other time then?"

The anticipation in his voice that surprised her and she gave a slight nod. "Yes, some other time."

While Maura and Georgette stitched curtains several hours later, Maura recounted what had happened at the mercantile earlier in the day. Georgette plunged her needle into the fabric, and hiked a shoulder. "I think he realizes what a prize he lost."

"I doubt he'd ever think of me as a prize. He probably has just come to the realization that although I can't move as quickly as others, I did provide him a measure of assistance. At least he could leave the store for short periods of time when I was there." Maura lifted one of the curtains to the dining room window. "What do you think?"

"They're going to be ideal." Georgette bobbed her head. "I'm glad you chose this heavy lace fabric. I wasn't sure when I first saw it, but it's exactly what we need."

Maura returned to her chair and picked up her needle and thread. "I think dark green tassels on the curtains, along with the dark green tablecloths, will set off the oak furniture to perfection."

"I agree. You made an excellent choice." Georgette hesitated a moment. "Michael Blanchard asked me if I would attend a gathering at the minister's house Friday night."

The news didn't surprise Maura. Of late, Michael had been having difficulty hiding his interest in Georgette. "How exciting. You told him you'd go, didn't you?"

"No. I told him I wasn't interested in any type of courtship."

Maura gasped. "Georgette! Why did you say that? He's been so kind to us, and he's a nice man."

She shrugged and looked away. "I told you a few days ago that I'm not interested in men right now. I have Becca and you and our new business venture."

"You're also entitled to a little fun in your life. Just because he occasionally escorts you doesn't mean that you're obligated to enter into a courtship. So long as he knows all you're interested in is friendship, what's the harm?"

"I'm a mother, and I need to be with Becca. What will I say if he asks about my circumstances?"

"Tell him in a kind manner that you don't care to discuss your personal business, and I'm sure he'll honor your wishes. As to needing to be with Becca, you'd be gone only three or four hours. Becca won't even know you've left the house, and I hope you would trust me to care for her."

Georgette frowned. "I wouldn't feel right leaving you alone, especially during the holiday season. It seems improper for me to go out enjoying myself while you would be here caring for my baby."

"I want you to go and have some fun, Georgette. Tell Michael you'll go as long as he doesn't interpret your acceptance as anything more than friendship."

"Well...if you insist. It really does sound like fun." Georgette exhaled a sigh.

"Good. Now, tell me what they've planned for the evening."

Georgette's eyes shown with excitement. "We're going to have a taffy pull and make popcorn. Then later everyone will gather around the piano and sing carols. Michael said that he went last year and it was great fun."

"It sounds like a wonderful holiday celebration. I'm glad you've agreed to attend."

Georgette glanced toward the hallway. "It appears we've reached a good stopping point for this evening, and I think I hear Becca's familiar cry."

"You go ahead. I'll finish folding these, and then I'll be going to bed, also."

"You're such a wonderful person, Maura. I thank God every day for sending you into my life," Georgette leaned down and hugged Maura.

Maura returned the hug and then gestured toward the bedroom. "Thank you, Georgette. You and Becca have been a blessing to me also, and the three of us are going to be just fine. Hurry now and feed your baby before she thinks you've deserted her."

During the following days, the women fell into a routine of caring for Becca, cleaning, sewing, and testing the recipes they would place on their menu, both the regular fare and the daily specials they wanted to offer. It proved to be great fun, although several of the dishes had ended up as dinner for the large tan dog who had recently adopted them and now made his home outside in their backyard. They had named him Waffles, partly because of his pale brown coloring, but mainly because the first meal he'd received had been a batch of burned waffles they'd thrown out the back door. He'd eaten every bite, and the women had been calling him Waffles ever since. He'd follow them whenever they didn't scold and send him back home. But the dog seemed particularly protective of Becca. His tail would wag continuously when Georgette carried the baby outdoors, and if Becca cried, the dog would yelp until she was quieted. If a stranger approached the back door or he thought anything unseemly was occurring near the house, he barked profusely until Maura or Georgette assured him everything was all right.

Maura and Georgette had discussed the possibility that Waffles might present some problems once they opened the restaurant, but for now his presence was welcome.

When Friday evening arrived, Maura eagerly assisted Georgette as she prepared for the party. The dress she had chosen was a cherry red tissue silk with a bertha of ivory lace-bordered gauze. The cuffs and skirt were embroidered in a deep green diamond design, and Georgette fashioned her hair into a chignon of pale blond curls fastened by a deep green ribbon and small red roses. She was a beautiful young lady, and the excitement of an evening out had added a touch of color to her cheeks.

When a knock sounded at the front door, Georgette turned to Maura. "Are you sure you don't mind staying with Becca?"

"For the third time, it is my pleasure to take care of Becca." Maura gestured toward the front porch. "I'd better answer the door before Waffles wakens the baby." Maura hurried down the hallway and opened the door. Waffles was stationed between Michael and the entrance. "Waffles! Stop that barking before you wake up the baby! You know Michael. Maura waved Michael forward. "I'm sorry for Waffles's greeting, but at least he didn't jump on you and ruin your suit. Georgette will be down in just a moment."

At the sound of footsteps, Michael turned and watched Georgette come down the staircase and into the foyer.

"You look—" but he stopped midsentence, obviously recalling Georgette's warning that she didn't want a suitor. "—very friendly," he finished.

All three of them burst into laughter. "Thank you, Michael. You look very friendly also." Georgette giggled.

Michael held her brown velvet-trimmed cloak as Georgette slipped her arms inside. Looking into the hallway mirror, she carefully tied the matching velvet bonnet, then placed a kiss on Becca's forehead. Georgette and Michael bid Maura good-bye and headed off toward the Wilsons'. Maura watched through the opalescent glass window until they were out of sight and then placed the sleeping baby in her cradle. Pulling her rocking chair closer to the fireplace, she began to sew the last set of curtains for the dining room.

Chapter 7

Georgette and Michael made a most striking couple, although there was little competition. In fact, she and Mrs. Wilson were the sum total of the women at the gathering. Mrs. Wilson divulged that she'd invited Luther, hopeful that he'd bring Maura, but he had politely declined. In a town the size of Placerville there were few women, and the remainder who had been invited were unable to attend for one reason or another.

The older woman's lips tightened as she surveyed the room. "I probably waited until too close to Christmas. Next year I'll have it earlier."

There was, however, no shortage of male guests. It seemed that the single men of the church were more than available to enjoy an evening of homespun holiday festivity.

"Your house looks lovely, and the tree is quite beautiful." The branches were void of any ornamentation.

"Thank you, Georgette. I thought we'd make a few decorations this evening and decorate the tree if our guests wanted to help. Most of the men don't have an opportunity to participate in the familiar holiday activities they were accustomed to during childhood, so I thought they might find it fun. Mr. Wilson said he doubted they'd want to participate." Concern shone in the older woman's eyes.

"I don't know about the men, but it sounds like fun to me." Georgette beamed at the woman and hoped her words would offer a bit of encouragement.

Mrs. Wilson motioned to her husband. "Charles, since you and the men are gathered at the fireplace anyway, why don't you begin making some popcorn? When it has cooled—and if you gentlemen haven't eaten all of it—we'll string some for the tree."

It was obvious that Edith Wilson was an organizer. Pulling out strips of wrapping paper that she had painted, she set several of the men to work making chains. Next she produced a large bowl of cranberries to be strung and a large container of gingerbread men and stars that she had baked the day before. Another container held cornucopias she'd made out of an old box. They'd been decorated with ribbon, lace, and velvet scraps, ending up as pretty ornaments. Yet another box contained candle holders that her father had hammered out of tin and given to her for her first Christmas tree after she'd been married.

"I've used them every year. Now that Papa's dead, they mean even more to me." Mrs. Wilson cradled one of the candle holders close to her heart.

I wonder what she'd think of my father's last gift to me? A one-way ticket out of his life. Much easier than dealing with the embarrassment of a daughter who was pregnant out of wedlock.

"How did you happen to come to Placerville?"

Georgette jerked to attention. It was as if the older woman had been reading her thoughts. She hesitated and before she could speak, Michael came up behind her. "I'm here for a lesson on how to get the string through these gingerbread men." He sat down beside her with a gingerbread man in one hand and a string in the other.

"How did you come to choose that particular task?"

"I figured I'd get to eat the ones I break." He gave her a sheepish grin.

"I believe there must be a small part of little boys that never quite turns into men." Mrs. Wilson chuckled. "You instruct him, Georgette, while I see if there's going to be any popcorn left to string for the tree."

"Are you having a pleasant time?" Michael watched as Georgette used her needle to enlarge the hole Mrs. Wilson had made while baking the cookies. Carefully she threaded the string through the hole and tied it in a knot.

"Yes, I'm having a wonderful time." She handed him a needle and piece of string. "Now, let's see if you learned anything,"

When his first attempt resulted in a decapitated gingerbread man, she giggled. "You can't push quite that hard."

"While I'm eating this one, perhaps you should give me another lesson."

Georgette shook her head and laughed. *It feels so good to laugh over such a simple thing as a broken cookie.* She deftly used the needle to enlarge the holes in ten of the cookies.

When she continued, Michael leaned toward her. "Aren't you going to leave any for me?"

She nodded toward one of the cookies. "I think your talents may run in other directions. Why don't you see if you can pull the string through the top without breaking any more"

"I think this is merely a plot to keep me from eating the cookies."

He'd whispered loudly enough for the entire group to hear his lament. Although they laughed along with him, none of them offered him any compassion. They were busy stringing popcorn and attaching the candle holders with only each other for company. No doubt it was difficult to sympathize with the only unmarried man in the room who had escorted a beautiful woman to the party.

When they had finished decorating the tree, the group moved into the kitchen to begin pulling the taffy that Edith had made and placed on the table to cool just a bit.

"Georgette, put this apron over your dress. I don't want this taffy pull to be the cause of staining that beautiful gown." Mrs. Wilson held a sateen apron with ribbon embroidery.

"This apron is as pretty as my dress, Mrs. Wilson. I don't think I want to chance staining it, either. Don't you have an old one I won't worry about?"

"Of course she does." Mr. Wilson removed a faded cambric apron from a hook near the back door.

"Charles! Don't offer her that old apron."

"Oh, we don't need to put on airs. Georgette will be just as happy in this old apron as your fancy holiday finery." He stopped beside his wife and pecked her on the cheek.

"He's right, Mrs. Wilson. Now I feel like I'm ready to get to work on that taffy."

Georgette wasn't sure why, but by the time they had finished the candy, a nagging uneasiness had begun to plague her.

She removed Mrs. Wilson's apron and hung it back on the hook. "I think I should leave now that we've finished the candy."

"Oh, please don't go so early. We're going to light the candles on the tree and sing carols. The decorations look so pretty, and once we light the candles, there's a whole different atmosphere. I'm sure Maura is delighted to have some time with the baby; in fact, I know she'd want you to stay for the very best part of the evening." Mrs. Wilson curled her lips into a tiny pout. "Besides, I've made a chestnut pudding that you haven't even tasted."

Georgette glanced at Michael and arched her brows.

"It's up to you. I'd like to have you stay and enjoy yourself, but if you're feeling anxious, we'll leave whenever you're ready."

She had hoped he would make the decision for her. Obviously he was wise for his years and realized that if he said they should stay while something was amiss at home, she'd hold it against him. On the other hand, if he said they should leave and everything was fine at home, it would be his fault that she missed the most meaningful portion of the evening.

Georgette sighed. "I guess I'm just being silly since this is my first time away from Becca for more than an hour."

"So you'll stay?" Mrs. Wilson clapped her hands like a small child.

A sudden rush of warmth enveloped Georgette when she realized how much she was actually wanted. "Yes, I'll stay."

Before she could change her mind, Edith decided they should have dessert and then sing carols before returning home. She carried a beautiful silver tray bearing her glazed chestnut pudding into the dining room and was greeted by the expected ohs and ahs of all in attendance. The pudding had been baked in a fluted mold and inverted on the platter and was now covered with a delectable-looking punch sauce and surrounded by waxed holly leaves and berries.

"My sister sent me the chestnuts from back East. I wrote her last spring telling her I longed to have our mother's famous chestnut pudding for Christmas, and low and behold, a box arrived just last week. I had nearly given up on receiving them." Mrs. Wilson glanced around the group of gathered guests as she dished the pudding onto china dessert dishes.

One of the men waved his spoon in the air. "It tastes even better than it looks."

Georgette licked her lips after trying a bite of the delicious confection. "I don't believe I've ever heard of chestnut pudding, Edith, but it is luscious. Perhaps you'd be willing to share your recipe with me, and if we're fortunate enough to find a supply of chestnuts, we could serve it at the restaurant."

Edith beamed at the idea. "First you boil the chestnuts just long enough to peel them easily," she began. "Once you've gotten them peeled, you want to cook them in milk—not a lot of milk—just barely enough to cover the chestnuts, and you must be sure to add half a cinnamon stick to the milk. . ."

Her husband tapped the side of his dessert dish with his spoon. "Perhaps it would be easier for Georgette to remember the recipe if you'd write it down for her tomorrow." He nodded toward the piano. "Why don't we move over to the piano, and I'll light the candles while the rest of you begin singing?"

"How silly of me, prattling on like that. The men don't want to hear me recite a recipe, but I'll be sure to write it out for you." She looped arms with Georgette as the two of them walked toward the piano.

Mrs. Wilson sat down at the piano and struck the opening chords to "O Little Town of Bethlehem." Soon all of them were singing while Mr. Wilson carefully lit the candles. "Silent Night" was followed by "We Three Kings" and "Joy to the World."

A short time later, Georgette lightly nudged Michael. "I really must be leaving. The tree is so pretty and it's been such a joyous evening, but it's getting late."

Without saying a word, Michael moved from her side, gathered her cloak and bonnet and brought them to her, while the others continued singing.

"Must you leave us?" Mr. Wilson drew near as Georgette was tying her bonnet.

"I must get home, but it's been one of the most wonderful nights of my life." Impulsively, she walked to where Edith sat on the piano stool and gave her a hug. "Thank you, Edith, for making me so welcome in your home."

"It was my pleasure." She gestured to the men. "We'll sing you out the door." She'd struck the first chords of "God Rest Ye Merry Gentlemen" when a pounding sounded at the front door.

Luther worked late Friday night, just as he had most nights since Maura had moved out. There were a few town folks that were doing a bit of Christmas shopping or buying necessities to make their gifts while others would come in later in the day when their other chores were completed. Some of the miners who were in town for supplies or just to get drunk came to the store whether it was day or evening. If they saw so much as a lantern burning, they figured the store was open.

After Luther and Maura had married, she had been responsible for completing the paperwork and performing the accounting for the mercantile each evening after dinner. However, when she moved out, Luther was once again required to assume these thankless tasks. Instead of doing the paperwork after returning home, he preferred to work on it at the store as he had time between customers and stocking the shelves. Sometimes, on nights like tonight, when most of the decent town folk were at home preparing for Christmas or over at the Wilsons' enjoying a holiday gathering, he'd work late and finish up before returning home for the night.

I probably should have asked Maura, he thought to himself as he tallied a column of figures, but knew he didn't want to take the chance of being rejected. He'd attended the Wilsons' annual gathering every year since he'd arrived in Placerville, but it was different this year. He was afraid someone might question him about his marriage if he were in a more relaxed setting. Luther was all business while in his store, and people immediately sensed that about him. They never attempted to probe into his personal life while he was working, and he liked it that way. In fact, he didn't want people delving into his personal affairs at any time, but he knew in a small town that was impossible.

It was ten-thirty when he finally decided to close the store and make the brief walk home. However, he had walked only a short distance when he heard the eerie howling of a dog in the distance. It stopped and then began again. As he continued down the crooked street, he glanced toward the house that Maura and Georgette had purchased. It had become a habit. He despised himself for it, but hard as he tried, he couldn't keep from looking toward their new home each time he left the store.

There appeared to be an oil lamp burning, but that wasn't unusual. Maura's probably still sewing on her tablecloths and curtains, he thought. He had learned that she was an ambitious woman, rising early and staying up at night until all of her chores were done. Probably learned that at an early age, what with it taking her longer to do things, he reflected.

A sudden movement on the front porch caught his eye as he turned toward the house one last time. Straining his eyes, he attempted to make out the figure stirring about on the front porch. And then it came to him. The howling was Waffles, the stray dog that had attached himself to the women shortly after they'd moved into the house, and he was pacing back and forth on the front porch.

Luther quickened his pace and then broke into a run toward the house. As he drew closer, he could see that the glass in the front door had been smashed and the door was now standing ajar, but there was no sign of Maura or Georgette. As he ran up the first two steps, Waffles bared his teeth and emitted a low guttural snarl.

Great! Luther thought. *How am I supposed to get past this dog and see if anything's wrong?* After several attempts at coaxing the dog into allowing him past, he became completely exasperated.

"Waffles, sit!"

Immediately the dog retreated into a sitting position and allowed him to enter the house. Becca was crying, and as soon as Luther entered the house, Waffles ran ahead of him to the bedroom. The dog seemed to sense Luther would help. Spotting Becca in her cradle, Luther quickly judged the infant appeared to be in no apparent danger. Except for the cold air that had been drifting in through the front door, nothing seemed out of order. Luther grabbed a quilt from Georgette's bed and placed it around the baby. That would have to do until he could find Maura.

"Where is she?" He looked at the dog, his unease rising to new heights.

Luther startled when the dog took off running up the stairs toward one of the bedrooms. Following Waffles's lead, he raced up the steps but momentarily stopped in the doorway, overcome by the sight. The room had been completely ransacked. Maura was on the floor, with a small pool of blood by her head.

Stooping down, he carefully lifted her onto the bed and felt for a pulse. Her breathing seemed shallow, but she was alive. *Where is Georgette?* The two women were seldom far apart.

"Is Georgette here?" The dog tipped its head to the side and looked up at him. Luther silently chided himself. Had he expected the dog to answer?

Waffles didn't move from Maura's side, a likely sign no one else was in the house. And then he remembered the Wilsons' party. Michael Blanchard had mentioned that he would like to ask Georgette to the party. Afraid to leave and yet not sure when Georgette would return, Luther mentally weighed his options.

"I guess you're it." He pointed at the dog and used a commanding voice. "Stay!" He hoped the animal would remain with Maura long enough for him to find Georgette. Relieved when Waffles didn't rise to follow him, he hurried downstairs. Scooping up the baby, he wrapped the heavy quilt around her for protection and headed toward the Wilsons' parsonage.

He could hear the strains of "God Rest Ye Merry Gentlemen" as he approached the house and banged on the front door.

Chapter 8

*L*uther! What's happened? What's wrong with the baby?" Panic seized Georgette when she caught sight of Luther carrying Becca in his arms. "Where's Maura?"

"Give him a chance to answer." Michael gently touched her arm.

Luther thrust Becaa into Georgette's open arms. "There's no time to explain—Maura needs a doctor. I've got to return to the house. I left her there alone. One of you men go for Doc Simmons—and tell him to hurry!"

After descending the steps, Luther stopped and turned. "The baby appears to be fine, but you might want to remain here with Mrs. Wilson for a while."

Georgette clasped the baby tight to her chest. "I think I should go back to the house." Georgette looked at Michael and Mrs. Wilson for confirmation.

Mrs. Wilson shook her head. "It's safer for you and the baby to remain here, my dear, at least until we find out what's going on."

"That's just it! I can't stand not knowing how Maura is and if there's some way I could be helping her." The baby whimpered and then burst into a lusty cry.

"Michael, why don't you go to the house and check on the situation? By the time Georgette has finished feeding the baby, you should be back with a report for us." Mrs. Wilson waved the young man toward the door.

"Oh, that's a wonderful idea, Edith!" Georgette bobbed her head. "Would you do that for me, Michael?"

"Of course, he will." Edith didn't give the young man an opportunity to answer. Instead, she grasped his arm and guided him toward the door. Once they were on the front porch, Mrs. Wilson leaned close. "If the news is bad, don't tell her all the details immediately. We'll need to soften the blow a bit so that she doesn't become overly anxious."

Michael nodded his head in understanding and pulled his coat tightly around him as he hurried away.

Georgette lifted the heavy quilt from around the infant. "Becca is soaking wet."

"Don't worry, dear. I have some soft white tea towels. You can use one of those. Becca will never know the difference." Edith hurried to the kitchen and returned with a substitute diaper.

"Thank you, Mrs. Wilson." Georgette glanced at the woman, but her thoughts remained on Maura's condition.

Edith peered over Georgette's shoulder. "Oh, look—her wrapper is soaked, too. Let me see what I can find."

The older woman hurried off and soon reappeared with two pieces of soft flannel and a blanket.

She handed the items to Georgette. "I'm afraid I don't have much in the way of baby clothes, but why don't you wrap her tightly in these pieces of flannel? Then we can use the larger blanket to keep her snug."

In spite of her concern, Georgette offered the older woman a weak smile. Edith was fluttering about like a mother hen taking care of a brood of chicks.

Edith arched her brows. "Did I say something amusing?"

"No, I was just watching you scurry about helping me. I'm so appreciative of your kindness." Georgette completed changing the baby's diaper and swaddled her in the flannel fabric. "Do you think it's a good sign that Michael hasn't returned yet?"

"He hasn't been gone more than twenty minutes, dear. You must remember that until Maura is able to talk, there won't be much to tell. It may take the doctor a while before he can give us any kind of prognosis. I know you feel very helpless right now, and so do I. But the two of us can do the most important thing of all. We can pray."

And pray they did! From the moment Edith made the pronouncement until they heard a stirring at the front door.

Charles Wilson led Michael and two of the other men into the parlor, all of them sober-faced.

"Tell me!" Georgette jumped up from her chair, her stomach clenching in a tight knot. "Tell me that she's all right, please."

"She's alive, but she hasn't regained consciousness just yet." Michael moved to Georgette's side. "The doctor said there was only superficial bleeding, but he couldn't be sure that there wasn't some internal bleeding or trauma to the brain itself. It appeared that she was struck with some type of blunt instrument, and we don't know how long she was lying there unconscious."

Mrs. Wilson frowned. "Michael! There's no need to go into all the unpleasant details. It will only cause Georgette to become overly anxious."

Michael's face turned crimson at her reproach; he looked toward

Georgette, his eyes revealing deep remorse.

Mr. Wilson shook his head. "She's not a wilting flower, Edith. If anyone has a need—in fact a right—to know what is going on, it's Georgette. I think she'd be more upset at Michael for withholding information from her, wouldn't you, child?" The pastor looked toward Georgette, obviously seeking her confirmation.

Georgette was torn. She understood both the pastor and his wife were trying to protect her. Having to side with either of them would prove uncomfortable.

After a quick glance at the older couple, Georgette attempted to form a diplomatic response. She turned toward Mrs. Wilson. "I think it's probably best that I know the full extent of Maura's injuries and what awaits me when I return home. Hearing the news, although upsetting, is easier to bear while I am here surrounded by such loving friends."

Mrs. Wilson patted her hand. "Well, of course, dear. I was just afraid that if you became too upset, Becca would sense it and become fretful. But I see you are of a stronger character than I thought."

Georgette smiled at the older woman before turning to Michael. "She's going to need me there to care for her. How soon will the doctor be leaving?"

Michael cleared his throat. "To be honest, the doctor has already left. He started home at the same time we did."

"What? Get my cloak. How could you leave her alone like that?" She frowned at the group of men standing in the parlor.

Michael drew near. "Georgette, you need to calm yourself. Surely you know we wouldn't have left Maura alone. Luther is with her. The doctor gave him a list of instructions, and he insisted that he would remain to care for her. When we left, he had pulled the rocking chair close by her bed, and Waffles was curled by his feet."

"Luther? You left Maura to Luther's care? What were you thinking—or were any of you thinking?"

"He's her husband, Georgette. He's the one who should be with her," Michael said.

Georgette flinched at his remark. "He may be her husband, but as far as I'm concerned, he doesn't act like one. Besides, come morning his primary concern will be the Buchanan Mercantile—not his wife! Michael, you can escort me or not, but I am going home right now!"

No matter what any of them said, she wouldn't be dissuaded.

"I'll get your cloak." Michael immediately hastened to fetch her wrap.

"And I'll get the baby." Edith pushed to her feet. "I'd be happy to come along and remain at the house with you—in fact, we both would, wouldn't we, Charles?"

"Wouldn't we what?" Her husband looked up and blinked his eyes.

"Charles! We wouldn't mind staying over with Georgette and Maura tonight, would we?" She repeated the question with a look that implied she expected his agreement.

The pastor gave a slight nod. "We wouldn't mind, but Luther is there, and I don't think they need a complete houseful of people upsetting their routine."

Edith turned her attention to Georgette. "What do you think, my dear? Would you like us to stay with you?"

"Thank you for the offer, but Pastor Wilson is right. Luther is already at the house and—"

Mrs. Wilson didn't give Georgette an opportunity to finish before interrupting. "But what if the baby is awake during the night so that you can't get any rest? Come morning, if Luther leaves to tend the store, you'll be tired and with no help to care for Becca and Maura."

"Why don't you go along, Edith? I don't think there's any need for me to intrude."

It was obvious Mrs. Wilson wasn't going to relent. Not wanting to waste more time arguing, Georgette acquiesced. Mrs. Wilson smiled before she hurried out of the room. Moments later, she returned with Becca in her arms.

Georgette extended her arms and cradled the baby close. "Thank you, Mrs. Wilson." She glanced down at the baby. "Michael is going to escort me home now. Once you gather a few belongings you'll need for the night, you come to the house."

"Charles will escort me—it won't take me but a few minutes." She'd barely spoken the final words before she scurried out of the room to begin her preparations.

Charles offered a weak smile as they reached the front door. "Edith means well."

"Of course she does, and I'm sure I'll be glad that she insisted on keeping me company." Georgette hoped her words would set the pastor's mind at ease. "Thank you for all your help, and thank you for the wonderful evening. I'm sorry it had to be marred by this tragedy." Georgette hesitated for a moment and glanced toward the piano. "Strange, but it seems a lifetime ago that we were singing carols, doesn't it?"

Michael grasped her elbow and escorted her down the steps. As they neared the house a short time later, Georgette's steps began to slow. "What's that covering the window?"

"The window was broken out in the front door. Luther put boards over it until the glass can be replaced,"

"You mean whoever broke into the house also broke out the window?" A chill climbed up Georgette's spine.

"Luther doesn't think so. He believes Waffles broke it out."

"Waffles? Where did he get an idea like that?"

"Seems the dog had a pretty good-sized lump on his head and some cuts around his face and front paws," Michael said. "Course, nobody's sure of anything right now."

She nodded her head as they walked up the front steps and cautiously entered the house.

"Who's there?" Luther appeared at the top of the steps.

"It's me, Luther, Georgette—and Michael is with me." She moved to the bottom of the stairway so he could see her. "I'm going to put Becca in bed. Would it be all right if I come up to see Maura?"

He nodded his head. "You leaving?" Luther turned his attention toward Michael, then nodded toward the door.

"In just a few minutes. I plan to wait and bid Georgette good night." Michael frowned. "You'd think this was his house."

"What did you say?" Georgette asked.

"I was just telling Luther I'd be leaving as soon as I bid you good night."

"Oh. I thought I heard you say something about the house," she said.

Michael shook his head. "It wasn't important." He gestured toward the upper rooms. "I know you want to get upstairs and see Maura, so I won't keep you any longer, but I wanted to tell you how much I enjoyed spending the evening with you at the Wilsons'. I'm just sorry all this unhappiness had to occur. I hope you'll allow me to stop by and see how all of you are doing and permit me to do anything I can to help."

Georgette didn't miss the hopefulness or sincerity of his words. "Of course, please stop by. I can't promise perfect hospitality, but I'm sure that under the circumstances, you'll understand." She walked beside him to the front door. "Thank you for this evening, Michael. I'm sorry to rush you off, but I do want to get upstairs and see Maura."

"I understand." He touched his hand to the bolt on the front door. "Be sure to lock the door after Mrs. Wilson arrives."

His protectiveness warmed her like a ray of summer sunshine. She nodded and then turned and ran up the steps.

Quietly she tiptoed into the room. Waffles came toward her, wagging his tail and looking a bit the worse for his experience. She leaned down and started to pat him but stopped short, not wanting to hurt him.

"Good dog, Waffles." He stopped by her side and licked her hand.

"Maura?" she whispered. "Maura, it's me, Georgette. Can you hear me?"

"She's still unconscious," Luther said. "She moved a little just before you got here, but that's been the extent of it. The doctor said not to be overly concerned unless this continues for another day or so. I'm trying to believe him."

Luther was gently running his thumb back and forth over Maura's left hand. Strange, Georgette thought. He could barely stand to look at her withered arm before, but now that she's in a state of trauma, he's sitting here stroking it as though he loved her—flawed limbs included.

"Mrs. Wilson insisted on spending the night. I tried to discourage her, but she wouldn't hear of it. Under the circumstances, it will prevent any idle gossip that might arise. She should be here soon, and I can sit with Maura while you get some rest. When Becca needs to be fed, you can come back and sit with Maura, and then I'll get some rest. If she should wake up, I'll come and get you immediately." Georgette hoped he wouldn't disagree. The last thing she wanted was an argument with Luther.

"I guess that would work. I know you want to be with her, and I'm sure you'll be more comfortable if I'm not around. I'm sure you don't hold me in very high esteem."

"This isn't the time for us to discuss what I think of you, Luther. Right now, all I care about is that Maura gets the best care possible. I can put aside my feelings to ensure that." She'd barely uttered the words when a rapping sounded at the front door.

Startled by the noise, Waffles barked and skittishly ran in and out of the bedroom door.

"Hush, Waffles."

Luther and Georgette turned toward the bed. The soft command had come from Maura's lips, but she didn't appear to have moved, and her eyes were still closed.

Luther leaned close to the bed. "Maura!"

"Maura—can you hear me? Oh please, Maura, answer me." Georgette stepped to the foot of the bed.

But Maura didn't move; in fact, not so much as an eyelash fluttered.

They looked at each other, questioning whether they'd really heard anything; then the rapping at the front door sounded once again. This time, however, Waffles remained calm while Georgette went downstairs to answer the door.

Edith entered the house and apologized the minute she bustled into the room. "Just point out where I should put these things and tell me what you want done." She fluttered her hand toward her husband. "You can leave, Charles."

Ignoring his wife's dismissal, the pastor moved toward Georgette. "Has there been any change?"

"Not really. Luther and I both thought we heard her speak a few minutes ago when you knocked on the door, but I'm beginning to think our imaginations got the best of us." She offered him a weak smile.

"I'll be praying. I'm sure that God is going to see both of you through this just fine. I'll be on my way, now." He leaned to the side and gave his wife a kiss on the cheek. "Good night, dear, I'll check on you in the morning."

Mrs. Wilson walked her husband to the door where they exchanged a few more words before he departed.

"Would you lock the bolt on the door, please?" Georgette motioned to the older woman as she closed the door. "I'm going to sit up with Maura until the baby wakens for her feeding. Why don't you sleep in my room since I may have difficulty hearing her when she wakens?"

Mrs. Wilson nodded. "You go right ahead. I'll come to get you when she's hungry,"

It seemed only minutes had passed when Georgette awakened Luther from a restless sleep.

Georgette stood in the doorway. "I'm going downstairs to feed Becca and rest for a while. Do you want Edith to sit with Maura? She's still sleeping."

Luther pushed up from the large overstuffed chair where he had been sleeping. "No, I want to sit with her. You go and get some rest." He rubbed his eyes as he walked toward Maura's bedroom.

Inside the bedroom, he stared down at his wife's motionless form. He had treated her shabbily, and he knew it. *I've become as cruel and heartless as my father.* The small oil lamp on the bedside table cast a flickering glow upon the pages of Maura's open Bible. Hoping to find comfort in the passages, he sat down and picked up the Bible.

"'God is our refuge and strength, an ever-present help in trouble.'" The words seeped into his soul as he read them aloud, and then looked at his wife. "I'd guess you've been asking God for strength all your life—strength to deal with people just like me. People who judge you before ever giving you half a chance." Tears stung his eyes.

"Now me, I've spent the last five years dwelling on my past, constantly attempting to prove my father wrong. It appears, however, that in my zeal to prove him incorrect, I've become just like him—an unrelenting taskmaster, void of love or compassion." A tear rolled down his cheek and he swiped it away.

Dear God, forgive me, he silently prayed as he continued his vigil.

Chapter 9

*a*fter two long days and nights, Luther agreed to reopen the store. Pastor Wilson and several others had offered to volunteer their time to keep the mercantile open, but Luther knew it would be utter chaos. None of them knew his stock or prices; moreover, his inventory lists would be botched in no time, to say nothing of what would happen to the bookkeeping system without proper accounting at day's end.

Georgette sighed a breath of relief as he walked out the door. "I know he's trying to help and it's his place to be with Maura, but I'm glad to have him out from underfoot for a while." Georgette glanced at Mrs. Wilson as the two of them began to clear away the kitchen dishes.

The older woman nodded. "I know, dear, but we must remember how distressed he must be to have his wife in such a condition. I can't even begin to think how I would feel if that were Charles."

"Mrs. Wilson! There is absolutely no parallel between your marriage to the pastor and Maura's marriage to Luther. Quite frankly—and I know I shouldn't say this—I wonder why he's even here. He didn't want to be around her when she was healthy." When Mrs. Wilson's eyes widened in surprise, Georgette gasped. "Oh, I'm sorry, I shouldn' have said that."

"You don't need to apologize, Georgette. I know that you are deeply concerned about Maura; besides, you're worn out from lack of proper rest. But let me share with you one thing I've learned in my life—we humans give up on things a lot faster than the Lord does. He is so much more creative than we could ever imagine, and believe me—His plan will be revealed in His time.

"Luther and Maura are both Christians, and I believe that God will restore their marriage. It may not occur in an uncomplicated manner or in the near future, but when it happens, it will transpire because both of them have looked to Him for their answer. Now, I guess I'd better get upstairs." She sighed and wiped her hands on a dish towel.

"Thank you for those words, Mrs. Wilson. I've not been very charitable to Luther. In fact, I've been downright rude at times. You've convinced me that I need to be praying for Luther rather than judging his behavior." Thoughts of her own past rushed to the forefront of Georgette's mind.

"We'll both pray for him! He won't be able to resist if we're both soliciting God's help." Mrs. Wilson chuckled as she prepared to depart for home. Before leaving, she carried Becca's cradle upstairs for Georgette.

The older woman had been gone for several hours, and Georgette now sat stitching on the last of the tablecloths as Becca slept. Waffles was curled up on the rug by Georgette's feet, keeping vigil, when a loud rapping sounded at the front door.

Startled by the noise, Georgette jumped from the chair, her sewing basket and contents falling to the floor and frightening the dog. Instantly Waffles barked and wakened Becca, whose lusty cries nearly drowned out the dog. The knocking sounded again, and Waffles howled another chorus of barks while Becca continued to wail.

"What in the world is going on?" Maura's eyes shone with surprise. "Why is Waffles in the house, and why is everyone in my bedroom?"

"Maura! Oh, Maura, are you all right?" Georgette questioned, attempting to be heard over the barking dog and sobbing child.

Again the rapping began.

"Georgette, please go answer the door so that Becca and the dog will settle down." Maura waved toward the bedroom door. "Here, I'll hold Becca." She reached forward to take the baby.

Confusion clouded Maura's eyes when Georgette hesitated. "What is wrong with you, Georgette?"

"Let me answer the door, and then I'll be right back to explain." Still holding the baby, Georgette rushed downstairs. She didn't know who was more perplexed—her or Maura. Waffles, the ever-ready protector, raced behind her and skidded to a halt in front of the door.

"It's just Pastor and Mrs. Wilson. Now stop your barking." Georgette motioned for the animal to sit.

"I was beginning to get worried." Mrs. Wilson stepped inside and lifted Becca from her mother's arms. "Did our knocking waken her?"

Georgette chuckled. "I'm not sure if it was the knocking or my dropping the sewing basket or Waffles barking." She drew closer to the older woman. "You're never going to believe this, but all the commotion seems to have awakened Maura. I need to get back upstairs right away."

"Here, Charles, you take the baby, and I'll go up with Georgette." Mrs. Wilson passed the baby to him and directed him to try rocking her in the parlor. "I'm sure she'll be just fine."

Mrs. Wilson returned downstairs a few minutes later with Georgette following behind. "Charles!" Edith hurried into the parlor. "You're just not going to believe this, but Maura is back with us and seems fit as a fiddle. Here—give me the baby and go fetch Luther." She extended her arms toward the child. "I'm sorry, Charles. I'm so excited that I've forgotten my manners. Would you please go to the store and give Luther the news?"

"Of course, I will." He grinned and kissed her cheek. "No need to apologize. I learned to live with your enthusiasm years ago."

"Enthusiasm. Now that's a nice word for it, isn't it?" She smiled at Georgette. "Charles always did have a way with words. I think that's one of the things that makes him such a fine pastor."

Luther was squatted down stocking shelves at the far end of the room when the bell over the front door jangled. Moments later, Pastor Wilson called out to him.

"Luther pushed to his feet and motioned to the preacher. "I'm over here."

The pastor doffed his hat and waved it overhead. "I've good news."

"What? What's happened?"

"Maura has regained consciousness, and Edith sent me to fetch you. I'd be happy to watch after things here at the store, if you'd like." Luther hesitated at the preacher's offer. "Or I guess you could put a sign on the door for a while."

"What? Oh, no, I've no problem with you tending the store—in fact, I appreciate your kind offer. It's just so—" Luther stopped short, unable to find the proper word.

"Miraculous?" The pastor quirked an eyebrow.

Luther nodded. "Yes—that, too." He wasn't sure that miraculous was quite the word he had been searching for, but what had happened truly was a miracle. "If you're certain that it's not an imposition, I would like to see her. I won't stay long."

Charles patted him on the shoulder. "Stay as long as you like. I think I'll be more adept at running your store than performing several of the other chores Edith has thrust upon me lately."

Luther hurried as quickly as his feet would carry him. He entered the front door a short time later, and rushed upstairs. Maura and Mrs. Wilson appeared entranced as Georgette regaled them with an account of Waffles heroic deeds.

Luther removed his cap and turned toward the women. "Didn't

figure there was any need to knock on the door and cause one of you to run downstairs. Charles came over and told me the news, but I guess you know that."

Mrs. Wilson was the first to respond. "Perhaps we should give you two an opportunity to talk alone. Why don't you sit here?" She pushed up from the chair and stepped away from Maura's bedside.

"Thank you, Mrs. Wilson." Luther nodded at the woman before he sat down.

"Isn't it about time to feed Becca?" Edith nudged Georgette.

"No." Georgette remained seated, but when Mrs. Wilson frowned, she popped up from her chair. "Ohhh, you're right, she may be hungry."

Together, the two women departed the room.

"It was kind of you to come so quickly," Maura said, though not sure why Luther had hurried to her bedside.

"I've been very concerned about you, Maura. In fact, I didn't return to the store until this morning when Georgette and Mrs. Wilson insisted. I don't know what Georgette told you before I came in, but you gave all of us a real fright. Do you recall any of what happened the other night?"

She touched her head with her fingertips. "I think so, although I almost wish I didn't."

He reached forward and grasped her hand. "Will you tell me?"

Startled, she pulled away.

"Maura, did he—did he hurt you?"

She shook her head. "Not in the way you're thinking." He'd obviously misinterpreted her reaction to his touch. "Georgette tells me that you're the one responsible for finding me and getting help. Thank you for what you did."

"I'm just thankful that Waffles was making such a racket and caught my attention out there on the front porch. Do you feel up to talking about it?" His voice was tender and kind, unlike the Luther she remembered.

Perhaps that knock on my head caused a memory lapse of some sort. Maura stared at him, unable to reconcile Luther's current behavior with the man she remembered.

"I'll just sit here quietly." He settled in the chair as though he intended to spend the remainder of the day at her bedisde.

She shifted in the bed. "I feel well enough to talk about what occurred. I don't believe my memory is impaired—although you're not acting like the man I remember, so perhaps it is."

Without further hesitation, she related the events that had occurred several nights earlier.

"Michael and Georgette left for the party at the Wilsons' and Becca was asleep in her cradle. I wanted to finish hemming the tablecloths and decided to stay up until they were completed. Besides, I didn't want to leave Becca downstairs, but I couldn't carry her cradle up—well, that doesn't matter. Anyway, I heard someone outside on the porch; then there was a tapping at the front door. Before I could get to the door, a man burst in and—"

His features tightened into a frown. "You mean you didn't have the door bolted?"

"No, I didn't have the door bolted." She stiffed at his question. "I didn't know when Georgette would be coming home, and I didn't want her to stand outside waiting for me to answer the door if I was in the bedroom with Becca. Besides, we never bolt the door until retiring for the night. Neither of us has had any cause to be frightened."

"Maura! With all the men coming through town, do you think that two women alone are safe?"

She sighed. "Do you want to hear what happened or lecture me on my susceptibility to strangers in Placerville?"

His frown softened. "I'm sorry. Go on with your recollections."

"As I was saying, a man burst in the front door and told me to be quiet. As soon as he got inside, he slammed the door behind him. When I asked what he wanted, he said he was down on his luck, telling me he'd been searching for gold without any success. I offered him work roofing the house, but he just laughed and asked me why he should work when he could just take my money. When I told him I didn't have any money, he became angry and threatened me." She inhaled a deep breath, as memories of the event flooded over her.

"Becca awakened and I was afraid he would hurt her, so I told him I might be able to find a little money upstairs. He followed me, and I took what money I had in my reticule and offered it to him. Angry because it was such a small amount, he began cursing and yelling, his voice growing louder and louder. Then he began pulling out drawers and slamming the furniture about, all the while shouting he was going to kill me if I didn't show him where my money was hidden. I screamed back at him, and the next thing I heard was glass breaking. Suddenly Waffles came running into the room and attacked the man—"

Luther leaned forward. "Did he actually bite the intruder?"

"I'm not sure, although he had his teeth bared and was growling when he lunged at the man. I don't recall anything after that." She dropped back onto her pillow.

He shook his head. "I've tired you out too much. It was too soon for you to go through the ordeal of recounting the events."

"No, it's probably better this way. I might have forgotten or distorted some of the events if I hadn't told someone, but I am feeling somewhat weak. Perhaps Mrs. Wilson could bring me something light to eat. I think that might help."

"Of course. How thoughtless of me. You haven't had any food in close to three days now. It's no wonder you're weak. I'll go down and see what they can rustle up for you." He rose from the chair.

"Thank you." She offered a weak smile. "And, Luther—you need not feel obligated to visit. I'll be fine. Georgette and Mrs. Wilson won't allow me to starve to death, and you have your business to look after."

"Does that mean I'm unwelcome?" His voice hitched and his eyes shone with pain.

"It doesn't mean you're unwelcome. It means merely that I know you have come out of your feeling of Christian duty and responsibility because I am your wife—at least by the letter of the law—"

He held out his hand to stay her. "And in the eyes of God."

"Definitely in the eyes of God, Luther. Just not in your eyes or your heart." She turned away from him.

He crossed his arms over his chest. "How can you become a wife in my eyes and heart if you won't even allow me to visit?"

"Whenever you want to visit me out of more than pity or a sense of duty, you are welcome. Until then, it's best you stay away." She wouldn't give him further opportunity to hurt her.

"I didn't want to intrude, but I thought you might be hungry. Oh, Luther! I almost ran into you." Mrs. Wilson approached the doorway where Luther stood with his arms still folded against his chest.

Luther glanced at the older woman. "I was just coming down to tell you that Maura was hungry."

Edith stepped forward and placed the tray on Maura's bedside table as Luther moved around her. "Don't let me rush you off. I'll be out of here in a moment."

"I was leaving anyway. Take care of yourself, Maura. If there's anything you need, send word." The thumping of his footsteps and slamming of the front door provided the final evidence of his departure. Had he changed? Did he truly care or had he appeared only out of Christian duty? She doubted him. Even more, she doubted her own judgment. Luther Buchanan hadn't proved he was a man to be trusted.

Maura quickly regained her strength; and although the women agreed that the restaurant would not open until after Christmas, they couldn't forego the opportunity to entertain with a dinner party on Christmas Day. The Wilsons, Ballards, and Bergmans, as well as Michael and Luther, were all invited. Stanley Ballard operated the livery stable, Samuel Bergman was the new president of the Placerville Bank, and all of them regularly listened to Pastor Wilson on Sunday mornings. Georgette left a short time earlier to personally invite each of the couples and Michael.

Georgette bustled into the house and removed her dark blue bonnet and matching cape. "I didn't stop by the store. I thought you'd want to invite Luther personally."

Maura inwardly cringed at the announcement.

"Was I wrong?" She turned to face Maura.

Maura shrugged. "He'll probably turn me down. To be honest, I'm not sure I can handle the humiliation."

"Maura Thorenson! I don't want to seem unkind, but I wonder how he felt when you told him he didn't need to bother visiting you. Seems I remember some passages from the Bible that we studied before I became a Christian. You're the one who taught me about forgiveness and God's grace. Do you remember what you said when I asked you how you could ever associate with the likes of me?"

"Of course, I do. I told you that it was always a privilege to be associated with another child of the kingdom. But those circumstances were completely different. You had just accepted Jesus as your Savior and were feeling so unworthy. On the other hand, Luther has been a Christian for years, but look at how he's treated me." Maura frowned at Georgette.

"Seems I recall something else you told me. Didn't you say that sometimes Christians are so unforgiving and critical of each other that Satan can just sit around and enjoy the chaos they create for themselves?"

"Georgette, I think you're manipulating some of my teaching, trying to make it fit a totally different situation!"

Georgette stepped across the hallway and hung her cape and bonnet on the hall tree. "Then why are you getting so upset? You've been a Christian for years, too. It would appear to this newborn Christian that you both need to take a look at yourselves. I love you, Maura, but you're just as wrong as Luther. He's hurt you, and now you're not going to be happy until you've made him suffer for what he's done."

Maura flinched at the girl's retort. "You've become quite an authority, haven't you? Let me tell you something, Georgette. You don't know what it's like to be different. You stand in front of me with a beautiful, whole body that any man would love. You haven't lived through years of being stared at and whispered about—children pointing you out to their parents as if you were some type of monstrosity. You've received looks of adoration while I've received stares of disdain. It's easy for you to tell me I shouldn't worry about receiving further humiliation from my husband." Her voice had risen a full octave during the recitation.

"I'm sorry, Maura. What was I thinking of? Here I am upsetting you, when the last thing you need is to become distressed. I'll go and ask Luther, and if he says anything that makes me think he's coming out of pity, I'll retract the invitation." Georgette quickly retrieved her cape from the hall tree and placed it around her shoulders. "I'll be back in just a few minutes. Please look after Becca for just a little longer." She grasped her bonnet and rushed out the front door before Maura could say anything further.

The cool air felt good against her cheeks as Georgette walked quickly toward the general store. *Why did I say those things to Maura? She's the only true friend I've ever had, and now she'll probably never speak to me again.* Georgette grimaced at the thought.

When she walked into the store, Luther arched his brows. "You look like you just lost your best friend."

"Perhaps I have."

"What'd you say? Couldn't hear you." He stepped toward her.

"Oh, nothing." She dare not relate what had happened with Maura. "I was just deep in thought. Maura and I were wondering if you would like to join us for Christmas dinner. The Wilsons, Ballards, and Bergmans have all agreed to attend, and, of course, Michael will be there, too."

His lips curved in a broad smile. "Sounds like you've gathered most of the businessmen and their wives."

"Not quite. The majority of the businesses in Placerville will be open on Christmas. I don't think the saloons and gambling halls ever close their doors, do you?"

"Not if there's any chance of making money, they don't. And I imagine you're right. A lot of the miners will be feeling melancholy and will come to town hoping to drown their holiday loneliness in liquor."

Georgette shook her head. "That's such a shame." His comment caused an idea to form. "You know, Luther, it would be wonderful if there were an alternative—something for those men to do besides get drunk."

He hiked a shoulder. "I don't know what it would be. That's usually the high point of coming to town—getting to the assay office and then the saloon."

"What if they could come to the restaurant—Maura's and mine— and join us for dinner? Free of charge. We could put Mrs. Wilson in charge of entertainment in case they wanted to stay for a spell after dinner. You know how she loves to see folks have a good time. What do you think?" An air of excitement had overtaken her earlier downcast spirit. This could be a wonderful opportunity to share the real meaning of Christmas.

"I'm not sure why you're asking me. I think Maura and Mrs. Wilson are the ones you should be talking to."

She leaned forward, determined to gain a response. "But do you at least think it's a good idea?"

He gave a slight nod. "It's a real nice idea, Georgette."

Once he admitted her plan was worthy, she decided to push him even further. "And would you be willing to help if we needed you?"

He shook his head and laughed. "You are one insistent woman! You talk to the others, and if they're willing, you can count on me. Just remember, my skills in the kitchen need a lot of improvement."

"Don't worry. There will be lots of things you can do. I'm going to go and talk to Mrs. Wilson and Maura right away." She hurried toward the door before he could change his mind.

"By the way, Georgette, is there some special reason why you came to extend my dinner invitation instead of Maura?" Luther's voice boomed across the room.

She stopped, frozen in her tracks. Why did he have to ask that? How should she answer? She wanted to tell the truth, but she certainly didn't want to cause any further breach in the quickly fading marriage of her friend.

She drew in a deep breath. "Because Maura asked me to. I've extended the invitations to all our guests." It was the truth, pure and simple. Now if I can just get out of here before he questions me any further. She reached for the door handle.

"Does she really want me to come?" He crossed the room and stopped at her side, obviously intent upon receiving an answer.

"She put your name on the list of guests." Georgette would leave the rest to his imagination. "I really must be going, Luther. If Maura agrees to my idea, we'll need to begin planning right away."

He moved aside and she hurried outdoors where she could finally breathe a sigh of relief. She marched toward home with only one thought in mind: *Maura's not going to put me in that position again.*

The minute Georgette arrived home, Maura approached her. "What did he say?"

"If I didn't know that you had more important things to do, I'd think you were watching out the window for me." Georgette arched her brows and grinned. "He said he'd be here, but he also wanted to know why I was the one doing the inviting instead of you!"

"What did you tell him?" Maura's voice was shrill.

"I told him the truth." Noting the alarm that shone in Maura's eyes, Georgette patted her shoulder. "Don't panic, I told him you had placed his name on the list of guests and that I had delivered all of the invitations. Then I rushed out before he could question me any further."

"Thank you, Georgette."

"You're welcome. However, I made up my mind on the way home that I'm not going to do your bidding again—not where it concerns Luther. It's too uncomfortable. I don't want to cause additional problems for you and Luther, but I don't want to lie, either. You two are old enough to discuss matters without a go-between."

Maura nodded. "I know that was unfair of me, but I don't think I could have withstood further rejection from him."

"Let's forget about it for now. Guess what?" Georgette didn't wait for a response. She was too excited about her plan to truly expect Maura to guess. She inhaled a deep breath. "While I was inviting Luther, I had the most wonderful idea. Want to hear it?"

"Of course! Your ideas are usually quite remarkable." Maura gestured toward the kitchen. "Let's sit down and you can tell me all about it."

Georgette followed her into the kitchen, but rather than sit down, she paced around the table. "Instead of having a dinner just for the folks we planned on, why don't we invite any of the miners who come into town for Christmas? They'll end up in the saloons trying to drink away their loneliness because there isn't anything else for them to do. What do you think?" She plopped onto the chair opposite Maura.

Maura shook her head. "Oh, Georgette, I don't know. That would be—"

"I know it's a lot of work, but Luther said he'd be willing to help, and you know how Mrs. Wilson loves to entertain. She'd be playing the piano and singing carols—why, she'd probably even have Pastor Wilson give a short sermon. If everyone helps, it won't be that much work, and there probably wouldn't be that many guests." She'd been surprised by the hesitation in Maura's voice. She'd expected her to be thrilled with the idea.

Maura offered a weak smile. "It is a generous plan. There's no doubt about that. But—"

Georgette hurried to interrupt, unwilling to hear anything but a positive response. "Oh, thank you, Maura! I was afraid you would give me a whole list of reasons why we couldn't do it. However, I should have known better, for you don't want all those poor men drinking in a saloon any more than I do."

Maura placed her hand on the table. "Do you realize how little time there is to plan for such a meal?"

"We've already planned it. All we need to do is prepare more."

"Have you talked to anyone except Luther about this idea?"

"No—I thought I should talk to you first. But as soon as I feed Becca, I'll go and talk with the others." She could barely contain her enthusiasm.

Maura smiled at her and nodded. "I suppose it won't be so difficult if we have enough help. And you're right—it certainly would provide a nice alternative for those men. I do believe you've been blessed with a charitable heart, Georgette."

Chapter 10

The small group had worked diligently, preparing for the dinner and festivities to be held on Christmas Day. Shortly before midnight on Christmas Eve, Michael arrived to escort Georgette and Becca to midnight services at the small church. Although his invitation included Maura and she knew it was sincere, she once again felt like the extra—"the fifth wheel on the wagon."

I hate feeling this way. Why can't I just be thankful that I have friends who are willing to include me in their plans instead of resenting my situation? She removed her woolen cape from the small bedroom closet and pulled a pair of black kid gloves from the dresser drawer. Suddenly, a knock at the front door sent Waffles bounding down the steps in a fit of ferocious barking.

"That dog is going to break his neck flying around the corner and down the steps like that." Maura shook her head and descended the stairs expecting to see Michael.

"I think he's determined to protect the three of you." Luther grinned at her. "I stopped to see if I could escort you to Christmas Eve services."

"Oh, how nice!" Georgette clapped her hands together. Noting Maura's stare, she quickly dropped her arms to her sides. "I'm sorry. I guess I'm meddling in your business." She looked back and forth between the two of them.

Luther smiled in her direction. "That's all right. It's good to have someone excited about the invitation."

Did he truly believe she could forget all the hurt he'd inflicted and be thrilled to have him appear without notice? Her stomach cinched in a knot. "Perhaps I'd be more excited had you invited me in advance rather than showing up at the door unexpected."

Luther's jaw clenched. "I'm sorry. I didn't realize that an engraved invitation was necessary to accompany one's spouse to church."

"Well, I just think it's lovely that the two of you will be spending Christmas Eve together in God's house." Georgette clasped her hands together and smiled at them.

The two of them turned toward her simultaneously.

"Who asked you?" They spoke the question in unison.

Georgette's eyes brimmed with tears. "I wish you could see your-selves. If so, perhaps you'd have a change of heart." She turned and strode toward her bedroom.

"Georgette!" Maura followed after the girl. She could feel Luther's stare as she limped into the parlor. Glancing over her shoulder, she saw him watching her.

"Is that pity or disgust I see in your eyes?"

"Neither—it's astonishment. Astonishment at how something that seemed so right could turn out so wrong." He shook his head as he walked toward the door.

How could one evening turn into such a disaster? She needed to set things aright with Georgette. Before she could say a word, another knock sounded at the door.

When Georgette stood, Maura shook her head. "I'll go. I'm sure it's Luther returning to apologize."

Waffles ran along beside her as she entered the front hallway and opened the door. "Merry Christmas." Michael's face was alight with expectation. "Everyone ready to go?"

"Just about." Maura hoped he hadn't heard the disappointment in her voice. She had been certain that it would be Luther. *I should have known better.* She straightened her shoulders and let her disappointment give way to anger.

She returned to Georgette's room. "It's Michael. I should have known that Luther wouldn't return."

"Why should he? And why would you want him to?" Georgette gaped at her as though she'd lost her senses. "I'd think you would have had enough dissension for one evening. Personally, I'd like to go to church without any further upheavals. Are you going to join us or not?"

The sting of Georgette's words hit their mark. Maura nodded. "I apologize for my undignified conduct. I don't want to spoil your holiday."

"You don't owe me an apology, Maura, and it's not the holiday I'm concerned about. It's you—you and Luther and—"

Maura took a backward step and gestured toward the parlor. "We're keeping Michael waiting." She turned and continued down the hallway. Any further discussion would only lead to more words spoken in anger—words that couldn't be taken back.

The services were just beginning as they entered the church and slipped in a pew near the back. The candles at the front of the church offered only a dim glow, which made it impossible for Maura to spot Luther.

He probably went home. She leaned toward Georgette in an attempt to gain a better view.

"Don't you have enough room?" Georgette whispered, scooting a bit closer to Michael.

"I'm fine." Hoping Georgette wouldn't realize that she'd been looking for Luther, she forced herself to keep her eyes focused on Pastor Wilson throughout the remainder of the sermon.

As Mrs. Wilson struck the opening chords of "O Little Town of Bethlehem," their individual candles were lit, filling the church with a shadowy, flickering light that trailed out into the night as they left for their homes.

"Do you still want me to help tomorrow?"

Maura turned, startled to see Luther standing behind her. "I thought you'd gone home earlier."

"No, I was sitting up front. Would it be better if I didn't come tomorrow? I'll do whatever you prefer. I don't want to be the cause of ruining all the hard work that's gone into your dinner plans."

"Of course we want you to come! Besides, we need your help." Georgette stepped forward before Maura could say a word. "I think we're going to need every pair of hands we can get! At least that's my opinion."

Maura nodded. "I agree. We'll need all the help we can get." His attendance might make her uncomfortable, but she could withstand a bit of discomfort in exchange for the extra help.

"In that case, I'll plan to be there." He tipped his hat. "Good night to all of you."

"I'll be down early in the morning to help you carry that lumber up to the house, Luther." Michael's message echoed in the crisp evening air.

Luther waved his hand in reply as he continued on his way. Maura didn't miss the fact that there was a bit of a slump to his shoulders and a slowness to his stride.

The three of them walked home in silence; even Becca remained silent, the cool air apparently not disturbing her sleep. When they reached the house, Maura extended her arms to take the baby from Georgette.

"I'll put her to bed. You two go ahead and say your good nights."

"Thank you." Georgette placed the baby in Maura's arms.

Becca was soon snuggled into her cradle beside Georgette's bed. After giving the infant one last kiss, Maura returned to the parlor.

"You two appear to be deep in conversation. However, I was going to retire for the night. It's late, and we'll have to begin preparations early tomorrow." Maura glanced at Michael. She shouldn't leave the two of them alone, but the day's events had left her weary, and they were adults who knew right from wrong.

"There's no need for you to remain up. We had a few matters to discuss, but we're almost through. Michael will be leaving momentarily." Georgette smiled and turned her attention back to Michael.

"Good night." A lump began to rise in her throat as she ascended the stairs.

Why am I feeling sorry for myself? I could be sitting downstairs holding hands with Luther or living under the same roof if I chose. She unbuttoned her dress and prepared for bed. Why do I feel so miserable, and why am I so jealous of anyone else who has a relationship? She unpinned and brushed her long auburn hair, stroke after stroke, until her arm began to ache.

"You need some changes in your heart," a small voice whispered inside her head. Overcome by the unexpected message, Maura sat looking in the mirror.

"I need to change. Me! It's always me that's wrong; it's always me that must give in and overlook the way others treat me," she murmured aloud. "That's not fair. Why doesn't anybody else need to change?"

"Me, me, me. Poor me," came the small voice once again. *"You can either change your heart or turn into a bitter old woman, unloved and wallowing in self-pity. Luther will meet you part way, if you'll only give him a chance. It might help to have a positive approach instead of a negative attitude when you're around him."*

Slowly Maura walked to the bed and got down on her knees. "Is that You talking to me, God?" A trickle of tears escaping her eyes "I know you're right—that I've become bitter through the years. Even more so since marrying Luther. I wanted to have a good marriage—like Daniel and Amanda's—is that so much to ask?"

There was no answer—only the stillness of the cold starry night. "I'll try, God. If that's what You want, I'll try." She rose to her feet, the promise fresh in her mind as she drifted off to sleep.

Morning arrived all too quickly. Although Maura had been the first to bed, she still hadn't come downstairs. Luther and Michael had already arrived, she'd fed Becca, and Waffles was barking at each knock on the door.

Georgette strode to the bottom of the stairway. "Maura, are you awake?"

A few moments passed before she heard the opening of a door. "I'm sorry. I've overslept. I'll be down shortly."

Georgette returned to Michael's side. "That's a first."

"What's that?" Michael glanced over his shoulder.

"Maura oversleeping. I've never known her to do that."

"She was probably exhausted from all the trouble she caused Luther yesterday." Michael grinned at her.

Georgette frowned. "Michael! If that was the case, they'd both have overslept because Luther was dishing it out just as fast as Maura."

"What are you two talking about? Thought I heard my name mentioned." Without waiting for a reply, Luther pointed his thumb in the direction of the store. "You want to help me with that lumber?"

Michael looked at Georgette. "You think we ought to get the makeshift tables and benches set up?"

"Why don't you just carry the lumber up here, and we'll wait until we need them? There are quite a few tables and chairs in the dining area already, and I'm not sure how many men will actually show up. Besides, it will save having to fight our way around all that extra 'furniture' until closer to dinnertime."

A short time later, Luther led Michael to the storage barn behind the store, and the two of them chose pieces of lumber to place in the wagon. "We'll take those wider ones to use for tables; the narrower ones will make good benches." Luther gestured toward some barrels. "I think we can use those smaller barrels under the benches, and I've got lots of the big ones to use under the tables."

"Good idea." Michael crossed the short distance and picked up one of the barrels. "How many you think we'll need?"

Luther shrugged. "Don't have any idea, but even with rearranging, that dining room is only going to hold two of these setups. If there are too many guests, either they'll have to wait their turn or, if it's not too cold, we'll see if Maura and Georgette want to put a couple tables outside."

When they'd finished loading all the necessary items for the makeshift seating, they hitched up the team and led the horses up the street and to the rear of the restaurant. Once the horses had come to a complete halt, Luther deftly unhitched the team and walked them back around to the front of the house.

"I'm going to take the horses back down to my barn. No sense in having them hitched up here all day," Luther said.

"Good morning, Luther."

Luther turned to see Maura waving at him from the front porch. He nodded. "Mornin' and Merry Christmas to you." After her behavior last night, the pleasant greeting surprised him.

She descended the porch steps and walked toward him. "You want some company walking the horses back?"

"I can take 'em—unless you're anxious for some exercise." He wasn't certain why she'd want to walk with him, and he sure didn't want to begin the day with another argument.

Her lips curved in a cheery smile. "I'll probably get all the exercise I need today fixing and serving dinner, but I wouldn't mind the company."

The smile and lilt in her voice caught him off guard. "In that case, come along." They'd gone only a few steps when Luther glanced at her. "You know, Maura, you're a hard person to figure out. Last night you were so angry that I didn't know if you wanted me to come over here and help out today. And now, this morning, you act like there's nothing you enjoy more than being in my company. Am I dense or missing something here? To be quite honest, I just don't understand you."

Luther waited, uncertain she'd respond to his comment.

She sighed. "I'm sure you don't—and I'm not sure I understand you, either. But if we're ever going to begin understanding one another, I think we need to call a truce. That's why I wanted to be alone with you for a few minutes." She walked into the barn by his side.

Luther didn't respond as he uncinched the gray dapple workhorses. He didn't miss the fact that his silence had caused Maura to fidget, but he wasn't yet sure what she had in mind when she mentioned a truce. He removed the horses' leather collars and, when he had finished, he walked over and positioned himself behind the railing surrounding the stall where she stood. Resting his arms on the top wooden board, he leaned forward until they were eye to eye, "What kind of truce did you have in mind?"

His warm breath tickled her neck and sent shivers racing down her spine. An undeniable heat warmed her cheeks as her thoughts rushed back to their wedding day and the passionate kiss Luther had placed upon her lips. Unconsciously, she traced a finger across her mouth. Not wanting him to know the effect he was having upon her, she dared not move.

She silently chastised herself. Before meeting with Luther, she should have decided exactly what to propose. "I thought perhaps we could try speaking to and treating each other with more kindness."

"Is that all you thought?" Once again, he leaned close to her before he spoke.

She swallowed hard. "No, but it's a starting place."

He moved from behind her and walked around the stall. When he stood directly in front of her, he placed his hands on either side of her waist and lifted her onto a nearby crate. She didn't resist but gave him a questioning look.

"I want to see your eyes when you talk to me." His hands remained on her waist. "Instead of all those vague answers you've given me, why don't you tell me what you really want—from me, from this so-called marriage, from life itself."

Discomfort assailed her. She hadn't anticipated being placed in a position in which she might have to reveal her inner thoughts to him.

"I'm not sure we have time now for such a deep conversation. I need to assist with dinner preparations. Besides, everyone will be wondering where we are." She wanted to escape his pointed questions until she had time for a bit of thoughtful contemplation—time to carefully prepare.

Luther continued to hold her in place. "There are enough folks in that kitchen that they'll be falling all over each other. Besides, I told Michael we might be gone for a while. He'll be able to answer any questions that might arise regarding our whereabouts. Since we are married, there's certainly no need to worry about any impropriety in our being alone, is there?"

"Well, no. . ." She couldn't think of any other excuse to escape the moment.

"So tell me, Maura Buchanan, what is it you want?"

Maura Buchanan. The name sounded foreign to her ears. She still thought of herself as Maura Thorenson.

"When you think of yourself, you think of Maura Thorenson—not Maura Buchanan. Am I right?"

Her head snapped up at his remark. How did he know what she was thinking? There was a twinkle in his inquiring mahogany eyes.

"It makes you uncomfortable that I have some idea of what you're thinking, doesn't it?"

Before she could reply, he bent his head and pulled her to him, his full lips gently caressing hers and then quickly giving way to the urgency of his passion. She responded, leaning forward and placing her arms around his neck, her breath shallow as his lips explored hers with an unrelenting hunger.

When their lips finally parted, he looked deep into her eyes. "You were thinking of that, too, weren't you?"

Her knees had turned weak. Fearing she might slip off the barrel if he released her, she leaned against the railing.

"Yes." She couldn't deny she'd longed to once again feel his lips on her own.

"And what else were you thinking?"

"I want a devoted husband who is affectionate and tender. A husband who will allow me to share his life, who admires my strengths and overlooks my imperfections. I want a husband who loves God and wants the kind of marriage God intended for His children." Surprisingly, Luther's kiss had erased her fears. "I usually hide my true feelings. It's a way to protect myself from the pain others can inflict."

He smiled at her, tenderly lifted a strand of hair, and then tucked it behind her ear. "The problem with hiding your true feelings from your marriage partner is that you never receive the full joy God intended. I realize that being honest makes it easier for others to hurt you. But when you are open and honest with the person you love, it gives him the opportunity to fulfill your hopes and dreams instead of leaving him guessing how to please you."

She nodded her head but wasn't sure she was willing to go quite that far.

"For instance, there is nothing improper about a wife telling her husband she would like to be kissed. Husbands don't automatically know those things." He grinned at her.

"I would like that." She lifted her head and closed her eyes.

He broke forth in a laugh. Pain sliced through her like a sharp knife. When he leaned forward to kiss her, she turned her head.

On his second attempt, she again turned away. Luther sighed and he shook his head. "Maura, you misinterpreted my laughter. You can't always assume the worst when people laugh. I am pleased that you want me to kiss you. Truly, I am. I laughed only because I was using the statement about kissing as an illustration and you took it literally. I'll try to be more careful in the future if you'll try to be less sensitive. What do you say?"

She glanced up at him and didn't miss the pleading look that shone in his eyes.

"I think I would still like a kiss." This time he didn't laugh as he gathered her into his arms.

When he finally released her from his embrace, he lifted her down from the crate. "We have a lot more to talk about, but I suppose we should get back to the house."

Maura draped her shawl across her arm as they walked from the barn.

"I believe it's getting cooler." Luther lifted the shawl from her arm and placed it around her shoulders.

Maura nodded and smiled at him. "I think I'd like for you to keep your arm around my shoulder."

"I think I'd like that, too." He placed his arm around her and pulled her close while they made their way down the street.

She couldn't remember the last time she'd been so content— or so happy.

Chapter 11

*M*aura! Where have you been?" Georgette frowned as her as she and Luther walked into the house.

"Luther and I returned his horses to the barn." She smiled when Luther winked at her.

"Well, don't just stand there. We'll have guests arriving soon, and the rest of us have been hard at work while you've been gone. We planned on having you here to help us." Georgette's frazzled appearance and curt remarks didn't surprise Maura. She had tried to warn the girl that the dinner preparations would be more work than she could imagine.

Luther shook his head. "Maura was exactly where she needed to be, so please don't be harsh with her. It's really my fault for keeping her away, but there were things we needed to discuss. Things I felt were more important to our future than the dinner. She wanted to return, but I assured her there were plenty of hands to prepare the meal."

Georgette shifted her eyes back and forth between the two of them. "So you two have been talking. That's music to my ears." She grinned. "Did this talking have an amiable outcome?"

"I would say it did. Wouldn't you agree, Luther?" Maura looked up at him and wished she could ask for another kiss.

"Most amiable, although we didn't have enough time to resolve all of the issues we wanted to discuss. Did we, my dear?" He tipped her chin and placed a fleeting kiss on her forehead.

"No, not everything." Once again, he'd known what she was thinking. The idea was most disconcerting. She'd have to be careful what she thought!

Georgette stood momentarily transfixed. "God certainly can work miracles." With a baffled look on her face, she turned toward the kitchen.

"You go and help her, my sweet, and I'll see what I can do to help Michael." Luther leaned down to kiss her cheek.

My sweet, he called me "my sweet." The words echoed in her mind as she walked into the kitchen. However, it didn't take long for the culinary mayhem to push all thoughts of Luther from her mind. A quick survey of the situation made it quite clear that no one had organized the group of women. Everyone was scurrying about, but very little had been accomplished.

"Ladies!" Maura banged a ladle on the wooden table to gain their attention. "It appears that we need a bit of teamwork if we're to prepare and serve this meal on time. I think the easiest plan would be to make assignments. Is that all right with all of you?" She didn't wait for an answer. Instead, she waved to Georgette. "You're in charge of the meat, Georgette; have Michael help you with carving when you're ready. Mrs. Wilson, you're in charge of the stuffing and sweet potatoes—"

The older woman frowned. "But the turkeys have already been stuffed. Don't you want me to do something besides the sweet potatoes?"

"You can prepare the mashed potatoes also, but remember you'll need to help Georgette unstuff those turkeys when they're ready." Maura sent a fleeting smile in the woman's direction.

And so it went. Maura assigned the tasks and each of the women was responsible from beginning to end for those particular foods or tasks. Earlier they had placed signs about town informing folks of the dinner, but Maura thought it would be a nice gesture to personally invite folks so that they would feel genuinely welcome. Luther would be a perfect choice to help.

"Luther, there you are." She smiled at her husband as she entered the parlor where he and Michael were tending Becca. "I think it would be hospitable to go to the saloons and gaming parlors and invite the men to dinner. They may not see the signs; besides, some of them may not be able to read."

Luther leaned back in the sturdy oak chair, balancing on the back two legs and holding himself steady with the tips of his toes resting on the floor in front of him. His lips curved in a slow grin.

"Maura, my dear wife, do you have any idea how the owners of those saloons and gambling halls are going to react when I walk in and invite their customers to leave for a free meal?"

"No." She shook her head and waited.

He let his chair drop forward and then rested his arms across his thighs. "They are going to be very unhappy. This is one of the busiest times of year for them. In fact, the men spend most of their money trying to drown or forget their loneliness during this time of year."

"Well, I know that, Luther. That's why we planned this get-together!" His answer confused her, and she blew out an exasperated sigh. "I thought you were going to reveal some really good reason why you couldn't go invite folks."

He stared at her and then looked at Michael as though he needed help.

Michael looked as though he was trying to swallow a smirk. "Go ahead, Luther. You're doing fine. Explain it to her."

Luther rubbed his jaw. "Let me put it this way, my dear. If I go into those businesses and ask the customers to leave and come over here for free food and festivities, the owners of those businesses may never speak to me again. They're going to be angry because we'll be the cause of their losing money." He arched his brows. "Does that help you understand?"

"Well, if that's the only problem, invite them, too. Tell them we'd be happy to have them join us."

Luther pushed back in his chair, obviously intent upon ignoring her request. "I think perhaps those who want to attend will come without a special invitation."

"If you don't want to go, I'm sure that Michael would be willing to assist." Maura turned toward her new prey for her holiday mission.

"You know I would do that for you, Maura, but Georgette told me that I dare not leave this parlor. She said she'd be more than a little upset if she had to stop her work to tend to Becca. And I need to be here to carve the turkeys. I promised Georgette." He appeared pleased to have a negative response at the ready.

"I see." Maura gave a firm nod and turned away. Saying nothing further, she returned to the kitchen, certain she'd heard the two men congratulate each other on sidestepping her request.

It had been only a few minutes when she returned with Amelia Bergman in tow. "Amelia is going to tend Becca for the rest of the afternoon." She lifted the baby from Michael and placed her in Amelia's capable arms.

"You sure she's old enough to look after a baby?" Michael asked, a sense of foreboding in his voice.

"Of course, she is. She's fifteen years old and has seven younger brothers and sisters. She's had loads of experience, haven't you, Amelia?"

Amelia nodded her head in affirmation and walked toward the bedroom carrying her young charge.

"Now then, gentlemen, I think we've been able to work out a plan." She smiled as the two men looked at each other with obvious apprehension.

She turned to her husband and leaned close. "I am doing as you requested earlier, Luther. I'm being open and honest with you in order to allow you the opportunity to fulfill my expectations."

"This isn't quite what I had in mind when we talked. . ." Luther's voice faltered.

She straightened and met Luther's gaze. "Well, we never know when an opportunity will present itself, do we? In any event, it would make me extremely happy if you and Michael would go and extend a personal invitation around town."

"But—" Michael began.

Maura waved him to silence before he could offer further protest. "No need to worry about carving the turkeys, Michael. Georgette said she wouldn't need you to carve the turkeys for at least another hour."

The two men exchanged a look of doom. "Guess we'd just as well get this over with, Michael." Luther rose from his chair, and Maura followed behind them as they walked onto the porch and down the steps.

She called his name and Luther turned and walked back toward her. "When you return, I think I would like a kiss."

"I'll be happy to meet that expectation." He grinned and hurried to catch up with Michael.

A little over an hour had passed when Michael and Luther returned to the house. Georgette quickly rushed Michael into the kitchen to assist her with the turkeys. Maura walked into the parlor and caught sight of Luther.

"I see that you're back all in one piece." She placed her hand on her heart. "I'm glad none of those men did you harm."

Without a word, he swept her into his arms and kissed her soundly. Breathless, she slowly pulled away from him.

"I am all in one piece, my dear, but just remember that you are the one who sent me out extending invitations."

She arched her brows at his comment. "Did the business owners become angry?"

"They weren't overly pleased, but I guess they'll get over it." He nodded toward the kitchen. "By the way, how many did you say you'd planned on serving?"

"I'm not sure, but I think we'll have plenty of food. Why do you ask?"

He didn't answer but merely pointed his finger toward the front window. She peered out and gasped when she caught sight of the throng of people headed toward the house. She looked from the street toward Luther and then back again.

"Are they all coming here?"

"Yep!"

Surely he was joking. "All of them?"

"Yes, all of them. After Michael and I had visited a couple of the saloons, the owners got together and decided that the best thing to do was just close down and let their employees as well as their patrons attend your dinner. You're going to feed everyone from the miners to the dance hall girls." He grinned. "I hope you ladies are up for the task."

"This is more than I expected, and I know it's more than Georgette expected." She attempted to tamp down her rising fear. What if the crowd turned angry if there wasn't enough food?

He turned toward her and smiled. "Like you said earlier, you never know when an opportunity will present itself. Just look at this as an opportunity, Maura. In fact, you may never get another chance to minister to this many unsaved folks at one time."

"But there are so many." Her words came out in a breathy gasp.

"Hopefully those turkeys and hams will stretch as far as the loaves and fishes." He placed a protective arm around her. "We'll manage,"

Maura returned to the kitchen as fast as her legs would allow, though her left hip and leg had begun to ache. She'd been on her feet all day, and her limp always worsened when she began to tire.

Maura waved Georgette to her side. "Our guests are arriving. Many more than we anticipated."

Georgette bobbed her head. "I know. Michael told me. What are we going to do?"

"We'll just have to organize ourselves. I think if we set up a line and have them come through with their plates, not only can we control the portion sizes, but also it may control seating. By the time the ones at the beginning of the line are done eating, they can free their places for the others. If we run out of food, we'll apologize and let them know we'll plan for more guests next year." She hiked a shoulder. "That's the best I can come up with at the moment."

Hastily issuing instructions to the men and women assisting, Maura gave the dining room one last glance. It was chilly, but at least the weather was bearable. At the last moment Maura asked Michael and Luther to move the small piano onto the front porch so that Mrs. Wilson could play Christmas carols. If anyone could keep a group in good humor, it was Mrs. Wilson.

Assuring Maura she was up to the challenge, Mrs. Wilson delightedly took her place at the piano. Before long, the strains of "Silent Night" being sung by the crowd filled the house, and soon the dinner was being served.

Maura's plan worked. Their guests didn't seem to mind the wait once they reached the kitchen and were served the finely prepared meal. The biggest problem turned out to be keeping enough clean dishes; however, once again Maura convinced Luther and Michael to aid the women who were rushing to wash, dry, and replace the plates, cups, and silverware. They helped with the chore until several of the dance hall girls asked if they could assist. Maura quickly accepted their offer and put the men to work at other chores.

After all of the guests had been served, the kitchen cleaned, and the rest of the group had departed, Maura, Luther, Georgette, and Michael sat down in the parlor before the glowing fire Michael had started a few hours earlier.

Luther and Maura were seated on the tapestry-covered loveseat. His arm was draped around her shoulders and her head rested against his arm. Michael and Georgette were deep in conversation regarding the events of the day when Luther leaned down and kissed Maura's ear.

She looked up and smiled sleepily.

"Come home with me?"

"I am home, Luther." She felt him stiffen as soon as she said the words.

"Your home is with me." His voice was no more than a whisper.

"Well, yes, that's true enough. But, Georgette and I bought this place. You know that. I can't just walk off and leave her alone." She kept her voice low so Michael and Georgette wouldn't hear.

Michael leaned toward them. "Would you like for us to leave you alone?"

Maura shook her head. "No, it isn't necessary."

The words had barely escaped her lips when Luther overrode her response by saying they'd appreciate a few minutes of privacy.

As soon as they'd left the room, Luther turned toward Maura. "I want you to come home and begin our life as husband and wife, Maura. We've begun to work out our problems, and we need to be together if we're going to make our marriage succeed."

"I know there is truth in what you're saying, but there is so much left for us to discuss and, as I said a few minutes ago, I can't just walk out on Georgette."

He sighed and leaned back on the settee. "You didn't seem to have much problem walking out on me."

"You've told me to be honest and open with you. I'm going to try and do that, Luther, and I hope I won't regret it." She turned to look at him and grasped his hands in hers. "I believe it would be best if we at least discuss our problems and how we can resolve them before I return. I won't deny my feelings for you—I'm sure you've already guessed how much I care for you, but you've hurt me deeply. I don't want that to happen again. Let's take a little time and do this right."

"Just because we wait six months or six years doesn't assure we'll be happy," he said, obviously referring to the six-month waiting period she'd invoked prior to their marriage.

"I'm not talking about six months, Luther. Just enough time to discuss some of the problems we face and how to resolve them. And whether or not you want to acknowledge it, leaving Georgette and the baby living alone is different from when I left you. She'd have to find someone to stay at the house with her, at least during the night. She'd be scared to death to stay alone, and after what happened to me, I certainly wouldn't want to place her in such a precarious position. Of course, I'd be here during the day to help her with the restaurant, but that isn't the same as living here."

His mouth dropped open. "You plan to continue the restaurant venture? Even after you return home? I don't think that would ever work."

"You see, Luther, there are many things for us to resolve. I want our marriage to succeed, probably more than you can imagine. But it would be folly for me to return now." She gently squeezed his hand, hoping he'd see merit in her suggestion.

"Then I suppose there's nothing left to say." He pushed up from the divan.

"That's just it, Luther—there is everything left to say." What could she say that would change his mind? "Please tell me that you're not angry and that we'll talk further." She didn't want to beg, but she would do so, if necessary.

"You've misunderstood me again, my dear. I merely meant there was nothing further to say about your returning home tonight. We will talk and we will resolve our differences and you will return home." His voice was filled with confidence.

"You sound very sure of yourself."

"I'm not sure of myself, but I'm sure of God's plan for us, and I'm sure that I love you, Maura Buchanan." He extended his hand to her.

She rose to meet his waiting arms and feel the warmth of his kiss. They walked toward the front door and, after they kissed good night, she watched him as he walked down the street. Surprising her, he turned, blew her a kiss, and called out, "Merry Christmas."

"Merry Christmas, Luther." She stood on the porch for a few

minutes, her thoughts racing. *You're a complex man, Luther Buchanan.* She turned toward the door as Michael and Georgette stepped outside.

Michael glanced toward the street. "Luther gone home for the night?"

"Yes, for the night." Maura smiled and then returned indoors, leaving the couple to say their good nights.

Chapter 12

*M*aura rose early the next morning and had finished preparing breakfast before Georgette awakened.

"Aren't you the early bird." Georgette walked into the kitchen as Maura removed biscuits from the oven. "You ought to enjoy these last few days before we open the restaurant—sleep in while you can." Georgette shifted Becca into her other arm as she eyed Maura's breakfast preparations. "Are you planning on serving breakfast to the whole town or are you extra hungry?"

"I thought I'd take Luther's breakfast down to him." Maura did her best to avoid Georgette's watchful gaze.

"That's a first, isn't it?" Georgette sat down and balanced the baby on her lap. "It appears that the two of you are getting things worked out. It was nice to see you snuggled together last evening—just like a married couple should be."

"Luther has told me that he wants the marriage to work and that he cares for me." She filled a plate for Georgette and turned to look at her friend. "I believe him, but we need to resolve some of our differences before we make another attempt at living together."

"Living together! I hadn't given any thought to that. When the two of you get your problems resolved, I'll be left alone."

Maura wasn't surprised to hear the panic in Georgette's voice. "Please don't worry, Georgette. I won't leave before we make suitable living arrangements."

"You're not going to desert me, are you? And what about our business? I can't do this on my own, Maura. I need you." Fear shone in her eyes and she reached for Maura's hand.

"Georgette, please don't cry." Maura enveloped her friend and hugged her close. "We'll work this out. I promise—and I take my promises seriously. Now, you finish eating, and I'll take this food down to Luther and be back shortly."

The bell over the mercantile door announced Maura's entrance, and Luther immediately strode toward her. His gaze fastened on the wicker basket she carried over her arm.

"Did I arrive in time, or have you already had breakfast?"

"I haven't eaten yet, but even if I had, there'd still be room for your cooking." He patted his stomach.

She placed the basket atop a small table and emptied the contents before glancing toward the door.

Luther gestured toward one of the chairs. "Please don't rush off. Sit down and visit with me for a while."

"I told Georgette I'd be right back." Maura sighed. "When she saw that I had fixed breakfast for you, the realization that we might get back together hit her." He flinched at the remark, but she stayed him with her hand. "Don't misunderstand—Georgette wants nothing more than for us to be reunited—but she's fearful of her future. I promised her I wouldn't move out until we could make satisfactory arrangements."

"That could take a long time, Maura. Perhaps you shouldn't have made such a promise." Concern laced his words.

"The Lord will provide a way when the time is right. I'm sure of it." She picked up the basket and returned it to her arm. "Is there a time today when we could talk further?"

"Why don't you come here? That way Georgette won't feel as though she's confined to her room while we're talking. As soon as I've closed the store, I'll come and fetch you." He cut a piece of ham and grinned at her. "This looks delicious."

She chuckled. "You go ahead before it gets cold. Why don't you come for supper, and we can leave afterward."

"That sounds good." He nodded and smeared butter onto one of the biscuits.

"I'd better be getting back. Just bring those dishes along when you come." She hesitated and returned the basket to the table. "It will be easier to bring them in the basket."

He laughed. "You're right. I'll even wash the dishes. Thank you for breakfast." He dipped one of the biscuits into the creamy white gravy.

Her heart swelled with delight as she walked out of the store. "You are most welcome."

She'd not gone far when Mrs. Wilson rushed toward her calling her name.

Fear gripped her. "What is it? Has something happened to Georgette or the baby?"

"No, no, they're fine. I stopped by to see you, and Georgette said you were at the store with Luther. She said to tell you she was taking Becca for some fresh air. Do you have time for a visit?"

Relieved, Maura clasped a hand to her chest. She needed to remember that Mrs. Wilson had a flair for the dramatic. "Certainly. Come back to the house, and I'll fix a fresh pot of tea."

Once they returned to the house, Maura lifted two china cups and saucers from the walnut cabinet in the dining room and carried them into the kitchen. While she waited for the water to boil, she arranged biscuits on a china plate and placed it in the center of the table alongside a small crock of strawberry preserves.

"What brings you visiting so early this morning?" Maura removed the kettle from the stove and poured water into the teapot.

"You'll be so pleased to hear my news—I just couldn't wait to come tell you." The older woman bubbled with enthusiasm. "After Charles and I returned home last night, we had a visitor."

She said nothing further, and Maura knew that she was expected to encourage her. "And who was that?"

"One of the dance hall girls, the one with the black curls. Her name is Marie McTavish. She said you visited with her for a short time while she was washing dishes."

"Yes, I remember her." Maura poured tea into Mrs. Wilson's cup. "A pretty girl. She asked me several questions about why we were hosting the dinner. When I told her we wanted to give folks an option other than gambling or drinking to celebrate Christ's birth, she seemed genuinely touched. However, I didn't have time to visit very long, and when I returned later, she was gone."

"Well, she came to our house last night at about nine o'clock. Said she wanted to ask some questions about being a Christian. Charles was so good with her, explaining things carefully. He revealed the plan of salvation and then read to her from Romans 10:9-13. She became so excited when Charles assured her that God would forgive her sins. It truly brought tears to my eyes hearing her. When I was listening to her talk, it was apparent that the poor girl thought no one else in the world had ever been as sinful as she had been. After several hours of talking and praying, she accepted Christ as her Savior. Can you believe it? God gave us a miracle yesterday!"

Maura smiled. "I think He probably gave us more than one, but that is certainly wonderful news. I'm sure that the angels are rejoicing for Marie, and I'm happy that you came and shared the news with me."

"It's true that I wanted you to hear the news right away, but there's a little more we need to talk about." There was a note of reticence in Mrs. Wilson's voice.

"What's that?"

"Needless to say, Marie doesn't want to return to her previous life-style and, well, I don't think she'd be happy staying with Charles and me. Besides, I'm not sure that the parishioners would agree to that type of arrangement on a long-term basis. So, after I went to bed last night, a thought came to mind that perhaps. . ."

Edith left the sentence dangling while she took a sip of tea.

When Maura said nothing, Mrs. Wilson quirked a brow. "Well, what do you think?"

"About what? You said that a thought came to mind, but you didn't tell me what it was." Apparently the older woman had expected Maura to read her mind. Either that, or she was playing some sort of game.

Mrs. Wilson frowned. "Well, I was hoping for an invitation for Marie to move in here with you and Georgette. I thought it would be quite obvious, but it seems I was wrong,"

Maura gasped. "You can't be serious! We don't even know her." How could Mrs. Wilson think such an arrangement would be acceptable?

"Know who?" The two women turned to see Georgette standing in the doorway.

"Marie McTavish. She's one of the dance hall girls that attended the dinner—" Edith began.

"She was converted last night, and now Mrs. Wilson has come to ask if she can move in with us." Maura couldn't believe this discussion was going to continue any further.

"Move in with us?" Georgette's voice had risen several octaves. "A dance hall girl?"

"A converted dance hall girl," Edith corrected.

"Good heavens, I don't know how you could even ask such a thing. I have a young daughter, and I certainly don't need the influence of a woman of ill repute living with us." Georgette pinned the older woman a stern look.

"'Let he who is without sin cast the first stone.'" Mrs. Wilson folded her arms across her chest. "This young lady has accepted Jesus Christ as her Lord and Savior. She needs the support and affection of Christians, not judgment and derision. However, I've obviously made an error in judgment. Please forgive me." She pushed away from the table.

"Wait, Mrs. Wilson." Maura grasped the older woman's hand. "You must realize the fact that you've caught us completely by surprise with your request. I'm not saying it's totally out of the question, but Georgette and I really need to discuss this. Why don't you come back after lunch, and we'll talk further?"

"I'll be happy to do that." Mrs. Wilson's earlier enthusiasm had disappeared and had been replaced with a look of dejection.

No sooner had she left the house than Georgette turned on Maura. "How can you even consider such a thing? She's an immoral woman. What kind of message would we be sending to the community if we harbored the likes of her?"

"Listen to yourself, Georgette. Christ forgave you when you became a Christian, He forgave me when I became a Christian, and He forgave Marie when she became a Christian. Who she was and how she supported herself in the past has no bearing on the conversation at hand."

Georgette dropped onto one of the nearby chairs. "Oh, really?"

"I seem to recall you repeating a certain statement to me awhile back. It was a comment I'd made to you about Christians being so unforgiving and critical of each other that Satan can just sit around and enjoy the chaos that they create for each other. Do you remember that?"

Georgette nodded. "Of course, I remember. But we were talking about you and Luther. It was a totally different set of circumstances."

"I see. So you think we should be able to pick and choose the circumstances to which we apply God's principles?" Maura didn't want to anger Georgette, but the girl needed to reconsider her position.

"Well, not exactly, but I think this is different." Georgette shoved her lower lip into a pout.

"I don't want to hurt you, Georgette, but please tell me how you've come to such a decision. You needed refuge and assistance when you were pregnant with an illegitimate child. I felt it was my Christian responsibility to help you, and God has blessed me with a wonderful friend because of the help I offered to you and Becca. How can you now so quickly dismiss another woman in need?"

"You make me sound like a wretch." Georgette bowed her head. "Deep down I know that we should help her, but I'm so afraid of bringing unwanted attention upon myself or Becca. I don't want people to find out about the circumstances of her birth. In fact, I haven't even told Michael. You and Luther are the only ones that know, and I live in daily fear that he'll tell Michael. I know that it's selfishness on my part, because I don't want to face the ugliness of my past."

Without a word, Maura placed her arm around Georgette's shoulder and gave her a reassuring hug.

"We all have things in our past that we're ashamed of, but we can't let that be a deterrent to helping others. Satan uses that old scheme a lot."

Georgette placed her palm over her mouth. "I know what you say is right, but I don't want things to change." Her words were barely audible.

"Life is full of changes, Georgette. Nothing stays the same. Besides, most changes are exciting and fun if we keep an open mind about what God has planned for us."

"What's fun about all of this?" She pursed her lips together.

Maura patted her friend's hand. "Maybe I should rephrase that. Sometimes changes are exciting and fun—other times they may be painful. What I do know is that God always leaves us with a message through those changes, and those messages are exciting."

"I suppose it wouldn't hurt to talk to her. If we do agree, where is she going to stay? The only furnished bedrooms are yours and mine."

"I think the Wilsons would be willing to have her remain with them for a short time, at least until we can make adequate arrangements for furniture. Mrs. Wilson's concern was that Marie have some type of permanent living arrangement in place, not that she move her out immediately."

"If that's the case, perhaps we could ask Michael about making a bed."

Maura smiled at Georgette, who had gone from one extreme to the other in a matter of minutes. First she had wanted nothing to do with Marie, but now she had Michael making a brand new bed.

"Why don't we meet with Marie? If we find her personality agreeable, perhaps she could come over during the days and help us get ready for the opening of the restaurant. If we all get along and it appears that we could live together, we'll make plans for furnishing a bedroom." Maura squeezed Georgette's hand. "What do you think?"

"That sounds reasonable. We can certainly use her help with the restaurant—if she has any talent in that direction. I'm sorry. That was an unkind remark." Georgette's cheeks flamed.

Maura grinned. "Well, we already know that she can wash dishes, and that's a beginning."

Mrs. Wilson returned several hours later with her typically bubbly personality intact. She fluttered into the house and never ceased talking until Georgette placed a cup of tea and plate of cookies in front of her.

"Oh, thank you, my dear." She picked up an applesauce cookie and took a bite. "These are wonderful." She wiped the corners of her mouth with the linen napkin Georgette had supplied.

"Why don't you enjoy your tea, and I'll tell you the plan we have in mind." Maura sat down as Edith took another bite of cookie.

The older woman nodded her head in agreement as she sipped the cup of tea.

"Since we have only the two bedrooms furnished—"

"Oh, well, we can—" Mrs. Wilson interrupted.

Maura touched the woman's hand. "Please let me finish,"

"I'm sorry." Edith ducked her head, obviously realizing she needed to control her enthusiasm.

"As I was saying, since we have only two bedrooms furnished, Georgette and I thought that Marie could come here to work alongside us, preparing for the opening of the restaurant during the day. Then at night, she would return to stay with you and Charles. During this time of becoming acquainted, we would see about furnishing one of the other upstairs bedrooms. If we find ourselves harmonious—and we will make every attempt to do so—we will then offer Marie a home with us. What do you think?" Maura leaned back and awaited the woman's response.

Mrs. Wilson had lost some of her earlier animation and sat quietly for a moment as she finished the last of her tea.

"I don't suppose there's much choice, if that's what you think best. I had hoped you would welcome her immediately." Her voice held a lingering note of persuasiveness.

Maura shook her head. "Now, Edith, don't try to make us feel guilty. We already had a discussion about guilt earlier this morning. I think our decision will prove best for all three of us. If we find that we're incompatible, it will be kinder to Marie if she hasn't already moved into the house. You would agree with that, wouldn't you?"

"Well, yes." Though she said the words, her posture told another tale. She'd obviously expected them to accept Marie into their home this very day.

"Why don't you bring her over first thing in the morning, and we'll see how things go from there?"

"You're probably right. I realize adding another person to a household can change the whole complexion of things and I'm asking a lot of you two. But I don't think you'll be sorry. She's a lovely girl." Mrs. Wilson pushed away from the table.

"We're sure that she is." Georgette glanced at Maura and smiled.

"I suppose I should get home and discuss this with Charles and Marie. I haven't said a word to them yet, and I'm about to burst a seam holding it in." She giggled as she stepped toward the hallway.

The other two women laughed at her last remark. Edith was such a sweet and generous person, but truth was truth: she would probably explode if she didn't tell them soon.

Maura walked behind Mrs. Wilson toward the door. "Please keep in mind that Marie may not be interested in this plan. Working in a restaurant may be the last thing that she wants to do with her life."

"Oh, don't be silly, Maura. She'll be delighted." Mrs. Wilson lifted her hand in a dismiss gesture, then retrieved her blue shawl from the hall tree. "Marie and I will be here early tomorrow morning."

"Not too early!" Maura stood beside Georgette on the front porch, the two of them watching the older woman as she bustled toward home.

"We've had quite a day, and it's not even dinnertime. I don't think I can take much more excitement." Georgette sighed and turned toward the door.

"Oh, my goodness. Dinner!" Maura rushed ahead of Georgette.

"You needn't get too excited. It's just the two of us, and I'm in no big hurry to eat. Besides, we can have something simple."

Maura stopped short. "In all this commotion, I forgot to tell you that I'd invited Luther to dinner this evening. When I took his breakfast this morning, we agreed to meet after supper to further discuss some of our problems. And when he suggested that we meet after dinner, I told him to join us and we could talk afterward."

"Well, I'm sure that he's not expecting a feast, especially after all the work we performed yesterday. Why is he being so pushy? Can't this wait? I'll walk down to the store and tell him that we've had some unexpected business today so you're too busy to entertain this evening." Georgette followed her into the kitchen.

"No—I want to talk to Luther. I just need to decide upon something to fix for dinner."

"I see." Georgette pursed her lips in a pout. "He's already got you playing to his tune."

"Now what is that supposed to mean? You've encouraged me to try and resolve our problems, but now that we're making progress, you're acting like a spoiled child."

Georgette lowered her head. "You're right. I have no business interfering. It's just my fear of losing you—of being alone—that makes me so quarrelsome. Forgive me, Maura. You know I want you and Luther to be happy. If you'll let me help you, I'm certain we can have something prepared for dinner by the time he arrives."

Maura had been pleased with the evening thus far. Luther appeared to enjoy visiting throughout dinner, and had even asked if Becca would soon be awake so that he could see her.

"Why don't you two go into the parlor and visit? I'll clean up the kitchen," Georgette said when they had each finished a second cup of coffee. When neither of them moved, she gestured toward the other room. "I'll bring in dessert when I'm through."

"We had planned to go to my place and visit. That way we won't be interfering with you and Becca," Luther said.

Noting Georgette's wounded expression, Maura said, "Besides, Edith may stop over—you know how impulsive she can be."

"Oh, of course. How silly of me! You two go along. I'm sure that you'd like to have some privacy." Georgette's attempt to sound cheerful fell a bit flat.

Luther stood and retrieved his gray blanket-lined jacket from one of the pegs by the kitchen door.

Luther nodded toward Maura's lightweight cape hanging near the door. "I think you'll need something heavier than your shawl this evening."

"What? Oh, yes, I'll get my wool cape."

Georgette continued working in the kitchen, while Maura hurried upstairs to gather her warmer cloak.

Upon her return to the kitchen, Luther held Maura's cape for her. She glanced up at Luther. "I think she's upset," she whispered.

He smiled and leaned close to her ear. "She'll be fine."

"We're leaving, Georgette. Come lock up behind us, please." Maura hesitated in the hallway.

"My hands are wet. You go ahead and I'll lock it in just a minute," she called.

Luther leaned forward to open the door, but Maura frowned and glanced over her shoulder. As if realizing that Maura would not leave until the door was locked behind them, Georgette appeared in the hallway, drying her hands on the blue calico apron tied around her waist. Georgette's red eyes belied the cheerful countenance she attempted to present, and had Luther not steered her out the door, Maura would have insisted that they remain.

"I don't like seeing her upset." Maura placed his arm around her as they descended the front steps.

Luther nodded. "I know you don't, but this isn't about Georgette, it's about our marriage."

"You're right, but it's still difficult." A quiver of pleasure shot through her when he tightened his hold to keep her close while they continued to his home.

Once inside the house, he placed his hands on her shoulders. "Let me take your coat, and you can make yourself comfortable over there on the sofa."

Maura carefully positioned herself at one end of the carved oak sofa, which had been upholstered in warm shades of brown and tan. Luther soon returned and sat down close beside her.

"I was so eager for us to resume our conversation, I could hardly wait for dinner time to arrive." He leaned down and placed a light kiss upon her lips.

The kiss caught her by surprise. Although she enjoyed Luther's touch, his romantic fervor could easily sway her emotions. And, right now, she needed clarity of thought. Perhaps a change of topic was in order. "Did I tell you that Edith came looking for me when I was bringing your breakfast?"

"Oh? And what was our good pastor's wife doing out and about so early this morning?"

"It seems that Marie McTavish, one of the dance hall girls who attended the Christmas dinner, went and talked to Charles last night. She wanted to know more about Jesus, and after he explained the plan of salvation, she accepted the Lord," Maura explained.

His lips curved in a broad smile. "Well, then, I'd say that the Christmas dinner was a successful ministry. I can just imagine Edith bustling about to spread the good news."

"That wasn't the only reason she came visiting. She was thrilled about Marie, of course, but she was also interested in finding suitable living accommodations for the new convert."

His eyes gleamed with excitement. "And the perfect solution is with Georgette."

"With Georgette and me," she corrected. "Edith's idea was that Marie come and live with us and help in the restaurant."

"But, Maura, don't you see? This must be God's answer to our problem. Marie needs a place to live, and Georgette needs someone to live with her, which frees you to return home. This is wonderful news." He pulled her into a warm embrace.

"Not so fast, Luther." She placed her hand against his chest and leaned back. "I can't just move out and leave Georgette living with a complete stranger."

He shrugged. "Why not? You two were strangers not so long ago."

"Not really. We had developed a friendship while on board the ship and during the time we lived here with you. There was no question that we could compatibly live under the same roof, and we had a vested interest in making the situation work in order to support ourselves," she reminded him.

"She and this Marie can become friends, and they'll both realize the fact that they need to get along. After all, nothing is going to change their need to support themselves. At least not right away," he again rebutted. "When is Marie moving in?" he asked, his voice filled with excitement.

"Well, we haven't agreed that she can—at least not yet. We—"

"Why not? It's a perfect solution for all of us," he interupted.

Maura shook her head. "We want to see if we're compatible first. Marie is coming to meet us tomorrow. If the meeting goes well, she will come to work for us during the days and return to the Wilsons at night. Then—and only then—will we suggest that she move in with us. We did agree to begin furnishing an additional upstairs bedroom for her."

"Wait a minute! What's all this talk about we? Georgette's the only one who has to get along with her, and I'm sure that she'll make more effort if she knows you've decided to return home. The two of them should be deciding how they want to operate the restaurant and if they want to begin furnishing additional rooms. It will only complicate matters if they begin to rely on you—Georgette already does too much of that. Besides, Marie can have your room." He pinned her with a solemn look. "This is the answer to my prayers."

"It may be the answer to my prayers as well, Luther. But I think we're going to need time to make sure. We have several differing ideas that we need to resolve—"

"You could move back tomorrow. I can bring the wagon over first thing in the morning, and I'm sure that Michael and Charles will be glad to help. You can run the store while we're doing that." A look of complete satisfaction written on his face.

He was completely ignoring everything she'd said. Truth be told, he'd likely not even heard a word she'd spoken. She frowned and shook her head. "No!"

"No?" He arched his brows high on his forehead. "What do you mean, no?"

"I want to take the time to effect a lasting reconciliation; I've told you that. Luther, I don't plan to give up my interest in the restaurant. The money we used to purchase that home was an unexpected inheritance from Mrs. Windsor. It was her dream to open a restaurant and boarding house in California. Georgette and I are fulfilling that dream not only for ourselves but also in memory of Mrs. Windsor. That may be hard for you to understand, but I'd like to think that we are being good stewards and providing a much-needed service to this community, as well as supporting ourselves." She wanted him to understand that the boardinghouse was more than a whim on her part.

"You don't need to support yourself any longer. That's my job, and I want to do it. Let Georgette and Marie fulfill the dream. It doesn't have to be you. Besides, you won't have time for working at the restaurant." He pulled her close and attempted to capture her lips.

She was right—he wasn't listening to her. She ducked her head to avoid his kiss. "No, Luther. We won't solve our problems by everything being exactly as you say and then your quieting me with a kiss. My resentment would begin to rise, and eventually your kisses would become bitter. I don't want that to happen."

"What is the answer, then? We do everything as you say so that you'll be happy?" A hint of irritation laced his question.

"No. If we did that, you wouldn't be happy. After a while, you probably wouldn't even want to kiss me," She tipped her head to the side and looked into his eyes. "I don't want that to happen, either."

"So? What do we do?"

She hesitated, her thoughts racing as she attempted to come up with a reasonable solution. Finally, she met his gaze. "Would you object if I planned the menus and ordered the supplies for the restaurant?"

He stroked his jaw for a moment. "Well, no. That would probably work. Perhaps you could arrange to go over menus with Georgette and help at the restaurant two or three mornings a week, as well."

She looked deep into his eyes and smiled. "I would like a kiss."

He laughed heartily before gathering her into his arms and kissing her soundly.

"Now, for the next matter." She moved from his fervent hold. "We need to come to an agreement about when I will move back home. I know you want it to be tomorrow. However, I think three months would give us enough time to be sure that Georgette is comfortable with the new arrangement."

"Absolutely not!" he bellowed. "I'll not wait three months—one month is the absolute maximum I'll agree to!"

"Six weeks?" she questioned.

"The first day of February. You will sleep under this roof commencing the first day of February and not a day past. Do I have your word?"

His folded arms and furrowed brow gave evidence that he would brook no further argument.

"You have my word. Shall we seal it with a kiss?" She grinned at him.

"If anyone had ever told me that you would totally capture my heart and mind, I would have laughed. Just look at me—a complete fool over the woman I felt obligated to marry. Do you know how much I love you?" He pulled her toward him.

Before she could answer, his lips were upon hers with an urgency and obvious desire that soon inflamed her whole being. Returning his passion, she surrendered her lips and returned his kiss with mounting ardor. His hand cupped the nape of her neck, which pulled her even closer and held her captive to the intensity of his yearning.

"We must stop this." Reluctantly, she pushed away from him.

"Why? We are married." He gently attempted to pull her closer.

Resisting him was difficult, but he needed to hear the truth. "But I don't feel married, Luther."

Sorrow lingered in his gaze. "I'd like to change that! It's you who's not willing."

"I'm willing, Luther. But I believe that it would be better to wait until I've moved back home and we are truly living together. A new beginning to our marriage, with both of us eager and willing to share our lives. Does that make sense to you?"

He waited for what seemed an eternity and then turned toward her with a smile emerging upon his face.

"Why don't we really start over? Let's have a church wedding, like you dreamed of, with our friends there with us. I'm sure that Charles would be pleased to perform the ceremony, and it would give Edith another project to oversee. What do you think?" His excitement was palpable.

She bobbed her head with enthusiasm. "And we could have a small reception at the restaurant." How long had it been since she'd felt such delight? "Oh, Luther, it would be grand. Thank you for being so thoughtful," she said, spontaneously giving him a hug.

"Let's go tell Georgette." He stood and extended his hand to her.

"I probably should get back home, but I'd rather wait to tell Georgette. I think she'll accept it more once she's gotten acquainted with Marie."

"You're probably right. Just remember this: you agreed to move back by the first of February at the latest."

"What do you think of January twenty-ninth as our wedding day?" She glanced over her shoulder at Luther as he helped her with her cape.

"It sounds fine. Is there something significant about that particular day?"

She nodded and smiled. "Yes. It's my parents' wedding anniversary, and they've been married almost forty years. Perhaps it will be a good date for us, also."

"Then January twenty-ninth it is."

Chapter 13

*M*arie McTavish invaded the lives of Maura, Georgette, and Becca with an enthusiasm and joy that nobody could ignore. The gifts of her newfound salvation and friends were a seemingly constant source of delight to her, and she expressed it in every way possible. Having left seven brothers in Ohio, she was immediately captivated by Becca's many charms. In fact, it seemed as if the baby were always riding on her hip.

"You're spoiling her," Georgette mildly scolded as Marie walked into the kitchen early one morning with Becca in her usual position, resting on Marie's hip.

"Love doesn't spoil children. It makes them blossom—just like flowers. Untended flowers soon wither and die; untended children do the same. Maybe not a physical death, but in other ways that damage and scar them for life. I won't indulge her whenever the time comes that she needs correction, but she hasn't reached that time in her life just yet," Marie's eyes shone with pain.

Georgette silently chastised herself. Perhaps her words had been too harsh. "I've never seen you so serious, Marie. I'm sorry if I upset you."

Marie gathered the ingredients for buttermilk biscuits and placed them on the table. "It's all right. Guess I'm just thinking about my own childhood,"

"Tell me about it," Georgette said.

"Nothing much to tell. Too many kids, too little money. I watched my ma turn into an old woman by the time she was thirty. She died shortly after my youngest brother turned two. I was the oldest child and the only daughter. Guess that says it all." She hiked a shoulder. "I had to give up going to school when Ma died. All my time was taken up cooking, sewing, doing farm chores, and tending my brothers. When I turned sixteen, I told Pa he'd better find someone else to take over. He didn't take too kindly to the idea, but I stuck to my guns. I figured he'd never look for a wife as long as he had me around, and I sure didn't plan to die like Mama. Soon he found him a widow lady to marry. The day she moved in, I moved out."

"Where did you go?" The tale fascinated Georgette. Her own family was not wealthy, but they had never wanted for the basics in life.

"I hate to admit it, but I took the egg money and used it to pay for my passage to St. Louis. However, without any education or experience, I found that there weren't many jobs available. So I went to work cooking in a restaurant. One day the owner of a saloon down the street asked if I wanted a job making twice as much money. Unfortunately, I jumped at the chance." She shook her head, obviously sorry for the choice she'd made.

"You were young and made a mistake; we all do. What's important is that we learn from those mistakes," Georgette consoled.

"I'm afraid I was a long time learning! I saved enough money to get myself to California, hoping to get a fresh start. Trouble is, I used up all my money getting here. I told myself I'd work in a saloon only for a little while, just long enough to get some money together and figure out what I wanted to do."

Georgette gathered the baby from Marie's arm. "What city were you living in?"

Marie mixed the ingredients and then placed the dough on the table.. "Here. In Placerville. Jake Grisby, the owner of the saloon, was in San Francisco the day I arrived. He goes there whenever he needs to hire new girls."

"Why?" Georgette stepped closer.

Marie picked up the rolling pin and rolled the biscuit dough. "To watch for new female arrivals. He has quite a line—but let's not go into that. Anyway, I came to Placerville and ended up worse than when I'd been in St. Louis. Jake always found a reason not to pay us. He figured if we ever got ahold of any money, we'd take off—and he was right about that. You can't just walk to another town from Placerville—at least not one where you could make a living."

"I'll bet you've had lots of men asking for your hand. Women are scarce around here. Why didn't you accept one and get out of that place if it was so bad?"

"Oh, sure. I had marriage proposals. But most of the men that came in the saloon couldn't support a wife. Besides, what little gold they found was used to buy liquor and more supplies because they were determined they'd strike the mother lode the next time they went out in the hills. And the few men of means that came around weren't about to marry a saloon girl. Believe me, there wasn't an easy answer. At least not until I listened to Pastor Wilson," she explained.

"I'm so glad that you came to our Christmas dinner. Just think, if Jake hadn't closed the saloon Christmas day, you'd most likely still be working for him. I'll bet he's been seething ever since." Georgette giggled.

Marie wiped the flour from her hands. "I think you're probably right. I'm hoping I can save up enough money to help a couple of the other girls get out of there someday. Working there is a poor excuse for a life."

A gust of cold air followed Maura as she entered the back door. She shivered in spite of the warmth in the kitchen.

"It's getting colder, isn't it?" Georgette bounced Becca while Maura hung her coat on one of the pegs by the back door.

"Yes." Maura walked to the fireplace to warm her hands.

Marie smiled in Maura's direction. "What took you out so early this morning?"

"Luther and I wanted to meet with Pastor Wilson to go over our wedding plans. You know how Luther is—he didn't want to leave everything until the last minute."

Georgette's lips tightened into a pout. "My goodness, Maura, you've got almost three weeks. How much can there be to discuss?"

Maura had little doubt that Georgette hadn't totally adjusted to the upcoming changes. While the girl voiced her support of their reconciliation, her actions revealed she hadn't yet accepted the fact that Maura would soon be moving out. "Luther just wants everything to go smoothly."

"He just wants to be sure that you don't back out."

"Back out? Georgette, I'm already married to Luther. This wedding is more for me than Luther. He wanted me to have the kind of wedding I've always dreamed about. One I could remember with fondness." Maura had done her best to understand Georgette's feelings, but her words were beginning to sting.

"Right now, Luther Buchanan would do anything to get you back to that store. He's probably already figuring how much more money he's going to make having you there working all the time." Georgette stuck out her lower lip.

Maura couldn't refrain from breaking into laughter at Georgette's dramatic exhibition.

"Just what are you laughing about?" Georgette frowned.

"You!" Maura said. "I'm surprised that you're not stomping your feet. Honestly, Georgette, you're acting more childish than a two-year-old."

"Is that right? Well, perhaps if you were in my position, you'd be stomping your feet, too! I'm about to lose my best friend, and it's not a very pleasant feeling." Georgette's voice warbled.

"Lose your best friend? You're not losing me, Georgette. I'm only moving down the street," Maura said. "I think we need to have a talk. Let's go in the parlor. Marie, would you mind looking after Becca?" Maura didn't wait for an answer before ushering Georgette toward the other room.

Once they'd stepped into the parlor, Maura pointed at a chair. "Sit down."

Georgette plopped down into the wooden rocking chair and began to furiously rock back and forth.

Maura sat down opposite the girl. "You know, Georgette, I remember a young girl I met on a ship sailing to California. She became my friend, and I thought she wanted only the best for me. It appears that what she really wanted was what was best for me—as long as it was what was best for her also."

"That's not true." Georgette jumped up from the chair. "I still want what is best for you, but I'm not convinced that going to live with Luther is what's best."

"Georgette, it's not been so long ago that you were seeing the kinder, gentler side of Luther. But now that we've made progress in reconciling our differences, you've changed your mind. Your attitude makes me think that you're more concerned about losing my help in the restaurant than anything else."

"I'm hurt that you could even think such a thing." Tears formed in Georgette's eyes. "I suppose the real truth is that I've come to rely upon you, Maura. If—I mean, when—you leave, it's going to be like leaving my family all over again. I'll be alone."

"Georgette, Luther has agreed that I can continue to help here at the restaurant. And I plan to do just that. Besides, you must remember that you have Becca and Marie. Marie is such a dear, and the two of you are already getting along famously. I truly believe that the Lord has sent her to us for this very reason."

Still unwilling to concede, Georgette shook her head. "The Lord knows my heart, and He knows it's you I want here."

"The Lord knows what we need, and He provides. Nowhere in the Bible does it say that He provides what we want. Remember that,

Georgette. It's a difficult lesson—one that most of us don't fully master in a lifetime."

"I'll try to be happy for you, Maura, but I want you to remember that if things turn sour again, you've always got a home here."

Maura embraced the girl. "Thank you, Georgette."

"I must admit that I'm surprised that Luther has agreed you can continue to help with our business," Georgette said.

"I think he realizes how important the restaurant has become to me, and he also knows how much I'll miss being with you and Becca. He truly has changed, Georgette. In fact, now I don't doubt his love for me. We've both had changes of heart, and I think we're going to begin our marriage for all the right reasons when we have our wedding in a few weeks."

"I hope so, Maura. The last thing I want is for you to be hurt again."

Georgette sighed, obviously unconvinced that Luther's motives were genuine.

During the next week the weather turned colder, and on several mornings the Placerville inhabitants had awakened to a light dusting of snow. This morning, however, it had continued. Maura glanced out the window, watching as the large, wet flakes began to accumulate, the tree branches already laden with the additional weight.

Marie walked into the kitchen and poured a large mug of coffee. "Why the worried look?"

"Luther left for San Francisco yesterday. I tried to convince him to wait until the weather cleared, but he said that would mean holding off until spring." Maura pushed the cream pitcher across the table toward Marie.

"He'll be fine." Marie picked up the pitcher and poured a splash of cream into her coffee. "I'm sure that he's been making the trip for quite a few years now and knows how to take care of himself. Quit your worrying! It'll do him no good, and it certainly won't do you any good."

"You're right, but it's easier said than done."

Marie smiled and placed an arm around her new friend. "If the three of us commit to keep him in our prayers until his safe return, perhaps it will be easier for you."

"Thank you, Marie. It would mean a great deal to know that you and Georgette are praying for Luther's safety. I'll be doing the same," she said. "By the way, have I told you how pleased I am that God sent you to us?"

Marie grinned. "Well, not exactly. However, Georgette has told me that I'm God's answer to Luther's prayers."

Maura chuckled at the remark. "I think you are God's answer to many prayers. But, in addition to that, I am very pleased to be counted among your friends and am happy that you've come to live here."

"Thank you, Maura. I'll be forever in your debt—and Georgette's." Marie's tone had turned serious.

"You're not in my debt, Marie. You've more than earned your keep around here. Without your help, it would have been several more weeks before we could open the restaurant. And now look at us—we've been in full operation for almost two weeks."

"Speaking of which, I'd better get busy. We'll have customers expecting breakfast soon." Marie pushed away from the table, just as the front door slammed shut.

"Georgette! Where have you been? I didn't even realize that you'd left the house." Concern etched Maura's fine features.

Georgette knocked the snow from her boots and then moved toward the kitchen stove to warm herself. "I wanted to remove some of the snow from the front steps before our customers begin arriving," she said. "It's really coming down, so my efforts will probably be in vain." She glanced out the window as she removed her heavy wool coat and gloves.

Maura shrugged. "We may not have many customers if it's that bad out there."

"Don't count on that," Marie said. "The men around here have become used to a hearty home-cooked breakfast. Believe me, they'll be here. I'd better get out back and bring in some more wood." She reached for her wool coat hanging by the kitchen door.

"Michael tells me that it looks as if this promises to be the worst storm in several years." Georgette stepped to the fireplace and rubbed her hands together. "He said anyone caught out in this weather would be fortunate to survive."

Maura's chest tightened with fear. "Michael thinks it's going to be that bad?" She attempted to hide her growing concern, but panic had already seized her.

"He said it looks like we're in for a good one, and there's no telling when it might stop. A couple of the old-timers that have been around these parts for years told him from the look of the skies, we'll probably be snowed in for quite a while. I hope Luther's got his supplies well stocked," she said.

"Luther's gone." Maura's voice was no more than a whisper.

Georgette wheeled around to face her. "Gone? Gone where?"

"San Francisco."

"San Francisco? Why on earth did he leave this time of year—with so little time before your wedding? Did he have supplies coming in?"

"He didn't tell me much. I asked him to wait, but he said he had to go. I know it wasn't for supplies because he didn't take the wagons. He was going alone on his horse and said he should be back in plenty of time for the wedding."

"Isn't that just like him? That man is so selfish—always thinking of himself and causing—"

Maura frowned. Rather than listen to Georgette berate her husband, Maura needed encouragement and support. Anger and pain mixed with anger and welled inside her chest. "Georgette, I really don't want to hear your unkind remarks. I'm concerned about Luther, and what would help me is to know that my friends are praying for his safe return rather than criticizing his mysterious actions."

Maura had barely uttered the words when Marie bustled in the back door with an armful of wood, her hair turned temporarily white from the trip outdoors. "The men are on their way, ladies."

In spite of the snow, the breakfast crowd arrived and the morning passed quickly. It was shortly after ten o'clock when Maura noticed Georgette sitting with Michael. He'd apparently returned for another cup of coffee and a break from his work. This arrangement had become a recent habit, and Maura was pleased to see the two of them forming a caring relationship.

Maura had neared the front door when Georgette called out to her. "Where are you going, Maura?"

She paused and tied the ribbons of her heavy wool bonnet. "I promised Luther that I'd take care of the store during the afternoon while he's gone. I'll be back to help with supper, and things are well underway for the noon crowd. So I don't think you'll need me. If you do, send word to Charles, and I'm sure he'll relieve me at the store so that I can return."

"Wait, Maura. I'll go with you. It's treacherous walking out there, and we sure don't want you falling down," Michael said.

She gestured for him to remain seated. "No, no. I don't want to take you away. I can make it just fine."

Michael shook his head and jumped up from his chair. "I'll hear nothing of the kind."

Once they were out the door, she was glad to have Michael's assistance. Walking in the wet snow was nearly impossible, and the high winds made it difficult to see so much as a hand in front of one's face.

"It's a real white-out," Michael shouted as they pushed against the wind.

Maura didn't attempt to reply. It was taking every ounce of strength she had just to remain upright for the short distance. In fact, it would have been impossible without Michael's help. Once inside the store, she removed the "Closed" sign from the door and carefully lit several of the oil lamps.

"I'll get a fire going for you before I leave." Michael strode toward the stove. "By the way, Georgette didn't seem to know why Luther had ventured off to San Francisco in the middle of winter. Did he confide in you before leaving town?" His gaze remained fixed on the wood he was stacking in the fireplace.

"I really don't know, Michael. He said he had some business that had to be taken care of and he'd be back in time for the wedding."

She was chilled to the bone, and although she could have mustered the strength to get a fire started, she was thankful for Michael's help. She remained a short distance away as he adeptly laid the wood in place and set a match to the tinder. She smiled as the fire began to lick upward toward the larger logs.

"It ought to warm up in here pretty soon. Why don't you sit close by and dry off." He surveyed the sparse wood pile by the stone hearth. "Looks like I'd better bring in some more wood before I go so it'll be good and dry before it's needed."

"Thank you, Michael. I appreciate your help." She sat down in the chair he'd pulled close to the fireplace. She had hoped he would say something to bolster her spirits and help assuage the growing fear in the pit of her stomach, but he didn't.

He rubbed his gloved hands together. "I'm glad to help, Maura. I just wish that Luther wouldn't have taken off in this kind of weather. He knows better."

She nodded, but felt the need to defend him. "It wasn't snowing when he left."

"No, but he knows enough about this country to realize there was a possibility of something like this." Seeing the pained look on her face, he quickly added, "Luther knows how to take care of himself. I'm just glad he's traveling on horseback instead of with wagons. He stands more of a chance of getting through without wagons. Besides, he's made more trips to San Francisco than anyone else around Placerville. If anyone can find his way through this storm, it'll be Luther. I'll get that wood and then I'd better get back to work."

A short time later, he returned with a pile of wood, laid it out so it could dry as quickly as possible and then tipped his hat on the way out.

"Thanks again, Michael."

He nodded. "I'll come back around four o'clock and fetch you." A rush of cold air and a light layer of snow entered the store as Michael left.

Doubt there will be much business here today, she thought as she began walking about the store and deciding what tasks would keep her busy during the next several hours.

Placing a pot of coffee over the fire, she was heartened when two old miners came wandering in to sit by the hearth and play a game of checkers. They were familiar faces, men who now spent more time in town than they did mining. Maura had learned that when their funds ran low, they'd go back into the hills until they'd accumulated enough gold dust to keep them going a while longer.

They drank steaming coffee from large tin mugs and talked with each other, commenting from time to time on the weather and shaking their heads in obvious disgust.

A couple of hours later, they stood and prepared to leave. One of them turned toward her. "Luther say when he'd be back?"

She shook her head. "He didn't say exactly."

"Did he take the wagons?" the other man inquired.

"No, he didn't go for supplies," she said.

"How 'bout I go out there and take care of the animals for ya? Was he planning on you doing that, or did he make other arrangements?"

"I'm not sure," she replied, having given no thought to the horses that probably should have been tended earlier in the day.

"Don't you worry, missus. We'll take care of 'em while he's gone. Luther's done plenty for us in the past, so it's the least we can do."

"I sure do thank you," Maura said. Once the men departed, Maura whispered a prayer of thanks. Once again the Lord had provided her with the assistance she needed.

Michael reappeared shortly after four o'clock and escorted her back to the house. The savory aroma of beef stew and cornbread, together with the warmth from the kitchen, greeted them as they opened the back door.

"Why'd you come clear around back?" Marie wiped her hands on her apron as the couple entered.

Maura stomped her feet in an attempt to clear the snow from her shoes. "I convinced Michael to come around here so that we wouldn't track all this mess into the front."

"You shouldn't have been concerned about that." Georgette's lips curved in a weary grin as she entered the kitchen. "I've spent a good part of the day wiping up the mess created by this snowstorm."

"Well, I hope that we've saved you a little work." Maura leaned forward and gave her friend a hug.

"I'm glad you're back here. If this snow keeps up, I'm not going to hear of you going back to that store tomorrow," Georgette warned. "Michael agrees with me, don't you, Michael?" Georgette pinned Michael with a look that said he'd best agree.

"Well, I don't think it would be wise." Michael's tone was more cautious than Georgette's

"Let's wait until tomorrow before we make any decisions." Maura decided it might prove best to change the subject. "What needs to be done toward finishing dinner?"

"Everything's ready, but I'm not expecting much of a crowd tonight," Marie said. "I didn't prepare near as much as we normally do. Hope I didn't misjudge folks."

Maura removed several serving bowls from the cabinet. "We'll find something to serve them if we run out of stew, Marie. Folks are more likely to come and eat when they have to be out and about early in the day. Once they get home, they're probably going to stay put."

The next morning the snow had stopped, but the winds continued gusting, causing large drifts to form in their wake. Maura peeked out the parlor window and was greeted by dazzling snowdrifts along the front of the house that completely covered the lower half of the windows.

We're really snowed in, she thought, sure that they couldn't possibly open the front door without being prepared to tunnel through the five-foot-high drifts. Marie walked into the parlor and positioned herself alongside Maura.

"Guess we won't have to cook for anybody except ourselves today, will we?" Marie shot a pensive look in Maura's direction. "He's going to be just fine." Marie patted Maura's arm. "I just feel it in my soul."

"Thank you, Marie." Maura turned and removed a cup from the shelf. "I think I'd like a cup of coffee." She didn't want to think about where Luther might be. If she did, she was afraid where those thoughts might lead her.

During the weeks that followed, the snow and winds finally abated. Through the combined efforts of the townspeople, they had finally dug themselves out. Although the weather remained frigid and the sun couldn't seem to emit enough heat to melt the snow, life returned to a semblance of normality. But still no word was received from Luther, and the few new folks who came to town had seen or heard nothing of the man whom Maura doggedly described to them.

"I don't know what you can be thinking, Maura. You're only going to cause yourself further distress and heartache. Please tell me that you'll cease this nonsense immediately." Georgette tightened her lips into a thin line.

"You'd just as well stop badgering me, Georgette. I've made up my mind."

"This is utter foolishness!"

"You need not take part if that's the way you feel. Just stay here and carry out your chores as usual. I'll not hold it against you," Maura said as she placed an iron kettle filled with water over the fire to heat.

Georgette sighed. She longed to be supportive of her friend, but this was pure foolishness. Maura was setting herself up for further heartbreak. "Do you really believe that he's going to magically appear just because it's January twenty-ninth?"

Maura turned to face her. "We set January twenty-ninth as our wedding day, and I'm going to be there—on time—for the wedding."

Against Georgette's wishes, Maura placed a notice on the front door of the restaurant for the last three days stating that they would be closed for business today. The two of them had argued about the circumstances: She did not want Maura to be disappointed or embarrassed when Luther failed to appear, whereas Maura was sure that the wedding would turn out as planned. Only Marie remained silent.

Once the water was heated, Marie assisted Maura in filling the tub and then left her to enjoy a warm bath, the soothing fragrance of lavender oil filling the room.

"Why don't you try and talk some sense into her," Georgette whispered to Marie as Georgette exited the kitchen and entered the hallway.

"No, I don't think it would be proper for me to become involved in this. Besides, Georgette, Maura is a grown woman. I'm sure she understands that Luther probably won't be at the church. However, if she feels this strongly about keeping her commitment to the wedding plans, why are you so determined to stop her?"

"It's just silly. After all, they're already married. Why should she put herself through this added pain?"

"I'm not sure why she's so stubborn, but I'll certainly not be the one attempting to stop her." Marie's tone was firm. "I've got to get upstairs. I told Maura I'd help her get dressed. Are you going to get ready or not? She's planning on you being her attendant."

Georgette sighed. "Oh, there won't be any wedding. But if she's going to get ready, I guess I will, too. Have you seen Michael this morning?"

Marie glanced over her shoulder. "No. Isn't he supposed to stand with Luther?"

"Yes." Georgette shook her head as she followed Marie up the stairway. "I wonder if he's going to go to the trouble of getting ready or if he has more sense than the rest of us."

Maura allowed the warm water to envelop her as she slid into its depths, pushing all thoughts from her mind as she soaked in the sweet-smelling fragrance. When the water finally turned cool, she stepped out of the tub and dried herself in front of the fire. Wrapping herself in the warm quilt that Marie had left for her, she made her way upstairs to her bedroom.

Marie looked up as Maura entered the bedroom. "I don't think I've ever seen such a beautiful wedding dress."

"Thank you, Marie. I'm quite fond of it myself and feel quite fortunate. How many brides are able to wear their wedding dresses more than once?"

"Not many, I'm sure," Marie said.

Maura didn't miss the concern than shone in Marie's eyes. She wanted to set the girl's mind at rest so she drew close to her side and smiled. "You don't need to worry about me, Marie. I'll be fine. Even if Luther doesn't make it, I'll be fine, but I need to keep my promise."

Marie glanced toward the hallway and kept her voice low. "Georgette cares about you very much, Maura. At first I thought she was jealous you were leaving, but now I think she's truly concerned that you'll be deeply wounded if the wedding doesn't take place."

"I know Georgette means well. Georgette is a dear girl whose friendship I treasure, but she must realize that I'm keeping things in proper order—God first, Luther second, and then others. I must at least try to honor my word to my husband. I hope that she'll understand my reasons, and you need not worry—I'm not angry with her. How could I be? I know she's merely trying to protect me." Maura touched her fingers to the fine lace on the wedding gown. "Would you help me with my dress?"

Marie bobbed her head, and carefully held the gown as Maura stepped into the ivory and lace confection.

Georgette sighed as she walked into the room. "You look lovely. I had forgotten just how beautiful your dress is." She touched the lace accented sleeves as she walked in a circle around Maura.

"Thank you. You're quite a sight yourself." Georgette had donned the deep green silk gown that the two of them had sewn especially for this occasion. "That color is lovely with your hair and skin. You should wear it often."

"Thank you, Maura." Georgette leaned forward and lightly kissed Maura's cheek.

"Let me get your shoes." Marie hurried across the room and retrieved the low-heeled ivory shoes decorated with tiny lace bows.

"Would you like me to fashion your hair in finger curls like last time?" Georgette didn't wait for an answer before picking up Maura's hairbrush.

"I'd like that very much." Maura sat down and lifted her head to enjoy the brushstrokes.

After several attempts, Georgette and Marie finally agreed that the bride's hair passed inspection. Carefully, Georgette placed the coronet headpiece of crystal-beaded flowers and waxed orange blossoms that held the lace veil on Maura's head.

Maura met Marie's forlorn gaze in the mirror. "You have no bouquet to carry."

"Of course she does. Wait until you see it. Maura's mother made it, and it matches her headpiece. It's absolutely stunning." Georgette had hurried to answer before Maura could say a word.

"Where is your bouquet?" Georgette glanced about the room.

"In the second drawer of the chiffonier." Maura turned and watched as Georgette pulled the small bouquet fashioned from ribbons, lace, and waxed orange blossoms and leaves from the depths of the bureau.

"Oh, Maura, it's lovely." Marie traced a finger down one of the ribbons that bedecked the delicate arrangement.

"Thank you, and thank you both for your help." After a final glance in the mirror, Maura turned towardt her friends. "I think we're ready, with time to spare."

"I just hope that Michael gets here with the buggy." Georgette had barely finished her sentence when a knock sounded at the front door. Waffles bounded from the room and raced down the steps, his instinctive barking at any intrusion now expected by the residents of the household.

Georgette followed the dog downstairs. Moments later, Maura stepped into the hallway. Michael stood inside the front door dressed in his best dark blue suit. No doubt, the buggy was parked and waiting in front of the house.

"Is she ready?" Michael's question drifted up the stairs to where Maura stood.

"Yes, but believe me, I tried my best all morning to dissuade her. She wouldn't hear of it." Although Georgette whispered the remark, Maura didn't miss a word. She shouldn't be listening to their conversation, but she'd wanted to know if there was any word from Luther before she walked downstairs.

"I haven't seen anything of Luther, and I think if he were in town the store would be open or there'd be some sign of him. I stopped by the Wilsons' place earlier today, but they hadn't heard from him, either. However, Charles and Edith said they'd be at the church as planned. I'm afraid everyone's going to be there except Luther. I hope this isn't going to turn into a disaster for Maura."

Michael's voice was filled with such compassion that Maura couldn't continue to listen any longer. She stepped to the top of the stairs and pasted a bright smile on her lips. "Hello, Michael. Thank you for being so prompt."

Michael looked up toward her as she descended the stairs. "My! Don't you look lovely. How fortunate can a man be? Escorting such lovely ladies doesn't happen very often. This is truly a pleasure. Let me help you with your wraps."

"I'll go and get Becca." Marie hastened down the steps while the others retrieved their coats.

The three of them smiled when Marie returned with Becca in her arms. Marie had gathered the baby's downy fuzz together and placed a tiny bow on her head.

"She's dressed for the occasion, too." Marie handed the baby to Georgette while Michael assisted Marie with her coat.

The brief ride to the church seemed even shorter today. Maura strained to catch sight of Luther or glimpse any evidence that he might be present at the church. But she didn't see any sign of his horse or the buggy that he used on Sundays and special occasions. From the number of carriages tied outside the church, it appeared many of the folks from town had braved the cold.

"Looks like you're going to have quite a few folks celebrating with you," Michael said as they pulled to a stop at the back of the church.

Maura merely nodded her head and allowed him to assist her down from the buggy. She wasn't certain whether having so many guests would prove a good or bad thing. If Luther didn't appear, she hoped those in attendance would show compassion.

"I'll take you in and come back for Marie and Georgette. I'm sure you'll want a few minutes to talk to Charles before it's time to begin." Michael escorted her into the back of the church and toward the small room where she was to meet with the pastor.

The tinkling sounds of the piano lingered in the air as she entered the room. Pastor Wilson was there—alone—sitting in one of the chairs and reading his Bible.

"Maura, don't you look lovely. What a beautiful bride you are." He stood and placed his Bible on the small oak table sitting between two of the chairs.

"Thank you, Charles. Have you seen anything of Luther yet?" She'd attempted to withhold any sign of expectancy, but failed.

"I'm afraid not, my dear. But there's still time. The service isn't due to begin for another fifteen minutes, and I'm not opposed to waiting a bit longer than that if need be."

"Luther believes in punctuality. If he's not here at the appointed time, he'll not be coming." She spoke the words with assurance. If she'd learned nothing else about her husband, she knew he abhorred tardiness.

"Now, now, my dear. Occasionally life can cause delays. We can't always adhere to the ticking of a clock. Why don't you sit down, and we'll read some scripture and pray a bit." The pastor gestured toward one of the chairs.

Maura carefully backed toward the chair, the whalebone stays causing her no small amount of difficulty in maneuvering. She smiled. "I think I'd rather stand, if you don't mind. It took a great deal of time getting in and out of the buggy, and I don't think I'm up to the challenge quite so soon."

"Certainly. I understand." He leafed through his Bible and then tapped a page. "Are you familiar with the words of Matthew 6:25, Maura?"

"Would that be a passage about worry and anxiety?"

"Exactly," he said with a smile. "Would you like me to read it aloud?"

"Please." Slowly she began to relax.

Charles settled into the chair beside her and quietly began to read. Maura listened carefully as he recited these words: "Behold the fowls of the air: for they sow not, neither do they reap, nor gather into barns; yet your heavenly Father feedeth them. Are ye not much better than they?"

Both Charles and Maura turned as a voice behind them continued, "Which of you by taking thought can add one cubit unto his stature?"

"Luther!" Maura stood and rushed to his outstretched arms. "Oh, Luther, I was so worried. You should never have made that trip. Were you caught in the blizzard?"

He smiled down at her and reached into the embroidered blue satin waistcoat he had worn for their wedding in San Francisco. Pulling out his watch, he clicked it open and chuckled. "I'm afraid we'll have to wait until after the wedding for explanations if we're going to begin on time."

Maura grinned at the preacher. "I told you he believes in punctuality."

"There's time for just one thing before we go into the church." He reached into the breast pocket of his coat and pulling out a black velvet box. "This is why I went to San Francisco." He carefully lifted the lid.

She gasped at the beauty of his gift to her. "Oh, Luther."

"Do you like it?" His eyes twinkled in obvious delight.

"How could anyone not like it?" She lifted the beautiful brooch from the ivory silk that lined the box. The circular silver pin was set with a hexagonal emerald surrounded by six sparkling diamonds.

Once the piece of jewelry was in her hand, Luther gestured to her. "Turn it over."

Carefully, she turned over the pin and saw the engraved words on the back. *Maura, you have changed my heart forever. I'll love you always. Luther.*

Her voice caught. "Thank you." She traced her finger over the words. Turning the pin over, her finger caught on a tiny clasp and the pin snapped open to reveal a delicate watch.

"I thought you might like to have a watch to make sure that I'm punctual, since I'm always checking the time." He beamed at her.

"Oh, Luther, what a wonderful gift. You couldn't have chosen anything that would have pleased me more."

The preacher leaned forward and eyed the gift. "It would appear that you'd better pin that on her gown, or we're going to be late in spite of those timepieces."

This time, her wedding was everything that Maura had originally hoped for. Most important, their vows were exchanged in love with hope for their future together as husband and wife. When Pastor Wilson announced that Luther could kiss his bride, it took no prompting from Maura.

After Luther pulled her into his arms, his lips sought hers with a fervent desire that touched the depths of her soul. She leaned into him and returned the kiss with an intense longing. A longing to begin her life anew as his wife—her life as Maura Buchanan.

Judith McCoy Miller was chosen as a favorite new author in the Heartsong series, and her historical novels have ranked high among readers. In her first contemporary novel, *A Trusting Heart*, Judith drew on events in her own life to make the story come alive. Her other books draw from her fascination with history. She makes her home in Kansas with her family.

Mail-Order Husband

by DiAnn Mills

To James and Mimi Wigington.
Your devotion to each other is an inspiration to all.

Prologue

Central Nebraska, 1880

Lena Walker stiffened and glared into the face of the man before her. "I will not marry you, Dagget Shafer. Not now, not tomorrow, not ever."

His small, dark eyes narrowed, and despite the thick black beard covering most of his face, skin as bright red as a cardinal's feathers shone through. "You will change your mind, Miz High and Mighty. You can't run this farm by yourself and rear those two younguns. You'll either starve or get sick and die."

"I can work this land and raise my children just fine by myself," she said with a lift of her chin. Perspiration beaded her forehead and trickled down her back as she fought her rising temper.

"I dare say you'll live to regret your decision not to marry me. A woman needs a man to take care of her and tell her what to do," he said. "And if you had the sense to look around, you'd see there ain't many eligible men in these parts." He turned to face the entrance of the sod dugout, used as a barn, then whirled back around. "Of course, now I see you'd make a bad wife. I need a woman who knows the meanin' of doin' what her husband says and where her place is, not some sassy, purdy face. Miz Walker, you ain't got what I need. You ain't fit for any man."

Swallowing another sharp retort, Lena glanced at the bucket of water in her hands and, without thinking, tossed the contents into Dagget Shafer's face. Probably the closest thing he'd seen to a bath in a year. "Get off my land." Venom riddled her voice. "We don't need the likes of you."

For a minute she thought Dagget might strike her. She dropped the bucket, grabbed the pitchfork leaning against the dugout wall, and silently dared him to step closer.

Dagget must have sensed she meant business, because he plodded toward his mule, muttering something she couldn't make out.

Lena started to challenge his view of her fitness to be a wife but held her tongue. She'd run him off, and that's what she'd intended. How could

403

he think she'd be interested in a man who never bathed, had the manners of a pig, and refused to step inside a church? Her heart ached for his six children who no longer had a mother, but her sympathy didn't extend to marrying their unbearable father.

"Mama, you all right?" eleven-year-old Caleb asked, peering around the corner of a horse stall.

She took a deep breath to settle her pounding heart as Dagget rode away, his legs flapping against the sides of the mule. "Yes, Son. I'll be fine."

He picked up the empty bucket. "I'll go fetch some more water."

Lena nodded and laid her hand on her son's shoulder. "Thanks, Caleb."

He glanced up through serious, sky-blue eyes. "I'm glad you're not marryin' him, Mama. We do just fine by ourselves."

Suddenly the whole incident seemed funny. The thought of Dagget standing there with water dripping from his greasy beard to his dirty overalls, nary saying a word, was priceless. Caleb took to laughing, too, and their mirth echoed from the sod barn's walls.

"We do need help," Lena finally admitted. "But it will be by God's hand, not by Dagget Shafer or any of the others who seem to think I'm begging for a husband."

"We work good together, Mama," Caleb insisted.

She smiled into the face of the boy who looked so much like his departed father, with the same dark brown hair and tall, lanky frame. "Right now, you, Simon, and I are doing all right, but tomorrow may bring something else. God will provide; I'm sure of it. But I need to talk to Him about the matter."

That night, after the embers from the cow chips no longer produced a flicker of orange-red, and the only sound around her was her sons' even breathing, Lena prayed for guidance.

Oh, Lord, what do You want me to do? This place needs a man to run it, and the boys are too young. I know the men who have come asking me to marry them could run this farm proper, but, Lord, none of them were fit. She shook her head in the darkness, dispelling the visions of the other two farmers who had indicated a desire to marry her. One of them was old enough to be her father, and the other reminded her of a billy goat—with a disposition to match.

Lord, Dagget made me awful angry today, and I'm sorry to have lost my temper. I'll apologize the next time I see him; I promise. It's my pride, I know. I'm sorry, and I'll do better.

Life simply didn't seem fair. Men could come looking for a wife, even place a notice in one of those big newspapers back east. They took advantage of women who had no one to help them when circumstances took a bad turn.

Suddenly an idea occurred to her. If a man could find himself a bride by placing an advertisement, why couldn't she find a husband that way?

Chapter 1

Wanted: Christian husband for widow with two young boys. Must be of high moral character, refrain from drinking spirits, be even-tempered, and be able to run a farm in central Nebraska. Interested gentlemen apply by mail. Please allow two to three months for reply.

*G*abriel Hunters smoothed out the wrinkled *Philadelphia Public Ledger* advertisement. He'd read it several times during the past three days and had committed the words to memory. Tonight he'd crumpled it, certain the foolish notion would pass once the paper crackled in the fireplace.

But Gabriel couldn't rid himself of the hope bubbling between the lines of the print. He snatched the newspaper clipping from the sputtering flames, as though the words were more valuable than silver or gold.

Something foreign had occurred to him, something contrary to his hermetic way of life. He actually wanted to respond positively to this widow. A big part of him believed a home and family might fill the emptiness in his heart. Shaking his head, Gabriel suspected God had plans for his perfunctory existence, and the thought brought a surge of unusual emotions. He felt a strange and exhilarating strength in considering a home beyond Philadelphia. Many times he'd wondered what lay outside his world of private bookkeeping, a place where gossip and malicious speech didn't prevail.

Glancing about the sparsely furnished room, he concluded nothing really held him in Philadelphia. Mother had passed away two years prior, and his best friends—his books—could be taken with him. God could be providing a way to obliterate the past and start anew. Certainly a pleasurable thought.

Allowing himself to dream a trifle, Gabriel closed his eyes and imagined the tantalizing aroma of beef stew and baking bread, the sound of children's laughter, and the sweet smile of a woman who loved him.

He studied the newspaper clipping again. What did he know

about being a husband and rearing children? He'd never courted a woman or known his own father. After much thought, he realized men had been husbands and fathers for thousands of years. Certainly it came naturally.

Another thought occurred to him. Jesus was not much younger than Gabriel when He embarked upon His ministry. Perhaps this stood as a sign from God to answer affirmatively to the widow's notice. He could do this; the Bible would be his guide.

The dilemma lay in farming. He rubbed his hands together. Soft. No calluses. Mother had insisted upon a small garden behind her establishment, but all he'd done was pick a few tomatoes and green beans. The girls had managed the rest. All the work he'd ever accomplished amounted to dipping his quill into an inkwell. Gabriel grinned. The *Farmers' Almanac* provided all the knowledge he might ever need to till the land. How difficult could it be to milk a cow or plant seeds and harvest crops? After all, men had tilled the earth since Adam and Eve. He'd spent most of his life submerged in books and had learned volumes of vital information, and he felt confident in his savvy. This new venture merely challenged his intellectual appetite.

Gabriel stood and stepped away from his oaken desk. He surmised Lena Walker must not be endowed with qualities of beauty, or she wouldn't have had to resort to advertising for a husband. It didn't matter, for he certainly had not been given eye-pleasing traits either.

A husband and father. Something he'd secretly dreamed of becoming but had never thought he'd share in the blessing.

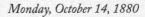

Monday, October 14, 1880

Lena pulled her frayed, woolen shawl around her shoulders as a north wind whipped around the train station. She shivered, not relishing an early winter, but at least she'd have a husband to keep the fires burning and a helpmate to share in the work. How pleasant to think of conversation with someone other than two young sons—not that she didn't appreciate their willingness to talk—but sometimes she felt hauntingly alone.

"Mama, I hear it," Caleb said, glancing up from where he'd bent his ear to the train track.

"I do, too," six-year-old Simon chimed in.

Lena felt her heart pound harder than the rhythmic sound of the

Union Pacific making its way toward Archerville, a small town north of Lincoln and not far from the Platte River. Fear gripped her. What had she done? Ever since she'd accepted Gabriel Hunters's aspirations to marry her and be a father to her sons, she'd begun to have serious doubts. Up until she'd posted her reply, the idea had sounded like a fantasy, a perfect solution to all of her woes. Of course she'd prayed for direction and felt God had led her to Mr. Hunters, but could she have misunderstood God?

Her stomach twisted and turned. This man could be a vagrant or, worse yet, an outlaw intending to do harm to her and her precious sons. Advertising for a husband now sounded foolish. Accepting a man's proposal sight unseen sounded even worse. She'd be the laughingstock of the community, and that didn't help her prideful nature.

What had happened to her faith? Hadn't she heard clear direction from God about the matter? She'd received more than twenty replies from interested men, but none had piqued her interest like the man she expected on board the train. With a name like Gabriel Hunters, he must be the strong, burly type. In fact, his name lent itself to that of a lumberjack. Yes, a rugged wilderness man who lived by his cunning and wits.

Swallowing hard, she forced a smile in the direction of her lively sons. *Oh Lord, make Mr. Hunters a likable man who'll love my boys. They can be a handful, but oh, what joy.* Both looked identical to their father, but Caleb leaned more to a compassionate nature, while Simon always ran with the wind and whatever notion entered his mind.

"It's getting closer," Simon said, nearly squealing. "I wonder what Mr. Hunters looks like."

"I'm wondering if he'll be friendly," Caleb said in a chiding tone. "That's more important."

"He'll be whatever the good Lord desires for us," Lena said. "And the Lord only wants the best for His children."

She felt her mouth grow dry as the train chugged down the tracks, slowly coming to a halt and carrying the inevitable. Naturally, if the man proved to be less than she expected, she'd refuse to wed him. They weren't to be married until three days hence, which gave both of them time to consider what the future held in store. She wanted to pray with him and talk about everything. No surprises for Lena. Mr. Hunters might be taking on a ready-made family, but he was also getting a farm.

Remembering his letter tucked inside her pocket, she fingered it lightly. His penned words echoed across her mind.

Dear Mrs. Walker,

This correspondence is in regard to your advertisement for a husband and father for your sons. I am thirty-six years old and have never been married, but I believe God will show me through His Word how to be a proper husband and father. I abstain from strong drink and tobacco, and I welcome the opportunity to share in your family's life and teach your sons what little I know.

I've studied agricultural methods and am prepared to be of assistance in this endeavor. I'm a modest man and not easily persuaded, but God has put our union in my heart.

Sincerely,
Gabriel Hunters

Lena assumed Mr. Hunters had an excellent education from his choice of words. How magnificent for her sons. She felt truly blessed and exhilarated—until the train's whistle sounded, the steam billowed with a *spwish*, and the train screeched to a halt.

Lena well knew her ability to act hastily. *Oh Lord, I'm afraid I've made a terrible mistake. Please give me a sign.*

A man stepped down from the train, a tall, stout fellow who hadn't been able to fasten his jacket. A gust of wind caused him to suck in his breath. Wiry, yellow hair, resembling straw, stuck out haphazardly from beneath a tattered hat as though he might take flight. A patch of the same barbed-wire hair sprang up from his eyebrows, ample jaws, and chin.

Lena covered her mouth to keep from laughing, but then she saw no other man exiting the train. Oh my, what *had* she done?

The man set his bag beside him and removed his hat, clutching it close to his heart. His hair lay matted like wet chicken feathers. "Mrs. Walker," he said, approaching her with a concerned frown. "Are you Mrs. Lena Walker?"

"Yes, I am," she replied and extended her hand. He grasped it lightly. It felt cold and clammy. Lena dare not look at Caleb and Simon for fear she'd burst into laughter—or tears.

"I'm Gabriel Hunters," he said with a gulp, his words jumping out like a squeak.

"It's a pleasure to meet you, Mr. Hunters." She released her hand and gestured toward her sons. "This is Caleb; he's eleven. And this is Simon; he's six."

Oh Lord, help them to remember their manners. Help me to remember mine!

Mr. Hunters bent his portly frame and offered his hand first to Caleb, then to Simon. "It's an honor to meet you, Caleb and Simon Walker. I'm looking forward to an auspicious relationship."

His voice trembled slightly, and Lena felt compassion tug at her heart. She hadn't considered he might have reservations about their meeting.

Simon's gaze shot up at his mother. "Are we in trouble, Mama?"

Lena gathered her shawl closer to her; the wind had taken a colder twist. "I don't think so, Son." She took a deep breath, hoping her ignorance didn't show through. "Mr. Hunters, Simon isn't sure of the meaning of *auspicious*."

Still bending at the knee, he nodded and turned his attention to the small boy. "It means successful or promising."

Simon's blue eyes appeared to radiate with understanding. "Mama says a word like that when she thinks Caleb and I are doing something we shouldn't."

"Suspicious?" Mr. Hunters asked.

"Yes, sir. That's it. Do you like chores, Mr. Hunters? Me and Caleb get real tired of 'em, and we're sure glad you're here to help." He reached out to shake Mr. Hunters's hand again. "I see you like to eat a lot, sir, and your clothes appear a bit tight, but never you mind. Our mama cooks real good, and she can fix your clothes when they tear."

"Simon," Lena gasped, horrified. Hadn't they talked about proper introductions all the way to Archerville?

Mr. Hunters stood and tugged at his gaping jacket. "I apologize if my corpulent body is offensive."

"No, sir. Not in the least," Lena replied before one of the boys could embarrass her further. She assumed the meaning of *corpulent* had something to do with his size. "Kindly excuse my son's bad manners. Caleb, would you like to carry Mr. Hunters's bag to the wagon? We can all get to know each other on the way home, and I'll cook supper while you boys show Mr. Hunters around the farm."

Mr. Hunters stared anxiously at the train. "I have another bag, but it's extremely cumbersome. Several of my books are packed inside."

As if hearing the man's words, the conductor scooted out a fairly large trunk. "Right heavy this is," he said, massaging the small of his back.

Mr. Hunters reached for his belongings and stumbled with the weight. Lena dashed forward with Caleb and Simon, but the man fell flat on his back with his bag quivering atop his chest and rounded stomach.

Instantly, the conductor stood by his side and removed the trunk, then helped the dazed man to his feet. Simon began to chuckle, followed by Caleb. Despite Lena's stern looks, the two boys laughed even harder. She found it difficult to contain herself, wanting to give in to the mirth tickling through her body. *Oh Lord, surely I misunderstood!*

"Oh dear, are you all right?" she asked, trying desperately to gain control of her wavering emotions.

Mr. Hunters shrugged his shoulders and dusted off his clothes. "Ma'am, this is definitely not the proper image I wanted to present you. I sincerely apologize for my blunder."

"No need to fret about it," she said, and for the first time she caught a glimpse of his eyes—coppery brown, much like the color of autumn leaves, unusual for a person with blond hair. A second look reminded her of a frightened animal, cornered with no place to run.

Poor Mr. Hunters, and we're laughing at him. Immediately, she sobered. "I hope you don't mind, but I scheduled the wedding for three days hence. I thought we could use the time to get accustomed to each other."

His face turned ghastly white. "Ma'am—"

Lena gathered what had shocked him. "Sir, I intended to have you sleep in the barn until our wedding." Her face grew hotter than a Nebraska sun in mid-July.

He released a pent-up breath. "Those arrangements sound perfectly fine to me."

They moved awkwardly toward Lena's wagon. Caleb and Simon struggled with one bag, and Mr. Hunters heaved with the trunk. Moments before, Simon had embarrassed her with his endless prattle. Now no one uttered a word.

"You must be quite fond of books," she said, groping for something to say.

"Yes, ma'am. I hope you don't mind, but I took the liberty of having the rest of them sent here in a few weeks."

"Of course not. The winter nights approaching us will provide you with plenty of reading time."

"Will you read these books to us, sir?" Caleb asked, struggling with the heavy bag.

Mr. Hunters's shoulders relaxed. "I'd be pleased to, along with the Bible."

Lena swallowed. Mr. Hunters might not be what she'd envisioned, but this part of him was a relief.

They reached the wagon and, after much difficulty, loaded the trunk and bag. Caleb and Simon climbed into the back, curiously eyeing the outside of Mr. Hunters's baggage.

"Do not touch those," she reminded them.

Lena turned for the man to assist her onto the wagon seat, which he did with much effort. Huffing and puffing, he attempted a smile.

"Would you like to drive us west toward my home?" she asked, smoothing her dress.

His shoulders sank. "Ma'am, I've never driven a wagon before in my life."

Chapter 2

*G*abriel wanted to step down from that wagon and make a running leap to board the Union Pacific back to Philadelphia as fast as his round and aching legs would allow.

His entrance into Archerville had been met with one disaster after another—and this last occurrence would surely conclude his demise. The boys, his future sons, had been beset with amusement when the trunk landed him on his backside, and his future wife had just learned he knew nothing about driving a wagon.

Defeated and exhausted from the laborious trip to middle-of-nowhere Nebraska, Gabriel realized he'd made a terrible mistake. And in three days' time, he might make an even worse one.

Oh God, why did I think You willed this for my life? Am I once again to be made a laughingstock of a community?

"Don't concern yourself, Mr. Hunters. I've driven this wagon more times than I care to remember," Mrs. Walker said, but he couldn't tell if she sounded annoyed or simply tired—most likely the former.

He didn't blame her; he wasn't pleased with his lack of dexterity either. In less than ten minutes, he'd discovered that not all knowledge came from books. Apprehension rippled through him at the likelihood of the next twenty-four hours revealing a generous amount of his ignorance.

"Mr. Hunters," Caleb began, "what did you do while in Philadelphia?"

Obviously, he didn't drive a team of horses.

"Bookkeeping," Gabriel replied. When he saw the rather confused look spreading across the boy's face, he added, "It's arithmetic. I help business establishments add and subtract what they earn and what they spend."

Caleb nodded. "Like when Mama sells a cow, then pays our bill at the general store?"

"Correct, and what's left is profit."

"We don't have any of that," Caleb said with a much-too-serious look for a boy. "We simply pay what's owed and start all over again."

Gabriel saw a muscle twitch in Mrs. Walker's face. Farming a

160-acre homestead and raising two boys must be a real hardship. No wonder she needed a husband. At least she knew how to survive. His former confidence in farming had ended at the railroad station.

"But the Lord provides," Lena said quietly. "We have a house, clothes to wear, and food. Some folks aren't as fortunate."

"I pray I'll be able to make you more prosperous," Gabriel said firmly.

"Thank you, Mr. Hunters. I—"

"Are we going to be rich?" Simon asked, tugging on Gabriel's coat-tail. "I know 'zactly what I want."

"Simon," Mrs. Walker scolded. "Mind your manners. Now, you boys leave Mr. Hunters alone for a while. He and I have things to discuss."

The boys scooted back to the end of the wagon and dangled their feet over the edge. They minded well. A good sign. He'd seen his share of misbehaved boys and the damage they could do.

Gabriel glanced at the sights of Archerville behind him as they pulled away from the small town. One dusty street was lined with a few necessary businesses: a general store and post office; a jail; a barber and undertaker; a saloon; and across from the liquid spirits and worldly entertainment, a freshly painted church—for a dose of the Holy Ghost.

The odor staggered him. Horses, pigs, and cows wandered through the town and contributed their droppings wherever they saw fit. Certainly nothing resembling the cleanliness or the hustle and bustle of Philadelphia. A burst of wind whipped around a barrel outside the general store, sending it teetering to the ground. A shiver wound its way around Gabriel's spine. As much as he'd looked forward to leaving the city, this new environment settled upon him like questionable figures in a ledger.

He'd been lonely before with people everywhere, but now he felt alone and afraid. Yes, fear did have a strangling hold on him, fear of the unknown and fear of the future. God did lead him here to Archerville, of that he had no doubt, but that thought did little to calm him.

Gabriel studied Mrs. Walker's horses. They appeared fine to him—shiny coats and not at all swaybacked. He'd expected mules. His gaze trailed up the reins to her hands, callused and deeply tanned. He'd never seen a woman's hands that weren't soft and smooth. Another oddity. Well, he didn't intend for his wife to work herself into an early grave. Wetting his lips, he stole a quick glance at her face. With all the commotion at the train station, he hadn't afforded a good look at his future wife.

Oh no. Shocked and disgruntled, he instantly changed his focus to the surrounding countryside, flat, bleak, and uninviting.

Lena Walker was comely, and he couldn't trust an attractive woman.

She'd betray him just like his mother and the other girls. For weeks since he'd received Mrs. Walker's agreement to the marriage, he'd prayed for a plain woman, one who matched him in appearance. A man could build a life with a woman who'd never stray. He'd never have to worry about her participating in the activities his mother had.

Suddenly, Gabriel fought the urge to shake his fist at God. The One in whom he'd put his faith and trust had tricked him. He'd journeyed all this way only to find a woman who would hurt him more deeply than his mother. Although his mother had died and he'd forgiven her, he was smart enough not to fall into the same well again.

What should he do now? *Lord, cruel jokes are what the bullies did when I attended school. I can't believe this is from You. Even if she might be different, she'd never love the likes of me. Have You forgotten what I look like?*

"Mr. Hunters, forgive me. I had so many things to ask you, but now I can't seem to figure out where to begin." Mrs. Walker offered him a slight smile, then quickly stared ahead at the road.

Perhaps you're disappointed; can't blame you. "We're strangers, Mrs. Walker. We have much to learn about each other."

"Yes, that's true. Could we begin by calling each other by our given names and talking about ourselves?"

He nodded, although he wasn't so sure he wanted Lena Walker to know more about him. "Certainly, if it suits you."

She took a deep breath and sat straighter as though summoning courage for an arduous task. "My name is Lena Jane Walker. My family came to Nebraska from Ohio when I was a girl. I'll be thirty-one years old come February." She paused and urged the team of horses to pick up their pace. "I've been a widow for three years. I'm strong and healthy, and so are my sons. The Lord guides my life, but I do tend to make mistakes more often than not."

"We all do," he said solemnly, regretting the moment he'd considered her advertisement for a husband. Why hadn't she told him what she looked like?

"My biggest fault is my temper," she continued, as though bound by some unexplainable force to confess her worst. "I'll do my best to curb it, but I thought you should know."

When she looked his way again, the intensity of her green eyes captured his heart. Their gazes locked, and he could not pull away. Truth and sincerity with a mixture of merriment radiated back at him. The combination caused Gabriel to rethink his former conclusions about comely women. *Help, I'm so confused.*

Could it be Lena Walker held no malice? He knew God intended the best for him, and for a moment, Gabriel had forgotten His goodness. He'd proceed with caution, remembering more than one of his mother's girls had looked as innocent as a child.

Mrs. Walker averted his scrutiny. "I want you to know the real reason why I contacted the Philadelphia newspaper."

"I'd be obliged if you would. Naturally, I assumed you needed help with your land and your sons."

"Yes, but I never thought a man would be interested in coming all this way, and when you did, I took it as a sign from God that this was His will. You see, two farmers asked me to marry, but I couldn't tolerate them. I felt advertising for a husband made more sense. I wanted God to send what I needed."

His stomach lunged. "Why didn't you wed one of the men who proposed?"

She shrugged. "They weren't God-fearing, or bathed, or good to my sons. When they came around asking, I threw them off my land. Guess they got a taste of my temper."

A mental picture of this woman tossing a grown man off her farm leaped from his mind. It sounded incredibly funny, and he stifled a laugh.

"You can laugh," she said, shaking her head. "Most folks around here do anyway. They think I've lost my mind by refusing to marry up with a man who'd take care of the farm." She stopped talking abruptly, as though she suddenly felt embarrassed.

Gabriel thought about Lena's confession, and a cloud darkened his mind. "Ma'am, are you desiring a husband who allows you to direct his ways?" *I may not be handsome or successful, but I believe a man is head of his household.*

Lena abruptly reined the horses to a halt. Her face paled. "By no means. I believe in the biblical instructions for husbands and wives—a husband guides and directs his home."

"As do I. A marriage must follow every God-given precept."

"Precisely. Now, tell me about yourself."

The tension seemed to grow worse. He didn't want or see a reason to reveal much about his person. He deemed that a willingness to do right by her was all that held importance. "You already know quite a bit about me from our correspondence. My complete name is Gabriel Lawrence Hunters, and I've lived my whole life in Philadelphia."

"Are your parents living?"

"Mother passed on some two years ago."

"So your father is still in Philadelphia?"

Gracious, woman, how much do you need to know about me? "I have no idea." He prayed for a diversion, anything to stop the questioning. "This is magnificent country."

She smiled. "Yes, it is. In late summer, prairie grass can grow taller than a man."

He studied the landscape in curiosity and in avoidance of Lena's inquiries. In the distance all he could see was flat land with miles of prairie grass, now limp and brown. According to his findings, this river valley hosted dark brown soil. Farmers near the Platte River grew mostly corn, but they also raised oats, barley, and wheat. Although Mrs. Walker's land lay farther south, he assumed the farming methods were the same. He tried to envision what fields of ripe corn looked like. From his research, he gathered tall green stalks with green shoots and a cap of brown silk-like tassels. He'd find out in the months to come.

Gabriel remembered Lena's mentioning in one of her letters about a few head of cattle, but he'd neglected to find out how many or what kind. He should have asked, since he'd be working with the beasts.

A hint of excitement, a rather peculiar sensation, spread through him as he considered this adventure. For the first time in his life, he'd watch things grow: corn, cattle, pigs, a garden, and two freckle-faced boys. He'd learn how to farm properly; after all, he'd read the books.

Three white-tailed deer leaped across the road from the tall grass, such wondrous creatures. My, how he admired their gracefulness. The call of a flock of geese perked his ears. Staring up into the sky, he watched their perfect V formation head south.

Winter. Philadelphia was frigid in the winter, but he'd heard Nebraska received bitter temperatures and several feet of snow, and that wasn't long in the making.

"It's all so serene," he whispered really to no one.

"Yes," Lena agreed, "but the same things making it peaceful can also turn on you if you're not careful."

"I don't believe I understand," he replied.

"Nature," she said simply. "Just when you think everything is perfect and a bit of heaven, it turns on you by throwing a twister over your land in the summer, or a prairie fire destroying everything in its path, or a blizzard to blind you in winter."

Like a beautiful woman. Gabriel studied her features beneath a faded bonnet. This time he took in the oval shape of her face and large, expressive eyes framed by nearly black hair. Her pursed lips reminded him of a rosebud. If only Lena Walker appeared a bit less lovely. Those looks could defeat a man—drive him to lose his principles. He'd seen it done too many times.

The regrets about Lena again plodded through his rambling thoughts. A plain woman whom no other man might covet had been his heart's desire. If blessed with any children, they might not look especially pleasing, but he'd teach them how God examines the heart for true beauty.

Already Gabriel didn't trust Lena, and they hadn't even completed their nuptials.

Chapter 3

*L*ena shoved a lump back down her throat. She'd made such a fool out of herself in trying to soothe Gabriel's humiliation. The laughter she'd felt for him back in Archerville had quickly turned to regret when she couldn't utter a single intelligent word.

They should be discussing the farm or arranging a time to talk about Caleb and Simon. She and Gabriel would be married in three days; they should be spending this time getting to know each other.

Fear gripped her like the time she'd sighted a cloud of grasshoppers descending on the fields ready for harvest. Gabriel Hunters was nothing like she'd pictured: He didn't look like he'd ever spent a day in his life on a farm. Well, she simply had to know the truth.

"Did you grow up on a farm?" she asked.

"Not exactly," he replied after a moment's pause.

The fright subsided to a rising anger. "Where, then, did you learn about farming?"

"From books," he said simply, staring straight ahead.

His reply shook the very foundation on which she built her values. "From books? How can you feel the soil between your fingertips from a book? How can you tell the color of ripe wheat?"

"The written word is a valuable asset. I place complete trust in what I've read and studied." His ample chest rose and fell, while the buttons on his jacket threatened to break free. "Man has farmed since the beginning of time. If it were a difficult process, then human beings would not have survived."

I refuse to lose my temper. She clucked the horses to venture a tad faster. *I refuse to lose my temper.* "Many people have died due to crop failures or the natural hardships arising from living here. I hope you read *that* in your books."

"I have."

"And your conclusion, good sir?" She gritted her teeth to keep from adding a vicious retort.

"I have determined to be a farmer. There are many things for me to put into practice from the books I've read. If I had thought this undertaking an impossibility, I would not have answered your advertisement."

Mercy. What have I done? Lena glanced back to see Caleb and Simon still dangling their feet from the wagon. God had entrusted her with those precious boys, and she would guard them with her life. She'd see them grow to manhood and have children of their own. They needed a father—a man who had experienced life and knew its pitfalls. Somehow she doubted if Gabriel Hunters could fulfill those qualifications. She'd clearly heard God's affirmation of this strange union, but why? God must be punishing her for her pride and temper.

"Ma'am," Gabriel said, just loud enough for her to hear, "I'd be grateful if you'd give me an opportunity to be the husband and father you need."

Gabriel believed he had lowered himself as much as he could without some consolation in return from his future intended.

"I want to give you a chance, but you must understand how much I need a man who can work the land," Lena said, her eyes moistening.

He did not miss her tears, and immediately he wanted to whisk them away. "I will not disappoint you."

She hastily glanced away and pointed to a shadowing of buildings in the distance. "Up there is the farm. Besides the two horses, we have a mule for working the fields, a few pigs, chickens, ten cows, and a bull. Hopefully we'll have more cows in the spring."

Gabriel's first view of his new home and its outbuildings fell far below his initial ideas of a rural home. He'd seen the great farms in Pennsylvania, the clapboard homes and the well-kept barns and sheds. The conditions here ranged close to the shanty life on the poor side of Philadelphia. Bleak. Desolate.

The cabin had been constructed of sod brick made from dried prairie grass and dirt. He remembered from Lena's letter that the cabin was called a soddy. These structures kept out the heat in the summer and shut out the cold in winter. Gabriel couldn't keep from wondering if the soddy carried a smell. However, the structure did have two windows with real paned glass.

The roof looked like the same weathered sod laid over some type of wood. From the bare spots with shoots of plant life sprouting up from them, he assumed the roof leaked. Obviously, carpentry would be his first priority, or whatever else he deemed necessary to make the home comfortable. Using a hammer and nails shouldn't be too arduous, if those tools were required. He hadn't seen any trees, and the fact puzzled him. Where did one find wood?

What Lena referred to as a dugout more closely resembled a cave dug out of a hillside with a portion of the front built with the same sod bricks. With his keen insight into the world of mathematics, he should be able to calculate the length and width of sod necessary for repairs. Come spring, perhaps they could locate lumber to have hauled in for a good, solid barn.

Lena pulled the wagon to a halt. The boys jumped from the back and fell into the welcoming embrace of a mangy dog that had emerged from out of nowhere. Barking and wagging its flea-bitten tail, the animal eyed the newcomer suspiciously. . .and growled.

Gabriel hesitantly stepped to the ground. He didn't care for dogs. He'd never owned one or knew anyone who did, but he'd been bitten once when he'd bent to pat a dog while walking to the Philadelphia library.

"Just let him sniff you," Caleb said when the dog growled at Gabriel the second time. "Turnip, you need to make friends with this man. He's going to be marryin' our ma."

The dog's name is Turnip? "We don't have to do this right now," Gabriel replied as he deliberated whether to help Lena down from the wagon or wait to see if the dog took a bite from the seat of his trousers.

"Put Turnip in the barn," Lena said to her son. "Gabriel can make friends later."

Once the dog followed the boys into the dilapidated dugout, Gabriel offered her his assistance. Immediately, he noticed her firm grip—stronger than his.

"You have a fine-looking place here," he said.

She frowned. "Don't add lies to your deceit. Everything is falling apart, and you know it."

"I'm not by nature an egregious person," he replied.

Lena planted her hands on her hips. "Gabe, let me tell you right now. Those big words don't mean anything to me. Here in Nebraska, we don't have time to learn the meanings of such nonsense. Using them will only upset folks, make them think you are better than they."

Is she always this petulant? And the name Gabe? No one has ever called me anything but Gabriel.

Lena whirled away from him. He saw her shoulders rise and fall before she faced him again. "I'm sorry, Gabriel. This is not how I wanted our first meeting. We're supposed to be getting to know each other, not quarreling. Will you forgive me?"

He wondered the extent of Lena's sensibilities, for he'd certainly seen a gamut of them in the brief time they'd been together. Could he endure a lifetime of irrational emotions? Of course, he must. His mother could flare at a moment's notice, then turn her sweetness toward an unsuspecting victim. His integrity lay foremost in his mind, and he'd made a commitment to the woman before him. After all, God had given him clear direction. Hadn't He?

"I can most assuredly forgive you and take into consideration your emotions. I'd be a fool not to comprehend that my credentials do not meet with what...with what you anticipated. But rest assured, I will curtail my vocabulary to something more acceptable. Making good friends is important, and a proper image is quite desirable."

"Thank you, and you can start right now. I never thought I was an ignorant person, but I'm having problems following your words."

Were all women so particular? His mother had been his only example, and she always had her mind set on business—and on her disappointment in him. Lena flashed her troubled gaze his way. He could make a few concessions, since she had more to lose in this endeavor than he. "I'll do my best," he said, carefully guarding each word. "I've never been called Gabe, but it does have a pleasant sound to it."

She brightened. "You like it? Wonderful. I know Gabriel in the Bible was a messenger, and I'd like to think of you in the same way, but shortened seems to fit you."

At last she appeared happy. He inwardly sighed. Now, on to other things. "Perhaps we can talk later after your sons are in bed?"

"I'd like that very much."

He could quickly grow accustomed to Lena's smile. He offered one of his own, then quickly turned to secure his trunks from the wagon. "Where shall I put my things?"

"Inside the cabin, in the boys' room for now." She folded her hands in front of her as though searching for the courage to say something else. "I hope the barn is all right for a few days," she finally said.

"Most certainly," he replied, lifting the massive trunk into his arms. He'd ache tomorrow from this work.

"I'll fix us some supper. I hope you like venison and carrots and potatoes." When he nodded, she continued. "The boys have chores and milking to do, so we'll eat as soon as they're finished."

Gabe felt the call of a challenge. "And I'll assist the boys as soon as these are inside."

His first view of the cabin, or rather what he could see of it, astounded him. It was dark even with two windows, but the sod bricks were nearly three feet thick, which made for a wide window ledge. Lena had a few dried wildflowers sitting in a crockery jug alongside a framed picture of an elderly couple.

"Your parents?" he asked, adjusting the trunk in his arms.

"Yes." She tapped her foot on the earthen floor, then pointed to a quilt near the back. "That's Caleb and Simon's room."

He maneuvered through the meagerly furnished dwelling: a rocking chair in front of a fireplace, two small benches positioned around a rough-sawn table, and two other ladder-back chairs. A small cookstove rested in the corner, where a few pegs held two cast-iron pots and a skillet. Glancing about, he saw a good many household items hanging from the walls. Lena was a tidy woman. Another quilt separated the main living area from what Gabe assumed was her bedroom. He tried not to stare at it, feeling his face redden at the thought of sharing a bed with this woman. The plastered walls were a surprise to him; he'd assumed they would be covered with newspapers.

The boys' room held a chest and two straw mattresses, and he noted not much room for anything more. The earthen floor came as a shock. He'd been accustomed to wood floors with a soft rug beneath his feet. A bit of dried grass had fallen from the roof to the floor. *Surely this leaks.*

A short while later, he plodded out to the dugout, the old twinge of excitement fading to an uncomfortable knot in the bottom of his stomach. A distinct, disagreeable smell met his nostrils. *How sad; one of the boys must surely be ill.*

As Gabriel entered the darkened dugout they referred to as a barn, a horrific stench took his breath away, and he covered his nostrils. This was worse than Archerville. "Caleb, Simon, is everything all right?"

A voice replied from the shadows. "Yes, sir. We're back here. Just starting to milk."

He recognized Caleb and ventured his way. "I'd like to help. What is that dreadful odor?"

Simon rushed down to meet him. "I don't know, 'less you're smellin' the manure."

Ah. Why didn't I detect it? "I'm sure you're right."

"It's powerful bad," Caleb said. Gabe had yet to make out the boy, because his eyes were having trouble adjusting to the faint light. "Tomorrow we have to clean out this barn before Ma thrashes us."

"Perhaps I can be of assistance?" Immediately, he regretted his words.

Hadn't he already decided to make repairs to the various buildings?

"Oh yes," Caleb replied, a bit too enthusiastically.

By this time, he'd made out where the young boy knelt on his knees, leaning into a brown-and-white cow. A *ping*ing sound alerted Gabriel to milk squirting into the bottom of the pail. *So Caleb squeezes those conical attachments to discharge the milk.*

"When's the last time you milked a cow?" Caleb asked, grinning into his half-filled bucket.

Gabe refused to reply. "Do you have a stool?"

"He can have mine." Simon stood and peered up at him curiously. "I have one, but it's a little wobbly. Try balancing yourself with your leg."

The endeavor didn't look too difficult. He stepped over beside Simon's cow, but the stool, which was really a rickety nail keg, appeared a bit precarious. The youngest Walker bolted from his position, making room for Gabe. About that time, the cow made a woeful sound as though lamenting the milking process.

"Hush," Simon ordered. "And don't be kicking over the bucket either."

As soon as Gabe eased onto the keg, it gave way and shattered into a mass of wood pieces and a splintered seat.

"Goodness, Mr. Hunters," Simon said. "You've gone and done it now. Ma will have a word to say about this."

"You hush, Simon," Caleb said. "He couldn't help the keg breaking with his weight and all. Ma knows the difference between an accident and an on-purpose."

God help me, Gabe silently pleaded. "Boys, I can milk this cow in short order as soon as we can find a suitable stool for me."

"Ain't none," Simon said. "You'll have to bend down on your knees."

Gracious, is anything easy here? "I shall need to construct a new milking stool, but for right now I'll do as you suggest."

Gabe gingerly touched the cow. Its bristled hide felt strange, reminiscent of the short-haired dog that had bitten him years ago. He wondered if cows bit.

No matter. He'd see this task to the end. All of a sudden, the appendages hanging from under the cow's belly looked rather formidable. Did he grab them one at a time or use both hands? Rubbing his fingers together, he realized the time had come to show his initiative. He reached out and grabbed an udder. It felt soft. Not at all like he'd imagined. Gabe squeezed it, and a stream of milk splattered his jacket.

"In the bucket, Mr. Hunters," Simon said impatiently. "Ma says waste not, want not."

"And she's so right," Gabe replied. "I'll not be shirking my duties." His next attempt sent the milk into the pail. He sensed such satisfaction, but the twisted position of his body made it difficult to breathe.

"I bet you never did this before either," Lena said, towering over him.

Chapter 4

Somehow Lena restrained the doubts and ugly retorts threatening to spill out over supper. Ever since she'd entered the barn with the suspicion that Gabe Hunters knew nothing about milking and discovered she was right, her mind had shaken with anger.

How had he lived for over thirty-six years without learning the basics of life? Even city folks had to eat and survive. No matter if God had been involved with this husband mess she'd gotten herself into, come morning she'd be sending Mr. Gabe Hunters packing.

To make matters worse, she'd told Caleb and Simon to clean out the barn three days ago. The smell would make a person throw up their shoes. Lena tilted her head thoughtfully. After a night in the barn, Gabe would be more than willing to leave.

"Good food, Mama," Caleb said, breaking the silence.

The fire crackled, providing all the sound Lena needed while she ate. "Thank you. Most times we have corn bread, beans, and sorghum molasses," she added in explanation to their guest. "Tonight was. . .supposed to be special. In the morning—"

"We'll get right on cleaning the barn after we deliver the milk," Gabe announced.

Lena said nothing. She had learned a long time ago about letting her temper simmer rather than letting it boil over. That method didn't always work, but tonight, laced with prayer, her angry, racing thoughts were subsiding.

"I agree with Caleb," Gabe continued. "The food is delicious."

"Thank you, Mr. Hunters." She didn't dare lift her gaze to meet his for fear she'd give in to temptation and tell him just exactly what she thought about his book learning. Maybe it was enough to know he had the company of animals tonight.

"When did you want to hold our discussion?" he asked, taking a big gulp of coffee.

She swallowed a piece of molasses-soaked corn bread. "As soon as the boys go to bed. Normally, we have Bible reading before their prayers."

"May I do the honors of reading tonight and conducting prayers?"

You're going to need it by the time I'm finished with you. She bit her tongue and tried to respond civilly. "Sounds like an excellent idea. I look forward to what you'll be selecting."

"What have you been reading?"

"Job," she said.

"Mama, I don't think Mr. Hunters wants to read about a man who had sores all over his body and his family died," Caleb said. Upon meeting her scrutiny, he quickly added, "Of course, what he reads from the Bible is his choice."

"Job is fine," Gabe said. "There's something for us to learn in every piece of scripture."

Lena glanced at his barely touched food. From the looks of him, Gabe seldom refused a meal. She lifted her coffee cup to her lips. She hadn't much of an appetite either—too many emotions floating in and out of her mind. Feeling Gabe studying her, she lifted her gaze to meet his. Kindness poured from those coppery pools and along with it a sensation akin to hurt and desperation. Her father had given her a cat once that looked at her in the same way. The animal had been beaten and left to fend for itself until her father brought it home.

A smile tugged at Lena's lips. After all, she could be kind and show him Christian hospitality until she told him there wouldn't be a wedding.

To her surprise, Gabe suggested all of them help Lena clean up from supper. Soon the dishes were washed and the debris that had fallen through the roof whisked away from the floor. A moment later, he disappeared into the boys' room and returned with spectacles in his hand.

"Here's the Bible," Lena said, handing him James's weathered book with its turned-down pages. Someday she'd give it to Caleb. All of a sudden, she wanted to jerk it back. This man had no right to take James's chair for Bible reading. She choked back a sob. "We sit by the fire, and I read from the rocking chair."

"You have to be real careful," Simon said, finding his position on a braided rug. "If you don't say the words right, the devil will pounce on you while you're in bed."

"Simon," Lena scolded. "Where ever did you hear such a thing?"

He glanced at his older brother with one giant accusing glare.

Gabe chuckled, surprising her. "Well, Simon, I haven't been able to do much since I arrived here with any expertise, but I *can* read. And the devil doesn't come after you when you're sleeping just because you can't pronounce a word correctly."

Caleb found his spot near his brother and said nothing. Lena would deal with her older son later. The two boys faced Gabe, warming their backs against the fire. If Lena hadn't been so upset, she'd have treasured the sight of her precious sons looking to a man for scripture reading. She pulled a chair from the table, hoping he hadn't lied about knowing the Bible.

"We're near the end of Job," Lena said. "I have it marked. Oh, it's the last chapter."

Gabe carefully put on his spectacles and cleared his throat. "Job, chapter forty-two. 'Then Job answered the Lord, and said, I know that Thou canst do every thing, and that no thought can be withholden from Thee.'"

Lena felt a knocking at her heart. *I know You can do everything and that no thought can be kept secret from You.* She shifted uncomfortably. *Lord, I do know You are all-powerful.*

Gabe continued. " 'Who is he that hideth counsel without knowledge? Therefore have I uttered that I understood not; things too wonderful for me, which I knew not.'"

This is about Gabe, isn't it? Lena knew in an instant her belittling thoughts about him had not honored God, especially when she'd doubted the Father's hand in Gabe's coming to Nebraska. She didn't understand any of it.

But he doesn't know a thing about farming. Having him around and having to teach him will be like having another child underfoot.

Lena fidgeted; the sweltering realization of being under conviction brought color to her cheeks. She glanced Gabe's way, his reading perfect against the stillness around them. Even if she had to show him how to farm, how ever would she get used to looking at him? She peered into the fire. James had presented a striking pose, and his hearty laughter had brought music to her soul. But Gabe? Although he had nice eyes, she'd have to look at his portly body and pallid skin for the rest of her life.

" 'Wherefore I abhor myself, and repent in dust and ashes.'"

Lena wanted to scream. *All right, Lord.* She wouldn't tell Gabe he had to leave. She'd teach him how to farm and tend to animals. She swallowed and choked on her own spittle, causing Gabe to halt his reading until she was all right. Yes, she'd marry him. But for the life of her, she didn't understand why, except God had ordained it, and He had a plan.

"What do you boys think about Job's life?" Gabe asked once he'd finished reading.

Simon balanced his chin on his finger. "Hmm. Pick better friends?"

Gabe smiled and ruffled his dark hair. "That's one thing. Caleb?"

"I'm not sure, Mr. Hunters. I think we're not supposed to get mad at God when bad things happen."

"Yeah," Simon piped in. "The devil might be out looking for someone to hurt and give you a wife who wants you to die."

Lena hoped the warmth in her face didn't show. Her whimsical son always saw things in a different light, and he wasn't afraid to voice his feelings.

"You're both right," Gabe said. "We don't always understand why things happen, but we can always trust that our God is in control."

Lord, You've already made me feel awful. There's no need to do it again. "Gabe, would you lead us in prayer?" she asked, hoping he didn't hear the turmoil in her voice.

He nodded. "Father God, thank You for bringing me here to this fine home. Bless Lena, Caleb, and Simon. Guide them in Your infinite wisdom, and keep them safe in the shelter of Your almighty arms. Amen."

"Amen," Caleb and Simon echoed. They glanced at Lena expectantly. When she nodded, they bid Gabe good night and followed her to their small bedroom behind a blanketed curtain.

All the while she tucked them in and planted kisses on their cheeks, Lena considered the man sitting by the fireplace. She'd made a commitment to God. Now she had to echo that same promise to Gabe.

She'd rather plow her land without a horse.

Gabe twiddled his thumbs while he awaited Lena's return. He felt certain his heart would leap from his chest. What a fool he'd been to think he might belong here. Would she simply order him off her farm or tell him sweetly to take his fancy words and books back to Philadelphia? Not that he considered either request in poor taste. All his life he'd been labeled a failure, and circumstances were not about to change overnight. Learning new things and fitting into a family would take weeks, even months. Today, he'd ruined every opportune second he'd been given.

What now? *Lord, I wanted this to work. I could have learned how to farm and help Lena with those boys. I know she's not what I envisioned, but I don't think I'm what she expected either. I could have put my despicable past behind me and found confidence in being a husband and father. Oh, I know my confidence is in You, but is it a sin to desire a loving family?*

Turnip growled. Another member of the family against him. "You want to send me back on the next train, too?" he whispered. He stared at the dog, trying to initiate some semblance of friendship with the mongrel.

The dog turned its mammoth head as though attempting to understand the man creature before him.

"We could have pleasant times together," Gabe continued, momentarily shoving aside his current disturbing situation with the members of this household. "Why don't you sniff at me a bit? I need a faithful companion."

Turnip focused his attention on the fire. Perhaps he contemplated Gabe's dismal mood. At least the dog wasn't growling.

"Gabe?" Lena asked quietly, interrupting his thoughts. "Would you like another cup of coffee while we talk?" She wrung her hands and offered a shaky smile.

"I'd like that very much."

"With milk?"

"I believe milk is just fine."

She felt her insides flutter while she poured the hot brew into a tin cup. "I guess we have much to talk about."

Gabe raised his hand. "Lena, I know I've failed miserably today, and I surely understand your aversion to me. I'm riddled with compunction. Let me simplify the matter. I'll leave in the morning, but I need to trouble you for a ride into Archerville."

"What is compunction?"

"It means I feel guilty and ashamed for building up your hopes, then disappointing you."

She inhaled sharply. "No. . .I'd rather you stay. . .and we follow through with our original plan."

"To marry? After I deceived you?"

She handed the coffee to him and slipped into the chair beside him. "I'm sure I have disappointed you."

Only by being lovely. "You are exactly what God intended for me. God does not issue unfitting gifts."

His reply must have moved her, for her eyes moistened. "What sweet words. I must admit I had my doubts until you read from the Bible, but now I am sure we should marry as God put into both of our hearts—unless you have changed your mind."

He leaned forward in the rocking chair. "No, ma'am. I came here to marry and help you, and that is what I still need to do."

She stared into the fire, and he turned his attention to the flames devouring a cow chip. Silence invaded the empty space between them.

"The preacher is expecting us day after tomorrow," Lena said quietly.

"I'll be ready."

Silence once again reigned around them.

"Caleb and Simon want to know what to call you," she finally said.

Gabe had pondered this ever since he boarded the train in Philadelphia. "I believe for now, I'd like them to call me Gabe. When and if they ever feel comfortable, they can call me something more endearing."

"Like Pa or Papa," she finished for him.

He smiled. "Yes. Our arrangement is not unusual, but I want Caleb and Simon to feel some sort of affection before choosing a fatherly title."

Again, Lena appeared moved as she brushed a tear from each cheek. "I'm pleased, Gabe."

He felt his heart lifting from his chest. "Now, I must seal our relationship properly." He slid to the front of the rocker and dropped to one knee in front of her. The effort caused him to take a deep breath. "Lena Walker, would you do me the honor of accepting my proposal of marriage? I promise to cherish you for as long as I live and to always consider Caleb and Simon as my sons." His heart softened as tears flowed more freely from her eyes. He prayed they were shed not in sadness but in hope of a blessed future together. "I have much to learn, and I will always do my best."

Lena bit into her lower lip and smiled. "Yes, I will marry you."

Chapter 5

*G*abe slowly moved toward the barn, or rather the dugout, dreading the night before him. The thought gave a whole new perspective on cave dwellers. He carried a kerosene lantern in one hand and two quilts in the other, but the darkness didn't bother him, just the smell permeating the air.

"Why don't you let me make a pallet by the fire?" Lena had suggested just before he stepped out into the night. "I hate for you to sleep in the barn. The odor gags me, and I'm used to it."

"No. It simply wouldn't be appropriate. I refuse to cast any doubt upon your name. The barn will suit me until we're married."

Glancing up at a clear, star-studded night, he shoved away the unpleasantness of the sleeping arrangements by focusing on the various star formations. As a child, he'd studied them while he waited for his mother to come home. Usually he fell asleep before she stumbled in.

"Gabe," Lena called.

He turned to see her slight frame silhouetted in the doorway. The fire behind her filled his senses with a picturesque scene. An unexpected exhilaration raced up his spine. This woman would soon be his wife, and she'd been given the opportunity to negate the agreement. Maybe not all lovely women were the same. Maybe he'd been given another chance to make his life amount to something worthwhile.

"Gabe?" she called again. "No one will ever know you slept by the fire."

"I'll know," he replied, then waved. "Good night, Lena. Tomorrow I'll help the boys clean out the barn."

He whirled around, feeling a bit giddy. For one night, he could endure most anything. Then the smell violated his nostrils like a hot furnace. What manner of insects crawled in the hay? Would the animals bother him? It would be a long night.

"All right, boys," Gabe said the following morning at breakfast. "We have a full day of work ahead of us, but I understand you have milk to deliver first."

"Yes, sir," Caleb replied, reaching for a piece of corn bread.

"We share our milk with Mr. Shafer and his six children," Lena added. "He doesn't own a cow, and I promised his wife before she died that I would keep an eye on the children."

How commendable. "All right," Gabe said, turning back to the boys. "I'll go with you if your mother doesn't mind."

He glanced at Lena, whose pallor had turned ghastly white. "You might not want to go to the Shafers'. Dagget is not the sociable type."

"Mama threw him off our land 'cause he got mad when she wouldn't marry him," Simon said. "He don't like us much, but the others are friendly."

"Simon," she uttered, her face reflecting the humiliation she must have felt. "Son, can't you ever leave well enough alone?" She stared into Gabe's face. "I feel sorry for his children since their mother died. The oldest girl, Amanda, has her hands full taking care of her brothers and sisters and dealing with her father. Caleb and Simon take the extra milk, but I don't ride along, and I don't think you would want to either."

Gabe had seen the surly type before; he'd go another day. "I'll take your advice and get started on the barn while they're gone."

Lena sighed. "I'll help until they get back. It's a nasty job." She gave the boys a stern look. "And it will never get this dirty again. Right, boys?"

"Yes, ma'am," they chorused.

Gabe hadn't slept a wink last night, but he'd never admit it. Every time he moved, the broken ends of what little fresh hay he'd found jabbed his body like tiny needles. Before daybreak he'd nearly jumped through the roof when a rooster crowed his morning call right beside him. Then he'd discovered some sort of bites all over him. He didn't want to think what might have caused them. Although the manure smell curdled his stomach, the unaccustomed sounds of the animals—both inside and out—had also kept him awake. He'd have to ask the boys about the birds and animals in the area and how to recognize their calls. The possibility that the animals were predators flashed as a warning across his mind, not that he believed himself a fearful man, merely cautious.

In the morning light, he'd seen that the structure housing the animals not only needed repairs but also existed in an overall sad state of disarray. How did they locate anything without designated areas set aside for tools, feed, harnesses, and such? This project would take more than one day, but he wouldn't be working on it tomorrow. That was his wedding day.

He glanced down at his newly purchased working clothes, thinking he should have obtained another set in Philadelphia. By tonight he'd be emitting the same stench as those animal droppings. With a shrug, Gabe headed outside, eager to begin his first day as a Nebraska farmer.

Lena took extra pains to prepare a hearty meal the morning of her and Gabe's wedding day. She hadn't slept the night before because of the anxiety about the day swirling around in her head.

"I don't believe I've ever had such a delectable breakfast," Gabe said.

His clothes were wet. Surely he had not tried to wash them last night.

"Lena, your cooking certainly pleases the palate. Thank you. I apologize for not complimenting you sooner."

Simon eyed Gabe curiously. "How can a pallet please you? I'd rather sleep in my bed."

Lena turned her head to keep from laughing.

"Palate, p-a-l-a-t-e," Gabe said slowly, giving the boy his utmost attention. "It means your mother's food tastes good. A pallet on the floor is p-a-l-l-e-t. It's a common mistake, because the words sound the same but are spelled differently."

Simon shook his head. "Sure can stir up strange things in a person's head. Whoever came up with words should have thought about what he was doing."

Gabe smiled. "I believe you have a valid point." He turned to Lena. "Caleb said he and Simon haven't attended school since last spring." He scooped a forkful of eggs and bacon into his mouth, then bit into a hot piece of corn bread oozing with butter.

"The schoolteacher quit after the spring session, and Archerville hasn't been able to find another," Lena replied. "I try to teach them reading, writing, and some arithmetic, but they really need someone more educated than I. I know we were lucky to have a teacher when other farms farther out have nothing."

He reached for his mug of coffee. "I'd be honored to assist in Caleb and Simon's fundamental studies."

Lena recalled Gabe had been too tired to eat supper the night before after working all day in the barn. He'd barely made it through the scripture reading before heading to bed. How would he find time to teach the boys?

"You're welcome to do whatever you can," she said.

"Perhaps in the evenings after our meal and before scripture reading."

"Are you sure that won't be too much trouble?" Lena asked. "I'm thinking with you here, I should have more time to devote to their book learning."

Gabe rested his fork across his plate. "Their schooling is as important as food and shelter. I'll not neglect their education. The future of this country belongs to those who aspire to higher learning. How rewarding to someday see Caleb and Simon attending a fine university."

I'd never considered them going to college. Gabe is good for them. Thank You, Lord.

An hour later, alone in the house while the boys delivered milk and Gabe prepared for the ride into Archerville, Lena pondered the day ahead, her wedding day. She wiggled her fingers into a pair of ivory-colored gloves. At least they would hide her work-worn hands. She stared at her left hand and remembered not so long ago when her ring finger was encircled by a wedding band. Only when Gabe had informed her of his arrival date in Archerville had she removed it.

Mixed emotions still battled within her. Today she planned to marry a man she did not know or love. At least she knew James before they wed. A lacing of fear caused her to tremble. Although she believed God's hand was in this marriage, she still felt like a scared rabbit.

Smoothing her cornflower-blue Sunday dress, she examined her appearance in the small mirror above her dresser. She pulled on a few wispy curls around her face, then pinched her cheeks. Inside her pocket, she'd already placed a few mint leaves to chew before the ceremony so her breath would be sweet for her wedding kiss.

A slow blush crept up her neck and face, and a chill caused her to massage her arms. She felt sordid, as though remarrying meant she no longer valued her vows to James. But that wasn't true. He would have wanted her to remarry a good man. James had been so handsome—tall, darkly tanned, muscular, and he always made her laugh. An image of Gabe flashed across her mind: his fleshy stature, the wiry straw-colored hair, and his pale skin. How could she ever learn to love and respect him? He knew nothing about living on a farm, and she questioned if he knew anything about marriage.

Yesterday, with the boys, he'd cleaned out the entire barn and organized tools and equipment, which hadn't been done since before James's illness and not ever to the extent of Gabe's high standards. He'd planned on Friday, the day after their wedding, to build another milking stool and make roof repairs to the barn. The stool would have to wait, since lumber was too dear. Gabe had looked happy, satisfied with what he'd accomplished. She felt relieved about this part of him. Goodness knows what she'd have done if he'd been a lazy sort.

"We want to call Mr. Hunters Gabe," Caleb had announced. "I'm not so sure he knows how to be a father. Why, Mama, I had to tell him what some of the tools were used for."

Oh Lord, I know You are in this. Help me to be a good wife and not compare Gabe to James. Hold on to my tongue and help me to be sweet-tempered.

Lena heard the door to the soddy open. "Mama," Caleb called. "It's time to go."

Chapter 6

*K*indly take the bride's right hand," the Reverend Jason Mercer instructed. He towered over Gabe as he cleared his throat and continued with the wedding ceremony. "Repeat after me."

Although he shook with thoughts of the future, Gabe repeated the vows word for word. "I, Gabriel Hunters, take thee, Lena Walker, to be my wedded wife, to have and to hold from this day forward, for better or for worse, for richer or for poorer, in sickness and in health, to love and to cherish, till death us do part, according to God's holy ordinance; and thereto I plight thee my troth." Nervousness tore at his whole heart and mind—to say nothing of what it was doing to his body. He stared into Lena's incredible green eyes and saw the same trepidation.

Poor lady, she said little on the ride here, and now her hand trembles like a fall leaf shaking loose from a mighty tree. How arduous this must be for her.

Standing alone in the church except for his soon-to-be family, the reverend, and a friend of Lena's, Nettie Franklin, Gabe appreciated that no one else gawked at them. He desperately needed solace.

"Repeat after me, Lena," the reverend said.

"I, Lena Walker, take thee, Gabriel Hunters, to be my wedded husband, to have and to hold from this day forward, for better or for worse, for richer or for poorer, in sickness and in health, to love and to cherish, till death us do part, according to God's holy ordinance; and thereto I plight thee my troth." Her voice quivered. Gabe held her hand firmly, understanding her fears for the day and tomorrow because he had just as many if not more. Only God could ease their uncertainty.

"Do you have a token of love?" Reverend Mercer asked.

"Yes, sir," Gabe replied in a voice not his own. He reached into his jacket pocket and pulled out his mother's ring, a striking red ruby set in gold, not gaudy but dainty and elegant. It was the only thing he'd kept of her possessions, because it once belonged to his great-grandmother.

As they joined their right hands, Gabe held his breath until he slipped the heirloom onto her left ring finger. *Thank You, Lord, for allowing Mother's ring to fit.* She'd left him something of value after all.

Behind Lena, Caleb and Simon stood solemnly. No doubt Caleb, acting on behalf of the family, had misgivings about Gabe's qualifications as a provider. These first two days had been such a disappointment, and Gabe had to ask the boys about everything. He looked like a simpleton.

The two youngsters stared at him in a mixture of disbelief and confusion. From the looks of them—thick, mottled brown hair and wide, dark eyes—Lena's deceased husband must have been a dandy. Now she had a man who held the same shape as a potbellied stove—painted white.

"By the power vested in me, I pronounce you man and wife. What God hath joined together, let no man put asunder." The kindly young reverend paused and smiled. "You may now kiss your bride."

I've never kissed a woman before. How am I supposed to do this? Should I have rehearsed or found a book?

Gabe stepped closer, his bulging midsection brushing against Lena's waist. He lightly grasped her thin shoulders and bent ever so slightly. She quivered with his touch, and he prayed it was not from aversion. Her lovely features settled on him in a most pleasing manner, reminding him of an angel depicted in a stained-glass window at his church in Philadelphia. To him, Lena had given beauty its name. Maybe God had given him a woman he could trust after all.

"Thank you, Lena, for giving this lowly man your hand," he whispered.

Tears graced her eyes, and he seized the moment to offer a feathery kiss to her lips. "I am most honored."

The seal of their commitment, Gabe's first kiss, tasted warm and sweet with a hint of mint. Quite agreeable. In fact, he could easily grow accustomed to this endearment.

"Congratulations," Reverend Mercer said in a booming voice. Over the few years he'd served as clergy, the reverend must have repeated a thousand "amens," but none as meaningful as the one Gabe interpreted as a blessing upon this ceremony.

"Thank you," Lena said quietly to the reverend.

Nettie, a pleasant-looking young woman, reached out to hug Lena. "I'll be praying for you every day," she said.

The two women's eyes flooded with tears. "Don't make me cry. This is a happy occasion," Lena said, dabbing at her eyes.

"Yes, it is, and you deserve all the good things God can give," Nettie replied, offering a smile.

Gabe offered Nettie his hand in a gesture of friendship. "Thank you for witnessing the ceremony. I'm grateful."

"I'm sure you will be very happy," the reverend continued with a nod. For a young man, his hair had rapidly escaped its original seating. He grasped Gabe's hand. "I have a good feeling you will make a splendid husband and a fine father."

"I don't know about that, Reverend Mercer," Simon said with a deep sigh. "Mr. Gabe needs to learn some farmin' and how to ride a horse first."

Gabe glanced into the little boy's face, seriousness etched on his features. How should he respond when the boy spoke the truth?

Lena whirled around to face her youngest son. "Simon, you apologize this instant." She met Gabe's gaze. Her face had transformed from ashen to crimson in a matter of a few moments. "I am so sorry. I'll properly discipline him when we get home."

"No need," Gabe said as gently as possible. This was his family, and he needed to take control but not exhibit harsh or domineering ways. "I have a better idea, if you don't mind."

When Lena said nothing, he lowered to one knee and eyed Simon. "No one knows more than this man before you all the items I need to learn and experience, but you could have voiced your concerns in a more mannerly fashion. So while you are feeding the animals this afternoon by yourself, Caleb will be teaching me the fine art of bridling, saddling, and riding a horse. When you're finished, you can offer any helpful advice."

Simon's eyes widened, and Caleb muffled a snicker. "Yes. . .sir."

"Good." Gabe stood and caught a glint of admiration in Lena's eyes. "Is this suitable?" he asked her.

"Most definitely." Lena smiled, and his heart turned a flip.

Oh Lord, help me to be worthy of this woman. If only she weren't so comely. Ignoring the misgivings pouring through his mind, Gabe offered her his arm. "Mrs. Hunters, may I escort you to our carriage? I will then take care of the monetary arrangements with the good reverend and drive you home, with your careful instructions, of course." He shot a glance at Caleb and Simon, who thankfully chose to say nothing.

She linked her arm with his. Her touch exhilarated his spirit. *I'm a married man, and I have two sons!*

Lena listened to the sounds of her sons' laughter coming from the barn while she lowered the bucket into the well. She caught sight of the ruby ring, thinking once more how beautiful its brilliance and how out of place it looked on her weather-beaten hand. Gabe's mother must have been a highly educated and sophisticated woman.

"Mama," Caleb called from the barn.

She turned to see Gabe riding the mare toward her with no assistance. He sat erect in the saddle, and his hands held the reins firmly. Without his hat, the late afternoon sun over his shoulder picked up the pale blond of his hair, reminding her of ripe corn. *Gabe Hunters, I believe with a little physical work and the sun to darken your skin, you just might strike a fine pose.*

Immediately, she detested her impetuous thoughts. The Bible clearly stated the measure of a man dwelled in his heart, not in his looks.

"How quickly you learn," she said, drawing up the water and setting the bucket aside.

"I believe my ability to progress is due to Caleb's excellent instructions," Gabe replied. He'd pulled the mare to a halt and talked to her while leaning from the saddle.

Crossing her arms, she laughed. "Mr. Hunters, you do catch on fast. Why, you look like you were born in a saddle."

Gabe joined in her laughter. "We'll discuss my riding ability after I learn how to trot and gallop. Perhaps in time we could ride together."

"It's been a long while since I've enjoyed riding," she said wistfully. An image of her and James riding across the plains so many years ago flew across her mind.

He dismounted, a bit clumsily but successfully. "You work too hard," he said, grasping the reins in one hand and picking up the bucket in the other.

"That's life on a farm," she said simply. His nearness served to remind her of the vows they'd shared earlier in the day. For a moment she'd forgotten, not really wanting to think about it all. Then she remembered the night and her wifely duties. . . . The unknown had always been frightening, and though farm life seemed insurmountable before, now she had a husband who knew less about toiling the land than her sons.

"I want to do all I can to make your land profitable."

His words sounded as though he'd read her thoughts. "Thank you." She glanced again at her left hand. "My ring is far above anything I've ever owned," she murmured. "Is it a family heirloom?"

"My great-grandmother's passed to my mother." He smiled. "I'm glad you're pleased."

"I've never owned anything so fine."

"It reminds me of you and the thirty-first chapter of Proverbs. 'Who can find a virtuous woman? For her price is far above rubies.'"

Lena felt the tears spill swiftly over her cheeks. The precious gems flowing from Gabe's mouth came so naturally. His words touched her heart with a special warmth and beauty of their own. *Must be from his books, and I can barely keep up with the boys' schoolwork.*

"Have I upset you?" he asked, his strawlike eyebrows knit together.

"No." She shook her head. How could she tell him, this stranger— her husband—all the fears, doubts, and questions racing through her mind about him and this ruse of a marriage?

She'd entered into this with only thoughts of herself. She'd wanted a farmhand and a model for her sons. Not once had she considered this person might have feelings and emotions. The very thought he might be sensitive with the potential of caring very deeply for a new family had never really occurred to her.

I am so selfish. Gabe doesn't deserve a woman like me. Rubies? Lena thought the verse about throwing pearls to swine best befit her.

"Lena," he whispered.

She knew her eyes held her turmoil when she should be happy this first afternoon of their marriage. Unbidden droplets of liquid pain coursed down her cheeks.

"I think it's best if I continue to sleep in the barn."

"Why?" Had she hurt him so badly he could not bear being with her?

Gabe moistened his lips. She'd learned in the three short days they'd been together that he often did this before he spoke of important matters. "We do not know each other, and of utmost importance is for us to be friends." He cleared his throat. "Affection should be present before we live as man and wife, don't you think? And how else can we develop a fondness for each other unless we first appreciate our strengths and talents?"

Oh Lord, is Gabe a saint or simply terribly wounded by my initial reaction to him?

She detests me. My inadequacies have destroyed any hope of respect. Gabe wanted to place a hand on her shoulder, but he dared not see her recoil. Lena's tears moved him so deeply he feared if he didn't turn away, he, too, might weep.

All of his doubts about her beauty and possible unfaithfulness surfaced and drowned in his inward grief. He had spoiled what could have been great joy. In all of his grandiose ideas of learning to live on a farm and all it entailed, why had he foolhardily thought he could experience the knowledge by reading books? Now the theory burst in his face. As his mother always said, "Gabriel, you are an utter disappointment. I can't love anyone who is such a fool. Live your life in your books; see where it gets you. Nowhere, I tell you. Nowhere."

"I want what you want," Lena said, between sobs. "If this is how you believe our lives should begin, then so be it." She lifted her tear-glazed face. "Perhaps we should have corresponded more before your trip here."

Gabe felt his heart plummet. If they had written numerous letters, she would have detected his deception. "I'm sorry for allowing you to believe I knew about farming and living by the sweat of my brow. But I will learn—"

"I know you will," she interrupted, taking the bucket of water from his hand. She paused, staring at the water as though it offered the answers to the dilemma plaguing them. "Do you want to leave?"

Gabe refused to answer, carefully forming his words. He took in a panoramic view of the farm—the work it needed, the work he didn't know how to do. He should give her and the boys an escape from the community's ridicule. They need not be the victims of his idiocy. Defeat wrapped a black hand around his heart and strangled the utterances he believed proper and fitting for the situation.

"No, Lena, I don't want to leave. I came here to start a new life, and I want to stay."

Chapter 7

*L*ena marched down the front of Archerville's Gospel Church, where only four days earlier she and Gabe had spoken their vows. Nervousness had attacked her then, but not as much as the sense of every eye in the building studying her and Gabe now. What a sight they must present—Lena shivering like a new bride, her husband carrying his traveling hat with his wild hair and filled-up suit, and her barefoot sons pretending they weren't embarrassed by it all. To make matters worse, Riley O'Connor sat on the aisle seat midway down.

Oh Lord, I'm so sorry, but I feel like the whole church is laughing at me. She glanced at her new husband and offered him a shaky smile. Gabe might not give the appearance of a Nebraska farmer, but he certainly had treated her and the boys well. Unless something changed, he was a giving man and anxious to learn about farming. But those resolves didn't help her face the forty people attending this Sunday morning service.

"Good morning," Amanda Shafer whispered. Unlike her father, Dagget, Amanda was a sweet, pretty sixteen-year-old who loved the Lord and took the best possible care—under the circumstances—of her brothers and sisters.

"Mornin'." Lena hooked her arm into Gabe's. "Amanda, this is my husband, Gabriel Hunters. Gabe, this is Amanda Shafer."

"A pleasure to make your acquaintance, Miss Shafer," Gabe said, his every word pronounced perfectly...and sounding foreign. "Or is it Mrs.?"

"Miss," Amanda replied. "And these are my brothers and sisters."

After Amanda politely introduced her siblings, she added, "We're neighbors and see Caleb and Simon 'most every day."

"Amanda is a big help to her pa in raising these children," Lena added hastily, eyeing an empty pew two rows up from where they stood.

"Your father must be very proud of you. Is he here that I might introduce myself?"

Amanda's face flushed pink. "No, Pa is at home today."

He needs to be here with his family.

Reverend Mercer greeted Lena and Gabe as he made his way down to the front of the sod-bricked church. Thankful for the interruption,

Lena urged her family to the empty bench near the front. At least there she wouldn't have to endure the stares from the rest of the congregation.

Lena attempted to concentrate on the sermon, but the topic caused her to cringe from the moment Reverend Mercer read from the Bible about God's looking at a man's heart rather than his physical appearance. *All right, Lord. You shamed me, and I know You're right.* Sitting up straighter, she patted Gabe's arm and focused her gaze on Reverend Mercer, although her ears didn't take in another word.

At the close, Reverend Mercer stood before his small congregation and teetered back and forth on his heels. "I have an announcement to make. This past week I had the pleasure of marrying Lena Walker and Gabriel Hunters. Let's all take a moment to congratulate this fine couple. Mr. Hunters is from Philadelphia and welcomes the task of farming in our fine country." He motioned for Gabe and Lena to stand and face the people. Slapping on a smile, she nodded at the well-wishers and ignored the snickers. Caleb and Simon stared straight ahead at the door, and she wished she could do the same.

"Mr. and Mrs. Hunters, would you and the boys kindly join me in the back so each one of these fine people can greet you?"

Oh no. Dagget may not be here, but Riley O'Connor is. Knowing that man's quick tongue, he's liable to say anything after I refused his improper advances. Sure glad I walloped him when I could. Instantly, Lena felt sorry for Gabe. He'd be caught like a snared rabbit, unsuspecting in the least of Riley's insults.

Gabe greeted each face with a smile. He appreciated the sincere welcomes from most of the people and their desire to be friends. But he also saw the wary expressions and mocking stares from a few. How well he knew the judgmental type, whether they lived in Archerville, Nebraska, or Philadelphia, Pennsylvania. If you didn't wear the clothes they wore, converse in their familiar words, or come from an acceptable family, then you were cast at the bottom of their list. He'd seen it too often and well recognized the characteristics.

Fortunately, he had an opportunity to prove himself capable and responsible to those who mattered—Lena and her sons. God valued him and had given him the distinction of being a part of this community. By His hand, he'd succeed.

"Good to have you here," a wrinkled elderly lady said after stating her name. She patted his hand and gave a toothless smile. Slivers of gray peeked beneath her bonnet. "Lena is a fine woman, strong and determined."

"Thank you, ma'am. We'll be happy, I'm sure."

"Pure pleasure to meet you. Glad you're here," a balding man said. Dressed in a little better attire than most folks there, he introduced himself as Judge Hoover. "I'd like for you to meet my wife, Bertha." A round woman smiled prettily, but before Gabe could respond, the judge continued. "This is a growing town, and I praise God for each newcomer." He swung his arm around Reverend Mercer's shoulders and ushered him outside into the fall sunlight with his quiet wife behind him.

Then Gabe met the eyes of a tall, slender fellow who eyed him contemptuously. "Hunters, eh?" He kept both hands on a tattered hat in front of him. "Sure don't look like a farmer to me. Ya won't last here."

Remember, sir, we are in God's house. Gabe had dealt with this type of person longer than he cared to remember. "Looks are often deceiving, as the reverend so eloquently established this morning," Gabe said. "The good Lord willing, I will succeed at my endeavors."

If the ill-mannered man could have spit in church, Gabe surmised he'd have done so. Furrowing his brow, the fellow turned his attention to Lena. Immediately, he became charming in every sense of the word.

"Lena." His words dripped with honey. "You look right pretty this morning." He smiled broadly, revealing a row of perfectly white teeth— not a common sight, and certainly an edge for any man wishing to impress a woman.

Gabe ran his tongue over his own teeth—fairly straight and not discolored from tobacco. *Have you forgotten she is my wife?*

Lena lifted her chin and glanced at the door. "Riley O'Connor, your horse is waiting for you."

"How soon before you get bored with this city feller?" he asked just loud enough for Gabe to hear. Leaning a little closer to the new Mrs. Hunters than Gabe deemed proper, Riley turned to Gabe and sneered. "She never minded my kisses. In fact, she asked for more."

Lena lifted her hand as if she might strike him.

"It's all right, Lena," Gabe soothed, not once taking his gaze from Riley. He feared she was ready to unleash her temper, not that he wouldn't enjoy seeing this rude fellow with freshly slapped cheeks, but God didn't ordain this type of behavior and fighting as a means of settling disputes.

"Mr. O'Connor, I am currently overlooking your deficiency of manners, but when issues pertain to my wife, I thank you kindly to refrain from indecorous speech."

Riley issued him a snarl.

"In other words, Mr. O'Connor, Lena Hunters is a married woman and does not desire to hear your crude remarks." Gabe turned to Lena. "Is that a correct assumption, dear?"

"Yes, it is," she replied and dismissed Riley in one seething glare. A young woman carrying a baby stood behind Riley. "Martha, your little girl is growing like a weed, and look at those sky-blue eyes. Can I hold her?"

Riley stumbled down the steps in a huff and headed straight to a horse tethered beyond the wagons.

Once the receiving line for Archerville's Gospel Church had diminished, Gabe expelled a long breath. He leaned down to Caleb and whispered, "How did I do?"

Caleb pressed his lips together in an obvious gesture to suppress his mirth. "You did right well. Judge Hoover shook your hand, which means he likes you, and he can be rather bad-tempered. And. . .you put Riley in his place."

"Thanks," Gabe replied. "I do believe I'm ready for the peace and quiet of our farm."

He glanced at Lena, whose face resembled a color somewhere between gray and flour white. *Did she and Mr. Riley O'Connor court before I came? Was his arrogance a result of being a jealous suitor?* Rolling the conversation with Riley around in his jumbled mind, Gabe could only dispel the despairing thoughts with a shiver.

"Shall we go home?" His question sounded weak.

"Please," she uttered, once again hooking her arm into his.

Outside the sod church, Reverend Mercer lingered at the Shafer wagon while holding a little girl who hid her face in his jacket.

"Excellent sermon this morning," Gabe called to him.

The reverend turned and waved enthusiastically. "Thank you. Mighty glad to have you with us. See you next week?"

"We'll be here," Gabe assured him.

"Has someone invited you to dinner?" Lena asked the reverend.

Are you not wanting to be alone with me. . .because of Riley?

"Yes, ma'am."

Her shoulders relaxed. "We'd love to have you come next Sunday."

The reverend smiled and thanked her politely before handing the bashful child back to Amanda Shafer.

Seeming to ignore Gabe and Lena, Caleb and Simon chattered in the wagon, caught up in their own world of trapping animals and teasing each other.

"Are you displeased with me?" Gabe asked softly. He held both reins firmly as had been his instructions.

She gasped. "Oh no." Shaking her head, she adjusted her sunbonnet. "I'm so sorry about what happened."

"You mean the saturated infant I was asked to hold?" He didn't want to upset her if she truly felt bad about Riley.

Her gaze flew to his, and she blinked back a tear.

Now I've truly upset her.

"Riley O'Connor," she uttered, as though his name were a curse. "I'm so sorry for the things he said to you."

"To me? Ma'am, he insulted you."

She shrugged and stared up at the sky. "He insulted both of us, Gabe. I want you to know that I never courted him. Not ever. I wouldn't allow him near me, which is probably why he was so mean today."

"You don't have to explain it to me—"

"But I want to! He asked me to marry him, and I refused. He's been like that ever since."

Another thought needled at Gabe. "Should I have challenged him outside? Did you expect me to engage him in a fistfight?"

"Goodness, no. You handled him much better than I ever could have."

When she sniffed, he yearned to extend consolation to her. "The situation is over and done. Perhaps he won't trouble you again now that we're married."

"I hope not." She forced a laugh. "I nearly blacked his eyes. Oh, I wanted to, Gabe."

Gabe laughed heartily. "I saw. I'll be sure to avoid making you angry."

And she joined him, laughing until the boys begged to know what was so funny.

Chapter 8

Lena rocked gently in front of the fireplace, enjoying its familiar creaking like an old friend. She loved these moments: quiet, peaceful times while she tended to mending. The only sounds around her came from the mantel clock's steady rhythm and the comfortable rocker. Usually Gabe taught the boys their lessons during this time and then treated them all to a chapter in some magnificent book. Nightly he read from the scriptures and led in prayer.

Tonight the men in her family had hurried from supper to make sure the animals were all secure. The temperature outside had dropped considerably during the afternoon, and the wind whistled about their soddy like a demon seeking entrance. Snow clouds hovered over them all day, and she knew without a doubt that the sky planned to dump several inches of snow—possibly several feet—before morning.

Inserting her needle into Caleb's torn drawers, she worked quickly to patch the knees. He'd most likely need the clothing tonight. Fall had passed with no hint of Indian summer; suddenly the warm days of early September changed to a chilling cold in October and now November. The dropping temperatures alarmed her, and she prayed the winter would be easy. Usually the frigid weather waited to besiege them until at least December, with the coldest days landing in January and February.

Lena paused and stared into the crackling fire. A smile tugged at her lips. This past month as Mrs. Gabriel Hunters had been good and ofttimes humorous. Gabe was indeed a fine husband—maybe not exactly what she'd wanted or envisioned—but God knew best. Such a tenderhearted, compassionate man, but he had his unique moments. When he decided to complete a task, he refused to give in to the cold, the time of day, mealtime, or a lack of knowledge. Tenacious, he called it, but she knew better. Gabe had a stubborn streak as clear as she knew her name.

My, how she appreciated having her husband around. Praise God, Gabe hadn't mentioned the unfortunate incident with Riley again. Riley hadn't been back to church—for which Lena was grateful, especially given that hearing God's Word had done nothing to improve the man's disposition.

The sound of Gabe's hearty laughter and the giggles of her sons caressed her ears as if she'd been graced by the sweetest music ever sung this side of heaven.

"Mama, we're ready for a winter storm," Caleb said once all three had made their way inside.

"I'm glad," she called from the rocking chair, smiling at her sons, then meeting a sparkle in Gabe's merry gaze. *He enjoys this work. Seems to thrive on it.*

"If you don't mind, Lena," he said, "we went over our arithmetic in the barn. So I'd like to work on our reading tonight."

"A story?" Simon asked. "When we're all done with our lessons?"

Gabe chuckled. "I imagine so, providing your reading expertise surpasses my expectations."

Caleb placed his coat on a peg by the door and turned to his younger brother. "That means we do well."

Simon crinkled his forehead. "I know what it means. I study my vocaberry words."

"Vocabulary," Caleb corrected. "The correct pronunciation of the English language is a declaration of our appreciation for education." He nodded at Gabe as though reciting before a schoolmaster.

Lena stifled a laugh. Caleb, who had not shown much interest in schooling before, had blossomed under Gabe's instruction. He actually looked forward to his schoolwork.

"I don't need to know how to say words as proper as you," Simon said between clenched teeth. "I'm just going to be president of the United States, and you're going to be a doctor."

"Both are worthy callings," Gabe said. "No point in brothers becoming adversaries. Neither profession is above the other or requires less expertise. Education is vital to any man's vocation."

"Even a farmer?" Caleb asked.

"Absolutely. A farmer needs to know how and when to till the soil, take care of the animals, make repairs, and a host of other necessities too numerous for me to mention."

Simon shrugged and sighed heavily. "Sounds like I'll be tending to my lessons until I'm an old man."

"Precisely," Gabe replied and ruffled his hair. "We never stop learning; that's why God gave us eager minds. Now, gather your slate so you can inscribe any words of which you don't comprehend the meaning while I read."

Thank You, Lord, for directing this man to my sons. I've never heard such wisdom.

"And what will you be reading this night, providing the boys master their work?" Lena asked, not wanting Gabe to see her enthusiasm at the prospect of another exciting tale.

Gabe thrust his hands behind his back and teetered on his heels. "I think a new book, *David Copperfield*, by Charles Dickens. I believe the boys will enjoy the tale of a young boy in England and his adventures. There is much to learn about life and England in this novel."

Lena caught his gaze, and a faint shimmer of something she had not felt in years swept through her. *Lord, what a blessing if I learn to love this man.*

Gabe settled in beside her on a rag rug. He'd begun teaching the boys in this manner, saying they learned more when they shared eye contact. Obviously, he was right.

"Are you weary tonight?" he asked her quietly.

Her heart hammered. Why did Gabe ask her this? "No. Is there something that needs to be done?"

"Only my hair needs to be cut before church tomorrow. It reminds me of straw, and the longer it grows, the more unruly it becomes until I look like an overstuffed scarecrow."

She calmed her rapid pulse. *Oh my. I nearly had a fright.* They still remained as friends, with Gabe sleeping in the barn. For a moment, she'd wondered if he'd decided to claim his rights as her husband. "I'd be glad to. Perhaps I can help you, since it wants to go its own way."

"I'd be much obliged," he replied. "I've never been able to comb my hair so it would lay smoothly."

Once Caleb and Simon finished their lessons and they all heard the first chapter of *David Copperfield*, the boys scurried off to bed amid the rising howl of the wind outside.

"I'll bring in some more chips from the porch and a few corncobs for the cookstove," Gabe said, reaching for his coat. "You know better than I do how much snow may fall, and I want to be prepared."

"Maybe a few inches, but most likely a few feet." Lena pressed her lips together. Snow always frightened her, more so than the other threats of nature. James had become ill in this kind of weather, then died of pneumonia. "I can cut your hair when you come back inside."

A short while later, she pulled a chair beside the fire, where Turnip rested with his face on his paws. Pulling her scissors from her apron pocket and securing a comb from the bedroom, she waited for Gabe to dump an armload of chips near the dog.

Once seated, he shook his head. "Only a miracle or losing all of my hair could help."

Lena laughed lightly. "I don't think you will go bald anytime soon." She dragged a comb through his thick hair, all the while pondering its wildness and his wiry eyebrows. "Have you ever tried combing it in the direction it grows?"

"You mean straight up?"

She joined him in another laugh. "Not exactly, but do you mind if I try something?"

"Whatever you can do will be an improvement."

She touched his shoulders and felt him shudder. For certain, she hadn't been this close to him since he'd kissed her on their wedding day. "I'll do my best," she managed, remembering the shiver she'd felt with his gaze earlier. "Do you mind if I wet it a little?"

"Uh. . .well. . .certainly."

Odd, he's never been at a loss for words. Makes me wonder if something is happening between us. Lena shook her head. *Of course not; we've barely known each other a month.*

All the while she dampened Gabe's hair, she saw chill bumps rise on his neck. "I'm sorry this is cold. I used warm water."

"You're. . .you're fine," he said.

She glanced at his face—red, too red even for their position in front of the fire. *I can't stop now. What will he think?* Swallowing hard, she continued combing his hair, easing the coarse strands in the direction they wanted to go—straight back rather than to the side. The change amazed her. His face looked thinner, and his eyes seemed larger—like huge copper pennies.

"Have you not combed your hair back before? Why, it looks wonderful," she said. "I can trim it a little, but, Gabe, you look positively dashing."

His face now resembled a summer tomato. She hadn't meant to embarrass him, but he did look. . .well, striking. With a snip here and there, his hair rested evenly over his head. She couldn't help but run her fingers through the thick blond mass. Instantly, she realized what she was doing and trembled. Whatever had she been thinking?

"Do. . .do you mind if I cut a bit of your eyebrows, since they tend to stick up, too?" she asked.

He shook his head and moistened his lips. *This is hard for both of us!*

Once completed, she excused herself long enough to fetch her hand-held mirror from her bedroom. "Just look, Gabe."

He took the mirror, and their fingertips met—a gentle touch, but it seared her as though she'd stuck her hand in the midst of a hot flame.

Shakily placing the mirror in front of his face, he leaned closer. "You've worked wonders," he mumbled.

"No, I haven't. You have beautiful hair; it simply has a mind of its own."

He examined his image more closely, turning the mirror from side to side to catch every angle. "Even without a hat, it won't stick out like a porcupine."

She laughed and moved to face him. "Your hair looks good, and your face is pleasing, too." *Now, why did I say that?*

"Uh, thank you, but I believe you've been isolated on this farm too long. It's affecting your judgment." He avoided her gaze, and she, too, felt terribly uncomfortable at her brash statements. "I think it's time I ventured to the barn."

Lena nodded, but another whistle of the wind alarmed her. "Gabe, the barn is simply too cold for you to sleep out there. Why, you'll freeze to death."

This time his ears reddened. "Nonsense. I will be snug and warm."

"I refuse for my husband to sleep in a barn when this soddy is where you belong."

He stood and strode across the room for his coat. "And I say the barn suits me fine." He reached for the latch. "I have two warm quilts out there."

"Would you like a comforter?"

Gabe stared at her incredulously, and she grasped his interpretation in horror. "I mean a third blanket."

He hesitated. "If it will not inconvenience you."

On unsteady legs, Lena made her way to the blanket chest in her bedroom and brought him a thick new quilt. He thanked her and opened the door. An icy gust of wind hurled its fury at them.

"Please, Gabe, stay inside tonight."

"No, this is what I committed to do until we are ready to live as man and wife."

Your stubbornness will make you ill. She grabbed her coat and muffler. "Then I'm going with you."

Chapter 9

$\mathcal{M}$ ost certainly not!" Gabe replied, a little louder than he intended.

"If you insist upon freezing to death, I most certainly will join you," Lena replied, shrugging into her coat.

Completely frustrated, Gabe toyed with the proper words to convince her of her absurdity. He'd tried so hard to refrain from using the vocabulary that confused those around him, but his mind spun with the terms familiar to him.

"See, you can't even argue against me." She swung her muffler around her neck and face.

"What must I do to convince you of this foolishness?" he asked with an exasperated sigh.

"Be sensible and sleep inside by the fire."

I'll agree until you fall asleep. "All right. I concede to your pleas, but I must get my quilts from the barn."

"If you aren't back in ten minutes, I'm coming out there."

Gabe nodded, speechless. He knew Lena meant every word. He lifted the chain deep inside his overalls pocket holding his pocket watch. From what he'd seen of his wife with Caleb and Simon, he dared not proceed a moment past her ultimatum.

Odd, he used to have to tug on that chain to retrieve his pocket watch. Glancing at the small clock on the fireplace mantel, he double-checked the time.

"I'll be waiting," she said, folding her hands at her waist.

He'd seen that menacing look on her face before. The lightning stare didn't occur often, but he understood the flash occurred before the thunder. Truth of the matter was, he enjoyed Lena's feisty moments. She'd told him right from the start about her temper, but he'd yet to see it vex him. The few times she'd lashed out at the boys, they'd needed an upper hand.

The frigid air nearly took his breath away—a raw-bone cold that sought to solidify his blood. Gabe buttoned his coat tighter around him. Used to be the outer garment didn't fasten. Another oddity.

Loyal Turnip braved the cold with him. "Thanks," he said to the dog. "I believe we men need to form lasting bonds." Moments later he returned with his quilts, after giving himself enough time to check on the livestock.

When he glanced at the roaring fire, he saw she'd made a soft pallet before the burning embers. All those less-than-comfortable nights in the barn plodded across his mind. The smells there were still offensive, but he'd grown accustomed to them, and the sounds of animals—both inside and out—no longer jolted him from his sleep. With the cold came the likelihood of fewer insect bites.

Then he saw Lena. She'd removed her outer garments, but she'd been busy.

"What are you doing?" he asked at the sight of her constructing a second pallet beside his.

"I'm staying here beside you until you go to sleep," she replied, not once looking his way. "Gabe, you're a determined man, and as soon as you hear my even breathing in the next room, you'll be out the door and to the barn. Won't happen if I'm here. I sleep like a cat."

Have I met my match? We'll see who falls asleep first.

"And why are you so insistent about my sleeping arrangements?" He chuckled.

She wrapped her shawl about her shoulders. "The boys' father stepped out into a blizzard and caught pneumonia. Before two months passed, he died."

Gabe frowned. "I'm sorry, Lena, but I'm overly healthy. Just take a look at my portly size."

"If you haven't noticed, you're losing weight." Her features softened. "I don't want to lose another husband."

With elegant grace, Lena slowly descended to the floor, sitting on the rag rug where he'd taught the boys their lessons. She pulled her knees to her chest and wrapped her arms around the faded blue dress she wore every day but Sunday. An intense desire to draw her to him and kiss her soundly inched across his mind—just as it had earlier when she'd touched him. He couldn't have this. Gabe Hunters had made a commitment. He'd feign sleep, then creep to the barn.

"Shall we talk?" he asked. "I'm not ready to retire."

"I'd like that," she replied quietly. "Is there anything you need? The pillow is nice and soft."

"No, I'm fairly comfortable, thank you."

Gabe studied her, this enigma before him. This puzzling, confusing, perplexing woman who bore his name. So unlike his mother, Lena had a spirit graced with compassion and tenderness, even when angered. He didn't want to learn to love her, not really. A part of him didn't trust, or rather refused to trust a woman as lovely as Lena Hunters. But. . .in quiet moments like these, he allowed himself to dream of this genteel woman loving him.

"You are an excellent teacher for the boys," she said, resting her chin on her knees. "They are learning so much."

He smiled, recalling their impish grins and eager minds. "They are teaching me as much, if not more."

"We've been married a month," she said, glancing his way.

"A good month. An abundance of work has been done."

"Some days, I think you work too hard."

"Nonsense. I must compensate for all the skills I lack in farming."

She sighed, and her shoulders lifted slightly. "I'm impressed with what you've accomplished. You're making yourself into a fine farmer." With lowered lashes, she stared back at the fire. As though mesmerized by its brilliance, she blinked and took another deep breath.

She's exhausted. My poor Lena, and she's concerned about my welfare.

"You need your rest," he urged.

"I will when you fall asleep. Shall I read to you?"

He pondered her question. "I believe so, then I'll read to you."

She nodded and reached for the Bible. "What would you like to hear?"

"I don't have a preference. Why not your favorite passage?"

So close he could see a shimmer on her fire-warmed cheeks, Gabe listened to Lena read the book of Ruth. No wonder she chose this accounting of such a godly woman. Ruth, like Lena, was a widow who put her faith and trust in the almighty God. He delivered Ruth from her poverty and blessed her in the lineage of Jesus Christ. How wonderful if Gabe could be Lena's blessing.

He listened to every word, concentrating on the musical lilt of her voice. She was tiring; too many times she shifted and straightened to stay awake.

"No matter how many times I hear Ruth's story, I'm impressed with her devotion to Naomi," he said when she was finished. *I shall not say a word about the weariness plaguing her eyes.* "Now, I will read to you. Perhaps a novel?"

"Not *David Copperfield,*" she whispered, covering her mouth to stifle a yawn. "The boys will be jealous. More of the Bible sounds fine, perhaps the Psalms. They are so soothing at the end of a long day."

"Excellent choice. I'll start with Psalm 119." Gabe thumbed through the pages, noting she grew more tired as time progressed. "'Blessed are the undefiled in the way, who walk in the law of the Lord. Blessed are they that keep his testimonies, and that seek him with the whole heart. . . .'"

By the time Gabe reached verse sixty, Lena had drifted asleep, her head resting on his left shoulder, her body completely relaxed. Being careful not to disturb her, he wrapped his arm around her frail shoulders. She snuggled closer, bringing a contented smile to his lips. He'd won in more than one way this night. Although he needed to quietly slip out to the barn, right now he wanted to close his eyes and bask in the joy of having her next to his heart.

He delighted in her face flushed with the firelight and her lips turned up slightly as if she enjoyed some wonderful dream. Tendrils of black had escaped from the hair carefully pinned at the back of her head to frame her oval face, and the thought of seeing those long silky tresses drape down over her shoulders filled him with pleasure. Such a sweet, altruistic soul. He felt dizzy with the moment, painfully aware of her nearness. Surely his sensibilities existed in an ethereal realm.

Daring to lean his head against hers, Gabe fought the urge to kiss her forehead. For the first time in his life, he felt protective. *Oh Father, is it so wrong of me to pray this angel of a woman might someday love me? I've vowed not to care that deeply, but she is breaking my will—or is it You acting on my behalf?*

How much longer he sat with Lena snuggled against him, Gabe did not know, only that this timeless moment must certainly be a glimpse of heaven.

Slowly he began to nod. As much as Gabe resisted allowing the closeness between him and Lena to fade, he had to put her to bed. With more ease than he anticipated, he gathered her lithe body in his arms and slowly rose to his feet.

Lena didn't stir, nor did her breathing alter. *I thought you slept like a feline.* As she lay against his chest, she sighed. Gabe wanted to believe she felt content because of him. Glancing down, he saw her face looked as smooth as a young girl's. She must have been a beautiful child.

He couldn't help but pull her closer, cradling her like he'd seen mothers carry their babies. He prayed she wouldn't waken, not because of his vow to sleep in the dugout, but because he wanted to relish the softness of this sweet woman for as long as possible.

Gabe moved slowly into the bedroom. He clutched his wife with one arm and pulled back the quilts with the other. Gingerly he laid her on the straw mattress. The thought of removing her shoes crossed his mind, but he feared waking her. Instead, he covered her completely, tucking the blankets around her chin. No point in Lena Hunters falling prey to an illness.

Gabe studied her face. Even in the midst of darkness, he could see the peacefulness on her delicate features. It took all of his might to turn and leave, knowing the bitter cold of the barn awaited him.

"James," Lena murmured in her sleep.

Gabe shot a glance over his shoulder.

"James," she repeated barely above a whisper. "I miss you so much when you're gone."

Chapter 10

*G*abe felt as though the bitter temperatures outside had taken roost in his soul. His reaction to Lena's honest emotions vexed him. How mindless of him to consider she might one day grow to care. He, Gabriel Hunters, the illegitimate son of a woman who once owned Philadelphia's largest brothel, would never compare to a decent man like Lena's deceased husband. How foolish for him to attempt such an inconceivable feat. He should have remained in Philadelphia, living in solitude and managing the monetary accounts of others. There his books were his friends, and they neither demanded anything of him nor ridiculed him.

Defeated before he even stepped foot on Nebraska soil, Gabe determined it best to return to the life he'd left behind. He could shelter himself from the cold, from people, and from the elements and live out his days in peace.

"Is that really what you want?"

Shivering, Gabe ignored the inner voice.

"Do you remember how My people grumbled after I delivered them out of Egypt from Pharaoh's cruelty? Were they not afraid and ready to return to slavery when they couldn't see My plan? Do you want freedom or a life enslaved in bitterness and loneliness?"

Gabe's deliberations only took a moment: Caleb, Simon, and, yes, Lena promised more liberty than a ledger with worrisome numbers. Straightening, he turned his gaze into the fire. He could make an impact on these people's lives and learn how to farm. He could contribute useful information and encourage them in their spiritual walk with the Lord. Allowing the resentment from the past to take over his resolve meant the evil forces in this world had won. God hadn't promised him this family's love; He'd simply instructed Gabe to follow Him to Nebraska.

Turnip tilted his shaggy head as if understanding Gabe's silent turmoil. His tail thumped against the clay floor, offering no advice, only the gift of loyalty.

"Come along with me," Gabe whispered. "You and I have more in common than what others may cogitate." Slipping into his coat, he silently grimaced at the thought of one more night on a straw mattress.

But with renewed confidence, he rolled up the three quilts for the trek to the barn.

Silently he made his way to the door with Turnip right behind him. The latch lifted with a faint *click*.

"And where do you think you're going?" Lena quietly demanded.

Gabe's gaze flew in her direction, and he stiffened. *Caught.* "To the barn to sleep," he replied firmly.

In the shadows, his dear wife lifted a shotgun—the one that normally hung over the door. "I said that I did not intend to bury another husband. I know how to use this."

Gabe buried his face into the quilts to keep from laughing aloud and waking the boys or angering his wife. His earlier worries and fears, especially about James, contrasted with her resolve to keep him from the barn now seemed incredibly funny. He knew Lena's gun wasn't loaded. "Well, Mrs. Hunters, if I mean that much to you, then I shall surely sleep by the fire with Turnip at my feet."

The following morning, three feet of fluffy white snow banked against the dugout and house and halted any plans to attend church. Lena gazed out at the dazzling display of winter's paintbrush. Smiling like a child with the first glimpse of a winter treat, she thought how much the boys would treasure playing outside this afternoon. She might even steal a moment with them.

Gone were the howling wind and the threat of a death-chilling blizzard. In their wake, a quiet calm of white blanketed the land. The pure innocence in the aftermath of the storm reminded her of giving birth.

She watched Gabe trudge from the barn to the soddy. What had possessed her last night to pull the shotgun on him? This temper of hers had to be put to rest. *My goodness, what if he had refused?*

Once Gabe had resigned himself to sleeping by the fire, she'd crawled back into bed. Soon his laughter roared from the ceiling. In the next breath, she'd joined him, apologizing and holding her sides at the same time. If the boys woke, she never knew it, or maybe they simply enjoyed hearing the sound of merriment.

He is a delightful man, Lord. Why he puts up with my disposition is beyond me.

Leaning her forehead on the frosty glass window, she reflected a moment on the differences between James and Gabe. She hoped her contemplations were not wrong and quickly scanned her memory of the Bible to see if God would be disappointed in her comparisons. No particular verse came to mind, so she allowed her musings to continue.

James had enjoyed teasing her, sometimes unmercifully. After last night's episode, she realized Gabe possessed a delightful sense of humor, too.

James didn't take much to book learning. He claimed nothing equaled the education of living life and taking each day as it came. Gabe placed a high regard on books and the importance of learning. Lena thought both men were right, but if she allowed herself to be truthful, she wanted her sons to have the opportunity to seek professions other than farming if they so desired.

James sometimes grew so preoccupied with the workings of the farm that he neglected her and the boys—not because he didn't care for them, but because his love took the form of providing his very best. Gabe put his new family right under God. She'd seen him stop his work to give Caleb, Simon, or herself his undivided attention.

James's deeply tanned skin and dark hair had turned the heads of many women. Gabe's light hair and pale complexion reminded her of an albino mare her father once owned. With that horse, one had to look a little closer to find the beauty—but oh, what a gentle spirit lived inside. Lena had asked for the mare, and her father had consented, saying she recognized the value of a kind heart.

She held her breath. Remembering the albino and her father's words jolted her senses. Was there much difference between the mare and Gabe? A tear trickled down her cheeks as she realized the beginnings of love nestled in her heart.

How strange she could see so much of Gabe in such a short time. James and Gabe were notably different—each with their own strengths and weaknesses—equally good men. Before last night, she'd believed she'd never love another like James. But this morning's reflections caused her to think otherwise.

Gabe had carried her to bed, covered her, clothes and all. Not many men were that honorable. She sighed deeply and whisked away the tears. Now she understood the wisdom in Gabe's desiring them to feel affection for each other before they consummated their marriage.

The latch lifted, and Lena waited expectantly for him to enter. Her heart fluttered, and she didn't attempt to stop it.

"Ah, Lena," he greeted, stomping his feet before stepping inside. "The boys and I have been conversing about all of this snow, and we'd like to take a stroll. Would you care to join us?" A sparkle of something akin to mischievousness met her gaze.

"Splendid," she replied.

He turned to leave, then added, "Leave the shotgun inside unless you think there's a wild beast that might threaten us."

Her eyes widened, and she giggled. "Oh, I don't know, Gabe. A nice wolf's pelt sounds like just the right thing." She pulled on her boots, then grabbed her coat, mittens, and wool muffler while he waited.

"Naturally, you'd need ammunition to protect us." They shared a laugh. "I do plan to take the rifle," he added. "Beauty can be deceiving."

"Yes, sadly so," she replied, feeling utterly content.

"In what direction is the school?" he asked a few moments later, as the boys chased each other in the snow.

Lena pointed northwest and squinted at the sun's reflection on the snow. "About two miles from here. Do you want to see for yourself?"

He nodded slowly. "Indeed."

"I imagine the soddy is in bad shape, being left empty and all. It needed repairs before we lost the teacher."

"Any prospects?"

She shook her head. "I don't think so. Haven't heard, anyway."

They trudged along, stepping in and out of drifts. Gabe walked beside her, helping her through the deep piles of snow.

"It's unfortunate no one desires the teaching position," he said.

"Oh, the Shafer girl would love to fulfill it until a suitable person is found, but Dagget refuses. Says he needs her at home. Truth is, he's right."

"Is she capable?"

"I believe so. Amanda has a quick mind and certainly knows how to handle children."

"Hmm," Gabe replied, lifting the rifle to his shoulder. "This matter will take some thought. Perhaps I should pay a visit to Mr. Shafer in the morning when the boys deliver the milk."

"He'll run you off," Lena warned, her pulse quickening at the thought of how loathsome Dagget could be. "He's mean and selfish—almost as bad as me." She laughed, then sobered. "Really, Gabe, he is not a good father—works all of those children much too hard. I know our staple diet is corn bread and sorghum molasses, but he could butcher some meat for those children instead of selling his livestock to buy whiskey. Wouldn't take five minutes for you to see he doesn't care about them or their schooling."

Gabe lifted a brow. "But I don't give up easily, and if his daughter would make a fit teacher—"

"Good luck," Lena said. "He's as contrary as a sow with pigs—and just as dirty."

The crispness of the afternoon nipped at their breath and stung their cheeks, but Lena felt warm inside. For the first time in a long time, she felt safe. . .and content.

"Mama," Simon called.

She glanced in his direction and saw three white-tailed deer at the edge of a snow embankment. Like statues in the landscape, the deer suddenly leaped and bounded away—so graceful and lithe.

"You should have shot one, Gabe," Simon said. "Since Mama showed you how to use the rifle."

"Another day," Gabe replied. "Today is for pleasure, and I don't want to be killing an animal just for the sake of drawing blood. We have smoked venison at home."

Simon studied him curiously, then shrugged and took out after his brother.

"I'll take the boys hunting soon," Gabe said. "One at a time, though, so I can establish individual rapport. And if I haven't said it before, I appreciate your meticulous instructions on how to care for and use this rifle."

"You're welcome. I was amazed at your marksmanship after only a few tries." She smiled in his direction. "Of course, the Winchester is only as good as the one who fires it."

"Well, we shall see how skillful I am after a hunting expedition." Gabe chuckled. "Do we have elephants and lions out here? I sort of fancy myself as a hunter of ferocious beasts."

"Not likely, but we had a band of outlaws pass through here a few times."

He cringed, no doubt for her to see. "I'll take to bringing down a few geese or rabbits, if you can show me how to remove their outer coatings."

She shook her head. "We *skin* animals, and we *pluck* feathers from birds."

"I'll be sure to remember that."

Lena gasped and clutched Gabe's shoulder. "Oh no. Dear God, no."

Chapter 11

Gabe's attention flew to Caleb and Simon. They stood motionless, paralyzed by a pack of wolves slowly encircling them. He heard the growls, saw the bared teeth.

Lord, no books ever prepared me for this. Help me. Help me, I beg of You. A quick assessment of Lena revealed a colorless face.

Wordlessly, he took careful aim at a wolf closest to Simon. "Pray, Lena," he said, shielding any emotion. "God must deliver this bullet." Although tense, he focused on Lena's careful instructions from the past and all he'd read about the capabilities of the rifle.

"Don't move, boys," he called evenly. From what he'd read, running could prove disastrous. Holding his breath, he squeezed the trigger. A sharp *crack* splintered the air and startled the predators. One wolf howled and fell onto the snow, its blood staining the white ground.

"Steady," Gabe called to the boys.

Breathing a prayer of thanks and noting none of the animals had inched closer, he sited another one, fired, and missed. He swallowed hard, looking neither to the right nor to the left. Again the wolves took a few steps back, and he squeezed a third time in hopes they would disperse. "Get out of here," he shouted.

Help me, Father. Lena couldn't bear losing Caleb or Simon—and neither could I.

He dug his right-hand fingers into his palm, then released them before lining up a wolf straying too close to Caleb. This time, the bullet sunk into the wolf's neck. The cries of the injured animal pierced the air. In the next instant, Gabe fired at another one and missed. The rest of the pack moved beyond the circle, then one broke and raced in the opposite direction.

"Go on, get!" Lena cried. "Leave us alone!"

"Move back slowly," Gabe said to the boys. "Keep your eyes on those wolves, and do not panic." He fired another shot.

The animals watched Caleb and Simon's retreat, then turned and chased after the other lone wolf, disappearing into the scenery. Gabe studied the two he'd shot to make sure he'd killed them. One moved, and he sent a bullet into its skull.

"Thank You, Lord," Lena uttered.

Gabe heard her soft weeping and longed to comfort her, but she needed to embrace her sons and feel their young bodies safe and secure.

Simon and Caleb didn't show the emotion Gabe felt, but youth had a way of bouncing back after adversity. Once Lena had hugged them until they complained, Gabe dropped to one knee and wrapped his arms around them both. Tears filled his eyes, and he didn't strive to disguise them.

"I ain't—I mean, I'm not calling you Gabe anymore," Simon said. "You're my pa now."

Joy beyond Gabe's comprehension filled his very soul. *I never thought I'd be good enough. Thank You.*

"Some good shooting," Caleb said, staring at the dead wolves. "I don't think I'll ever forget today for as long as I live."

Tears coursed down Lena's cheeks. Gabe caught her gaze and her whispered words of gratitude. "Praise God for you, Gabe Hunters, and I bless the day you made me your wife."

He stared speechless, a rarity for him. Finally, he choked back a lump in his throat. "I think we can visit the schoolhouse another time," he said with a sniff. "I'd like to skin those animals—if one of you can tell me how—for new hats and mittens for you boys. Let's tend to it and move toward home. I'm in the mood for a snowball fight." He hoisted the rifle onto his shoulder and tossed a smile in Lena's direction.

Simon grabbed his free hand. "You might not know a lot of things, Gabe—I mean, Pa. But you stopped them wolves from eating me, and the other things don't matter."

Gabe couldn't reply for the overwhelming emotion assaulting him. He'd gone countless years without shedding tears, but today he'd made up for lost time.

"Listen to me, boys, while it's this cold and those wolves are venturing close, you won't be delivering any milk without me along, and I don't want you wandering far from home," he said.

"Yes, Sir," Caleb said with a smile. "Do you suppose you might teach me how to shoot, Pa?"

Gabe slept by the fireplace that night. Once Simon cried out with a bad dream, and Lena crawled into bed with him. Gabe surmised she needed her arms around the boy as badly as Simon needed the affections of his mother.

Unable to sleep, Gabe rose early to milk and feed the animals. He felt a new confidence about his role in the family—a position he'd desperately craved but certainly hadn't wanted at the expense of yesterday's ordeal.

Today he'd approach Dagget Shafer. Hopefully the man wasn't as formidable as the wolves.

"I don't have a good feeling about this," Lena said as Gabe lifted the pail of milk into the wagon. "Dagget has no respect for anyone, including himself."

"A friend might redirect him. Does he claim to be a Christian man?"

"Gabe, he refused to attend his wife's funeral because it took him away from his farm." A torch flared in her eyes. "He treats those children horribly."

And he wanted you to marry him? "I'm pleased you decided to accept my proposal instead of his, even if you had to run him off with a pitchfork." He chuckled, knowing the teasing would ease her trepidation.

She lifted a brow. "And how did you know about that?"

Gabe leaned over the side of the wagon and smiled into the face of this woman, this woman who had touched his heart like no one had before. "I'm having difficulty remembering. Perhaps it was the unsigned notice I received in Philadelphia warning me about your temper, or possibly the animals during those nights I slept in the barn—"

"Or Caleb and Simon," she interrupted. Covering her mouth, she shook her head, no doubt attempting to stifle her glee.

"But I have the distinction of you persuading me to your manner of thinking with a shotgun," he whispered.

She sighed and tilted her head. "Will you ever forget what I did?"

Gabe climbed up on the wagon seat and laughed heartily. "I rather doubt it. It's my ammunition." Calling for the boys to board, he picked up the reins and urged the horses on. "We'll return shortly, Lena, most likely a little better than an hour, since I have business with Mr. Shafer."

"Do you have the rifle?" she asked as they pulled away.

"Yes, ma'am. Danger won't find me unaware." At least he hoped not.

Gabe drove the team, a task he'd come to enjoy, while Simon chatted on about everything. Caleb, on the other hand, merely watched the landscape.

"You're quiet this morning," Gabe said. "Is a matter perplexing you?"

"I'm praying," the boy replied, picking at a worn spot on his trousers.

"Anything particular?"

He shrugged. "I don't want you to die like my pa. You didn't fit in so good in the beginning, but you do now."

Gabe realized the boy spoke from his heart. "A man doesn't choose what day God calls him home, but I have no intentions of doing anything foolish to quicken the process."

"I know that, but asking God to watch over you seems fitting to me."

"And I thank you. Life's been difficult since your father died."

"Yes, sir." Caleb stared at the snow before them.

"Taking on the role as head of a household can be taxing."

"Yes, sir."

Do I dare force his feelings out, Lord? Poor Caleb looks so miserable. "I'm sensing you didn't weep at the funeral."

A muscle twitched in Caleb's cheek, and his lips quivered.

Gabe continued. "My assumption is you knew your mother needed you, and so you pushed your grief aside."

Long moments passed with Simon's incessant talking to absolutely no one. A solitary tear slipped from Caleb's eye.

"Would you like to grieve the loss of your father now?" Gabe whispered.

Caleb nodded, his face so filled with sorrow that he threatened to burst. Gabe pulled the reins in on the horses and brought them to a stop.

"What's the matter?" Simon asked.

"Hush, Simon," Gabe chided gently. He turned to the older boy and enveloped him in his arms.

Caleb's tears began quietly, then proceeded to heavy sobs as his body heaved with the agony wrenching at his heart. *What do I say?* When God did not give him any words, Gabe remained silent.

For several minutes he held the boy, allowing him to spill out every stifled tear he'd ever swallowed. Gabe knew the healing power of physical grief; he'd been privy to it a precious few times when only God could comfort him. When Caleb withdrew from the shelter of Gabe's chest, he seemed humiliated.

"Don't ever regret showing emotion," Gabe said. "A real man attempts to experience all the happiness and sorrow the world contains. Only then can God use him in His perfect plan."

The boy offered a grim smile. "After today, He'll be using me for something big."

Meeting his smile, Gabe gathered up the reins and urged the

horses on. *Is this what a father does? Lord, I'm exhausted from yesterday and today. . .but my spirit is exhilarated.*

The Shafer property bordered Lena's about forty minutes away, but instead of a sod-bricked soddy, the family's dwelling was a dugout—at least that's what it appeared to be. Many folks used this type of home, and Gabe understood the majority of homesteaders didn't have time to construct a soddy when they first arrived. Preparing the fields for crops took priority, and dugouts were quickly constructed for shelter.

The Shafer home and the two dugouts used for barns fell short of being called in shambles. All looked as if the roofs would cave in at any moment. A pig had climbed the snow-packed hill forming the home's roof. Gabe envisioned it falling through in the middle of a meal. Didn't sound like a good dinner guest to him. More pigs rooted up next to the house, leaving their droppings outside the door—a sharp contrast to the white landscape. Gabe had no tolerance for the lack of repairs, filth, or shabby clothes of the youngsters who met them.

"Mornin', Simon. Mornin', Caleb," a thin, pale boy said. His feet were bound with rags, and he didn't wear a coat.

"Mornin', Matthew," the boys chorused. One scratched his head, and the other spit, reminding Gabe of old men ready to sputter about the weather and their rheumatism.

"This is our new pa." Simon lifted the bucket of milk from the wagon.

Gabe climbed down and offered Matthew his hand. "Pleased to make your acquaintance. My name's Gabe Hunters."

Matthew didn't appear to know how to respond. He lightly grasped Gabe's hand and muttered something inaudible.

"Is your father available to speak with me?" Gabe asked, once again taking in the boy's tattered clothing. "I'd like to introduce myself."

"He's with the pigs." Matthew pointed to a dugout nearby.

"Thank you." *I can follow the smell—even in the cold.* Gabe rounded the dugout. He heard a list of curses much like he used to hear from his mother's customers. Already he didn't care for Dagget Shafer.

"I told you to take care of this sow before breakfast, and it still ain't done," Dagget shouted. "Guess you need a beatin' to learn how to mind."

Echoes of yesterday assaulted Gabe, causing him to tremble with rage. "Mr. Shafer," he called out, forcing himself to sound congenial.

Another string of curses was followed by an "I don't have time to see callers." Dagget shuffled toward him, smelling like the animals he tended. "And who are you?"

Once again Gabe stuck out his hand. "Gabe Hunters. I'm your

neighbor. Lena Walker's husband."

The man narrowed his brows and ignored Gabe's gesture of friendship. "Lena, ya say? She must have been looking for money, 'cause you don't look like a farmer to me."

And you don't possess any qualities resembling a decent human being. "I'm learning. I just thought it was about time I introduced myself."

"Why?"

"To be friendly, neighborly."

By this time, a little girl about three years old emerged from the shadows. She appeared clean from what he could tell, but her thin sweater and even thinner dress caused the child to shiver. In the shadows, a dark discoloration on her cheek indicated a bruise. Gabe didn't want to think how she might have been injured. The vile image of this man inflicting the blow brought back a myriad of his own beatings.

Bending, Gabe stared into the little girl's face. "Good morning," he said softly. She looked fearful and stepped back. "I'm Gabe Hunters."

The child recoiled as though he intended to harm her. She raced from the dugout, her sobs echoing behind her. Dagget broke into raucous laughter, further irritating Gabe.

"I'm sorry if I frightened your daughter," he said, still confused with what he'd witnessed.

"Aw, she thinks yer taking her to the Indians," Dagget said between offensive guffaws.

"Why would she believe such a thing?"

Dagget wiped his face with a dirty coat sleeve. "I told her she'd best be ready in case I sell her to a man who'd trade her for blankets from the Indians."

He doesn't deserve any of these children. "What right do you have to tell a child such a terrible story?"

"It ain't no story. I'd do it in a minute. She ain't worth nothing, and it's none of your business nohow."

Gabe stared into the haggard face. He seldom grew angry, but causing terror in a child incited a fury so great that it alarmed him. "You're right. Your daughter is not my concern, but I'm wondering why you don't pick on someone who can meet you as an equal."

Dagget narrowed his brows. "Like you? I'd make manure out of you in less than five minutes."

"Probably in less time than you might think, but I will say this. If you want to get rid of that child and any of your others, just bring them to our home. We'll take care of them in a proper manner."

Gabe whirled around and marched back to the wagon. What an insufferable beast and an even poorer excuse of a human being. No wonder Lena had refused his marriage proposal. He glanced at the dugout with an earnest desire to gather up every one of those children and take them home. Dagget would no doubt come after them once he needed work hands. Gabe looked to the heavens for answers. The thought of another child suffering through the same ordeal as he'd known infuriated him.

Lord, I know I utilize more of Your time than appropriate, but I'm pleading with You to look after these children. I've only met two of them and heard about four more, but You have them sealed in Your heart.

He'd met some wonderful hardworking people here in Nebraska—good citizens who loved the Lord and demonstrated their devotion to Him and each other in everything they said and did. Then there were a choice few who wouldn't know how to model the Lord if their lives depended on it. Gabe refused to dwell on Dagget another minute. He and Riley O'Connor were a matched pair.

Caleb and Simon stood near the wagon, still talking to Matthew. "Let's go, boys," Gabe said. "We have plenty of matters to tend to at home."

"Don't you be coming around here no more," Dagget shouted with a string of curses. "Them boys can bring the milk without the likes of you sticking your nose into my business."

Gabe took a deep breath and faced Dagget. "My sons will no longer be delivering milk. I will bring it each day but Sunday. If you want the milk for your family, then you'll deal with me."

He joined Caleb on the wagon seat, while Simon climbed onto the back. He released a labored breath and turned the horses toward home.

"I've never seen you mad," Simon commented a few moments later.

"I've never been so infuriated," Gabe replied. "Dagget Shafer places no value on his gift of children or the importance of the example he gives to them."

"I heard what you said to him back there," Caleb said. "I thought he was going to tear into you."

Gabe smiled grimly. "One punch would have flattened me, but I didn't care."

"I'd have helped you," the older boy said firmly. "We'd have done fine together."

Gabe wrapped his arm around Caleb's shoulders. The bond he and Caleb had formed felt good. *A father's love for his children.* "Your mother would have disciplined us severely for fighting, I'm sure."

"Naw," Simon piped up. "She doesn't like the way Mr. Shafer treats his children either. We don't tell her the things he says to us in the mornings."

A new surge of anger bolted through Gabe's veins. "Well, he won't have the opportunity anymore, now, will he?"

Chapter 12

*Y*ou're right, Gabe. It's snowing too hard to attend church tonight," Lena said with a disappointed sigh. Already at midday, she could barely see through the window for the driving snow. "I'd looked forward to driving into Archerville for the Christmas Eve services."

"We can conduct our own," Gabe replied with a reassuring smile. "It won't be the same for you, because I know how you enjoy visiting with the other members, hearing the sermon, and singing, but we'll honor the Lord's birth just the same."

"Oh, I know you're right, and you've looked forward to tonight, too," she said. "I've noticed how you enjoy the minister's company." She tilted her head. "Seems like Christmas Eve should be spent with others, but we'll make do just fine."

"Of course we will. I'd like to involve the boys in our own little service, and I do have something for each of you."

"You do?" *When did he purchase gifts?* The occasions they'd ridden into Archerville for supplies, she'd been with him the entire time.

He offered a wry grin. "I purchased gifts in Philadelphia before boarding the train there."

"Mine are very small," she said, "and not fancy."

Gabe reached for her hand—an infrequent action for him. "You, Caleb, and Simon are my Christmas treasures. With you, I am the wealthiest man alive."

His words moved her to tears, for she knew without a doubt he meant every word. Although no mention of love had crossed their lips, she felt it growing as each day passed.

"Gabe, I have never met a man with such a giving spirit. I feel as though you know our needs before we speak them."

His gaze met hers, sealing those words she wanted to say but couldn't—not until he spoke them first. "Next to God, my family is my life."

Oh, my dear Gabe. I never dreamed I could learn to love you, but you have made it easy.

That night after a hearty supper of ham, turnips, white-flour biscuits—which were a rare treat—and a pie made from dried pumpkins, they gathered around the fireplace to hear the Christmas story. Pushing back the rocker, all four sat on the rag rug. Caleb and Simon read from Luke, and Lena led in singing Christmas carols. Outside, the wind whistled as it often did during snowstorms, but somehow it didn't sound threatening as the story of Jesus' birth unfolded before them.

"I have an idea," Gabe said, "one I think you'll enjoy. Caleb, I want you to pretend you are a shepherd boy. You've heard the angel's proclamation of Jesus' birth and are hurrying with the other shepherds to see the baby. Unfortunately, you must assist an aging shepherd who has difficulty walking. All the others leave you behind."

Caleb stared into the fire for a moment. He nibbled on his lip, then turned to Gabe. "Knowing me, I'd feel sad the other shepherds would see the baby Jesus before me."

"Only sad?" Gabe asked.

"Well, probably a little angry." Caleb glanced at his younger brother. "Sometimes when I have to wait for Simon to tag along with me, I get mad. He can't help being slow, like the old shepherd. Maybe I could talk to the old man so the walk would go faster."

"Very good." Gabe patted Caleb on the shoulder. "How do you think the old shepherd felt when the younger one had to help him walk to Bethlehem?"

Caleb brought his finger to his lip, seemingly concentrating on Gabe's question. "He might remember when he was young and didn't have to lag behind. I think he'd feel bad for the shepherd boy, too."

"What would the two discuss along the way?"

"The angel's message?" Caleb asked without hesitation.

"Probably so," Gabe said.

Caleb took a deep breath. "And maybe how they all had been frightened when the angels appeared in the sky."

Lena listened in awe at the way Gabe taught the boys without their ever realizing it. *Caleb's always so serious. I wish he'd learn how to enjoy life before he's an old man.*

"And you, Simon?" Gabe continued. "What if you were the young shepherd boy?"

"Since the angels came at night, I might be a little afraid of wild animals."

"Much like the day with the wolves?" Gabe asked.

Simon's face grew serious. Nightmares had plagued his little mind since the incident. Many nights his cries awakened them all. "Yes, sir."

"Don't you think if God cared enough for the world to send His Son as a baby that He might be watching out for all frightened boys?"

Simon gave Gabe his attention. "I think so. Do you think God cares about my bad dreams?"

Gabe ruffled Simon's hair. "I'm sure He does." He looked at each member of his family. Love clearly glowed from his gaze. "We all need to pray for Simon's nightmares until God stops them."

"I will," Caleb responded. "Those wolves were scary."

"Bless you, Son. We all need to pray for each other, in good times and bad." The room grew quiet, then Gabe spoke again, his tone lighter. "And now I have a gift for you."

The boys' eyes widened.

Gabe rose from the floor and walked to his trunk, where he stored his books. The fire crackled, and Turnip rose on his haunches, his ears erect. "Easy, boy. It's just the wind searching for a hole to get inside." Gabe retrieved a leather pouch and brought it back to the fire.

"You really did purchase these before you left Philadelphia?" Lena asked. "Why, you didn't even know us."

Gabe smiled, warming her heart. "I believed the future held something wonderful. . .and it did." He pulled out a small brown paper parcel. "This is for you, Simon."

The young boy grinned at his mother, then eagerly took the package. Inside, two carved wooden horses with soldiers mounted atop poised ready for a little boy to play with them.

"Thank you," he breathed, turning the toys over and over in his palm. A broad smile spread from ear to ear.

"And you, Caleb," Gabe said, handing him another parcel.

Lena watched her elder son slowly untie the string wrapped around his gift.

"A compass," Caleb whispered, moistening his lips. He peered up at Gabe with an appreciative gaze. "I will take good care of it always. I promise."

Gabe nodded. "I know you will. I know both of you take excellent care of your possessions." He turned to Lena. "And now for you." He strode over to the chest and pulled out a much larger package and handed it to her.

Oh my. Has Gabe spent his money on something extravagant for me? It's large, too. He gingerly placed the gift in her lap. "Open it, please," he said.

Lena swallowed a lump in her throat and slowly unwrapped the package, savoring the thought of Gabe's generous spirit more than what was inside the package. She gasped, and her fingers shook as she lifted a cream-colored woolen shawl for all to see. "It's beautiful," she uttered, staring into his face. Never had he looked so handsome, so beloved as tonight. Every day his unselfish devotion amazed her, and every day her love for him grew. "Thank you so much. I've never had a shawl so grand."

"You're welcome." He smiled. "There's more for you." Gabe took the shawl and placed it around her shoulders.

Lena turned her attention to the remaining items in the package. Neatly folded yard goods in colors of light green and a deeper green plaid felt crisp to the touch. "How perfect," she whispered, examining the fabric and relishing its newness.

"I believe there's an ample amount of calico for a dress and jacket," he said.

"Oh yes." She blinked back the tears. What was it about this man that drove her to weep for joy?

Gabe rubbed his hands together. "On our next visit to Archerville, I'd like to purchase the necessary items to make all of you new coats. And I believe new shoes and mufflers are also in order."

This time Lena did cry. She hadn't known where the money would come from to purchase the needed clothing for the boys. They grew so fast, and Caleb tended to wear out his clothes before Simon had an opportunity to wear them. "Oh, Gabe, you spent too much. Thank you, thank you ever so."

He lightly brushed his fingers over her hand. "I have a little put aside for our needs."

If only I could give to him what he's given to me and our sons. He loved her and the boys, of that she felt certain.

Lena hurried to the bedroom to fetch her own small packages. She'd saved for Christmas since last summer. For Caleb and Simon, she had bought peppermint sticks and had sewn them warm shirts. The ones they wore for everyday use were thin and had been patched many times. The boys thanked her and dutifully placed a kiss on her cheek.

She handed Gabe his package, believing he'd like it but nervous nevertheless. Slowly he unwrapped the gift, and at first she feared he was displeased.

"Not a day passes I don't wish for a journal," he said, running his fingers over the leather cover. Still staring at it, he continued, "Humorous and serious bits of conversation, happenings I refuse to forget, something new I've learned, lessons our Lord has taught me. . ." He glanced up at her. "Memories are what keep us alive. Thank you, Lena. I'll treasure this always."

Her heart leaped to tell him those precious words, but she couldn't—not yet.

"Stop it, Caleb!" Simon shouted as his face got thoroughly wiped with snow, courtesy of his older brother.

"What's the matter with a little snow?" Caleb asked, holding Simon down with one hand and reaching for another handful with the other.

"You know what I'm talking about." Simon sputtered and tried to punch him, but Caleb was faster and simply laughed. He coated Simon's face with the cold snow.

"Tell me," Caleb taunted.

"Pa," Simon hollered. "Caleb keeps hitting me in the face with snow that the cow did her business in."

Gabe groaned. *What would those two do next?* "Caleb, leave your little brother alone."

"Do you want to hear what he did to me this morning?" Caleb protested.

Not really, but I guess I will.

"He locked me in the outhouse for nearly an hour."

Gabe looked away to muffle his guffaw.

"You called me a runt," Simon retorted. "And took my quilt last night and wouldn't give it back."

"Boys, I have the perfect solution to this," Gabe said, wishing the boys could get along for one whole day without picking on each other. "Your mother is taking advantage of this cold weather by mending and such. The last I checked, she was preparing to darn socks—something each of you need to learn."

Simon stared at him incredulously. "That's woman's work!"

I feel a lesson coming on. "I believe your mother worked like a man before we married."

"That's right," Caleb said with an exasperated breath. "But since you've been here, Ma doesn't have to do that anymore."

Gabe lifted a brow. "Then show your gratitude. Inside, boys."

"Yes, sir."

"Yes, sir."

Caleb and Simon plodded to the soddy. Gabe grinned and turned his attention back to rearranging the tools inside the barn. He wondered what they'd think of next.

Had four months really passed since Gabe arrived in Nebraska? The days flew by, each one blending into the next. He loved every moment of it, not once ever considering the natural demands of his family and farm as a hardship.

As had been his habit since the first morning, Gabe woke at the hint of dawn. He'd grown accustomed to sleeping on the tamped earthen floor by the fire, long since comprehending he had the warmest spot in the soddy, but this morning an eerie shriek of wind woke him. The howls carried a sense of foreboding, different from other bouts with high winds that ushered in heavy snowfall. Gabe's concerns mounted for the livestock. They had a goodly stock of supplies and provisions, but he feared losing any of the animals to the cold. When the temperatures had plummeted in the past, the dugout had provided sufficient protection to ensure the warmth of the horses, mule, and chickens. But the cattle in the fields could not huddle close to a warm fire.

After slipping his overalls over his trousers and pulling his suspenders up, Gabe quickly added chips to the fire. *Thankfully, we can keep the soddy warm.*

"You're up earlier than usual," Lena said quietly. "I'm afraid we're in for a bad storm." In the shadows her silhouette and soft voice comforted him. His love for her abounded in moments like these. The freshness of sleep on her lovely face tempted him to reveal his heart. Fear of her rejecting him always halted his confession. He believed she cared and often saw something akin to affection in those green eyes, but he could be mistaken.

"Winter winds are attacking us again," he said, making his way to the peg holding his outer garments. As he shrugged into his coat, he fretted over past snows. "Lena, how did you survive the winters alone? How did you deal with all of the work and responsibilities of this farm?"

"By God's grace," she answered. "When the wind tore around the soddy and snow banked against the door, or when in the heat of summer, tornadoes raged, I simply prayed." She walked across the room and took his muffler from his hands. Wrapping it around his neck, she smiled. "God's never failed me. Somehow I managed to make it through one perilous situation after another. Then He sent me you." Her last words were spoken barely above a whisper.

Gabe warmed to his toes. Was she conscious of what her sweetness did to him? The emotion bursting inside him sought to surface. He longed to take her into his arms and declare his love. *Oh Lord, dare I?*

"Tonight, after Caleb and Simon are in bed, I'd like to discuss a matter with you." Gabe instantly regretted his choice of words. He sounded as though he wanted to propose a business transaction. "I mean, do you mind talking with me for a while?"

"Is everything all right?" she asked, pulling her shawl around her shoulders.

"I believe so." He dipped his hands into each mitten. "It's not a topic you need to worry about, just a personal matter about which I wanted your opinion." He offered a smile and grasped the latch on the door. "Come along, Turnip. We have work to do. From the sound of the wind, I may be blown to Archerville."

She laughed lightly. "I'd come looking."

Would you, my love? "How far would you venture?"

"As far as Philadelphia, and if you weren't there, I'd look some more."

Chapter 13

*O*utside, the biting cold and wind whipped around Gabe's body with a fury he'd never experienced. He fought to stand and instead fell twice to his knees. The very thought of Lena and the boys existing in this ominous weather filled him with dread. Surely God had watched over them.

Once the animals were fed and cared for, he gathered up the quarter pail of milk and trekked back to the house before dawn. Only one of the cows had not gone dry, and the others had been turned out to pasture when they'd stopped producing milk. He caught a glimpse of the winding smoke from the fireplace, and he knew his family welcomed him inside. As always, Lena would have coffee ready.

Although the faint light of morning tore across the sky, he couldn't study the clouds for the curtain of snow assaulting him from every direction. He'd studied clouds in his books and, together with Lena's teachings, had learned to read nature's map. This morning spelled blizzard, and already all he could see of the cabin was the fire twinkling through the window. Suddenly the wisp of smoke from the chimney vanished.

The Shafers would miss their ration of milk today, but he dared not risk losing his way in the snow. He'd missed bringing them milk before, and they had fared well. Obviously, this was a day to advance the boys in their lessons.

"Turnip," he called. Normally the dog came bounding. "Turnip." Gabe released a heavy sigh. He pondered looking for the animal. However, once he ventured out into the blinding snow and ferocious wind, he abandoned his purpose, setting his sights on the beacon in the cabin window.

Turnip is probably in the house, lying by the fire all snuggly warm. Deserter.

Each step took his breath and cut at his face. He contemplated resting the pail on the snow and pulling the muffler tighter around his face but feared spilling the contents. If the blizzard raged on, they might need the milk.

"Gabe!" Lena called.

He glanced toward the cabin.

"Gabe!"

"Yes, I'm making progress," he replied, the wind stinging his throat. "I see the firelight in the window."

"I'm waiting for you."

The dearest words this side of heaven. He'd stumble through ten blizzards for that endearing sound. "Don't linger in the cold," he called to her. "You'll be ill."

"Not until you get here."

Stubborn woman, and I love her for it.

Once he reached the front door, she opened it wide. A gust of wind sent it slamming so hard on the inner wall of the cabin that he feared the house would crumble. She stood covered from head to toe with the new coat, mittens, and muffler he'd purchased in Archerville. She reminded him of an Egyptian mummy he'd seen in a book.

"I should have given you a rope," she said, shaking the snow from her coat.

"To tie about my waist and to the house?"

She nodded. "Don't leave again without it. You could wander around for hours and freeze to death."

He chuckled. "I know you've expressed concern over that condition before." He hung his outer garments on the peg beside hers. The aroma of coffee mixed with frying cornmeal flapjacks filled his nostrils.

"Ready for coffee?" she asked as if reading his thoughts.

"Absolutely." He walked to the fireplace and glanced around for the dog. "Isn't Turnip inside?"

She whirled around and stared at him. "No. He left with you."

Where is the dog? He shivered, both from the bitter cold and from the prospect of Turnip caught in its grip. "I need to find him."

"Later, Gabe. You need to get out of those wet clothes." She hesitated. "You've lost so much weight I believe you could wear James's clothing. Let's take a look. We can deal with the dog after breakfast."

He followed her into the bedroom, feeling slightly uncomfortable with the unmade bed and the fresh scent of her lingering in every corner. If he were to wake up tomorrow and find himself blind, he'd live out his days with her face in his mind.

Lena pulled a trunk from beneath the rope bed and sorted through it. Gabe stood back, uncertain if he should invade her personal treasures.

"Here's a shirt and overalls," she said, handing him the carefully folded clothing. "I'm sure they will fit."

"Will this plague you or the boys? Seeing me in his attire?"

She shook her head. "He'd be pleased they'd come to good use, and so am I." She stepped from the small room and pulled a curtain separating the bedroom from the main room. "Do you mind if I let the boys sleep?"

"Let them," he replied, examining the shirt and overalls. He felt oddly disconcerted by the knowledge that they'd belonged to Lena's deceased husband. "Not much for them to do today with the blizzard." *And I need to find Turnip.*

Gabe donned the clothes and caught sight of himself in Lena's dresser mirror. *I look so different—not at all like the Gabriel Hunters who left Philadelphia. What happened to my portly body?*

In the midst of his second cup of coffee and a third flapjack smothered in molasses, he looked up to see Caleb making his way through the blanket separating the boys' room from the fireplace and cookstove.

"Mornin'," he greeted through sleepy eyes. "Sounds like we have a blizzard. Strange, we haven't had one all winter."

"We do, Son," Gabe replied. "My first Nebraska blizzard, and it's everything this family has warned. We'll all stick close to the fire today; maybe do a little extra reading."

Caleb grinned. "Sounds good to me." Glancing about, he gave his mother a puzzled look. "Where's Simon and Turnip?"

Lena's face turned a ghastly shade of white. She swallowed hard and called out, "Simon, are you using the chamber pot?"

No answer.

"I woke up, and he wasn't there," Caleb said softly. "He wouldn't have wandered outside, would he?"

Gabe rose and made his way to the boys' room. His coat. He prayed Simon's coat hung on the peg beside his pallet.

"Simon?" Lena called, her voice anxious. . .and scared.

"He's not here." Gabe hurried to the front door. He couldn't face Lena. First he'd lost Turnip, and now Simon had disappeared. "I'll find him," he said as he grabbed his winter garments. By the time he'd pulled on his mittens and wrapped the muffler around his face to bar the frigid cold, Lena had a rope.

"Tie one end around your waist and the other around one of the porch posts," she said shakily.

He couldn't avoid eye contact any longer. "I'll not disappoint you or Simon." Not waiting for her reply, he stepped out into the blizzard, praying harder than when he'd faced the wolves. At least then he could see his son and the face of danger. He felt his way to the right post anchoring the porch.

"Simon, where are you?" he called, but the wind sucked away his breath, and the words died in his throat. Securing the rope, he plodded toward the barn.

I've always had a keen sense of direction, but not even a compass could assist me now. Oh Lord, be my feet and lead me to Simon.

"Simon, Turnip," he tried calling again. The roar of the wind met his ears.

After what he believed was several minutes, he bumped into the well. He'd walked in the opposite direction! Making his way around it until he could grab the well handle, Gabe closed his eyes and turned in the direction of what he believed was the barn. Every second became a prayer. On he went, his feet feeling as though they were laden with weights. The way seemed endless, and ofttimes he fell.

"Pa." He strained to hear again. "Pa, I'm scared and cold."

Praise God. Simon must be in the barn. Guide me, Lord.

Gabe tried to speed his trek, but the elements slammed into him as though an invisible wall had been erected. "I'm coming, Simon. Have faith."

With his chest aching and each step an effort, Gabe at last touched the side of the dugout where he believed Simon awaited inside. "Simon, I'm by the barn wall."

Nothing. Not even the hint of sound indicating the boy rested safely inside.

Gabe repeated his words. *Keep him in Your arms. I beg of You.* Rounding the barn, he found the opening. A few moments later, he stepped inside and scanned the small area. A pair of arms seized him about the waist. Gabe wrapped his arms around Simon, wanting to shelter him forever from the cold and wind.

"You came," Simon said between sobs. "I thought I'd die here with Turnip and the animals."

Turnip's tail thumped against Gabe's leg. Never had the dog looked so good. "I heard you calling for me," Gabe said, carefully inspecting him from head to toe. Luckily, the boy had dressed warmly before leaving the cabin.

Simon shook his head. "I didn't call for you. I just waited and talked to God about being scared."

Thank You, Lord, for sending Your angels to minister to me and keep

Simon safe. Joy raced through Gabe's veins while he hugged the boy closer.

"You're the best pa ever," the boy said, clinging to Gabe's snow-covered body.

"We must give the credit to our Lord," Gabe replied, tucking Simon's muffler securely around his neck and face. "Oh, Simon, what made you decide to come looking for Turnip?"

"I didn't. I heard you get up early and wanted to help with the chores, but with the blizzard, I couldn't find the barn. Turnip guided me here, but you were already gone."

The dog nuzzled Gabe's leg, and he patted him. No doubt God had used stranger-looking angels than a mangy dog.

"We need to head back. Your mother and brother are very worried. First, let's check on the animals and pray."

And they did, thanking God for taking care of Simon and sending His angels to help Gabe.

"Ready?" Gabe asked, dreading the walk ahead.

Simon nodded. "Don't let go of my hand, please."

"I'll do better than that. I'll carry you." Although Gabe wondered how he'd make it back with the extra load, he knew God hadn't brought him this far to desert him now. He'd follow the rope. Gathering up Simon, he whispered, "Keep your head down against the wind, and pray."

"Yes, Pa. I love you."

Lena could wait no longer. Gabe had been gone an hour, with every minute taking a toll on her heart. She had to do something.

"Caleb, I'm going out there. I'll follow the rope, so don't worry." Pulling on her heavy clothes, she ignored her son's protests.

"Then I'm going with you," he said stubbornly, reaching for his coat.

"I won't lose two sons in this blizzard."

"And I won't lose my ma, pa, and brother either."

Bravery doesn't need to be so dangerous. "I want you to stay here, please."

Caleb stood before her dressed for the weather. "I'm going with you." He lifted the latch. "We'll both follow the rope."

Lena made her way to the post, but the rope was gone. She searched the other side of the porch. Nothing. She kneeled on her hands and knees, frantically searching for the loose end. She felt certain Gabe had secured his end to the right side. Caleb joined her. The wind stole her breath, but she refused to give up. The snow could have covered the rope in a matter of moments, but without it, Gabe would never find his way to the cabin. She prayed and wept—for Simon, Gabe, and the love she possessed for both of them.

Caleb tugged at her coat. She ignored him. He tugged harder and began to drag her back. "I found it," he shouted.

Lena wrapped her fingers around the frayed ends and clung to it as though she held the hand of God. She and Caleb managed to crawl back onto the porch and to the door. Securing the rope around the porch post had proved useless. She'd not let it go until she saw her family. *Help them, Father. Bring them back to me.*

"I'll stay out here and hold it," Caleb shouted above the wind.

"No, I'm stronger. Go back inside."

"I'm nearly twelve, Ma, and I'm staying."

He sounded so much like James, so much like Gabe—so much like a man. She didn't argue.

Lena's whole body grew numb with the cold. Every so often she stomped her feet and forced her body to move. Caleb followed her example. *Where are they?*

Then the rope moved. Perhaps the wind had grasped it and toyed with her mind. She felt another pull and grabbed Caleb's arm.

"They're coming! I can feel it." She laughed and cried at the same time, simply believing Gabe had Simon. After all, he'd said he would bring back her son—their son.

The minutes dragged on before she caught sight of Gabe trudging through the snow, carrying Simon with Turnip beside them. For a moment, she feared her eyes might deceive her, but then Caleb called out to Gabe, and he answered. Tears froze on her cheeks.

Once the wind and snow lay outside and she saw Simon and Gabe were safe, Lena threw her arms around Gabe's snow-laden body and sobbed on his chest.

"Simon's fine," Gabe soothed. "He was in the barn with Turnip staying warm with the animals."

"I was afraid I'd lost you both. Oh, you dear, sweet man, I love you so."

Chapter 14

She. . .she loves me? Surely I'm mistaken. She must mean Simon. Gabe pushed Lena's show of exuberance to the far corner of his heart. Later he'd contemplate those words when solitude embraced his mind and body.

A shiver rippled through Gabe's body, and he suddenly noticed that his teeth were chattering uncontrollably. Practical matters had to be addressed first.

Gabe thought he'd be freezing till the day he crossed over the threshold from earth to heaven. . .and poor Simon. Even sitting by the fire and cocooned in a blanket, the boy still shivered.

A teasing thought passed through Gabe's mind. "When I was in Philadelphia, I read about this doctor who believes we all would be healthier if we took a bath every day rather than once a week."

Caleb and Simon's eyes widened in obvious disbelief.

"Might be a little cold to start that today, don't you think?" Gabe asked and caught an amused glance from Lena. "Although, if you want, I could bring in enough snow to melt for the tub."

"Not today," Simon replied. "I'd rather work on my lessons all day until it's dark."

Laughing, Lena kissed Simon's cheek. "Drink this," she said gently.

"What is it?" He stared at the cup of brown-colored liquid.

"Tea with honey. It will help you get warm on the inside."

Simon peered up at Gabe as though looking for his approval. "Yes, drink it. You'll be glad you did. I'm having plenty of coffee to warm me up. Our insides are cold, Son."

The boy nodded and reached through the blanket for the tea. Gabe smiled. Lena was right when she said Simon usually did the totally unexpected. He'd never offered to help with chores before. And to venture out on this horrendous day? No one in this household would ever doubt the presence of God. Gabe carefully recorded the story in his journal to read when the problems of life seemed overwhelming. After he'd told Lena about thinking he'd heard Simon's voice call out to him, she'd cried again.

Her endearing words when they entered the cabin still nestled deep in his heart. Had she really meant them, or was she simply filled with gratitude? Emotion often guided a woman's response to external stimuli, and he fully understood if she'd simply overreacted in her enthusiasm to find Simon safe. But he desperately wanted to believe otherwise.

She handed him another cup of coffee. "Are you doing all right?"

"Yes, thank you." Her very presence intoxicated him.

"Do you still want to talk to me about something tonight?"

Even more so. "If you're not exhausted."

She smiled and laid her hand on his shoulder. "I have a topic of my own, if you're not too tired."

Simply listening to your voice fills me with joy. "We'll have a good evening together." Speaking more softly, he added, "You are an excellent wife, Lena. As I said on our wedding day, I'm honored."

She blushed, and her reaction surprised him. Clearly flustered, she rose and wrung her hands. "Ah, Caleb, would you like to get the Noah's ark from the chest under my bed? I think Simon would enjoy playing with it."

"And when you're finished, I'll read to you," Gabe added. "I have a new book I believe you will enjoy."

"It's not about snow, is it?" Simon asked, holding his cup with both hands. "Or wolves?"

Gabe chuckled. "No, Son. The book is called *Moby Dick* by Herman Melville. The story is about a whale and a sea captain."

Simon grinned before taking a sip of tea. "I can hardly wait."

"Me, too," Caleb echoed from the other room. "A real adventure. Might I read a bit of it aloud?"

"Most assuredly." In times like these, Gabe forgot the boys' pranks and mischievous ways and dwelled on his intense love for them and all they represented.

The day passed quickly with quiet activity. While Gabe read, Lena sewed by the fire. When evening shadows stole across the sky, she prepared corn in one of the thirty different ways she knew to use it. The challenge had become a joke to them, especially when they all grew tired of corn bread, mush, flapjacks, and molasses.

Lena possessed a radiance about her that he didn't quite understand; perhaps her glow came from the fact that Simon had not frozen to death. These past four months had seen both lads in perilous circumstances. Was this the way of raising children? He'd rather think not, but the logical side of him told him otherwise. No wonder parents' hair grew gray. He'd always attributed it to wisdom, but now he credited the color difference to the hardships of parenting. In reflecting on his past, Gabe knew without a doubt that he wouldn't trade one moment with his family.

God, You have blessed me beyond my most secret thoughts. All I can say is thank You.

Once the boys were in bed, Lena tended to her sewing while Gabe wrote in his journal, recording every moment of the day.

I thank the Lord for His deliverance today, he concluded. *Now, I cannot let the words of my heart stay imprisoned any longer. I will tell Lena this evening of my love for her. To hold it back any longer would be to deny my very own existence.*

He closed the book and set it aside. Now that the words were in print, he must brave forward.

"Would you like another cup of coffee?" Lena asked.

He studied her cherished face as he mustered the courage to begin. "No, thank you."

She drew her rocker closer to his chair. "Are you plenty warm?"

"Yes, I'm content." His heart began to pound more furiously than drummers in a parade. "You mentioned your desire to speak with me about a matter."

She nodded and stared into the fire. Her cheeks flushed, kindling his curiosity.

"You're not becoming ill, are you?" He leaned forward in his chair to view her more closely. The thought of touching her forehead crossed his mind.

"Oh no. I'm perfectly fine," she hastily replied.

Easing back, he folded his hands across his once-ample stomach. "Go ahead, I'm listening."

She rose and paced back and forth in front of the fire. "Do you remember what I told you this morning when you returned with Simon?"

She's full of regret. I surmised as much. "Yes, I do remember." With great effort, he stared up into her face.

Slowly, she removed her apron and laid it across the rocker. Inhaling deeply, she sat in front of him on the rug. "I meant every word," she whispered.

Gabe thought his heart had stopped.

She moistened her lips. "I've known for weeks, but I didn't want you to think of me as brash." Lowering her head, she picked at a loose tuft on the rug.

Have I heard correctly? Is this a dream? But when he glanced at the top of her head, he dared not lose his nerve. Gently he lifted her chin and smiled into those green pools he'd grown to cherish.

"And I have loved you for weeks, but I was uncertain of your response."

She looked innocent, fragile, her lovely features silhouetted by the fire, her pursed lips equally inviting. Gabe bent and kissed his wife. It was a soft kiss, a tender kiss, but a luxury that invited more. . .and more.

"I do love you, Lena," he whispered. "You are my life and my joy. I never dreamed I'd be so blessed."

She drew back from him. With a sweet smile, she pulled the pins from her raven-colored hair and allowed the long tresses to cascade down her back. Taking his hand, she said, "I believe it's time we became man and wife."

Lena woke and wiped the sleep from her eyes. Sometime during the night the winds had stopped. Gabe had risen in the wee hours of the morning and tried not to stir her, but she knew the instant he'd climbed out of bed. For two weeks now, they'd been true husband and wife, and she treasured their tender relationship.

"Go back to sleep," he'd whispered earlier. "The snowstorm is over, and I want to check on the cattle."

"I'll go with you," she said, unable to bear the thought of him leaving her side. She'd become unashamedly possessive.

He'd leaned over and kissed her. "No, my dear. I won't be long." For the first time in years, she felt loved and protected. Her eyes closed. How wonderful to love and be loved. Surely this would last forever.

Now, as morning graced the skies and the shades of rose and amber ushered in the dawn, Lena met the day with happiness and hope for the future. She had a husband who cherished and adored her—and considered her sons as his own. What more could she ever ask?

This morning he planned to ride over to the Shafers to make sure they had fared well during the storm. Most likely the snow held drifts in some places higher than the cabin. She and Gabe had already experienced the snow drifting to the top of their door, holding them captive within their home.

Lena sighed and listened to see if Caleb and Simon were up. She should go with Gabe. Dagget despised her husband, ridiculing him each morning when he brought milk. Gabe had asked him one day why he didn't buy a cow if he detested his presence so much. In any case, the children wouldn't get any milk today until the wagon could get through.

As she dressed, her thoughts drifted back to those first few weeks when Gabe had tried so hard to learn everything he could about the farm. He'd hammered his thumb, spilled a bucket of milk, spooked the horses while learning to drive the wagon, and nearly gotten sprayed by a skunk. The dear man did not give up, even when drenched by a downpour in the midst of patching the dugout roof. She admired his courage and stamina. Every day a new adventure brought them closer—even the unpleasant and frightening challenges. There had been a time—and not so long ago—when she'd believed no man could ever take James's place. How wrong she'd been. God had indeed brought her the best.

God had indeed brought Gabe the best. He treasured his family and their relationship. Two weeks ago, he and Lena had confessed their love for each other, and now he actually felt like a married man. Never had he dreamed his life might contain such fulfillment. Oh, there were disagreements here and there, and Simon would always be unpredictable, but to have his heart's desire fulfilled. . .well, he simply couldn't put a price on what it all meant to him. When Lena looked at him with her impish smile, he melted faster than the snow in spring.

This morning, he had a job to do. Neither the cold nor the snow could stop him from braving the elements to reach the Shafers. He worried about the Shafer children, especially when he noted the many times that sour old Dagget had been drinking by the time he arrived with milk. He'd seen the scurvy sores on the children's thin arms and faces, and Lena had sent dried fruit and vegetables to add more nutrition to their diet. Caleb and Simon had passed their old coats, mittens, mufflers, and hats on to them, but Gabe doubted if Dagget even noticed.

The Shafer children were mannerly, and Gabe had allowed Amanda to borrow a few books. She always thanked him, eager to report on what she'd read and often pointing out confusing words for his explanation. He appreciated her willingness to educate herself, especially in this part of the country where most women lived to bear children and work the farms. Amanda had done her best to school her brothers and sisters with a McGuffey Reader, but she didn't have any slates or chalk. Gabe found extra in his trunk so she could teach them to write and learn arithmetic.

Smoke curled above the dugout in the distance. He breathed a sigh of relief. He'd feared their home had caved in with the weight of the snow. An abundance of it had fallen in the last two weeks, so much he'd climbed onto the roof of his house and barn to clean them off.

The image of the little Shafer girl with her bruised face and obvious terror haunted him. Not once had he seen her since she ran from him, Dagget's repugnant laughter echoing through the barn.

Dismounting his horse, Gabe saw the door had more than three feet of snow banked against it. Not seeing a shovel, he used his gloved hands to scoop a path wide enough for the door to open. He knocked soundly. Amanda answered, her eyes red. A whimpering child could be heard in the background.

"Good morning, Mr. Hunters. I'm glad to see you are all right from the storm."

Something is wrong here. "I came by to see how you were faring after the snowstorm. I apologize for not having milk, but the drifts are too high for the wagon. I believe the cow is about to go dry, too."

Amanda's round face, pale and rigid, looked distracted. "Thank you, but we are warm and have plenty of chips for the fire."

"And food?"

"We will manage. I appreciate you stopping by." She hesitated, then whispered, "I can't let you in, Mr. Hunters. Pa would thrash me for sure."

He smiled in hopes of easing her nervousness. "I understand, Amanda. Is—"

"Amanda, whata ya doing?" Dagget's slurred voice bellowed.

She glanced behind her. "It's Mr. Hunters."

"Shut the door!" A string of curses followed.

"I'll not keep you," Gabe said to Amanda. "Let us know if we can be of assistance."

Amanda's eyes pooled as she slowly shut the door. Gabe offered another reassuring smile and ambled toward his horse.

"Wait," Amanda called from the doorway. "We do need help. Mary is awful sick—burning up with fever."

Gabe whirled around. "What have you given her?"

"I don't have anything but a little ginger tea, and I've applied a mustard plaster. Pa had me give her whiskey and a little molasses, said it would cut the cough and put her to sleep. Mr. Hunters, did I do the right thing? Ma always said spirits invited evil."

"Amanda, get in here now! I'll teach you to mind me."

Dagget had been drinking, that was obvious, but Gabe wasn't about to ride home and forget the little girl lying sick. He strode back to the door and entered the small dugout. It smelled rank from whiskey, vomit, and unkempt bodies.

The little girl stared up from a straw pallet with huge, cavernous eyes, the same child from the barn incident weeks before. She coughed, a deep, ragged sound that rattled her chest. Her little body shook, and she barely had enough strength to cry. Nearby, Dagget sat sprawled in a chair with a bottle of liquor in one hand and the other clamped around Matthew's wrist. In the shadows, three boys ranging from about Simon's age to probably fifteen sat motionless.

Gabe clenched his fists and fought the rage tearing through him. He swallowed his anger, realizing a fight with Dagget would solve nothing. "A good father would put down that bottle and see what he could do about nursing this child."

Dagget lifted a brow. "She ain't none of yer business. So ya'd best be leaving before I find my shotgun."

"Not yet," Gabe said quietly, edging closer to view the child's pallor.

Dagget staggered to his feet and took a swallow from the bottle. Finding it empty, he threw it across the room. The pieces landed dangerously close to the boys huddled in the corner. "Git me my gun, Charles."

Chapter 15

*T*he older boy emerged from the corner, a strapping young man, tall and muscular. He glanced at his little sister suffering through another gut-wrenching cough, then at Amanda. "No, Pa. I'm not getting you the gun."

Dagget swung his arm wildly. He released Matthew and stood to stagger toward Charles. "Boy, you'll know this beatin' for a long time."

Lord, why are there such animals in this world? "You'll not harm him," Gabe said, surprising himself with his firmness.

"It's all right, Mr. Hunters," Charles said. "He's too drunk to do anything but talk, and we've all had enough. Truth be known, I could take him on, but I don't like the idea of fighting my own pa."

"Why, you—"

Gabe grabbed Dagget's arm and shoved him back down onto the chair—the first time he'd ever touched a man in fury. "Stay put, because I intend to make sure this child is properly tended to."

"If only the doc didn't live so far away," Charles said, bending to feel Mary's forehead while Amanda wiped her face with a damp cloth.

"It would take four days or more to get him," Gabe replied, thinking Dagget was angry enough without Charles adding more rebellion by leaving. "She needs attention now, and that's a rough journey for a grown man."

"No disrespect meant, but it's time I acted like a man and took better care of my brothers and sisters. Pa never acted like this when Ma was alive, and he treats Mary like a pitiful dog." Charles shook his head. "It's not her fault Ma died giving birth to her, but Pa expects her to pay for it every day."

"Seems like she doesn't want to fight this sickness," Amanda added. "It's as though she's given up."

"I have to do something." Without another word, Charles reached for a thin coat on a peg beside the door. "I need to get help somewhere."

"Go to Lena. She has more tea and some herbs to nurse your little sister." Gabe began to pull off his own outer garments. "Here, take my coat. It's warmer. And my horse is already saddled."

491

Charles hesitated.

"Do take the coat and Mr. Hunters's horse," Amanda insisted. "You don't need to be ill, too."

Reluctantly, Charles accepted the clothes. A handsome lad with light hair and strong features, he stole another glimpse at Mary. "Thank you, Mr. Hunters, and I apologize for not expressing my gratitude in the past for the milk."

"It's quite unnecessary," Gabe said. "Hurry along. The snow is deep, and it will take you a few hours to get there and back."

Nodding toward his father, Charles asked, "Do you want me to tie him up?"

Excellent idea. "No. I can handle Dagget just fine."

After he left, Gabe greeted the other children. They appeared a bit leery of their father, who only stared into the flames. He didn't bark any orders or curse. He simply sat.

Amanda made Mary as comfortable as possible, wrapping her in another blanket and moving her closer to the fire, while Gabe scooted Dagget's chair away from it.

Nearly three hours later, Lena and the boys arrived. Simon rode on the horse, while the other three traveled on foot. Charles carried food, ginger for tea, and a potion of dried horseradish to brew for Mary. Lena and Caleb carried dried elderberries, salt pork, a little milk, and a blanket.

"None of us wanted to wait at home when we might be of use here," Lena said. "The walk felt refreshing after being inside all day yesterday."

"I'm glad I didn't know you were trekking across the snow, but I'm glad you're here." Gabe helped her remove her coat and kissed the tip of her nose—so natural a gesture, so easy now that she'd revealed her heart and accepted his love.

Lena's presence eased the heaviness threatening to overwhelm him. To him, anger had always been a characteristic of the weak and a trait he'd refused to succumb to. The sins accompanying loss of control were vile. *I've never felt so angry. I don't know whether to apologize to Dagget or try to make him comprehend what he's doing to his family.*

Caleb and Simon urged the younger boys to head outside with them. Gabe surmised the Shafer children didn't share the luxury of free time very often, but their lack of proper clothing tugged at his conscience.

"Check on the hogs," Dagget bellowed. "And feed my mules."

Gabe said nothing for fear he'd strike the man. Every muscle in his body tensed, ready to shake him until what few teeth he had fell out.

He definitely did not feel like the model of a godly man.

"Why?" Dagget asked of Gabe a few moments later. "You bring milk 'most every day. You're ready to fight me over—" He pointed to Mary.

"Can't you say her name?" Gabe asked, the ire swelling inside of him again. *Lord, I'm being self-righteous here. Dagget is wrong, but it's not right for me to condemn him.*

"She killed her ma." Bitterness edged Dagget's words.

Gabe glanced at the child. If she died, God would lift her into His arms in heaven. If Dagget died, what would be his fate? "God took your wife home and left you a gift. In fact, He left you with six treasures. Maybe it's time to cease your complaints about the children He's entrusted to you and start taking care of them before you lose them all."

"Easy for you to say," Dagget sneered.

Pain wrenched through Gabe's heart as he remembered his own childhood. "No, it's not easy for me to say. I understand little Mary's plight." Gabe stood and towered over Dagget. "Look at your daughter. She's not fighting the fever; she has nothing on the inside of her to want to live. Unless you give her a reason, she won't survive."

A bewildered expression spread over the man's face even in his drunken stupor. Gabe turned his attention back to Mary, disgusted at the drunken excuse of a man before him.

"Pray for me, Lena," he whispered. "I'm incensed with Dagget. I think I could tear him apart with my bare hands."

She lifted her gaze from Mary and touched his face. "You're a man who loves his family and doesn't understand why Dagget fails to see his blessings. I'll pray for you and Dagget." She studied Mary's face. "And this poor baby suffering here."

"If only Pa loved her," Amanda softly whispered. "Sometimes we hide her from him so he won't beat her."

"We won't let him hurt her ever again," Charles vowed. He took a deep breath. "I think I'll check on the animals."

Gabe stood. "I'll go with you. Staying inside is making me irritable."

Lena watched Gabe leave, her heart heavy with the sadness etching his features. She wanted to offer comfort, but the right words slipped her mind. Her childhood had been happy and full of wonderful memories, but she'd come to know something terrible had happened to Gabe as a child—something that weighed on him like a heavy yoke. Perhaps she should ask him about it when all of this was over.

She'd never heard Gabe raise his voice, and he really hadn't shouted at Dagget, but his anger had spilled over like a boiling pot. How well she understood the guilt of an uncontrollable temper. Each time she forgot her resolve to contain hers, a matter would irritate her, and her mouth acted before her Christianity set in.

Of course she understood giving it all to God would help, but Lena wanted to end it all on her own—to show God she could please Him. She hadn't been able to curb her unforeseen anger by herself yet. She glanced at Dagget. Drunk. Mean. Hurting those he loved, or should love.

I'm not like him. I'm a good mother and wife. I don't hurt anyone or use horrible language. I love my family, and they love me.

Lena unwillingly recalled the days following James's death when her heart had hardened against God and all those around her, even Caleb and Simon. She'd despised James for leaving her alone to raise two children and manage the farm. Her tears of grief had turned to hate for his abandonment. The turning point came when Caleb asked her why she didn't like him or Simon. Lena had cried and begged God and the boys' forgiveness. Since then, she'd managed her temper fairly well—but not to her satisfaction.

Obviously, Dagget felt the same way about Mary. Unfortunately, he hadn't recognized the poison brewing in his soul.

Lena pushed aside her disturbing thoughts. At present, Mary deserved all of her attention. She bent and kissed the little girl's feverish cheeks. *I'd take this child in a minute—all of them—and give them a proper home where they'd know the meaning of real love.*

"Do you think she will be all right?" Amanda's voice broke into quiet sobs. She sat on the other side of her sister and adjusted the quilt for what seemed like the hundredth time.

"Are you praying?" Lena asked quietly.

Amanda buried her face in her hands. "I don't know what to pray for. I've been Mary's mama since the day she was born, and I love her so very much. I even named her Mary Elizabeth after Ma, but Pa has made her life miserable. Perhaps she should be with Jesus and Mama. At least she'd be happy and loved."

Lena moved alongside the young woman and held her while she wept. "We all want what's best for Mary, and only God in His perfect wisdom knows the answers. He loves her more than we can imagine, and He knows our hearts."

"I want her to fight this and get well," Amanda said, lifting a tear-stained face. "I don't want to lose my little Mary." She turned to the child. "Please get well. I promise to take better care of you. None of us will let you be hurt again."

Lena cried with her. Children shouldn't ever have to suffer for adults' mistakes. "We must pray for God's healing. He can work miracles." Lena took a sideways glance at Dagget, who stared at them. In his slouched position with his chin resting on his chest, huge tears rolled down his face.

"Have I killed my little girl?" he groaned.

Lena recalled Gabe's earlier words. "She needs to hear you love her and want her to live."

Dagget curled his fingers into a ball and trembled. "Amanda," he said softly. "Do we have any coffee?"

"Yes, Pa."

"Would you mind getting me a mug full?"

Amanda tore herself from Lena and brought her father the coffee. Although steam lifted from the hot brew, he downed it quickly. All the while the tears washed over his dirty cheeks. He stared at Mary, wordless. Lena didn't know if his drunkenness had brought on the emotion or if he sincerely regretted the way he'd treated the child.

Mary's breath grew more ragged, and she cried out, delirious in her half-conscious state. Lena tried to give her more tea, but the little girl couldn't swallow it.

"Oh, Jesus, please save this precious child," Lena whispered.

An instant later, Dagget scrambled to the floor beside his youngest daughter. He pulled her hand from beneath the quilt and held it firmly. "Mary, I want you to live. I know I've treated you bad, but if you'll give me a chance—if God will give me a chance—I'll make it up to you and your brothers and sisters."

The door squeaked open, and Gabe walked in with Charles. The youth had aged years in a matter of hours. Weariness and a hint of sorrow settled on his features. Gabe's gaze flew to Lena, questioning, wondering, and fearful.

"Charles wants to ride for the doctor, but I've explained the trek is too dangerous with all this snow. As long as there's sunlight, he can find his way, but on a cloudy day, he'll get lost."

Lena nodded in agreement and turned her attention back to Mary. She saw the sorrow on Dagget's face as he held Mary's hand and shed one tear after another. Each time the child coughed, her whole body shook.

"There's a bottle of paregoric under my bed," Dagget said. "Would that help?"

Paregoric. Lena knew it contained opium, and some folks got so they had to have it all the time.

Gabe cleared his throat. "I've heard of its being used for cough before, although its primary use is for stomach ailments."

"Would it hurt her?" Amanda asked.

"I knew of a woman who became addicted to laudanum—a mixture of opium and alcohol—but we could try a little of the paregoric," Gabe replied. "It's up to you."

Silence resounded from the walls of the small dugout.

"I think we should try anything that might help," Charles finally said. He ran his fingers through his hair. "We have to do something."

Gabe moved to Dagget's bed and pulled out the small bottle from beneath it. "Let's give her a dose. In the meantime, why don't we call in the other children and pray together for Mary?"

A short while later, they all gathered together while Gabe prayed. "Lord Jesus, all of us have asked You today to spare this child and heal her. Now, we all are praying together. Hear our voices. We look to You for strength. Amen."

Later that afternoon, with no change in Mary, Gabe realized the necessity of making arrangements for Caleb and Simon. Pulling Lena aside, he shared his thoughts. "The boys ought to get home. I'd like to escort you back. Then I'll return to spend the night here."

"Would you mind if I stayed the night instead?" She stared at the unconscious child, still and dangerously hot. Not once had she left Mary's side with Amanda and Dagget.

"Of course not," he replied. "Whatever happens, Amanda will need you."

She reached for his hand, and he assisted her to her feet. "I'll walk you outside."

While Lena pulled on her coat, Gabe stepped around to Dagget's side. "I'm going home with the boys, but Lena is staying the night."

He nodded. "Uh. . .uh, thank you for. . .today. I'll not be forgetting it."

Gabe grasped the man on his shoulder. "I'll be by at daybreak."

Gabe and his family stepped out of the dugout. Once the door shut behind them, Gabe voiced his concerns to Lena. "Do you think Dagget is harmless?"

"Yes, I believe so. Right now regret is eating him alive."

"Do you think it will last?" Gabe remembered all his dealings with Dagget, and the thought of the man tossing his foul words at his precious wife alarmed him.

She shrugged and wrapped her arms around her. "I hope so. These children need him."

"But he's so mean, Mama," Caleb said. "I don't think he'll ever change."

"We have to give him a chance, just like the good Lord does for us," Lena said.

Gabe hugged her and planted a light kiss on her lips. "I love you, Lena Hunters. Now, hurry on inside, before you get too cold."

Caleb and Gabe trudged through the snow back to the farm, while Simon rode the horse. They all were quiet, including Simon, and the silence offered an opportunity for Gabe to reflect on the Shafers. Oh, how he wanted Mary to live, and how well he understood her desire to die. Children needed love to grow and flourish. Without it, they grew inward, as he'd done. Fortunately for him, he'd come to know a heavenly Father who'd changed his whole life.

"Pa?" Caleb asked.

Gabe gave him his full attention.

"Would you take all six of the Shafers and love them like us?" Caleb asked.

"What do you think?" Gabe responded.

"I believe you would."

"Do you feel my sentiments are wrong?"

Caleb did not hesitate to reply. "No, not at all. I think it's mighty fine."

"Of course, what is best for those children is for their father to love them."

"I'm sure glad we have you for a pa," Simon piped up.

"Me, too," Caleb echoed. "We got the best pa in Nebrasky."

Lena had dozed by Mary's side, while Amanda slept off and on. Every time Lena awoke, she saw Dagget staring into his little daughter's face. He didn't eat the supper of salt pork and corn bread that Lena and Amanda prepared and refused anything to drink. The boys did their chores and silently went about their business until time for them to sleep, although Charles sat near the fire, watching Mary. The vigil continued with only the sounds of the younger children's soft snoring and Amanda's quiet weeping.

Just before four o'clock the next morning, Mary stirred. "She feels cooler," Dagget said. "Don't you think so, Lena?"

Immediately, Lena touched the child's forehead. "The fever's broken. Praise God."

Amanda and Charles awakened and scooted closer.

"Mary," Dagget whispered. "Can you talk to me?"

Through half-closed eyes, the child whispered, "I'm so tired."

"Sure you are, honey. Now you just sleep, and I'll be here when you wake up."

"Are you my Jesus?" Mary asked a moment later.

Dagget sucked in a ragged breath. "It's your pa, Mary. I'm so sorry for being mean to you. I. . .I love you, child."

Lena blinked back her tears. God had answered many prayers this night. What a dear Lord they served.

Chapter 16

*L*ena ladled the freshly churned butter into a small bowl and proceeded to rinse it thoroughly before packing it lightly into a yellow mound. Gabe loved his bread and butter. Even when Caleb and Simon complained about the endless meals of corn bread, Gabe never said a word. Instead, he'd reach for a second hunk. At night, he loved to sit before the fire and feast on leftover corn bread with milk and molasses. Didn't take much to please her husband.

The snow this March came lightly and in inches rather than feet. A few more heavy storms might fall upon them, but the likelihood lessened as the days drew closer to spring. Lena loved the seasons, but she'd had enough of snow and ice.

What a winter, Lena mused, but a much easier one with Gabe to share each day. He'd changed so much since the first time she'd seen him at the train station in Archerville—and not simply in appearance. That alone proved startling enough. He'd shed all the excess weight, and the work outside had tightened his muscles and darkened his skin. One glance at his copper-colored eyes could leave her breathless, and his thick blond hair, well. . .

In short, Gabe Hunters had transformed into quite a handsome man, but his heart had won hers from the moment he reached out to her and the boys.

I'm a pretty lucky woman to find a man who loves me as much as I do him.

So much had happened in the last month. Dagget had given his permission for Amanda to teach school, and the area farmers had pitched in to make the soddy presentable. Gabe had offered his assistance in helping Amanda form a schedule and arrange the classes. He'd been guiding her through basic reading, writing, and arithmetic much like she'd done with her brothers.

Today, Gabe had gone hunting while the boys were in school, much to Caleb and Simon's regret. They'd have gladly gone along, skipping their lessons with Amanda in light of a few hours in the wilds. Gabe had taken to regularly bringing in game, and today he had his sights on taking Dagget with him. How strange that these two different men had grown to be such good friends.

"Hello," a voice called.

Lena strained her ears. She didn't recognize the voice. Her gaze trailed to the loaded shotgun hanging over the door.

"Hello, Lena?"

She peeked through the window. Dread washed over her.

"Lena!"

She opened the door to see Riley O'Connor dismounting his horse. *Gabe will not be happy about this.* "My husband's not here," she said, crossing her arms.

Riley shot her a wide grin as he tied his mount to the porch post. "I hoped he'd be gone."

"Why?" she snapped. Remembering that Riley's temperament when challenged equaled her own, Lena rephrased the question. "I don't understand why you need to see me."

"I think you have a good idea." He loped toward her, offering an easy smile. "I wanted to see you."

She didn't like him, not one bit. "Unless you have business with Gabe, then you don't have any reason to be here."

"You and I have unfinished business," he said in a low voice, standing dangerously close.

Lena stepped back and took a deep breath. *Hold your temper. He's bigger than you.* "We have nothing to talk about."

"I asked you to marry me, you refused, and now you're married to that city feller."

"Then everything is settled." Lena lifted her chin in hopes he understood her silent dismissal.

Riley's eyes narrowed, and he lifted one worn boot onto the porch. "You never gave me a chance."

"For what?"

"To win you back."

"You never had me. Riley, please, just leave. I am a happily married woman. I love my husband very much, and he's going to be upset when he finds out you've been here."

"Good. I'd like the chance to fight 'im."

She closed her eyes and fought for control. Anger bubbled hotter than a pot of lye and tallow. "My Gabe has better things to tend to than fighting you. In case you've forgotten, you and I never courted, never kissed—unlike what you told Gabe—never anything. As I remember, you rode up one day and stated you were planning to marry me. I said no then, and I would say no again, even if you were the last man in the world!"

Riley's foot slipped from the porch, leaving a clump of fresh manure on the edge.

"Aw, Lena, just let me come inside for a spell. I'm sure you'll change your mind."

"Get out of here."

"You're making a terrible mistake. Lots of women think I'm good to look at."

She gritted her teeth. "I don't. Take your charms to one of them."

A wry smile spread over his face. "Why don't we just see?"

Quickly, Lena stepped inside the open door and slammed it. "You'd best leave, Riley. I have a shotgun in here, and I'm not afraid to use it."

"I'm goin'! I feel sorry for your husband. You ain't worth the trouble."

Latching the door, Lena peeked through the side of her window's calico curtain to watch Riley gallop off. She closed her eyes and touched her pounding heart. *I've got to tell Gabe.*

That evening, while the boys tended to chores and Gabe skinned three rabbits—Dagget had brought down a deer—Lena stole over by the well where Gabe hunched over the animals.

"What's wrong?" he asked, lifting a brow. "You look upset."

She nodded and wrapped her shawl closer about her shoulders.

"It's too cold for you without a coat, Lena. Why don't you stay warm by the fire, and I'll be there momentarily."

"You don't mind?"

He smiled. "I'm finished, and I rather enjoy the opportunity to catch my wife alone."

A few moments later, Gabe joined her at the table. She poured both of them a cup of freshly brewed coffee and sat across from him, her mind spinning with Riley's unpleasant visit. For a few tempting seconds, she thought of not telling him at all. *Who would know the difference? No, that's wrong.*

Taking a deep breath, she blurted out, "Riley O'Connor paid a visit while you were hunting with Dagget." It didn't sound at all as she intended. Trembling, she wrapped her fingers around the mug of hot coffee.

Gabe stared at her, emotionless. "What did he want?"

"He was up to no good, saying things that weren't true."

"What did he want, Lena, and what did he say?"

Suddenly, she burst into tears. "Gabe, if that man ever shows up on our land again, I'm going to fill his backside with buckshot!"

"I'd like to know what happened." The cold tone of Gabe's voice nearly frightened her.

"He just talked about him and me. . .insinuating we used to court. I hurried back into the cabin and told him to leave or I'd get the shotgun after him."

Solemnly, Gabe rose from the table. "I believe I need to pay Mr. O'Connor a visit. I won't have this in my home."

She grabbed his suspenders. "No, Gabe, please. That's what he wants. I told him I was happily married and I loved you." She glanced up at him through blinding tears and repeated the conversation word for word.

Sighing heavily, Gabe lowered himself onto the chair. A distant look filled his eyes, and for a moment, she saw a stranger before her. "I'm glad you told me," he finally said.

"I couldn't keep anything from you. We're supposed to share every-thing." *This is not like Gabe. If I didn't know better, I'd swear he didn't believe me!*

A shadow of something she didn't recognize swept over his face. "I'm not sure what to do."

"Nothing, Gabe. I really don't think he'll be back. I made him plenty mad."

This time his gaze captured hers, and the grim look changed to the one she cherished. "Let's hope it deterred him, for if there is a next time, I'll be forced to take drastic measures. No one, I repeat, no one will accost my wife."

Lena said nothing as Gabe snatched up his coat from the peg and headed outside. A sick feeling swirled around her stomach. Why did she feel he doubted her?

Gabe finished skinning the rabbits with a vengeance that frightened him. Dagget Shafer. Riley O'Connor. How many other men had vied for Le-na's attention? Had she encouraged them? Was she still seeing Riley? Why did she have to be so beautiful? He knew the degradation of men when they became consumed by a comely woman. Jealousy enveloped their lives. One sin led to another. Drunkenness. Fights. Murder. Fami-lies destroyed and a host of other atrocities.

And I'm traveling down the same highway of destruction. My jealousy has to cease, or I'll shatter my marriage. He'd fall victim to the same wick-edness he'd sworn never to enter. Gabe swiped at a single tear coursing down his cheek. His relationship with Lena ranked second to God. Only a fool would destroy something as good as the Father's gift.

Dropping the knife, he wiped his hands clean on the snow. If only he could eliminate the bitter memories as easily as he'd just washed his hands. Gabe stood and took long strides back to the cabin.

The moment he opened the door, he could see Lena had been weeping. He hated what he saw, knowing his insensitive response had ushered in her tears.

"Lena." He crossed the room and took her into his arms. "I apologize for not understanding how today affected you. All I could dwell on was Riley coming after you."

"You have nothing to be jealous of," she whispered, stroking his cheek and no doubt seeing his single tear. "You are what is most important to me—you and our sons."

He held her against him, his fingers running through her dark silky hair, her breath soft and warm against his neck. "I'm so fortunate to have you in my life. Please forgive me."

"Oh, Gabe. Don't be so hard on yourself. Riley O'Connor is a difficult man. You reacted like any man who'd been insulted."

"It's no excuse for me to be difficult, too. We have so many fine friends, and I don't need to make a fuss over one ill-mannered scoundrel."

"I love you, Gabe Hunters. Nothing's going to change my heart."

He held her close, chasing away his fears and bitterness. Someday, he'd have to tell her about Mother and the others, but not now. For this moment, he wanted to simply cherish the woman in his arms.

Chapter 17

*W*inter slowly melted into the Platte River, and Gabe eagerly looked forward to spring. At last he could plow the fields and plant corn and other grains for a fall harvest. He wanted to help Lena plant a sizable vegetable garden, knowing she'd have to preserve the food while he worked in the fields. He'd learned so much about Nebraska since last October, and this new season promised to teach him even more. Without a doubt, the cold winter months had given him and his family time to get to know each other. They'd played in the snow and gone hunting, and Lena had taught him how to ice skate.

It has been a good season, he wrote in his journal. *My family is affectionate, and I am deeply grateful for their devotion. I believe we would not have grown this close if the winter had not closed in around us. Now I'm eager to do the work that will provide for my family.*

In the mornings, after milking and chores, Gabe listened for the birds. Through Caleb, he'd learned to distinguish the soft coo of a mourning dove, the unique call of the bobwhite, the obnoxious cry of the crow, and from time to time, the gobble of a turkey, which reminded him of chattering women. Near the river, ducks and geese abounded, and occasionally, he and the boys would bring one down for a fine meal.

Once he'd sowed the crops, Gabe wanted to take Caleb and Simon fishing. Of course, the first few times the boys would have to teach him how to properly operate a pole, line, and bait. No doubt he'd provide yet another source of amusement—but he didn't mind.

Dagget and his family worked through their differences. Little Mary never left her father's side, nor did he object. Dagget had even bought a cow, which ended Gabe's morning visits. Still, a few times a week, Gabe ventured toward the Shafer farm just to keep his mind at ease. Shoots of spring plants weren't the only things thriving at the Shafers'.

Lena and the boys had shown Gabe how to read the tracks of the white-tailed deer, coyotes, foxes, rabbits, and a host of other animals. He looked forward to seeing prairie dogs, for Simon found them quite interesting.

The wolves hadn't bothered them since the incident with Caleb and Simon, although Gabe still looked for them from time to time. He'd lost a few head of cattle over the winter: three to hungry wolves, two others to the cold.

Gabe wouldn't trade his new life for the biggest mansion in Philadelphia—or anywhere else for that matter. He thought being a husband, father, and farmer surely must be God's richest blessing.

Today he'd begin the plowing. Like a child eagerly awaiting a spectacular event, Gabe hadn't been able to sleep all night.

"Gabe, it's hard work," Lena warned. "Your shoulders will ache. In fact, your whole body will hurt. You'll fall into bed dead tired only to get up before dawn and start again. I think I should help—Caleb, too."

"Maybe Caleb—later," Gabe replied with a frown. "But not my wife. I'm the provider."

Before the sun offered a faint twinge of pink, Gabe hurried through his chores, then hitched up the mule to the iron plow. He slipped the reins over his shoulders and offered a quick prayer. Grinning like a lovestruck schoolboy, he took out across the earth, all the while envisioning fields of waving corn and grain just like he'd seen in his books.

After one length of a field, Gabe realized the truth in Lena's words. Plowing was hard work! He looked behind him and saw his beloved wife watching. Waving wildly, he gestured to the completed row. Turning the mule, he began again. No point in letting her know she'd spoken correctly in her assessment of the plowing.

Tonight he'd be one sore man.

Midmorning, Lena brought a crockery jug of cold water wrapped in burlap and a cloth to wipe the sweat from his brow.

"Admit it, Gabe. This is hard work," she said while he drank deeply.

Not yet, maybe never.

When he refused to reply, she laughed. "I'm sure your books on farming didn't talk about the sweat pouring off your face or the way your back feels like it's breaking in two."

He tried to give her a stern look, but one glimpse of her sweet face melted his resolve. "The endeavor is satisfying," he said, clamping his lips so she wouldn't hear his chuckle.

"Are you ready for me to help? Or can I send the boys as soon as they get home from school?"

"No, ma'am. I'm a Nebraska farmer, and I'm excited about plowing my own fields."

"And you're sure about this? Caleb will be disappointed, since he wanted to help."

He leaned over and kissed her. "I made it through the fall and winter—wolves, Dagget, blizzards, and Riley. Now I'm ready for the spring and summer and whatever comes with it."

She wrapped her arms around his neck. "Tornadoes. We get some nasty twisters in the summer. Prairie fires, too." She tilted her head. "Back in '73, we had a horrible drought, and in '74 the worst plague of grasshoppers ever seen—ate everything to the ground. Even the trains couldn't run because the tracks were slick with 'hoppers."

"I'm ready." He grinned.

"I see you are." She stepped back from his embrace and laughed with him. "I'll bring you food and water in a few hours. Besides, you're beginning to smell like a farmer."

By noon, Gabe wondered how many days it would take to complete the plowing. It had taken him half a day to till one acre. No doubt by the time he finished, he'd be strong and muscular. He grimaced at the mere thought of Lena guiding the plow over the rough terrain and supporting the reins. No woman should work like a man.

After devouring dandelion greens and corn bread at noon, Gabe fought the urge to stretch out on the blanket where Lena had set their meal and sleep a few moments before submitting himself to the plow again.

I am a farmer. We don't shirk in our work.

"Close your eyes for a little while," she urged, coaxing him to lay his head on her lap. "The plowing doesn't have to be finished today, and you were out here before the sun barely peeked through the clouds."

"Now I understand how Samson felt," he said. "Next you'll want to know where I confine my strength."

She stroked his cheek with her fingertips. Intoxicating.

"I'm a farmer, not a lazy city man," he mumbled. "I'm going to call you Delilah."

She combed her fingers through his hair; soon her touch faded into memory.

Lena woke with a start. She'd fallen asleep! She'd planned for Gabe to rest before finishing the day's work. Shielding her eyes from the sun, she saw him in the distance struggling with the mule. Why, he'd gotten so much done. How long had she slept? From the sun's position in the sky, she must have napped for over an hour.

"Gabe Hunters, you tricked me!"

He heard her call and took a moment to wave. She wanted to shout at him, but the incident suddenly struck her as funny. Looking about, she saw he'd gathered up the remains of their meal and packed it nicely into the basket. Only the quilt beneath her needed to be folded and placed with the other items.

"Gabe Hunters, you never cease to surprise me," she whispered. Beneath her fair-haired husband's smile and gentle ways rested more courage and grit than in any man around. *He's a warrior,* she thought. *The best there is.*

Humming a nondescript tune, she walked back to the house. The boys should be home from school by now and seeking out mischief if she guessed correctly. Perhaps her strong-willed husband would accept Caleb's help.

As darkness covered the farm and stars dotted the sky, Gabe came trudging in for supper with Caleb and Simon behind him. Although they'd washed at the well and their cheeks glistened from the scrubbing, the lines in their faces and their hunched backs betrayed their exhaustion.

"I have beef stew," she said brightly, "and a dried chokeberry pie with fresh cream."

"I'm starved," Simon moaned, dropping into a chair.

"I don't know why," Caleb said with a glare. "All afternoon you and Turnip chased rabbits, while Pa and I took turns at the plow."

"You didn't work that much," Simon replied. "I saw Pa do more rows than you."

Mercy, let's not argue. Gabe is tired enough without settling the boys.

Gabe ruffled Caleb's hair. "You both worked equally hard, and you spent a good part of the day in school. Caleb, you were a great help in the fields, and, Simon, thank you for completing the evening chores without assistance."

"Why don't we eat so you men can get to bed," Lena said, filling their plates with the hot stew and a slab of buttered corn bread.

"It smells delicious," Gabe said. He chewed slowly as though every motion took all of his strength. "Do you boys mind if I postpone our reading of *The Last of the Mohicans* until tomorrow night?"

Caleb sighed. "I'm too tired to listen."

Simon agreed.

Shortly thereafter, the two boys headed for bed with promises to say their prayers before drifting off to sleep. "School is just too hard for me," Simon said.

Lena captured Gabe's gaze and smiled. Their youngest son was not about to admit the afternoon's venture had worn him out. She watched the two boys disappear into their small room.

Gabe slumped into a chair, and she immediately stepped behind him, massaging the shoulder muscles she knew were tight and sore. He winced. "And so what has made you so tired?" she whispered.

He pulled her around and down onto his lap, offering a light kiss. "All the good food I ate today. Plowing is fairly simple."

She shook her head. "I suppose the pain I detect is a bee sting?" she asked with a tilt of her head and a smile she could not hide.

"Not exactly." Gabe tossed her a most pathetic look, reminding her of a little boy seeking sympathy.

"Is that the way you peered at your mother when you needed something?" Lena asked, pretending to be stern.

Immediately, Gabe stiffened. *What have I done?* She knew he never spoke of his mother, except to discourage a conversation.

"Maybe I should go to bed."

Lena despised her foolishness. "I'm sorry. I know you don't like to talk about your mother."

He gently lifted her from his lap. "It's all right. My mother behaved rather uniquely with her maternal instincts."

"She really hurt you," Lena said, wanting to touch him but slightly fearful. The regret and anger in his face had occurred only once before—when he'd dealt with Dagget Shafer the night Mary nearly died.

Shrugging, he chewed at his lip. "I'm a grown man with a fine family. I determined a long time ago to rise above my circumstances. Revisiting the past is pointless." He stood and grasped her arms. She could feel him trembling. "Lena, I don't want to speak of my mother ever again. She's buried, and everything about her is best forgotten."

"I'd be glad to listen. It might help how you feel."

"No!"

Chapter 18

*L*ena woke the following morning to discover Gabe had already left for the fields. She'd slept soundly, not her normal manner of doing things, but she'd had a difficult time falling asleep the night before. She'd cried before coming to bed, and not once had Gabe apologized or attempted to hold her when she crawled in beside him. This morning she was furious.

When she finally climbed out of bed, she discovered Caleb and Simon were outside doing their morning chores before school, and she hadn't prepared their breakfast or lunch buckets. Even with time pressing against her, the memory of Gabe's final words last night seared her heart.

Slapping together corn bread and molasses sandwiches, Lena roughly wrapped the lunches in cloth and tossed them into the boys' buckets. She turned her attention to the boys' breakfast. Anger raced through her veins as she heated the skillet for fried cornmeal and eggs. *Look at all I've done for him, and this is how he treats me! Where would he be if I hadn't married him and taught him about farming?*

Without warning, Lena felt her stomach roll. *Now look what Gabe's done—made me sick with his rudeness.*

"Who has made you ill?"

The gentle whisper penetrated her soul. She'd allowed her temper to upset her, the evil poison she'd sworn to overcome. Gabe had nothing to do with her churning stomach. Pulling the skillet from the fire, she dashed outside to rid her body of whatever had revolted in her stomach. Sick and feeling the pain of remorse, Lena realized she couldn't go on with the rage inside her.

After the boys left for school, Lena picked up the Bible. Oh, how she needed the Lord this day. Every part of her wanted to crumble in memory of her horrible temper. She remembered her thoughts the day when Mary hovered between life and death and how Dagget's ugly temperament had nearly killed the child. *Am I any different? Would I lose Gabe and the boys if they knew the horrible things I was thinking?*

Praise God, Gabe and her sons had been outside and not witnessed her tantrum. The One who really counted, the One she'd given her life to, had heard every thought and seen every deed. Lena rubbed her arms; the guilt of her sin made her feel dirty. She thought she could resolve her temper without bothering God. One more time she'd failed. How long before she destroyed the affections of her family with her selfishness?

Opening the Bible, she leafed through page after page, reading the notes and underlined passages. Some scripture she had marked; other notes came from Gabe or James. Remembrances of all the nights by the fire listening to her husband read and pray settled upon her as though she'd crawled up into God's lap.

Choking back her tears, Lena continued turning the pages of the Bible, allowing His Word to soothe her troubled spirit. The book of Romans graced her fingers; the first verse of chapter eight she had memorized as a girl: "There is therefore now no condemnation to them which are in Christ Jesus, who walk not after the flesh, but after the Spirit."

But I am walking after the flesh by not turning over my anger to the Lord. My rebellion is displeasing to the One who has given me life.

Catching her breath, Lena shivered. How could she expect to please God on her own? She must give Him her struggles at this very moment.

Heavenly Father, You have blessed me far more than I could ever imagine. I'm sorry for not giving You my problem with anger. In the whole six months Gabe and I have been married, not once has he ever raised his voice or initiated an argument. It's always been me. Take this burden from me, I pray, for without You, I will only sin more and more. Amen.

Closing the Bible and laying it on the table, she proceeded to tidy up from breakfast. Peace lifted her spirit. No longer did she feel sick or angry, but instead, she prayed about the problems plaguing Gabe in regard to his mother. The woman must have hurt him deeply for him not to want her mentioned. Poor Gabe. Such a good, sweet man. He'd given her, Caleb, and Simon his devotion without asking for anything in return.

With a new resolve to live every moment of her life totally for her Father, Lena determined never to confront Gabe with any questions about his past. Let him come to her if he desired to talk. Until then, she'd pray for peace in his soul.

At noon she carried a basket of corn bread, newly churned butter, apple butter, boiled eggs, and a slab of ham along with a jug of buttermilk and another one of water to the fields. Gabe must be starved by now. They'd fared well during the winter with plenty of food—although they'd all gotten tired of cornmeal and molasses. With spring here, she could gather fresh greens, elderberries, and chokeberries. Later on in the summer, fresh vegetables would add variety to their diets. And as always, everything would be dried for the next winter.

During the morning, Gabe had plowed with a vengeance, completing more rows than he thought possible. Dagget said the corn should be planted by the twentieth of May to ensure its being knee-high by July fourth. At this rate, he'd be done with time to spare.

All the while he deliberated on the way he'd spoken to Lena the previous night. She'd meant nothing by her innocent remark, and he'd lashed out at her unfairly. If he admitted the truth, Lena should be told about his mother. The woman who had given him birth might have gone to her grave, but the wounds still drew blood. Not a day went by that he didn't ponder something she'd said or done. This pattern of action made him think he hadn't truly forgiven her.

Lena had allowed God to work through her. She said and did the right things to instill self-confidence in everything he did. Every day he looked forward to what God had planned for him and his family. Lena loved him, and he loved her. The doubts he'd experienced in the beginning about her fidelity grew less and less as he viewed her true spirit. She trusted him, and he needed to trust her.

Gabe chuckled despite his grievous thoughts. His Lena had a temper. Feisty, that one. She'd warned him repeatedly about her outbursts, but he hadn't seen much of them. He enjoyed her free spirit. *I bet she's boiling over this morning.* The thought saddened him. Any repercussion from last night clearly was his fault.

He had to apologize, but in doing so he had to reveal the truth of his past. *Can I tell a portion of my life without revealing the entire story?* The answer came as softly as the breeze cooling his tired face. Truth didn't mean dissecting what he comfortably could and could not state.

Gabe stretched his neck and stared at the sun straight up in the sky. Glancing toward the house, he saw Lena edging toward him, carrying a basket. Bless her. He didn't deserve her bringing him food. An urgency knocked at his heart.

Lord, I'm afraid I haven't given You the past—not completely. I realize now if I had allowed You to share my pain, I would have been able to tell Lena about Mother. Take the bitterness from me and use my past to Your glory.

Shifting the reins around his shoulders and giving Turnip a pat, he proceeded to plow the row that brought him closer to his wife. Suddenly, the burden didn't seem so heavy.

Lena and Gabe met at the end of the row—she with her basket of food and he wearing an apology on his lips. Halting the mule, he dropped the leather pieces to his side and approached her. She wore a timid smile, a quivering smile. He felt lower than the dirt he plowed to submission beneath his feet.

"Lena," he said, "I apologize for the way I spoke to you last night, and in my self-pity, I neglected to tell you good night or kiss you properly."

She nibbled at her lip. "Would you like to kiss me now?"

"I smell of sweat and the mule."

"That's a farmer's smell." Lena offered a half smile. "I love my farmer." She set the basket onto the ground and reached out for him.

Gabe enveloped her in his arms, and she clung to him as though they'd been apart for days. He bent to claim her lips, tenderly at first, then more fervently than their first night together. At last, he drew himself back. "I never meant to hurt you. You are the sunshine to me each morning and the vivid colors of sunset each night."

"I wish I could state things as wonderfully as you," she whispered. "You make me feel special—pretty and pleasing."

"And you are; you always will be."

Her shoulders fell, and she shook her head. "I'm sorry for all the wicked things I thought about you," she whispered. "And the things I threw."

He could not disguise his smile. "What did you throw?"

She swallowed hard. "A ham bone, but I picked it up and brought it for Turnip."

Gabe roared with laughter.

"No, please," she said, her eyes misting. "You don't understand. That bone is what brought about my prayer giving God my horrible temper." She stared up at him. "I did it, Gabe. I surrendered my anger to the Lord."

Once more pulling her close, he realized he had not been the only one to confess sin this day. "His ears must be filled with the Hunters from Nebraska. The Lord and I had a talk of our own."

She waited patiently, a look of curiosity and love glowing from the luminous green pools of her eyes.

He lifted the basket. "Let's eat, and I will tell you all about it."

The food tasted wonderful, and the talk between them was light and flirtatious. Gabe knew he masked the serious conversation about to evolve, but the Lord promised to be his strength.

"Are you ready to hear a story?" he asked, wiping a spot of apple butter from Lena's lip.

"I always like a good story."

"This one has a remarkable ending."

"I'm ready, Gabe, for whatever you want to tell me."

He nodded and lifted his gaze to the heavens for a quick prayer before he began with the story only his heavenly Father knew. "My mother never knew my father. She worked at a brothel in Philadelphia. . .an exquisite woman whose parents were from Norway. I remember she had hair the color of the sun and eyes the fairest of blue, but her disposition didn't match." He paused, and Lena reached over to take his hand.

"Mother gave me the last name of Hunters, although I have no idea where she found it. I was an inconvenience and an irritation to her. . .well, her business transactions. At an early age, she left me alone while she worked. She drank to drown her own pain, which only made her even more disagreeable. She took her disappointments with life out on me, and so did many of the gentlemen she brought home. I quickly became their whipping boy. The tongue-lashings and beatings were unbearable until I learned to believe I deserved them for whatever reason they gave me." Gabe covered the hand touching his. "I know you've seen the scars on my back, and I thank you for not mentioning them before."

Huge tears rolled down her cheeks, and he hastily added, "Don't cry. This has a happy ending, remember?" With a deep breath he continued. "As I grew older, I became absorbed with learning. School was the perfect diversion for the abuse at home. However, when the other students discovered where I lived and what my mother did, I became the brunt of their ridicule. So I buried myself even deeper into my books. I grew infatuated with words. Their meanings gave me power, and that's when I started using them to fight back. No one else might have comprehended their meanings, but I did. It gave me an opportunity to consider myself better than the ones who shunned me.

"About the time I turned sixteen, Mother purchased the brothel and became the madam of the largest establishment of its type in Philadelphia. She enlisted me to work there, do her books, and keep her records straight. Also at the same age, I received a Bible from a well-meaning group of ladies from a nearby church who aspired to reform everyone living within the confines of the brothel. The women didn't want the book, so I began reading it." He paused, and she said nothing, as if knowing he would continue.

"Shortly thereafter, I started attending church. No one knew or cared, for they were all sleeping off the escapades from the night before.

"When I turned twenty, Mother developed a cough. The doctors couldn't find a cure. Her only temporary relief came from medication that she began to rely on as much as the alcohol. Remember when Dagget asked about giving little Mary paregoric, and I told him about the woman who became addicted to laudanum? That was Mother. By the time I reached thirty, she had to be nursed day and night."

"And you took care of her?" Lena asked.

"Yes. She depended solely on me. I resented it at first, but the Lord kept dealing with me until I forgave her—at least I thought I did. But the bitterness stayed with me." He squeezed her hand. "That's why becoming a husband and father meant so much to me. I had to make up for what had been done to me."

Lena nodded, the tears glistening on her face. He brushed them aside. "I understand, Gabe. I really do. You are a wonderful father."

"But a true miracle happened right here on this farm—the blessings of love. You have no idea of the joy that filled my soul the first time Caleb and Simon called me Pa. I would have died a happy man right then. But your love has been the finest treasure of all. God gave me all these gifts, but I could not release my resentment until this morning." He reached up to touch her cheek. "And my story has such a beautiful ending. I have the richest of blessings at my fingertips."

Chapter 19

*L*ena wept with Gabe until they began to tease each other about their puffy and reddened eyes. *We are a pair, Gabe Hunters, you and I.*

"You look like you've been in a fight and lost," Lena accused, blowing her nose on his clean handkerchief—one of the items from Philadelphia that he still insisted upon carrying.

He lifted a brow. "And who rammed their fist into your face, Miss Blow-Your-Nose-Like-a-Honking-Goose?"

She wiggled her shoulders to feign annoyance. "My nose, sir? I thought we were talking about your eyes. Maybe Turnip threw the punches."

He drew her into his arms and kissed the tip of her nose. "Promise me we will always have laughter," he whispered. "I want us to talk, to cry together, even to argue from time to time, and always to laugh."

Laughter. Yes, what a true blessing. He'd never laughed so much in his entire life.

"I'll do my best," she said with a smile. "You are much more handsome with a smile on your face." She took a deep breath. "Although today was necessary, too."

"I agree," he replied. "I'm insistent about urging the boys and you to discuss your thoughts and feelings, but I'm not always so quick to adhere to the same advice."

"I really am sorry for your unhappy childhood," Lena said seriously. "We had our good times and bad, but my memories are sweet."

He stared at the fields, at the cabin, and then at her. "When I reflect on it, I can't help but see the good resulting from those days."

"You mean your compassion for people? For children?"

"Yes. I could have easily drifted into Mother's manner of living and not come to know God."

"Did she ever accept Jesus as her Savior?"

He picked up a clod of dirt and sent it soaring across the plowed field. "I don't know if she ever asked Him to rule her life or not. I talked to her about the Lord and read to her from the Bible, but I never knew if she actually made a decision."

Silence held them captive. Lena felt eternally grateful for the day. They'd both shed ugly garments that threatened not only their relationship with the Lord but also their happiness as husband and wife.

"I have something else to tell you," Gabe said. "I hope when I've finished you won't feel I have deceived you in any way."

She stared at him curiously.

"Mother died a wealthy woman, which meant I inherited the brothel and an exorbitant amount of money. I dissolved the business, in case you wondered." He glanced teasingly at her. "And I donated the building to a church, which now uses it as an orphanage. After praying through what God wanted me to do with the rest of the funds, I gave to several churches and deposited the balance in a Philadelphia bank. When the time comes, we will be able to provide funds for Caleb and Simon's education. There is plenty there to expand the farm when we're ready and for other unforeseen expenses. Someday, I'd like to take you on a trip, anywhere you want to venture."

Lena felt the color drain from her face. "Why ever would you want a poor widow when you could have had so much more?"

"God had a plan, dearest. A very pleasant one, I might add. However, I do believe I gained more than money from my adventure in Nebraska."

"I'm so very lucky," she whispered.

He gave her the smile meant only for her. "Nonsense. I am the fortunate one."

My dear, sweet husband. You try so hard. "Want to know my thoughts and feelings right now?" she asked.

"Most certainly."

She closed her eyes. "I want a kiss, a very nice long one."

"I can oblige."

"Not just right now, Gabe. I want one every day for the rest of our lives."

"I can still oblige."

"Even if we've quarreled or the things around us threaten our joy in the Lord and in each other?" she asked, tracing his lips with her fingertip. "No matter if snow blizzards keep us inside for days, or rain forgets to fall, or grasshoppers eat the very clothes we wear, or Caleb and Simon disappoint us?"

"I promise to oblige."

"Good; let's begin now."

"How far is this town you're talking about?" Gabe asked, teasing Caleb and Simon about the three-mile walk to see a prairie dog town. They'd gone to church earlier, and the boys had been pestering him for days to visit this spot. "Is there a hotel? A sheriff? I'm really thirsty, too."

Lena giggled. He glanced her way as they walked and captured a loving gaze. She still looked pale from being ill that morning, but the color had returned to her cheeks. She'd been perfectly fine the night before. The idea of his precious wife—or any of his family—falling prey to one of the many illnesses tearing through this land alarmed him. He squeezed her hand, sending love messages from his heart to hers.

A year ago he'd received her first letter. So much had happened since then. God had transformed him into a new man, taken away his selfishness, and worked continually to mold him into a godly husband and father. *Thank You, God, for the gift of family and their love.*

"It's not much farther, Pa," Caleb said. "We have to be quiet, because once they sense we're around, they stop chattering and disappear."

"And what do they say?" Gabe asked. "Don't believe I've ever had a conversation with a prairie dog."

Simon frowned and shook his head. "You don't understand what they're saying; you just know they're talking to each other."

Lena nibbled at her lip, no doubt to keep from laughing. "Simon, why don't you tell him what they look like?"

"That's right. I haven't seen a good picture in one of my books." Gabe grinned. "Are they as big as Turnip?"

"No, sir," Simon replied. "Be glad we left him at home 'cause he'd scare them down into their holes."

"They live in holes? I thought they lived in a town."

Simon shook his head in what appeared to be exasperation. "Prairie dogs are smaller than rabbits. They live under the ground, but we call them towns. When you see them, they sit on their back legs and wave their front legs like arms. Then they talk to each other. Remember how Miss Nettie Franklin used her arms when she talked that Sunday in church about drinking whiskey being a sin?"

How well I remember. I thought Judge Hoover would burst since he owns the town's saloon. "She was quite demonstrative that day and quite successful in gaining everyone's attention."

"Gabe," Lena whispered. "Let's not encourage Simon."

He winked at his wife. "Go ahead, Simon."

"Well, that's how those prairie dogs look when they are talking to each other, flapping their arms as if they are pointing out something that really matters."

"Hush, Simon," Caleb said. "We're almost there, and I don't want Pa to miss them."

The four moved ahead, being careful not to make a sound. In the distance, Gabe heard chattering—like a squirrel convention. As he inched closer with his family right beside him, he saw the humorous stance of the peculiar animals. They *did* resemble Nettie, and he stifled a laugh. What a town, indeed!

Suddenly, the animated creatures detected humans and dived into their burrowed homes. Nothing remained but the doorways into their dwellings.

"Doesn't appear to be a good town to ride through," Gabe remarked a short time later, "especially if your horse stepped through one of those holes."

"True," Lena replied. "Of course, there are a few people towns too dangerous for decent folk to walk through, too."

"Is my philosophical nature rubbing off on you, dear?" Gabe asked, slipping his hand from hers to wrap it around her waist.

"Oh no," Simon moaned. "Does that mean Ma is going to start using all those big words, too?"

"I might," she said with a tilt of her head. "Do you mind?"

The little boy's eyes widened, and he stared at his brother. "What do you think, Caleb?"

"Might be all right. Ma could take over teaching school for Amanda." His eyes sparkled mischievously, so much like his mother.

"That wouldn't do at all," Simon quickly replied. "Pa needs her at home. She wouldn't be happy teaching school, and then she'd be too tired to cook supper."

"And I'd miss her," Gabe added. "Amanda will have to keep the job until the town finds someone else."

Chapter 20

*G*abe stared up at the sky. Black clouds swirled, and the rumble of distant thunder with a flash of lightning intensified nature's threat. Storms and high winds he could handle, and he'd learned that when it rained, the household items had to be shifted from one side of the cabin to the other—depending on the direction of the rainfall. But the green color spreading across the horizon bothered him.

Glancing at the barn anchored deep into the earth, he wondered if Lena and the boys would be safer there than in the soddy. Although the walls of their home were nearly three feet thick, a twister could still do a lot of damage.

With a heavy sigh, he wished Caleb and Simon were home from school. He focused his attention to the east, straining to see if they were heading this way. Nothing. A gust of wind nearly toppled him over. *This is not merely prairie winds, but a malevolent act of nature.*

Gabe wondered if he should set the mule and horses free to run with the cattle until after the storm, but if his family were safer in the barn, then those animals would be, too. The cattle were contained in barbed-wire fencing. Of course, that could be easily blown down.

With a heavy sigh, he realized they'd had a good spring. The corn stood more than a foot high, and they'd been blessed with ample rain. He hadn't considered he might lose a crop. Suddenly, all those days of work twisted through him. Lena's words about the Lord providing for their needs echoed through his ears.

This spring, tornadoes had always managed to venture far from them—until now.

Drenched in sweat, he stepped outside and studied the southwest sky. In a matter of minutes, the temperature had dropped, and the wind had increased its velocity. *Where are Caleb and Simon?* Then he saw his sons racing home against a background of a hideous green sky. The closer they came, the better he felt.

Thank You, Lord. I didn't mind You taking care of them, but I feel much better knowing where they are.

"Gabe," Lena called from the doorway. "This looks bad, and I'm worried about the boys."

"They're coming," he replied above the wind. "I see them. Are we safer in the barn?"

"I think so." She scanned the sky, then shouted, "Hurry!" to Caleb and Simon, although Gabe doubted the boys could hear their mother's call. By the time they'd all scurried into the barn, huge droplets of rain pelted the earth. Ear-splitting cracks of thunder resounded, and jagged streaks of lightning split the sky.

"I saw a twister touch down in the distance," Caleb managed to say, trying to catch his breath. "Looked to be heading this way."

Gabe skirted his family to the farthest corner of the barn cradled deep into the hill. He positioned the horses and mule in front of them in case of flying debris. The structure had been built facing the east, which gave him some comfort in their safety. He moved to the opening, seeking some sign of the twister. "It might miss us," he said, watching the wind tug at the roof of the cabin.

"We'll know soon enough," Lena shouted. "Gabe, please don't stand out there. You don't have any idea how the wind could snatch you up."

"I'm being careful." His gaze fixed southwest to where a dark funnel cloud moved their way. The fury of nature left him in awe. One minute it showered his crops with water, and the next it threatened to beat them to the ground.

As the twister soared across the fields, a roar, like the bellowing of a huge beast, sent a tingle from his neck to his spine. This was not a time to stand outside and challenge the wind. Foolishness invited a loss of life—his own.

"Gabe!" Lena called frantically.

"I'm coming," he replied, moving back.

Huddled against his family, Gabe listened to the creature spin closer. "I hope all of you are praying," he said. "Not only for us, but for others in the twister's path."

They didn't reply. His request didn't warrant one. In the shadows, he couldn't see the emotion on their faces, but from the way Lena, Caleb, and Simon trembled beneath his arms, he knew fright penetrated their bones.

"Aren't you afraid, Pa?" Simon whispered shakily.

"Of course I am. But God is in control, and at times like these we have to hold on to our faith."

"Wish I could see Him," Caleb said.

"You can, Son. God's in the quiet summer day, the blizzards last winter, and the wind outside. Close your eyes, and you can feel Him wrapping His love around you."

Lena squeezed his hand, and he brushed a kiss across her cheek. "I love you," she said. "Seems like you always say the right things to make us feel better."

He forced a chuckle. "I'll remember that the next time I slip and use those long words you so despise."

A deafening crash of thunder caused Simon to jump and snuggle closer. "If I had known we all were going to be this close, I'd have taken my bath before Saturday night," Gabe said.

Caleb laughed in reply. *Thank You, Lord, for Your comfort. Keep us in the shelter of Your wings. Peace, be still. Amen.*

As ferocious as the storm sounded, the wind finally ceased to howl and left only a steady fall of rain in its wake. Gabe released his family. He was grateful they were unharmed. Now he needed to see what had been done outside. Swallowing hard, he made his way to the front of the barn. Although the rain continued to fall, he could see the cabin stood with only minor roof damage. He glanced to the fields surrounding them. They looked untouched except for one in the direct path of the tornado. The corn planted there bent to the ground as if paying homage to a wicked wind god, but perhaps the stalks might right themselves in the next few days. Even if that didn't happen and the field of corn perished, they'd survive.

Sometimes he thought his optimism masked good sense, but he always tried to buffer his decisions with logic. Leading his family was often. . .

Gabe searched for the proper word. Glancing back at the boys, he knew exactly what fit. Hard. Just plain hard. What a relief to know God held the world in the palm of His hand.

He felt Lena touch his shoulder. "Do you suppose we should check on the Shafers?"

He nodded. "I also need to make sure the cattle fared well, but I can do that on the way there. Any chance of the twister changing directions and heading back this way?"

She sighed. "Doubtful, though I've seen two touch down in the same day."

"We'll wait until the sky clears." He clasped the hand on his shoulder. "The Shafers' dugouts are in bad shape. I know Dagget plans to build a soddy once harvest is over."

"Amanda told me. She's very excited. Dugouts don't last much longer than seven years, and Dagget built that one ten years ago."

"Sure hope the twister didn't step up his plans," Gabe said, glancing at the distant sky in the Shafers' direction. It looked menacing in a mixture of dark blue and green.

The tornado had laid waste to the dugouts and fencing of Dagget's farm. From what Gabe could tell, the wind had hit them as if they were a child's toys.

"Hello!" he called, stepping down from the wagon. "Dagget, it's Gabe and Lena and the boys."

A pool of water streaming from the door indicated the inside trench used to keep out the abundance of water had overflowed. What a mess for them to endure.

The door swung open, and Amanda stepped out along with some of her brothers and Mary. "We're all right," she called, "but Pa and Charles rode out this morning to check on fences and haven't returned."

Gabe's insides twisted with fear. He didn't like the sound of those two out in that storm. Dagget had changed considerably since their first encounter. He'd become a caring man and wouldn't endanger his family. "Which way did they go, Amanda?"

She pointed to the southwest. "That way."

Lena nudged him. He hadn't noticed when she'd climbed down from the wagon. "I'll stay and see what I can do here. Why don't you go look for them?"

Their gazes met. She obviously felt the same concern he did. "The wagon might be necessary," he said.

She nodded, her thoughts evident in the lines of her face. "Do you want to take Caleb?"

Gabe studied the growing boy, now twelve years old. In some cultures he'd be considered a man. Still, he'd like to shelter him for as long as possible from the ugliness of the world.

"I'd like to go, Pa," Caleb said. "I'm nearly as tall as you, and I could help."

Placing a hand on the boy's shoulder, Gabe silently agreed. Life's lessons could be a difficult lot, but he'd rather they occur while Caleb was with him than for the boy to learn on his own.

The sheared path before them looked like someone had taken a razor to the field. To the right, barbed wire stood untouched. Cattle grazed peacefully on their left.

"Do you suppose Mr. Shafer and Charles are dead?" Caleb asked as the wagon ambled on.

Gabe's heart plummeted. "I don't know, Son, but we'll deal with whatever we find. Dagget and Charles know this country, and I'm sure they read the signs of the twister."

"I remember when my first pa died," Caleb went on. "He just went to sleep and didn't wake up."

I hope if God has taken them home, we don't find their bodies mangled. A vision of the wolves crossed his mind. He had the rifle. By now the sun shone through the clouds, and the sky gave no hint of rain or the earlier violence. Calm. Peaceful.

Within the hour, Gabe spotted Charles on the trodden grass, bending over his father. "I believe we've found them," he said, breaking the silence.

"Mr. Shafer must be hurt," Caleb said. "Sure hope he's all right."

Gabe merely nodded. Charles had not moved, and he surely had seen and heard the approaching wagon. Once Gabe pulled it to a halt, Charles lifted a tear-stained face.

"Pa's gone," he said with a heavy sigh. "We tried to outrun the twister. I didn't know he'd fallen."

Gabe surmised what else had happened. "Are you hurt?"

"No, sir."

"Can I take a look at your pa?"

Charles swallowed hard. "When I looked back, the twister had picked him up. Then it slammed him into the ground. I thought it had knocked the breath out of him, but his head hit hard."

As Charles moved aside, Gabe saw the blood rushing from Dagget's crown. "Caleb, stay in the wagon for now."

From the looks of him, Dagget had died from the blows to his head. Charles dried his eyes, and together the two lifted Dagget into the back of the wagon while Caleb minded the horses.

Charles said nothing as they drove back to his home. Sorrow etched his young face. Upon seeing his family's farm, he finally spoke. "He's been a good pa since last winter. Before that, I don't know if I'd have grieved so much."

"Now you have good memories," Gabe replied softly.

"I want to bury him beside Ma. He missed her terribly."

"I understand. We'll get the minister and have a proper burial."

Charles wiped his nose with his shirtsleeve. "Thank you, Mr. Hunters. You're a good neighbor."

Gabe startled at the sight of the minister already there when they arrived. He'd ridden out once the twister blew through.

Odd. Why here at the Shafers'? Gabe wondered until he saw the way the man looked at Amanda.

"I should have guessed the reverend would be riding out to check on things," Charles said. "He's taken a fancy to Amanda."

God had already made provision for the Shafers. It appeared to him that Jason Mercer needed that family as much as they needed him.

"Glad you had the foresight to come," Gabe said, shaking the reverend's hand.

"I couldn't let a moment pass without riding out," he replied. "I had a notion something was wrong."

The following morning, Gabe, Charles, and Caleb dug the grave for Dagget. The ceremony was short but meaningful to his family. Dagget had died a good man, filling his life with the things that mattered most— God and his family. Little Mary plucked some goldenrod and laid it atop the mound of dirt.

"For you, Pa," she whispered. "I'll always love you."

Lena edged closer to Gabe and took his hand. He felt her body shudder. For the first time he understood why she fretted over him and the boys. Love didn't stop death; it simply made it harder to say good-bye.

Back at home, Gabe dipped his pen in the inkwell and wrote his reflections about the tornado, then ended his entry with Dagget's death.

Dagget was a good friend. Although we didn't start out this way, the Lord saw fit to bring us together. Lena believes Dagget learned a lot from me, but the truth is he taught me a few valuable lessons. Aside from hunting techniques, which I sorely needed, my friend confided in me about how it felt to love a woman, then lose her. I selfishly pray that when the Lord calls Lena and me home, we go hand in hand. The idea of ever having to part with her sears my soul. And yes, I know God would comfort me, but I'd hate to consider such a separation. This morning as we laid him to rest beside his wife, I wondered if I had thanked him enough for his companionship. Aside from my beloved Lena, Dagget Shafer was my first real friend. God bless him.

Chapter 21

*L*ena finished covering the rhubarb cobbler with a cloth. Caleb had taken a ham and a beef roast to the wagon, and Gabe carried a huge pot of greens. She corked the crockery jug filled with fresh buttermilk and glanced about to see if she'd missed anything. Spotting the quilt she'd set aside to spread out for their lunch, she snatched it up and wrapped it around the jug.

Taking a deep breath, she massaged the small of her back and blinked back the weariness threatening to creep into the eventful day—to say nothing of the queasiness attacking her stomach. *I have to tell Gabe soon. As observant as he is, I can't believe he doesn't already know.*

"Is there anything else?" Gabe asked from the doorway.

Instantly she drew her hands away from her back to gather up the food. "Just what I have here."

"You certainly look pretty this morning. Do weddings and house raisings always brighten your cheeks?" He warmed her heart with his irresistible smile.

I'm pregnant, Gabe, and tonight I'll tell you. "My, how you toy with a woman's affections, Mr. Hunters. I'm overcome with your flattery."

He winked and snatched up the jug and cobbler. "I'll remember those sentiments."

She blushed and giggled. For a grown woman, sometimes the way Gabe made her feel like a schoolgirl nearly embarrassed her.

Today promised to be such fun. Amanda Shafer and the Reverend Jason Mercer were married yesterday morning, just one month after Dagget had died. The young minister declared his intentions shortly after the funeral, promising all that he'd see to raising the Shafer children. Today the community gathered together to build them a sod cabin.

Lena tingled with excitement. The mere thought of visiting with the women all day long pushed aside the sickness that had plagued her since earlier that morning. She'd stopped telling Gabe about the morning wave of illness until she knew for sure she carried their baby. The poor man didn't suspect a thing. She touched her stomach. The thought of new life, another child for Gabe, filled her with anticipation. But along with the joy came the reality of how lucky she'd been to give birth to two healthy boys who had aged beyond the critical years. She prayed her new baby would also thrive in this hard country.

Enough of these silly worries! Gabe will be so happy!

The wagon ride to the Shafers', now the Mercers' and Shafers', seemed bumpier than usual, or perhaps the jolt rocked her queasy stomach. She continued to smile, praying her stomach to calm. Caleb and Simon hadn't done this to her. Perhaps she carried a girl. What a sweet, delicious thought.

With the musings rolling delightfully around in her head, she pushed away the sickness threatening to send her sprawling into the dirt. She could hear Gabe now—crowing like a lone rooster in a chicken house. And the boys, they'd be wonderful big brothers.

"Are you feeling all right?" Gabe asked, reaching over to take her hand into his.

Does he know? "I'm very happy," she replied.

"Happiness doesn't make one pale—or get sick."

Sometimes. "I'm perfectly fine," she assured him and reached over to plant a kiss on his cheek. "Today will be such fun. I can hardly wait."

"I agree. You can socialize with all the women while we men build Amanda and the reverend's new home."

She laughed. "Are you wanting to trade places?"

"Absolutely not. Besides, you spent three years laboring in man's work, and I plan to do everything in my power to make sure your life never involves that again. Women's chores are difficult enough."

"You're too good to me. I'm not so sure I deserve you." She grinned up at the early morning sun. Birthing babies was hard work, but it was a whole sight easier than farming or building cabins. "I hope it's not too late when we get home today."

"It's hard to tell, Lena. Being new to this, I don't know how long it will take to construct the cabin, but I imagine a good many folks will show up to help."

She nodded, busily forming the words she'd use to tell Gabe about the baby. *"Have you ever thought about a child of your own?"* No, he considers Caleb and Simon his own. Maybe, *"Wouldn't it be grand to have a little one?"* Or, *"Do you think you could build a cradle?"* The thought of holding an infant again and watching him or her grow filled her with joy. God certainly had blessed her over and beyond what she'd ever imagined.

Gabe and Lena were among the first workers at the building site. Amanda and the reverend had chosen an area beyond the dugout to construct their home. Like so many other farmers, they planned to use the dugout for a barn as long as it stood. Gabe didn't think it would last beyond another winter.

Eager to get started, Gabe helped Lena unload the wagon.

"Go on, get going," she said with a laugh. "Simon can help me. Never saw a man in my life who loved work more than you."

He leaned closer. "Oh, there're a few things I enjoy more."

She blushed and glanced about them. "Gabe Hunters, someone will hear you!"

Gabe grinned at his wife and watched her and Simon unload food onto a makeshift table. He grabbed two spades for himself and Caleb and trekked toward the other men busy at work. The sod house would be approximately sixteen feet wide by twenty feet long, the size of most all the sod houses. Amanda claimed it would be a mansion in comparison to what she and her siblings were accustomed to.

"Mornin', Gabe, Caleb," a neighboring man greeted.

"Morning," he replied. Riley O'Connor walked with the man, but he didn't acknowledge Gabe or look his way.

I'm going to try to be civil. He can't help being lonely.

They hurried to a field of thick, strong sod where a few men turned over furrows for the sod bricks. Gabe watched in earnest, for he wanted to build a barn in the fall. He and Caleb helped trim the bricks to three feet long and two feet wide, understanding they must be equally cut to ensure straight, solid walls.

"Sure glad you taught me how important it is to know arithmetic," Caleb said, measuring a sod brick with a piece of string Lena had cut for the occasion.

"Never underestimate the value of education," Gabe replied, tossing his elder son a grin. "Although experience is important, too."

They shared a laugh, and as they worked side by side, Gabe reminded Caleb of the fall and winter and all the lessons the family had to teach him. There had been so much for Gabe to learn, and plenty more remained ahead.

The cabin raising went fairly quickly. The first row of bricks was laid along the foundation line, with younger children and some of the women filling the gaps with mud as mortar. Every third layer was laid crosswise to enforce the structure and bind it all together. They set in frames for a door and two windows and put aside sod to secure them later on. Shortly after noon, the walls stood nearly high enough for the roof, but tantalizing aromas from the food tables caused them all to stop and eat.

"Are you enjoying the day?" Gabe asked Lena, handing her his tin plate. He'd eaten in a rush so he could get back to work. As soon as all the men were finished, the women and children would share in the food.

Her eyes sparkled. "This is better than a church social. We've all brought Amanda gifts for her new home, and she's so very happy."

"What has she gotten?" Gabe asked curiously.

"Food, scented soap, embroidered pillowcases and handkerchiefs, a corn husk basket, and some fabric scraps for a quilt. The poor girl has never known anyone to care for her like the reverend, and combined with the cabin and all, she's a little beside herself."

He stood and brushed the corn bread crumbs from his hands. "My compliments to all the women for their fine cooking." He winked and brushed her cheek with his thumb. How lovely she looked, his Lena. Her cheeks were tinted a rosy pink, reminding him of wildflowers blossoming in the sun. The sky had seemed to dance with color, but not nearly as brilliant as the light in her eyes. "I love you," he whispered.

She wrinkled her nose. "I have something to tell you."

"And what is that?"

"Well, I—"

"Hey, Gabe, if you're done, how about giving me a hand with framing the roof?" a neighboring farmer called. "Since the preacher's gone to the trouble of having lumber hauled in, the least we can do is get it up right."

"I'll be right there." Gabe glanced at his wife, waiting for her to speak.

"I'll tell you later." Lena laughed. "The news can wait."

Gabe saw Caleb eating with a young man, laughing and talking, but at the sound of the neighbor's voice, Caleb glanced up.

"Finish your meal, Son. You've worked hard today." He remembered his own longing for a companion when he was Caleb's age and how much he valued the friendships in Nebraska. Yes, he was a fairly lucky man, as they said in Nebrasky.

Leaning against the wagon, Lena crossed her arms and fought a wave of dizziness. She hadn't been able to eat all day for fear of being sick. Mercy, those boys hadn't made her ill like this, but soon she'd be four months along, and the sickness should leave.

"Are you all right?" Nettie Franklin asked. She'd helped Lena put her things back into the wagon.

"I'm fine," Lena assured her.

"You're pale, and I see you didn't eat a thing."

Lena nodded, nearly overflowing to tell someone about the baby. "Can you keep a secret for a day?"

The young woman quickly moved to her side. Her large, expressive eyes widened. "On a stack of Bibles, I'll keep a secret."

"I'm pregnant," Lena mouthed and looked around to make sure no one else had heard.

Nettie giggled. As the local midwife, she had a right to know about future babies. "So Gabe doesn't know?"

"Not yet. I started to tell him a few minutes ago, but Hank Culpepper hollered at him to come help with the roof." Lena wiggled her shoulders; the excitement of actually telling someone about the baby made her want to shout. "But I will tonight—if I don't bust first."

"Have you been sick much?"

Lena squeezed shut her eyes. "Every morning. What amazes me is Gabe usually doesn't miss a thing, and he has yet to question me. I can't believe he hasn't guessed it."

Nettie hugged her shoulders. "I'm so happy for you. What a blessing."

Suddenly, Lena felt her stomach roll. "What is that horrible smell?"

They looked to the cooking fire where a kettle of beans still simmered, but with the offensive odor Lena felt certain they'd burned.

The two scurried to pull the kettle from the fire. Another whiff of the beans sent Lena's stomach and head spinning. She swallowed the bile rising in her throat and blinked repeatedly to stop the dizziness. Blackness surrounded her. Nettie screamed for help just as Lena's world grew dark.

Gabe wiped the sweat from his brow with the back of his shirt. Water would quench his powerful thirst. Besides, he was curious over Lena's news. He looked about and saw there was a lull in the work right now, too. Maybe he could take this opportunity to satisfy both desires.

"Be right back," Gabe called out, thinking how his vocabulary had shrunk since last October. But he fit in with these farmers, because now he belonged.

Lifting his hat to cool his head, Gabe headed toward the spot where he'd left Lena. Some kind of commotion had drawn the ladies' attention. Rounding a group of wagons, he moved closer.

Suddenly, Gabe felt the color drain from his face. All of his worst nightmares and misgivings about his wife were realized vividly in front of his eyes. Rage seethed from the pores of his flesh.

Lena lay in the arms of Riley O'Connor.

Chapter 22

hat is going on here?" Gabe bellowed. He clenched his fist, ready to send it through those pearly white teeth.

The crowd of women around Lena and Riley instantly hushed and made way for Gabe to reach his wife. He'd tear Riley apart with his bare hands. So this was Lena's news! All those words of love and endearing smiles meant nothing to her. *Lord, help me!*

"Riley, what are you doing with my wife?" he shouted.

Riley looked up. Surprise swept across his face. Gabe took a glimpse at Lena, who moved slightly in Riley's arms. She looked pale, ghastly pale, but no wonder. She'd been discovered.

"Answer me, man." Gabe pushed his way through the mounting crowd. The women gasped. If they wanted to see a fight, then he'd give them one.

"Listen, Gabe. It's not what you think."

He held his breath and attempted to control his rapid breathing.

Nettie rushed to his side. "No, Gabe. This is not what it seems. Lena fainted, and if it hadn't been for Riley, she'd have fallen into the fire."

His head pounded. Had he heard correctly?

"That's right, Hunters," Riley said. "I caught her before she fell. Nothing else."

"Gabe," Lena moaned. "Where's Gabe?"

Emotion clawed at his throat and threatened to choke him alive. Riley lifted Lena into Gabe's arms without a word. She felt light, fragile. "Lena, are you all right?" He didn't care that most of Archerville gawked at him. He'd already made a fool of himself—not once thinking about Lena, but only of himself. "I'm so sorry I shouted."

"I didn't hear a thing," she said and wet her lips. "I don't remember what happened to me, just got dizzy."

"Well, I'm getting you home and to bed. Tomorrow I'm riding to North Bend for the doctor. No more of this."

"No. It's not necessary. I'm fine, really." She stirred slightly, but he could see through her ploy. "This is natural, Gabe. The sickness will pass."

"What do you mean, the sickness will. . ." He heard Nettie laugh, then slowly the other women began to laugh. "Are we? I mean, are you?"

Lena smiled and reached up to touch his face. "Yes, Gabe. We're going to have a baby."

"Ah, wh–when?"

"Mid-December."

He let out a shout that resembled a war whoop he'd heard at a Wild West show back east.

"Gabe Hunters," she said with a laugh. "You sound just like a Nebrasky farmer."

On December 10, Gabe paced the cabin floor while Caleb and Simon stared into the fire. Lena had labored with the baby for nearly four hours, and he'd had enough. She didn't cry out, but he'd heard her whimperings. Outside, the night was exceptionally cold, although only a sprinkling of snow lay on the ground.

"How much longer?" Caleb asked, breaking the silence from the ticking clock above the fireplace.

"Soon," Gabe muttered. "Can't be much longer."

He went back to pacing, keeping time with the clock. In the next moment, he heard a cry. He stopped cold and stared at the quilt leading into their bedroom.

"You have a girl, Gabe Hunters!" Nettie Franklin called. "A healthy baby girl!"

"Can I come in now?" he asked, frozen in his spot. "I want to see my wife and baby."

"Not just yet. Give me a moment," Nettie replied. "Oh, she's right pretty, but no hair."

Gabe waited for what he believed was an hour. Suddenly, he couldn't contain his excitement a moment longer. He pushed through the quilt, his gaze drinking in the sight of his lovely Lena and the red-faced baby in her arms.

"She's beautiful," he whispered, tears springing to his eyes. "And you're beautiful." He kissed Lena's damp forehead, then her lips, before kneeling beside the bed.

Lena glanced up from staring into the baby's face. "Thank You, Lord," she whispered.

"Amen," he said, gingerly picking up a perfect, tiny hand. The awe of this miracle left him speechless. He memorized every bit of the tiny face, then kissed the baby's cheek. "I love you, Lena. You never cease to fill my days with joy."

"And I love you. She looks like you."

"Oh, I want her to look like you."

"Nonsense. She has your eyes and chin. They're just like her father's. I certainly hope she doesn't have my temper."

Gabe chuckled. "I want my daughter to have spunk."

"I'll settle for spunk. What shall we name her?" Lena asked.

He pressed his lips together. "Hmm. How do you feel about naming her after our mothers?"

Her eyes widened. "I think that's a wonderful idea."

"I've been thinking the best way for me to honor my mother is to name my daughter after her. What was your mother's name?"

"Cynthia."

"Cynthia Marie. What do you think?"

"Perfect," Lena said with a smile.

"Caleb, Simon. Come on in and meet Miss Cynthia Marie Hunters, your new sister."

Gabe's eyes pooled with joy. The Lord had showered him with so many blessings—surely something he'd never have known from books. The intensity of his feelings for Lena and his family spread through him like sweet molasses. Never had he expected the love of such a fine woman, or two strapping sons, or the sweetness of an infant daughter. He was happy. He was content. He'd given and received the greatest gift of all.

DiAnn Mills is a bestselling author who believes her readers should expect an adventure. She combines unforgettable characters with unpredictable plots to create action-packed, suspense-filled novels.

Her titles have appeared on the CBA and ECPA bestseller lists; won two Christy Awards; and been finalists for the RITA, Daphne Du Maurier, Inspirational Readers' Choice, and Carol award contests. Library Journal presented her with a Best Books 2014: Genre Fiction award in the Christian Fiction category for Firewall.

DiAnn is a founding board member of the American Christian Fiction Writers; the 2015 president of the Romance Writers of America's Faith, Hope, & Love chapter; a member of Advanced Writers and Speakers Association, and International Thriller Writers. She speaks to various groups and teaches writing workshops around the country. She and her husband live in sunny Houston, Texas.

DiAnn is very active online and would love to connect with readers on any of the social media platforms listed at www.diannmills.com.

Forever Yours

by Tracie Peterson

Dedicated to all the would-be writers out there,
with three supportive suggestions that were once offered to me,
and one extra that I would like to add.

1. Write what you know.
2. Learn what you don't know.
3. Never give up on the dream.
4. Colossians 3:23

Prologue

*R*iotous changes, for which the young country was already famous, ushered in the turn of the century in America. As the 1900s quickly added years and headed into their teens, a fascination grew for things mechanical and complicated. America was hungry for change and innovation, and her people were only too happy to comply.

Among those changes were some that would drastically alter the course of history. Skeptical crowds viewed automobiles and airplanes, never believing the contraptions would retire the horse and buggy. Meanwhile, the warm wonder of electric lighting spread like a fire out of control and soon engulfed the young nation. New carbonated drinks, rising hemlines, and a variety of contraptions and conveniences that baffled the mind were part of the flood that swept the country into young adulthood.

The world was, of course, not without its problems. Racial hatred ran rampant, especially in larger cities in the East. Leonardo da Vinci's "Mona Lisa" was stolen in August of 1911 and not recovered until two years later. And in 1912, the nation mourned in stunned dismay the sinking of the *Titanic*.

In an almost frantic frenzy, Americans pressed forward at such an alarming rate that old-timers questioned the sanity of those younger. Where would it all lead? And how could it possibly be good?

In the unspoiled innocence of the recently admitted state of New Mexico, things were no different from the rest of the country. A hunger was growing for the wealth and wonder of all that their sister states enjoyed. Perhaps the old-timers weren't panting for change like the younger citizens, and maybe the natives looked with contempt on the destruction that always accompanied progress. But in the growing town of Bandelero, New Mexico, the children of its founders were now coming of age, and with this came bold ideas for the years to come.

Chapter 1

*D*aughtry!"

The voice sounded loud and clear from outside the adobe stable.

"In here, Daddy!" a young, auburn-haired woman called. She finished cleaning the hoof she held between her slender, jean-clad legs before making any move to greet her father.

Garrett Lucas bounded into the stable with a look of determined frustration on his face. Now in his mid-fifties, Garrett was still lean and muscular from his years of ranch work. His hair was a salt and pepper brown that he fondly told his children was growing whiter by the minute due to their antics.

"Where have you been?" he asked.

Daughtry patted the back of her horse Poco and moved to put away her grooming equipment. "Daddy, you know very well that I ride before breakfast every single morning. Then I come back here and see to Poco, just like you taught me."

Relief crossed Garrett's face before he nodded to his daughter. "I think you ought to have one of the hands ride out with you," he advised. "Or at least you could ask one of your brothers."

"Daddy! I'm twenty-three years old. When are you going to realize that I'm fully capable of taking care of myself?" Daughtry's voice betrayed the frustration she felt with her father's constant overshadowing protection.

"Just because you're grown doesn't mean I stop worrying about you," Garrett offered by way of apology.

Daughtry sighed and brushed the dirt from her pants. "I know and I'm glad you love me, but I have to have some room to breathe. You have one of the largest ranches in New Mexico to run, so why not concentrate on that and let me go my own way?" Daughtry paused and looked at her father seriously. "Sometimes you and the boys are just more than I care to deal with. I don't know how Mother stands it."

Garrett grinned. "I keep your mother too busy to worry about it. Besides, she likes my keepin' an eye on her."

"Well," Daughtry said, coming forward to place a quick kiss on her father's cheek, "I'm not Mother."

She walked past her father and kept moving toward the adobe-styled ranch house. For all her life Piñon Canyon Ranch had been her home, and all her memories, both good and bad, were enclosed by its boundaries. Now, it seemed more like a prison. The world was changing out there, but here, time seemed to stand still. Her family didn't have electricity, telephones, or automobiles, and often Daughtry had the dreadful feeling that life was passing her by.

"I wish you wouldn't wear your brother's clothes," Garrett said from behind her.

Daughtry stopped in her tracks and turned, and her father quickly covered the distance between them. She fixed an expression on her face that she hoped would prove her determination. They'd argued this before, but she was willing to argue it again.

Garrett sighed. "Okay, I give up. Wear jeans when you work around the ranch. But I better never catch you wearing them into town. They're too revealing, and I won't have every guy there drooling and following you around."

Daughtry laughed. "Oh, Daddy. You are impossible. No man is ever going to drool over me, because you're always two steps behind or in front of me. No gentleman can get close enough to ask my name, much less ogle me."

"Good," Garrett said, putting his arm around his daughter. "Let's keep it that way."

Inside the ranch house, a flurry of activity was managing to create absolute chaos. This was typical of breakfast at the Lucas table, and Maggie Lucas took it all in stride. Maggie was still a fine-looking woman, with a shapely figure and dark auburn hair, and Daughtry so closely resembled her mother that people often mistook them at a quick glance.

When her husband and daughter came into the dining room, arm in arm, Maggie couldn't help but smile. Then, just as quickly, a frown crossed her face as she caught sight of her daughter's grim expression. Garrett was obviously making himself a pest again.

Maggie knew why, but it didn't help matters any. Her own heartfelt grief at the loss of their daughter Julie, almost four years earlier, caused her to sympathize with her husband. When Julie had ridden out on a cold December morning, no one thought that only hours later she would lie dead at the bottom of an icy ravine. Her horse had lost its footing, and Garrett had never forgiven himself for letting Julie ride out alone. Truth be told, Garrett had never stopped blaming himself for the tragedy and had become incessantly more preoccupied with Daughtry's safety. Indeed, his concern had rapidly approached a level of grief all its own, for he knew his inability to protect Daughtry from all of life's many dangers. His grief and frustration threatened to drive Daughtry away from her father and their home.

Daughtry's brothers swarmed around the room. Dolan and Don were arguing, as was typical for the seventeen-year-old twins. Joseph, sixteen, was trying to snag pieces of food off the plates as Anna Maria and Pepita hurried around the table to avoid his reach, and fifteen-year-old Jordan, Jordy to everyone except when he was in trouble, was reading as he walked. No doubt another western. Jordy loved to read them and point out the inaccuracies. There was only one author he held any esteem for and that was Zane Grey.

Finally, Gavin, the oldest of the boys at twenty-one, entered, gave his mother a peck on the cheek, whirled her in a circle, more to clear her out of his way than anything, and took his seat at the table.

"I'm starved!" Gavin fairly roared, then grinned up at his mother who was shaking her head at him.

"Well, if we can get everyone to take a seat," Maggie said, "we'll have breakfast." Nearly in unison, four boys took their seat, leaving Garrett and Daughtry standing.

"Well, come on Sis, Dad," Gavin said, reaching out to take hold of his mother's hand. "Let's pray and eat."

Garrett took his place at the head of the table, while Daughtry went to sit across from her mother. Everyone joined hands, while Garrett blessed the food. When his brief prayer ended, the chaos which had existed earlier died away to civility and calm. Maggie Lucas would tolerate no rowdiness at her table.

Daughtry picked at her food, while all around her, her brothers ate as though they were starving. She was hungry, or at least had been until that morning's episode with her father. How could she ever get him to stop worrying that she was going to die tragically like her sister?

"Aren't you hungry?" Maggie asked her softly.

Six pairs of eyes followed their mother's gaze to see what Daughtry's response would be. Sometimes, she felt as though she held the entire ranch hostage, awaiting her answers. But most of the time, Daughtry felt like she was the hostage.

"I'm fine," she muttered under her breath and continued to pick at the biscuits and gravy on her plate.

"We've got a heap of work cut out for us today," Garrett was telling his sons, and Daughtry let her mind wander, knowing that this would keep everyone occupied for a spell.

Why can't I just get away from here? Her mind reeled at the unspoken question. What she wouldn't give to leave Piñon Canyon. At least for a little while. *I've never even been out of New Mexico,* she thought. *There's a whole world out there that I only know from magazines and books. Will I ever see it? Will I ever be able to enjoy the things other people do?* She was twenty-three years old. An old maid by some standards, not that her father cared. If he had his way about it, she'd stay unmarried and lonely until her dying day.

The boys all seemed to be talking at once, and Daughtry nearly laughed out loud at the thought of being lonely. *How could anyone claim such a feat in this house?* she wondered. But she was. She was lonely and bored and unhappy with her life. She prayed about it often. She read her Bible. She even sought the advice of their longtime family friend, Pastor David Monroe, but nothing seemed to help.

David had suggested she mingle more with people her own age, but every time she tried to do just that, her father would come looking for her. She'd hoped that after a little time had passed and the pain of Julie's death had dimmed, her father and brothers wouldn't be quite so possessive of her. But, if anything, it was more of a problem than ever.

What made matters even worse was that Daughtry and Julie had never been that close—and now Daughtry felt as though her sister was to blame for all her misery. That only managed to add guilt to the loneliness and frustration that already smothered Daughtry.

I miss her, too, Daughtry thought. *Even if we didn't see things eye to eye, she was my sister, and I loved her.* Daughtry looked around her at the family she cared for more than anything or anyone. *I love them all,* she argued with her heart. *But they're killing me!*

"What are you going to do today, Daughtry?"

"Huh?" Daughtry's mind fumbled to recall the question.

Garrett seemed undaunted. "I was just asking what you had planned to do today?"

"Oh," Daughtry said and glanced at Maggie. "I guess Mother and I are going to finish sewing our dresses for the fair."

Garrett nodded. "Sounds like a good idea. The fair's in two days and I wouldn't want my favorite ladies to show up looking shoddy."

Maggie rolled her eyes. "You wouldn't care if we wore potato sacks, as long as you had one of us on either side of you."

The boys snickered, but Daughtry didn't. Her mother spoke the truth. Except maybe dressing in potato sacks was pushing the boundaries a bit.

"I guess you're right," Garrett said with a smile and leaned over to place a kiss on his wife's temple. "I'd go anywhere with you, Mrs. Lucas, and you could indeed be wearing potato sacks and still outshine everybody else." His gaze betrayed his pride and passion for the woman at his side.

"Well, I for one will not be wearing potato sacks," Maggie replied. "Nor will Daughtry. We have some very special dresses planned. You just wait. There won't be an eligible bachelor in town who won't sit up and take notice of our daughter."

"Not that it would do any good," Daughtry said before she could check the thought.

"What's that supposed to mean?" Garrett questioned. All eyes turned once more to her for an answer.

Daughtry pushed back her chair and got to her feet. "It means just what you think it means. No one is going to look at me twice because my daddy might take offense at their forwardness and put them in their place. And if not him, then one of the mighty Lucas brothers. I'm so tired of being treated like I'm five years old. Did it ever once dawn on any of you that I'd like to meet a nice young man, fall in love, and move away from here?"

Everyone stared at Daughtry in surprise. She had never before given such an outburst of criticism for what they perceived as their dutiful love for her.

"Daughtry!" her mother gasped. "You apologize to your father and brothers, this minute."

Daughtry leaned against her chair and considered the situation for a moment.

"Sorry," she muttered and turned to leave. Stalking down the hall, she added in a whisper for her ears alone, "Sorry that I live in this house and will probably die in this house, too!"

When the boys had finished with breakfast, leaving their parents alone, Maggie couldn't help but try to ease the tension between her husband and daughter.

"Daughtry does have a small point," Maggie began. She tenderly ran her fingers across the back of Garrett's hand. "She is grown up and does deserve to settle down with her own husband and family."

Garrett's eyes flashed anger, as though Maggie's declaration was one of betrayal. "I just want to see her with the kind of man who's going to respect her and love her. He needs to know what's going on with this world and how to make a living that will support her. You've never taken her side over mine before. Why now?"

Maggie sighed. "I'm not taking sides, Garrett. It's just that I see something in Daughtry these last few months that worries me. I'm afraid if you don't find a way to work it out, Daughtry will put a permanent wall between the two of you. You don't want that, Garrett. You've already lost one daughter."

Garrett stormed from the table without another word. Maggie stared after him for a moment, tears brimming in her eyes. "Help him, Father," she prayed. "Help Garrett to heal before it's too late."

Chapter 2

*D*aughtry remained silent on the ride into town. The growing community of Bandelero was overflowing with people due to the fair, and Daughtry tried to put her feelings behind her and smile. At least she was away from the ranch and she was wearing something pretty.

She glanced down at the lavender dress she'd helped to make. It had a pleated bodice with hand embroidery and lace to edge the scooped neckline. At the waist, a darker lavender ribbon trimmed the gown and tied in the back to show off her very feminine form. Outlandishly gaudy hats were the rage these days, but Maggie and Daughtry had found little use for them on the ranch. Instead, they had ordered less complicated arrangements from Sears and Roebuck. Her mother predicted the simplicity would do more to turn heads, and, when it did, Daughtry could only hope that her father wouldn't be anywhere nearby.

As Garrett brought the carriage to a halt outside of a two-story adobe house, a sudden ruckus caused the horses to rear and prance. Everybody waited for the smelly, noisy automobile to pass by before even trying to dismount.

"Useless things!" Garrett declared, finally settling the horses. "You won't ever see me in one. I'll stick with horses."

"I think they look like fun," Dolan said from the back of his horse. "I hear they actually have races with those things. They go for days and days, and people even get killed."

"How awful!" Maggie exclaimed, taking her husband's hand as she exited the carriage.

Daughtry stared past her brothers to the street where the car was rapidly disappearing. She silently wished that she could be one of the happy passengers.

"Daughtry, you daydreamin' up there?"

Daughtry looked down at her father and smiled. *If he only knew,* she thought. As she stepped from the carriage, however, they were bombarded with friends, and she was distracted from her thoughts.

"Garrett! Maggie! I'm so glad to see you all," Lillie Monroe called from behind a swirl of people.

"Where's Dan?" Garrett asked, while Maggie embraced her lifelong friend.

"Had to set a broken arm," Lillie said with a shrug. "That's all part of being married to the town doctor. You always have to share him. I'll be glad when he takes a partner."

Lillie's sons, John and James, joined them and soon were catching up the Lucas boys on all the news. Sixteen-year-old Angeline Monroe was nowhere to be seen, much to Daughtry's relief. Angeline only reminded Daughtry how old and outdated she'd rapidly become under Garrett's overprotective hand. Angeline was young and just beginning to live, while Daughtry felt her life was over.

"The fair is going to be a great deal of fun," Lillie was saying, while Garrett and Maggie kept stride with her. Daughtry took advantage of the moment to slip out of sight and wander around town alone. Heaving a great sigh, she rounded the corner and ran smack into the broad chest of a stranger.

"Excuse me," she said, looking upward into soft brown eyes.

"I'm afraid the fault is mine," the man returned. "I just came to town for the fair and I don't know my way around."

Daughtry laughed. "It's not all that difficult, believe me."

The man smiled appreciatively. "Maybe you could show me."

"I'm not sure that would be proper," Daughtry said, glancing around for her father or brothers. "I don't even know you."

"Bill," he replied and extended his hand. "Bill Davis."

"Daughtry Lucas," she replied and extended her small gloved hand to take his.

"There," he said confidently, "now we're no longer strangers. Would you do me the honor of introducing me to your fair city?"

Daughtry laughed, glad to be free for once. "Of course."

The rest of the day passed much too quickly for Daughtry. She ran into Jordy once, but he seemed unconcerned that his sister was on the arm of some stranger. Later, Daughtry narrowly avoided a confrontation with Gavin, when she and Bill happened into a knot of people who stood laughing and talking, blocking the street. As the crowd thinned a bit for them to pass by, Daughtry found Angeline Monroe to be the focal point of the group. Laughing and enjoying the attention, Angeline didn't so much as nod when she caught Daughtry's eye.

"Do you know her?" Bill questioned after they'd managed to slip past the gathering.

"Yes," Daughtry replied, hoping Bill wasn't going to ask to be introduced.

"She seems awfully young to be flirting with so many men. You ought to have a talk with her folks," Bill said, surprising Daughtry with his words.

"People have been trying to tell her folks for years," Daughtry laughed. "But she's very spoiled."

"Unlike you," Bill said, his sincerity clear in his voice. Daughtry blushed furiously but said nothing as she kept walking.

With Angeline just a memory, Daughtry cast sly upward glances at the sandy-haired man who walked beside her. He was as tall as her father, and the width of his shoulders was also nearly the same. He was dressed in jeans and a light brown shirt, but it all seemed rather regal to Daughtry. Perhaps Bill was her Prince Charming, and he would whisk her away from the stifling life she'd known.

"So how come a pretty thing like you hasn't up and married?" Bill asked her while they walked the festive avenue of carnival games.

"Truth? Or would you rather hear some fabulously devised story?" Daughtry asked, completely serious.

Bill studied her for a moment and laughed. "Truth."

"It won't appeal to you," she said, glancing around her for the millionth time.

"You looking for someone?" Bill asked her softly. "I mean, ever since this morning, you've been looking over your shoulder and down the street. What's the problem?"

Daughtry sighed. "The same reason I've never married. I have a very possessive father—and five brothers who feel it's their duty to fill in for him when he can't be there to do the job."

"I see," Bill said, and Daughtry thought he sounded a little nervous. "Are they the killing kind or just the wounding and maiming type?"

Daughtry laughed out loud, catching the attention of several people around them. Stifling her amusement, she waited until they'd walked away from the listening crowd. "I've only known them to be the ranting and raving kind, actually."

Bill grinned. "Ah, that won't bother me then. My ears can tolerate the hollering."

"Don't be so sure." Daughtry glanced at the railroad depot clock and sighed. "I'd better get back. I've been gone way too long."

"I'll walk you," Bill said and tucked her arm around his.

Daughtry wanted to tell him no, but the truth was, she was enjoying herself too much. Maybe God had decided to smile down on her and allow her to meet a respectable young man after all.

"Daughtry, I've been looking for you." Her father blocked their path, and behind him stood three of her brothers.

Garrett was frowning fiercely at Bill, and the scowl was so intimidating that the younger man immediately dropped his hold on Daughtry.

"I've just been seeing the sights and enjoying the fair," Daughtry said, trying to control her temper. Then, hoping she could smooth matters, Daughtry turned to introduce her friend. "This is Bill Davis. Bill, this is my father, Garrett Lucas, and my brothers, Gavin, Dolan, and Joseph."

Garrett was barely controlling his temper as he reached out and yanked Daughtry by the arm. "Evening, Mr. Davis. You'll have to excuse us now."

Daughtry was livid. Garrett continued pulling her down the street, while her brothers firmly discouraged Bill from trying to interfere.

When they were back in the solitude of the Monroe backyard, Daughtry dug her heels in and stopped.

"How dare you!" she exclaimed, and the hurt in her eyes changed quickly into rage. "I can't believe you would embarrass me like that."

Garrett looked at her for a moment. "Daughtry, I was only looking out for your best interest. You don't know that man, and he had no right to be handling you."

Daughtry shook her head. "Enough is enough. I've had all I'm going to take. You may be my father, but I'm of age and old enough to make my own choices. Good night!"

Garrett called after her, but Daughtry ran into the house without so much as a glance over her shoulder. She knew they were spending the night with the Monroes, but she had no idea where she was to sleep. Gratefully, she ran into her mother.

Tears were blinding her eyes, but Daughtry didn't want to talk about it. "Mother, where am I supposed to sleep?"

Maggie noted her daughter's state of mind. "Daughtry, what's wrong?"

"The same old thing. Now, I just want to go to bed. Where am I sleeping?"

Maggie led her daughter to the small room she was to share with Angeline. "I'm sorry, Daughtry. I don't know what has happened, but I hate the fact that it's hurt you so much." She reached out and hugged her daughter close.

Daughtry wrapped her arms around her mother and sobbed. "I can't stand it anymore, Mother. I love you all so much, but I have to be allowed to grow up." She abruptly released her mother and turned away. "I just want to go to sleep now, please."

Daughtry knew that she hurt her mother when she shut her out, but she could see no sense in discussing the matter any further. Silently, she undressed and slipped into bed for a good cry before going to sleep.

Morning light dawned, and Daughtry woke with a new determination and outlook on her life. During the night, after hours of praying and pleading with God, she'd decided to run away from home. At least that's what she called it, though she doubted that someone could actually run away at her age.

Angeline still slept peacefully, and because Daughtry knew the girl had come to bed quite late, she tiptoed around the room collecting her things. After dressing and pinning up her hair, Daughtry made her way downstairs.

"Morning, Daughtry," Lillie called to her from the kitchen. "Did you sleep well?"

"Yes, thank you." Daughtry struggled to sound pleasant.

"Are you hungry? I've fixed enough food for a small army. Of course with your brothers and James and John, it very nearly resembles just that."

Daughtry smiled. "Are Pastor David and Jenny coming over this morning?" Daughtry questioned, referring to Dr. Monroe's brother and his wife. "I was hoping to talk to them before we left for home."

"I think they plan to stop by," Lillie responded. "Did you not get a chance to see them last night?"

"No," Daughtry replied. "I didn't."

"Did you need to talk to them about anything in particular?"

"Yes," Daughtry murmured, "but it's rather, well, personal." She thought maybe David or Jenny could offer some help or suggestions on where she could go.

Lillie smiled and nodded. "That's quite all right, I understand."

Within moments, the quiet talk was forgotten as the room filled with the bodies of young men all rivaling the other for the center of discussion.

Daughtry managed to slip outside with her plate of food. She ate with a ravenous appetite, suddenly remembering that she hadn't had any supper the night before.

"I brought you a peace offering," Garrett said, coming up behind her. Daughtry looked up but said nothing. Garrett held out a newspaper. "I knew you'd want to catch up on what was happening around the world. I managed to latch onto this copy of the *Denver Post*."

Daughtry took the newspaper from her father. He was trying so hard to make up for his behavior, and even though she had no intention of changing her mind about leaving, Daughtry couldn't treat him badly.

"Thank you, Daddy," she said softly and glanced briefly at the headlines.

"I really am sorry," Garrett said.

"I know," Daughtry replied. *You always are.*

Seeing that she wasn't in a mood to talk, Garrett left Daughtry to finish her breakfast alone. Daughtry knew that he wanted her to laugh and think nothing more about the events of the previous night, but that wasn't possible for her.

Flipping through the pages of the paper, Daughtry came across an advertisement. It was like no other she'd ever seen. This was an advertisement for a wife. Quickly scanning the lines, Daughtry read:

> *Wife wanted to share the dream of building a ranching empire. Looking for a hard-working woman who isn't afraid to love and live with a man who will provide a home and remain forever yours in the eyes of God and man.*

It was signed N. Dawson, with an address in care of the post office in a small town in eastern New Mexico.

How romantic, Daughtry thought as she reread the ad. The days of mail-order brides were a thing of the past but, from time to time, people did still seek a mate through that unconventional manner.

Daughtry began to get an idea. A very serious idea about answering the advertisement. She folded the paper and stared at it for several minutes. *It could work,* she thought to herself. It could be everything she'd prayed for.

Back at Piñon Canyon, Daughtry penned a response to the man she could only address as Mr. Dawson. She wondered as she wrote what his first name might be. She imagined Nicodemus or Nathaniel—maybe even Navin or Ned, although those names didn't appeal to her sense of romance.

She stared at the blank paper for several minutes, then began to pour out her thoughts.

Dear Mr. Dawson,

I am responding to your advertisement and would very much like to receive more information about the marriage and dream you propose. I have grown up on a ranch and thus have spent my entire life working at the same dream you seem to have. I would be happy to correspond with you regarding the matter. Please address your reply in care of the Bandelero, New Mexico, Post Office.

Daughtry Lucas

Almost as an afterthought, Daughtry picked up her pen again and added a postscript indicating that she had enclosed a picture of herself. Then, scouting through her desk drawer, she managed to find one that had been taken recently at a church picnic. She thought the photo did her justice.

Slipping the letter and picture into an envelope, Daughtry addressed it and made plans for how she would get away the next morning to mail it. This was a great adventure, she thought to herself, and, for once, she looked forward to the next day with less dread.

N. Dawson, she thought with a smile. *Maybe, just maybe, he will be my answer to prayer.*

Chapter 3

*D*aughtry had nearly given up hearing anything from N. Dawson when, much to her surprise, she found a letter awaiting her at the post office. Giddy with excitement and grateful that she'd ridden in alone for the mail, Daughtry tore open the envelope.

She wasn't prepared for the many pieces of paper that accompanied the letter. Reviewing the items, Daughtry was shocked to find legal documentation for a marriage by proxy, a train ticket, and photograph. The picture was face down and Daughtry decided to leave it that way until after reading the letter. *This way*, she thought, *I won't be influenced by looks alone.*

Carefully opening the letter, Daughtry eagerly read the contents.

Dear Miss Lucas,

I was enchanted by your photograph and letter. I would like to say that I believe you are a Godsend. My faith being firmly rooted in Him, I can say without a doubt that you are the woman I am to marry.

Daughtry reread that line several times before continuing. A strange feeling was coursing through her, and it made her hand shake ever so slightly as she read on.

Enclosed you will find a train ticket to bring you to me and a legal document which will allow you to marry me before you make the journey. It is most imperative that you marry by proxy by the twenty-fifth of September, otherwise the documents will be null and void.

I hope this answers your questions, and I hope the enclosed photograph will put your mind at ease regarding my appearance and age.

Forever yours,
Nicholas Dawson

"Nicholas!" Daughtry breathed. "His name is Nicholas." Gingerly, she refolded the letter and turned the photograph over. Her breath caught in her throat. He was clearly the handsomest man she'd ever seen. She studied the man who casually sat for the photograph. He was dressed in a smart suit, with dark hair and even darker eyes staring back at her. His eyes seemed to twinkle, if that were possible, and his lips were curled upward.

"Oh my," she said breathlessly. "He's wonderful."

She lost track of time, studying the picture as though trying to memorize each and every feature of the man. Finally, when a train whistle blew and broke her concentration, Daughtry realized she would have to be heading back to the ranch.

After another quick examination of the document and train ticket, Daughtry replaced the papers in the envelope and tucked the letter into the deep pocket of her split skirt. Without much thought, she tossed the rest of the mail into her saddle bag and mounted Poco.

"What have I done?" she questioned aloud. All around her the rich cobalt blue sky stretched out to the purple haze of mountains. The noise of Bandelero faded, leaving Daughtry with only one pounding question in her mind. *What do I do now?*

She felt the side of her skirt to reassure herself that the letter hadn't been dreamed. "This man is serious, Poco," she said, as though the horse might offer her some insight. "He's sent me a train ticket and the means by which to marry him before coming to his place." The horse kept a steady trot, mindless of its owner's ramblings.

"Dear God," Daughtry finally prayed, looking upward to the cloudless sky. "I didn't mean to cause trouble, but maybe this is the direction You're leading me. The man says I have to make up my mind before September twenty-fifth." Daughtry paused in her prayers. "Father, that's only ten days from now."

A trembling started anew in Daughtry. Ten days! That's all the time she had to make a lifelong decision. She argued and reasoned with herself all the way back to Piñon Canyon. How could she leave her home and marry a stranger? Even if he were a very nice looking stranger? On the other hand, Daughtry knew she was going to leave this place, one way or another. She had no idea how she would care for herself alone, and marriage to anyone would be better than dying an old maid, she thought.

Three days later, Daughtry was still mulling over her proposal. She'd re-read the letter until it was well-worn and she knew every word by heart. Always, she came back to the picture and lost her heart a little more. "Forever yours, Nicholas Dawson," she sighed and stared at the dark eyes of the man who wished to marry her. Only seven days were left.

Daughtry had never been a person given over to moments of spontaneous decision. She always thought things out and, inevitably, reasoned away any urge to do something foolish. This was no exception, and as time passed, Daughtry recognized too many good arguments against accepting Nicholas's proposal.

"I can't hurt Mother that way," Daughtry thought aloud. She had taken Poco out for her routine morning ride, grateful to escape the escort her father thought necessary. Pulling back on the reins, Daughtry slipped down from Poco's back and walked alongside the gelding for awhile. "I can't just walk away from my responsibilities," she continued. Poco seemed more interested in the patches of fading green grass than in his mistress's declarations.

"I've always been a good girl," Daughtry said firmly. "I've always been dependable and reasonable. I'll just have to make it clear to Daddy that I need to be allowed to court and marry and eventually leave Piñon Canyon to make my own home. He'll come around in time."

Daughtry studied the landscape for a moment. The rocky western slopes of their property headed upward into the Sangre de Cristo mountain range. Soon snow would cover the magnificent crests and Piñon Canyon would be blanketed in white.

Another winter, Daughtry thought to herself. *And in January, I'll be twenty-four.*

Daughtry walked on in silence. She had to do the right thing, she reasoned. She had to trust God and endure the situation as best she could. When she got back to the house, she would simply write to Nicholas—no, Mr. Dawson—and tell him that she couldn't marry him.

She was about to remount Poco when a cloud of dust in the distance caught her attention. Riding hard and fast across the open plain was her father. Daughtry remained on the ground until a worried-looking Garrett reined up beside her.

"You're on foot," he said, looking Daughtry over from head to toe. "Is something wrong?"

"No, Daddy," Daughtry said, taking a defensive tone. "I'm just enjoying the morning."

Garrett frowned. "Why didn't you bring someone with you?"

"Because I'm a grown woman, and I don't need an escort. I like to spend time on my own, and I don't want to have someone following me around all the time. It's bad enough that you won't leave me alone."

Garrett's eyes revealed his hurt, but Daughtry was rapidly growing angry, and her father's pain was furthest from her mind.

"Daddy, you and I have to talk about this," Daughtry said firmly. "Why don't you walk with me a spell."

Garrett quickly complied and joined his daughter on the ground. He started to speak, but Daughtry held up her hand. "Please let me say what I need to say," she began. "Then you can tell me what you think and we'll go from there."

"All right."

Daughtry swallowed hard and took a deep breath. She prayed that God would give her the right words to say. "Daddy, I know how much losing Julie hurts you. I hurt too. I miss her, and I wish that she would never have gone out riding that morning. But the truth is, she did, and I can't change that and neither can you. You can't change it by smothering me or watching my every step. You can't do God's job, Daddy."

Daughtry stopped and looked at her father for a moment. He was still a young man, vital and strong, and Daughtry knew he was perfectly capable of providing for his family. He'd helped her with so many things in life. He was the one who had helped her find Christ as her Savior. He was also the one who had taught her to ride and shoot and a hundred other things that pertained to her life on the ranch.

"I love you, Daddy," Daughtry said, looking deep into his eyes. "But I want to get married and have a family. I want a life of my own, and I want you to let me go."

Garrett looked at her blankly for a moment. "Have you found someone?" he asked softly.

Daughtry smiled ever so slightly at the thought of Nicholas. "I thought I had, but now I'm not sure. I do know, however, that it's what I want for my life, and I believe it's what God wants for me, too. I don't want to go to school or hold a job or make a great splash in society. I just want to be a wife and mother. I don't want to grow old taking care of you and Mother. You're supposed to care for each other, and we children are supposed to leave the nest." Garrett nodded, and Daughtry thought he finally understood. Feeling a bit of relief, she offered him a smile.

"Who is it?" Garrett asked without thinking.

"Who is who?"

"Who were you thinking about marrying?" Garrett questioned, and Daughtry could see the determination in his eyes.

"It isn't important," Daughtry said in exasperation.

"Well, why don't you let me be the judge of that."

"Because I'm a grown woman and you aren't the judge of my life," Daughtry stated in anger. "I'm the one who will decide whom I marry and when. This isn't the Middle Ages, Daddy, and I'm not going to be like Momma and let my father decide for me." Daughtry stormed past him and remounted Poco with a fury in her eyes that Garrett had never before seen.

"You're still under my authority, Daughtry," Garrett said, swinging up into his own saddle. "That gives me a say in what you do."

Daughtry gripped the reins tightly. She tried to steady her voice before she spoke. "Daddy, you're making this very difficult. Will you allow me to make some choices for myself? Will you stop shadowing everything I do in the fear that I will end up dead, like my sister?"

Garrett looked at her for a moment before silently shaking his head. "I can't, Daughtry. God made you my responsibility."

Daughtry refused to answer. Instead she dug her heels into Poco's sides, something she rarely did, and flew out across the ground for home. By the time she'd headed into the stable yard, Daughtry had made up her mind. No matter what else happened, she was going to marry Nicholas Dawson! She would have the last word on this and no one, especially not her father, would stand in her way.

Chapter 4

a t a few minutes before three o'clock in the morning, Daughtry led Poco from his stall. She walked him out past the stables and corrals and moved silently toward the open range. She prayed that she was doing the right thing by leaving, and a part of her sincerely thought she was. She remembered her mother saying on more than one occasion that God often expected a person to step out in faith. Mounting Poco in the New Mexican darkness, Daughtry figured this was as big a step of faith as she could possibly make.

The ride into town was uneventful, and when Daughtry arrived, she quickly tied Poco up outside of the church, knowing that Pastor David would recognize the horse and get him back to Piñon Canyon. She wished she could take Poco with her. At least then she'd have something to comfort herself with at the end of her trip. But arranging to take Poco would require her making her presence known to the freight agent, and he would no doubt remember where she had gone when her father came looking.

Knowing the church would be open, Daughtry took her two heavy bags and slipped inside the dark protection of the sanctuary. Quickly, she pulled on clothes she'd borrowed from Pepita in order to board the train and not be recognized. She pulled a heavy shawl over her head and secured it under her chin. Then, taking her bags in hand, Daughtry made her way to the train depot.

Only a handful of people waited for the five-thirty eastbound. Gratefully, Daughtry didn't recognize any of them. She waited in the shadows, however, just in case one of them recognized her. When the train whistle blasted through the early morning silence, though, Bandelero was just coming awake, and no one Daughtry knew was anywhere to be seen.

Daughtry grew fidgety waiting for her turn to board, but as soon as she took her place on the nearly empty train car, she began to relax. Freedom, she thought to herself, came at a high price, but she was sure it would be worth it.

Looking out the soot-smudged window, she nearly ducked down

at the sight of Dr. Monroe, or Dr. Dan as she affectionately called him. He was hurrying down the street, however, black bag tucked under his arm and a look of determination on his face, and he never glanced at the train. No doubt another medical emergency, Daughtry thought.

Soon the train began its journey, and Daughtry breathed a sigh of relief. When they reached the town of Springer, the conductor announced an hour wait while they took on several carloads of cattle. Daughtry realized this would be the perfect opportunity to find a minister and have the proxy marriage ceremony performed.

Hurrying through the town, she wondered to herself what minister in his right mind would marry two strangers together. *What if I can't find someone willing to do the job?* Worry flooded her soul. What if she had to turn back, or worse, meet Mr. Dawson without the marriage in place as he'd requested?

Daughtry's worries were for naught, however. The first minister she approached was more than happy to take her offering of five dollars to perform the proxy service. Armed with marriage papers in hand, Daughtry made her way back to the train, ten minutes before it pulled out and headed east to her new home.

Staring out the window, Daughtry felt something akin to excitement and foolish regret, both at the same time. She was a married woman! She was no longer Daughtry Ann Lucas. Now, she was Daughtry Dawson, wife of Nicholas.

Taking out the photograph of her husband, Daughtry tried to imagine what type of man he was. He looked tall, and she could see that he was broad-shouldered. He looked strong and healthy, maybe even older than she. She realized with a start that she had no idea how old her husband was. Nor did she know whether he'd ever been married before or if he had children.

"What have I done?" she questioned softly, then glanced around quickly to make certain no one else had heard her.

When the train finally arrived at Daughtry's destination, she panicked. Nicholas wouldn't know she was coming. She hadn't sent a telegram or tried to telephone or anything else that would let him know of her arrival. She'd brought a small amount of money with her, enough to rent a room for the night, but fear gnawed at her like a hungry animal. Daughtry had never been on her own before.

She stepped from the train and immediately signaled a man to assist her. "Do you know where the Nicholas Dawson ranch is located?" she asked the man.

"No, Ma'am. I can't rightly say I've ever heard of the man."

Daughtry's face fell. Just as she was about to ask the man who might know, another voice sounded from behind her.

"Did I hear you say you were lookin' for the Dawson place?"

Daughtry turned and met the eyes of a dust-laden stranger. The man was older than her father, but his shoulders and chest were massive.

"Yes," she managed to say. "I need to get to Nicholas Dawson's ranch."

"Well, you're in luck," the man said in a noncommittal way. "I'm on my way out there with this load of freight. I just have to finish picking up the rest of it and we can be on our way."

Daughtry sighed aloud. "You, sir, are an answer to prayer."

The man snorted at her declaration and pointed to his wagon. "You just wait over there and I'll be with you directly. These your bags?" he questioned, glancing at the luggage beside Daughtry.

"Yes."

"That all you brought?"

"Yes," Daughtry replied and ignored his look of curiosity.

Without another word, the man took the bags, threw them up into the freight wagon, and went off in the direction of the train. Daughtry hurriedly planted herself by the wagon and was relieved when the man returned fifteen minutes later to finish stacking the cargo.

The afternoon was late when Daughtry and the freighter finally arrived at the Dawson ranch. The man had offered her no name, and, in return, Daughtry hadn't explained who she was. Now, as the man unloaded his wagon and stacked lumber and supplies inside a rather run-down barn, Daughtry glanced around nervously for her husband. When the freighter finished and Nicholas had still not appeared, Daughtry grew frightened.

"Are you certain this property belongs to Nicholas Dawson?"

"Sure as I am of anything," the man replied. "I've been bringing supplies out here for weeks now. He's gone a lot, which would explain why he isn't out here to greet us now. I notice his horse is gone, so there's no telling where he is or when he'll be back. Did he expect you?"

"No. Well, yes." Daughtry tried to answer reasonably. "He didn't know what day I would get here. Tell me, what else do you know about Mr. Dawson?"

The man eyed her suspiciously for a moment. "Don't know much. He's new to these parts. Took this old place off the hands of Widow Cummings and declared he wanted to turn it into a fine ranch again.

Other than that, I don't guess I know anything else."

"You have met him though?"

"Sure," the man said and scratched his head. "I take it you haven't?"

Daughtry shook her head. "No, I haven't met him yet. I have his picture and a letter, but that's all."

"You kin of his?"

"No," Daughtry replied and smiled weakly. "I'm his wife." The man burst out laughing, and Daughtry felt foolish for having mentioned the matter.

"Well, I'll be. I heard he was after gettin' himself hitched. Didn't find any prospects in our little town though, and I heard tell he advertised in the papers for one. Is that how you came to marry him?"

Daughtry felt completely stupid. "Yes," she managed to whisper, "that's how it happened."

"Well, I wish you the best, Mrs. Dawson," the man said, climbing up into the wagon. "Here." He turned to rummage under the seat of his buckboard and handed her something down. "You might want to order something, then I'll have a reason to come back out this way."

Daughtry stared down at the Sears and Roebuck catalog the freighter had just handed her. Daughtry greatly needed his gesture of kindness. "Thank you," she said softly. "You have been so very kind. What do I owe you for the ride out?"

"Not a thing, pretty lady. Not a thing." He retrieved his hat, tipped it to her, and moved his horses back out to the road. Within minutes, the dust of his wagon faded into the distance, leaving Daughtry all alone in the middle of nowhere.

"I've brought this on myself," Daughtry said, squaring her shoulders with a look of determination. "I've just got to make the best of it."

She took her bags in hand and headed toward the rundown house. Staring at it in the soft glow of early evening light, Daughtry realized it was sorely neglected. No wonder Nicholas needed a woman who was willing to work hard. *Well*, Daughtry thought to herself, *this will be a challenge, and I will meet it head on and with a light heart.*

Her resolve lasted as long as it took to get through the back mud porch and into the kitchen. She could see well enough to realize that the place was hopelessly filthy and in need of more than just a little attention.

Setting her mind to the work at hand, Daughtry decided to do as much as she could to put the place in order before her husband returned. She quickly lighted several lamps and explored the rest of the house in order to determine what should be done first.

Through the kitchen, Daughtry found a small but promising dining room. This connected to a small parlor, and this in turn came out onto a short hall that blended into a vestibule of sorts that ended at the front door. Crossing the hall, Daughtry found a larger sitting room filled with an assortment of odd looking crates, furniture, and a wood stove that had been used recently but not cleaned in a long time. Finding more lamps here, Daughtry lit another and left it to radiate a cheery glow in the room, while she continued to explore.

Back in the hall, she turned and opened the door to a small closet. Farther down, she noticed two more doors and opened one into a small room that looked as though it had been a sewing room at one time. Hadn't the freighter said the ranch belonged to a widow before Nicholas bought it?

The other door opened into the bedroom, and Daughtry became suddenly aware of Nicholas's masculine presence. Several articles of clothing lay around the room in disarray. Putting the lamp on the nightstand beside the four poster bed, Daughtry picked up a black suit coat and held it in front of her. The shoulders were broader than she'd even imagined. Nicholas must be quite a large man, Daughtry surmised, by the look of his coat.

She picked up other items and stared at them, as if hoping they would answer her unspoken questions. Picking up a pair of discarded jeans, Daughtry held them against her, trying to get an idea of how Nicholas' size might contrast to her own. She'd worn her brothers' clothes on many occasions, but they'd always been old clothes they had long outgrown. These were the clothes of a man, not a boy, and Daughtry knew there was no comparison.

Realizing that the sky was getting darker and feeling the need to relieve herself, Daughtry went back down the hall and made her way outside. She instantly spotted the outhouse and started across the yard.

For a moment, she paused to take in the beauty of the sunset. The sun looked like a ball of molten scarlet against the fading colors of the sky. Lavender, so dusty and dark that it was nearly purple, blended into streaks of blue and amber. Daughtry hugged her arms against her body and thanked God for the wonder of it.

"Only God can paint the sky like that," she sighed.

Back in the house, Daughtry realized she could do little about the house's untidiness so late in the day. She found a can of peaches and a tin of crackers and made her supper on these. Morning would surely prove to offer her more understanding of her new home.

When she'd finished with the meager provisions, Daughtry extinguished all the lamps but the one she carried with her. She took her bags and made her way to the bedroom. Her only thought was to get a good night's sleep, but when she was actually in the room once again, Daughtry grew uncomfortable. Should she sleep in his bed? What if he came home in the night?

She was about to make a pallet on the floor, when a mouse scurried across the room and out the door. With a shriek of fright, Daughtry's mind was made up. Nicholas or no Nicholas, she was sleeping in the bed!

Chapter 5

$\mathcal{D}$aughtry tried to ignore her concern for the absent husband she'd never met. Three days had passed since she'd arrived at the ranch, and Nicholas had still not come back. Trying to soothe her worry, Daughtry set up Nicholas's picture on the small table in the kitchen and, as she worked, she talked to him as though he were there.

"I'm going to have to start bringing up wood," she said absentmindedly. "It's getting considerably colder and pretty soon it's bound to snow. I used the last of the coal, or at least what I could find, so I guess I'll just have to go down to that grove of trees and see what I can find there."

Daughtry had worked wonders with the place and, in spite of her nervous state of mind, she was pleased with the way things were shaping up. She'd inventoried the supplies and managed to find a pantry just off the kitchen that she'd not seen in her first day of exploring. Nicholas had laid up quite a store of canned goods and smoked meats, as well as plenty of flour, sugar, soda, and salt. Daughtry nearly cried in joy at the sight of so much food.

Her first project had been to clean the kitchen. She reasoned that if she could have this one room in perfect order, she could easily work with the others at her leisure. Going around the room, she noted what was worth keeping and what was plain and simple trash. The curtains were still in good shape but needed to be washed, so Daughtry removed them and began heating water in the biggest pot she could find.

Piece by piece, she emptied the room, until nothing remained but the dirty black stove and the empty ice-box. She found soap in the supplies that the freighter had left in the barn, as well as brushes and a well-made broom. Taking these, she scrubbed the grime from the walls, floors, counters, and cabinets, until everything was spotless. After this, she tackled the stove, washing it thoroughly until she was satisfied that she could cook food without fear of catching something from the filth.

Bit by bit, the room took shape, and Daughtry continued to talk to Nicholas as though he were there, relating her plans as she continued.

She went to work cleaning the small table and chairs that had set in the kitchen, as well as the pie saver and jelly cabinet that she'd taken outside. She was just about to move them indoors, when she remembered something in the barn.

Setting out across the yard, Daughtry opened the barn door and went inside. After several minutes of searching, she returned to the house with a bucket of white paint and a brush. Maybe Nicholas hadn't planned on the house being painted inside, but Daughtry thought a fresh coat of whitewash would help matters a great deal. If he were mad at her, then she'd just have to apologize and try to fix the matter. That was, if he ever showed up.

More nosing around revealed a wealth of useful household goods, and Daughtry began to take courage from the way the house shaped up. The kitchen was actually attractive now with its freshly painted walls and cabinets. The shelves were lined with sparkling dishes from sets that Daughtry had found in crates in the large sitting room, and the pots gleamed from her hours of scrubbing.

Every night, Daughtry went to bed more exhausted than the night before. After the second day, she'd made notable progress with the bedroom, feeling that this was the next place to be put in order. After wrestling the mattress outside and beating it until the entire yard looked like the middle of a dust storm, Daughtry scrubbed down the room and furniture. Finally, she washed every article of clothing and all of the linens before deeming the bedroom acceptable.

She didn't have long to wonder what she'd need to turn her attention to next. When it rained on the second night, Daughtry learned quickly that the roof was leaky. Steady drips fell from the ceiling in more than one place, and Daughtry knew that her job in the morning would consist of trying to repair and reshingle her roof.

She barely had time to worry about her husband. For all she knew, he didn't even exist, except that she had papers that told her otherwise. Every day, she tried to make ready for his return. She wanted very much to prove herself worthy in his eyes. And oh, what eyes, she thought as she drifted into sleep. Dark, dark eyes that seemed to laugh at some private joke. Dark eyes that Daughtry prayed would behold her with love and devotion.

Daughtry rose early, thankful that the storm had passed early in the night. She pulled on the set of boy's clothes she'd brought with her from home, finding them much easier to work in, and planned her day.

She set bread out to rise and made herself some breakfast before considering the roof. The kitchen was chilly, and Daughtry was grateful for the warmth of the stove. She reminded herself that leaky roofs could be lived with as long as she could keep a fire warming the house. With that in mind, she decided to bring more wood up to the house before worrying herself with anything else.

The day was rapidly getting away from her, and the sky was clouding up again. Daughtry knew she should at least try to check the roof out and see if she could do anything about the leaks, just in case it rained again that night.

Making her way to the barn, Daughtry found an old wooden ladder and took it with her to the house. She climbed up on top, noting several very soft spots, and began picking away at the tattered shingles. She was used to adobe houses, but this clapboard house she now called home was very similar to some of the other buildings at Piñon Canyon. Daughtry had helped her father and brothers on more than one occasion with roofing, repairing, and building. She had loved working alongside her family and learning every aspect of how to make the ranch run prosperously.

This was the first time Daughtry had allowed herself to remember her family and tears came to her eyes. Were they worried about her? Of course they were, she chided herself. Her father would be frantic, even though she'd left them a long letter explaining her need to get out on her own. Would they ever forgive her for stealing away in the night? Would she ever be welcomed back?

Exhaustion overwhelmed Daughtry as she climbed into bed that night. How she longed for a bath in a tub of hot water. But for now, she had to settle for washing out of the kitchen sink, where she poured pans of heated water. Perhaps she could talk Nicholas into purchasing a tub—if he ever showed up.

She drifted immediately into sleep, succumbing to the strain of the days that had passed in heavy, never-ending work. Daughtry dreamed of dark eyes and a handsome face, wondering where her husband was and why he'd not returned. The picture of Nicholas faded into that of her father's angry image, and Daughtry tossed restlessly as she sought to escape his rage.

Then the dream took another path, one that Daughtry had never before envisioned. She was being held safe and warm in muscular arms. Snuggling closer, Daughtry felt a hand run through her long hair. Sighing, she relished the dream. This would be what it was like to be held by Nicholas, she decided.

Then, to her surprise, Daughtry felt warm lips against her cheek. They trailed down to capture her lips, and Daughtry returned the kiss.

In the foggy uncertainty of sleep, Daughtry struggled to open her eyes. A part of her wanted to go on sleeping so that she could enjoy the dream, but another part of her was being beckoned. She could almost hear someone calling her name.

Daughtry tried to concentrate on the voice but it faded, and as it did, she became more awake, until she suddenly realized that she wasn't alone. Opening her eyes wide, Daughtry stared into the amused dark eyes of Nicholas Dawson.

For a moment all Daughtry could do was stare. Was she dreaming or was this real? The shocked look on her face caused the man beside her to chuckle.

"I–I—" Daughtry couldn't speak a coherent word to save herself. Shyly, she pulled her arms from the man's neck and tried to ease away from him, as if he wouldn't notice.

Nicholas sat up and Daughtry could see he was fully clothed and sitting atop the covers she so carefully clutched to her neck. With a grin he spoke. "I sure hope you're my wife."

Daughtry saw nothing amusing about the situation. She was trembling from head to toe, and whether it was from the shock of finding Nicholas in her bed or from the passion he'd awoke in her, Daughtry wasn't sure.

In a flash, Daughtry leaped from the bed and ran for the door. She knew her long flannel nightgown wouldn't offer her much coverage, but she wasn't about to stop and retrieve her robe on the way out the door. She reached for the handle and had just turned it, when Nicholas was beside her.

"Don't go. I'm sorry I scared you. It wasn't very nice of me, but I couldn't help myself." His voice was rich and warm, just as Daughtry knew it would be. Daughtry let her hand slip from the handle, but she couldn't bring herself to face her husband.

Slowly, as if dealing with a terrified child, Nicholas turned her to face him. "I'm Nicholas Dawson, although I'm sure you've already figured that out. You look just like your picture."

Daughtry lifted her face to meet his. "You too," she whispered.

Nicholas smiled and his eyes lit up. "I never figured on getting such a beauty for a wife. I wasn't even sure you'd agree, what with me in such a hurry and all. I'm sorry I wasn't here when you arrived. I had to be away on business, and I just got back this morning."

Daughtry nodded and looked away. Her senses were suddenly raging with all that she was seeing, hearing, and feeling. As if realizing she needed space, Nicholas stepped back and waited for her to speak.

"I'm Daughtry Lucas, I mean, Dawson," she said nervously. She took a deep breath to steady her nerves. "I didn't know when you'd be back. I took some liberty with the house. I'm sorry if I overstepped my rights, I mean, I didn't know what you'd expect of a wife, and I, well. . ." Daughtry stopped as she realized she was rambling and twisting her nightgown.

Nicholas just grinned at her, making the whole situation even more uncomfortable. Daughtry glanced at the bed, and her face flushed crimson.

Noting where her gaze ended, Nicholas reached out and touched Daughtry's cheek. "I really am sorry for startling you. I should have waited until you woke up good and proper, but I haven't always used the sense the good Lord gave me. What say you get dressed and come on out to the kitchen and we'll talk?"

Daughtry was mesmerized by the way his thumb was rubbing her jawline. His fingers were on her neck, and the warmth of their contact against her bare skin sent tremors through Daughtry that she couldn't control.

Surprising them both, Daughtry jumped from the door and moved back to the end of the bed. "I've got my things in here," she said motioning to the wardrobe. "If you'll wait in the other room, I'll get dressed."

Nicholas nodded, the smile never leaving his face. When he had gone from the room, closing the door firmly behind him, Daughtry's knees gave out and she crumpled to the floor.

"Dear God," she prayed in a whisper, "I've really done it this time. Please help me to know what to do and say, and please don't let Nicholas be mad about the paint. Amen."

Getting dressed as quickly as she could, Daughtry laughed to herself. *Paint? I'm worried about paint?*

Chapter 6

*D*aughtry hurried into the kitchen to find her husband sitting comfortably at the small table. She pulled her apron from a hook near the door and tied it around her trim waist. Nicholas watched all of this in complete silence, surprised at the control Daughtry seemed to have managed to regain in her few minutes alone.

He watched her as she put wood in the stove and got the fire going. He was more than a little impressed at what he'd found upon his return. Truth be told, he nearly walked back out the door, fearing that he'd entered the wrong house. A double take confirmed that he was indeed in the right house but that a transformation of tremendous proportions had taken place. Now looking at the petite and delicate woman he'd married, Nicholas was even more surprised.

Daughtry put a pot of coffee on the stove and turned to question her husband.

"What would you like for breakfast?"

Nicholas smiled to himself. He hadn't had someone to wait on him since leaving home and that seemed a million years ago. "Whatever you're having," he replied and leaned back against the chair.

Daughtry looked thoughtful for a moment. "Well, I have fresh bread and of course there are the canned foods. I wasn't able to locate any eggs or potatoes, so I can't really do you justice with anything grand. I could make tortillas and heat up some of the meat from the pantry." She fell silent and shrugged her shoulders. "I was just going to have toasted bread and jam."

"Sounds fine for me as well."

Daughtry nodded and went back to work, while Nicholas continued his silent study. He figured she was about five feet, four inches tall. Surely no taller, and she couldn't weigh more than one hundred pounds. She had pulled her hair up into a loose bun of rich copper. He liked the shade, never even imagining from her photograph what color her hair might be. She had a sweet face. Almost angelic, he thought. In fact, she looked so childlike that Nicholas suddenly sat up with a start.

"How old are you?"

"A lady should never reveal her age, Mr. Dawson." Her smile was brief and Nicholas caught her teasing tone. "However, because you are my husband and entitled to know full well what you've saddled yourself with, I will admit that I'm quite old."

Nicholas laughed at this, and the amusement lingered in his eyes. "How old?"

"I'm twenty-three. I'll be twenty-four in January," Daughtry said with something akin to regret in her voice.

"A mere baby," he chided and was rewarded with a look of sincere appreciation in his wife's eyes. Had someone honestly told this slip of girl that she was old?

Daughtry brought the toast and coffee to the table, then retrieved two mugs, a knife, and the jam before sitting opposite Nicholas.

"Would you ask the blessing?" she asked rather timidly.

"Certainly," he said without a second thought and bowed his head. "Father, thank You for this food and the hard labors of this industrious young woman. I ask that You would bless this house and this union between Daughtry and me and let us live our days devoted to You, Amen."

Daughtry looked up filled with wonder. "That was a beautiful prayer. Especially asking God to bless our marriage." She paused for a moment, then jumped right into the matter. "We do have a rather strange arrangement here, don't we?"

Amused, Nicholas reached out and took several pieces of toast. He liberally slathered jam across each piece and handed two to Daughtry before replying. "Strange doesn't half seem to explain it."

Daughtry poured the coffee and began to feel at ease. "I've always been a very straightforward kind of woman, Mr. Dawson."

"Please don't call me Mr. Dawson. Call me Nicholas or Nick, but not that."

Daughtry smiled. "All right. As I was saying, I like to be honest about things and I don't like to play games, at least not people games. Do you know what I mean?"

"I think so," he said with a gentleness in his expression that further dispelled Daughtry's anxieties.

"I've never been the kind of person to jump into things without real regard to the consequences, but this time seems to be an exception. I'm not sure I did the right thing in marrying you, but it is done and I don't believe in divorce or annulments. I just wanted you to know that I take our marriage very seriously." Nicholas stared at her soberly while she continued. "I intend to make you a good wife. I will work hard, and I know a great deal about ranching. I'm not weak or fragile, and I've spent most all of my life working outdoors alongside. . ." Daughtry stopped abruptly. "Well," she continued hesitantly, "I've spent a lot of time working at the kind of things that will build this place into a respectable and profitable ranch."

A smile played at the corners of Nicholas's lips. "Anything else?"

Daughtry put her coffee down and took a deep breath. "I suppose I should say that I'm a Christian. I believe in walking close with the Lord and reading the Word every day. I like to go to church and fellowship with other believers, and I will never do anything willingly that goes against the laws of God."

"I see."

Daughtry pressed on lest she lose her nerve. "I'm a very devoted person to those I love and care for. I will endeavor to be whatever you need me to be." She was blushing profusely at this point. "And, while I know very little about you, I am very teachable and happy to learn."

Nicholas reached out and put his hand over hers. "What about children?"

Daughtry's eyes flashed up to meet his. "I love children."

Nicholas patted her hand and smiled. "Good, because I do too and hope that we can fill this house with a dozen or more."

Daughtry's eyes widened at his boldness. "Well, I don't know if I love them that much." Her teasing was clearly evident and Nicholas laughed.

"I think I'm going to enjoy being married to you, Daughtry. I, too, have had my misgivings about marrying a person of which I knew nothing more about than the fact that she had beautiful penmanship and took a lovely picture."

Daughtry started to thank him for the compliment, but he continued to speak. "I did, however, pray about this matter and felt that God's answer was found in your letter. I worried that perhaps my desire to rush the marriage would put you off, but again I prayed and asked God to intercede and bring the event about. And, well, here you are, and I must say that I am more than a little bit impressed with the answer God's given. Not only are you the loveliest woman I've had the pleasure of knowing, but you're intelligent, witty, and very charming. Not to mention that you've accomplished in a few short days what I believe would have taken most men weeks to do."

Daughtry remembered the paint and grimaced. "I used your paint," she said, still not sure why it upset her so much. "I saw it with the supplies in the barn and, while I was cleaning the kitchen, I thought it looked like it could use a good coat. I hope you aren't upset with me. I didn't mean to use something without permission."

Nicholas stared at her rather sternly for a moment before replying. "What I have is yours, Daughtry. How could I possibly fault you for benefiting us both? That's just another thing I like about you. You're willing to just get in there and do what needs to be done. That's to your credit. You aren't one of those sad little women who sit around all lost and doe-eyed, waiting for their husband to instruct them in what they should do next. I like what you've done here, so stop fretting." Daughtry relaxed, realizing he was completely sincere.

"I do have some questions, though," Nicholas said, surprising her. Daughtry nodded to show her willingness to answer but was even more surprised with the topic of his question. "Have you ever been in love?"

Daughtry thought back through her life, especially the years before Julie had died. She'd found more than one cowboy fascinating company, but only on friendly terms. She couldn't honestly remember feeling anything akin to what she was feeling for Nicholas, however, and that gave her reason to believe that she'd actually fallen in love with her husband.

"No," she answered softly.

"Me neither," he offered. "I just wondered if there were any ghosts that needed to be laid to rest. You know, broken hearts, lost loves, that kind of thing."

Daughtry shook her head. "I can honestly say there was no one."

"Why were you inclined to answer my advertisement?" he continued.

"I guess," she began, "that your advertisement intrigued me. I thought the whole notion sounded, well, rather," she hesitated and looked away, "romantic."

"I've never been called romantic before."

"I find that hard to believe," Daughtry replied without thinking.

"Why's that?" Nicholas questioned, honestly wanting to know what was going through his young wife's mind.

Daughtry shifted uncomfortably. "Do I have to answer that?"

Nicholas laughed. "I'd sure like it if you did."

"Very well," she murmured and tried to reason out her words before speaking. "You strike me as a very considerate man," she began, "a man who would be most sought after by the ladies of his community. You are very. . ." She swallowed several times, then took a drink of coffee.

"I am very what?" He sensed her discomfort but was completely captivated with what she had to say.

"You are very handsome," she said. "I was very taken with your photograph and the way you signed your letter."

"The way I signed my letter?"

Nicholas leaned back in his chair and waited for her to explain. If she took all day, he wanted to hear exactly what she had to say.

Daughtry blushed and confusion filled her mind. "Forever yours," she whispered. "You signed your letter, 'Forever yours.'"

Nicholas smiled. He'd purposefully chosen that very ending after remembering it from one of his father's letters to his mother. His mother had told Nicholas once that the phrase was more than mere words, it was a pledge of sorts, and she had cherished it greatly. Now his own wife seemed to savor the words for the exact same reason.

"Something I learned from my father," he explained.

Daughtry used that introduction to Nicholas's past to question him further. "Tell me about yourself."

Nicholas shrugged. "Not much to tell. Nobody ever baked me bread as good as this, that's for sure."

"I'm serious," Daughtry said, pouring more coffee into her empty cup. "What about your family?"

"What about yours?"

"I'm alone," Daughtry replied.

"Me too," her husband replied and furthered her frustration.

"How am I to get to know you, if you won't tell me about yourself?" questioned Daughtry softly.

Nicholas leaned forward and smiled, revealing gleaming white teeth and eyes that fairly danced. "We have a lifetime to get to know one another," he answered. "I just don't think we need to do it all at one time. I'm going to enjoy getting to know you, little by little."

Without another word, Daughtry got to her feet, left the room for a moment, and returned with papers in hand.

"These are the marriage documents," she said, handing them to Nicholas.

Nicholas read them over and cast a glance upward to meet Daughtry's eyes. "Our wedding day was the twenty-first of September?"

Daughtry nodded.

"Wish I could have been there. I'll bet you were something to behold." Daughtry laughed at this, and Nicholas smiled broadly at her. "Did I say something wrong?"

"No, it's just that I look a whole sight better now than I did that day. Later, I'll show you what I was wearing."

Nicholas got up and went to the front sitting room where he retrieved a lock box, which he promptly brought back with him to the table. Taking a key from his vest pocket, he unlocked the box and carefully put the papers inside. Daughtry noticed when he did that her picture and letter were also inside the box, along with a large amount of money.

"They should be safe here," he announced and held up the key. "If you need anything, money or such, or you want to put something in here, just holler."

Daughtry nodded. "Just a minute, please," she said and went to the bedroom.

When she walked back into the kitchen, she thrust some money into Nicholas's hands. "I'd like to add this to your savings," she whispered. "It's all I had left after the trip."

Nicholas took the money and met Daughtry's eyes. He knew what she was doing and felt what she was trying to say without even hearing the words. He nodded, placed the money with his own, and shut the box. "Our savings," he said, locking the box and handing Daughtry the key. It was his way of meeting her trust with his own.

Daughtry reached up, but instead of taking the key, she simply closed her hand around Nicholas's and smiled. "I'm content for you to have control."

Chapter 7

*D*aughtry felt as though she lived a lifetime within a single day. Nicholas asked her to share with him all that she'd done in his absence, and Daughtry happily complied. He seemed especially impressed with the large stack of wood she'd positioned near the back of the house.

"I couldn't find any more coal," she explained, "so I did the next best thing."

"Those must be some arms you have," he teased and reached out to gently caress her upper arm. "Hmm, you don't feel like a lumberjack."

Daughtry giggled and looked at him shyly. "I felt like one, and I think I probably got as dirty as one. I went down to that grove of trees by the creek," she said and pointed. "There was quite a bit of dead wood there, and I just made good use of it."

"I have a load of coal coming," Nicholas said, reluctantly removing his hand from her arm. "It ought to get here tomorrow or the next day at the latest. I also arranged for the ice man to deliver here until the creek freezes. I figure I can manage to keep us supplied through the winter."

Daughtry felt her skin tingle long after Nicholas had stopped touching her. She barely heard his words as he continued to speak of his arrangements for the ranch.

"I thought we might go into town tomorrow. We could purchase some of the things we'll need for the winter and also get some staples that I didn't have on hand. Milk and eggs ought to be readily available."

"A milk cow and chickens would suit us better," Daughtry said without thinking.

"I suppose that's true enough," Nicholas said thoughtfully, "but with winter coming on and us not having the ranch really prepared for livestock, I thought maybe we'd just rely on store bought."

"I guess that makes sense," Daughtry replied, walking with slow even strides beside her husband.

They paused at the broken down corral, and Nicholas leaned against

573

a piece of fencing. The wind had picked up a bit and blew wisps of Daughtry's hair across her face.

Daughtry noticed the look of hesitancy in her husband's eyes, and she couldn't help but wonder if he were hiding something from her. How could she know what type of man he'd been before or what type he'd be now? Mother had once said that people always proved their true nature by their actions. Well, so far Nicholas's actions had given Daughtry little to fear.

"What do you suppose we should do first?" he asked her seriously.

Daughtry's introspection was released as she shrugged. "It all depends on your plans."

"What would you suggest?"

Daughtry smiled. "Well, being a woman, I suggest the house be put in order first. When I was trying to repair the roof the other day. . ."

"What? You were up on the roof?" Nicholas interrupted.

Daughtry felt her face flush. "Not exactly ladylike, was it?"

Nicholas laughed. "Ladylike or not, I'm amazed at your abilities. Did you actually get up there to fix the roof?"

Daughtry nodded, feeling rather proud. "I was inspired. The second night here it rained so hard that I had puddles all through the house. I can't say I accomplished much, but it was a healthy start."

"I guess that's what I'll do first then," Nicholas said with a thoughtful glance back at the house. "What else?"

Daughtry smiled. He genuinely wanted her to have a say in the matter. "Well, I'd like to cart everything out of the house and clean it good before winter sets in," Daughtry admitted. "As you could see, I only managed to set the kitchen and bedroom to rights before your return."

"Two very important rooms, if I do say so myself," Nicholas remarked.

"I figured it that way too," Daughtry said and, without thinking of the implications, added, "after all, I figured most of my time would be spent in one place or the other." The words were no sooner out than Daughtry realized how they sounded. She clapped her hand over her mouth.

Nicholas laughed until he doubled over, and Daughtry turned crimson, knowing he must think her terribly forward.

"I didn't mean," she started to justify herself, then realized she would only make matters worse by continuing.

Nicholas straightened up and tried to control his mirth. "That's quite all right, Honey," he said with tears of laughter gleaming in his eyes. "I pretty well figured what you meant."

Daughtry had to turn away to hide her embarrassment at her own statement. *Sometimes,* she thought, *I say the stupidest things.*

Nicholas sobered as if he'd noticed her discomfort. "So we empty the house," he said matter-of-factly, "and we wash it all down. Then what?"

"We put it all back inside," she answered softly. "Of course, if we don't want something back in the house, we can store it in the barn. I don't really know where you want things, so it might be nice if you had a part in the sorting through."

"I'm not sure what's even in there," Nicholas admitted. He stared at Daughtry's back for a moment before continuing. "I bought the place as is from a widow woman who wanted to move back East to live with her daughter. She'd let the place run down to this state and was barely able to feed herself. I heard from the sheriff in town that they were considering trying to force her out for her own good, so I came out here and we made a deal. She left a lot behind, but I have no idea whether it's useful stuff or just junk."

Daughtry nodded and finally turned to meet Nicholas's gaze. "I uncrated the dishes," she said, "but I didn't go through much else. I guess we can do that together, if you like."

"It would be my pleasure. Now, why don't you tell me about our grove of trees. Did you see anything of value there?"

"There were several apple trees, and I think I recognized a plum or two. Would you like to walk down there?"

"Yes," Nicholas replied. "I'd like that."

Daughtry began to walk at a fairly good pace. She was disturbed for some reason by the feelings Nicholas brought about. She thought back to the days she'd spent with nothing more than his picture and realized how much she'd lost her heart to him. *He can't possibly feel the same way,* she scolded herself. *Men are much more level-headed about such matters.* Nicholas obviously needed a hard-working wife, and he probably hadn't wanted to waste his time with romantic notions and courting.

Daughtry was so lost in these thoughts that she didn't pay any attention to the ground she was covering. Before she could tell what was happening, she lost her footing on a large rock and fell forward.

Nicholas's arm shot out in a flash and encircled her waist protectively. He pulled her upright, then, as though he were doing the most natural thing in the world, he pulled her close against him.

Daughtry stared up into his face, knowing he would kiss her. She saw the questioning look in his eyes, as though he were asking permission. Without thought, she reached her hand up to the back of his head and pulled his face down to meet hers.

Nicholas needed no more encouragement. He quickly captured her lips with his own and kissed her so ardently that Daughtry forgot for a moment who and where she was. When he pulled away, Daughtry uttered the first thing that came to mind.

"I love you, Nicholas! I have ever since seeing your picture." Daughtry no longer cared that the declaration sounded like that of an infatuated teenager. She meant the words with all her heart. She really did love this man.

Nicholas held her at arm's length for a moment. The troubled look on his face brought Daughtry back to reality. Somehow, she had offended him.

"I'm sorry," she whispered and walked backwards a step. "That must sound insincere. After all, we've known each other for such a short time." She turned to go back to the house, wanting to run away and hide from her feelings and the man she'd so clearly startled.

Nicholas crossed the distance between them and halted Daughtry from going any farther. "I don't believe you could be insincere if you tried," he whispered.

Daughtry lifted her face, revealing all the emotion and misgivings she felt. "Please don't be angry with me. It's just that I haven't had much practice at things like this. Maybe it's because I've never felt this way before." She shrugged her shoulders before continuing. "My mouth gets a little ahead of itself sometimes, as you've witnessed before."

Nicholas shook his head. "I'm not angry. Surprised, yes, but not angry."

Daughtry nodded and tried to think of something she could say to negate her declaration of love. Short of lying, however, she didn't know what she could say. She meant her words of love. As crazy and untimely as it seemed, Daughtry knew they were truer than anything else she'd said to Nicholas.

As if reading her mind, Nicholas took hold of her hand and squeezed it gently. "Just answer me this. Now that we're not in the middle of a kiss, did you mean it?"

Daughtry knew exactly what he was asking of her. "I meant it," she barely whispered. "I know it sounds impossible, but it's true. I never would have married you otherwise."

They walked back to the house in silence, but Daughtry felt the awkwardness between them. She knew Nicholas was taken aback by her statement, but she sensed that something more than just that was troubling him.

Without a word, they sat down at the table and stared at each other. When Nicholas finally did speak, Daughtry felt her heart skip a beat.

"Tell me about your family, Daughtry."

The soft request shouldn't have caused her such fear, but Daughtry felt confident that Nicholas would never allow her to stay if he knew the truth. And more than ever now, Daughtry didn't want to lose her husband and new life. She didn't want Nicholas to send her back home.

"I grew up on a ranch," she said carefully. "I learned just about everything there is to know. I can ride, shoot, rope, brand, mend fence, whatever. I've nursed sick calves back to health, assisted with birthings, medicatings, and even helped to drive the herds to market. Ranching isn't just something I learned," she admitted. "It's something that's in my blood."

"But that doesn't answer my question. I want to know about your family. You said that you were alone, but there must have been someone with you at one time or another. What became of your father and mother? Do you have brothers or sisters?"

"I had a sister," Daughtry said, feeling it safe to speak of Julie. "She died several years ago when her horse slipped on an icy trail and went over the side of a ravine."

"I'm sorry. That must have been terribly hard on your folks."

"Yes, it was," Daughtry admitted before realizing that Nicholas had led her where she didn't want to go.

He was looking at her intensely now, expecting her to continue, but Daughtry knew she couldn't. "I don't want to talk about it anymore," she whispered and quickly left the room.

Nicholas stared at her chair for several minutes. What was she hiding and why did she look so fearful whenever he mentioned her past? Frustration began to build into anger at her distrust, but then Nicholas caught himself and realized that he had no room to express such thoughts. He was just as guilty of hiding from the past as she. Maybe it was what had brought them together. Maybe it was what God expected them both to deal with.

Chapter 8

The weeks that passed were the happiest Daughtry had ever known. She worked at Nicholas's side, laughing, teasing, and falling into a comfortable routine of being Mrs. Dawson. At night, they snuggled down under handmade quilts to share each other's warmth. Beneath the covers, they talked and dreamed about the future.

Daughtry loved it all. Not a single part of her new life caused her regret, except that she had to avoid her past. She started having nightmares about her father coming to tear her away from Nicholas's strong arms, but she choked back her fears and refused to let them surface. She couldn't risk losing all that had come to mean so much to her.

But, try as she might, Daughtry couldn't forget her family, nor could she dispel the building anxieties that haunted her every waking moment. All she could do was pray and ask God to forgive her and guide her steps, convincing herself that nothing else needed to be done.

Sundays were always a joy to Daughtry. She prepared for church with great enthusiasm, though today the sniffles from a passing bout with a head cold caused her some discomfort.

Nicholas popped his head through the bedroom door with a grin as broad as the barn door opening. "You need help with the buttons, Mrs. Dawson?"

Daughtry looked up and shook her head. "You can't appreciate what we women have to go through in order to look just right for our men."

Nicholas rolled his eyes. "You always look just right to me, even when you're wearing those boys' jeans you seem to favor."

"Sometimes I wish I could wear jeans to church," Daughtry said with a giggle. "Especially when the wind whips up and comes blasting across the open range."

"Well, I'd better never find you wearing those things off the property. It wouldn't be decent to have all the townsmen following you around with their tongues hanging out."

"You sound just like my father," she replied without thinking. The words were no sooner out than she realized her mistake.

Coming to her, Nicholas pulled Daughtry into his arms. "Why are you so afraid to tell me about him? Did he hurt you?"

Daughtry shook her head.

"I promise to understand. Whatever it is—whatever he did to you. . . ." His words trailed into silence.

"He was a wonderful father," Daughtry said, still trembling beneath Nicholas's touch. She would say nothing more, though, and in frustration Nicholas released her.

"I'll get the wagon," he said and stalked out of the room.

Daughtry knew she'd hurt him by refusing to deal honestly with him. She comforted herself by remembering that Nicholas refused to share any real details of his own past with her. They were both hurting and hiding, she decided. They might as well do it together.

Daughtry was glad that Nicholas wasn't a man given to holding a grudge. By the time they headed into town he was laughing and joking about first one thing, then another.

After church they enjoyed a leisurely ride home, and Nicholas shared his plans to buy Daughtry a horse. Good horse flesh was something to get excited about, and Daughtry squealed her delight at the news and threw her arms around Nicholas's neck.

"You really mean it?" she asked, hugging him so tight that he had to stop the horses in order to control her.

"Yes. Yes," he said, laughing at her enthusiasm. "Who would've thought that a little ol' horse would have gotten me so much attention?"

"It's just that I've really missed riding," Daughtry said happily. "Back home, I used to ride every day. I had the most wonderful gelding named Poco. He was about fifteen hands high and had the most beautiful gray coat." She stopped talking because Nicholas was looking at her strangely.

Daughtry jumped back and hung her head. She'd done it again. She couldn't keep from bringing up her family and the home life she'd once loved. "He was a good horse," she finally said, when Nicholas wouldn't speak.

Nicholas remained silent and, when Daughtry said nothing more, he snapped the reins and sent the horse down the path to home.

Daughtry tried not to think about her family that night as she curled into her husband's arms. The day had brought on too many memories, and more than once she'd nearly told Nicholas everything just to be rid of the burden.

"Nicholas?" she whispered against his ear.

"Yeah?"

"I love you." Her voice sounded like a child's trying to get on the good side of an adult.

For a minute, Nicholas said nothing. He tightened his grip on her and sighed. "I don't think you can love me and not trust me," he finally replied.

Daughtry stiffened in his arms. "What would you know about it? You don't love me. At least you've never said that you do."

Nick chuckled at her little girl-like voice. "Never said I didn't, either."

Daughtry tried to ease away, but Nicholas would have no part of it. "Daughtry," he whispered her name and it sounded like a song. "Don't leave me."

Daughtry wanted to cry out that she'd never leave, but in the back of her mind that one thing spread panic through her like no other. She might not ever leave of her own accord, but what if her father forced her to leave?

"Never!" she declared in a whisper and settled down into his arms again.

Daughtry faded into a deep sleep, but soon she found herself in the middle of a most realistic nightmare. Her father had learned of her marriage to Nicholas, and now he had come to face him in some sort of showdown, straight out of the frontier days she'd heard so much about.

Tossing from side to side, Daughtry fought with the images, pleading with her father to leave things as they were. He was furious and unyielding, promising to take Daughtry back home where she belonged and to hurt Nicholas if he dared to interfere.

He quoted the Bible to her, as Daughtry fell to her knees at his feet. "Children are to obey their parents," she heard him say. Turning in her dream to face her husband, Daughtry cried out at the betrayal and pain she saw in his eyes.

"You can't be my wife, Daughtry. You are his daughter," Nicholas told her through the misty fog.

"No," Daughtry moaned softly in her sleep. "No."

"Daughtry!" Nicholas exclaimed and gently shook her shoulders.

"Oh, Nick," she cried and fell limp against him as though all of her strength had been drained away.

Gently, he eased back against the pillows, taking her with him. "Why don't you stop all of this and tell me what's wrong. Tell me what you're keeping from me that causes you to have such fitful nights."

Daughtry looked up at him in surprise. Nicholas just shook his head. "This isn't the first time, you know. You nearly flail me to death night after night. It's only getting worse, so you might as well deal with it here and now."

Daughtry knew he was right, but the fear in her heart caused her to hesitate. "You won't like it," she whispered.

"Why not let me be the judge of that?"

"Because I can already tell," Daughtry replied. "You're so serious about everything, and you handle things in such a mature way that I'm afraid this will make you very angry with me."

"Daughtry," Nicholas said, reaching out to touch her cheek, "I could never be angry with you. Tell me."

Daughtry wiped at her tears with the back of her sleeve, took a deep breath, and got up on her knees. "I ran away from home to marry you."

"What?" Nicholas's eyes widened in surprise. "Don't tell me you're really sixteen or something."

Daughtry laughed. "No, I'm honestly as old as I said. A woman wouldn't joke about a thing like that."

"Then why do you say you ran away?"

Daughtry folded her hands. "My father was devastated after my sister died. It will be four years this November—but he only gets worse with each year that passes. Julie's death caused him to become overprotective of me. Everywhere I went, either he or one of my five brothers was there to shadow my every step. He wouldn't let me meet anyone or court. That's why I never fell in love with anyone else. You have to understand, I love my father and brothers, but they were smothering me to death. Even my mother understood how I felt, but she couldn't seem to reason any sense into my father."

Daughtry could not bring herself to look at Nicholas's face as she continued. "We had a terrible argument the night before I learned of your advertisement. When I saw your ad in the paper, I thought it just might be my way out. I decided to write to you and at least learn more about you, but then you wrote back with the proxy and the train ticket." She paused. "And your picture."

She looked up to see that Nicholas had put his hands behind his head and was studying her intently. Fearing what he might say, she hurried on. "I was going to write to you and refuse the proposal. I thought I could reason with my father, but when I tried to ask him nicely to give me more space—to let me grow up and fall in love—he refused. I was so angry, that I wrote them a long letter and slipped out in the middle of the night to come to you. I didn't let them know I was marrying you, and I didn't say where I was going, only that I would be taken care of and safe."

She sighed. "I'm really sorry, Nicholas. I thought I was doing the right thing, or at least I thought it would work out to be the right thing. I saw it as an opportunity and I took it. Now, I keep having these horrible dreams that my father and brothers come to take me back. They're always so angry and ugly, and I never have a chance to save you."

By now she was crying and Nicholas could no longer remain aloof. "Five brothers?" he asked, his forehead wrinkling up in disbelief.

Daughtry only cried all the more and nodded her head. "I don't want to leave you. I don't want them to take me away." She nearly wailed the words, and Nicholas began to chuckle.

"No one is going to take you away from me, Daughtry. Especially not now, not after all this time has passed between us. You're a grown woman, and you made your choice. You're a married woman, and you belong with me." His words forcefully placed the boundaries for Daughtry to see.

"What's done is done," he added. "You can't let them worry about you, though. And you can't go on having nightmares every night. I have to believe that this father of yours must be someone pretty special. Otherwise, it wouldn't upset you so much. Tomorrow we'll go to town and you can telephone them, or we'll send a telegram. Either way, you have to let them know what you've done and that you're all right."

"You aren't mad at me?" she asked through her tears.

Nicholas opened his arms to her with a smile, and Daughtry nestled down eagerly. "How could I be mad at you?" he whispered and reached over to turn down the lamp. "I love you."

Chapter 9

*D*aughtry felt November's chill air breathe down her damp back. She was working to pull out the last of the brush that had once surrounded her house. Rising up and stretching, Daughtry relished the sun, mild as it was, and put her face upward to catch every single ray. Winter was soon to be upon them and, by all the signs, Daughtry feared it might be a difficult one.

Nicholas watched his wife from his vantage point in the barn loft. She grew more beautiful every day, and every day he knew he loved her more. How good of God to throw them together. He observed her as she went back to work, thinking back to the day they'd gone to the post office and mailed the letter to her father and mother.

"I don't think I can do this, Nicholas," she had said in a pleading tone that begged him to let her forget the whole thing.

"You have to," he'd insisted firmly. "Nothing bad will come of it, Daughtry. If your folks come here, they'll see how happy you are, and they won't even want you to leave."

At least Nicholas hoped things would work out that way. He continued to watch Daughtry, but he was thinking now of his own parents. They'd be livid if he'd pulled such a stunt, but then they were always critical of the choices he'd made in life. If it weren't for them, however, he might never have met and married Daughtry, and that would have been a pity.

Turning his attention back to the work at hand, Nicholas was surprised when Daughtry called up to him in a frantic voice.

"Nicholas! Someone's coming!"

Like he'd done as a child, Nicholas jumped from the loft to the stacked bales of hay, then to the floor of the barn. He bounded out quickly to note the three horseback riders approaching from the west.

"Oh, Nick," Daughtry whimpered. "I just know it's my father and brothers."

"At least he only brought two," Nicholas said with a smile. "Go on in the house. You wait there for me, and I'll talk to them first. You'll see, Daughtry. It's going to be all right."

Daughtry did as she was told, not because she felt overly obedient, but because she was a coward. She had no desire to hear the things her father would no doubt have to say to her husband. "Why, God?" she prayed aloud. "Why couldn't I have just done things the right way?"

In only a matter of minutes, angry voices rang loud and clear. Daughtry tried to cover her ears, not wanting to know what was said. What if her father said something really ugly? What if Nicholas refused to let them see her?

Daughtry started to pace. A part of her was certain that she should go outside and try to smooth over the situation. Maybe once her father saw how happy she had become and how wonderful Nicholas truly was, he'd let things be and go back home.

She reached for the door, just as things quieted considerably. A horse whinnied nervously, and Daughtry pulled back. Nicholas had told her to wait inside. She at least had to show him that she could follow his instructions. She might have misled him regarding her family, but that was all behind her now and she wanted to be a good wife.

Just as she'd convinced herself that everything was going to be all right, shots rang out, and Daughtry felt her knees turn to jelly.

"They've killed each other!" she gasped and ran to the window.

Outside, two men lay on the ground holding their bleeding arms, while one man remained on his horse with his hands raised high in the air. Daughtry didn't recognize any of them. She breathed a sigh of relief and turned her attention to her husband.

Nicholas stood with his feet fixed and a rifle leveled at the third man. The rage in his face was terrifying, and Daughtry saw blind hatred in his eyes. She stared at her husband's face and thought, *Who is this man?* He certainly didn't resemble the gentle one she'd married. Daughtry clutched her apron to her mouth to keep from screaming.

Her mind whirled. Who were these men and why had Nicholas shot them? Furthermore, where had he gotten the rifle to do the deed? She'd never seen a gun of any kind on the grounds, although she wouldn't have been surprised had there been one.

Staring at the scene outside her house, Daughtry couldn't hear a word that was being said. She watched the third man dismount from his horse and stare down the barrel of Nicholas's rifle. She couldn't watch anymore.

Daughtry moved to the far end of the house and cowered in the corner. She was wavering between tears and out-and-out hysteria. The more she thought about the scene, the more frightened she felt. A nervous laugh escaped her as she shook her head. Had Nicholas killed the two men? She sobbed and drew a ragged breath. Suddenly, she felt more terrified than she'd ever been in her life. She would have gladly welcomed the sight of her father and brothers at that moment, but she knew she could hope for no such reprieve.

The kitchen door banged, and Daughtry knew someone had come into the house. Trembling, she backed into the corner even tighter.

"Daughtry!" Nicholas called out to her as he moved from room to room. "Daughtry, where are you?" His voice sounded worried, almost panicked.

When he came into the front room, he sighed when he saw her. "Why didn't you answer me? Are you okay?"

Daughtry couldn't say a word. She stared at him, trying to force herself to calm down. It was an impossible task.

"Daughtry, come here, Honey. It's all right now."

Daughtry shook her head, not really seeing him. She saw instead the man who'd held the rifle in black rage. She saw a killer in her mind and felt her breath quicken.

Nicholas stepped forward with his arms extended. When he came to her, Nicholas reached out his hands to pull her into his arms. Daughtry went wild.

"No!" she screamed and fought his grasp. "Don't touch me!" She doubled up her fists and flailed them in the air at his face and chest.

With stunned realization, Nicholas understood that Daughtry was terrified of him, not the men he'd tied up in the barn.

As gently as he could, Nicholas pinned her arms to her side and physically carried her to the sofa. Daughtry was crying and yelling incoherently, begging him not to hurt her. Nicholas thought he'd die inside.

"It's all right, Daughtry. Honey, don't do this," he whispered. Holding her against him with one arm, he began to stroke her face with his other hand. "Daughtry!" He nearly yelled the name, and she immediately settled.

Raising her blue eyes to meet his dark, almost black ones, Daughtry couldn't hide the fear she felt. All of her foolishness in running away, marrying, and hiding here with a stranger had suddenly come home to her. Gasping for breath, she strained against his touch, while at the same time she heard his gentle words.

"Daughtry, those men are outlaws—a part of my past catching up with me. They meant to hurt us. I only did what I had to do in order to protect us. I was only defending myself."

Daughtry let the words sink in. Reason drove out the fear, and she began to relax in his hold. "Who—who—" she stammered, "are they?"

"It's not important. They're wanted by the law, and later I'll take them into the sheriff. I have them tied up in the barn, and they can't hurt you." He softened his expression and loosened his hold ever so slightly. "But then, you aren't really worried about them hurting you, are you?"

Daughtry couldn't answer him. She felt so foolish for her behavior.

"Daughtry, have I ever given you reason to fear me?"

"No," she managed to whisper.

"I'm not a bad man, Daughtry. I know there's things I can't tell you just yet, but trust me. I understood about your secrets, now I'm asking you to understand about mine."

She felt her fears give way to sympathy, then relief. He had only defended himself, she thought. Slumping against him, completely spent, Daughtry clung to his shirt. "I'm sorry," she said softly.

Nicholas brushed back her hair with his hand. "It's all right. I can honestly understand your misgivings."

"Why can't you tell me about your past?" she questioned. "I told you about mine."

Nicholas sighed. "It's a long story, but for now I'm just begging you to trust me and to trust God to work it all out. I love you, Daughtry. Please, don't doubt me on that."

"I don't," she replied and sat up. She studied the worry in his eyes. It went beyond concern and seemed like something that bordered fear. Was he afraid she'd stopped loving him?

"Oh, Nicholas," she said and kissed his face several times, "I was so afraid you'd be killed. Then when I saw you with that gun and you were so angry—well, I just didn't know what to think."

"I know, Honey, and believe me, I would have saved you from having to go through it if I could have."

Daughtry nodded. It was all right, she told herself. Whatever his past consisted of, she no longer cared. She only knew that she loved him and that she would stand by him no matter what.

Leaning down to put her face on his shoulder, Daughtry spoke. "We'll just trust God to get us through this," she pledged.

"That's my girl," Nicholas said and leaned back against the sofa.

Chapter 10

*D*ays later, Daughtry had nearly forgotten the unpleasant incident. "Are we really going to get the horse today?" she asked eagerly. Securing her bonnet, she waited for Nicholas's reply.

"Yes, for the millionth time," he said laughing. "I've never seen you so excited about anything in our two months of marriage."

"Well, there was the time that rat got in the house," Daughtry said with a grimace. "Or wait, what about the bathtub? I got pretty excited about the bathtub."

Nicholas's eyes twinkled. "Yes, yes, you did. I seem to recall having some very fine apple cake that evening. Wonder if I'll get another one for buying the horse?"

"We'll see," Daughtry said with a smug look of satisfaction. "Depends on how good the horse is."

"Now, while we're in town," Nicholas said, bringing the wagon to a halt, "I want you to get whatever you think we might need. We've got to make sure we're stocked up for the winter, just in case we have trouble getting into town."

Daughtry nodded and pulled out a small list. "I wrote down things for the kitchen." She glanced up and down the street which was already teaming with people. Several suffragists stood at one end of the street expounding on the necessity of women having the vote. At the opposite end of town there seemed to be an unusual amount of traffic at the railroad depot. "We seem to have come on a busy day."

"Looks that way." Nicholas helped her from the wagon and put a finger under her chin. "Get yourself some warm clothes while you're at it. I was looking through the things you brought into this marriage and you aren't at all well supplied." His mouth curled into a grin, and Daughtry returned his smile.

"Do you need anything?" she asked. "I can sew, you know, and we still have Mrs. Cummings's old sewing machine. I'm sure I could get it in working shape."

"I could use some heavy shirts for winter," he said, then placed a light kiss on her forehead. "But don't worry about me. I want you to make sure you have everything you need. Everything, understood? Even if you worry that I might think it frivolous. I've never had a wife before, so I wouldn't be knowing what one might need."

Daughtry was touched by his generosity. "I'll try to be thorough. Where will you be?"

"Oh, here and there. I have to get the horse and there's a few other things I need to attend to. I'll pick up the mail, so you don't have to worry about it. Now, here's some money, and if that's not enough, tell them to hold whatever it is you want and I'll pay them before we head home."

Daughtry watched as Nicholas took off down the street. He was so kind and loving. Gone were the images of the hateful man with the rifle. All Daughtry could see was the man who touched her heart.

She was headed across the street to the general store when she happened to glance once more at her husband's retreating form. Surprised, she noticed he'd headed to the sheriff's office. Watching him go into the small building, Daughtry quickly made her way down the street to follow him. She wanted very much to know if her husband were in some kind of trouble.

"But why would he come here if he was an outlaw?" Daughtry wondered aloud. Biting her lip, she looked around quickly and was grateful to find herself alone on the boardwalk.

The town was much too small to have a very grand affair for a jail. Daughtry knew from what folks had told her on the train coming here that this was a one saloon, one cell kind of town. She would have been just as happy had they told her it had no saloon, but then, the world wasn't perfect.

Leaning close to the window, Daughtry could see her husband in deep discussion with a man she could only guess was the sheriff. She couldn't hear anything from this vantage point, however. Quietly, she made her way around the building and up the alley. She came to the window nearest the two men and paused. This one had the shade pulled down on the inside. She could see nothing, but she pressed her ear to the glass after a cautious glance down the alleyway.

"You go far enough back with these men to be related," she heard the sheriff saying. He said something more, but his words were garbled and Daughtry couldn't begin to understand.

Then Nicholas bellowed in a voice so loud Daughtry had no trouble distinguishing every word, "I didn't ask them to look me up. They rode in looking for trouble and I gave it to them."

The sheriff, equally enraged, ranted back. "Well, you made your bed this time for sure. You brought it all on yourself!"

Daughtry wondered silently what Nicholas had brought on himself, but she was unable to continue listening at the window because someone was coming down the alley. She made her way down the street, crossing to avoid the suffragists and their battle cries.

She quickly entered the general store and furiously began her shopping. Her mind was filled with ugly images and worrisome thoughts. What if Nicholas had once been an outlaw? Maybe he was once partners with the men who sat in the jail cell. She shuddered at the thought. That just couldn't be possible. Or could it?

She toyed with several bolts of flannel material and finally settled on a dark blue plaid and a solid brown. She ordered the yardage and sought out buttons to match, planning in her mind to make Nicholas two good shirts before winter set in. Remembering his instructions to her, Daughtry went through the material a second time and chose several colors of wool to make herself some simple skirts. She finished by securing some plain white cotton and two calico prints for blouses, before turning her attention to colorful skeins of knitting yarn.

She paid for the goods, certain that she'd overspent what Nicholas had given her, but found to her surprise that she had plenty of cash left over. Seeing that she still had enough money, Daughtry quickly instructed the store owner to throw in several pairs of long underwear for her husband.

"What size?" the man asked her as he went to retrieve the goods.

"Oh, my," she said in surprise. "I don't know."

"Well," the man said looking at the blushing woman, "is he bigger than me?"

Daughtry sized the man up for a moment. "Yes," she determined quickly. "He's at least this much taller than me and about this much wider," she said, holding her hands out to indicate the size. Just then, Nicholas came into the store and Daughtry motioned to the storekeeper. "That's him."

The man behind the counter smiled and nodded. "Morning, Mr. Dawson. I didn't know this little lady was your wife."

"We're newlyweds," Nicholas said, coming up behind Daughtry. "Now what did you mean 'That's him'?"

"I was just buying you some. . ." Daughtry blushed again, unable to talk about underwear in the presence of her husband.

The storekeeper quickly brought the requested product to the counter and added it to the stack of things Daughtry had already paid for. "Will these do?" he asked, looking at Nicholas and not Daughtry.

Nicholas had to hold himself in check to keep from laughing out loud at Daughtry's sudden embarrassment. "She thinks of everything," he said with a wink over Daughtry's shoulder to the storekeeper. "They're fine."

Daughtry handed the storekeeper the remaining amount due, while Nicholas put his arm around her lovingly. "Did you get everything you needed?"

"Yes, and then some. I certainly can't complain about your generosity, Mr. Dawson."

Nicholas picked up their supplies and led Daughtry to the door. "Would you like to get something to eat while we're in town?"

"That might be fun," Daughtry replied, looping her arm through Nicholas's. "But it's also a bit frivolous. We're going to have a great many expenses come spring and. . ."

"Madam," a deep, but clearly female voice called out, "you are a victim of our society."

Daughtry and Nicholas both stopped directly in front of a sour-faced woman who was dressed in black with a white sash that clearly identified her suffrage cause. The woman continued before either Nicholas or Daughtry could comment.

"This man seeks to enslave you! You needn't be chained to him like a dog. The men of America seek to make women their possessions. They want to control them. He," the woman said, sticking a bony finger in the middle of Nicholas's face, "wants to control you. He wants to dominate your every living moment."

Daughtry stared up at Nicholas as if contemplating the woman's words. Nicholas just shrugged and raised a questioning brow.

"That's right," the woman continued. "This man would just as soon see you bound to him—fit only to serve his pleasures and bear his children!"

Daughtry smiled broadly at the woman. "I know. Isn't it great?"

At this, the woman sputtered and stepped back in horror, while Nicholas threw back his head and roared with laughter.

"You, young woman, are the very reason women are oppressed. You are the reason we can't voice our opinions and vote for our own representation," the woman called to Nicholas and Daughtry as they made their way down the boardwalk.

"You certainly made a spectacle of yourself, Mrs. Dawson. Probably set back women's rights a hundred years," Nicholas said, helping her down from the boardwalk.

"Oh dear," Daughtry said in feigned concern. "I suppose that means I'll be bound to you even longer now."

"Only forever," Nicholas said with a gentleness in his voice that warmed Daughtry's heart.

Daughtry stared up at her husband, all the love she felt for him shining clear in her eyes.

"Well, are you going to just stand there or are you going to tell me what you think of your new horse?" he questioned.

Daughtry's eyes widened and she quickly looked around. Standing there, tied to the back of the wagon, was a beautiful chestnut mare, complete with western saddle. "I thought you might like to ride her home," Nicholas whispered against her ear.

"Oh, she's beautiful! Of course I want to ride her home. Oh, Nicholas, thank you!" She threw her arms around her husband, nearly causing him to drop their packages.

Helping to set things back in place, Daughtry composed herself a bit, but the delight was evident in her eyes.

"You're welcome," he said and happily deposited the packages in the back of the wagon before turning to lend Daughtry some help in mounting.

"Does she have a name?" Daughtry questioned, running her hand along the mare's sleek neck.

"She does. The owner called her Nutmeg."

Daughtry cooed and talked to the mare, whispering the name several times. "I think we'll be good friends, you and I," she said to the horse.

Nicholas helped her up into the saddle, then took his place on the wagon. "You sure you want to ride her home?"

"Of course I'm sure," Daughtry replied indignantly. "I could ride before I could walk, at least that's what my father used to say." She frowned only briefly at the reference before moving Nutmeg forward.

Nicholas pulled up alongside her once they were on the road out of town. "It's going to be all right, Daughtry. You can't be worrying all the time about what might or might not happen."

"I know, but it's been awhile since we sent the letter. I figure it won't be long before. . ." She couldn't finish the sentence, but Nicholas understood and conveyed his sympathy with his eyes. Taking a deep breath, Daughtry reminded herself that she had Nicholas's love and that he would protect her. Then an earlier scene crossed her mind and Daughtry grimaced. *But who's going to protect Nicholas?* she wondered. *Who will protect him when his past catches up with him again?*

With the sheriff's words still reverberating through her head and her own imagination running wild, Daughtry couldn't help but fear the truth. She worked almost mindlessly around the kitchen that evening, putting the finishing touches on supper, waiting for Nicholas to reappear after seeing to the horses. She pulled a peach cobbler from the oven and smiled. At least she could offer him a good home-cooked meal. Cooking was one thing her mother had insisted Daughtry learn.

"Umm, smells mighty fine in here," Nicholas said, coming through the mud porch into the kitchen. "And it's warmer in here, too."

Daughtry came to him and helped him off with his coat. "It does feel a lot colder," she replied, feeling the chilled night air as it followed him through the open door.

"No sign of snow just yet," Nicholas added, giving his hat a toss to a hook beside the door. "It might just go around us."

Daughtry nodded. "Supper's ready."

"I can see that," he said, staring appreciatively at the table. "You're going to make me fat," he laughed but eagerly took a seat.

"I baked you a cobbler," Daughtry said proudly. She brought the bubbling concoction to the table in order to show it off. "It ought to taste even better with the fresh cream we brought home."

"I'm going to have to keep buying you presents, I see."

"Maybe you could just share secrets with me instead," she replied soberly.

"What do you mean?" he asked, knowing full well what she wanted.

"I just think it would be nice to know more about you. Like those men the other day. I can't just forget about them. Who were they and why did they want to hurt you?" Daughtry sat down to the table and waited for Nicholas to speak.

"It's nothing," Nicholas snapped and began putting food on his plate. Softening his tone, he looked at her with pleading eyes and added, "Nothing that needs to concern you."

"But I heard the sheriff yell at you," Daughtry said without thinking. She bowed her head, ashamed to admit she'd spied on her husband.

"Don't nose into this, Daughtry," he replied sternly, the first time he'd ever sounded angry with her.

"I have a right to know," she protested, lifting her face to meet his.

Nicholas's eyes narrowed slightly. "Stay out of it. I mean it!" He slammed his fist down on the table, causing all the dishes to rattle. Daughtry stared at him for a heartbeat, then got up and ran from the table.

She was out the back door and running past the barn before she realized he was calling after her. Pride wouldn't let her slow down, however, and Daughtry continued until she came to her favorite place. The little grove of trees by the creek offered her a safe haven, but not much warmth. Shivering uncontrollably under the full moon, Daughtry began to cry. Why had he been so mean?

She knew he'd follow her, but when he wrapped his arms around her and pulled her close, Daughtry jumped back in fear.

"Don't," she said between chattering teeth.

She could see the pain in his face. Pain of rejection and fear of loss. "I'm sorry, Daughtry. I didn't mean to lose my temper."

She said nothing, wondering at the strained apology. Did he think that was enough? Just an "I'm sorry?" *What do you want him to say?* Daughtry asked herself and could think of no answer.

Nicholas reached out to her again, and this time Daughtry didn't push away. "I really am sorry," he whispered against her ear. "It's just that the whole episode with those men unnerved me. I can't help but worry that we aren't safe here anymore. I can't help but worry that I've exposed you to something harmful and ugly. Before, when it was just me, I didn't have to worry about things like that. I prayed and asked God to ride with me, watch over me, and take me home when the time came. But now, there's so much more. There's you and. . ." He fell silent. What was the use? He couldn't explain it.

Daughtry's heart softened toward him. His worry for their safety concerned her more than she wanted to admit but, right now, all she wanted to do was comfort him.

"It's all right, Nicholas. I'm sorry to have pressed the matter, and I'm sorry that I spied on you. I do love you and I trust you, so from now on, I'll leave the matter be."

Chapter 11

Thanksgiving drew near and with it the haunting reminder of Julie's death. Daughtry found herself thinking about her sister, even when she didn't want to. Julie would have been eighteen. Thoughts of her naturally turned Daughtry's mind to her father. She was both worried and relieved that he'd done nothing to interfere in her life. Was he so angry that he no longer cared?

"It's a beautiful day out here, Daughtry!" Nicholas called from just outside the back door.

Daughtry made her way outside, wearing only her dark green wool skirt and long-sleeved calico blouse. "Yes," she murmured, relishing the reminder of summer. "I think I'll do the wash outside today."

Nicholas mounted his horse and gave her an admonishing look. "Don't overdo it and don't stay outside if it turns cold. I don't want you getting sick."

Daughtry grinned at his fatherly words. "I'm surprised you're willing to leave me here alone."

"I'm not very happy about the idea," Nicholas said, "but you're insistent on having fresh turkey for Thanksgiving, and since the Shaunasseys offered to sell me one of their birds, I guess I'll just have to overlook my discomfort."

"Oh, go on with you now," Daughtry said and reached out to smack the horse on the rump. Instead, Nicholas caught her hand and lowered his lips to her fingers.

"Please stay out of trouble," he whispered. "I've grown very fond of you, Mrs. Dawson."

Daughtry's heart warmed to his words. "And I, you, Mr. Dawson."

With nothing more said, Nicholas took off for his five-mile ride to the Shaunasseys, while Daughtry went back inside to ready her laundry.

With most of the wash done by noon, Daughtry was just putting away her wash tub and scrub board when the unmistakable sound of a wagon caught her attention. Peering around the house, Daughtry was pleased to see the freighter, Tom O'Toole, making his way up the long Dawson drive.

She quickly hurried inside to put on coffee and arrange a plate of cookies, while Tom completed the trip to the barn. He was bringing in the last of their ordered supplies for winter, and Daughtry was hopeful that he might have thought to bring the mail as well.

"Afternoon, Mrs. Dawson," the man said, jumping to the ground.

"Afternoon, Tom," Daughtry replied. "When you finish there, I've got hot coffee and cinnamon cookies for you."

"That ought to make my work pass quicklike," he announced. Pulling down a heavy crate, Tom motioned. "This here is a bunch of them canned goods you asked for last time. It just came in from Denver."

"Oh, good," Daughtry replied. "You can bring that on up to the house, and I'll get to work putting it away."

Tom nodded and followed Daughtry into the house, where he deposited the crate, requested a hammer, and pulled the nailed lid off. Daughtry immediately went to work, while Tom made his way back outside.

Humming to herself, Daughtry felt good about their filled pantry. There was more than enough food to tide them over for a great many months, if necessary. Nicholas, however, seemed to think that even if heavy snows buried them, a good strong prairie wind would most likely clear a path to town. With that in mind, Daughtry didn't worry much about the distance.

She was nearly finished when Tom gave a heavy knock on the door and bounded into the room. "All done out there," he said, and Daughtry poured him a mug of coffee and pointed him to the chair.

"You just rest awhile and help yourself to those cookies. Nicholas has gone over to the Shaunasseys' to get our Thanksgiving turkey."

"Me and the missus are planning on heading up to Raton for Thanksgiving. She's got a sister there and nieces and nephews, and since it wasn't that far by train, we thought it might make a nice trip before the snows set in."

"It does sound like fun," Daughtry said half-heartedly, for, in truth, she loved her little hideaway home and didn't desire to travel away from it, even to visit her family.

Tom drained his coffee and reached for a third cookie. Daughtry started to refill his cup but he waved her off. "I still have two more deliveries to make, so I'd best be on my way." He got to his feet, and Daughtry followed him out of the house.

"This weather is sure enough pleasant," Tom said, making his way to the wagon. "I could do without the snow for awhile."

"Me too," Daughtry replied. "Well, take care, Tom." She waited while he climbed up into the worn wooden seat of his freight wagon.

"Oh, I plum forgot," he said, reaching under the seat. "I brought the mail for you."

Daughtry's face lit up, hoping that maybe a newspaper or magazine might be included in his delivery. Nicholas had ordered several magazines for her when they were last in town, and Daughtry was beginning to think they'd never arrive. To her disappointment, though, Tom handed down only a single envelope.

"This one's for you," he said and picked up the reins. "I'll be seeing you, Mrs. Dawson." He snapped the reins and took off on his route while Daughtry stared at the unmistakable handwriting of her father.

With shaking hands, Daughtry forced herself to open the letter. She waited until she made it back to the kitchen table, however, to read it. She was feeling weak in the knees and almost green with anxiety by the time she unfolded the single page.

Daughtry stared down at the words in disbelief. Her father was coming! She read the brief statement of when he planned to arrive and found that the date in his letter matched the one on the calendar. Her father planned to arrive today!

Daughtry dropped the letter on the table. If her father showed up and Nicholas were not there to prevent him from taking her back, what would she do? Feeling sick inside, Daughtry got up from the table and began to pace.

"Dear Lord," she whispered, "I know that sinful nature got me here. I know that I was out and out disobedient, but, Father, I love Nicholas and I don't want my father to take me back to Piñon Canyon. I want to stay here and be Nicholas's wife." She paused and realized her prayer was more the uncontrollable babblings of a rebellious child. She folded her hands together and took a deep breath.

"Show me what I need to do, Father. Show me how to make this right. Please forgive me for going against my father's wishes, and help my father to understand why I did what I did and to forgive me for hurting him. Amen."

Daughtry felt only marginally better. She knew that God was in charge and would take care of everything. She even knew that He'd already forgiven her for her willful disobedience. Daughtry couldn't wash away the feelings of helplessness, however.

A quick glance at the clock on the wall started Daughtry panicking again. *He plans to arrive today,* she thought, *but when?* Finally, Daughtry decided she'd ride over to the Shaunasseys' and get Nicholas. She could face anything with Nicholas at her side.

Despite the nice weather, she put on heavy wool stockings and a wool, split skirt. She pulled on her riding boots and grabbed a warm, fitted jacket to throw in her saddle bag in case the weather turned cool. Then suddenly, without really knowing that she was packing, Daughtry found herself throwing together gloves, a bonnet, her jeans, and one of Nicholas's thick flannel shirts. When she'd gathered these things, Daughtry took two wool blankets and rolled all of it together into a pack that would fit behind her saddle.

Somewhere in the midst of her worry, Daughtry knew she was running away again, but her mind wouldn't let her reason out the truth.

"I can't go to Nicholas," she said aloud, "or I might pass Daddy on the way." The thought of being already en route when her father caught up with her made Daughtry believe he'd have just that much easier of a time forcing her home.

Running with the pack into the kitchen, Daughtry laid out provisions for herself, including matches, a small pot, and a generous amount of food. She stuffed as much as she could into her saddle bags, then leaving the kitchen in complete disarray, she grabbed her things and ran for the barn.

Nicholas was in a good mood as he made his way home that afternoon. He had a nice fat turkey confined in a crate on the back of his rather skeptical horse and two warm loaves of pumpkin bread in the saddle bags behind him. His mood was founded on more than the food, however. He was going home to her. Home to his wife. Daughtry!

He hadn't realized how much he'd come to love her until he spent time away from her. This was the first time since she'd arrived that he'd spent nearly an entire day without her by his side. Even the time he'd had to take the outlaws into the sheriff hadn't amounted to more than a couple of hours.

Anxious to hold her in his arms and see her pleasure at the turkey, Nicholas urged his horse into a gallop and hurried for home.

Nicholas approached the house without giving much thought to the cloud of dust that rose to his right. He was preoccupied with his thoughts and didn't even see the riders until he was bringing his horse to a stop just outside the barn.

Nicholas thought to dismount but sat instead with his eyes fixed on the riders. Without being told, he knew they were Daughtry's father and three of her brothers.

"Well, Lord," he whispered against the silence, "I guess this is it. I'm about to answer for what I've done with this man's daughter. I could sure use some direction in how to come under my father-in-law's good graces."

The riders approached, slowing to a slow walk until they were directly in front of Nicholas. The older of the three pressed his horse forward until he was nearly nose to nose with Nicholas.

"You Nicholas Dawson?" Garrett Lucas asked from between clenched teeth.

"I am," Nicholas replied softly. "You must be. . ." He never got the words out, because Garrett flew across the saddle and knocked Nicholas off of his horse and to the ground.

Chapter 12

*A*fter two well-placed blows against Nicholas's face, Garrett's sons managed to pull their father off the stunned man. Nicholas refused to fight back and got to his feet slowly. Knocking the dust from his backside, he moved away a step, while Garrett strained at the resistance of his sons.

"You have to answer for what you've done!" Garrett declared. His face was reddened with anger.

Nicholas rubbed his jaw and a hint of a smile played at his bloodied lip. "I think I just did."

Garrett was livid and refused to be humored. "Where's my daughter? Where's Daughtry?"

"I would imagine in the house. As you can see for yourself, I just got back," Nicholas replied gingerly. He didn't believe his jaw was broken, but it hurt nevertheless.

"Dad, you promised to be levelheaded about this," one of the boys was saying. Nicholas watched as the other two nodded in agreement. Maybe Daughtry's brothers were able to see that their sister had a right to make her own choices.

"Don't tell me what I said, Joseph!"

"He's right, Dad. Daughtry told us in the letter that she's happy. Why don't we let her tell us otherwise."

Garrett seemed to relax a bit, and Nicholas took the opportunity to speak. "I'm sorry, I truly am. Not for having married your daughter, but for the way we went about it. I know what Daughtry put in her letter, so I know that you realize I was completely unaware of your existence when she married me. It's a poor excuse, I know, but I hope in time you will forgive me."

Garrett stared at Nicholas for several minutes.

"I'm Garrett Lucas," he finally said. "These are my sons, Gavin, Dolan, and Joseph."

"Pleased to meet all of you," Nicholas responded. He didn't offer his hand, feeling if he did he might be forcing the issue a bit. Instead, he motioned to the horses. "What say we tie these fellows up and you let me put my turkey in the barn, and we'll go inside and talk this out with Daughtry."

The other men nodded. Nicholas could see the boys speaking in low whispers to Garrett, while they tied the horses to the corral fence and waited for their host. They seemed like good men, he thought to himself, and he smiled. Of course they were good men; they were Daughtry's family.

Making his way to where they awaited him, Nicholas took the lead. "Come on inside."

Nicholas immediately sensed that all was not right when he entered the kitchen. Things were strewn about in a haphazard way that was not indicative of his wife's normal sense of order. For a minute he stood in the silence, while Garrett and the boys glanced around the room.

"Daughtry!" he called out, but in his heart, Nicholas knew she wouldn't answer.

He rushed from one room to the next, and when he saw the same disarray in the bedroom that had greeted him in the kitchen, Nicholas knew that she was gone. Panic filled his soul. Had friends of the men he'd jailed come for him and taken her instead?

The fear was clear in Nicholas's eyes as he returned to the kitchen. "She's not here. I'm going to check the barn and see if her horse is gone. You wait here," he instructed and ran out the back door.

Nicholas began to pray as he'd never done before. "Dear God, keep her safe. Please don't let any harm come to her. Oh, God, please help me find her."

When Nicholas realized the horse was indeed missing, he made his way back to the house with a heavy heart. Where was she? The light was fading and the wind was picking up, causing a chill to fill the air. Where was Daughtry?

The defeat on his face made it clear to Garrett that Nicholas was more than a little upset at finding Daughtry gone. "Where do you suppose she got off to?" Garrett asked, trying to keep his voice even.

Just then, Nicholas spied the letter on the table. He picked it up, praying that it might be some note of explanation from Daughtry.

"She's run away again," Nicholas muttered and handed the letter to Garrett. "She found out you were due to be here and, what with me gone, she was afraid."

"Afraid? Of me?" Garrett nearly growled in disbelief.

Nicholas nodded his head. "She's been in a real stew since we married. Always looking over her shoulder, wondering when you were going to come and take her by force."

"She was afraid of me," Garrett stated sadly as if all the wind had gone out from him. "I don't know why she thought I would try to make her unhappy."

"It's not important now. What is important is that we find her," Gavin offered, and Nicholas nodded.

"I just wanted her to make good choices," Garrett said, trying to explain himself.

"She's a good woman," Nicholas responded without hesitancy. "She makes good choices."

"Ha," Garrett sounded. "She doesn't seem to have made a very good one this time. She's out there somewhere, only God knows where, and she's alone. It's getting colder and. . ."

"I'm going after her," Nicholas said and turned to leave. "You make yourselves comfortable here, in case she comes back."

"No," Garrett replied, "I'm going after her. She's my daughter, and if I caused this like you said, then I'll find her."

"She's my responsibility now," Nicholas said a bit more forcefully than he'd intended.

"And I say she's still under my authority and protection," Garrett replied, coming to stand only inches from Nicholas. "I was there when she came into this world, and God gave me charge over her."

"But I married her, and that authority now falls to me," Nicholas replied softly. "I love her as much as you do."

"You may love her," Garrett answered, "but she's still my daughter. Flesh of my flesh and blood of my blood."

Nicholas nodded. "I know. But she's my wife, and she's carrying our child."

Garrett's mouth dropped open at this sudden declaration. A part of him wanted to fight Nicholas all over again, while another part of him stood in awed amazement.

"A baby?" he questioned in disbelief.

"Yes," Nicholas replied.

"Why don't we stop this nonsense," Gavin finally spoke up. "We should go together. With all of us looking, we're bound to find her sooner."

"He's right," Nicholas said, seeing the change in Garrett. "Let's all go. I've a feeling she won't be all that far."

"Yeah, but we're talking about my sister," Dolan joked. "She's very stubborn, and who knows where that'll take her."

Nicholas grinned. "She's had good training, though. I know Daughtry can take care of herself." Grabbing his coat, he added, "I'll tell you about her fixing the roof while we ride."

Daughtry had found the perfect place to make camp for the night. She had ridden for several hours before coming to a rocky wall barrier. As she paralleled it for a short time, the sky began to grow dark, and Daughtry realized she'd have to stop and take shelter. She also noticed that the air was getting cold.

At the first sound of water, Daughtry felt a bit of contentment wash over her. She'd have a good camp for both Nutmeg and herself. Bringing the horse to a stop by the stream, Daughtry quickly went to work, and before the last few glimmers of late autumn sun had faded behind the mountain peaks, she had a nice fire going.

She thought how beautiful the night was and how the tiny pinpricks of light that were millions of stars in the sky seemed to keep her company through the loneliness of her vigil. "I know I've brought this on myself, Father," she prayed. "But I just didn't know what else to do. I wanted to trust You to work it out. I wanted to have faith that everything would be all right, but I was so frightened."

The wind picked up a bit, and Daughtry hugged a blanket close to her. Foolish or not, she was out here alone and had to make the most of it. Garrett Lucas had raised his children to be capable of caring for themselves outdoors, and Daughtry was certainly no exception to that rule. As the fire began to die down, she tossed several large logs on the coals and settled down for the night.

"Oh, Nicholas," she sighed against the haunting sounds of the canyon winds. "I need you."

Chapter 13

*D*aughtry tried to sleep but couldn't. Perhaps the hour was just not late enough, she reasoned; after all, the sun had only been down for an hour, maybe two. In frustration, she sat up and leaned back against the rock to contemplate her actions.

In the distant night she could make out little noises, but nothing that offered either comfort or fear. She thought of her life and all that she'd known.

This region of New Mexico was still very rustic. They didn't have electricity to the outlying houses, and while most of the towns sported not only electricity but running water, telephones, and automobiles, Daughtry's world hadn't consisted of any of these things. She felt as though she stood between the past and the future, not really taking hold of either one.

She smiled to herself as she thought of Nicholas building the small addition off the kitchen to house the bathtub. He'd seemed so happy when he realized how much pleasure it gave Daughtry.

They were a strange couple, Daughtry thought. "How could two people who had never before met be so perfect for each other?" she questioned the air. Clearly, the hand of God had been working in spite of human rebellion and disobedience.

Daughtry frowned. Her father was no doubt at her house right this very minute. What a coward she was to leave Nicholas to face him alone. She hugged her knees to her chest. *Oh, God,* she prayed, *please help him. Help Nicholas to deal evenhandedly with my father, and help my father to keep his temper under control.*

She must have dozed, or so she figured, because suddenly the sound of horses clipping at a slow, even pace caused her to jerk upright. Getting to her feet, Daughtry was further stunned to see her husband, father, and three of her brothers ride casually into camp as though they were there for supper.

Standing with her mouth open and her eyes wide, Daughtry was speechless. Nicholas jumped down from his horse, throwing the reins to Joseph, while Garrett dismounted and handed his to Gavin. Before she could utter a single protest, Nicholas had her in his arms and was turning her around as if to inspect every single inch of her.

"She looks to be in one piece," she heard her husband mutter.

Still Daughtry could say nothing, and not until Nicholas completely shocked her by handing her over to her father to continue the examination, did Daughtry finally voice her protest.

"Stop this at once!" she exclaimed and pushed away from her father. "I'm not a helpless child, you know. I'm perfectly fine—or at least I was until you all got here."

She looked from the two men at her side to her brothers. "How dare you interfere in my life this way! I'm old enough to know my own mind. You can't just waltz in here and think to control me!"

Garrett glanced at Nicholas and received one of his lazy, I-told-you-so grins. "I think you should spank her," Garrett said with a slow drawl.

"Sp—sp—spank me?" Daughtry sputtered, completely enraged. "You think he should spank me?"

"That's right," Garrett replied.

"If he doesn't want to do the job, I'll do it," Gavin called down from his mount.

"You're all insufferable." Daughtry put hands on her hips and struck a defiant pose. "I'm a grown woman and. . ."

"You may be a grown woman, but you haven't got a lick of sense," Garrett replied.

"I have plenty of sense."

"Then what are you doing out here when you have a perfectly fine home?" Garrett questioned.

Daughtry looked to her husband for help, but Nicholas looked away as if to keep from laughing.

Daughtry crossed her arms. "I wouldn't be out here at all if it hadn't been for the way you treated me. I may have run off, but you forced me to make that decision."

"I know," he said in a dejected tone that immediately softened Daughtry's heart.

Garrett pushed his black Stetson back and drew a deep breath. "I know I've been unfair to you, Daughtry. It's just that ever since Julie died, I guess I felt like I had to keep a better eye on you. I couldn't get past feeling that if I'd only watched her closer, made her take someone with her when she rode, that maybe she'd be alive today. You'll feel different when you have your child. You'll know just how much a child means to a parent."

Daughtry reached out to touch her father's cheek. "I know. I miss her too. And I also feel guilty."

"Guilty for what?" Garrett asked in complete surprise.

"For being angry with her. Angry that she died. Angry that because of the way she died, I had to bear the consequences." Garrett grimaced at the latter, but Daughtry continued. "We all miss her, but overprotecting me won't change the fact that she's gone to heaven and we're still here."

"You're right, of course," Garrett answered and opened his arms. "Will you forgive me?"

Daughtry melted into her father's embrace. "Of course," she sighed. "I forgave you a long time ago. If it hadn't been for our confrontation, I might never have met Nicholas—and, Daddy, I do love him. I didn't just marry him to get away from home. He's a good man, and he loves God."

Garrett glanced over her shoulder at Nicholas.

"I'm glad you love him, Daughtry."

As if reading her father's feelings, Daughtry pulled back. "I'll always love you too, Daddy. Please forgive me for the way I've done things. I know I was wrong. You and Momma brought me into the world and raised me up to love God and my fellow man—and now it's time for me to go on and live my life with Nicholas."

Garrett nodded. "I know. Just as Julie's death isn't the end, I know that your marriage is just the beginning of many wonderful things. Nicholas helped me to see that. He helped me to realize that life and death are just a part of the circle that makes us who we are. Julie may be gone, but now there's your baby and life starts anew."

Daughtry dropped her hold on Garrett and stepped back a pace. "My *what*?" Her mouth dropped open in stunned silence.

Garrett looked at Nicholas. Nicholas stepped forward with a sheepish grin.

"I think Daughtry's been a bit preoccupied these last few weeks even to realize that she's expecting," he offered by way of explanation. "But I feel very confident that she is."

Daughtry felt her face flush. She calculated the days of their marriage, her monthly cycles, and felt a strange knowledge settle over her. "A baby!" She looked up at Nicholas who seemed quite pleased to have known before even she did.

Without warning, she felt her knees buckle and she fell forward into her father. Garrett managed to take hold of her under the arms, and, looking at Nicholas with a telling smile, he unceremoniously handed the unconscious Daughtry over to him.

"Good luck," Garrett said with a laugh. "You're going to need it."

Quite awhile later, Daughtry and Nicholas made their way to bed. Garrett and the boys had taken up residency in the front sitting room, refusing to let Daughtry and Nicholas even think of giving up their room.

Daughtry brushed her long coppery hair and thought of the news that she was to be a mother. How could she have been so caught up in her guilt and fears that she hadn't realized she was with child? She was almost humiliated that her husband had to be the one to point the news out to her.

Just then Nicholas came in, deposited his boots, and got ready for bed. Daughtry turned and stared at him for a moment. He was so very handsome with his dark hair and broad shoulders. She liked the way he moved with catlike grace and confidence.

Realizing that she was watching him, Nicholas turned and smiled. Daughtry's hand automatically went to her stomach in wonder. How could it be that they were to become parents? Why had God chosen to bless their union so early on with such a miracle?

"How?" Daughtry questioned, getting up and slipping into bed. "How did you know?"

Nicholas shrugged and eased into the covers. "I'm not stupid. I know all about women. I have a mother after all. Not to mention my sisters."

"Imagine that," Daughtry said rather sarcastically. "You have sisters."

"Yes, I have two sisters and a brother," Nicholas replied. "I am the oldest."

"I see."

"Lance is twenty-eight," Nicholas continued, knowing her unspoken questions. "Natalie is twenty-five and Joelle is nineteen. So, you see, I am more than a little familiar with things that pertain to the female species."

Daughtry blushed and shook her head. "I can't believe that I didn't realize what was happening."

"I thought maybe you did," Nicholas replied. "But when we went to town and I told you to get anything you thought you might need, and you only worried about my underwear—well, then I knew that you didn't know."

Daughtry laughed. "You must think me pathetic."

Nicholas opened his arms to her, and Daughtry slid into them eagerly. "I would never think you pathetic," Nicholas answered softly. "You are most precious to me."

Daughtry leaned her head against his chest. "You aren't angry, are you? About the baby, I mean."

"Why would I be angry?"

"Well, it certainly happened a lot quicker than I anticipated, so I figure it must be just as shocking for you."

"It did surprise me," Nicholas admitted, "but once I realized that it was most likely true, I kind of liked the idea."

"It's just so amazing and wondrous," Daughtry said, her hand going again to her abdomen. "But, I couldn't bear it if you were unhappy." She lifted her face to his, her eyes huge pools of blue.

"I couldn't be more happy about it," Nicholas replied and kissed her forehead. "If you'll recall, I was the one who planned for a dozen or so."

Daughtry laughed. "Well, one down and eleven to go."

Nicholas joined her laughter with his own, then suddenly grew sober. "Daughtry, you have to promise me that you'll be more careful. I nearly died when I came home and found you gone. I know you were scared, but so many things could have happened to you out there. Not to mention that I'm still not all that sure we're safe from my past."

His words both startled and frustrated her. Why wouldn't he tell her what past it was that he was running from?

Daughtry eased up on one elbow to study him for a moment. She was about to protest his silence when she saw something in his eyes that made her want to comfort him. She placed her hand on his chest and smiled. "Whatever you decide is fine by me. If you need to leave this place, you'll do so with me by your side."

"No questions asked?" Nicholas whispered, staring hard at his wife.

"No questions asked."

Morning light brought the blended family together at breakfast. For the first time, Daughtry used her dining room table and chairs and enjoyed preparing a feast fit for an army. Nicholas spoke about the ranch with her father and brothers, while Daughtry made sure that all the cups were filled with steaming coffee and that no one went away hungry.

"I've got a great deal to learn," Nicholas confessed. "But Daughtry's been a tremendous help."

"She ought to be. She's grown up ranching all her life. Piñon Canyon is probably the largest ranch in New Mexico, although I've never concerned myself with such things. We do a good business in beef and horses," Garrett said between forkfuls of food. "There's certainly enough business there, and I always presumed it would pass equally to all of my children." As he spoke, an idea came to Garrett and he put down his fork.

"What say you and Daughtry come live at Piñon Canyon for the winter? I could teach you firsthand all that you'd need to know to get this place running, and, come spring, I would send you off with a starter herd of the best cattle this side of the Mississippi."

Daughtry looked at her father in surprise, then to Nicholas. What would he think of the offer, she wondered? She didn't have long to contemplate as Nicholas raised his eyes to hers. They both thought back to the day of the shootout, and Daughtry nodded as if in answer to Nicholas's unspoken question.

"I think we'd both like that," Nicholas replied, and Daughtry nodded and continued seeing to her brothers' plates.

Garrett couldn't have been more surprised or grateful. "Good," he answered, feeling the first real peace since Daughtry left home. "I don't think you'll be sorry."

"I'm sure we won't be," Nicholas replied. "We won't need to do much here, maybe just board up the windows so that no harm comes to them. We'll take our horses with us, and there's no other livestock or obligation to contend with."

"What about our turkey?" Daughtry asked with a grin. "I can hear him out there even now." Everybody laughed, having heard the turkey's protests through much of the night.

"We'll take him with us," Garrett announced. "We ought to be home in time for Thanksgiving, and he'll make a great main course."

Chapter 14

*N*icholas stared down at the mammoth ranch that spread across the endless valley. Nestled between the mountains was Piñon Canyon, the home where Daughtry had grown up. He looked in awe from the empire below, to the man who owned it all, and finally to his wife.

"Like it?" she questioned with a grin. "You should see it in the springtime when all the grass is newly green and the wildflowers are blooming."

Nicholas nodded. "I can only imagine. It's easy to see why you love it." Daughtry smiled. She'd only recently told Nicholas of her fondness for her childhood home.

Her father and brothers moved ahead on the trail, leaving Nicholas and Daughtry to themselves. "When I left," Daughtry said, remembering her escape, "I thought I was leaving a terrible place. A prison. Now I can see that it was more the way I perceived things inside and not at all the way it really was."

"Can you be happy here again?" Nick questioned, reaching out to touch her arm.

Daughtry gave him a radiant smile, and, in spite of the blustery cold winds that came down from the mountain, she was warm and content. "I can be happy anywhere that you are."

Maggie Lucas fussed and pampered her daughter from the moment she got down from her horse. Arm in arm, they walked off toward the house, while the men saw to the horses and gear.

"He's very nice looking, this Nicholas Dawson," Maggie said, bringing Daughtry a steaming cup of hot chocolate.

"Yes, he is. He's also very kind and considerate, and he's a Christian, Momma."

"That's good," Maggie said, and Daughtry heard the unmistakable sound of relief in her voice.

"I'm truly sorry for the way I acted." Daughtry put the cup down and looked up at her mother. "I know I must have just about broke your heart in two, and I can't live with myself any longer. Will you please forgive me for running off and hurting you like I did?"

Maggie put her arms around Daughtry and hugged her close. "I could see how bad things were. I only wanted you to be happy, but I knew how miserable you were. I tried to talk to your father, and he only snapped at me. There's nothing to forgive. I knew in my heart, after learning that you'd left, that God was with you and that He'd guide you safely. It gave me a great deal of peace, even when I didn't know where you were."

"Why did it take Daddy so long to show up?" Daughtry suddenly asked.

"He was mad and real hurt. Mostly because he knew he was responsible for your actions. At first he refused to even deal with it but, as time passed, I could see the anger burning inside him like a spark just waiting for kindling to feed its flame. One day, he marched in here, told Gavin and Dolan to saddle up, and announced he was going to find you and this man who'd stolen you from him."

Daughtry smiled and pulled away from her mother. "I take it Joey went along to keep the peace."

Maggie nodded. "You know Joseph." This time Daughtry nodded, while Maggie continued. "That's what happened here. How about what happened at your end?"

"I got Daddy's letter and it spooked me. I'm sorry to say I ran away again, because Nicholas was at a neighbor's house and wasn't due home for awhile. I had no idea how soon Daddy would arrive, so I packed a horse and left. I figured I'd rather camp out in the cold than face his wrath alone. Besides, I was so scared he'd take me away and I'd never see Nicholas again."

"What happened then?"

Daughtry laughed. "They all came riding into my camp as big as you please. Nick was sporting a bruised face, and Daddy was wearing skinned knuckles. I heard later that Nick wouldn't even defend himself. Just let Daddy have at him, then asked him to forgive him for marrying me."

"He is quite a man," Maggie said in surprised awe.

"You don't know the half of it," Daughtry said with a mischievous twinkle in her eye. "I have a surprise for you."

"What?" Maggie cocked her head to one side as if trying to figure out what her daughter would say next.

"Daddy asked us to live here for the winter, so that he could teach Nicholas all about ranching."

"And your husband agreed?"

"He did," Daughtry said with great happiness. "But we're going home in the spring, and Daddy promised to send us with some prime stock to start our own herd."

"Well, I am impressed," Maggie said, taking a seat beside her daughter.

"And," Daughtry added, reaching out to take hold of her mother's hand, "I have one more surprise. I'm going to have a baby."

"A baby!"

Her mother looked as though she might faint, and Daughtry squeezed her hand. "I was so worried about Daddy coming to take me away that I didn't even know it myself, until Nicholas pointed out the obvious things."

"A baby," Maggie said again, this time more steadily. "I'm going to be a grandmother. Wait until Lillie hears this one."

Daughtry laughed. "You'll no doubt have me knee-deep in sewing projects, and before the winter is over, I'll have enough clothes for triplets."

The women were still laughing when the men came in the room. Maggie got up and received a heartfelt kiss from her husband, while Nicholas went to Daughtry's side and waited to be introduced.

"Momma, this is Nicholas, my husband," Daughtry said proudly.

Maggie surprised Nicholas by brushing aside his extended hand as she threw her arms around him in a motherly hug. "Welcome home, Nicholas," she said with love. "I'm so glad to have acquired another son."

Nicholas spent most of his waking hours with Garrett and Daughtry's brothers. He worked harder than he'd ever worked in his life and knew that he was in many ways facing up to whatever tests Garrett could put him through. At night he collapsed into a tub of hot water, which Daughtry always saw was ready for him, then he would crawl into bed, more asleep than awake.

More than one night, Daughtry would lie beside her husband and watch him. His dark black hair would curl just at the collar and beg her touch, but Daughtry was always careful not to disturb him. She knew her father was working him too hard, but she reasoned that both men had something to prove and, for now, she'd not interfere.

Daughtry settled into the routine with misgivings. She missed the days when Nicholas had belonged just to her. Their ranch hadn't been so demanding, and Nicholas could take plenty of time to stop and talk or hold her. Now, however, she rarely saw him until dinner time, and by then he was so tired he didn't care whether he was married or not.

At dinner one night, the family finally began to feel comfortable enough to ask Nicholas questions, and one of the first was about his family.

"My mother and father are both still living. They live near Kansas City, where my father handles investments."

Daughtry hung onto every word but tried to appear as though this was all old news to her. She wasn't about to inform her family that Nicholas hadn't seen fit to confide in her.

"And do you have brothers and sisters, Nick?" Maggie questioned and Daughtry jumped in to reply.

"He has a brother and two sisters," she said confidently before Nicholas could get a word in edgewise. She looked over at her husband, daring him to say more, but Nicholas just grinned and went on eating.

"I guess I still don't understand how you could just up and marry a fellow after you read about him in the paper," Jordy said and turned to Nicholas. "No offense, I think you're as good a man for a brother-in-law as any, but my sister's always been rather picky."

Everyone laughed at this but Daughtry. "I'm not picky, just cautious."

"So cautious you answered a stranger's letter out of the *Denver Post* and sneaked away in the night to marry him? He could have been three times your age and given to fits of rage for all you knew," Gavin said.

"He is given to small fits," Daughtry laughed.

"So what made you do it?" Jordy pressed his luck. "I mean, other than getting away from here?"

Daughtry put her fork down and stared at Nicholas for a moment. "I fell in love with his picture."

Garrett and the boys thought this hysterical and started laughing and slapping the table. Nicholas looked across the table at Daughtry and winked at her blushing face, while Maggie cleared her throat loud enough that the others quieted down.

"That's a silly reason to get married," Jordy replied.

"Sure is," Garrett seconded. "Imagine, marrying someone just because you've fallen in love with their picture. Why, for all you knew, he hadn't even sent you a picture of himself. It could have been anyone's picture."

"I seem to recall," Maggie began slowly, concentrating on moving the food around her plate, "a certain love-sick cowboy who fell in love with a 'spitfire of a girl' as he called her. This man had never met this girl," Maggie continued, "but her father had a portrait of her hanging in his house and that cowboy fell in love with her after staring many hours at it."

Everyone fell into silence as all eyes were drawn to Garrett. Garrett looked across the table at his wife and smiled. Their romance had begun very nearly as she said, and now their daughter had gone and fallen for her mate in much the same way.

"Is it true, Daddy?" Daughtry asked with a hint of laughter in her voice.

"No," Garrett said, surprising Maggie. Her eyes narrowed questioningly, but he quickly continued. "I fell in love with her the first time I saw the portrait, not after hours of studying it." Maggie's smile broadened, and the boys broke into laughter.

"What about you, Nick?" Don suddenly asked.

All heads turned and waited for Nicholas to reply. Even Daughtry couldn't imagine what he might say, and her hand froze in mid-air, her water glass clutched in her fingers, as she waited for his answer.

"I prayed a lot about a wife," Nicholas finally answered. "I was never much the courting type, and even though I had plenty of women giving me the chase, I just wasn't interested in settling down. But I guess I started to see the benefits of having a partner, and so I prayed, then put the advertisement in the paper." His eyes never left Daughtry as he spoke. "Then your sister answered and sent her picture—and while I thought her a remarkably good-looking woman, I can't say that I fell head-over-heels just then."

"What was it then?" Jordy piped up to ask.

"I guess I was intrigued by her letter," Nicholas responded, seeing the disappointment that flickered across Daughtry's face as she lowered her head to drink. "Of course, once I met her I knew she was exactly what I needed. She's everything a man could want in a wife."

Jordy thought the answer reasonable and continued the conversation by telling of a letter he'd received from some girl in town. The laughter around her did little to revive Daughtry's spirits. Something in Nicholas's response troubled her, and while she couldn't quite figure out what it was, it remained between them nevertheless.

Chapter 15

*D*aughtry let her frustration boil until morning when she had no other recourse but to vent her emotions at Nicholas. She'd had too much time to think about things and her imagination was running wild.

"Why did you marry me?" she questioned while Nicholas was dressing.

"What?"

"You heard me. Why did you marry me? Why did you push for a quick wedding by proxy? Why didn't you just come here if you wanted a fast wedding?"

Nicholas stopped buttoning his shirt and stared at Daughtry for a moment. He recognized the barely controlled anger in her eyes. "What happened to no questions asked?"

"What happened to sharing your life with me?" Daughtry asked simply.

"What's this all about?"

"It's about us," Daughtry replied rather indignantly. "It's about who you are and why you wanted me to marry you. It's about you being intrigued by my letter, but not in love with me."

"But I love you now," Nicholas offered.

"I want to know the truth, Nicholas. I want to know what you are hiding and why you refuse to trust me."

Nicholas winced at her words. He stared blankly at the wall behind Daughtry for a moment, then in a sad voice said, "Proverbs 19:13 says, 'A foolish son is the calamity of his father; and the contentions of a wife are a continual dropping.'"

"Are you calling me contentious? Just because I ask for the truth?" Daughtry appeared truly hurt, and Nicholas wished to ease her pain.

"No," he shook his head and replied. "I use that verse in reference to myself." Then he grinned and tried to ease the tension between them. "However, if you're feeling guilty. . . ."

Daughtry put her hands on her hips and started to say something but held her tongue. Nicholas saw the softening in her eyes. "Why do you call yourself a foolish son?" she finally asked.

Nicholas ran his hands back through his hair and sighed loudly. "You'd better sit down," he said, coming around to her and pulling out a chair from a nearby desk. Daughtry did as he told her, her eyes never leaving his face.

"I did my share of wild oat sowing when I was young. My folks, good people, saw that I was headed into trouble and began working on me, but I already knew it all, or thought I did, and sought my own way instead. Around the turn of the century, I struck out on my own and hooked up with the wrong crowd. I never really did anything myself, but I was always with one of them when they did something. My name started getting just naturally linked to the kind of bad men that could cause me some major entanglements with the law."

"Are you a criminal?" Daughtry asked hesitantly.

"No," Nicholas said and sat down on the edge of the bed directly in front of her. "No, I always managed to stay just inside the law. I was finally taken aside by an older friend of the family and given a good talking to. As a result I ended up getting myself deputized and began working with the law. Unfortunately, my old friends saw it as a means of advantage for their schemes. They figured their old buddy Nick wasn't about to hand them a prison cell in exchange for the good times they'd showed me."

"Were you a Christian when all of this was going on?"

"I thought I was. Thought I knew about the Gospel and how to live. But I was just as lost as those outlaws when it came to salvation for my soul. Anyway, years like this went on, and my folks were getting more and more worried about me. My brother had married and so had my sister Natalie, and here I was outrunning bullets and breaking up outlaw gangs." He paused for a moment to see how she was taking the news.

"Those three men," Daughtry whispered, "the three you had to turn over to the sheriff, were they. . .?"

"Part of the old Chancellor Gang."

Daughtry gasped, and Nicholas realized that she knew full well who and what that notorious group represented.

"A couple of the gang died in prison, but most of them were paroled just months before you and I married. Everybody was afraid if I stuck around Missouri, they'd locate me and kill me like they promised. Guess nobody gave them much credit for tracking me down out here."

"Kill you?" Daughtry hadn't heard a word past those two.

Nicholas reached out and took her shaking hands into his own. "God helped me to see that I needed more than a casual relationship with Him. When I started thinking about my own mortality and how one of the outlaws I'd helped to put away could just as easily get out and come gunning for me, I knew I wasn't ready to die.

"My father and mother were beside themselves, however, even before the Chancellors got out of prison. My father cornered me when I turned twenty-eight and told me that he was through giving me free rein to do as I wished. He offered to take me into his investment house, but I knew that wasn't for me and I refused. So he told me I had until I was thirty to settle down—or else."

"Or else what?"

Nicholas smiled a little sadly. "He said he'd disinherit me for my own good."

Daughtry looked at him rather puzzled. "Your own father would do that to you?"

"He knew what he was doing," Nicholas replied. "He knew that it would shame me into obedience even at twenty-eight. I didn't want to lose out on the money but, more than that, I didn't want to alienate myself from the family. I knew there would be a full-scale war between him and my mother, not to mention my sisters and brother if they thought Dad was picking on me."

"So what did you have to do to meet his demands?" Daughtry said, suddenly feeling fearful of the response. "What constituted settling down?"

"I had to get a reliable profession, a home in one place, and. . ." He paused, unable to finish the sentence.

"And a wife?" Daughtry asked, her eyes wide.

"Yes."

"And you had to do all of this before you turned thirty?"

"Yes."

"And when did you turn thirty?"

"September twenty-fifth," Nicholas replied softly.

Daughtry stared at him in shock for several minutes. "That was the day the proxy would no longer be any good. That's why you pressed me to hurry and marry you before coming to the ranch."

"Yes," Nicholas said and held her hand tightly. "I had to fulfill my father's requirements. It was important to me. Not just for the inheritance, but because his approval meant a lot to me. I wanted to make him proud of me. I bought the ranch and went about looking into how to be a rancher, then, before I knew it, time had slipped up on me and it was almost too late to get a wife."

"You used me," Daughtry said, suddenly feeling ill. The look in her eyes reflected the betrayal she felt.

"Now, wait just a minute," Nicholas said and took hold of her shoulders firmly. "Isn't that a bit like the pot calling the kettle black? Did you or did you not answer my advertisement in order to escape your overprotective father?"

"That's not why I married you!" Daughtry exclaimed. But even as she said it, she remembered only too well having decided not to marry Nicholas. Not until her father had refused to listen to reason did she change her mind, and she knew that was one truth she couldn't escape.

"And why did you marry me, Daughtry? Surely not because you were head over heels in love with me from all the courting and flowery words I'd spoken. Maybe it was the hours of evening walks by the river or the cards and flowers." His tone was much too sarcastic for her to bear.

Daughtry jumped to her feet. "I loved you when I married you. I'd fallen in love with your picture and your letter. I thought you'd fallen in love with me as well."

Nicholas stood and spoke calmly. "I did fall in love with you. I told you the truth when I said that. I can't help it that I didn't fall in love with your photograph or letter. I can't help it that I felt desperate to meet a deadline and didn't give the matter as much consideration as I should have. I did pray about it, though. I had a good peace about it too. Daughtry, I know without a doubt that God intended us to be together."

Daughtry tried to grasp all that he said. "Just when did you fall in love with me?"

Nicholas smiled, hoping that her question meant they were making headway. "I'm still falling in love with you," he answered softly, "but I think I first knew it when I came into the bedroom that morning and found an angel asleep in my bed. You know, we've never talked about that."

"Yes, I know," Daughtry said, suddenly feeling a bit uncomfortable at the memory. Everything had happened so quickly. Her marriage, getting to know Nicholas, finding herself with child—it had all come on so fast.

Nicholas pulled her to sit with him on the bed. "I came back to the ranch and all I could think about was that you might or might not be there. I knew I wouldn't have much hope of finding another wife, even though I had two other replies."

"You had other replies?" Daughtry asked, sounding like a little girl.

Nick grinned. "Yes, I did. But yours was the only one I answered."

"Oh."

Nicholas continued, "You can't imagine what I thought when I'd seen all the work you'd done. I figured at first maybe you'd lied about yourself and sent me someone else's picture, because there was no way that I figured a little thing like you could accomplish so much in so little time. Then when I walked into the bedroom. . ." He fell silent, closing his eyes to revisit the memory. "When I walked in and found you asleep in my bed, it was like Christmas morning. I knew then that you'd married me by proxy and that my obligations to my father were fulfilled. But," he said, putting a finger to her lips as she started to protest, "I was completely captivated to know that you belonged to me."

He pulled her close to him and breathed in the sweet scent of roses and lavender. "You were so beautiful, just lying there asleep." His words were warm, and Daughtry felt them relaxing her against her will. "Your hair was spilled out across my pillow, and when I reached out to touch it, I just naturally found myself climbing onto the bed. I couldn't believe how God had blessed me, Daughtry. I still can't. I love you with all my heart, and I am forever yours. I want to be a good husband to you. I've told you everything, and I hope you'll find it in your heart to forgive me."

Daughtry looked at him, his dark eyes revealing a conflict of emotions from within. "I can forgive you," Daughtry finally said, "but I don't know if I can forget." She pulled away from him and got to her feet. A shadow of hurt still lingered in her eyes.

Nicholas came to her, but Daughtry held her hand out. "Please don't touch me. I need to think."

"Daughtry, even God forgets the past when we ask Him to. I'm not only asking, I'm pleading with you. This isn't a matter between just you and me now—we have a child to consider as well."

"I know."

"If you can forgive me, then please forget what I've done to hurt you. Just put it behind you. It's insignificant and unimportant."

Daughtry's eyes flashed anger for just a moment. "It's important to me," she said and stormed from the room to contemplate what her husband had revealed.

"Lord," Nicholas prayed even as Daughtry's footsteps echoed down the hall, "help her to see that I love her. Forgive me for the deception, and help her to forgive me. I love her, Father, and I know that You've brought us together for a purpose. I don't know what the future will hold in store for us, but You do, and I'm asking You to direct me so that I don't mess things up again. Amen."

Chapter 16

*D*aughtry pulled on her coat and made her way to the barn. She had to get away from the house and Nicholas in order to sort through her feelings. Grabbing a bridle, Daughtry went to the corral, intent on singling out Nutmeg for a ride.

Nutmeg saw Daughtry and whinnied softly, but Poco, after months of neglect and an absent owner, was the one that came to Daughtry. The horse snorted once, then pushed its muzzle against Daughtry's neck, almost pleading.

"So you want to go for a run, do you, Boy?" Daughtry asked softly while stroking the velvety nose. She looked across the corral at Nutmeg, then secured the bridle on Poco and led the horse to the stable to be saddled.

Several of the ranch hands immediately offered to assist her. She started to refuse, but because of her condition and her own uncertainty as to what she should or shouldn't do, she finally relented and accepted their help.

Once on Poco's back, she headed out for a trail she'd ridden most of her life. The air was cold and snow had fallen on the high mountains the night before. The open valley in which the ranch was situated had received only a dusting of snow, though, nothing that Daughtry concerned herself with. Instead, she took the opportunity to pray and think about what Nicholas had said.

"Dear God," she whispered with a glance heavenward, "I think I need to talk about this. You're the only One I can explain it all to, because You're the only One who truly knows what I did and why."

Poco was used to years of such prayers and kept plodding along as though this were perfectly normal.

"I realize," Daughtry continued, "that I did wrong in marrying Nicholas the way I did. I wronged him, I wronged my folks, and I wronged You. I made pledges that I shouldn't have—but now that they're made, there is certainly no turning back."

The words of Ecclesiastes 5:2 came to mind. *Be not rash with thy mouth, and let not thine heart be hasty to utter any thing before God: for God is in heaven, and thou upon earth: therefore let thy words be few.*

Daughtry pondered the scripture for a moment before resuming her prayer. "I did speak rashly and without any real thought of the consequences," she admitted. "But I'm not trying to take back my pledge in marriage and my vows to You. I just need to understand them. I need to know what my marriage really and truly means."

Not that I can do anything to change the past, Daughtry thought to herself. She noted that Poco had followed their old trail high into the rocks, so she slowed the steed down, still contemplating her life before God.

"I love Nicholas," she told God, "but I'm afraid we both married each other for all the wrong reasons. He needed a wife to please his father and keep his inheritance, and I needed to escape my father's ever-watchful eye." She laughed at her choice of words and glanced heavenward again. "I suppose You know all about children who try to escape Your watchfulness."

Back at the ranch, Nicholas began to worry about Daughtry. He searched through the house and when he found her gone, he tore out, barely grabbing his coat, and headed for the barn.

"Daughtry?" he called as he entered the empty stable. There was no answer.

"Daughtry!" Nicholas called again, coming from the stable. Just then Garrett rounded the corner.

"What's wrong?" he questioned, seeing the concern on Nicholas's face.

Nicholas gave a sigh. "Daughtry is upset with me. She stormed out of the house, and I haven't seen her for about an hour. I thought maybe she went for a ride, but Nutmeg is right there in the corral."

Garrett quickly surveyed the horses and shook his head. "But Poco's not."

"Poco?"

"Her horse and favorite traveling companion before she left home. Nobody else would be inclined to ride him." Nicholas saw the apprehension in Garrett's eyes.

"I'd better go find her," Nicholas replied and went to saddle his horse.

"I'm coming too," Garrett stated.

The men were saddled and ready to ride within minutes, and without telling anyone else where they were headed, Garrett and Nicholas rode out side by side.

Daughtry felt renewed by her prayers. She could see now that though both she and Nicholas had made mistakes, the focus needed to be taken from the past and placed on the future. They had both been wrong in their actions, but they could easily put those things behind them and start anew. Of this, Daughtry was confident.

Realizing she'd been gone for a considerable amount of time, Daughtry turned Poco around and headed for home. Nicholas had asked her to forget the past and forgive him, and Daughtry intended to do just that. Somehow, together, they would put aside the circumstances under which they married and build a marriage that would be strong and faithful. A marriage that would bind them together, forever.

Daughtry smiled and began to hum to herself. She let Poco pick his way through the narrow canyon path and thought absentmindedly about what she would say to Nicholas. She was so deep in thought that the first few bits of rock falling from the steep canyon wall didn't even attract her attention. They did, however, cause Poco to stop and prance back a step or two.

Poco's actions caused Daughtry to snap to attention just as a huge rock slide covered the path directly in front of them. The loose rock combined with small amounts of snow gained momentum and rushed downward to block the passage through the canyon.

"Easy, Poco," Daughtry whispered and stroked the animal's neck to offer comfort. "We're okay." Daughtry glanced around behind her and knew that she would need to dismount in order to get Poco turned around.

Daughtry slid to the ground and reached out to take Poco's reins just as another slide captured the horse's attention and caused him to rear up and whinny nervously. Daughtry barely managed to avoid the pounding hooves.

While backing away from Poco, she lost control of him and the scared horse seized its freedom and ran.

For a moment, all Daughtry could do was stare after Poco's retreating form. "Great!" she muttered. "Now, I'll have to walk home."

Daughtry picked her way through the rubble and moved past the slide area. She knew she would need at least two hours to make the trek home, but what else could she do except begin walking? No one knew where she was, and only Nicholas knew that she was upset. He might even presume that she needed the extra time to sort through her feelings about him. Walking with determined steps, Daughtry would have laughed at herself had the whole situation not been so infuriating.

"Do you have any idea where she might have ridden?" Nicholas asked his father-in-law.

"She has her favorite places. One path in particular," Garrett responded and pointed to the west. "There's a secluded path that winds up into the rocky foothills. She always liked to take that route."

"Let's check there first," Nicholas replied.

"Look!" Garrett pointed to the ground. "Tracks! I'd stake my ranch that those belong to Poco."

The two men followed the tracks that led them in the same direction Garrett had suggested. With a smile, Garrett turned to Nicholas. "Daughtry can be pretty predictable."

"So far, I haven't been privileged to see that side of her."

Garrett laughed. "I think you have. Isn't this about the third or fourth time you've been involved in her running away?"

Nicholas grinned. "I guess I hadn't thought of it that way. She does seem to favor running rather than dealing with issues head on."

"She can be quite stubborn," Garrett agreed. "So can her mother."

The men had progressed along the path for nearly half an hour when they heard the unmistakable sound of horse hooves pounding through the canyon.

Garrett gave Nicholas a fearful look. "She wouldn't be riding like that unless something were wrong."

Just then Poco cleared the canyon and came into view. Nicholas felt his heart in his throat, and Garrett turned ashen at the sight of the riderless horse.

"Dear God," Garrett whispered, "let her be all right."

Nicholas pressed forward to halt Poco while Garrett watched in stunned silence. The horse whinnied and snorted at Nicholas, rearing back twice before finally settling down to allow the man access to the reins.

"What do you think?" Nicholas questioned, turning to Garrett.

"In truth, I don't know what to think. I don't like to think about it at all. It reminds me of Julie."

Nicholas nodded. "But the horse is unhurt. Maybe he just got spooked and threw Daughtry."

"That girl would have to be unconscious to be thrown from this horse. They're too comfortable with each other. Most likely something happened to cause Daughtry to dismount."

Nicholas looked hard at his father-in-law. "Have there been any strangers around lately?"

"None that I know of. Why?"

Nicholas shook his head. "It's nothing. I just wondered if someone could have made her dismount."

"I doubt there's anyone around these parts that would want to do harm to Daughtry. Years ago we had banditos to worry about, but they moved off to the south as Bandelero grew. Most likely she got off Poco to see to nature's call—or some other perfectly logical explanation." Garrett was trying hard to sound convincing, but in truth, he was desperately frightened for his child.

"You're probably right," Nicholas admitted, but the words did nothing to comfort him.

Nicholas tied Poco to his saddle and urged his own mount forward. Before he could go very far, however, Garrett called out to him, "Nick, would you pray with me?"

Nicholas turned to the man who had once wanted to beat him for stealing his daughter. The minute his eyes met Garrett's, a silent bond was formed. Each man acknowledged, without regret, the position the other held in the life of Daughtry.

With a slow nod, Nicholas waited until Garrett came even, then bowed his head and prayed for his wife.

Chapter 17

*N*icholas and Garrett proceeded together, each praying silently and fervently hoping that Daughtry would be found unharmed. In the back of Garrett's mind was the lifeless body of his fourteen-year-old Julie, only four years earlier. Meanwhile, Nicholas was envisioning the remaining members of the Chancellor gang trying to force his hand, using Daughtry as bait.

Neither man was of a mind to talk.

As the canyon narrowed and they could no longer ride side by side, Garrett edged his horse forward. "I'd better lead," he told Nicholas, "since I know the lay of the land." Nicholas nodded and brought up the rear, with Poco trailing behind.

At least in the canyon they were more secluded from the December wind, which was blowing hard and cold across the open valley. High mountain snows capped their surroundings in white, while the red-or-ange and sandy brown of the rock walls bore only minuscule traces of winter's impending touch.

Nicholas thought of their own ranch to the east. There they had no mountains to contend with—but no barriers against the harsh snows either. He wondered if they'd made the right decision in coming to Piñon Canyon. While he'd learned a great deal more in the few weeks since they'd arrived than he'd hoped to learn all winter, Nicholas was troubled.

Where was she? Where was Daughtry?

Nicholas' mind was so absorbed in thoughts of his wife that he had to glance up to see why his horse had suddenly stopped. Directly in front of Garrett were two men, both with guns leveled at his head.

"What's the meaning of this?" Garrett called out.

"Ain't none of your affair, Mister," a man dressed completely in black called out.

"Well, then, just whose affair is it?" Garrett asked, the irritation evident in his voice.

The other man, a short, squatty character, spit out a stream of tobacco juice and wiped his mouth with the back of his hand. "Well, Nick, it's been awhile, but I guess fate just throwed us together again. You ain't looking too bad for a man about to die."

Nicholas's eyes narrowed, and the scowl on his face was enough to make the man rethink his words. Garrett glanced back at his son-in-law and wondered about the connection between him and the men.

"Jeb, for a man who just spent the last years of his life in prison, I wouldn't think you'd want to throw yourself right back into a cell again," Nicholas replied, never taking his eyes from the man.

The man in black cursed Nicholas's smugness, but Jeb was the one who addressed the issue. "I don't care if I do get throwed back in. It'll be worth it just to say I had the honor of stringin' up your miserable hide."

"So you intend to hang me? I figured that'd be too much work. Why not just put a bullet in me here and now and be done with it?" Nicholas took a gamble with his words, knowing that Jeb answered to his older brother, the ringleader of the gang, Aaron Chancellor. With Aaron nowhere in sight, Nicholas hoped he could buy himself some time.

Jeb spit again before answering. His voice was full of anger and frustration. "I ain't going to do nothin' with you just yet. But when the time comes, I intend to see you suffer good and long."

"Still taking your orders from Aaron, eh?" Both outlaws scowled at the reference, but neither one said a word.

Garrett finally broke the silence and drew the attention of the men. "I demand to know what's going on and why you're even on my land." The men exchanged glances, and Nicholas knew immediately that they were up to no good.

"You own this here land?" Jeb questioned.

"I do," Garrett stated without hesitation.

Nicholas hoped to intercede and take Jeb's mind off of whatever he was plotting. "This man is nothing to you. Your war is with me."

"You've got that right, but I'll just bet there's some money to be made. This here landowner might be our ticket to Mexico."

"You can head on over to Mexico any time you want. It's not that far," Nicholas replied dryly.

"Shut up, Dawson," Jeb demanded. "Gus, what say we take the both of 'em and give Aaron a call. He can make the decision then as to what we do next."

"Doesn't he always?" Nicholas said, hoping to goad either one of them into immediate action.

"Tie 'em up, Gus," Jeb said, keeping his pistol leveled at the middle of Garrett's chest. With a smirk he added, "And gag Dawson if he so much as utters another word."

Daughtry had worked up quite a sweat on her hike back to Piñon Canyon. She knew she was still a couple of miles away when she heard the unmistakable sound of voices. Hoping that Nicholas or even her father and brothers had come searching for her, Daughtry climbed up on a rocky ledge to get a better look.

Easing into position, Daughtry gasped and flattened herself against the ground when she saw the men who threatened to shoot her husband and father. Immediately, her mind went back to the day when Nicholas had faced three outlaws alone. Were these men part of the Chancellor gang?

She struggled to make out what was being said but could only hear pieces of words. Try as she might, she was simply too far away to make any sense out of them. She lifted her head just enough to watch the scene below her. A man dressed in black handed his pistol to his partner, dismounted his horse, and took a length of rope from the horn of his saddle.

Helpless, Daughtry watched as the man first tied up Nicholas, then her father. In a matter of minutes the entire matter was completed, and the man remounted, claiming his gun and turning it once again on her husband.

"I have to get help," Daughtry whispered to herself. She watched as the men led Nicholas and her father off in the opposite direction from the ranch. Perhaps she could get back and tell her brothers before the men got too far.

Slipping noiselessly from her perch, Daughtry began to run as fast as she could move. She was panting heavily, unused to the activity, before she'd even crossed half the distance to home. She sucked in lungfuls of cold air, praying for strength to continue, and just when she felt her legs giving out, she caught sight of the corral fences and the orange adobe ranch house.

Dear God, she prayed, *please don't let them hurt Nicholas or Daddy.* The prayer continued, the same words, the same plea, over and over until Daughtry collapsed against the corral in order to catch her breath.

Gavin walked out of the barn in time to see his sister fall against the fence. Without hesitation, he ran as fast as his legs would carry him and scooped Daughtry into his arms.

"Are you all right?" he asked fearfully.

"No," Daughtry gasped, still breathless. "I. . .I have to. . ."

"Just be quiet," Gavin said, carrying her to the house. "You can tell me later."

"No," Daughtry said, putting her hand to Gavin's shoulder. "They have Nicholas and Daddy."

Gavin stopped dead and looked down at his sister. "Who has Nicholas and Dad?"

"I don't know, I think they might be part of the old Chancellor gang." Daughtry clutched her brother's neck tightly, the fear evident in her eyes.

"Why would you imagine such a thing?"

"Nicholas used to be a lawman. He was primarily responsible for putting the gang away." Daughtry drew a deeper breath. "You can put me down, Gavin. I'm okay."

Gavin shook his head. "No, we'd best get on in the house and let everybody hear the rest of this." He started walking again and spied Mack, his father's longtime ranch foreman. "Mack, something's happened, you'd best join us in the house." The dark-headed man nodded and followed Gavin inside.

"Mom!" Gavin yelled loudly. He put Daughtry down on a chair and yelled again, this time even louder.

"What is it?" Maggie questioned, coming into the living room. "I'm not deaf, you know."

"We've got trouble," Gavin explained. Maggie looked at Daughtry for a moment, noticing the redness of her face, as well as the dirt and disarray of her clothes.

"What trouble?" Maggie asked slowly and looked from Daughtry to Gavin and finally to Mack.

Just then, as if sensing that something weren't right, Daughtry's other brothers bounded into the room.

"What's going on?" Joey asked. The question was echoed by each of the others before Daughtry stood up to explain.

"Two men have taken Nicholas and Daddy. I went out riding this morning and a rockslide blocked my route home. I dismounted and Poco got away from me. I guess I took too long getting back, because Nicholas and Daddy came looking for me. I heard voices and came up over a rock just above where the canyon narrows. There were two men with guns, and they tied up Daddy and Nicholas and headed off in the opposite direction from the ranch."

"Who were they?" asked Dolan.

"Daughtry thinks they're part of the Chancellor gang," Gavin piped up. "Seems Nicholas used to be some kind of lawman, and they bear him a grudge."

"Daughtry, are you sure?" Maggie asked, trembling.

"I can't be positive. I couldn't hear what they were saying, but something happened awhile back, when Nicholas and I were on our ranch. Nicholas told me then that there was a good chance more of the Chancellors would come gunning for him."

"We'd better round up as many hands as we can," Gavin said to Mack. "Make sure everybody is armed and has what they need in the way of ammunition. Jordy, go get the guns from the cabinet in Dad's office. Don, Dolan, go saddle our horses and Joseph, get provisions for all of us. We don't know how long it's going to take or how far we'll have to ride." Without a word of protest, the brothers flew into action with Mack fast on their heels.

"I'm going too!" Daughtry exclaimed.

"Oh no, you're not," Gavin said, and the way he looked at her was so much like his father that Maggie had to laugh.

"But I can't just sit here," Daughtry protested. "I want to go."

Maggie came and put an arm around her daughter. "You're expecting a child, Daughtry. You have to think of more than just what you want."

"I suppose you're right," Daughtry replied sadly. The defeat in her voice caused Gavin to give her shoulder a reassuring squeeze.

"We'll get them back," he said, looking into both Daughtry and Maggie's eyes. "I promise you, we'll bring them back safe."

The women watched as their men mounted up and headed out. Daughtry felt hot tears slide down her cheeks. Would she ever get a chance to tell Nicholas that she was sorry and that she understood why he'd married her the way he had?

Jeb Chancellor led the way to the range shack, while Gus brought up the rear with Nicholas and Garrett sandwiched in between. Garrett immediately recognized the place as one they used only on occasion. It was well secluded and far enough away from the rest of civilization that no one would have any idea they were even there.

"This place belong to you too?" Jeb asked Garrett.

"Yeah."

"How much land you own, anyway?"

"Enough." Garrett was quickly realizing their game. "If it's money you're after, why don't you just name your price?"

"Just like that?" Jeb laughed. "What then? You gonna ride back to the house and write out a draft?"

"Is that what you want?"

"I don't know what I want yet," Jeb replied.

"Of course you don't," Nicholas sneered, "you haven't talked to Aaron yet. Big brother has to tell him what to think."

"I'm warning you, Dawson," Jeb said in a menacing tone. "Keep your mouth shut and you just might live to see tomorrow."

"He'd better live to see a whole lot more than tomorrow if you want any of my money," Garrett declared.

"What's he to you?" Jeb asked, halting his horse in front of the shack.

"He's family." Garrett's eyes met Nicholas's for a brief moment.

"Well, family or no, whether he lives or dies is up to Aaron. There ain't no amount of money what can buy back a man's years wasted behind bars." Jeb dismounted and slapped his reins around the hitching post. "Get 'em down, Gus, and bring 'em inside."

In spite of the way their hands were tied, both Garrett and Nicholas swung their legs over the necks of their mounts and jumped down unassisted. Gus poked Nicholas forward with the barrel of his gun pressed firmly in the small of Nicholas's back. In turn, Jeb motioned Garrett inside.

"Tie them to the chairs." Jeb took a defensive position with the gun leveled directly at Garrett, while Gus did as he was told. Once Nicholas and Garrett were securely tied, Jeb motioned Gus outside for a talk.

"Can you work the ropes loose?" Nicholas asked Garrett. Although they sat nearly side by side, Nicholas had to strain to get a look at the way Gus had tied Garrett's ropes.

"I don't know," Garrett whispered back. He strained against the hemp, feeling it chafe and bite at his wrists.

"I think, with any luck at all, I can work through mine," Nicholas replied.

"I think we'd best count on more than luck."

Nicholas grinned. "You do have a point there. I've been praying since we left to look for Daughtry." The smile quickly faded from his face. "Daughtry! I'd nearly forgotten." The agitation he felt was quickly mirrored in Garrett's eyes.

"It's in God's hands," Garrett replied. "I guess it always has been, except for the times I yank it back out." He smiled weakly at his son-in-law.

"I know what you mean. I guess I've pretty much messed up my share of living. I can't say that I've always done things to make my folks proud of me, nor can I stand on the memory of always trusting God to see me through." Nick paused for a minute, wondering if he should continue.

"Who are these men to you?" Garrett finally asked.

"Part of the Chancellor gang. I hung out with some of them before I became a lawman. They figured I'd overlook their shenanigans, for old times sake, I suppose."

"But you didn't?"

"No," Nicholas replied. "I couldn't. Like I told Daughtry, I grew up in a Christian home, and even though I felt the urge to spread my wings and buck up against the wind, I never broke the law. Bad thing was, I constantly kept company with those who did. Finally, a friend took me in hand and I became involved with working for the law instead of against it."

"Were you the one to put them away? Is that why they want to kill you?"

Nicholas took a deep breath and looked his father-in-law in the eye. "Yes. They tried once before back at my ranch. Daughtry unfortunately witnessed the whole thing. I hope you'll forgive me for bringing this on you and your family. I figured when you offered us a home for the winter that they'd lose track of me and give up the search. I guess they won't quit until they're all back in prison or dead."

"Don't be so hard on yourself," Garrett replied with genuine affection. "You've proven yourself to me more than once. I happen to think Daughtry made a good choice for a husband."

Nicholas's smile didn't reach the look of worry in his eyes. "If I only knew that she was safe."

"God's watching over her, Nick. We have to count on that. I guess I'm just now starting to see things more clearly. When Julie died, I figured I'd failed somewhere along the way. Now, I know better and my heart is cleared of the guilt. God's timing isn't always something we mortals can understand."

"I admire your faith, Garrett," Nicholas said honestly. "I hope some of it rubs off."

Garrett grinned. "I have a feeling your faith is greater than you know. Now, how are we going to get out of this mess?"

Chapter 18

*a*fter several hours, Daughtry had had her fill of waiting. As soon as she saw that her mother was amply occupied in the kitchen, Daughtry pled a headache and went to her room.

At first she didn't know what she'd do. All she really knew was that somehow, some way, she had to help. Without another thought, Daughtry began to discard her dirty riding outfit. Standing in nothing more than her heavy knit chemise and black wool stockings, she glanced into the mirror and smiled as a plan formed in her mind.

Racing to her clothes chest, Daughtry pulled out the bottom drawer and retrieved her brother's hand-me-down jeans. Disguised in boys' clothes, Daughtry figured she could ride into town and notify the sheriff, as well as the two Monroe families. This would get even more men looking for her father and husband and still wouldn't go against Gavin's instructions that she not join them in the actual search.

Rebraiding her hair, Daughtry coiled it around her head, then pulled on a dark brown hat and surveyed her appearance in the mirror. Noting the curvy appearance of her body in the jeans, Daughtry went to the wardrobe and pulled out one of Nicholas's duster coats.

The coat fell to just above her boot tops, but Daughtry knew it would be better than letting either her father or Nicholas catch her in town wearing boys' pants. With an apprehensive glance down the hall, Daughtry made her way to the front door.

Walking with determined strides across the corral yard, Daughtry took a rope and singled Nutmeg out of the few remaining mounts. Within a short time, she had the mare saddled and ready, grateful that no one had come to interfere with her plan.

Daughtry covered the distance into Bandelero in half the normal time. She knew she'd pushed Nutmeg to the limits, and as soon as the town was in sight, Daughtry slowed the mare to a trot. Nutmeg pranced nervously and whinnied softly at the sights and sounds. Daughtry was amazed at the way the small town was continuing to grow. What had started out as a handful of shops and services was now a bustling town, well on its way to becoming a city.

The sheriff's office was at the far end, and Daughtry knew she'd have to ride right through the heart of Bandelero before reaching her destination. Pulling her hat low, Daughtry urged Nutmeg forward, refusing to make eye contact with anyone on the boardwalks.

To Daughtry's utter frustration, the sheriff's office was closed without a single soul to explain his whereabouts. She heaved a sigh and made her way back to Nutmeg, just as a voice called out behind her.

"Sheriff's gone just now, but can I help you?"

Daughtry turned slowly to find Mr. Tate, owner of the hardware store. "I don't suppose you know where he's gone?"

"Daughtry Lucas! Is that you under that getup?" The man's shocked expression almost made her laugh.

"Yes, it's me, but the name is Dawson now. Do you know where the sheriff is?"

"Sure," Tate replied. "He's gone off looking for your father and some other guy."

"That would be my husband, Nicholas," Daughtry replied. She was relieved to know that the sheriff was already assisting in the search.

"Didn't know you got yourself married," the man said, scratching his chin. "Always figured you'd marry one of the local boys."

Daughtry couldn't be bothered with what Mr. Tate thought. Her real concern was what was happening to her husband and father. "If you'll excuse me," she said remounting Nutmeg, "I have things to do." Mr. Tate said nothing as he watched Daughtry settle into the saddle. "Good day, Mr. Tate." Daughtry urged Nutmeg back through town, wondering what she should do first.

Just as Daughtry had convinced herself that contacting Lillie and Dr. Dan would be the best choice, she pulled Nutmeg up short and gasped. The two men who'd taken her father and Nicholas were riding into town as though they were coming to Sunday meeting.

Without taking her eyes off of the two, Daughtry eased Nutmeg into a slow but steady walk. She had no idea what she was going to do, or how she could manage to capture the men, but Daughtry knew she had to do something.

When the men headed in the direction of the train depot, Daughtry felt herself grow frantic. What if they'd already killed not only Nicholas but her father as well? What if they perceived their job as finished and now they were taking the train back to—wherever?

When the men dismounted and tied their horses to the hitching post in front of the depot, Daughtry began to panic. *What do I do, Lord?*

She found her heart racing and, in spite of the cold wind, Daughtry felt sweat on her brow.

The men entered the building, and Daughtry quickly dismounted and tied Nutmeg several spaces away from their mounts. Glancing up at the double glass doors of the depot, she could see that the men were deep in conversation with the ticket agent. Without giving it another thought, Daughtry made her way to their horses.

"If they aren't going to leave by train," she mused in a whisper to herself, "they'll come back for their mounts. Either way, they'll be in for a surprise." She quickly slid her hand along the first horse and reaching under his belly, Daughtry loosened the cinch strap. Repeating this action with the other horse, she felt a bit of confidence in her mission. Somehow, she needed to find out what they were doing inside the depot, then she needed to get help.

Daughtry made her way around the building, peering in through the windows to catch sight of the two men. They seemed to be there to use the telephone, and the agent was somewhat disturbed by their request.

Daughtry watched intently, while one man pushed a handful of money across the counter to the agent and waited for his response. Daughtry knew the phone was on the track side of the building and that the agent's bay window was where she'd have her best chance of spying on the two men.

Slipping across the back, barely managing to avoid a man hoisting a heavy crate to the loading platform, Daughtry eased her way cautiously to the bay window. The window was positioned so that the agent could look up and down the track for some distance and Daughtry knew she'd have to keep to the wall beside it in order to avoid being seen. Thankfully, she noted that the two men kept their backs to her when they entered the room and that the telephone was opposite the side she'd chosen to be.

Daughtry felt herself trembling as she strained to hear what the two men were saying. Just then, the heavy blast from the four o'clock westbound blotted out all hope of hearing what the men were saying.

Glancing down the tracks, Daughtry watched as the train eased into the station, blowing off steam noisily. She felt more frustration than she'd ever known possible as she glanced back into the agent's office and found that the men were still on the phone.

"I have to find out what they're up to," she whispered.

People began to leave the train, while others crowded around her to take their place on board. Daughtry felt herself being pushed back through the comings and goings, until she lost her footing and fell forward.

With a shriek of fright, Daughtry found herself caught by strong hands and set back on her feet.

"Whoa, Son," a deep baritone voice called out.

Daughtry glanced upward and gasped, while the man staring down at her did the same.

"Sorry, ma'am," the man corrected his mistake, "I guess I mistook you in that garb."

Daughtry still couldn't speak. The man before her was the spitting image of her husband, only his hair was gray and his face betrayed his age. How could it be?

"I—I'm," she stammered. "It was my fault. I apologize."

The man smiled broadly, then reached out to take hold of the stately woman beside him. "No harm done," he said softly.

Daughtry stared in amazement at the couple. She looked at the woman for a moment, then back at the man.

"Is something wrong, Miss?" the man asked her, a look of concern replacing his smile.

Daughtry glanced back at the ticket agent's office and saw that the men were still there. Without hesitation she pushed back her hat and looked into the dark eyes of the stranger. "Do I know you?" she asked boldly.

"I doubt it," the man replied, and the woman at his side smiled.

"We're here to surprise our son," the woman said.

"Your son?" Daughtry barely squeaked out the words.

"That's right, perhaps you know where we could find him. His name is Nicholas Dawson. We received a letter from him saying that he's staying with his wife's family. I believe their name is Lucas," the man replied, then shook his head. "Forgive my rudeness, I'm Riley Dawson, and this is my wife Alexandra."

Daughtry stared up in dumbfounded silence at her father and mother-in-law. "Oh my," she finally managed to whisper.

"Are you all right?" Riley asked, seeing Daughtry pale at the news.

"I'm afraid so," she whispered, feeling faint. "I have a bit of a surprise for you," she said with a slight smile. "I'm Daughtry Dawson, Nicholas's wife."

Riley's mouth dropped open, while Alexandra's eyes widened and twinkled with amusement.

"You are Nicholas's wife?" Riley questioned.

Daughtry shifted her weight nervously and glanced back at the agent's office. "Yes, and the fact of the matter is, Nicholas and my father are in trouble, and I need your help."

Alexandra instantly sobered and reached out to Daughtry. "What is it? What's happened to them?"

Daughtry quickly explained to her in-laws why she was dressed as she was and how the two men inside the depot were responsible for their son's abduction.

"I need your help, Mr. Dawson," Daughtry said in such a way that Riley couldn't help but put his arm around her.

"Call me Riley," he said softly. "Look, I'll take care of this." He looked past Daughtry to his wife. "You take Zandy and go back to the ranch."

"Zandy?" Daughtry questioned.

"That's what most folks call me," Alexandra stated, trying to keep her voice calm.

"Oh," Daughtry replied with a nod. Then turning back to Riley she shook her head. "I'm not going back. I have to help Nicholas."

"Look, I know you want to help him, but we have no idea what we're going to run into," Riley said firmly.

"I know that half the county is out there looking for them. I can't just sit back and do nothing. Look, those two are leaving. Either help me capture them or stay out of my way." Daughtry's determination caused Zandy to laugh out loud, while Riley rolled his eyes.

"I see our son married a woman just like his mother. Stubborn to the bone and just as beautiful." Daughtry blushed at the half-compliment but turned to leave.

"Oh, no you don't," Riley said, taking hold of her arm. "You've got yourself a partner."

Daughtry turned and smiled. "Good. I loosened their cinch straps," she said with a grin. "They ought to just about fall into our arms."

Riley shook his head while, Zandy tried to refrain from laughing.

"They have guns," Daughtry said, while leading Riley and Zandy around the building. "But I figure when they fall off those horses, we might be able to get the upper hand, maybe even get their weapons away from them."

"You leave that to me," Riley said in a voice that made it clear to Daughtry he meant business. She nodded and halted when they reached the front of the depot. The men were still nowhere in sight.

"Alexandra," Riley said, turning to his wife, "you secure our bags and stay out of sight. I'll be hard pressed enough to keep her out of danger's way." He motioned to Daughtry who didn't like one bit that she'd gained yet another guardian.

Knowing the outlaws wouldn't recognize her or Riley, Daughtry motioned her father-in-law to follow her as the two men came bounding out of the depot. Without any time to lose, Daughtry and Riley flew into action as the men attempted to mount their horses. When the saddles twisted to the side and dumped the surprised men on the frozen ground, Riley quickly grabbed the revolver of the one dressed in black, while Daughtry put her booted foot firmly on the arm of the shorter, squatty man.

"Get up real slow," Riley instructed the men after he had Daughtry remove the other man's weapon. "Where's the jail, Daughtry?"

"Other end of town," she answered, feeling hope for the first time. "Come on, I'll lead the way."

Riley motioned the men forward, while Daughtry apprehensively moved out. The men weren't over their shock as they took hesitant steps forward, but the gun in Riley's hand left them little doubt that he meant business.

A crowd started to gather and follow Daughtry and Riley as they made their way to the sheriff's office. The mumblings and whispers were enough to unnerve Daughtry, but she took a deep breath and forced herself forward. *When this is all done,* she thought, *I may very well faint!*

Mr. Tate was there to greet them, and when Daughtry explained the need to put the two men into a cell, he rapidly produced a set of keys and led Daughtry and Riley into the jail.

Once they had the men behind bars, Daughtry sat down hard on a chair in the outer office, while her father-in-law began to question the men.

"You have my son and his father-in-law," Riley said with a menacing stare at the outlaws. He'd dealt with their kind plenty before, even if it were a lifetime before.

"What if we do?" the short man questioned.

"Well, the way I figure it, you can cooperate and tell me where they are, or I can start shooting parts of your body until you give me the information." Riley prayed his bluff would work.

The man stared at Riley as if trying to decide if he were serious or not. Daughtry held her breath, hoping and praying that Riley wouldn't have to shoot anyone.

"You wouldn't really shoot us," the man in black stated nervously. "Would you?"

Riley fired the revolver into the mattress just to the man's left. He glanced down at the gun as if carefully considering its benefits. "I'll do whatever it takes," Riley answered in a cool, unemotional tone.

Minutes later, Daughtry and Riley emerged from the jail to find the small crowd still lingering to learn what they could. Daughtry refused to listen to Riley's suggestion that he get another man to go with him.

"I know our land better than anyone here in town," she protested with hands on her hips. "And, unless you plan to lock me in a cell with those two, I'm going to find my husband and father."

Riley ran his hand back through his gray hair and stared at Daughtry.

"Remind you of someone?" Zandy questioned, coming up behind her husband.

"Frightfully so," Riley replied with a look at his wife that told her he really didn't mind the comparison. "Poor Nick." Zandy giggled at her husband's mock horror.

"Well?" Daughtry questioned. "Are you coming with me?"

"Of course I am," Riley responded. "Nicholas will have my hide over this and rightfully so, but I'm getting too old to fight the feminine wiles. Could you manage to stop long enough to arrange for Zandy to be taken to your folks' place first?"

"Certainly," Daughtry said with a smile. "My Aunt Lillie—well she's really not my aunt, but she and my mother are like sisters. Anyway, she lives in that house right over there. She's married to the town doctor, so there's always someone there. Just tell her who you are and what you need. She'll see to it that you get there."

Zandy smiled and nodded. Daughtry moved to retrieve Nutmeg's reins and motioned to Riley.

"You'd better saddle up one of their horses, Riley."

Riley gave Zandy a quick kiss, then did just as his daughter-in-law instructed. "Nicholas certainly has his work cut out for him," he muttered under his breath, and Zandy's laughter caused Daughtry to wonder at the murmured words.

Chapter 19

*L*ess than a half-hour after Gus and Jeb had ridden out for town, Nicholas had managed to free himself from the ropes. Crashing the ancient chair's rickety frame against the wall until it fell into pieces, Nicholas had managed to work his arms and shoulders loose.

"If you back up here," Garrett suggested, "I can probably pull those knots free with my teeth."

Nicholas nodded and pushed his hands, still bound behind his back, up to meet his father-in-law's mouth. Garrett worked at the ropes for only a moment before managing to pull the first knot apart. After that it was only a matter of teamwork and they had themselves free.

Rubbing his wrists and the spot in his shoulder that ached from the only sign of age he'd allowed himself—rheumatism—Garrett smiled at his son-in-law. "I guess we'll be quite a surprise for old Gus and Jeb."

"More than they can imagine," Nicholas said, returning the grin. "The way I see it, we'd be wise to lay a trap. There's no way of knowing if they'll come back alone, and I intend to round up every one of those good-for-nothings so I can get on with my life. I can't go on having to look over my shoulder every time a twig snaps, and I'll certainly not subject my wife and kids to it." Looking intently at Garrett for a moment, Nicholas grew sober.

"I'm really sorry for the danger this has placed you and your family in," he began. "I have to admit that one of the reasons I agreed to winter with you here was because I was worried something like this would happen at our place. I figured, and selfishly so, that they'd come around and find our place deserted, with no forwarding address or knowledge of where we'd gotten off to, and they'd give up and go home. I don't want to be responsible for killing any of them, but I won't let them kill my family."

Garrett reached out and put his hand on Nicholas's shoulder. "You did what you had to do. I would have done the same thing, and there's nothing to be ashamed of in thinking of Daughtry first." He grinned, breaking the tension between them. "I put her mother first, often to my detriment and, sometimes, my distraction."

Nicholas laughed. "Yes, Daughtry can be a real distraction too."

"Don't I know it," Garrett said, joining his laughter.

"What are we going to do about this?" Nicholas said, sobering once again.

"We'll have to take them when they come back. We can watch and see if more than just the two of them come back and judge the situation accordingly. The way I figure it, it's going to be about dark before they can make it back from Bandelero. We can use that to our benefit by leaving the place dark."

"Makes sense," Nicholas replied, sizing up the range shack. It was a single room, with little more than fireplace, table, and chair. The other chair, now good for little more than kindling, lay in a heap beside a small metal cabinet. "What's in there?" Nicholas questioned.

"A bit of food, some bandages, that sort of thing. No weapons, except maybe a knife." Garrett strode over to the cabinet and opened it. "Looks like Gus and Jeb cleaned it out. There's bandages and some liniment. Nothing else."

Nicholas nodded and continued to stare out the window. His mind immediately drifted where he didn't want to dwell. Daughtry was somewhere out there. Maybe she was alone and hurt or maybe she'd made it back safely to the ranch. Either way, not knowing was killing Nicholas.

"You love her a great deal, don't you, Son?"

Nicholas didn't even smile at the reference. "I do," he whispered. "More than I ever hoped I could love another person."

Garrett came up beside him and put his arm around Nicholas's shoulder. "Let's pray." With a nod, Nicholas felt hope return.

"We're about out of light, Daughtry," Riley called from his mount.

"I know, but we're nearly there," she replied in a breathless manner. "We'll just have to push them a little harder."

The horses, already more than a little weary from their continuous journeys, were sweat-soaked and starting to lather. Daughtry had never abused a mount in her life, but then, she'd never felt the urgency to save another person's life. Nicholas and her father might lie bleeding or half-dead, for all she knew. They just had to get to the ranch shack and see that they were all right. After that, she'd give Nutmeg a well-deserved rest, but not until then.

Daughtry felt a wave of nausea run through her, causing her to slow their pace a bit. She prayed silently that the feeling would pass, and when it didn't, Daughtry surprised Riley by pulling up quickly.

"Here!" she exclaimed, tossing her reins to Riley. She barely took four steps before losing the contents of her stomach.

Considerably more pale and slightly weak, Daughtry returned to her horse, ignoring Riley's shocked expression. She rinsed her mouth out, then took a deep drink from the canteen before remounting.

Meeting Riley's eyes, she nodded. "We're going to have a baby."

Riley's expression changed from shock to extreme concern. "You can't be out here doing this."

Daughtry shrugged. "That's what my brother said and no doubt what my father and husband will say. I can probably expect my father to suggest a spanking again—that seems to be his answer for wayward children."

"And rightfully so," Riley murmured, refusing to give in to Daughtry's dry amusement. "You could harm yourself."

Daughtry laughed. "I'm a little more concerned about what Nicholas will do when he sees me out here." Urging her horse forward, she grinned over her shoulder. "But I guess it's a little late to start worrying now."

Riley sat for a moment, still stunned by the news. Nudging the horse in the ribs, Riley caught up with Daughtry and spoke. "You amaze me," he said to her.

Daughtry was surprised to hear those words instead of a rebuke. She glanced up, still shaky from her bout of nausea. "Sometimes," she replied, "I amaze myself. I figure God has His hand most firmly on my shoulder, though. I don't doubt for a minute that He led me to town in order to find those two at just the right time. I was the only one who knew what they looked like." She paused, looking skyward. "God keeps pretty busy with me, but then I try to return the favor and keep myself pretty busy with Him."

Riley smiled. "Remind me sometime to tell you about how busy He had to keep with me."

Daughtry looked at Riley and nodded. "It's a deal."

The mountain peaks greedily sucked out the last bits of light, just as the range shack came into view. Daughtry and Riley did nothing to disguise their approach. They were hopeful that the noise they made would be welcomed by living, breathing souls.

Daughtry refused to listen to Riley's pleas that she let him enter the shack first. She raced across the ground without even securing Nutmeg to the hitching post. Riley did likewise and was on her heels.

Daughtry burst through the door into the darkness. She opened her mouth to call out to Riley, but someone knocked her down onto the hard wooden floor. While the beast managed to sit itself square on her backside, the cracking thud of a fist to a face left Daughtry little doubt that Riley had been properly subdued.

"Light a lamp," Nicholas called to Garrett who was now nursing his sore knuckles. Daughtry was so stunned she couldn't speak. She began to struggle furiously, which only made Nicholas twist around to clamp a hand to the middle of her back.

"Get off of me, you oaf!" she managed to gasp as her father struck a match to the kerosene lamp he held.

Nicholas's and Garrett's jaws dropped open with the stunned revelation that they'd managed to capture their rescue team. Without thinking to move, Nicholas stared at the crumpled body of his father, now stirring in the doorway. Daughtry started kicking her legs, but the duster wrapped around them sufficiently and saved Nicholas from any blows.

"Well, I'll be," Garrett finally said and motioned to where Riley was struggling to sit up. "You know him?"

Nicholas moaned, but still didn't move. "Yeah, he's my father."

"Figures," Garrett said, rolling his eyes upward.

"Nicholas! You're smashing me into the floor!" Daughtry exclaimed.

Finally realizing what he was doing, Nicholas shifted his weight and rolled to the side of his wife. Daughtry just lay there for a moment, trying to take in enough air to fill her lungs.

"I'd say while you have her down there like that—" Garrett began.

"Don't you dare!" Daughtry interrupted indignantly. "Don't you dare suggest he spank me. I'm not a child! If you two had bothered to look at who was coming. . ."

Nicholas interrupted as he took Daughtry into his arms and pulled her across his lap. "We did look. We saw that sorrel mare that Gus had ridden out of here and we saw two scraggly looking characters." Nicholas looked Daughtry over from head to foot, then glanced up at his father. "You gonna live, Dad?"

Riley rubbed his sore jaw. "Your father-in-law packs quite a punch."

"Don't I know it!" Nicholas exclaimed, and Garrett turned sheepishly to shrug. "How'd you get involved in all of this?"

Riley tried to smile, but his swollen lip wouldn't allow for it. "Your mother and I came to town to surprise you for Christmas. We ran into Daughtry at the train station where she'd pinned down your captors."

Nicholas turned to see Daughtry looking at him rather smugly. "You went into town wearing boys' pants? After I told you I didn't want to see you doing that?"

Daughtry groaned in exasperation and tried to free herself from Nicholas's grasp. He tightened his hold on her, leaving little doubt that the matter was far from settled.

"I saw the men take you and Daddy," Daughtry explained. "I ran back home and got Gavin and the boys. They're out there somewhere, even now, looking for you two. I couldn't just sit at home, and Gavin told me I couldn't go with them."

Garrett looked at Riley with a look that only fathers could share. "She's never been one to follow instruction."

"Well, she's going to learn real quicklike," Nicholas interjected. "Daughtry, you could have been killed. I could have busted you in the jaw like Garrett did Dad. Then what?"

Daughtry opened her mouth to speak, looking first at her husband, then her father, and finally Riley. Finding not even a shred of support, Daughtry crossed her hands against her chest and pouted. "I can't believe you aren't even grateful for the rescue."

Nicholas gently held her under one arm and got to his feet, pulling Daughtry up with him as if she weighed nothing. "I am grateful," he said softly, "but I'd be a whole lot more grateful if you were safely tucked away back at the ranch."

He looked at his father, shaking his head. "I don't suppose she told you that she's expecting?"

Riley chuckled. "She did. Right after she lost her lunch and we were nearly here. Reminds me of your mother," he added with such joy that Daughtry couldn't help but smile appreciatively.

"I will take that as a compliment," Daughtry replied. "Your wife is a wonderful woman. I imagine she would have come with us if I'd given her time to change."

At this Nicholas and Riley both laughed, and Garrett shook his head. "Sounds like Maggie. I'm sure if we don't make our way home soon, she'll be leading the searchers for us."

"Those horses are pretty spent," Riley said. "In fact, I think I'd better make sure they didn't wander off too far. In our hurry," he paused with a wink at Daughtry, "we left them to fend for themselves."

"I'll give you a hand," Garrett said, coming forward. "I hope you'll forgive the greeting."

Riley patted him on the back. "Forgiven. From now on, we'll fight on the same side."

"Agreed," Garrett chuckled.

When their fathers had gone outside, Nicholas pulled Daughtry to him so tightly she could scarcely breathe. "I was so afraid you were hurt," Nicholas breathed against her ear. "Thank God you're all right."

"I echo those sentiments myself," Daughtry whispered, lifting her face. "I couldn't just sit at home, Nick. I love you and I had to help. I couldn't have lived with myself if I'd done nothing and lost you."

Nicholas tenderly stroked Daughtry's dirt-smudged cheek. "I love you, Daughtry. My life wouldn't mean much without you in it." He lowered his lips slowly to hers, kissing her long and gently as though gaining reassurance from the action.

Pulling away, Daughtry sighed and leaned her head against her husband's chest. "I like your dad," she finally said. "He's just like you."

Nicholas chuckled softly. "I wouldn't have thought that a compliment a few months back."

"And now?"

"Now, I'm pleased you think it so. He's a good man, and I'm proud to be his son," Nicholas admitted.

"You'll work everything out between you?" Daughtry questioned. "I mean the demands he put on you and such. You won't hold a grudge or be angry with him? After all," Daughtry said looking into Nicholas's dark eyes, "it brought us together."

"No, I'm not angry with him," Nicholas smiled. "Grateful, but not angry."

Daughtry nodded and smiled. "And you aren't angry with me? I mean, I made a pretty big mess of things back at the house. I'm sorry for that too. I was riding back to apologize when I lost Poco. I just want you to know that it doesn't matter that you didn't love me when you married me. All that matters is that you love me now and that you'll always love me."

Nicholas kissed Daughtry lightly on the mouth. "I'll always love you, but I may have to tie you to a chair in order for you to bring our child into the world healthy and safe."

Daughtry laughed. "I promise from now on, I'll be good as can be."

"Uh-huh. Sure," Nicholas mused in disbelief, "until the next time."

Chapter 20

*C*hristmas Eve at Piñon Canyon had been a night of precious celebration as far back as Daughtry Lucas Dawson could remember. The house was decorated festively in pine boughs, red ribbons, wreaths shimmering with gold braided ribbons, and a tree that commanded the center of attention in the living room.

Daughtry lovingly touched the ornaments that hung on the tree. Delicate glass spheres, decorated with miniature paintings of the first Christmas, were among her favorites. They were nearly as old as she, and Daughtry remembered fondly, they were a gift from her father to her mother.

Laughter rang out in the dining room, where most of Bandelero, or so it seemed, had gathered to share in the festivities. When Daughtry's mother had come to New Mexico, soon to be wed to Garrett Lucas, she'd left behind her dear friend Lillie in Topeka, Kansas. But Lillie had soon followed and married Dr. Daniel Monroe, brother to the young pastor, David, who had an even younger wife, Jenny. They were more like a family of closely knit brothers and sisters, and their offspring had grown up in a togetherness that seemed natural and secure.

Daughtry had never known a Christmas Eve when they'd not all joined together to celebrate the birth of their Savior. She could still hear the years of gaiety ringing through her memories. She could still feel the warmth that wrapped around her tightly and made her feel that despite what else might happen, in this home, by these people, she was loved.

This year was even more special, Daughtry thought. Nicholas's family was with them. Added to this was the wondrous blessing that Daughtry was carrying her first child. She thought of Mary and how she must have felt as the birth of the Savior to the world approached. What an incredible feeling to know that she carried a life within her body. How much more must it have been for Mary, who carried the world's King.

The boys, now men really, talked boisterously from the dining room, breaking Daughtry's concentration. Anna Maria and Pepita had worked alongside Maggie and Daughtry to bake hundreds of tiny pastries and cookies for the party. Daughtry couldn't help but smile at the thought of her five brothers, not to mention Dr. Dan and Lillie's sons and Pastor David and Jenny's son, Samuel, digging into the intricately woven display of confectionery delights. No doubt they'd give little thought to the arrangement, but Daughtry knew there would be hours of praise for the taste.

Compared to the seeming army of men in the house, Daughtry knew there were only a handful of women. Besides their mothers, Angeline Monroe, Dan and Lillie's feisty daughter, and David and Jenny's quiet little Hannah, now eighteen and twin to Samuel, would round out the party of second-generation New Mexicans. The biggest surprise of all and most pleasant for the young gentlemen of the family, was Nicholas's dark-eyed sister, Joelle. She came by train only two days earlier and faced the wrath of both Riley and Nicholas at the announcement that she'd traveled alone.

It was of little matter, however, as all of Daughtry's brothers, as well as Samuel, and Angeline's brothers John and James, were quite taken with the beauty, leaving Angeline, who was normally the belle of the ball, with her nose slightly out of joint. No doubt Angeline would work through the competition and find herself the center of plenty of attention.

Daughtry stood alone in the living room and loved it all. She listened to the laughter, the voices, the happiness, and wrapped her hands around her still slender waist. Her child grew here, she thought and smiled. Two warm masculine hands fell over her own, and Daughtry leaned back into the arms of her husband.

"I wondered where you'd gotten off to," Nicholas murmured against her ear. "How's my baby?"

"He's fine."

"I meant you," Nicholas whispered huskily.

"I was just dreaming," Daughtry said with a smile.

"Are you sure you weren't trying to figure out what I got you for Christmas?"

Daughtry turned in Nicholas's arms and stared up innocently. "You aren't really going to make me wait until tomorrow, are you?" She batted her lashes coyly and put on her most alluring smile.

Nicholas chuckled. "I do love you, Mrs. Dawson. So very much."

"But you still won't give me my present tonight?" Her voice was pleading like a child's.

"Who can resist such charm and womanly wiles?"

Daughtry laughed and wrapped her arms around her husband's neck. "I promise to make you the very best wife, Nicholas. I will work hard beside you and together we'll build a ranch every bit as wonderful as Piñon Canyon."

"I've no doubt of it. You seem to make good things happen wherever you go."

"It isn't me," Daughtry replied with a knowing glance upward. "It's Him. God has made all the most wondrous things happen, in spite of the motives we humans attached to them in the first place. He's very good to look out for us that way."

"Yes, He is," Nicholas agreed.

With a tender kiss to Daughtry's forehead, he set her away from him and reached into his pocket. "I was going to wait until tomorrow, but since you are intent on celebrating early. . ." He fell silent and pulled out a small box. "I'm told this belonged to my mother's mother." He opened the box to reveal an elegantly styled ring. The wide gold band was intricately etched with scrolling and leaves. Set in the very middle was a dark red stone.

"It's a garnet," Nicholas said as Daughtry stared in dumb silence at the ring. He pulled the ring from the box and slipped it on Daughtry's still bare left hand. "I never even thought to send you a ring when I mailed you the proxy." He grinned at her, delighted with Daughtry's complete fascination. "Now you have one and no one will doubt that you belong to me."

"Oh, Nicholas," Daughtry replied, choking back tears, "it's beautiful. It truly is."

Nicholas nodded. "It's only part of the gift, however."

"Oh?"

"Yes," he whispered. "I've already talked with Pastor David."

"About what?" Daughtry asked curiously.

"I want us to marry again," he answered, taking Daughtry's hand to his lips. "Will you marry me in a proper church service, Mrs. Dawson? Marry me in front of all of our family and friends?"

Daughtry began to cry and, not finding the words to answer, she simply nodded her approval.

"Merry Christmas, Daughtry."

Daughtry reached up with both hands and pulled Nicholas's face down to meet hers. She kissed him earnestly on the mouth, her tears falling wet against his face. "Merry Christmas, Nicholas. I love you more with each passing day. I don't see how it is possible to love you more than I already did, but I do. I am yours, now and forever. Forever yours, no matter what the future holds in store."

Nicholas lifted her chin and glanced upward to the ceiling. "Forever His," he whispered in reply, "because He knows exactly what the future holds in store."

Tracie Peterson, bestselling, award-winning author of over ninety fiction titles and three non-fiction books, lives and writes in Belgrade, Montana. As a Christian, wife, mother, writer, editor and speaker (in that order), Tracie finds her slate quite full.

Published in magazines and Sunday school take home papers, as well as a columnist for a Christian newspaper, Tracie now focuses her attention on novels. After signing her first contract with Barbour Publishing in 1992, her novel, *A Place To Belong*, appeared in 1993 and the rest is history. She had over twenty-six titles with Heartsong Presents book club (many of which have been repackaged) and stories in six separate anthologies from Barbour. From Bethany House Publishing, Tracie has multiple historical three-book series as well as many stand-alone contemporary women's fiction stories and two nonfiction titles. Other titles include two historical series co-written with Judith Pella, one historical series co-written with James Scott Bell, and multiple historical series co-written with Judith Miller.

Also available from Barbour Publishing

A Bride's
Agreement

*Five Romances Develop Out of
Convenient Marriages*

Wherever Christian books are sold

Also available from Barbour Publishing

*Forever
Yours*

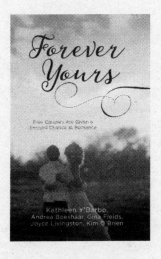

*Five Couples Are Given a
Second Chance at Romance*

Wherever Christian books are sold